Also by J. L. Larson

- **The Raid at Lake Minnewaska**

- **The Disappearance of Henry Hanson**

- **The Choices of Adam Bailey**

- **The Assumption**

The Accident at Sanborn Corners. . . .

And Other Minnesota Short Stories

J. L. LARSON

Ordering Information:

For orders and inquiries, please contact:
1-888-404-1388
www.goldtouchpress.com
book.orders@goldtouchpress.com

Printed in the United States of America

For your help and support:

MaryAnne, Charlotte, Megan, Tricia, Barb…and Matt

Contents

The Accident At Sanborn Corners 1

The Gas Lantern 66

Letting Him Go 128

What Becomes of a 'Corporate Animal' 142

The Mismatched Foursome At Lake Lindsay 193

The Girl on the Hill 259

Uncle Joe's Secret Life 321

The Encounter on the Lake 360

The Confrontation with Professor Grant 374

Sammy's Last Golf Ball 411

The Accident At Sanborn Corners

The fateful mishap occurred precisely at 11:00 P.M on a warm, humid Sunday night on July 12, 1970. The location was at a seemingly nonthreatening intersection in the surrounding flat farmland of southwestern Minnesota. The news of the serious car accident was naturally sad but to the locals in the area not surprising. This had not been the first time such a horrible collision had occurred at that junction. Accidents from fender benders to more serious disasters had been if not common then certainly a repetitive event in prior years and even decades before that night.

Anyone living in that part of the state the setting was simply referred to as Sanborn Corners. It was a crossing of two major highways on the relative flat farmland so prevalent in that part of the state. Long-term residents maintained a sense of foreboding about that intersection given the history of that crossing. With so many mishaps and tragic car and truck accidents, horror stories of death and destruction kept that scene notorious.

To the common traveler coming upon that crossroads on a sunny, clear day for the first time, there would be little hint of anything ominous ahead. A driver would not feel threatened; he'd be more apt to be yawning as he passed through the junction with his eyes tiredly roving over the repetitive cornfields and farms. Prior to his approaching Sanborn Corners no matter the direction he was approaching, the driver would see flashing lights and likely react that the warning seemed excessive considering the lonely singular forthcoming stoplight. Nonetheless, at least some uninformed drivers would become mindful that something wasn't as innocent as it appeared if there was such a blatant cautionary light so far in advance of the intersection. The general reaction was that most drivers would thankfully slow down with that kind of warning.

Still, if the driver was from out of the area, he be confused as he drove closer to the junction on that bright day. The dramatic warning made little sense given he could readily see in all directions of any oncoming or perpendicular traffic. Sure there were some slightly rolling hills, some pesky farm buildings and those seemingly whimsical locations of groves of trees momentarily blocking his view, but otherwise it was just another place in America where two major highways happened to intersect.

What was typical of that unaware motorist would be as he reduced his speed, he become more focused on the upcoming stoplight. If it was green, he would hope it would remain that color long enough for him to slip through the intersection without too much loss of speed. Within five hundred feet of the junction and the traffic light was still green, his probable choice would be to maintain his speed and blow through the crossroads even if the light turned yellow. There would of course be no decision if the traffic light turned yellow prior to five hundred feet. Though disappointed, he would unconsciously accept defeat and decelerate until stopped.

Sitting there waiting to proceed on green, he'd observe the worn looking structures on each corner. He'd glance at his fuel gauge deciding whether to fill his tank at the gasoline station on the corner before continuing his journey. He'd glance at the small café with three cars parked outside. He'd see a sign that read, "Get Gas Here" not knowing if it referred to the gasoline station or the eating establishment's food. His mouth would salivate for a moment, but he'd look at his watch and shake his head. The small restaurant with the gravel parking lot didn't look that inviting. He resolved that he wasn't that hungry anyway.

If he truly was not from the area, the driver might pan the scene while stopped and unconsciously thank his lucky stars he didn't have to live or work anywhere near such a remote and monotonous part of the country. Moving his head slowly from side to side to stretch his neck muscles, he'd anxiously begin moving slightly forward in anticipation of the light momentarily turning green. When the inevitable change to green finally occurred, he'd accelerate through the crossing slightly bothered by the delay and hardly glancing to either way for any cross traffic. There'd be no reason. He could see forever left or right on such a clear, sunlit day. Within half a minute he'd have his car back to ten miles an hour over the speed limit. Sanborn Corners would be in his rear view mirror and his mind would abruptly lose any memory of that isolated intersection.

On the other hand, if that same unaware driver made it through the junction on a green or yellow light, his speeding car would hardly have given him time to observe any of the few small businesses he'd just passed. Filling his tank or stopping by the café would not have been a thought. In fact, that sardonic thought about the luckless local people who had to live or work in the area would not have entered his mind. He more likely would have sailed through the intersection with but a glance at his watch as he calculated the time and distance to his next destination.

In either case that uninformed driver on such a beautiful, sun-filled day would never know he'd just driven through a junction that had earned a long history as a nasty and bloody death trap. Even if he'd heard something about the tragic legacy of Sanborn Corners, he would find the story hard to believe as he made the crossing.

The real curiosity was how those more informed drivers who lived in southwestern Minnesota and knew the bloody background of that intersection could become a statistic. Maybe it was the bland landscape. After so many trips through Sanborn Corners during good weather conditions, it was conceivable area citizens could get lulled into believing the dangerous crossing no longer warranted its dreadful reputation no matter the road conditions.

Unfortunately, whether oblivious or familiar, either motorist could well become prime candidates for misfortunes at Sanborn Corners when conditions were even slightly menacing. That first unacquainted driver would have no reason to think the evening haze or those snowflakes bouncing against his windshield or those pelting rain drops could be interfering that much with his vision. Sure, the intermittent groves of trees as well as the upcoming farm and business buildings were there, but they didn't seem to impede his ability to see other approaching traffic. And, that slight mound ahead just high enough to block an approaching vehicle traveling perpendicular would not be a thought. Moreover, seeing that green light ahead that driver might be confident enough to increase his speed so he wouldn't be inconvenienced if the light suddenly changed to yellow.

As for the motorist more familiar with the infamy of Sanborn Corners and facing poorer weather, he could still easily take his safety for granted. That evening's haze or those similar bothersome snowflakes or raindrops bothering his visibility could well be dismissed as an unimportant nuisance. He could be jaded to those flashing red lights warning of the upcoming stoplight.

It would be these types of drivers moving along in less than favorable weather conditions when Sanborn Corners and its foreboding history might abruptly show its teeth…like a python lying patiently waiting for its next meal to scurry by unknowingly and inattentively within inches of the snake's piercing bite. Certainly during serious inclement weather, any thoroughfare can be hazardous. Drivers will generally drive with more caution. However, this particular intersection never seemed to hold onto the cautious respect it had earned. Motorists definition of 'hazardous' varied whether drivers knew of its dire background or not. Sanborn Corners was just too isolated…too routine…and therefore too easy to forget past horrors.

And, that was the rub. When the weather was good coupled with daylight hours, there'd never been any mishaps reported of any consequence. It was just when the meteorological conditions deteriorated…and that didn't necessarily mean the worst circumstances. Too often it was in those in-between times and conditions…when the sun was setting blinding a driver, the rain was pelting but not a heavy downpour, the snow was falling but the incessant wind was blowing it across the roadway, or maybe some icy patches still existed on the highway. Then combine weather situations with those farm buildings, groves of trees, and that rolling hill close to the intersection one or all coincidentally blocking the driver's view, and the potential for disaster revved up dramatically.

Of course, not yet mentioned enough was the human factor. Alcohol played a big role on many of the accidents at that corner. Speedsters, whether young or old, trying to blow through the intersection on a yellow or just turned red light.

The carnage caused by high speed collisions was fairly obvious when witnessing what was left of the vehicles….and the victims….involved.

With these known factors the question can logically be asked why more wasn't done to limit so many ghastly and tragic accidents. After all, the tarnished reputation of this junction had history going back to the invention of the automobile. But, it wasn't as if the state patrol and the state highway department were oblivious just because the intersection was located in such remote and monotonous farm country. Many attempts at reducing the carnage had been put in place over the years…too often as a result of yet another horrifying car accident. But, the controls were rudimentary…as if no one truly believed Sanborn Corners should be that problematic or lethal. It was most often considered that the last accident at that junction was a fluke and there would be little reason to believe something so unfortunate could happen again.

Geographically, it was just two federal highways meeting at a point in southwestern Minnesota twenty-one miles south of Redwood Falls, eight miles west of Springfield, seven miles east of Lamberton, and two miles north of the village of Sanborn. The north and south running highway was Federal Hwy. #71. It started at International Falls on the very northern tip of Minnesota and ended at New Orleans close to the coastline of the Gulf of Mexico. The east and west roadway was Federal Hwy. #14. This highway ran across the United States through Minnesota and South Dakota before disappearing into the western plains of Montana. Easterly, Hwy. #14 ran through Wisconsin and disappeared into other Federal highway systems once it reached Chicago, Illinois. Both major highways just happened to cross on that seemingly innocent, non-descript tract of land in the middle of the gently sloping Minnesota farmland.

So why did Sanborn Corners continue to have so many cursed stories added to its lore? When conversations broke out about the dangers of Sanborn Corners… which was often in that part of the state…most agreed the remote countryside lulled most drivers into thinking they were safe going at high speed on either of the highways. The terrain was also falsely reassuring. Traveling day or night, the driver would feel he could see for miles in any direction. And, while there were patrol cars, drivers had some confidence they could spot a highway patrol soon enough to slow in plenty of time to prevent a speeding ticket. These factors could easily seduce most drivers into thinking they could travel fast and with impunity.

Exploring the background of Sanborn Corners, it was interesting how the very development of automobile transportation interrelated so consistently with the record of injury and death at Sanborn Corners. Going back to the decades of the 1910's and 1920's, speeding cars on the country roads raced virtually unchecked. During this time span automobile engines improved and were built with faster capabilities. Ghastly accidents were of course not limited to Sanborn Corners during that era. People learned rather quickly as they witnessed or read of daily death reports. Horrific damage could be the result of two or more speeding cars smashing into one another at a high rate of speed…and that destruction was not limited to the machines. It was the kind of tragic death that didn't happen a generation before. Rarely was there a collision of disastrous proportions of two horse-drawn wagons.

With the continuing advent of automobile, travel during those two decades, even the slower life of the rural folks would find the slaughter at a place like Sanborn Corners especially shocking…like a first time soldier seeing injury and death in his initial action in war. They weren't used to seeing life snuffed out by an invention in its infancy. But like today, that gruesome picture of destruction and mutilation would gradually fade as motorists moved on down the road away from the scene of death.

In the early days at Sanborn Corners before the two highways were paved, there were no stop signs at that intersection. As the numbers of Model T Fords increased, the lack of a stop sign at that crossing began to take its toll of traffic mishaps. It was decided in the early 1920's that a stop sign should finally be placed on at least one of the highways. Hwy. #14 was chosen to be the roadway required to stop. Cars on Hwy. #71 were not obliged to stop. To show their disdain, too often travelers on Hwy. #14 simply ignored their stop sign.

More deaths had to occur before stop signs were placed on all four corners. Of course, there was still the problem of drivers, including local folk, not taking the signs seriously. The remoteness still begged the question of the need. The accidents continued in surprising numbers despite these warning signs.

As the 1920's grew to a close, most people living in that region took more heed as they approached Sanborn Corners …and soberly if that was possible. Younger drivers, however, displayed little restraint. They often barreled through the intersection oblivious to potential death or injury Out-of-state drivers not familiar with the dangerous idiosyncrasies of this junction might slow slightly but generally sailed through the intersection. To them the four-way stop on such a flat, out-of-the-way intersection was ridiculous…at least those were the words communicated by the survivors of various accidents at that junction.

As time rolled on, there were more meetings and discussions about the continuing and increasing numbers of staggering accidents at Sanborn Corners. It was often discussed through the 1930's, 40's and 50's that automobiles were not mechanically ready to handle the high speed so many motorists were expecting of their cars. Braking systems were not sophisticated enough to halt a speeding car as promptly as a wayward driver would depend or expect. Seat belts were considered an inconvenience if they were even available. Windshields shattered more easily. Some vehicles were open air. On impact many victims had their final seconds of life be an airborne experience. Some continued their flight as angels…some did not!

After World War II, more and more studies were carried out nationally to further evaluate the causes of severe accidents and the particular brutality of collisions at such places as Sanborn Corners. Besides driving too fast, there were factors that were only beginning to become understood and respected. Inexperience at the wheel…

fatigue while driving…the impact of alcohol when driving a vehicle…and even road rage…all were becoming more acknowledged as problems. Still, these issues didn't carry the importance for too many years until more accidents…and deaths…caused more emphasis for better driver's education and more public safety messages.

Unfortunately what militated against these obvious reasons for car tragedies was how speed and drink were so much a part of American culture. It was manly to own a fast machine…in fact, the faster the better. As for alcohol, with generations of Americans convinced that booze was absolutely necessary to encourage a good time, drunk driving was just an accepted risk. In the decades immediately after World War II a fatal mixture of speed and alcohol just never reached a point in society important enough to limit. In fact, drinking and driving was usually more the subject of humor dating back to the first time a drunk got behind the wheel of a Model T. Driving while intoxicated might have been frowned upon, but it was accepted as a part of everyday life. There was a public attitude of bad luck where intoxicated drivers and speeding vehicles were the cause of death. It was believed that as long as the driver was conscious he should be able to control his driving enough to prevent an accident. If that same driver became unconscious from drink while driving, apparently that peril was not discussed earnestly.

When falling asleep at the wheel did become a more serious topic, whether induced by alcohol or exhaustion, Sanborn Corners often was used as a perplexing example. The early state highway department continuously expressed frustration over this fatigue issue. Studies were initiated to examine why this intersection could be so sinister. It was found with the roadways from all four sides being as straight as an arrow, the result could literally be hypnotic, especially at night. Highways on this type of landscape not only invited speed, speed, and more speed, but could as well become mesmerizing. The rhythmic sound of the car engine, the spellbinding stare against the setting sun, the melodic droplets of rain or snow against a windshield, or the mellow, sleep-inducing sounds of popular late night music on radio shows like Hobb's House broadcast across the state on WCCO-AM were all brought to the public's attention and awareness.

In the 1950's, larger stop signs with the red background were placed at all four stopping points at the devilish corner. People were ticketed more determinedly for going through stop signs. Of course patrolmen had to be there and see the infraction in order to ticket it. Nonetheless, this crack down on rural highway safety regarding more stop signs and setting some speed limits were given credit for holding down collisions.

Unfortunately, nighttime accidents did not decrease. Improved car engines and braking systems apparently gave drivers a false sense of security. The number of nighttime accidents…and deaths… at Sanborn Corners were as numerous as in previous years. Something more had to be done, especially after a particularly horrible wintertime accident ended in seven deaths. The gruesome collision wiped out an entire five-member family in one car and killed two of six in the other. Icy conditions were initially blamed, but the smell of alcohol was prominent even with the gasoline and oil spread out all over the snowy pavement. Both families were returning home from Christmas celebrations at relatives' homes.

In response, the state highway department decided that Sanborn Corners warranted the need for warning lights. A four-way blinking red light system was installed on each stop sign. These blinking red lights on all four corners did have some impact on the number of accidents and deaths at Sanborn Corners…finally! But, when shocking accidents still occurred, there was call for more precautions. Survivors often mumbled at the scene as they were being taken to the hospital in ambulances that they thought the vehicle from the perpendicular highway was going to stop so they could then proceed through the intersection. When both drivers thought that way, tragedy was the result. In too many cases it was a matter of travelers simply not knowing or adhering to the rules of the road.

After yet another devastating two-car pileup on a New Year's Eve night in the early 1960's, it was decided to put in a full four-way stoplight. There would then be no question when one car had the right to proceed and the other had the responsibility of stopping. Everyone from the highway safety department down to the local area folks believed that the stoplight would be the antidote for the high number of deaths at their infamous intersection.

That four-way stoplight, though difficult to prove, was given credit for saving countless lives. The only time there were some bad accidents was too often when young folks were trying to beat the yellow light while the crossroad hosted a driver who was anticipating the light turning green while driving too fast. "Beating the stoplight" and 'booze' continued to be the primary reasons for loss of life whenever the ghost of Sanborn Corners reared its ugly head.

By the middle 1960's an even more dramatic move was made to thwart further deaths at the notorious corner. Large blinking red lights were placed a half-mile before the intersection on each highway running toward Sanborn Corners as a further pre-warning of the upcoming stoplights. It was still not a fool proof method of holding down collisions, but short of having four patrolman standing out on the highways a half mile from the crossing of Hwy. #71 and Hwy. #14, the vivid red blinking light seemed close to the next best thing.

The results were good. For a couple years there were no deaths at that historically bloody junction. However, that record didn't last. When another fatal accident happened once again, alcohol and high speed were again judged the primary culprits. Not much a blinking warning light could do about a boozed up driver being too unconscious to take heed or feeling brave and wanting to blow through the yellow light.

To the end of the 1960's, there were continued efforts to discover any other reasons why Sanborn Corners was still recording an inordinate number of car mishaps even if they were relatively minor. Investigators began adding some other more subtle findings in their reports on the dangers of Sanborn Corners. There was repeated comment about how the perceived flat geography was deviously deceptive. That rolling hill momentarily blocking a driver from seeing oncoming perpendicular traffic was finally mentioned. The groves of trees at various places near the intersection were only cited as potentially problematic when combined with some light ground fog or the height of the corn crop in the summer or fall.

As for the small business buildings on all four sides of the intersection, their effect was only added under certain night time conditions. There were two gasoline stations, a feed and grain mill with a high storage tank and a café on the respective corners. There was concern that under the right circumstances...patchy ground fog or even minor rainy conditions...a driver's view might be obstructed just long enough not to see a vehicle moving crossways as that driver was making his decision to rush through the intersection as the stoplight happened to turn yellow.

These more subtle and understated factors would also be noted by any person who ever worked at one of those Sanborn Corners small businesses. Driving each day to that intersection, how could a worker not contemplate what the circumstances had to have been in the seconds before an accident that had occurred the previous day or night? He would already have heard the details about the probable cause or causes....maybe the slippery roads, possibly the smell of booze had permeated the crash scene...or less evil, perhaps the state patrol report might suggested a brake malfunction on one of the vehicles. Whatever the investigation found, would it not be probable that each worker would approach the 'corner' with even more scrutiny that following day trying to imagine any other possible factors for the collision. Since they'd driven to work in all types of weather, would they not consider the conditions of the previous night? Might they take some renewed notice of a certain grove of trees or of one of the structures at the intersection in combination with some hazy ground fog that might have interrupted a driver's vision?

And, there was always the human error factor. If there was no hint of alcohol found in the victims or in the damaged vehicles, the very next consideration had to be the decision-making of both drivers. Humans make their own judgment whether to abide by speed limit signs or warning lights, or even to heed precarious conditions on the road. For too many accidents at Sanborn Corners, the highway patrol could only attach the blame to the frailties and bad judgment of those who were in the driver's seat.

That would lead full circle to the repeated question of what might have contributed to the bad judgment even if no alcohol was present. Was it lack of driving experience...ill-health interrupting focus...maybe poor night vision... falling asleep at the wheel...or a momentary lapse in concentration? The human factor was always the great mystery of Sanborn Corners. State patrolmen or ambulance personnel on the scene would often just shake their heads mystified as to why sober and usually attentive victims could not have been more careful.

It was the locals in Sanborn, the community just two miles southeast of the deathly corner who were the primary followers of the fatal lore. The history of fatalities read like a sad tale of a long ago plague still infecting people in current days. And when they would hear that too familiar sound of screeching brakes, the reverberation would resonate over the generally flat terrain toward the village. The strident noise would be particularly clear in the evenings when the day had become quieter. Then, whether young or old, while sitting on their porches during the warmer weather or huddled up in their cozy homes in the dead of winter, they would momentarily stop any action and hold their breathes hoping and praying not to hear the possible accompanying next disastrous sound. If there was only silence following the squealing brakes, there was relief. They knew the individuals driving those cars had stopped in time and would live to see another day. There would be no other audible sound as one car would quietly yield to the other and the vehicles would continue their journeys. Both drivers would likely be applying a cold look at one another as they passed by the other at the intersection. Neighbors and families would then continue their lives in town thankful that a potential horror had been averted. A momentary flash of an unpleasant memory of a previous crash at the corner might materialize. With no ugly subsequent sound, that recollection mercifully would fade away in seconds.

Then there were the other times…the times that seemed too frequent…the terrible screeching sound surrendering to the most horrifying din of metal against metal. This momentary and sickening thud and the clamorous sound of broken glass would be like a small explosion. Local residents hearing this boom echoing across the farmland would bring back intense memories of previous accidents. They would visualize the horrible impact and wince imagining what that metal and glass had just done to human flesh.

The first thought was to call the local police or fire department. People would wonder if anyone else heard the sickening noise. The concern didn't need to be voiced. Even with the TV or radio on, that disaster could be heard by anyone in Sanborn with average hearing. In less than a minute the fastest caller to the police or fire department would have kick started the emergency process. Sirens would begin blaring and those crisis vehicles could be heard racing to the scene.

Most locals within ear shot would then gradually return to what they had been doing, but this time those memories of previous accidents would not go away. They would wonder how this mishap would compare to the many other accidents occurring at Sanborn Corners. They would think how precious life was and how it could be smothered out so abruptly with just a momentary lapse in judgment or concentration…or just plain bad luck. Depending on the hour, some would venture out onto their lawns and talk with neighbors as a way of purging their past nightmares of previous crashes. Some would talk about how long it had been since the previous accident. Others would recall and then describe the worst scene they'd ever witnessed at Sanborn Corners.

For these people it had taken just one horrible accident occurring at that junction for them to understand how violent a crash could be and how nauseating was the sight of the aftermath. Most everyone in Sanborn had witnessed the covered dead body after it had been thrown from one of the torn apart vehicles. In fact, too many locals had seen much worse than just a dead body. For certain there was little desire to see anything so ghastly again.

Still, there were some whose curiosity would not let them sleep. Depending on the hour of the day or night, an inquisitive Sanborn townsperson or area farmer might get into his car minutes after the disgusting sound of the accident and drive swiftly over to the intersection to get a better look at the deadly result… his justification being that he was there if needed, as if he had any actual medical background that could be called upon.

If the restaurant at that notorious junction was opened, the local person would try to appear casual by pretending to have coincidentally stopped by to satisfy his whim for something to eat or drink. Once inside the café, he could observe the mayhem as he sat there in the comfort of a booth while dipping a donut in a cup of coffee. That local could later claim he just happened upon the scene. As a witness to the post-accident trauma, he could enjoy a morbid sense of celebrity for the next few days as friends and neighbors might want to satisfy their dark desires for more detail.

But, mostly he was there to observe the devastation of the vehicles and take note of the skid marks on the pavement, to smell the spilling gasoline or the tell-tale odor of booze, to spot the possible sight of blood, and finally to watch the police and medical people carry out their jobs. And, certainly he wanted to see the victims…the dead covered by sheets, the seriously injured lying unconscious or in misery on a stretcher, or survivors with minor injuries sitting in shock on the pavement or in a squad car while holding a wet cloth over a head wound while being questioned by a patrolman or an emergency medical worker.

For this local, the sight of human carnage and disaster would be both appalling and intoxicating. This onlooker would feel a sense of good fortune… even elation… that he was not the casualty laid out on the ground covered by that sheet. Or, watching the unconscious victim being pushed on the gurney over to the ambulance, he might enjoy a feeling of liberation and appreciation that he wouldn't have to spend the night fighting for his life in some emergency ward. He could simply drive slowly back to his home and sleep the night away in his own bed. The next morning he could arise…in one piece…fill his lungs with fresh air, and be thankful to be alive. Whatever afflictions or pains he'd been suffering prior to the previous night would not hurt as much. Problems wouldn't be as serious. He was indeed in a better place than any of those people…dead or alive…who were involved in the previous night's accident.

As macabre as that man's thoughts might be, his reasons for wanting to see the outcome of another Sanborn Corners tragedy would be an answer to one very personal and secret desire. He was having his chance to feel elevated…to be able to cast his eyes down upon all the misery and misfortune of the previous night's disaster. He could feel contented that his life was better or even preferred over the lives of those victims…if for only a few hours or days.

That Sunday, July 12, a widespread thunderstorm had moved slowly and widely across that section of the state. There had been some damaging winds, but mostly it was the splendorous lightning and booming thunder that had people watching the panorama from the safety of their homes. The massive cloud system moving from South Dakota eastward had stretched from Windom up to Willmar. The general populace in that Minnesota farm belt…and not just the farmers…were quite happy with the one to three inches of precipitation, especially with no hail damage. There was only heavy rain. Anyone depending on a successful crop couldn't help but be pleased including the many small town businesses hinging on the farming trade. Only the kids in the various farm communities were discontent. Their late afternoon and evening time for play had been interrupted.

That summer the corn crop was progressing nicely. "Knee high by the fourth of July" had been a bromide of the past agricultural generation. With faster growing seed and improved farming technology by 1970, corn stalks were chest high in that part of Minnesota and even higher in many farms just south of Redwood Falls down to Sanborn along Hwy. #71. But, no matter how good the seed or the farming practices, water was necessary. It was always a concern having the right amount. Too much of a good thing could be destructive. That year the mix of rain and sunshine had been about right. Silent prayers were being answered. However, there were the beginnings of some furrowed brows up through that Sunday evening until the rain finally fell. The previous seven days there had been little measurable precipitation. That worry became moot for the time being with that evening's soaking rain…at least until the next perceived threat of a drought.

By 10:00 the system had blown through southwestern Minnesota. What followed was slightly cooler weather dropping the temperature from a high of eighty-two degrees earlier in the afternoon down to fifty-eight degrees as the lights went out in towns and farms for the evening. That decrease in temperature made the night quite comfortable although it did create enough condensation that produced some intermittent ground fog in the slightly lower areas of the rolling farmland. This periodic haze didn't appear hazardous since above the mistiness was the most vivid clear sky that followed the huge storm. With the decreasing ground light, the bright stars brought a mystic radiance to the surrounding countryside. The atmosphere around Sanborn Corners had such a mellow hue that any thoughts of an impending automobile tragedy would not be on anyone's mind. Truly, there would be so many other more dangerous days or nights for that type of misfortune to be more possible, particularly in the winter months with icy roads, pea-soup fog, or hard rain or snow storms.

So, on a seemingly gentle July night, caution might not be the first thing on a driver's mind. The sloping earth, the taller, silent ubiquitous corn stalks, the sporadic groves of trees, the periodic light reflections from the moon against that insidious ground vapor…all of this would give little hint that an accident of any magnitude could possibly happen on that particular evening.

Regarding Sanborn Corners, however, the conditions were ripening for peril. All it took was a few more coincidences of speeding, drunk driving, or poor judgment and the circumstances would become more and more ideal for a potential car accident. Then it would be only the luck of the draw whether the possible misadventure at the notorious intersection would be a minor mishap with few injuries…or a major scene of death and calamity.

As for the focus of this story…that 1970 car accident…veterans of the Sanborn Corners lore would always find it difficult to believe a collision of such proportions could have occurred that particular night. To the locals it would be remembered as a clear, star-filled night with only intermittent ground fog. Conditions were considered better than average. Furthermore, at that late hour on a Sunday night, car traffic was sporadic. Most Sunday nights people were home relaxing or at that hour already sleeping in order to get their rest for the coming week. In addition, all four blinking red lights a half-mile before the intersection from all directions were in full working order. What were the chances that a collision could occur when the setting seemed so benign?

While investigators generally ignored or downplayed the possible contribution of some ground fog, upon hearing of the tragedy, the locals realized they had been mesmerized by the beautiful night. Looking up they hardly considered that intermittent ground fog as precarious. With the humid conditions and the drop in temperature, those ingredients added to the potential peril. Still, most locals agreed that the conditions that late evening just didn't measure up to the more dangerous night time circumstances at other times in the year.

The highway patrol commented again and again how there were hardly any discernible skid marks leading up to the moment the cars collided. Normally there would be tire tracks before the point of contact as the vehicles tried to avert the inevitable. When this factor of no skid marks was reported, Sanborn residents and area farm families had no doubt why this horrific collision had caused such a pronounced reverberation. There was no screeching of brakes…only an explosion that lasted only seconds. That brief cringing noise woke up everyone for miles around except the hard of hearing. The lack of blackened pavement and the tumultuous sound indicated the obvious. The vehicles never slowed right up to the exact time of contact.

Alcohol consumption was certainly checked out. The strange thing was that no patrolman could detect the distinct scent of beer or hard booze in what was left of each vehicle. Of course the strong stench of oil and gasoline on the pavement could have masked the smell. Yet, experienced investigators knew the other tell-tale signs of alcohol usage by the drivers whether the odor could be detected or not. Remnants of broken bottles, aluminum cans, or pieces of cocktail glasses might be found. At that accident scene, no material evidence of that type was located.

It was the final report of this highway disaster, however, that made this scene definitely rare…and frankly quite upsetting. It was one thing to have such a major mishap on such a relatively moderate evening with little car traffic on the road. It was another thing that the victims were natives of southwestern Minnesota. They surely had to be aware of the tattered reputation of Sanborn Corners, especially if they were dealing with ground fog thicker than usual.

But, there was one other factor that made this crash scene more unique than any previous accident in that junction's history. In this one-of-a-kind catastrophe there were not just two vehicles involved. There were also not just the remains of three cars lying waste on the pavement or in the ditch. The real shock was that four vehicles met simultaneously at that intersection…all traveling at apparently mind-boggling speeds. One of the cars had a brief chance to avert the disaster by stomping on the brakes, but it had been to no avail. The skid marks were but five feet long. That car disintegrated into a cloud of flames, dust, and twisted metal along with the other three vehicles.

The report would further state that there were only four people involved… each one obviously a driver. Two of them were dead at the scene and two of the victims had survived at least to the point that they were taken by ambulance directly to the Redwood Falls Community Hospital. Both were unconscious and in serious condition when they departed the accident sight. One of the survivors died enroute to Redwood Falls. The other person's life was hanging by a thread upon arrival at the emergency ward. Thankfully there were no passengers found. Only the drivers were paying for their actions.

Investigators, emergency and medical workers…and on-lookers…were certainly hoping both survivors would live, so at least a description could be told of the unbelievably coincidental and alarming multi-car crash. When word came of the third driver's death…and that the final survivor was in a coma…hopes for any details were vastly reduced. It looked very likely this particular vehicular disaster was going to be filed as 'unexplained' in the lore of Sanborn Corners.

In the next twenty-four hours the accident scene would be cleaned up. One of the four damaged vehicles was placed in the front parking lot at one of the gas stations at Sanborn Corners. It was to act as a public service announcement for highway safety. This particular car was the only one of the four that had enough remaining 'body' to be discerned as an automobile. That vehicle became a local attraction. People from miles around stopped at that service station to quietly marvel over the devastating impact of the four-car pile-up.

Regarding the investigators, they had consumed pot after pot of the restaurant's coffee as they collated their findings. They eventually agreed the accident had been caused by 'reckless driving' and 'negligence' on all four drivers' parts. Whether not concentrating, or falling asleep at the wheel, or being unfamiliar with the dangers of the obscure corner, or taking their eyes off the road for an instant, or even one or more of the drivers simply having a death wish given the speed they were traveling, the resolution of this accident would always remain nebulous.

There was another factor that didn't come out in the final accident report, but was eventually shared or found out by the public. It was personal information about each victim collected over the weeks after the crash. The findings were supposed to be confidential. Too often, in situations like this one where there was so much general interest, privacy was disregarded. Investigators would interview the saddened family members who had fortunately not been passengers that night. Those interviewers upon sharing the notes of their conversations found certain oddities about each of the drivers…enough that the factor of 'state of mind' had to be considered as a very real contribution to the fiery catastrophe. These peculiarities suggested that each of the four had some behavioral issues that could have made each one…at times…careless or reckless. While these findings were very much after the fact, they were significant enough to be later added to the final report of the accident.

As for the victims, their experience in the mishap was short and instantaneous. One had flown through the windshield as if shot from a gun and landed in a ditch in front of the restaurant. He'd been impaled by one of the legs of a handmade sign inviting potential patrons to 'Get Gas….' The third word was indistinguishable covered in blood. That driver died on the way to the hospital. Two others had to be cut from the cars they were driving. Separating flesh, clothing, and metal was not a pleasant task. The lone other survivor was found groaning close to the center of the intersection having been apparently thrown straight up when the four cars met. Whether that driver flew through the windshield or out one side of the car was never fully discerned. Two of the patrolmen who served in World War II said the entire sight reminded them more of a bomb scene.

The identities of the injured were not immediately disclosed to the newspapers because verification was so difficult. As mentioned, the bodies were…in bad shape. Purses or wallets had been burned, destroyed or not found at the crash site until well into Monday. When a piece of wallet was found with a half-burned Social Security card, it was not much help. It was the same for the two personal licenses finally found in the mess. Again, both items were so damaged no letters of the victim's name or address could be distinguished. The only helpful identification found were the car license plates which didn't necessarily identify the driver.

News of the horrible accident…even one so late at night…flowed county by county like a tidal wave. By Monday morning most cafes in any sized community in that part of the state had heard about yet another score by that treacherous intersection. WCCO-AM radio in Minneapolis-St. Paul with listenership throughout most of Minnesota reported the news of the accident sparingly because of the lack of details.

Hearing that there was but one survivor, calls came into residents of Sanborn, Springfield, Tracy, and Redwood Falls from friends or relatives who hoped to get the latest news. They would only learn that the person was in critical condition and in a coma at Redwood Falls Community Hospital. Gradually identities were being found but held until there was certainty or until family members could be found. Newspaper reporters in towns around the area and used to finding local information, telephoned the Redwood County morgue hoping to find out the identities of the deceased. By orders of the state patrol, the morgue maintained a 'no comment' response until the next of kin were notified.

As Monday morning continued and it became more known that all four cars had met simultaneously at high speeds at the crash site, the interest amongst citizens smoldered. The grisly question persisted that by what gruesome stroke from the Almighty had brought each of these people to Sanborn Corners precisely at the same time Sunday night. There was further amazement as word spread that booze was not the key culprit in the horrible accident. Locals scoffed at that bit of news. Alcohol had seemingly always been part of car disasters over the years at the Hwy. #14 and #71 intersection. Townspeople in the area responded cynically that the investigators must have been drinking themselves not to have found traces of liquor.

But, the more serious-minded people in the towns around that area repeatedly asked the obvious question. 'What could cause four people to be so preoccupied that they paid little heed to warning signs, their speed, or even the reputation of the dangerous upcoming intersection?' Car license plates indicated the drivers were all from that part of the state. Surely they'd heard or read stories of the lethal history of this crossroad. What possibly could cause these four people to be so careless and unmindful?

As it approached mid-day on Monday, information about the victims was gradually being released, but not yet the key information naming the one driver still alive. People gathering at their small town cafes for early lunch heard the names of the four people involved. It was found that the victims indeed were residents of the general area of southwestern Minnesota, but they were not well known. In fact, as that day progressed, what locals did hear about the four drivers was particularly complimentary.

Area telephone lines flowed with gossip about each of the victims. As people ingested the various rumors while sipping coffee in their neighbor's home or back at that local café, a ghoulish reaction began to develop. Views began to be voiced about whom among the four victims most deserved to be that one survivor. It was pointless conversation and rather macabre, but those discussions grew more avid and widespread as the delay continued regarding that unknown person still clinging to life in the hospital. Who deserved to live developed into a sad but growing bi-product story beyond the unbelievable coincidence of four cars piling into one another at such a precise time.

Despite still being in a coma, the survivor's name was finally announced publicly Tuesday morning. There were too many expressions of displeasure that the wrong person was given the chance to live...as if their opinion on such a morbid subject actually mattered.

So, who was the survivor? Which one person involved in that horrible accident was causing so much curiosity. Though hanging onto life by a thread, why did this one survivor compel so many relatively sane people to make judgments why one driver might deserve a better fate than the other three? This grisly question now becomes the real subject in the remainder of this story.

Envision living in that area and Monday morning being caught up in the shear sorrow, shock and horror of yet another horrendous accident at Sanborn Corners. You've maybe witnessed some of the aftermath of one of the previous accidents... or, maybe your mind is recollecting vivid stories you've only heard regarding so many awful and too numerous collisions where lives were lost. Right away you'd be sickened by the tragedy...and disgusted that such reckless driving would again be repeated at that God forsaken intersection would culminate with more deaths.

Now picture your thoughts being fueled even more by mental images of any car accident injury or death scene you may have witnessed. Then consider your curiosity and concern being heightened as the names of the victims were delayed... and then finally announced later Monday. A few hours later you hear that one of those four poor souls is still alive and clinging to life at the municipal hospital... but his or her name is not being announced until next of kin can be reached.

Then, by Monday evening you hear some details about each of the crash victims ...basic background information mixed with some very negative rumor and innuendo. You listen to these adverse overtones. You may even believe some of them credible. After all, what could be positive about any person literally flying down a major highway at such a high rate of speed with little or no care for others as they approached the ill-famed Sanborn Corners?

Unfortunately, with the spread of this very negative gossip, could it be only natural to be slightly swayed by this disrespectful scuttlebutt. If might be difficult not to make some conclusions about those victims yourself? Then in the course of those hours on that Monday, you might hear some of your neighbors or friends make some surprisingly blatant comments as to which of the victims deserved to be that one survivor…as if the quality of these victims' lives…or lack thereof… had anything do to with their chance for survival.

Now let's say you were among those seemingly few citizens who were sickened by all these unsubstantiated and rumor-filled evaluations. You might walk away from such dribble….maybe even pointing out to some that loose opinions on such a morbid topic was just a waste of time and didn't matter anyway. Maybe you would even voice your disgust and suggest to your opinionated friends or relatives that they should be praying for all the victims and their loved ones instead of casting stones. In your more civil way of thinking, you would only want to eventually hear who the survivor was, be relieved for his or her family members, and feel great sympathy for the other three victims' kinfolk.

Except now, let's add a different and certainly unique dynamic to this story. Let's say you successfully discarded the gossip and rumor about these victims that Monday…at least for the most part. Let's pretend instead you were privy to each driver's state of mind and the circumstances in their lives as they carelessly sped toward their fates that Sunday night. Then the question might become… with this more valid and firsthand information…might you be tempted to make a judgment…even in the silence of your thoughts…to possibly lean in favor of one of the four to be that survivor…to be that one person more deserving to get a second chance at life.

This opportunity now presents itself. In the following vignettes you will be made cognizant of each victim's thoughts and lives prior to their disastrous meeting that Sunday night at Sanborn Corners. Then…if you are so inclined…contemplate with your inner self whether one of the drivers might merit your favor. Your preference will always be kept secret in the file of your own mind. Whether you reveal your morose partiality to anyone but yourself will of course be your choice.

Carol Brown
Pipestone, Minnesota

Carol Brown, Pipestone, Minnesota, perceived as a successful business woman …traveling east on Hwy. #14 from Lamberton just one mile west of Sanborn Corners – approximately 10:59 PM, Sunday, July 12, 1970. Visiting her mother that evening at a senior living center in Springfield, she'd already gone through Sanborn Corners a few minutes earlier on her way back to her home in Pipestone but had to turn back to retrieve something she'd forgotten in her mother's suite at the facility. She was furious having to retrace the nine miles back to Springfield.

Carol Brown was by most people's definition a woman who should have been happy and comfortable. As a professional business woman, she had the opportunity to set a fine example of how a female could effectively balance marriage, career, and motherhood. Originally from Little Falls, Minnesota, at forty-four years of age she had been one of the first women to reach the level of a bank vice president in the First National Bank System, a strong banking group based in the Twin Cities. During her career that spanned over twenty years, she had devoured every task, program and challenge thrown at her. At thirty-five she had completed her undergraduate program in Finance at Mankato State University. It took her six years to complete because of her full business and family schedule. Her life was busy beyond anyone's definition of the word. Most people had a distant respect for her. Interestingly, there was never anyone who'd ever voiced a desire to exchange places with her.

She had three children who understandably saw her only as their mother. Her work was not particularly important to them given their needs as budding teen-agers. They had grown to expect she'd be there for them when needed. That understanding had become less prevalent as she got more involved in her career. The kids tended to seek out their father for assistance or for answers to problems or needs.

Carol always perceived herself as the perfect parent and spouse. The kids had long since learned her delusion was not their illusion. They knew involving their mother in their lives would tend to make her irritable. Her patience at home was thin. She always had other things on her mind.

The art of parenting can be different things to different people. Some parents can be effective with seemingly little outward effort. Others perform the responsibility as if God himself is punishing them. In Carol Brown's case, her perspective leaned heavily toward the latter group. While gaining little joy in raising her kids, she still wanted to be observed and recognized as an effective, conscientious mother outside her home. Her ideal was to have her kids be an extension of the bank employees who reported to her. At work she didn't have to listen to her staff problems unless those difficulties reflected on her work or the effectiveness of the bank. She wanted the same in her family life. Her problem of course was that her kids couldn't be demoted or fired.

Carol typically worked twelve hour days…and most of the day on Saturday. With that schedule it didn't take long for her family to think of her more as a ship passing in the night. Her rationalization was that her parenting obligation would soon be over anyway once her kids went onto college. After all, the oldest was going to college that fall and the youngest was already thirteen years old!

She did show up to some of her kid's activities, but always with paperwork in her lap and her eyes incessantly looking at her watch. Leaving before the completion of the activity was typical for her.

Unfortunately, another habit she developed was her unremitting grumblings about her family. No one could understand why she complained about her kids' behaviors or her husband's shortfalls. Every family had challenges. Why did Carol Brown make it sound as if her family had the most problems and were giving her the least support for her hard work?

Her husband was not spared from her wrath. Again the joke was that her husband, Gerald, had never been forgiven for being the original cause of the children's births.

Her dissatisfaction with him made everyone uncomfortable. People wondered how long Gerald…a generally likeable man in the community…could put up with such treatment. It was he who coped with most of the everyday parental duties, i.e. driving the kids to friend's homes, to the doctor's office, to school, to events, and so on. Carol was always too busy. When Gerald did perform these parental obligations, he faced hell if anything went wrong. The fact that one of their children was diagnosed with any illness or even required a small cavity to be filled…to Carol somehow it was his failure as a parent.

Her dissatisfaction with Gerald was so apparent to family and close neighbors that there was talk how long the marriage could last…especially from Gerald's point of view. While he was always the model of patience with Carol and his kids, the verbal and subtle abuse from his wife was unending. No one could remember her ever saying anything nice about her husband in public. The only saving grace seemed to be that the two of them weren't seen often together.

Over time, her husband found other outlets to his less than sterling marital life. He stayed close to his kids by coaching in their sports, cooking their meals, and generally being there for the little things. His wife took little notice. Neighbors and friends of the Browns were impressed how stable and polite the Brown's kids were. Not surprisingly Gerald got the bulk of the credit.

If ever there was a reason for a male to stray from his mate, this was the marriage. But, surprisingly, Gerald had made his personal decision to keep the marriage alive for the sake of family unity. He even commented a few times with folks in his town how he was used to dealing with difficult issues in his business. As he said, he was not the type of person to walk away from a challenge.

In his own right he was reasonably successful as a local insurance agent for State Farm Insurance. It seemed as if everyone in town had Gerald handling their insurance needs. He was involved in his church, in a number of civic organizations, and was Vice President of the local Rotary Club. In his spare time he was always driving one of his kids someplace with a bunch of other young folks. His van could often be seen at the local Dairy Queen.

Sadly, Carol had little regard for her husband's career. If he had some business obligations and she was inconvenienced, she wanted him to feel guilty. He got so he knew better than to invite her to any social functions. Her whining about having to waste time socializing with people who couldn't do her any good made the effort ill-advised. As far as his volunteer duties, her attitude was, 'well, if I had the time, maybe I could do some of those nice things for people too.'

As far as Carol Brown's business life, though, her efforts and results were constantly being praised by her superiors. They appreciated her hard work and loyalty. She was credited for being highly effective in the handling of the large, important bank clients. To those clients, she had unlimited patience and provided conscientious service and worthwhile suggestions. She was on top of everything that could impact that level of clientele and typically handled these special business clients herself. In her mind she could not gamble on any incompetence within her banking staff. Delegating might create blunders. That could not be tolerated, since it might reflect badly on her.

With more satisfaction coming from her work, Carol found her most nourishing free time was spent when she could disappear alone to the family's lake home up near Ortonville. Over a weekend she could lessen the overload of paper work and even find time to read a book without being interrupted. This two-day break got her refreshed so she could continue working at her own high level of 'perfection'.

When she returned from the lake on those Sunday evenings, she was like a black cloud passing over the family home. She would invariably carp to her family that the weather at the lake was either too hot or too cold or too wet… and that her paper work dominated her entire stay at the lake. She would then nitpick about the general disorder in the house before retiring to her bedroom alone where she could seek more peace and tranquility before having to face the busy upcoming week.

If ever there was a woman buried in her own self-absorbed world, it was Carol Brown. She had become a bitter, unhappy woman. She had made a decision that life was hard, unforgiving, and without satisfaction.

On that Sunday of the Sanborn Corners tragedy, Carol had not gone to the lake but stayed at home to take care of some errands. She'd awoken lamenting about her full day and wishing the day was already over. Feeling obligated to join her family at church, she sat through the service only to impress others that she was both religious and a good mother. Her blood pressure was running sky high by the time the minister finally finished his sermon. Carol hissed to her husband that the pastor had taken extra time that morning for a baptism…and not reduced the time allotment for his homily.

That afternoon she had ten errands to run including an appointment for a haircut and shopping for some new business suits in Sioux Falls. Some of those items on her list could have been done by her children or her husband, but she wanted everything done right the first time. She had no trust in them.

The only other obligation she really had to do was later than evening visit her mother who lived at a senior living center in Springfield. There was a special Sunday evening dinner at the facility. Her mother wanted to introduce her to some friends. It was the last thing Carol wanted to do. But, she hadn't seen her mother for almost two months, so she felt compelled to make the trip to Springfield. With the time spent on the other errands, she had no time to get over to Sioux Falls. This put her in a particularly surly mood as she traveled the seventy-five miles to see her mother.

All the way over to Springfield she was moaning to herself about having to attend the dinner. Though driving alone, she was yelling in her car why her sister in Des Moines, Iowa couldn't live closer so both of them could share visiting her mother. Gerald had heard her complaint before she'd left and for once decided to stand up for the sister. He reminded Carol that her sister had been helping with her own husband's aged father.

Carol knew she was in the wrong, but rolled her eyes anyway. Her final response was mumbled just loud enough for her husband to hear. She said callously, "Well, if she can help him she should be able to help her own mother!"

When she saw that Gerald had already left the room, she rambled on louder, "I've got too much to do to be wasting my time going to a dinner at a senior living center. The food won't taste good anyway."

Gerald had learned how to deal with his wife's cynicism. His auditory nerve had been trained to shut down when she burrowed into one of her negative snits. It was just easiest to walk away from her.

Finally arriving late at her mother's living quarters in Springfield, Carol was naturally the last person to sit down for the dinner. There was much joking and merriment around the senior center dining room. However, when she entered the dining hall, her only feelings were that of sadness and hopelessness. She thought, 'Why should I work so hard? I'll just be one of these sullen people in a few years anyway.' Actually, there were very few brooding people at that dinner except for her.

She greeted her mother with a wisp of a kiss and perfunctorily asked her how she felt. Her mother told the same tales of her health woes and further put Carol into the doldrums. The dinner was as disappointing as Carol wanted it to be. Even though a local grocery store had donated the food fresh for the evening event and a local women's church group prepared a very satisfying meal, Carol's attitude would have made her displeased with a four-course dinner at a five-star restaurant.

As the dinner and social time was coming to an end, Carol could hardly wait to escape and return to Pipestone. Unfortunately, a major thunderstorm moved through the area causing the state patrol to warn all travelers to stay off the roads until the storm passed. 'Great', she thought, 'it's always me that gets the bad luck.'

The pounding of the storm on the roof of her mother's facility made her even more tired. She hadn't been sleeping well. Actually that had been the case for years, but especially in the last few months. She needed more than just a weekend of solitude at the lake to catch up on her rest. She could hardly wait for the coming week to be over so she could take off to the lake and be by herself.

As the storm continued, she could feel herself getting more fatigued. She thought how Gerald had offered to drive with her to Springfield, but she had told him 'no'. She'd said disparagingly, "Someone has to stay here for the kids… or didn't you think of that?"

Now she almost wished she'd taken him up on the offer so she could sleep in the passenger side of the car on the way home. But, it was his fault. He should have been more insistent in coming with her.

But, he had only done what he always did. Her sharp words made him shrug and retreat away from her. She hadn't meant to have been that curt, but once he left her she'd added another thoughtless remark by saying, "Besides, I need to be alone anyway. I've got a tough week coming up and I can't be bothered with idle chatter."

Unfortunately, he'd heard her last cruel, temperamental quip. His ears had not shut down soon enough.

As he went outside to play some basketball with his kids and some neighbor friends, he glanced back at the house and sighed. It was times like this one when he wondered how she'd become so adverse. She'd been critical and had a snide sense of humor when they married, but he was attracted to her by her energy and her quick mind. He'd just figured their budding relationship would give her plenty of reason to appreciate a better life and she'd tone down her discontent.

That had not been the case. Instead, she'd developed pessimism over time into an art form. He asked himself once again if it was something he'd done? He had no answer. He'd even asked her that very question a few years before. She just shook her head in exasperation and walked away saying she had no time to talk.

It was that very Sunday that the sting of her words before she left for Springfield finally provided the proverbial last straw. Gerald knew he could no longer ignore this preposterous situation. He had to insist that she seek some help…or have their marriage dissolved. While he didn't like to give up on anything, especially something so precious as a family unit, it was pretty obvious she had no interest in him and little interest in the kids. The situation had to be if not resolved, then at least discussed. He so wanted to believe that Carol had only to regain some focus on her personal life to make their marriage better.

At 8:00 that Sunday night, Carol was finally ready to leave the senior center in Springfield with the end of the ferocious thunderstorm. What she didn't know until she got outside was that a large tree had fallen barely missing her vehicle. She didn't appreciate that bit of good luck, only that her departure was now delayed because of some downed electric lines lying on the pavement by her car made it impossible for her to get into her car. It would take two and a half hours to get someone from the utility company out to that sight to shut off the power and make it safe for Carol to back across the wire and begin her return trip to Pipestone on westbound Hwy. #14.

By 10:45 she was fit to be tied. Of all the luck…hers was the only car being blocked by the downed power lines in the facility parking lot. And, she had so much work to do when she got back home. She shook her head and wondered why she was always chosen to have the worst luck of anyone she'd ever met. Carol Brown had her vehicle up to seventy miles per hour only blocks out of the Springfield town limits. She was swearing a blue streak as she barreled down the highway toward Sanborn Corners. The humidity was creating some mist on the road and out on the cornfields, but the sky was clear. She hoped to make it back to Pipestone before midnight.

It was 10:56 when she drove through Sanborn Corners earlier that evening on a yellow light. Heading west Lamberton was only seven miles away. She could hardly wait to see Gerald and relay all the things that had gone wrong in her life since she'd left the house earlier that evening. She hoped she could make him feel as miserable as she felt. Again she thought about the end of the week when she could disappear and be alone at their lake home. That sounded so relaxing. She needed a break. Everything was building up. Her kids were taking more time. Gerald wasn't pulling his half of the duties around the house. There was more pressure than ever at the office...especially being the only woman in the banking organization at her level. Yes, the lake would be a great opportunity to unwind. 'Of course,' she thought, 'it'll surely be raining the entire day up at the lake if her luck was what it always was.'

She looked down at her watch to see how long it would take her to get back to Pipestone. Her wrist felt naked. She didn't have it on! It was in her purse! She looked at the passenger seat. Where was her purse? She looked on the floor. Again...no purse!

When she realized where she'd left her handbag, a blue streak of swear words bounced off the interior of her sedan. The purse was on the bed stand of her mother's room back in Springfield. She'd been in such a hurry to leave, she'd practically run out of the senior center when the downed lines were repaired. She hadn't even said 'good night' to her mother in her haste. Carol felt no guilt. She'd be talking with her mother on the telephone the next day anyway. Her mother was always calling her.

But, she now had to face facts. She had to go back to Springfield and get her handbag. There was no alternative. Carol slowed down and did a quick u-turn right in the middle of Hwy. #14. No cars were coming. The night was like a still life painting. She saw no signs of life anywhere, especially with that continuous haze lazily hanging over the farmland around her. No lights were in any of the farmhouses save for the barn or porch light. Everyone seemed to have gone to bed at that late hour. Swearing once again over her bad luck and stupidity for leaving her purse, she stepped on the accelerator and headed back to the senior living center. She was two miles from Sanborn Corners and then it would be another eight miles from there to Springfield.

She increased her speed to eighty miles per hour as if the additional ten miles per hour would make a big difference in retracing her steps. She was seething as she looked ahead for the stop light at Sanborn Corners. She was re-tracing her travels now going east on Hwy #14 just over a mile from the fateful intersection. There was more ground fog now over the highway, but she paid little notice. She'd driven through that ground fog only three minutes before. All she could think of was how everything was wrong…and that she had been given the worst life ever created by God.

It was then 10:59 PM.

Jerome 'Romy' Jacobs
Luverne, Minnesota

Jerome 'Romy' Jacobs, Luverne, Minnesota…traveling south on Hwy. #71 only one mile north of Sanborn Corners — approximately 10:59 PM, Sunday July 12, 1970. Returning home from the Redwood Falls Invitational Golf Tournament, he had been unable to compete in the event due to extreme intoxication. People were surprised since Romy was customarily in a drunken condition. Despite being inebriated, he'd always made it to and from his golf destinations in the past and participated as best he could. That Sunday evening he was navigating his late model Ford Thunderbird across the flat southwestern Minnesota farmland to his home a hundred miles away in Luverne. His main goal that night was to use only his side of the highway to reach his journey's end.

Jerome 'Romy' Jacobs was the last one to leave the Worthington clubhouse the previous Wednesday night before the upcoming weekend golf tournament in Redwood Falls. It was Men's night at the Worthington Country Club, a perfect venue for him to get so plastered it wouldn't matter what score he achieved on the links. It was far more satisfying sitting at the bar relating stories of what he considered his previous fun-fulfilled life. That was what he lived for…to sit at a tavern, drink, and laugh. His audiences were few in number and only sat near him as long as he bought the rounds. Even with him buying the drinks, though, the most loyal lush found it difficult to keep listening. At times Romy was so drunk, he didn't realize he was talking and no one was sitting close to him.

Romy's father owned four men's clothing stores located in Worthington, Luverne, Sioux Falls, and Marshall. Romy didn't really have to work. He just had to give the impression he was involved in the family business. That had especially become necessary when his father finally retired and left the business in his supposedly able hands.

Romy had graduated from Arizona State University with some sort of degree at twenty-four years of age. He claimed it was a business degree, but there were few business courses on his transcript. Of course accuracy on his resume was unimportant, since he didn't need one. His guaranteed family job back in Minnesota was always there once he completed his degree. He was on the seven-year college plan at school and wished he could have extended the plan for another couple years. He liked having to return to Minnesota only during the warm months of the year.

While he'd worked some during his college summers, he'd mostly played golf tournaments around the state until returning to Mesa, Arizona each September. He never felt truly involved or even respected at any of the family-owned stores. However, with graduation completed he had to come back to a full year in the cold north. With that degree and his father perceiving a new maturity in his son, Romy actually took over the management of the Luverne and Sioux Falls stores with his father's guidance. He did have a modicum of success. His name was often in the newspapers because of the notoriety he was gaining in amateur golf tournaments in the area. With his name recognition offering free advertising, both stores he managed showed increased revenue for a couple years after Romy had become the manager.

He certainly enjoyed the his acclaim…and frankly got more satisfaction away from the stores than the time involved in running the businesses. When the golf season rolled around each spring, he was spending more and more time away from the stores. He was fortunate to be able to hand over the ordering, hiring, inventory and general operations to the two store assistant managers. As Romy told his two assistant managers, as long as they did their jobs well, he could involve himself in promoting the family business with community service work. The weekly lunches of the Rotary Club in the three Minnesota communities and in Sioux Falls…held at the respective local golf clubs…would be the extent of his community service. His staff at the stores knew by his deeply tanned face and arms his primary daily efforts were on the links.

As the golf season slowed each September, he spent more time at various bars. This activity became more his preference. As the years passed, his life style became ritual…a summer of golf and drinking followed by a winter of less golf and more drinking. As Romy approached thirty years of age, it amazed local golf club members how he could sustain his golf skills enough to be competitive.

By the time he had reached thirty-four years of age in 1965, his best golf was far behind him. He had taken over the family business completely the previous December with his father fully retired. Now, Romy no longer had to pretend to manage a store. The four family clothing stores were more in the hands of his CPA and his faithful assistant managers at each location. Luckily, those competent assistants did a masterful job of maintaining a profitable business. While Romy Jacobs didn't really have to show up at any of his stores ever, he felt some obligation to make what his assistant managers called 'a guest appearance' at one of the locations two mornings a week. The store managers knew it was more likely if there was a golf outing near their community that day. If there was no golf function that day in their town and Romy wandered into their store, those four assistant managers learned they were smarter to suggest lunch and then golf rather than allow him to walk around the store insisting on changes that might upset the staff. Though that assistant manager might have to blow an afternoon with Romy, the local operation would be better off in the long run with Romy out on the golf course.

Romy also contributed to the four stores' financial well-being by his taking up to two months off during the winter months for his annual trip to Arizona. His pretext was always to explore the idea of purchasing a possible clothing store opportunity near the ASU campus. Everyone knew it was just an excuse for Romy to get away from the Minnesota winter.

By the time he reached his thirty-ninth birthday, he had been married and divorced three times in twelve years and was being sought by gamblers on the golf courses in Arizona as well as the local courses in Luverne, Marshall, Sioux Falls and Worthington. His golfing skills had dramatically depreciated. He had become an easy mark.

As the summer of 1970 progressed, Romy continued his custom of playing the amateur golf circuit in southern Minnesota every weekend along with the many weekday corporate or benefit outings with his supposed friends. He was a terrific invitee at these functions since he was a big spender. All the locals had to do was to ignore as best they could his increasing bad manners and drunkenness.

By July his drinking had brought him to new lows. He was often dehydrated and was blacking out during rounds of golf when it was especially hot. When revived, he usually couldn't remember the last time he'd eaten. As for those weekend tournaments, he had finished only half of those events he'd entered that summer. He simply was too wasted by Sunday afternoon to finish the competition. The really sad spectacle was his deplorable conduct on the golf course…something that produced even more ridicule from his fellow competitors.

Still there were people who generally liked Romy Jacobs. Unfortunately these folks only remembered the past…that his father was a successful businessman and that his son would hopefully continue the trend….and that Jacobs was a skilled golfer when sober and a man full of funny stories when in his sanctuary at a barroom.

Whatever tournament he was in, the people who stayed close to him were locals who liked to drink. Picking up tabs at the bar was Romy's specialty. Oppositely, people who liked golf did not like Romy. He talked a good game, but that was as far as it went. His hands shook slightly and his concentration was superficial. Good golfers tried to stay away from having to play with him. He was apt to do anything on or off the golf course he thought was funny. He made a mockery of the rules of golf. It just was not fun to play a serious golf match with this man.

Once back at the clubhouse bar, he was the center of attention as he bought drinks for his fellow competitors and any reasonable looking female within voice range of his perch at the bar. Four hours on the golf course and six hours at the bar was a typical day with Romy Jacobs.

It was that Sunday, the last day of the Redwood Falls Invitational golf tournament that Romy really shined. He had not qualified for the Championship Flight on Saturday, so he didn't have to take his Sunday round of golf seriously in the lower Satellite flight...as if he would anyway. All non-qualifiers teed-off for their final round earlier Sunday morning mainly to complete their lesser important competition and get off the golf course to make way for the Championship flight golfers. Romy was supposed to be on the tee-box at 7:10. Considering he typically didn't leave the clubhouse at these tournaments until after 4:00 AM on Saturday night, an early tee time was too often missed. This tournament was no exception. In fact it was so near his tee time Sunday morning when he left the clubhouse that he saw little reason to return to his motel. He figured to sleep for a couple hours in his car. The activity of the other early Sunday morning golfers would certainly wake him up.

That Sunday morning all early morning competitors couldn't help but notice the passed out Romy Jacobs in the front seat of his Ford Thunderbird. The car was parked only fifteen yards from the first tee box. He was like a poster to all people walking by his vehicle on how not to live life. Golfers and spectators alike began to take bets whether Romy would be able to answer the bell when his foursome was scheduled to tee off.

It was 7:10 sharp when his group was introduced on the first tee box. Luckily, hearing his name over the loudspeaker had a magical impact on Romy. He opened his bloodshot eyes to the spectacle of sunlight, and three golfers looking into his driver's side window inquiring whether he was going to play.

Romy's response was unintelligible. He moved his tongue around inside his mouth trying to locate the rat that had died there sometime in the last three hours. To the small crowd around his vehicle, the fact that he was moving not only indicated he was still alive, but that he was going to give golf that day the old college try. He opened the driver's side door and fell out of the car. To witnesses, they figured it was a testament to his DNA that he was still breathing given the shape he was in.

The tournament could not wait. The other three players in his foursome teed off while Romy opened his trunk to find his clubs. His clothing, though stained and wrinkled, still looked better than most of the clothing worn by the other participants in the tournament. The big difference was that these men had showered, shaved, eaten, and brushed their teeth. These ordinary habits hadn't entered Romy's brain yet that morning primarily due to his blinding headache. Since he woke most days with that sensation, he couldn't see any reason not to play golf.

The grinding sound of the trunk clicking open made him wince. Pulling his clubs out of that trunk was painful to his ears and the noise brought shots of agony shooting through his body. The closing of the trunk exploded like a bomb. He'd been awake less than two minutes and the day was already getting off to a rough start.

With the announcer quietly repeating that Romy Jacobs was next on the tee, Romy was still fighting to get his golf shoes on. His playing partners were waiting impatiently already apologizing to the group who would be playing behind them. Finally, Romy dropped his large golf bag on the tee box joking that he'd never missed a tee time yet. His playing partners didn't react. They had already heard that he was notoriously late for his tee times…if he showed up at all. As far as they were concerned, they just wanted to compete that day and wished they didn't have to be an audience to a man who cared so little for his own health or the enjoyment of the competition.

Romy took a couple backswings and despite the pain in his joints seemed ready to address the ball. His hope in these situations was that he might be able to call upon his former skills to send his golf ball airborne. He figured it would just take a couple holes before he was finely tuned.

The announcer broadcast one final time that 'Romy Jacobs' was teeing off. Romy cringed at the piercing sound but was able to touch his visor to acknowledge the expected welcoming applause behind him. Unfortunately, there was only the silence of the morning doves softly whistling in the breeze. The secondary 'satellite' flight had few followers.

Romy reached into his pocket and pulled out a tee from the same pants he had played in the afternoon before. It served as another reminder about how long it had been since he'd eaten, showered, shaved, or changed clothes. He suddenly had a desire to tee off and get himself away from the public eye. He reached into his golf bag to get a golf ball trying to recall anything about the previous day. Saturday was now like a distant vague image that may or may not have happened. He had no recollection of even hitting a shot the previous day much less playing the Redwood Falls golf course. His mind was a complete blank.

Finding a golf ball, he held the ball and tee together and leaned down to tee the ball at his preferred height off the ground. As he bent over, the entire world started to spin. Every last drop of blood was flowing into his head. He couldn't bend anymore to stick the tee in the ground so he quickly straightened up to let the blood drain back away from his skull. It drained all right… it left his head feeling as if his brain matter had joined the blood flow that was now rushing to his stomach. He didn't want to throw up because he didn't want to lose what brain matter he had remaining.

The world began to spin very fast. He staggered toward his golf bag without taking a swing at the ball. Seconds later he was completely sprawled out on the ground as if his entire body had just quit functioning. For a moment no one moved. Most everyone thought it was the way Romy's day normally started… and waited for him to get up. Still others thought he had simply died and began wondering how the tournament volunteers were going to react to the inconvenience. Whatever the thinking of those present, no one seemed to care one way or the other about Romy Jacobs.

Yet, ever the stalwart golfer, Romy suddenly took a deep breath. He was still alive. Then, he rolled over and went to sleep on the side of the tee box. His snoring verified that he was still breathing. When Romy rolled a bit more onto his stomach his face rested in a small puddle of mud. One of the tournament volunteers had the decency to go over and move the passed out golfer's head to save Romy from drowning. One thing seemed for certain…it was quite evident the besotted golfer would probably not be playing golf that morning.

With other golfers and spectators waiting for word when the disturbance would end and the tournament could continue, the disgusted tournament director stood up, looked over at Romy's playing partners and waved them on to end any further delay. That whole episode would be much funnier later in the day when most people would finally hear the tale. But, at that moment to be an onlooker, the entire scene was more sickening and sad than humorous.

The tournament director then motioned for a couple volunteers to help gather up Romy Jacobs and assist him back to his automobile. The driver's side car door had been left open. There was cash on the seat along with his wallet, his car keys, and an unfinished can of beer. It was obvious Romy had been in deep slumber and was completely surprised when his name was announced over the loudspeaker. It was just a natural reaction for him to ready himself for his first swing of the day.

That tournament in Redwood Falls represented another milestone in the deterioration of Romy Jacobs. It was the first time he was so inebriated he couldn't even tee his ball up and make a swing at the golf ball. His body had finally rejected his natural reaction and impulse to go play golf.

As his would-be playing partners strolled by Jacobs being dragged to his car, there was relief written all over their faces. They would not have to put up with the antics of a drunk that day.

Romy regained some consciousness while being thrown into the front seat of his vehicle. At first he regaled against the assistance, but the shaking of his head made him dizzy. He felt himself slipping into unconsciousness once again.

When the car door was finally closed, he felt a calm overtaking him. The sudden silence allowed him to lay prostrate on the front seat and fall into a much needed slumber. Sprawled across the front seat of his brand new black Thunderbird, he did not move again for four hours.

As the morning progressed and the remainder of the tournament entrants teed off so close to the unconscious Romy Jacobs, there would be occasional tournament volunteers and spectators sauntering by the Thunderbird just to verify the story of the drunken man sleeping in the front seat of his car. If they didn't believe it, all they had to do was look through the windshield as if he were an animal at the zoo. They would see the dried mud on the side of his face and the drool coming out of his mouth onto the car seat and the soaked and soiled golf shirt and slacks he still wore from the round of golf the previous day.

Romy carried out a purpose that Sunday while lying in the front seat of his car. He was the perfect example of what life as a dipsomaniac could do to one's body, mind, and soul. Golfers and onlookers alike would walk by the car and just shake their heads.

It was high noon when the players he was going to play with finished their eighteen holes of golf. As if an alarm had sounded, Romy Jacobs awoke from his drunken stupor and sat up to evaluate not only what the situation was, but to come to terms with where he was and what day it was. By this time no one was paying any attention to him. There were far more interesting things than watching an embarrassing drunk try to regain some lost dignity.

The Championship flight of the tournament was about to tee off. That was what the gallery really wanted to watch. As the cloud lifted from his brain Romy realized he hadn't played golf yet that day. He looked at some of the leading golfers in the top flight beginning to gather at the opening tee box. Like a flash Jacobs was out of his car thinking that he must have made the Championship flight. He looked in the rear view mirror inside his car and saw the face of a man he almost didn't recognize. There was at least two days of beard growth to add to his matted hair. His clothing was in disarray…not something that best represented his family's clothing business.

Even Romy, given the horrible condition he was in, could recognize he might be experiencing one of the worst days of his life. He vaguely recollected trying to play golf that morning. By the stains on his shirt and pants, he'd obviously been lying in some mud. With his head woozy he finally made the only good decision of the day for himself. He decided to leave the parking lot so he wouldn't be so visible. His unsteady plan was to drive to the end of the parking lot where he hoped he could find some different clothing from his back seat, change in the car, and be ready on the first tee when his name was announced.

As he backed his car up he hit a post holding a corner of the tent where the tournament scoreboard was housed. As the corner of the tent buckled onto his car, event volunteers ran to the tent to save the entire assemblage from caving in. Romy just sat there in a daze taking for granted as he always did that someone would cover for him.

By this time the assemblage of people around that scoring tent and first tee box knew who Romy was and just wanted him to leave. Four of the volunteers directed him to back up carefully so he wouldn't take out any other object or human being during his exit. With that assistance Romy began his shaky route through the one lane parking lot hoping not to run into any of the tightly parked cars. It was the most pressure he'd felt in weeks. He barely managed to navigate his car to the end of the parking lot.

Unfortunately, there were no available parking spots. He was forced to continue away from the golf course to seek parking down the street in the residential area. Mercifully there was a parking spot large enough so he wouldn't have to parallel park. Still, he hit his right front wheel hard against the curb causing his car to stop abruptly…and preventing him from driving his Thunderbird up on someone's lawn.

In the silence away from the golf event, Romy found himself sweating profusely. Concentrating on driving his car had taken a lot out of him. Now all he had to do was find his golf shoes, change his shirt and pants, and carry his golf clubs back two blocks to the first tee. His belief that he was about to be called to tee off with the other players in the Championship Flight provided a kind of excitement and a slight sobering effect. He got out of his car bumping his head on the car door. Now, besides the headache returning, he was seeing stars. As he stood there trying to regain what composure he had, he felt his rapid heartbeat pounding overtime. Even he could tell he wasn't feeling well.

Hearing the loudspeaker down the street introduce the next Championship Flight foursome, he shook his head…slowly…and went into the back seat to grab some clean clothes. He found a new white golf shirt he'd taken from his Worthington men's store two days before. He figured a new shirt would give him a look of class that might cover up the beard growth and slimy hair under his golf cap. He pulled off his sweaty, smelly golf shirt. It looked like he'd just washed his car with the piece of clothing. He threw it on the ground and put the new white shirt on.

Immediately he felt a bit better.

Then he looked for a pair of pants. There was a convenient pair hanging up in the backseat. They were pressed and tailored to his liking. He pulled them off the hanger. With no place to change he just sat back down in his car pulling off his soiled pants and kicked them into the street.

The wind felt good on his milk white legs. He stood up with his two-day old underwear hanging loosely over his mid-section and then reached into the back seat for the freshly pressed pants on the hanger. He sighed loudly when he couldn't find them. As he crawled into the back seat trying to find the pants, it was then he saw his ever present cooler. His eyes lit up thinking of the three six-packs he hoped were still in that container. He dove across the seat to reach the cooler and opened it. It was the highpoint of his day so far. There they were. The three six-packs…and they hadn't been touched.

He heard the distant announcer welcoming another championship group to the tee off. He knew he had to hurry or he'd miss his tee time. He felt one of the six-packs. The ice had long since melted but the beer was still somewhat cool.

Romy's throat was parched. He figured he could have a couple beers while he looked for his pants. He snapped open a can and downed the beer without so much as a breath. The sensation of the drink sliding down his throat was just what his system needed. It relaxed him. If he could just find his pants, he'd be in tip top condition to walk the two blocks and tee off with the huge gallery ready to watch him perform on the golf course.

He could hardly wait. With no food since the previous day, he decided he should seek some kind of sustenance. But he was only wearing his new white golf shirt and his stretched out, slightly moist underwear. He had to find the new pants.

He opened another beer…and downed that one again without the need for a breath. That one stimulated his taste bud and seemed to lubricate his system lessening the need for food. He took another beer…then a fourth and drank them desperately. He just wanted to feel good again.

Suddenly he heard a person walking by his parked car. He quickly closed the door. He didn't want anyone seeing him with just a shirt and underwear on. What would they think with him being a championship caliber golfer and all? He waited until they disappeared before continuing his search for the freshly pressed pants.

With the door closed he no longer heard the announcer. He took the fifth and sixth beer and positioned himself in the back seat hoping no more people would be walking by his car. He laid back and took a deep breath. He at least wanted to be comfortable while he enjoyed his next two beers.

It was approximately 1:00 on that Sunday when Romy Jacobs fell asleep in the back seat of his car with four empty cans of beer lying on the floor of his car and two full cans at his feet waiting to be opened. He had taken another deep breath and barely felt his eyes roll up into his head. He would be passed out for the next five hours.

It was six o'clock that Sunday evening when Romy's eyes opened slightly. His brain felt like he was still unconscious even though he was aware what was going on outside his car. More people were leaving the golf course. It never occurred to him that the tournament might be over. He frankly had little memory of any golf tournament. After all, he'd spent most of the day sleeping in his car.

Then he heard some thunder outside. At least he hoped it was thunder. Otherwise there was something seriously wrong with his head. He laid his head back against the back seat and looked down. Then he saw his bare legs. He vaguely remembered he'd been looking for a fresh pair of pants to wear. He leaned forward and saw the new pair lying on the front seat of the car.

He grabbed them and slowly began putting them on. He now felt a sense of relief that he could now get out of his car without being embarrassed. As he opened the back door two unopened beer cans fell out onto the street. He kicked at them. He was thirsty, but not for a warm beer.

Romy nodded at some golfers rushing to their cars as more thunder sounded in the distance. He smiled thinking of the story he could tell some of his friends…

about being so wasted that he slept through a golf tournament. He began to laugh and farted as he latched his pants.

Looking skyward he finally realized the thunderstorm was pouring rain only blocks away. 'Well,' he thought, 'I might not be able to play golf anymore today, but no one else will either.' He felt some satisfaction in that belief.

As he got back in his car, the rain began to pelt down. He looked back down the two blocks to the clubhouse parking lot and decided to return to the post-tournament party inside the club. Usually there were some guys who hung around and had a few drinks before taking their journey home. He now wanted to join in that fun.

Romy headed back to the parking lot and drove up to the metal fence by the practice green. He misjudged the distance and banged into the fence before bringing the car to a complete stop. He looked around and hoped no one saw him knock over one of the fence posts. 'No harm, no foul,' he thought.

A golfer running in the rain toward his car glanced over at the small mishap. Romy got out of the car trying to make a joke out of the bent metal and the slight damage to the front of his car. 'Damn,' he chortled, 'why did they put that barrier out in the middle of the parking lot?'

Doubling over with laughter in the persistent downpour, Romy amazed himself how he could be so clever despite the weather conditions and still being half in the bag. The man running to his vehicle didn't react to the comment nor did another couple as they walked by under an umbrella to their car.

Romy dragged himself to the scoring tent to see who won the tournament. He saw the winning score and mumbled that he could have made that score blindfolded just a few years before. No one heard his comment. Most everyone had vacated the tournament grounds.

He then walked oblivious in the rain to the clubhouse. The smell of grilled hamburgers left over from the tournament was overpowering. Strolling by the mostly empty food table, he grabbed a formerly warm burger. With no volunteers around, he kept his money in his pocket. Nobody was the wiser as he gulped down the now cold, dried up hamburger in four bites. He got no particular satisfaction out of the food, but the taste did make him thirsty.

He dragged himself through the empty food area to the bar where there were a few guys still bellying up to the main bar. He recognized a couple of them from previous tournaments. They'd been drinking for some time and were feeling no pain. One of the golfers was particularly happy having gotten third place in the sixth flight while consuming a six-pack of beer on his last nine holes.

As Romy approached the bar, he bellowed, "Beer-tender, a round for my buddies. All six drinking buddies brightened up as they realized they had a guy who was ready and willing to pick up the bar tab.

Romy recognized one of the players as someone he'd gotten drunk with a few weeks before at a tournament in St. James, Minnesota. Romy couldn't remember the guy's name, but it didn't matter. All six of the men were three sheets to the wind. One of them had heard of Romy's exploits that morning on the first tee box and joked, "Well, if it's not Mr. Romy Jacobs returning from the dead. So… Romy…what score did you make today?"

The group exploded in laughter and slapped him on the back to make certain he knew they were kidding. After all, they didn't want to piss off a guy rich enough to keep them plastered until the club closed down for the winter.

It was three hours later that two of the remaining men at the bar assisted Romy Jacobs out to his car. They were laughing and wondering if Romy would be able to even turn his car on much less put his key in the ignition.

They pushed him into the driver's seat. One of the two men showed some concern saying, "Romy, why don't you take a little nap and sleep some of that beer off before you drive back to Luverne."

It was a good suggestion, but Romy didn't hear it. He was already sleeping with his head flopped back over the front seat. The two men then noticed the two remaining six-packs of beer in the back seat of the Thunderbird along with four empty cans. They grabbed the two six-packs rationalizing that it was a grand gesture so Romy wouldn't be tempted to drink the beers while driving home. Besides, if Romy was going to be stopped by the police on his way back to Luverne, having no beer discovered in his car would be in his favor. They even removed the four empty cans. It was the least they could do for a person who bought all those rounds of drinks back at the clubhouse.

Yet, in his condition they were generally certain he'd probably sleep in his car on this residential street far into the night. What they didn't know, of course, was that Romy had already slept in a drunken stupor through most of Sunday. He was no longer tired. He was just in a perpetual hangover.

It was 10:35 Sunday night when Romy jolted awake. His car was the only one in the golf course parking lot. There was only the outside light by the front entrance to the clubhouse shining brightly in the night. The golf tournament at Redwood Falls was history.

Romy shook his head slowly and tried to re-create his experience in that weekend golf tournament. He had no memory of his score on Saturday, but somehow remembered that he had played. The entire day of Sunday was non-existent in his mind other than he'd heard at some point that one of his drinking buddies…some guy named Earl…had won third place in the sixth flight. He couldn't recall who'd said it. For that matter, he couldn't remember what Earl looked like.

Romy Jacobs started his car. His head was in such a daze he could barely force his brain to make his arm shift the car into reverse. Strangely, though, his body wasn't tired. He figured if he could just clear out his mind, he could easily drive the one hundred miles back to his home. He hoped a bar he knew down by Windom might still be open if he needed a break on his way back to Luverne.

As his Thunderbird zoomed up the quiet street away from the golf course, he reached back and opened his cooler. He always kept the cooler well stocked.

He hoped to down a couple beers just to help him wake up. He was thirsty as a camel. But, his six- packs had disappeared. He shrugged. He didn't remember, but he must have drunk them already.

Five minutes later as he sped out of town south on Hwy. #71 his throat was so dry it actually hurt. He thought ahead to where he might get a drink. It was then he realized it being Sunday night made it that much more difficult to find a place open. He was only twenty minutes from Sanborn Corners as he left the lights of Redwood Falls in his rear view mirror.

The rainstorm had subsided while he had been drinking in the golf club bar, but there was still an intermittent haze along the highway as he drove along. But, the air was not as hazy as Romy's brain. The two lane road seemed like it was two feet wide. He was having trouble just keeping the vehicle between the shoulders of both sides of the highway. He figured if he met another car, he'd just have to slow down and maybe even stop to let the vehicle go by.

But, ahead there was only darkness, occasional ground fog, a dark, vivid sky, little if any traffic and a highway he thought was built more for a bicycle. If he could just have a drink, he'd feel a lot better. He figured he might give in and stop for a cup of coffee at the café at Sanborn Corners…if it was still open! He looked at his watch. It was either 10:45…or ten minutes before 9:00. He couldn't tell the big hand from the small hand on either his watch or the clock in his car.

He pressed harder on the accelerator hoping to get to the restaurant sooner if he went faster. He had to get there before 9:00…or 11:00…in case one of those times happened to be closing time at the cafe. A cup of coffee actually sounded good. He pressed the accelerator harder as he weaved down Highway #71.

Though he didn't know the correct time, it was actually a couple minutes before 11:00 when Romy Jacobs thought he saw the lights of Sanborn Corners far ahead. He was traveling about eighty-five miles an hour on the left side of the highway. His throat felt as dry as sand. He just had to get to that café. Maybe they had some beer in the back room. That sounded better than coffee.

Eugene Redding Jr.
Marshall, Minnesota

Eugene 'Junior' Redding, Marshall, Minnesota, was a fifth-year student at the local Southwest State College and a part-time bartender at a motel bar not far from the rural campus. He was traveling north on Hwy. #71 on Sunday, July 12, 1970. It was approximately 10:58 PM as he passed the community of Sanborn off to his left on the by-pass. Going around the town meant that

*he didn't have to reduce his speed. moving in access of 110 MPH,
Redding had already outrun a patrolman after leaving Windom
a short time before. He was looking to set his own speed record on
his return trip from Windom back to Marshall. He was feeling
very smug not only because he'd out-distanced the cop, but that
he'd completed yet another of his innumerable trysts with a lady
five years older than he living in Windom. What made it especially
cool in his mind was that the lady was married.*

That Sunday night twenty-three year old Junior Redding had just finished
dropping Mrs. Pamela Thomas off at her house in Windom and was hurrying
back to Marshall, Minnesota. He preferred his job as a bartender to going to
school, but he felt obligated to get some kind of degree…as if that piece of paper
would automatically put more money into his constantly depleted wallet. He
drove a Dodge Charger with an engine that made the horsepower on a patrol car
pale in comparison. Many a trouper had been outrun by that Charger. Redding's
late night exploits in racing back to school or to his parent's farm outside Lucan
were legendary…at least in his mind.

He had a penchant for placing himself in trouble and then being able to dash
away before anyone could catch him. As a result this reputation gave him the
confidence to take risks including his fondness for propositioning any female that
caught his eye. If she was wedded that was not a stumbling block. If a woman
was drinking alone at the bar where he worked, she was fair game.

He was the classic kiss-and-tell male sharing his conquests as freely and
easily as making the next gin cocktail. His stories made any male figure feel
as if he was missing something in his life. Male audiences to Redding's stories
never fathomed there was that incredible number of willing women living in
southwestern Minnesota. Moreover, how Redding found these willing females
was even more a mystery. Redding was a tall, good-looking enough guy, but he
didn't seem to have all that many lady killing traits to be so successful. His tales of
conquests were truly inspiring to anyone who would listen. Truthfully, though, it
was more astounding how so many of his friends never considered the possibility
that numerous of Redding's stories might be phony.

Pamela Thomas was one of those women that made at least one of his stories
quite valid. She was the wife of a man who owned a group of motels. He was
always on the road. The fact that her husband stayed at one of his motels so often
made her mind swirl with jealousy. She was certain he was being propositioned
by every single lady who happened to be staying at the motel he was residing.
That or he was doing the propositioning.

When Mrs. Thomas ventured up to Marshall to visit a friend on Saturday,
July 11, she ended up stopping by the motel bar where Junior Redding worked.
She had an hour to burn until her friend got off work. It took Redding behind

the bar exactly one minute to spot her and begin employing his practiced moves on the vulnerable looking thirty-three year old married lady.

As Redding learned her story, offered the proper sympathy at the right times and scattered effectively the small compliments about her judgment and of course her looks, she began to gaze at the young bartender with some interest. The three scotches and water didn't hurt in helping her lose her inhibitions either.

That weekend she never saw her friend. He offered to show her some fun if she could stay over. She got a room at the motel. As it turned out the two of them did not have a very early start to the next morning. They finally left the motel later that Sunday morning and ate brunch over in Lake Benton. Then they just did a joy ride around that part of the state. Redding knew southwestern Minnesota better than the original explorers and at least as good as the Indian tribes living there a hundred and fifty years before. As a result the two of them had three encounters that afternoon at various remote camping or picnic areas that Redding had sighted in his travels. As for Pamela she hadn't had that much attention from her husband in the last year. She could not believe the young bartender's interest in her and what she'd been missing.

Redding was equally pleased. He could not believe the good fortune he had in finding this experienced, good-looking married lady who didn't require him to tell her how much he loved her before each rendezvous. She was one of his best pick-ups.

She finally told him she needed to get back to Windom as she expected her husband to return to Windom later that evening. Junior finally kissed her good-by in the parking lot of the Marshall motel Sunday evening about 6:30. But, it would not be the last time she would see him that night.

To live up to his risky lifestyle, another hour later he was following the very path she took back to her home town. He wanted to cap this living dangerous weekend with one more tryst with the married lady. He figured to get to her house by 9:00, make love as long as she was willing, and be on his way back to Marshall before midnight. It would be a story he could boast about for months.

He arrived in Windom just after 9:00 and parked down the street away from her home. There'd just been a thunderstorm that had passed through the town. The dark clouds persisted making the night especially dark. That fit with his wishes. He figured he wouldn't be easily observed by any neighbors. Seeing there were no other cars in the Thomas' driveway, he finally knocked on the back door. The circumstance was even better than he could have fantasized when she opened the door. She had showered and was drying her hair while wearing a robe. Seeing him she seemed both bothered and complimented by his presence. It was the response he wanted.

Looking outside to see if any neighbors were watching, she grabbed him and pulled him into her house. Her heart was pounding for several reasons, but primarily because of nerves. It was all very exciting, but his youthful exuberance could not erase the terror she felt if her husband arrived home.

She laughed uncomfortably as he approached her. Pushing him away, she whispered, "Junior, what are you doing here? You can't stay. My husband could be coming down the street at any time."

Redding just looked at her with a wicked smile. She gazed into his sleepy eyes as she had many times that day…and finally succumbed to his urges. She just lost all caution.

An hour later Pamela jolted awake with Redding fast asleep next to her. She bolted to her bedroom window relieved that she saw nothing outside in the dark. Now her guilt and nervousness were growing by the minute. Junior Redding couldn't remain in her house one minute longer. If her husband returned, whatever was left of her marriage would be gone.

She rushed over to him and pushed him awake. "Junior, you have to leave. My husband is expected at any time. Please, you must leave!"

Redding woke quickly looking at his watch. It was 10:30. There was no reason to stay anyway. He smiled at her and kissed her while lazily saying, "Yeh…I'd better be on my way. No reason to make trouble."

He was up with pants, shirt and shoes on within thirty seconds. Pamela again went to the window and wistfully looked out. The neighborhood was still black, but she could see the moon starting to peak out through the clouds. She prayed Redding could exit without being seen. Having only two street lights at the end of each block eased her anxiety. At that hour, most of her neighbors had gone to bed. After all, it was a Sunday night. Most small town folks had to get up the following morning and go to work. She began to relax seeing the empty street. Holding back a snicker, it appeared she'd gotten away with a weekend to remember.

She noticed his car parked about a block away on the other side of the street. Thankfully, he knew how to disguise his visit. She mentally filed that valuable information for possible future tête-à-têtes. She liked Redding. He'd given her ample attention and many reasons to like him. She wondered why she couldn't get the same reaction from her own husband.

It was then the night changed. A car could be heard turning onto her street. Her heart leaped into her throat. The sound of the car was familiar. There was no doubt in her mind it was her husband. Pamela Thomas panicked. Redding was getting a soft drink from her refrigerator. Her husband would be driving into the driveway in the next fifteen seconds. She rushed to the kitchen shrieking that her husband was but one block away.

Redding smiled and swigged his soda. "No worry. I'll see you around."

Then he slipped out the back door as the husband drove into the driveway. Meanwhile Pamela rushed into the bathroom to take a shower praying that a heavy application of dove soap would erase any smells of Redding left on her body.

Junior Redding's blood pressure barely rose. This daring type of life style was exactly what he preferred. Walking casually down the alley away from the Thomas house, he drained his soda and threw the can at a neighbor's garbage can. He was proud of himself. He'd escaped another close call and had another amorous chapter to tell anyone who might want to hear about his exploits.

Trotting across a neighbor's side lawn, he arrived at his car. Jumping in the driver's seat, he caught the satisfied grin on his face in the rear view mirror. He loved this sense of adventure…this life of being on the edge. He knew in a few years this part of his life…the lying and deceiving…would likely be over. By then he'd have his degree in hand and likely be involved in a real job. But, he wanted to procrastinate that day for as long as possible.

He started his car. It rumbled with the horsepower he was certain could compete at the Indianapolis 500. He didn't know that for certain, but no one had ever questioned his claim when driving with him in his Dodge Charger.

It was sixty miles back to his folk's home outside Lucan or a few miles further to his apartment in Marshall. He decided he'd try to break his speed record back to his home. Forty-five minutes for the sixty mile trip became his goal. If there was a cop out on the road at that late hour on a Sunday night, that would be only a minor inconvenience. He figured he could keep his car in excess of one hundred twenty MPH on the straight-aways…plus he knew every side road. It would be futile for a cop to try and catch him.

He sped as quietly as his hot engine would allow through the neighborhood until he arrived at northbound Hwy. #71. His plan was to race north past Sanborn Corners to the Wabasso turn. Once he was on the back roads, he'd fly.

Hitting his accelerator, his car increased its speed to sixty-five MPH before he hit the edge of town. He was traveling almost twice the posted speed limit. Any thought of cops on the highway was no longer on his personal radar

The local police chief was coincidentally driving into Windom from the opposite direction as Redding's car accelerated to eighty-five miles per hour just outside the city limit sign as it whipped by the patrol car. Chief Marvin Anderson immediately did a u-turn in the middle of the highway. It angered him when some of these teen-agers had such little regard for the law. He figured he'd catch this kid and let him sit the rest of the night in the city jail house for reckless driving and possible drunk driving just to teach him a lesson.

As for Redding, he'd spotted the police car as he exited the town. He saw the blinking lights come on immediately as it reversed its course to come after him. His eyes lit up not being bothered in the least by the supposed challenge.

Pushing the accelerator to the floor, his Dodge Charger's back fender practically touched the pavement as an extra source of power propelled his vehicle to one hundred- thirty MPH. He knew what was under the hood of the cop car…and that car was no match for his own engine. He was at the top of a small hill north of town in no time…then on the straight flat pavement of northbound Hwy. #71. He felt as if he could be flying. Redding watched in his rearview mirror as the blinking lights of the patrol car got further and further… and further…behind.

Chief Anderson had his car at ninety miles per hour as he got on the straight away just north of Windom. As fast as he was going he was no match for the speeding car ahead of him. It took just one more mile for the chief to decide he was fighting a losing battle. For that kid to be traveling that fast, he deduced the young driver had out run many a cop in his day. The Windom police chief had better things to do than chase that kind of determination and experience. He'd let another local cop or state patrolman have the honors of arresting the young man further up the highway. With that, the police chief yawned, slowed his vehicle, and did another u-turn in the middle of Hwy. #71. His shift was going to end at midnight anyway. There was no reason to risk his life to make an arrest for a speeding violation. Chief Anderson was looking forward to the comfort of his bed within fifteen minutes after getting off work.

Redding mischievously grinned when he saw the police car's blinking lights shut down. The cop returning to Windom was the smartest choice. Redding whooped with his fist in the air as he chalked up another victory. Turning his AM radio dial to the Oklahoma City 50,000 watt radio station that broadcast rock music from Oklahoma to the Canadian border, he eased his car back to one hundred fifteen miles per hour as he flew north on Hwy #71.He had a good shot at making it to his folk's place outside Lucan in that record time… if he didn't run into any other obstacles.

For the next ten minutes he sang three top forty tunes at the top of his lungs as his speedometer maintained a speed of one hundred twenty-five MPH. When he finally rested his voice during a radio commercial, the time was 10:55. Junior Redding was less than eight miles from Sanborn Corners.

Pat Bryant
New Ulm, Minnesota

Patrick Bryant, New Ulm, Minnesota, a long time citizen of the community, was almost thirty miles from home that Sunday night as he sped toward Sanborn Corners in his 1965 tan Ford Fairlane. People hearing later about his involvement in a major car collision could not understand why or where he was going at that hour. He didn't even like to travel much out of town other than to go fishing along the Minnesota River. He normally was in bed by 10:30 PM. Bryant was as much a part of the town as the water tower. He was a head elder at the local Presbyterian Church and an employee of Brown County for over a quarter of a century. New Ulm was like a cocoon to him. All his views and his lifestyle were based on what

*he observed in and around his hometown, what he read in the
newspapers or what he saw on TV. Traveling west on Hwy. #14, one
mile east of Sanborn Corners' at approximately 10:59 PM Sunday,
July 12, 1970, he was moving at a high rate of speed away from his
community. His entire action that night was totally out of character.*

Pat Bryant had grown up in New Ulm, and except for a brief stint in the National
Guard, he'd never saw reason to leave his home town. If he wanted something
special he might drive over to Mankato just fifteen miles away, but he'd rarely
take the hour-and-a-half jaunt to the Twin Cities. He didn't like the traffic.

Bryant wasn't much interested in travel. He could read about other places in
books if he chose. And that was typical of Bryant…when he decided something
was right…then it was right. If he felt something was wrong…whether an idea, a
behavior, or someone else's belief…then it was wrong…plain and simple.

In his younger years he would remain quiet and not let a group or a person
know his feelings. However, as he matured and graduated into the position of head
surveyor for Brown County, Bryant became more verbal. In his work people could
not argue with the detail of his findings. This gave him extra latitude to appreciate
his own sense of power in his statements and beliefs. With his unfashionable close
haircut and his look of constant disapproval, he intimidated a high number of
citizens in the town and county. Over time his ferocious scowl along with his
aloof behavior left many people uncomfortable to be in his presence.

But, Bryant couldn't care less. He would never get fired from his job just
because people didn't like him. He was competent. As far as he was concerned,
that was all that counted.

Pat Bryant had married a local girl within a year after getting out of his six
months of active duty in the reserves. His wife, the former Diane Woodford, was
also a local girl who had graduated two years behind Bryant from New Ulm high
school. She had been taken with his confident air, his uniform, and his assurances
on what was right and wrong when she met him the first week he was home from
his reserve duty. She thought he looked like he should be someone in charge, like
a general… or at least a sergeant.

Bryant knew he had the type of girl he needed within a couple weeks of
meeting her. She was pleasant, respectful, docile, non-opinionated, and except
for her larger nose and protruding teeth, she looked all right. More importantly,
her response to him seemed positive. She often commented to him that he was
very consistent and dependable.

What was also important to Bryant was her faith. She was Presbyterian…
and that was how he had been brought up. To him that was the only religion that
counted. At the time he and Diane got married in 1946, Bryant disapproved of
couples marrying from different faiths…even different Protestant faiths!

It didn't take long for individuals to understand that Bryant had strong
feelings about most everything and didn't really want to listen to any opposing

views. As a result Bryant didn't maintain many friendships. Even worse, people tended to leave when Bryant entered a room.

The Bryants did add to the world's population. They had three children. Each child was brilliant according to Bryant. His wife initially appreciated his prejudice. However, his exaggerated claims about the abilities of his children caused her some problems with her friends. She sensed he was placing a lot of pressure on their off-spring.

As the kids grew, both Pat and Diane got very involved in their local church. Diane taught Sunday school. Bryant was on numerous committees and arrived first every Wednesday night for the pastor's adult bible study class. He especially admired the Presbyterian minister. Reverend George Reynolds was very articulate and knowledgeable about the bible and saw things very conservatively…as did Bryant.

The feeling of the minister towards Pat Bryant, however, was not mutual. Reverend Reynolds and his wife Rebecca would feel pressure to accept a dinner invitation at the Bryant's household once a year. He and his wife figured having dinner with Pat and Diane was the closest thing to hell within the community. Reynolds knew he would have to spend the entire evening listening to Bryant expound about his beliefs on a broad assortment of subjects. Rebecca got a reprieve by doing the dishes in the kitchen with the more pleasant Diane.

To Pat Bryant that annual dinner was the highlight of his year. He felt he was establishing a smoother street to heaven having the opportunity to sit down privately and talk with such a well-respected religious man as Reverend Reynolds. Bryant always liked that Reynolds didn't have much to say when the two of them talked while the ladies were chattering in the kitchen. If the minister didn't disagree with Bryant's thoughts and opinions, then Pat took it that he was on the right track for his eventual meeting with St. Peter.

It was an interesting perspective…one that would have astonished Reverend Reynolds who contemplated a career change every time he had to survive that annual dinner at the Bryant household. He considered it more a summons than an invitation.

As for Bryant, he was always concerned with finding an evening convenient for the minister and his wife. Those annual invitations had become very difficult to set up. Reverend Reynolds always had such a busy schedule.

Beyond his devout interest in his religion, Pat Bryant did have one other proclivity that one might think would make him more socially acceptable. He liked to play golf. He learned the game from a book and became one of the most mechanical swingers at a golf ball ever seen on the links. To play nine holes of golf with Pat Bryant was similar to waiting in a doctor's office with a sore throat sitting next to a coughing kid with an oblivious mother reading a six-month old *Redbook* magazine. It was tortuous.

Each golf swing to Bryant was like a work of art…and that meant the practice swings as well…all six of them before he hit the ball. Bryant at times might have heard comments about his own slow play, but disregarded them. He disapproved of rushing around the golf course. His belief was that if a person was going to participate in the game of golf, he…or she…should try to play the game correctly.

It was one Men's night event after Bryant's foursome completed nine holes in three hours with golf groups stacking up behind them that a special board meeting was called at the club to discuss how to approach Bryant about his ungodly slow play. He was actually destroying the fun of playing golf at the local club, but no one wanted to approach the irascible man about his deliberate play.

It was getting so people would call for tee times and ask specifically when Pat Bryant was going to play that day. If they couldn't tee off before him, they wouldn't play golf that day.

Two well-meaning board members finally visited Bryant at his office at the county building ostensibly just to have a cup of coffee. When the discussion eventually got around to their true purpose, Bryant stiffened up and reacted in his usual haughtily contemptible way. As far as he was concerned he did everything in life the way it was supposed to be done. He told them he was outraged they were asking him to do something in a manner he couldn't agree.

True to form, Bryant then stood up and informed the two golf club members that the conversation was over…that he had more important things to do. Furthermore, he stated, "Maybe some of you golfers would be wise to follow my approach on the golf course. What's the fun of rushing a round of golf?"

The two board members retreated in disbelief. They were astonished with Bryant's petulant, child-like behavior. They shared an uncomfortable laugh as they left the county building. One of them snickered, "If everyone played golf with the speed of Pat Bryant, there would be no golf."

The gist of the comment was how anyone could afford that amount of time away from their family and other responsibilities? What they didn't say to each other but were very much bothered was Bryant's hair-trigger temper. His flaming eyes and show of indignation revealed a very unstable man.

That office meeting nonetheless had some impact. The following Wednesday Men's day event was not blessed with Pat Bryant's attendance. The result was the return to an acceptable time to play nine holes for all golfers present that day. Those two club board members who faced up to Bryant had plenty of drinks brought to their table that evening from many very appreciative golfers.

There was a general feeling, however, that the result was too good to be true. Everyone knew Bryant was just stubborn enough to take on the entire membership over the issue of his slow play. Unfortunately for Bryant, his glacial pace on the golf course could never be accepted. No one would ever want to play golf with him.

And, sure enough, the next week there was Pat Bryant signing up to play another Men's day event. He showed no contriteness…if anything quite the opposite. He refused to talk with any of his fellow club members resulting in those players not wanting to play with him. As if expecting this response, Bryant had called ahead and insisted on a tee time at the height of the busy tee times, even if he had to play alone.

And, alone he played. Bryant in the height of men's day took almost three hours to play nine holes of golf. Golfers were up in arms playing behind him. Over quite a few beers that evening most of these members made a pact on how they would deal with this man who had become a thorn in the side of the entire local club membership.

What they decided to do set a new precedent in social behavior at a golf club. They simply ignored him. He was forced to play by himself. When out on the golf course, foursomes would be polite but they moved right past him as if he was bird watching and not playing golf. Some said a perfunctory 'Hello Pat'; most players did not. It was a type of conduct no member had ever seen being displayed on any golf course. But, Pat Bryant had to be dealt with in some way. This idea seemed appropriate and civilized and certainly would get their point across even to this very stubborn and unreasonable man.

On that next Wednesday Men's day, Bryant again played alone. As agreed, foursomes passed him while he took his interminable number of practice swings or stood motionless trying to decide what club to play. No intended disrespect was shown. Members continued their conversations as they walked by him as if he didn't exist.

At first Bryant showed anger. Getting no response, he played the rest of his nine holes in a dark funk. For the first time in his life, Pat Bryant was experiencing a collective group of people working publicly against him. They let him respond or behave any way he chose…and he could play as miserably slow as he pleased. All of it was disregarded as if he was a nonentity. He no longer was an albatross to the members trying to simply play a round of golf in a reasonable amount of time.

The following day, Bryant decided he'd really show his wrath. He cancelled his membership and demanded his full year's pre-paid dues returned. He found a check in the mail from the club for that full amount within days. From that point forward, he played no golf. Instead he found different interests. Fishing became his new resolve. The sport answered his needs much better than golf anyway. His time was his own. He could take as long as he wanted…and he could make it a family affair even if his kids and wife didn't particularly take to the pastime. It took one outing on a nameless, mosquito-infested farm pond for Diane and their kids to find other things to do on the weekends. From then on, Bryant fished alone.

As for Bryant's family, they were surprisingly normal. The kids were quiet, especially around the house. They weren't outstandingly intelligent, but they studied. As one might expect, there was pressure on the home front by their father for them to be honor roll students. The disapproving eye from their father for failing to get an 'A' was a fate each child dreaded. Bryant would not exactly ridicule the child, but he would show favoritism to the other children who earned better grades.

As a result the oldest child was always on the 'A' honor roll. That son took the easiest classes and invented new ways to cheat. The middle child, a girl, unfortunately had the worst features of both parents. She was neither popular nor pretty. Still, she studied hard and earned her good grades. She was known around the school for her perpetual frown. Teachers generally thought she was the saddest, most hard-working child they'd ever taught.

The third kid, another boy, was the rebel and the real problem child. He had some mental and social problems enough that classmates and teachers alike preferred to stay clear of this kid. His eyes too often showed rage. It seemed like just a matter of time before the powder keg would blow.

As each offspring finally left home in the late 1960's, all three were required to attend Mankato State University…less than thirty minutes from home. Bryant held the strange belief that this state school better known for training teachers was better than most of the top schools in the nation. People thought he was joking until he pulled out his own statistics to prove his point. The oldest boy and the middle daughter graduated and moved far away from New Ulm. The oldest decided to go to divinity school. The middle child became a teacher far north in Bemidji. She made it home for Christmas most years for two days. The youngest disregarded his acceptance at Mankato State University and signed up for the military the day after he graduated from high school without consulting either parent. He went to Ft. Bragg in North Carolina for basic training…and then literally lost contact with his family. He was stationed in Vietnam…and volunteered to remain every year when he could have returned stateside.

As far as Pat Bryant was concerned, once his kids left home, his job as their parent was done. Once the cost of college tuition, room and board, and books was completed, his offspring were on their own. His time was now invested in establishing himself as the best county surveyor in the state as well as involving himself even more in his church. With this highly competent, church-going image, Bryant considered himself a pillar in his community. To others he was an opinionated oaf who dominated conversations, and tolerated nothing that was not consistent with his beliefs.

So, that was the life Pat and Diane Bryant by the year 1970. All three kids were gone and showed little interest in even visiting back home. Bryant had no friends. The house was quiet. He still had his county surveyor work and his interest in fishing. And, he stayed active in his church. Diane kept busy with her day time work at the bank and then her evening church meetings, bridge clubs, and involvement with various civic organizations. She was gone most weekday evenings…and visited her mother on Saturdays or Sundays in Hutchinson. Bryant spent more and more time alone.

It was in that twenty-sixth year as a county worker, nineteen as a county surveyor, that some things began to happen that caused more unsettling times in the life of Pat Bryant. No one including his wife was close enough to the man to notice the changes.

In retrospect, Diane, when asked many years later, acknowledged that she should have taken more notice of his frustrations, especially after the new Presbyterian minister moved into town to replace the retiring Reverend George Reynolds. This new pastor, from Kansas, was going to be the fourth minister at the First Presbyterian Church in New Ulm since Pat and Diane were married. Being a long time elder in the church, Bryant had gotten to know all three ministers, but Reverend Reynolds most of all. He sincerely felt he had a close relationship and a notable influence with the longer termed Reynolds. That view had never been shared by the retiring minister.

The man of the cloth replacing George Reynolds was a much younger man. Bryant was not pleased this man had been chosen by a committee in the church. In Bryant's mind, the new reverend was too inexperienced to handle the job. Bryant felt a sense of weariness thinking about the time it would take him to help break in this questionable choice as the new leader of his church.

The supposedly verdant minister's name was Pastor Robert Sommerville. The previous three ministers all went by 'Reverend'. Robert Sommerville was only twenty-nine and wished to be called by the parishioners 'Pastor Bob'.

That preference didn't fit with Pat Bryant's belief system. Now approaching the age of fifty, he was as set in his ways as a marble statute. Bryant was head of the 'Elders' of the church and ran that group as if he were anointed to do so. One thing Reverend Reynolds was able to do before retiring, though, was establish a search committee for a new minister not including Pat Bryant.

In fact, Bryant had been waiting around to be named head of that search committee. When that expectation never materialized, he was supremely surprised and dumbfounded. When he approached the out-going Reverend Reynolds about the obvious oversight, Reynolds simply said that God had willed it that way, especially given Bryant's busy schedule as a surveyor. While entirely untrue, the deceptive response at least helped Reynolds have a relatively peaceful last few months of his tenure.

Bryant, though, was deeply hurt. No question those damaged feelings contributed to Bryant's ill-feeling toward the committee's final choice. Still, initially when Bryant heard some of the congregation on the committee touting the abilities and skills of the young minister, Bryant was ready to give the new pastor some slack.

He even accepted there could be some new ideas for the church. Bryant thought himself to be open-minded as long as Pastor Sommerville's changes were not too inventive and did not run contrary to Bryant's comfort in how the church and the services should be run.

The disagreements between Bryant and the new minister unfortunately happened almost immediately. In the first week on the job Pastor Sommerville stirred the pot too fast as far as Bryant was concerned. Sommerville's family was due to arrive from Kansas during the second week. Pastor Bob let it be known that his wife worked in real estate back home and she was looking forward to getting re-established in New Ulm. He further intimated how he and his wife were looking forward to serving the large congregation as well as updating the interior of the forty-year old manse.

The mention of his wife being a realtor caused a few wide eyes but none wider than Pat Bryant's eyes. He almost choked thinking that the wife of the new minister 'worked outside the home'! What kind of example would that set for the congregation? As far as Bryant was concerned, a minister's wife was supposed to be home raising any kids, maintaining the value system of a wife supporting her husband, and generally showing deference to the church and congregation. At least that was the way he interpreted what the church's doctrine said about minister's wives. No one ever asked Bryant from what 'book' he'd taken that excerpt.

It took Bryant six days from the time the Pastor Bob began his job at the church for a meeting to be scheduled. Bryant felt obliged to let the man get somewhat settled before he brought the young minister and his wife up to date with some of the hard and fast rules of their local church. Things were simply done differently and more correctly in New Ulm… than apparently what had been done at the Presbyterian churches in Kansas. Bryant felt that once he could put Pastor Bob on the straight and narrow, he was certain Sommerville would come around and see the light.

It was 4:00 on a Tuesday when Bryant strolled down to the church just a few blocks away. It was so conveniently located. The minister could walk up the street to Bryant's own office in the county building whenever a question had to be resolved.

Pastor Bob was busily getting his office set up when Pat arrived. He had some notes strewn on his desk likely getting ready for his first sermon the coming Sunday. It was a pleasure to see the young minister getting into the swing of things.

"Afternoon, Reverend," Bryant matter-of-factly said in greeting, "I'm Patrick Bryant."

Sommerville turned around and at first didn't recognize his visitor. That bothered Bryant initially. The two of them had met briefly two Sundays before when the new minister and his wife had met the congregation for the first time at an after-church social. Bryant figured Reverend Sommerville just hadn't realized one of the busiest, most important men in the church had just come into the church office.

Sommerville hesitated and finally smiled saying, "Ah….Mr.….Bryant. I'm sorry, I'm still getting used to names."

Bryant put a plastic grin on his face showing neither forgiveness nor irritation. That expression always seemed to intimidate so many people. He loved being daunting.

It was bothersome, however, that his look didn't seem to have any impact on the young man of the cloth. The pastor kept pulling things out of some boxes while pointing to a chair for Bryant to sit down.

Then Sommerville tried to correct something the head of the 'Elders' had just said. Politely looking at Bryant, he stated, "Please Mr. Bryant, call me "Bob…. Pastor Bob…or Pastor Sommerville…whichever you are more comfortable with. That's what I would prefer."

Bryant wasn't comfortable with any of the choices. 'His' minister was supposed to be referred to as 'Reverend'. This indicator was the most respectful and classic moniker with which a minister could be referred as far as Bryant was concerned. The thought suddenly dawned on him that maybe this young gentleman hadn't yet reached the point where he had earned the right to be called 'Reverend'. Maybe he should be called 'Pastor'…a reference to a minister Pat had rarely heard and therefore on a lower scale.

Bryant held that thought as he explained his purpose for stopping by the office.

"Yes…well…I just thought I'd stop by so we could get to know one another since I am the chairman of the 'Elders' in this church."

Pastor Bob suddenly laughed out loud. "Oh yes, of course. What is wrong with me! Pat…if I can be so bold…thank you for coming in to say 'hello'. I know we've shaken hands once before, but I've just met so many wonderful people in the congregation. They've all been very kind. Yes…it's good that we get a chance to converse."

Bryant showed his toothy, patient, but insincere grin. "No…we haven't had a chance to talk…and it's probably overdue."

Sommerville, saying nothing more, returned the grin. He'd heard about Mr. Pat Bryant from other parishioners on the committee. All the comments had not been complimentary…not one. They kept referring to Bryant as a church member who had expected to be part of the search committee. Because of his myopic, domineering style, he had not been asked. They all knew he would be looking for an older, conservative minister who kept things simple in his sermons, didn't say or do anything controversial, and above all wouldn't make too many changes.

Sommerville had been looking forward to meeting Bryant. In fact, he was going to give the man a call sometime that week. Unfortunately, Bryant just showing up at his office couldn't have come at a worst possible time. The pastor's wife and two young children were due in town within the hour. Sommerville wanted to be at the house to greet them.

Before Bryant got warmed up, the minister quickly forewarned him of the situation. "Mr. Bryant, I would love to talk with you now, but my wife and kids will be here shortly. Could we possibly rain check our conversation until tomorrow when I have more time?"

It was a matter of fact statement that should not have created the response Bryant was to give him. Bryant thought the statement was condescending and failed to show proper respect. After all, he was the leader of the 'Elders'. How could this brash young minister not put aside everything to talk to one of the top parishioners in his new church?

Bryant spoke curtly, "Well, 'Reverend' Sommerville, you can put off talking to me for as long as you want, but at some point you're going to have to understand how we run this church…and you'll need support from individuals in my position within this church."

Sommerville could not believe what he had just heard. Here was a man who had become so entranced with his self-importance he was practically expecting the new minister to bow before him. Sommerville had been selected by a very capable church committee. He had a master's degree in Divinity, but his degree and work experience for five years in Kansas obviously meant nothing to the supercilious Pat Bryant. The pastor fought standing up to the arrogant man. However, being a patient man, the minister made another attempt to mollify the situation. It might take less time to let Bryant say his peace and then leave.

"I'm sorry Mr. Bryant," he said, "I hoped you would understand my hurry since I haven't seen my family for a week. But, if now is an important time for you to talk with me, then they can wait. They've been to the house. They know where it's located. Let's talk right now."

Bryant felt better that he'd made his point. Still, he didn't like the way Sommerville took charge of the minor disagreement. Also, Sommerville hadn't apologized for his impudent remark about not having time to talk to Bryant. And as far as Bryant was concerned, this over-confident, advanced degreed minister was not going to control this church or any conversation with the head of the 'Elders'.

At that moment, Bryant decided he simply didn't like the new minister. Sommerville was too smooth. He was too self-assured. It infuriated Bryant. Yes, they would have a conversation, but it would be the minister doing the listening. If 'Pastor Bob' was pressed for time, it was too damned bad. Bryant was determined to tell this unqualified parson some of the ground rules. It would save everyone in the congregation including Sommerville a lot of time if he did things according to the old ways.

Bryant went at the pastor with an anger that bordered on a jealous rage. Sardonically he began. "Well, Rev..er..end, first of all, you should never have been put in this situation as a church leader for such an important congregation as this one in New Ulm. Maybe in another ten years you'd have the depth and background to handle such a responsibility. You'll see we have ways that we prefer in how we do our services, in how you characterize our church in this community, in what beliefs you portray in your sermons, and how your family is expected to represent our church as well. On that last point, maybe your wife had a business in Kansas, but she will be too busy being the minister's wife in our town."

Sommerville was speechless. He wished he could have this monologue recorded. He was listening to a man so far gone with his own importance, he was out of control. No wonder Bryant had become such a disliked person within the church. Listening to this worthless diatribe, would be something he'd never forget....nor did he hope he'd ever have to experience again. For this one instance, Sommerville didn't mind having his family wait a few extra minutes while he evaluated such maniacal behavior. It was something he was going to have to deal with as long as Bryant was a member of the church.

With every word out of Bryant's mouth, the pastor lost respect for this supposed leader of the 'Elders'. In fact he began to feel sorry for the man. Over the next few minutes, Sommerville wasn't listening to the wrathful words as he was trying to find a place he could interrupt.

Finally, Bryant paused for a breath and Sommerville leaped at the momentary quiet. "Mr. Bryant!" The name echoed in the room startling them both.

Lowering his voice, the pastor stated, "Mr. Bryant, I appreciate your views and I want to appease your fears. I'm certain this church will be ministered in the exceptional way you have been used to seeing it done by Reverend Reynolds. We have no disagreement in that regard at all."

Bryant flashed a self-satisfying grin thinking he was finally getting through to the unproven man of the cloth. His own voice was now much softer, almost avuncular, as he said, "Yes, as long as a young new minister like yourself will seek advice from people in the know at this church, your stay here can be very educational."

Sommerville sat there staring at Bryant in further disbelief while thinking, 'This guy is amazing. He is putting himself in the position of being a trainer.'

Bryant had no idea that Sommerville had been the first assistant minister at a church in Kansas twice the size of the church in New Ulm. The opportunity at New Ulm was to take charge of a still sizable church which would continue to round out his career as he moved up within the church organization. He was looking to stay in New Ulm for three or four years before he would move on. Of course, he didn't say that to the search committee. Even a Presbyterian minister can be politic.

Bryant continued, "Regarding your sermons, I can take time to go over some of the text to make certain you're getting the general ideas that our church professes. We wouldn't want to get any parishioners upset with any inconsistencies."

Sommerville couldn't help himself, "Inconsistencies, Mr. Bryant? Please give me an example."

Bryant knew he had gotten a bit over his head, but trudged on nonetheless. After all he had a son only a few years younger than this new minister. He rambled, "Well, we just want you to follow the intent of the verses and not put too radical of an interpretation on any of the words from the Bible."

Trying to keep his jaw from dropping, Sommerville simply nodded. "Please go on, Mr. Bryant, I'm finding what you have to say very revealing."

Bryant straightened up. He hadn't expected the parson to say 'revealing'. He'd expected him to say something more appreciative, like 'informative' or 'interesting' or 'enlightening'. Bryant stopped for a moment and asked, "Reverend, do you find what I have to say to be of any problem?"

Sommerville had his opening but chose not to light the fuse. It was just a question of time before this 'oaf' would eventually trip over his own tongue...as if he hadn't already done so. Somewhat icily, he gazed at his watch and replied, "No, Mr. Bryant...now is there anything else?"

Bryant thought for a moment whether to proceed with his "training' tips, but decided to stop. He'd made his point in their first meeting. There would be plenty of these conversations in the coming months.

Looking at his own watch, he replied, "No, Reverend, I believe that's all I have to say for now. I'll drop by later in the week if you'd like me to hear parts of your sermon before Sunday."

Flabbergasted, Sommerville only smiled. "No, Mr. Bryant, this sermon will be more of a greeting to the congregation, a chance for me to go over my background, and establish some of the new ideas...rather some of the minor changes... that might go on with me as the new 'Pastor'.

Bryant was ready to respond again to that word 'Pastor' but decided he'd wait until the next impromptu meeting to cover that subject.

They both stood up eyeing each other. Sommerville maintained a pleasant expression despite being astounded by Bryant's audacity and condescension. For an instance, the new minister wished he was still in Kansas.

Bryant gave Sommerville a hearty handshake exhibiting a confident sense that he'd scored some major points with the supposed new head of his church. Bryant was aware some things took time...as in raising children. That didn't happen in a day either.

The two men didn't see each other personally until the end of the following week. Not having been called for any assistance by the new reverend, Bryant felt compelled to stride over to the church to share some more of his thoughts with the untested minister.

Upon arrival, Sommerville was conversing with the church organist. Ms. Esther Goldhorn looked a bit subdued as she was hearing the musical selections Sommerville wanted for the upcoming services. She looked bothered...another indicator to Bryant why it was so important that he stay close and smooth out the difficulties caused by the new man.

Sitting in the front pew, he sat close enough so both the organist and Sommerville would see him, therefore being available to be brought into the discussion at any moment. By the furrows on his forehead, the minister hadn't expected the diffident organist to have so many problems with the few additional musical adaptations. He showed determined patience until she finally agreed to try the new music arrangement. When she acquiesced, Sommerville bared some audible relief. He was only human. Desperately he was trying to reign in his own irritability as he faced introducing some minor changes for his new congregation.

Seeing Bryant out of the corner of his eye, he knew he'd then have to deal with yet another predictably grim conversation with the haughty elder. Sommerville's voice could have been less stressed, but it wasn't. His tone was exasperated. "Yes, Mr. Bryant is there something I can help you with? As you can see, Miss Goldhorn and I were having a little meeting about the church music this Sunday. Could you and I meet later?"

Bryant again didn't like the attitude of the upstart minister. Gritting his teeth, he said, "Well, Reverend, I thought I might be able to help you…and maybe go over some of the ways we usually conduct our services including the music."

Sommerville took a deep breath and barely patient replied, "No, Mr. Bryant, we have the service well laid out. I believe you'll enjoy both the service and the music and I look forward to seeing you and your wife seated in one of the front pews this Sunday. Now, I really must finish this meeting with our organist."

Then he turned his attention again to Miss Goldhorn whose eyes were as large as wheel covers. She'd never seen Pat Bryant put in his place.

As for Bryant, he was apoplectic in silent fury. Not only was he summarily demeaned but he knew the church organist would spread word throughout the congregation that Pastor Sommerville had derailed a leading member of the congregation.

Spitting mad, Bryant marched the ten minutes back to his office with a black cloud over his head on an otherwise quite sunny day. During that walk, he'd made the decision to resign not only his flaunted position in the church, but take his church membership to another church that might appreciate his elevated experience and position.

Furiously whispering to himself, Bryant hissed, "No, 'Reverend Robert Sommerville', you will not see Patrick Bryant and his wife in the pew on Sunday. In fact, you'll never see the Bryant's darken the doors of your church ever again. I'm going to let you sink in your new job."

That night Bryant told his wife of the incredible disrespect the new minister had shown him. He growled, "I believe we need to be seeking a new church…one where we'll be appreciated." I think we should go over to St. Peter, Sleepy Eye, or even head towards Mankato to find a more appropriate church."

Diane Bryant knew her husband well. When he was in this kind of mood… and he seemed to be in this type of mood more and more recently…she just let him blow off steam and cool down. She remained silent…only concentrating on her knitting and some television quiz show in the background on the kitchen TV.

Unfortunately, Bryant was not capable of cooling down. He got in his car and for the next few hours just drove around the town. He felt lost. He felt disrespected. He felt old. He drove by his church a number of times and then by the parsonage three times in a half hour. On one trip he actually saw Robert Sommerville's wife and young children doing some work or playing outside their new home as the pastor himself was enjoying being with his family once again. It was a loving scene. Whether a minister or not, Sommerville had true unconditional feelings for his wife and kids. Bryant watched as the man hugged his children and then kissed his wife…way too long. Bryant had to actually look away. He wasn't used to seeing that kind of affection…and he wasn't certain he approved of it being shown so publicly.

Bryant drove from that scene with a new emotion he'd never felt. It was an extreme sadness that now combined with a loneliness that had become part of his existence in recent years. He felt envy. He couldn't remember kissing his wife that way. He could not recall his kids being overjoyed to see him…ever! His eldest son and daughter only made it back to their home once a year. Bryant wondered if his youngest boy would ever make it back to New Ulm.

Pat Bryant arrived home to an empty house that Friday night. He felt no energy. His wife had already prepared the same Friday night meal for him to heat up. Friday's was one of her bridge nights. The meal was roast beef, baked potatoes, string beans 'night'…just like always. He didn't understand why he felt so disappointed. There was nothing about the meal that should make him feel that way.

Bryant was asleep in front of the television when she got home around 10:30. Diane walked by him and asked how his day went…just like always. She only wanted to check if he'd returned to normal…at least to his 'normal'…before she went to bed.

She asked, "Do you want something else to eat?"

His voice was tired sounding but calmer as he gave her a one word response. "No." She then went to bed.

Bryant stayed in the family room and slept that night on the sofa acquired from an uncle in Litchfield who'd passed on fifteen years before. Bryant had built that extra space between the house and the garage sixteen years before by himself. Neither of his sons had helped. In his mind they weren't skilled enough.

He closed his eyes fitfully and soon fell into a non-restful sleep. He dreamed of the times in his youth when things were so much easier…how he went fishing whenever he desired…of those hikes along the Minnesota River, of hunting, and of being hungry to make money and getting ahead. He wondered why things seemed so difficult now.

That night he would periodically jerk awake wondering if he was still alive. It would take him a few seconds to discover that he was. Then those sad, lonely thoughts would reappear in his mind. He pondered whether there was anything else left in his future. Had he reached his pinnacle and now his ideas, the regard other people had for him, the love of his wife and children…was all that now in his past, if indeed those feelings had ever existed. He thought about the conflicts he was now more often having with people. Why didn't people respond to him like they reacted to other citizens in the community? Everyone seemed so irritated when in conversation with him…like they wished to get away from him. Further, why did he not have the kinds of friends others seemed to have? At the coffee shop in the morning or at noon, people would only nod a greeting and then move on very fast. Why was that?

Then he considered the real question. Who were his friends? He couldn't name a one.

Bryant slept fitfully in the family room until 5:00 AM. Then he awoke not able to sleep anymore. The horizon was beginning to show. He wanted to do something different…something he hadn't done in a long time. He sat up thinking what that activity could be. Like a flash, he thought about playing golf. That was it. It had been a long time. He now wanted to play golf. At that hour no one would be on the golf course, so he could play alone and at his own pace. It had been two years since he played the game.

He found himself kind of excited. Grabbing his dusty golf clubs in the garage, he threw them in the trunk and headed for the local municipal golf course. He was no longer a member, but at that early hour, who would mind.

Arriving, he headed for the first tee. His golf bag smelled musty, but the early morning air was crisp and invigorating. Bryant found himself enjoying the solitude.

Barely light enough to follow the flight of the golf ball, he took time to loosen up. Taking practice swing after practice swing, he was pleased how the memory of how he was supposed to swing had not left him. He must have made a hundred practice swings before he got a golf ball out of his bag.

When he finally teed off, it was ten minutes later. There was no one else including the greenskeeper at the golf club. He hit one ball…and only one ball. That was the way the game was to be played. He strolled down the short grass of the fairway kicking up dew as he strolled along. He didn't realize how much he missed playing the game. Beyond the shot making, being out on the golf course gave him a chance to take some fresh breathes of air, get some exercise, and test whether he could hit a good shot. Not once had he ever thought about the game being a way of making friends and meeting people.

Bryant's first shot had traveled almost one hundred yards…not far, but he'd made contact. As he took a ridiculous number of practice swings before swinging his seven- iron for the second shot, he heard the sound of someone else on the golf course. He looked over at the next tee box. There was a young man perhaps a hundred yards away hitting ball after ball at the par-3 second green.

Bryant was disappointed. He hoped to be alone at that early hour. Trying not to pay attention to the kid, he dubbed his second shot about forty yards leaving eighty yard remaining to the first green. As Bryant ambled toward his third shot, he glanced over at the golfer on the second tee-box. He was a young man likely in college or in the last year of high school. He was hitting shots like a machine… swoosh….swoosh…each ball taking off on a consistent arc toward his target. His swing looked youthful…so pure.

Bryant looked at his eighty yard shot and guessed the golf club that might go that distance if he hit the ball reasonably square. Choosing a seven-iron, this time he didn't take as many practice swings with that kid possibly watching him.

Finally hitting the shot, Bryant's ball sailed low hitting against a hill in front of the green. The ball bounced up in the air having much of its forward progress stunted by that small hill. Miraculously, the ball bounded onto the green and settled about twenty feet from the cup.

Marching more confidently toward the green, he hoped the kid had seen his shot. Bryant hadn't played golf for two years and he now had a par putt on the very first hole. He glanced back at the young man. The kid gave no indication that Bryant even existed. He continued just hitting shot after shot toward the second green... concentrating on his own effort....swing after swing...good hit after good hit.

Something inside Bryant suddenly made him discontented and disapproving. Bryant didn't like that the kid was digging up the next tee box with his constant practice shots. Worse yet, the teen-ager's practice shots were putting ball marks on those shots that hit the green on the fly.

Bryant's eyes narrowed knowing it would be his duty to let the young golfer understand the damage he was imparting on the tee box and the green. He was now more interested in hollering at the kid than finishing his par putt. Nonetheless, he invested the next five minutes concentrating on his putting stroke without hitting the ball. Other people might take some practice strokes and then just putted. Not Pat Bryant. It was not his way.

He studied the slope of the green for a few more minutes before finally addressing the putt. Finally he stroked it. It felt good coming off the club face. At least the ball was heading toward the cup. It was going way too hard, kicking up moisture from the dew as it sped for the flag he'd left in the cup. He winced remembering that he should have removed the flag stick. The ball slammed against the flag and just stopped dead on the edge of the cup. The result gave Bryant a momentary thrill...almost making a par on the very first hole he'd played in two years.

As he walked toward the lucky fourth shot...will wonders never cease... the ball actually fell into the cup! He had parred the hole after all! He broke out into a smile. It dawned on him he hadn't legitimately smiled or been happy for months...maybe longer. The fact was he really couldn't remember the last time. Life had just become so hard.

He took his ball out of the cup and energetically sauntered over to retrieve his golf bag. Filling his lungs with the morning air, he allowed his chest to protrude. He kept thinking, 'a par...after two years!' Marching toward the second tee box where the kid was still hitting practice shots, he thought again how his life had become so difficult. His decisions were being questioned on his job. That had never happened before. Was he no longer respected despite working the most hours of anyone employed in Brown County? Also, his work at the church was no longer appreciated. It still bothered him not having been chosen for the selection committee. And now look what the church got…a neophyte minister!

As Bryant got closer to the second tee box, the joy from parring the first hole had already disappeared. All the negative things going on in his life had taken over his thoughts once again. He looked up and the teen-ager was still hitting practice balls, not noticing another golfer approaching the tee off. Each shot the young man hit took turf from the ground. Each shot hitting the green left a pot mark that would have to be fixed.

The kid was in his own world. He seemed startled when Bryant approached the tee box saying coldly, "You mind if I go through?" He meant for his statement to come out sarcastic, but the kid didn't take it that way. He simply nodded and moved aside sitting on a bench beside the tee box. He was going to let Bryant hit and wait for him to complete the second hole before continuing his practice. It was proper golf etiquette even at 5:30 in the morning.

Still, Bryant didn't like the young kid's silence. It was not respectful enough. Bryant teed his ball up and began his pre-hitting routine of countless practice swings. Then he addressed the golf ball with a five-iron before stepping away. He stood there practically frozen in time thinking of all the things he needed to think about in order to make the perfect golf swing. In the middle of yet another practice swing, the kid let go with a slight cough…and then a sigh. Bryant tried to disregard the interruption, but his concentration had been ruined. Annoyed, he stepped away from his golf ball.

Again an interminable amount of time went by before Bryant was ready to take his backswing. The kid cleared his throat and sighed again.

This was too much for Bryant. He stopped, turned around toward the young man and barked, "Son, I'll be out of your way in a jiffy. Just please be quiet and let me hit my shot."

The kid didn't say a word. He just sat quietly. Bryant got ready to hit his shot. Again dozens of kids had been born in the Western Hemisphere before Pat finally took the club back and swung through his shot. The club actually made decent contact with the ball. The ball sailed toward the green. Pat was momentarily thrilled until the ball tailed off and caught the side of a hill and then careened into a sand trap some thirty yards from the green.

Bryant went from satisfaction to grumpiness in that second. He was certain his shot would have been better if the kid hadn't bothered him. He then remembered how he wanted to reprimand the young man for tearing up the tee box as well as the green with his shotmaking.

Retrieving his golf bag, Bryant snapped at the kid. "You know you're taking a lot of turf with each shot you hit. I'm sure you haven't thought about repairing the damage you're causing."

Bryant felt resurrected putting someone in their place, even if it was a young lad.

The feeling lasted only for seconds as the young man suddenly looked up showing no regard for Bryant's attempt at scolding him. Instead, the kid shrugged and responded, "And you sir are doing the same thing with the hundred practice swings you took before you finally struck you ball?"

Bryant was dazed by the response…another young teenager mouthing back at him showing no respect. He retaliated, "What about the holes on the green, son? Who's going to fix those marks on the green your golf shots have caused?"

The kid rolled his eyes and answered impatiently, "Me…of course. Why are you so concerned? You talk as if you're the only one who can think."

Bryant didn't like the answer. He kept at the boy saying, "So, I intend to report you to the golf shop. You shouldn't be hitting ball after ball at that green destroying both the tee box and the green."

The boy stood up looking a bit taller and even more confident. "Mister, do you start every day this grumpy? What gives you the right to yell at me for something that shouldn't concern you? I told you I would fix the green. In fact, I'd fix the green whether I hit balls onto it or not. I work out here. This is the only time I get to practice. I have been assigned to re-sod this tee box later this morning anyway. This is my quiet time. Why are you so determined to spoil my morning? Did God put you on this earth to make people miserable?"

Bryant was enraged with the glib response by the teen-ager. But, the kid wasn't done. "Besides, what gives you the right to talk with anyone out here or to get angry with me? You're not even a member of this club. I know most of the members and you're not one of them."

Bryant hated that the young man was correct. He was getting shown up. His anger was at the boiling point. Most people would shudder when Bryant was getting this furious. But the kid just stood there with golf club in hand giving him the most insolent look a teen-ager would ever have the guts to display to an adult.

Bryant was able to somehow rationalize the kid was nothing but an ill-mannered, impertinent little bastard. Bryant puffed his chest to his fullest and roared, "Well, first of all, young man, you should not be talking to your elders so disrespectfully. I asked you a simple question and you're reacting like a true snot-nosed kid. Your parents would be very displeased with your rude behavior."

The sound of his voice echoed in the morning air. Bryant was pleased with his angered and superior sounding retort.

Undaunted, the young golfer showed no signs of backing down…especially knowing he was mostly in the right. His voice was fearless. "First of all, mister, I'm a very respectful young man. I'm a good student. I'm a class officer. I'm leader of my youth church group. I plan on graduating in the top ten of my high school class. If you ask people at this club, I'm one of the nicest, most hard-working, and most cooperative kids they know. You are so far off base with your wild accusations that I know there has to be something seriously wrong with you. I believe you just got mad at me because you're either jealous that you're no longer my age…or you think you have the right to yell at people whenever you feel like it. Either way I feel sorry for you. I'll always remember you as an example of someone I'll never want to be."

Bryant was stunned once again. Bryant's belligerent comments and attitude were well-practiced. This young kid was ad-libbing his statements…and the comments cut deep.

He could tell his face was getting red and he was about to explode when he felt a twinge in his arm. He'd never felt such a pain. It caused him to lose his concentration if not his anger. Taking a deep breath, Bryant tried to keep the disdainful look on his face and the hardened tone in his speech pattern, but he knew he was wilting. It was as if he couldn't catch his breath. He'd just had something happen that had never happened before. He'd met his match in verbal conflict…and he'd been beaten by a kid!

Bryant couldn't let himself admit defeat even if he didn't feel so well. He indignantly scarfed, "Son, you've got a smart mouth……"

Again the young man interrupted him. "Mister, don't ever call me 'son' again. I would better be in hell than to be your 'son'. And as for having a 'smart mouth', let me just say that in the mood you're in, I could say 'Good Morning' and you'd take it the wrong way. I'm no more a smart aleck than you are friendly. I don't see your type very often, but you obviously are a very unhappy person. Again, I feel sorry for you."

The kid walked coolly over to his golf bag and looked back. "Now, mister, before we come to blows on this beautiful Saturday morning, I'm going to go retrieve my golf balls and get to work. If you leave now, I promise not to report you as playing on this golf course without a membership."

Then he paused for only two more seconds before adding, "I hope I never meet you or someone like you again. Good day!"

The young golfer then headed toward the second green to collect his golf balls and repair the green. He looked neither pleased with himself nor bothered.

For one of the few times in his life, Bryant was speechless. He picked up his clubs and simply walked back to the golf club parking lot leaving his ball out on the golf course. A broad range of thoughts were flowing through his mind. The boy had said so many things that were despicably mean and disrespectful…and uncomfortably truthful. Bryant felt as miserable as he'd ever felt in his life. And, for the first time he was seriously questioning himself…something he'd never experienced.

He then drove downtown to the café for an early morning breakfast. He didn't feel hungry, only annoyed and lost. He couldn't remember the last time he'd had breakfast at the restaurant on a Saturday. He was usually there only on the weekdays.

As he entered, it seemed like the atmosphere in the café got suddenly quieter. Only a couple crying kids with their parents were oblivious to his presence.

Bryant ordered a cup of coffee from a wide-eyed waitress he'd never seen before. He figured she was on the weekend shift. He paid for the coffee-to-go. The cashier said, "Thank you, sir." Her eyes hesitated looking at him, not as if she was scared of him, but more that she hoped he would just leave the café.

He wondered why she was displaying such nervousness as she turned away and serviced another customer.

Instead of leaving like he typically did during the week, Bryant decided to take his coffee over to a booth and rest for a moment. A *Minneapolis Tribune* was available on the bar. None of the café staff realized he had remained. Facing away from the cashier, he was virtually unseen as he sat in the corner of the small restaurant.

It was then the proprietor, Mabel Burgess, came out from the kitchen. Her voice was low as she whispered to the waitress, "Wendy, you know who that old fart was, don't you?"

Bryant's ears stretched as the café owner continued. "That was Pat 'my way or no way' Bryant. He's the most disliked man in town. When he comes in here, you're just better off to smile and don't say a word. He's always finding something wrong with the food or the way we do things at this café. I swear we can't even pour coffee properly according to him. We've learned to just smile and not respond to him. I've never seen him without that scowl on his face. I don't know how his wife puts up with him."

Bryant sat in the booth feeling beads of sweat dripping down his face. While he wanted to be angry, he was instead filled with self-doubt. The revelation that he was barely being tolerated by so many citizens in the community had never occurred to him.

He waited five minutes and then retreated out of the café after Mabel had gone back to the kitchen. As he trudged by the waitress who'd gotten him the coffee, he didn't look at her, but he could tell her eyes were bugging out. She was mortified that he may have heard her boss' comments about him.

In a stupor Bryant drove home. Diane was already gone. She volunteered at the Saturday morning Farmer's Market in Mankato. She wouldn't be back until early afternoon when she was then scheduled to work with friends at the church to prepare for the next day's welcome dinner for the new minister and his family. That evening she would bring home some chicken from a local franchise. That was their typical meal on any Saturday evening. He'd eat chicken in front of the television while she either talked on the telephone with friends or caught up on some housework. That had been their routine for as long as he could remember.

Bryant sat in his car in his driveway that Saturday morning for an hour. He wondered if his wife knew the reputation he carried around town. With no place to go and nothing planned for the day, he felt the most despondent he'd ever felt in his life. He thought about his kids. He had always wondered why once they left New Ulm they rarely came home. Now he had a clue. Even the previous Christmas, his oldest son said he had to get back to the Twin Cities by Christmas night because he had to work in the morning. His daughter stayed an extra day and went shopping in Mankato with Diane before returning to Bemidji. Her job at the school wasn't going to start for another week. As for his youngest son, the family hadn't heard from him in months…and then it was only a birthday card for Diane.

Bryant's mind then shifted over to his wife and how she had changed over the years…and maybe why she had changed. She was at least fifty pounds over the weight she was when they got married. Most of it was in her hips and legs. She now waddled…moving around like she was twenty years older than she actually was. Bryant had always reconciled that it was because of her particular type of job at the bank. Yet, the ladies working with Diane weighed much less and were more physically fit. If anything, they set a worthy example for good habits. Strangely, his wife no longer seemed to have the motivation to control her eating or show any interest in physical activity.

With the sun shining brightly that Saturday morning, Bryant tried to push the horrible events of the morning out of his mind. He decided to do something he might enjoy. He decided to gather his fishing equipment and try his luck on the Minnesota River. Within minutes he was back in his car and driving toward the river. However, given his state of mind that day, the excursion turned out not to be pleasant. He couldn't relax. There were too many negative thoughts passing through his mind. At one point he succumbed to the tiredness he felt, laid back on the ground and eventually slept along the shoreline. When he later awoke, the worm was still on the hook as he pulled in his line.

It was close to suppertime when he arrived home. Sure enough, there was the usual chicken dinner placed on the counter for him by his wife. She left a note saying she'd be at the church until later in the evening. His response was to toss the note aside in disgust. Hadn't Diane been listening when he told her they should start looking for a new church? How long had she been giving him a deaf ear whenever he talked about something really important?

He sat by the television with his chicken dinner for a couple hours looking blankly at the screen. The movie held no interest. He found himself extraordinarily tired, despite his afternoon nap while fishing.

When Diane finally made it home that night, she left him sleeping in the easy chair and went right to bed. She had to rise early to prepare for the church breakfast. She was as regular of a volunteer for church meals as were the pots and pans required to make the food.

Bryant and his wife were both up early as usual on Sunday morning, July 12. When Bryant shuffled into the kitchen, she was humming something soft as she prepared breakfast. They said hardly two words to each other as Bryant read the paper.

He had slept on all his gloomy thoughts from Saturday. As a result he was under a darker cloud than normal. In her case she was already dressed for church. Bustling around the kitchen and ready to leave, she showed no interest in any further discussions about changing churches or any other malevolent statements her husband wanted to make that morning. She figured his anger would go away…as much as it could…and he'd likely be in attendance at church later that morning.

He was about to confront his wife, but seeing her so eager to leave, his heart wasn't into what most certainly would be an unpromising exchange. Bryant was more bothered by her distant behavior. He felt if there was one person who should be loyal to his wishes, it should be his own spouse. The way she was humming and all dressed up for the day, there would be no expression of loyalty that day for him.

Oblivious to his depressed condition, Diane began carrying some items out to the car needed for the church breakfast. She had no idea his state of mind was any different than any other time. She'd become matter-of-fact about their relationship years and years before. While he was a decent provider and handy around the house, she had accepted those would be the primary reasons for them to remain husband and wife. They had little in common anymore. She often wondered if they ever had. He didn't abuse her verbally or in any other way. She hadn't thought about the word 'love' for so long it hardly scratched the surface of her mind. Truth was she didn't expect much of their marriage anymore. They would always just exist together because it was a marriage of convenience.

Out of habit, Bryant couldn't help but voice some irritation. When she was about to leave, he said, "Diane, where are you going this morning? I thought we had decided we were going to change churches."

Diane treated his statement with a disregarding wave. "Patrick, that's ridiculous. I didn't take you seriously. I have responsibilities for the church breakfast and the dinner. I have to go. People are depending on me. If you don't want to go to church this morning, that will be your choice. Now, I just have to leave. Between the morning breakfast and the welcome dinner later today, I'll maybe be home this afternoon, but not for long. We'll begin working on this evening's dinner at the manse starting at 4:00. So, be sure to clean up. I'll look for you in the back of the church fifteen minutes before the service like always."

Then she split out the back door. Bryant had no opportunity to counter with even a slight comeback. It wasn't like him to not have some snappy comeback. His mind felt dulled.

Pat Bryant did not go to church that Sunday. He instead drove one hundred miles north to an out-of-way rural lake and fished most of the day. He didn't catch much. He didn't see many people. He wondered if he was even missed at the church. He surely hoped so.

He arrived back in New Ulm around 10:00 Sunday evening after again falling asleep while fishing and then had taken another nap in his car in a rest area on the way back home. He'd never felt so perpetually tired. He had no energy.

Bryant was already anticipating what his wife would say to him when he walked through the door of their home. She would voice her disappointment that he wasn't at church. He wondered if she'd ask what he'd been doing all day. He hoped she might mention some of the people at church who might have expressed concern for him not being in attendance at church that morning. Even if they didn't mean it, just hearing those words might make him feel better.

On his way home he drove by the church. It was dark accept for some lights shining on the greenery around the front of the building. It irritated him that there was such a waste of electricity. He drove a couple blocks away to where the parsonage was located. There were still some lights on in the house and some cars out front. The Sommerville's were still entertaining. Bryant stopped his car and saw Diane's vehicle in the driveway. From his car he glanced in the front window and saw some of the people he knew. There was general laughter and merriment. Bryant couldn't believe people would still be at a party on a Sunday night. What was the church becoming…a place of worship or a social club? He was repulsed.

He was about to hit the accelerator when he saw Diane walking by the front window. She was laughing with someone. She was lively. It wasn't the personality he saw at home. He wasn't used to seeing her that happy.

At that moment, something seemed to snap in his brain. He sped forward and drove back toward his house. While driving he felt that same sudden pain down his left arm that he'd felt the previous morning during that altercation with that kid at the golf course. It was a dull ache but at times quite sharp. Arriving home he parked on the driveway and made his way into the unwelcoming, dark house. The atmosphere was colder than normal even though it was quite humid. He saw a note on the counter. It was from Diane. It read simply:

Patrick:

I'm at the dinner for the Sommerville's. They are such a nice family. Be back later.

Diane

His arm now ached even more…and his chest felt tight. The note made him feel forlorn. Never had he felt so distant from his wife…to say as much for everyone else in town.

Walking through the house, no lights were needed. He went down halls and into rooms from memory. He wondered why he was even there. He had nothing to do and nowhere to go. The house was like a morgue. He didn't feel like being entombed there that night.

There had been a storm in New Ulm while he'd been away. With the weather system having moved out of the area, the evening had turned into a cool, but starlit night. Strangely, though, he found himself sweating. He went back outside expecting the lower temperature to cool him off. Instead he just kept perspiring.

Feeling exhausted, he decided that a drive with the windows open might be the answer. The breeze might end his profuse sweating. Bryant retraced his steps to his car. It was 10:20 that Sunday night when he got back in his Ford Fairlane. Driving a few blocks, he sensed he needed a more pronounced breeze. Taking a left on west U.S. Hwy. #14, he headed for the edge of town. The wind whistling through the window made him feel better, but he still had that sharp pain in his arm.

He left the New Ulm city limits shortly before 10:30. His left arm was stiff and his chest felt strangely tight. He had things to sort out in his mind. Nothing seemed to make sense. He just needed to relax.

Shaking his arm to rid it of the numbness, he drove towards Sleepy Eye only fifteen miles away. The air coming through his open driver's side window was meant to cool him, but it only provided noise. He couldn't tell if he was feeling better or not; he just had this strong sense of being so tired. Out on the highway, he couldn't understand why he was driving so fast. He wasn't alert enough to be moving fifteen miles an hour over the posted speed limit. He had to slow down. He looked in his rear view mirror. If a state patrol was on duty and spotted the speeding Fairlane, a ticket would be issued for sure. Curiously that concern didn't slow him down.

Driving past Sleepy Eye towards the small town of Springfield he noticed the contrast of the clear night skies against the village lights in the distance. The night was so tranquil. Again he felt his forehead. Despite the huge rush of air blowing in through the window, he continued to perspire as if was running instead of driving. The noise inside the car was so loud, he couldn't hear himself groaning.

Looking out across the open farmland, he noticed the stars practically touching the horizon. It was a beautiful sight. He hadn't appreciated the beauty of a starry night for a long time. He also noted the patchy fog along the ground left over from the recently passing thunderstorm.

When Bryant reached Springfield, it was 10:51. The dull pain in his chest persisted; his left arm was completely numb. He tried to shake it, but it was heavy and only caused him more discomfort. Nonetheless, he felt more satisfied driving on into the night than returning home. When he left Springfield he was but eight miles from Sanborn Corners. There was some more ground fog as he left the town. Still, the sky was as vivid as a space view of the Earth in a Life magazine montage.

A mile out of Springfield Bryant's chest tightened even more. He hadn't realized the moisture he felt on his lips was sweat dripping from his brow. He sped up hoping to increase the rushing air through the opened window which in turn might blow away the perspiration. He tried again to shake his left arm, but it was not moving. He then noticed his shirt was now soaked. That was the first time he had to admit something might be wrong. Looking ahead into the black night, he recalled there was a café just ahead at Sanborn Corners. He figured he might take a break and get a hamburger and a cup of coffee.

Now his chest was really hurting. It was only a couple minutes before 11:00. He pressed down on the accelerator. The faster he got to Sanborn Corners, the faster he could get some food. Off in the distance he thought he could see the lights. He just had to get something to eat.

The speedometer now read over eighty-five miles per hour. Despite his pain, he thought back to how long it had been since he'd pushed his old Ford to that speed.

The lights were getting closer. He just had to keep his foot hard on the gas pedal to get to that café. Sweat was now getting in his eyes. He looked around. Things were blurry. There seemed to be even more ground fog. The pressure in his arm was now moving to his head inducing a severe headache. He realized that his vision was now so cloudy that the lights ahead were no longer very clear. The sky above was no longer as vivid as it had been. He couldn't tell if the lights at Sanborn Corners were close or still miles away.

And then Pat Bryant began to get sleepy…really sleepy. His only thoughts were about food and a cup of coffee. He prayed the café would still be open. He pressed the accelerator down even harder.

At just past 10:58 PM Sunday night July 12, 1970, Patrick Bryant's Ford Fairlane was going over eighty-five miles per hour moving west on Hwy. #14. Bryant had never gone that fast in that car or any other vehicle since he was twenty years old. He was less than a mile and a half from Sanborn Corners.

So, the tale ends as these four people and their vehicles propel forward at a shockingly high rate of speed before colliding so coincidentally and tragically at Sanborn Corners precisely at 11:00 PM on that humid Sunday night in July. The vehicles were so thoroughly demolished there was barely enough shape remaining to any of the four cars. That ritual over the years of leaving a damaged car on one of the corners after another Sanborn Corners pile-up almost came to an end that night. The vehicles were almost unrecognizable. Finally, it was decided to leave one of the chassis with part of the trunk still connected to be displayed in front of one of the filling stations. The driver and passenger seats had been completely ripped from the main part of the automobile and the front engine had ended up in a ditch. The other cars fared little better.

Not to be forgotten, however, was the other ghoulish part of the story… the delay in naming the survivor among the four victims. This part of the saga had caused countless coffee shop and neighborhood chats around southwestern Minnesota all through Monday after the accident. The chilling and ghastly part of this story were those conversations judging who among the four most deserved to be the one fighting for his or her life at the Redwood Falls Municipal Hospital…as if merit or how one lived his or her life had anything to do with being the fortunate survivor.

When the survivor was finally announced, most folks would never divulge they'd made any hideous judgments about which of the victims would be the one who most earned the right to live. Those that did never felt any particular guilt for any statements they might have made favoring one victim over the other. Their feelings changed to mostly empathy and grief for the families of the three deceased victims.

So, the question can now be brought back to you. You may have been one of those citizens who disapproved of the unfavorable or slanderous information being bandied about regarding those unfortunate victims that Monday. In fact, you may have been sickened by that loose talk and superficial judgments being made by some of your friends and neighbors.

But now, as promised, you have a more truthful and authentic picture of the lives of these four victims right up to the day and second of that hideous multi-car accident. It should be noted the actual survivor was transferred two days later from Redwood Falls Municipal Hospital to a large Minneapolis medical facility for six weeks of recovery and rehabilitation…and that this one surviving victim was contrite when interviewed by a reporter from the *Minneapolis Tribune* one month after the tragedy. In the ensuing article, this survivor claimed to have gained a new perspective on life while recovering. Promises of respecting others, wanting to be closer to family members, taking better care of personal health, and holding down speed on the open highway became the well-publicized life plan for that survivor. Maybe you could sense which of those four drivers might have made those humble declarations in the newspaper article. Maybe not….as it could have been a statement by any of them.

So…who was the person interviewed? Who was the driver who stared death in the face and survived? Which one was able to awaken from the ferocity of that hideous crash scene and gain a renewed appreciation for the preciousness of life? Which one would live on and have the motivation to transform his or her life? Most importantly, which one would be more apt to sustain such a dramatic personality and life style alteration whether that person deserved a second chance at a better life or not?

Considering that group of four people…their past lives…and who met so suddenly, so literally, so violently, and so coincidentally that night at Sanborn Corners, the question really becomes…..irrelevant. Did it matter which one survived?

The Gas Lantern

It was early…way too early…when I was jolted awake by an intrusive rap at the front door of my rustic lakeside cabin. It was just as well. My dream was going nowhere. The knock at least provided a nice reminder that I was still alive considering the mistreatment I'd done to myself the night before. The prior evening had been a classic early summer get-together with friends and neighbors…any excuse for a party. Actually my neighbor had two good reasons to celebrate. He'd finally completed his new dock…and secondarily it was the first day of his fortieth year on the planet. I hoped he was in better shape. My head felt as if it was in a vice.

I usually controlled myself at neighborhood bashes, but Dean and Carla Rutherford's party had been especially hearty. There had been a generous assortment of rich food, desserts, good wine and ice cold beer. I had been in a more festive mood than usual and I witnessed many of my neighbors over-partying. So, it wasn't just me. A storm had come through during the evening so many party-goers had stayed longer thereby eating and drinking more than they would ordinarily. I didn't customarily drink to excess, but the more smoked salmon I ate, the more beer I drank. Unfortunately, I consumed a lot of smoked salmon.

Now lying like a corpse on the daybed in my sunroom, I was paying the price for over indulging. Not only was I miserable, but I was a bit disgusted. I hadn't even made it down the hallway to my bedroom at whatever late hour I finally arrived home. While I assumed I'd recuperate, I still laid there wondering when the recovery process might begin.

As for the knock on the door, that minor interruption was already fading from my mind. The loud gurgling in my stomach was drawing more of my attention. I lay there trying to establish some kind of purpose to that Saturday. I considered getting out of bed would be a worthwhile goal. Then I'd have to open my eyes and the room would likely be spinning. What followed could be very unpleasant, especially with the bathroom so far away. Even twenty feet seemed distant.

Still not having moved a muscle, I was able to think without too much pain. I tried to recall how I had made it home. That memory was dim. The journey between my neighbor's cottage and my lake home was only the distance of a short city block, but I couldn't remember whether I'd retraced my steps home along the lake shore or if I'd walked along the roadway…a slightly longer route.

The heavy rainstorm then came into view in my cluttered mind. I remembered the party had been forced to move inside the Rutherford home. The rain had come down in sheets causing a few neighbors to leave in order to check that their windows were closed and their homes were secure. Given that amount of rain, would I have trudged home along the lake shore? The sand and mud would have been slushy and difficult to walk upon. I did remember Dean Rutherford saying as I was leaving the festivities that the weather forecast for the weekend was intermittent thundershowers and probable tornado warnings.

Another bang at the front door shocked me again out of my aimless thoughts. I was being brought closer to consciousness but not there yet. My mind returned to the previous night. There'd been a cool, overhanging mist following the storm. That cued my sleepy mind to remember that I'd chosen the sandy and muddy shoreline itinerary back to my cottage for no other reason than it seemed closer. As incoherent as I'd been at the time, it was lucky I'd made it home at all. But, there was something that had aided me. I had to think for a moment. Yes….there was a slight glow of light in that murky air in the direction of my cabin….like a harbor light along the ocean. I felt my forehead crease over the odd spectacle. I hadn't left any lights on in my home before leaving for the party. Where had that light come from? Even weirder, when I finally arrived at my dock and hobbled up the steps to my cabin, there was no light. There was only a pitch black lake home. What had become of the light?

My eyes began to dance around under my eyelids as if that movement might massage my brain. Suddenly there was too much thinking going on. My head felt dizzy. Worse yet my lower extremities were bubbling like a geyser waiting to blow. That brought another less appetizing image of what had happened on my way home. I'd also left the remains of some of that rich food and excessive drink in the tall grass along the shoreline. Involuntarily my tongue moved inside my mouth…a very unfortunate action. The horrible taste in my mouth suddenly brought my eyes to full width. I was certain my breath was lethal. Finding a toothbrush immediately moved to the top of my 'to do' list for the day.

That mysterious light at my place inspired yet another recollection of the previous night. There was something I smelled as I dragged my sorry carcass up the steps to my deck. It was an odor of gas. It had been quite pungent. I'd even been concerned. It reminded me of the whiff of a recently used portable gas stove or maybe a gas lantern. The funny thing was I didn't own a gas lantern. Still, the aroma momentarily had sobered me up long enough to check out my gas grill on the far side of the deck. I'd smelled and determined there was no leak.

I couldn't imagine where the smell had originated, but as fast as I smelled it, once I opened my sunroom door the stench magically dissipated. With the odor subsiding, I lost interest in the potential danger. My only focus was to find a place to lie down. That was the last thing I recalled. Obviously I hadn't made it very far once I got inside my sunroom. The daybed was a few feet away from the sliding glass door.

With my eyes tearing up from the wretched taste in my mouth as well as the morning sun slipping through the blinds in my cottage, I gave myself one final mental thrashing for being such a glutton at the party. Then I made an empty promise to myself never to eat or drink that much again.

Sitting up and rubbing my face left me still dazed. That was when another louder and more determined bang at my front door echoed through my cabin. My response was a more audible groan. Whoever the person was, he apparently was not going away. With my vision gradually returning, I surveyed the room to establish that I really was in the right house. Continuing to rub my face and combing my fingers through my hair, I prayed the intruder would leave. I was in no mood or shape to talk with anyone.

I then noticed my worn loafers by the patio door. They were still wet and grimy from walking along the lake on my return home. The mud and sand had partially dried on the tattered leather. That got me thinking about cleaning my shoes as a second project for the day. Between that and brushing my teeth, I figured I had two worthwhile goals.

Arising slowly I yelled out to the invader at my door, "Wait a minute…I'll be right there!" Immediately I was sorry for that action. The reverberations bouncing in my head brought more tears to my eyes. It occurred to me those eyes were likely bloodshot. I would certainly have understood if the moistness around my eyes was blood, not tears.

Taking a few steps, the room moved slightly until I took a deep breath. Then it was only the headache with which I had to contend. How I wanted to fall back on that daybed and bury my head in the drool-stained pillow. But, it was time to rise whatever time it was. It was not my usual routine to sleep away the morning, even if it was a Saturday. After a shower and a cup of coffee, there was no doubt I'd rally.

Unstably moving slowly toward the front door, I refused to look at the mirror hanging on the opposite wall. I had enough pride in my normal appearance not to confirm my worst fears. Trudging down the hallway, I contemplated whether I'd made an ass out of myself the previous night. I'd have to wait and hear reports on my behavior. I hoped the feedback would be kind, but I didn't expect it to be.

The sound of one last impatient knock ricocheted through my cottage. The noise made me hurry in hopes I wouldn't have to experience that racket one more time. This time, however, accompanying that clamor was the sound of a voice muttering, "Damn…nobody's home." What stood out was that the voice was that of a female…an unfamiliar and too uncommon resonance within the walls of my humble cabin.

I didn't want to miss this unique experience, so I hollered again, "Be right there!"

The resounding echo of my voice brought my hands to my ears. Then more quietly out her listening range, I mumbled, "Just a God damn moment. Keep your shirt on."

With a female at the door, I stepped back a few paces and entered my bathroom to throw water on my face and flatten the hair antennae on my head. I wondered what a female could be doing at my front door on a Saturday morning. Certainly she couldn't be soliciting for some volunteer organization. Maybe she was soliciting for herself!

I smiled. Despite my headache, I still had the willingness to make myself chuckle…and could take pride that my filthy mind was still intact.

When I opened the door, I really hadn't expected to see quite the vision of loveliness standing on my uneven, brick front stoop. I was ready to donate something to her cause whatever it was.

The sunlight temporarily blinded me, but as I shaded my eyes I could observe the funny smirk on her face. I tried to smile and only hoped I actually was. Judging by her looks, she'd been up for a couple hours doing some kind of outside work. Her blouse and work shorts were soiled with fresh dirt. She obviously wasn't going to ask me for a contribution in that get-up. The perspiration and grime on her face and arms certainly didn't detract from her looks. In fact, it made her all the more attractive.

While she obviously didn't know me, she respectfully couldn't help but kid. She grinned, "Whoa…if it was between you and last night's storm, I'd say the storm won."

She laughed at her own joke as a way of letting me know she did say something kind of witty. I gave her a smirk in appreciation for her attempt. Given my deplorable physical condition, I couldn't find the willingness to even chuckle. The strained smile was the best I could do.

Immediately, her face showed concern thinking that she'd gone too far with her barb. She quickly added, "Don't feel badly. The storm almost did me in too. I've been picking up leaves, branches, sticks, and broken limbs over at my place since early this morning."

In a feeble attempt at making her feel better, I muttered, "So…you came over for a cup of coffee as an excuse to get away from your yard work? I can respect that. Please come on in, if you'd like. I'll heat some up."

I'd just given her the usual casual lake country invitation, but she didn't seem interested. Shaking her head, she said she was in a hurry. It was better that she didn't, since the inside of my cabin was a mess. As badly as I felt, I still didn't want her to think of me as a complete bum. Why I felt that way was not clear. I'd known her for less than a minute.

While she made up some contrived reason for being too busy to stay and chat, it occurred to be that cleaning up my cottage should move up on my 'to-do' list right after brushing my teeth and scrubbing the muck off my loafers. As I recalled, that cleaning idea for my home had been on my list for at least two weeks.

I tuned back into what she was saying…something about the storm damage to her property. I wasn't paying close enough attention to understand why she was telling me her sad tale. Certainly that wasn't the reason she came over to pound on my front door. On the other hand, if that was the reason, it was fine with me.

As she spoke, my primary wish, besides imminent recovery from the previous night, was to somehow get a different angle from the blinding morning sun so I could recognize this female if I ever crossed paths with her again. Shading my eyes, it was very apparent I'd never seen her before. Her good looks wouldn't be easily dismissed.

She seemed momentarily embarrassed by her untidy appearance. She kept trying to control an unruly strain of hair that repeatedly fell in her face. I also noted the mud on her work shoes and a slight cut on her arm. I began to wonder if the storm had gotten the better of her as well. Considering I was not at my best, I decided not to try to be witty about her disheveled looks.

Suddenly there was silence. I thought, 'Christ, did she ask me a question?' I had no idea. In my swift attempt to be civil, I blurted out, "So…you've got a place near here do you?"

My heart was in my mouth as I watched her reaction. 'Damn,' I thought, 'maybe she'd already given me that information. Maybe she'd even said her name.'

I was relieved as she pointed across the lake. It was so bright outside my eyes wouldn't stop tearing. Even my large garage just thirty feet away was blurry. Nonetheless, I kept grinning and nodding my head.

She continued describing the assortment of repairs and clean-up needed at her residence. She talked as if her challenge was unique. All my throbbing head could muster was a barely patient and sarcastic thought of 'welcome to the club.' A lake home often required one to be perpetually involved in repair and maintenance. It made me wonder how long she'd owned her lake property. As far as I was concerned, cleaning up one's property the day after an evening rainstorm was standard.

When she'd completed her tale of woe, she finally appeared ready to explain why she'd been knocking at my door. Her speech pattern had been rapid… too hurried for me to follow. Her voice, though pleasant, still scrapped across my hearing sensors. It wasn't her fault. I was just overly sensitive to any noise above a whisper. Even the birds chirping were bothersome.

Oblivious to my inattentiveness, she went on, "I was taking inventory of the junk in my old boathouse and noticed a canoe leaning up over in the corner. It had "Hagen" carved on the side of it. I knew Mr. Hagen had owned this cabin for many years, but had sold it. I didn't know if you have any connections to him anymore, but I thought you might appreciate having it back in case it meant something to you or his family."

Her mention of 'Jim Hagen' brought me back to life. He was a name from my past. Thankfully I was able to respond without drooling. "Yes, I knew Jim Hagen very well. I'm the one who bought this lake place from him…well, actually from his son…a few years back. I used to come up here as a kid every summer for a week…sometimes two weeks. I was Hagen's son's best friend. His name was Johnny.

She paused, "Oh really. I may have met him once or twice during my high school or college years. I spent many summers up here during that time of my life. I'm curious…is Mr. Hagen still living in the area?"

That question left me blank. I just shook my head. Jim Hagen had finally decided to sell his place to me because his son had no interest taking over the family cabin. He knew I had an innate love for the lake life.

I hadn't thought about Jim Hagen for a long time. I'd heard he'd moved to nearby St. Cloud where he had a small place he shared with his brother along the Mississippi River. Her question made me sorry that I'd lost contact with the man. I'd heard he was not feeling well. I hoped he was still among the living.

The young lady brought me back to the present once again. "Well anyway, the canoe is leaning up against your garage in case you want it. If not, throw it away or call me and I'll have it removed. I just brought it over so you could inspect it and see if it's something you want."

Then she stepped back and headed for her SUV giving me a friendly wave as she said, "Anyway…nice to meet you. I'll probably be seeing you around."

The best I could do was nod and repeat practically the same words. Then, as she opened her driver's side door she seemed to remember something. "Oh yes, I almost forgot. I stopped by your place last night to ask you for help during the storm. Your home seemed to be my closest neighbor with a light on. I lost all the power at my place during the rainstorm. Seeing your lighted gas lantern just swaying on your porch, I hoped someone might be home. I drove over here, but you were out. Then I saw that gas lantern swinging in the breeze on the rope over your patio. I heard the party down the lake shore. I could have driven over there for help, but all I needed was a light."

Then she grinned playfully and said, "I kind of rationalized that your gas lamp could be a fire hazard the way it was rocking in the wind. So, I did us both a favor and took it back to my place. With the party going on next door, I figured your electricity was still on, so you wouldn't be in darkness when you got home."

A bit embarrassed she added, "At least that was my reasoning for stealing your gas lantern. And now here I bring you this old canoe and I forget to return the lantern. I'll get it back to you later today if that's all right. Besides, I need to buy one anyway. I heard there's another possible thunderstorm brewing tonight. I might as well get prepared for another power outage."

I'd followed her story about the canoe, but once she started talking about the gas lantern, I was lost. Not only would I have not left a gas light burning out on my porch during a windstorm, but I didn't even own a gas lantern. Besides, if I had needed some emergency lighting, I would have used some flashlights. I had plenty of those inside my house. I could only think she must have gotten mixed up in the dark, storm-filled night…and maybe borrowed someone else's lantern. Things like that happen often in a lake home environment. People borrow things and sometimes forget where they acquired them.

To save her any further awkwardness, I stayed quiet about not owning a gas lantern. I tried to be magnanimous. "Hey…don't hesitate to call me or stop by if you need anything. I know what it's like to get started in a new lake home."

My offer was a routine neighborly gesture…mostly empty but, in her case, certainly sincere. I couldn't imagine what tool she might need from the grimy and rusty contents of my garage. Nonetheless, I felt quite princely having made the offer. I hoped my attempt at generosity might improve her image of me.

Then I thought of something even nobler. "You know… since there's a possibility of more storms tonight, just keep the gas lantern for now. It's quite common to lose electricity in these parts during a storm. You may need it more than me, since I have a generator. Just keep it at your place. I'll get it back sometime down the road."

I was pleasantly surprised with my high-mindedness. I had a hangover that could kill a bull, but I was still decent enough to be civil.

Jumping into her vehicle, she gave me another wave. "Thank you. I appreciate your help. But, don't worry. I won't forget where I got the lantern."

With that she peeled out in her SUV. As quickly as she came, she was gone. Stumbling back inside the house, I tried to recall whether she'd given me her name. I definitely hadn't given her mine. Flopping back down on my daybed, I felt like a real dunce. Despite showing the manners of a farm animal, all things considered, I hadn't completely humiliated myself in front of the new neighbor. Next time I met her, there would be no way I couldn't make a better second impression.

I then laid back down on the daybed thinking that it might be a good idea to ask around and find out who the attractive female was and where she lived. I could take on that task after I did some cleaning in and around my cottage. With that I closed my eyes once more just to rest for a few more minutes.

It was a couple hours later when I finally woke for good. I hadn't slept until 11:00 since college about a dozen years before. Once I finally brushed my teeth and made a fresh pot of coffee, I was able to wander around outside surveying the damage from the previous night's storm. The coffee gave me a needed jolt. I was still languid but gradually returning from the dead.

Strolling down to my dock, the distant sounds of lawn mowers and power saws…and only a few motorboats…could be heard down the south shore of the lake. Other neighbors were wasting no time cleaning up and making the repairs on their properties. I saw the Rutherfords hacking at a fallen tree. They appeared no worse for wear from the previous night. We exchanged distant waves with me yelling, "Hey…great party. I'll be over later if you need help with the tree."

Then I added even louder, "….very much later!" They both laughed knowing my generosity was available only if they became desperate. After all, I had a clean-up project of my own to complete.

Walking onto my dock, the unsteadiness seemed even worse. It was apparent the dock repair might have to get moved up on my 'to do' list. At the far end, I sat down placing my bare feet in the water. The water always felt colder after a major rain storm. I loved relaxing on that dock enjoying the panorama of the vast lake. As a high school history teacher and basketball coach for the previous six years at a consolidated high school fifteen miles up the road, I felt fortunate I'd been able to afford where I was living. It fit the life style I'd always wanted.

Teaching was not my only profession. If so I'd probably never had the money to buy the lake home from old man Hagen. It was my seasonal sales job as a representative for a high school yearbook and graduation gift company based in Bloomington, Minnesota that provided me the supplemental income for some added comforts I might not otherwise have. Being able to concentrate on those jobs in addition to coaching the high school basketball team, I'd always accepted my bachelor status was preferred for someone like me. I liked being on the go whenever I wished…as well as being completely lazy whenever I wished.

Now at thirty-two I still saw no reason to alter my single status. I'd been asked numerous times if I minded living alone at the lake, especially during those long, cold, and lonely months during a Minnesota winter. Some people could be very uncomfortable just thinking about that part of living on a Minnesota lake. In fact, most of my neighbors had their primary homes at another more populated town or city. They rarely made it to the lake at all during the cold months. If they did it was only for a few hours to check how their second home was surviving the winter.

Fortunately for me, the winter months tended to be my busiest time of the year with teaching, coaching, and taking care of my side business. My weekdays ended late especially on Tuesday and Friday nights with basketball games. With basketball practices the other three weekdays followed by dinner at a few of my favorite local restaurants with my friends, I needed the weekend to unwind, catch up on chores, and prepare for the upcoming week. Those cold weather weekends were also the times I often drove to St. Cloud or down to the Twin Cities to meet college friends for dinner…and even date some ladies I knew. That had been my life style since moving to Lake Catherine. I was more than satisfied and didn't see the need to change that pattern.

A motorboat sped by bringing me out of my deep thoughts. Three teenagers were out for a joy ride escaping the obligation of cleaning their parents' properties. I immediately recognized them as part of my basketball team. They lived on the opposite side of the lake.

They waved while shouting out, "Coach…Coach," as if that was my first name. I wondered how long it would take them to call me by my first name once they got out of school. I'd no doubt always be 'Coach' to them in their memories.

I held my hands low indicating I wanted them to slow down so there wouldn't be any mishaps. For that I was serious. I needed those three kids on my team the following season. They laughed and then speeded up. Ruefully I smiled and shook my head knowing I'd probably have done the same thing when I was their age.

As the lake grew calm again, I panned my eyes directly toward the west side of the lake. There were less lake homes in that direction between my cottage and the far peninsula. In fact there were only two homes. They were much closer to my humble dwelling in size and style. That morning those two smallish lake homes took on the look of a serene painting given the inactivity on the two properties. That had been the rule since I'd moved into my cottage. Those two properties rarely saw their owners. In fact, I hadn't seen anyone there all spring.

Both lake places represented typical situations I'd seen before…the father had passed on and willed the property to his grown up off-spring. Those transfers of ownership assured that the two cottages would stay in the family name. However, that didn't mean the next generation necessarily had the time or the interest to use or maintain the lake homes. This was the case with both ownerships.

In the last three summers the off-spring and now their young children spent only a few weekends at the lake. Both families would arrive late Friday night, stay all day Saturday and then pack up and leave by noon on Sunday. It hardly seemed worth making the trip. In all, I'd met the owners of both homes twice. I doubt I'd recognize any of them if they walked by me. Even though we rarely crossed paths, there was still the neighborly camaraderie whenever they motored or sailed by on their respective boats. We'd exchange waves and some kind of greeting if they were close enough. Then they'd be gone. I wouldn't see them until later in the summer…sometimes not until the next year. They'd close their lake homes for the winter on Labor Day and open them on Memorial Day weekend the following spring. That was the way it was always going to be…at least until the lake homes were sold to someone else. As a result, I'd always felt a closer kinship to my neighbor further west down the shoreline at the peninsula.

That fact, in itself, was especially odd. The owner of that long admired home on the peninsula was no longer even alive. But, when he was living, I admired him tremendously. Even then, it was from a distance. My respect came from all the things I'd heard about him as well as the one time I met him. That meeting had been twelve years before when I was but twenty years old. At that time I had no idea I'd ever own a home on Lake Catherine. I was only visiting my friend, Johnny Hagen and his father, just like I'd been doing each summer since the seventh grade.

Given my familiarity with the background of Lake Catherine I'd learned about this neighbor at the peninsula from both Johnny and his father. Though that neighbor had been gone for almost ten years, well before I'd purchased the cottage from Jim Hagen, my remembrance of that one time we did meet remained as clear in my mind as if it was yesterday.

His name was Ray Lindstrom...and since buying the Hagen property I'd often looked to the west side of the lake wishing it was more than his spirit that lived on. Lindstrom had a much revered name in the Lake Catherine area. Even the ten years since his death, he was still talked about with great admiration. He'd developed a number of lake side properties while living at the lake. However, it was his home...the mansion on the peninsula on the west side of the lake...that was thought to be the most esteemed property on the lake for so many years.

As young teenagers, Johnny Hagen and I often fished in the quiet bay near the peninsula looking up the hill to that impressive Lindstrom house. We talked often how magical it would be to own something so stately and grand. To us it was so far out of our league, even dreaming about it seemed a waste of time.

Then, as often happened in other families, with Ray Lindstrom's death, the peninsula was left to his family. In this case the ownership was transferred to his two daughters who by that time were out of college and busy with their own lives. Taking care of the property and the mansion became a hardship. They had neither the time nor the desire to make Lake Catherine a priority. I wasn't around to see the gradual diminution of the property, but it happened similarly to the situations with the two lake homes nearer to me. The Lindstrom house... so highly regarded during the 1960's and 70's...was left uncared for and unlived in for almost five years prior to my moving to Lake Catherine in 1982.

When I took over ownership of the Hagen property, my only remembrance of the Lindstrom peninsula was my vision of it during its best years. It was a wonderful time.

As a youth every year I visited the Hagen's, Johnny and I would find numerous reasons to canoe, sail, or motorboat by that peninsula. And, every summer through my last weeklong visit during college, my friend would fill me in on the latest stories and hearsay of Ray Lindstrom and his fun-loving daughters.

Those wild and often exaggerated tales would be balanced by Johnny's father, Jim Hagen. He not only spoke highly of the Lindstrom family, but he gave me the background about Lake Catherine and what Ray Lindstrom had done to make the peninsula the most preferred on the entire lake.

Hagen described that west side of the lake before Lindstrom as an overgrown weed infested waste area with a small, dilapidated farmhouse built back in 1921 by a man simply referred to as 'Farmer Goblisch'. Farmer Goblisch didn't fish much, didn't own a boat, and considered the lake just a watering hole for his forty cows. In those early days when some lake homes were being built on the opposite and preferred east and south sides of the lake, the only scene conjured up in people's mind about the peninsula was the sight of many of those forty cows standing in the lake at the shoreline staying cool during the heat of the summer.

When Farmer Goblisch passed on during the 1950's, his property laid in obsolescence for years. His family had moved from the area and had little interest in returning to Lake Catherine much less to do anything with the property. To them the peninsula had little value. About 1960 Ray Lindstrom, a small town homebuilder from a community one hundred miles south of Lake Catherine, came exploring. He had been looking for some bargain-priced lake property in central Minnesota. He was just passing by the village of Lake Catherine on a Sunday afternoon in the late summer of that year when he saw a weathered 'for sale' sign pointing down a gravel road. By that time he was used to examining various nooks and crannies in that area of seemingly non-stop lakes. As he drove slowly along that barely visible farm road to some isolated pastureland along the quieter west side of the lake, he realized he might have found what he'd been seeking.

That Sunday afternoon he sought out the realtor located over at the county seat eight miles away to check out if this might be an opportunity or not. It all got down to the kind of a deal he might get if the sellers were in the mood to sell.

Lindstrom saw the pluses as many. The property was on the undeveloped side of the lake with most of the lake homes far across the water on the east side. He liked the solitude. He could picture himself fishing and not being bothered by too many boaters. Lindstrom also liked the location of the farm house on the hill. He visualized gutting the inside and eventually making the house bigger with a large protruding family room giving a three-sided view of the lake.

While Lindstrom saw opportunity, the realtor only saw worthless pastureland. It was a buyer's dream. Lindstrom practically bit through his omnipresent toothpick trying to get the selling information out of the disinterested realtor. The man had a hard time even finding in his files the main contact name of the Goblisch family. The realtor said he'd get back to Lindstrom.

Not one to let opportunity slip away, Lindstrom yet that afternoon eventually found someone in the Goblisch family living in the area. He got the contact number for the oldest offspring of Farmer Goblisch. He tendered a $100 an acre offer for sixteen acres and threw in some additional cash for the decrepit house. There was a bit more to the transaction than that, but as Jim Hagen told it, the Goblisch family was happy to pick up a few thousand dollars they hadn't expected and get rid of something that was of little importance to them.

Lindstrom's wife and kids were hardly surprised by the transaction. Ray had always been somewhat of a risk-taker. They wouldn't even see the property until the following spring, but they knew he was excited about his purchase…much the same way Farmer Goblisch's off-spring were about ridding themselves of the low-grade pastureland.

That same Goblisch family had to be astonished a few years later when their former peninsula became one of the more prominent properties on the lake. By then it was being called 'Ray's Peninsula' or the 'Lindstrom mansion'. The farmhouse was no longer recognizable. The addition to the back of the house boasted the aforementioned windowed, three-sided view of the lake. Lindstrom would build two other additions onto that basic farmhouse to give the house more balance.

While doing this he also built multiple homes at the far northern end of the peninsula out of the sight of his now quite substantial lake home. He also assigned his workers to upgrade the decrepit boathouse down the hill from the mansion. It soon boasted a small second story living area including a second level deck with connecting stairs to a very large main dock. It was the kind of place any romantic couple might imagine their next tryst. 'Ray's Peninsula' became the talk of the lakeside populace.

Lindstrom also had quite an impact on the area. The village of Lake Catherine, just four miles from the peninsula, had always been barely a spot on the map. It's only real repute had been gained by the folks who built lake homes on the east and south sides of the lake. Only one hundred fifty miles west of the Twin Cities, Lake Catherine had a local grade school, a post office, a Catholic church, some sect of Baptist church, and another strange church that no one really knew what faith it followed. There was also a gasoline station that was rarely opened and a general store that was rarely closed. Various types of repair businesses were based out of approximately ten home garages. These businesses focused on fixing cars, boats, farm equipment, snowmobiles, and lawn mowers. Five homes had perpetual signs nailed on a tree saying "Garage Sale" and there was one person with five cars parked in his front yard with a sign that said 'Darryl's Car Sales'. With the limited offerings of the village of Lake Catherine, most everyone drove the eight miles further down the road to the county seat for any serious shopping.

Through the decade of the 1960's Lindstrom built and sold twenty-two homes on the north side of his peninsula. In 1969 he bought more land in the Lake Catherine area. Thirty more lake homes were built. He sold them practically as fast as he finished them.

Mr. Hagen also mentioned that Lindstrom was very involved in the local church and community for a guy who lived a hundred miles away. He built a beach site at the peninsula and his daughters both gave swimming lessons to the area children. He also gave to the Catholic churches at Lake Catherine as well as the church at the county seat. At least a couple times there was damage caused by storms and Lindstrom sent his crew to the churches for needed repair work. Not many people knew of Lindstrom's generosity, but most assuredly the priests at both churches appreciated his bigheartedness.

Lindstrom was also a very private man. Stopping in either the general store in Lake Catherine or the café over at the county seat, he was often unnoticed. He didn't speak much unless spoken to first. When finally recognized, folks greeted him as if he'd lived there all his life. They wanted to be his friend. His responses were always short but cordial.

His wife understandably preferred to remain back at their yearlong community because of friends, family, church, town events and of course her bridge club. As the daughters grew older, they also spent less time at the lake because of weekday summer job commitments. Still, both daughters rarely missed a summer weekend inviting friends to join them at the peninsula.

As a result, Lindstrom was often alone during the weekdays over the summer. Local's vision of Ray Lindstrom was him sitting in an artificial leather and weather-beaten easy chair on the peninsula dock during the evening. He'd be casting his line in the calm waters in the bay again and again. When he wasn't sitting in that chair, it would be covered with a piece of canvas indicating it was not for anyone else's use. The chair was only removed from the dock when winter set in.

When fishing, it was said how his voice could often be heard echoing across the calm waters…as if he was alone in a conversation with God while his bobber floated aimlessly on the water. Folks thought him at times a bit unusual, but for all the good Ray Lindstrom was doing for the Lake Catherine area, locals respected his apparent need for privacy. As far as they were concerned, he had the right to talk with whomever he damn well pleased…whether the visitor was there or not.

It was Johnny Hagen who intimated to me how his father was the only real friend of Ray Lindstrom. The two older men had a strong bond with their love of fishing and their preference to stay out of other people's business. Johnny described seeing his father and Lindstrom often jawing away on the peninsula dock especially in the fall when life slowed after the tumult of summer. That told me Ray Lindstrom wasn't always talking to himself. I don't remember ever seeing Lindstrom sitting on his easy chair on his dock during my visits to Lake Catherine. Maybe it was because most of my stays at the Hagen's cabin were in the early summer when he was particularly busy.

As Johnny and I got older, we developed more interest in his two daughters, especially the older one who seemed nearer our age. Unfortunately, sightings of either daughter were rare. We'd occasionally see one or both of them running out to one of their vehicles to go someplace with their mother or father. They were always on the move. On the weekend when they had friends visiting, there was plenty of water skiing, swimming, and sailing going on by the peninsula. Where I wanted to go over and join in the fun, Johnny never wanted to take part. I always thought one of us might have missed an opportunity with that older Lindstrom daughter.

A fish jumped out of the water waking me out of my deep thoughts. I'd been sitting in that daze on my dock with my feet in the water for too long. It was time to do something to get my day rolling. Rising I glanced across the lake to the skies in the far northwest. It was a reflex action. It was the direction from which most weather systems materialized. That often dictated what plans could be made for the day. My attention froze for an instant as I noticed a vague outline of a wide cloud bank. More foul weather had been prognosticated for the later afternoon. It looked like the forecasters could be right. Still, the system was a long way off. If there was a possible thunderstorm moving toward Lake Catherine, it was a couple hours away.

Seeing the possibility of more inclement weather, I couldn't get too excited about cleaning up my property. I'd have to repeat the same effort the next day if the storm was as violent as the one the previous night. Whatever motivation I'd had now evaporated. I sat back down on the dock kicking the cool water on my leg ready to return to my trance-like journey back to those times as a youth when I was visiting the Hagen's and seeing 'Ray's peninsula' at its height. It now seemed so much longer ago than the almost ten years since Lindstrom had died maybe because of how aged the mansion and the property now looked with so little maintenance and care. What I'd seen as a teenager had deteriorated even more in the six years since I'd moved full time to Lake Catherine. Now the mansion on the peninsula was barely visible through the heavy brush, weeds and high grass at the shoreline.

I'd come to accept that the Lindstrom daughters were in the same predicament about the property as the Goblisch family had been back in the 1950's. Likely their lives were far from Lake Catherine as they pursued their own dreams. It was highly likely they were both married and might not even be living any longer in Minnesota. I sensed someone could get a hell of a deal if they had the time and money to invest in the peninsula. I definitely had the willingness if not the time. The money was another issue.

A whimsical gaze across the water at the faraway peninsula and my mind went back to Johnny Hagen and his salacious stories of the two Lindstrom daughters… but always with emphasis on the older sister. Starting from our teenage years, I recalled how Johnny would have new and better tales each summer when I arrived for my weeklong visit. I could tell he was smitten by her, but definitely considered her in another league. I kidded him that he wouldn't have the guts to carry on a conversation even if he'd run into in town. He never disagreed.

Admittedly, I was kind of enamored by that older sister as well. However, it was an abbreviated infatuation lasting only the week I spent at Lake Catherine each summer. Besides, I had so many other things I preferred doing at the lake with such limited time than fulfill a crush on a girl I'd only seen from a distance. Still, just knowing about her gave me fodder to tease my friend ceaselessly. I was always suggesting ways he should meet her. I never did convince him.

As our middle teen years passed, that Lindstrom girl while often in our conversation became less of a focus whenever I was at Lake Catherine. By that time Johnny seemed always to be lovesick over some girl back home. He'd waste time writing to her daily while complaining about having to live at the lake and being away from her. His pining made me sick. I only wished I could be in his shoes and live in that lake cottage all summer long.

As a result he was also disinterested in pursuing any other females around the lake. Disgusted, I told him loyalty to the girl back home was a bit misplaced since we weren't exactly going to propose marriage to any female at the lake…at least with our plans to begin college. There was no change in my friend. Those summer visits during my first two college years, I recall spending more time with his father working on the property or fishing with him than with Johnny.

There were times we boated past the peninsula, but that was as close as Johnny's interest got regarding that older Lindstrom daughter. Racing a motor boat by anyone was not a proven method of starting a conversation.

The curious part of being with Johnny was the displeasure he carried against both daughters of Ray Lindstrom. He was always questioning their reputations. He was convinced they were on the wild side…something I found quite winsome. His stories constantly backed up his claim. He'd note repeatedly and disgustedly how both daughters had no shortage of male companionship… and how the house on the peninsula was always buzzing with activity on summer weekends.

I eventually grasped the reason for his strange comments. His fragile ego… and he determined mine was similar…didn't have the strength to face that kind of competition.

He'd lamely tell me, "There are other fish in other ponds."

The last time I visited the Hagen's at Lake Catherine was that summer after my sophomore year in college. Finals had just been completed. I had a week break before I started my summer job back home and I spent it at Lake Catherine. How lucky I felt to be standing on the Hagen dock breathing in the fresh lake air once again.

I recall that last summer how I'd never thought about that older Lindstrom daughter when I was away from that lake. Upon arriving I'd pan my eyes across the lake and eventually settling my eyes on the peninsula. Then my curiosity erupted. I pestered Johnny for the latest details of the two daughter's lives at the peninsula.

He was of course indifferent, but willing to fill me in on some of the tales he'd heard since last I was at the lake the previous summer. As always I got the sense he was embroidering the yarns in an attempt to cast further aspersions on the Lindstrom daughters. He still considered either Lindstrom daughter more experienced and definitely in a different economic league than the two of us. In his mind those girls were the beautiful movie stars. He perceived the two of us to be stars as well, but more in the ilk of the original Tom Sawyer and Huckleberry Finn.

Mostly his narratives chronicled their broad assortment of beaus who clustered around them. He cited how these troubadours came up from the Twin Cities most weekends. They were so easy to recognize. Arriving early Saturday at Lake Catherine, their skin was often very white from not being outdoors. They'd stop down at the general store or the lone gas station to get directions to Ray's peninsula. Johnny described each male as loud, too energetic, funny acting…or looking…and wore what they arrived in the entire weekend…meaning a swim suit and a t-shirt. By the time they departed on Sunday night, they were not as energetic, very sunburned, well fed, and wishing they didn't have to leave.

He told of the guy who water-skied at dusk by a local picnic area near the village while wearing his swimming suit over his head and his supporter being the only thing that provided some modesty. Since it was Ray Lindstrom's motorboat, people wondered who drove the boat. Certainly not Ray! The hearsay was the driver appeared to have stuffed her longish hair under a baseball cap. That would have been the older Lindstrom daughter.

Another story had a guy waking up one Saturday morning in one of the daughter's beds much to the shock of Lindstrom's wife. Fortunately or unfortunately, as the case may be, both daughters had not made it up to the lake that Friday night. The guy had arrived after midnight and actually found Ray's peninsula and the mansion in the middle of a thunderstorm. Since cabins or lake homes were often left unlocked, the young man quietly slipped in through a back door of the lake house and simply found a bed and went to sleep. That next evening with both daughters having arrived at the mansion Saturday morning, the young man slept outside in a trailer. Lindstrom's wife wanted to be on the safe side.

Always Johnny's defamatory stories of Ray's daughters never reached the corrupt level he seemed to be striving. Their reputations always remained in intact. Both young ladies had an image of being respectful, friendly, responsible, and involved in the community life around the lake. Besides the swimming lessons they'd coordinated for the kids at the lake, they'd helped out in the recreation department over at the youth center at the county seat. Word was they were in church either Saturday night before they went out or Sunday morning no matter how late they had been out the previous night.

Still, Johnny described the Friday or Saturday night parties at the peninsula with plenty of insinuation. He always appeared irritable that two females could have such a host of males tracking them. He knew his non-competitive nature would never put him in the race.

I would find out years later that those supposed 'wild' parties at the peninsula had little to do with the daughters. These were social functions set up by the father for people he invited as possible prospects for lake home purchases. If a boyfriend or two showed up, they were just another plate at the table.

That last summer at the Hagen lake home, I had feeling it would be my final visit. Johnny told me privately he was thinking about quitting school and signing up with one of the military branches. He had no girlfriend and spoke of college with little interest. While we still ski'd, fished, and played some golf, our evenings were typically ending with him having too many beers at the local watering hole.

It was the night before I was going to drive back to my home to begin my summer job that Johnny and I had gotten back to the cottage surprisingly early from a bar. He'd passed out in his bed, but I wasn't tired at all. There'd been a quite serious hail storm when we were at the bar earlier. Despite the cool night, I was looking for anything to do…something memorable…rather than just go to bed.

It was just before 12:00 and the night was darker than normal with a mild haze over the lake and a persistent overcast sky. Knowing that night would likely be my last one at Lake Catherine, on an impulse I decided to take a joy ride in the canoe…alone… over toward the Lindstrom property. I had the weird idea of maybe sneaking onto the Lindstrom dock and sit in old Ray's easy chair. I just wanted to see what if felt like to observe life from his perspective. If his older daughter happened to see me and come down to the dock, then that would be an unexpected bonus. Of course that would be unimaginable. I expected no one to even see me on their dock from the house up on the hill.

As I launched the canoe off the Hagen dock, the haze from the earlier storm hung over the lake like a blanket. As I canoed, I had to stay close to shore just to keep my bearings. Within a half hour I was in the bay and closing in on the Lindstrom dock. Picking up the pace of my rowing, the fog suddenly got particularly thick. I was no longer certain I was going in the right direction.

And then, I saw a light. It seemed like it was moving but I couldn't get any perspective through the dense haze. Nonetheless, I paddled right for that light hoping it might be some kind of outside light at the Lindstrom boathouse.

As I got closer I could see the light flickering. It was some kind of gas lantern apparently left outside out on the dock. I stood up slightly trying to see better through the fog and that was when my head came in contact with a tree limb. I was closer to shore than I'd realized. The force literally knocked me over in the canoe. I was fortunate not to have fallen in the lake or upset the canoe. I found out later I was so close to shore I'd have landed in three feet of water if I had tumbled out of the canoe.

My half-conscious groans and foul language were heard. A voice yelled out, "Who's there? Are you O.K.?"

Though dazed, I answered in milder tones, "Yes, I'm all right. I just hit my head on an overhanging limb. I'm sorry. I didn't mean to scare you. I was just enjoying my last night at the lake. I'm a guest of Jim Hagen further down the shoreline."

The voice sounding more concerned than peeved then said, "Well son, row yourself over here towards the light, and let's see if you're as all right as you say. It sounded to me like you took quite a wallop."

I did as I was told. I slowly paddled toward the flickering light. I felt my scalp. No blood was dripping, but my head was woozy. When I got within a few yards of the light I found myself alongside the dock. Then as if opening a door, there he was…just as I'd heard him described. Ray Lindstrom was sitting in that chair on the dock with a fishing pole lying right beside it. I knew it was him. How could he be anyone else?

He got up and helped me onto the dock telling me just to sit down until I felt better. I remember thanking him for his help, but I don't recall exchanging names. Almost immediately, though, we just started talking. I sat on the dock while he sat back down on his easy chair a few yards away. Surprisingly he did most of the talking contrary to my impression that he was a very taciturn man. Or, maybe I was dizzier than I thought after the tree branch incident.

He said something about how he enjoyed the solitude of the evening and often came down and sat on his dock. He kept repeating how Jim Hagen was one of his better friends at Lake Catherine and that they often fished together. His chatter seemed unnatural. I guess he was paying more attention to my condition.

After a short time I felt better and entered more into our conversation. He learned that I was a college student and I'd been a guest of the Hagen's each summer since I was just out of elementary school. Our exchange then moved to fishing, a more interesting topic for both of us. He liked my enthusiasm about the sport and was impressed that I knew where the best spots were on the lake for catching bass. I noticed his fly rod lying by his chair and we talked about it. I told him I was going to get a good fly rod someday after I finally went out into the working world.

I don't know how long we talked. It could have been a half hour…maybe even an hour…until he sensed I was all right. Then he got up from his chair grabbed his fly rod and the gas lantern beside him. He stretched while mumbling, "Well, son, it's time for me to get up to the house before I fall asleep on this chair. I've enjoyed talking with you. The fog is lightening up a bit. You look in good enough form to make it back to Jim Hagen's place. Just paddle along the shoreline and keep your damned head down so you don't get knocked over again by some low hanging tree limbs."

I chuckled as he watched me making certain I held my balance He then quipped, "You sound like you've lived on this lake most of your life, not just a week or two every summer. With your love of fishing, I'm sorry we never got better acquainted. If you're ever around here again, stop on by. I've got a new fly rod in my boathouse. I'll let you try it out."

I shook his hand. It felt clammy from the humidity and the slight chill in the air. Then I slipped into my canoe and waved farewell. He gave me a cursory wave as he walked off his dock and then up the long stairs to his house. His body disappeared in the fog, but I could still see that flickering gas lantern moving back and forth as well as the scuffling sound of his shoes.

As I paddled away, I had the warmest feeling. I'd met the renowned owner of the peninsula and I was impressed with him. He was certainly kind and caring. What surprised me was his depth of thought. I'd wished I'd somehow gotten to know him much, much earlier than my last night at Lake Catherine.

When I finally arrived back at the Hagen dock, I quietly slipped through the door to the cabin trying not to wake anyone. I wasn't concerned about Johnny. He was sleeping off his drunken night. His father, though, was a light sleeper. As I passed his room, I heard his voice, unexpectedly clear, saying "Good night." He'd been aware I was gone from the house and had obviously been concerned.

I recall being shocked that it was after 2:00 AM. It hadn't felt I'd been gone that long. My head hurt only slightly. I remember being more exhilarated with meeting Ray Lindstrom than caring about my head.

Indeed those annual visits to the Hagen's lake home would end that night after eight years. During that next 1975-76 college year, Johnny would go into the navy and virtually disappeared from my life. The following summer...and the summer after... I found myself truly missing those visits to Lake Catherine. I would have periodic thoughts about my various experiences there, but that odd meeting with Ray Lindstrom always stood out as quite special. Regarding that older Lindstrom daughter, it was strange how any thought of her rarely materialized in my mind...as if she existed in no other place other than when I happened to be at Lake Catherine.

I'd always found it remarkable how one week each summer could be responsible for creating a dream. I was entranced with living my adult years in some kind of rustic, relaxing place on a Minnesota lake. But, once I left college that vision was so far away. In fact it was more a hallucination given my limited bankroll. I accepted a job teaching at a suburban St. Paul high school giving me the sense I would be traveling down a road taking me even further from that unrealistic dream.

Maybe that was why I took a second job with that high school yearbook and graduation gift company in Bloomington, Minnesota after my first year of teaching. I can't say I took the extra work with the conscious goal of buying a lake home...or even to attain some financial goals. My thinking was not that sophisticated. I was just looking for something that would make me good money and fill my extra time in the summer. At best I thought the extra pay would help me eventually afford a better apartment.

A little over a year after I'd started my teaching career in the Twin Cities, I did hear from Johnny Hagen. My boyhood friend and I hadn't talked but a couple times since the navy had taken him overseas. He was stationed in the Mediterranean Sea and had just returned to a base in Norfolk, Virginia. His phone call came from out of the blue. He'd thought enough about me to let me know that old Ray Lindstrom had died.

He told me his father had found Lindstrom a few days after Labor Day weekend slumped in his comfortable chair on the dock with his fishing pole resting in his hands. He had not been gone long. There was a bass on the end of the line when it was finally reeled in. Lindstrom had a peaceful look on his face and a toothpick hanging from his mouth.

I remember telling Johnny how much I appreciated his call...and to look me up when he got back home. That never happened...at least for the next three years. By then he was out of the navy and had decided to remain in the Norfolk, Virginia area. He hadn't been back to Minnesota but once in those three years. Even then he never called. The vision of us playing together as youths became as vague as the memory of my annual visits to Lake Catherine.

But, something mind boggling did happen in the spring of my fourth year of teaching at Roseville High School. I received a letter from Johnny Hagen. He was still living in Norfolk, Virginia. I hadn't heard from him since that sad phone call about Ray Lindstrom a few years before. His note started out more conversational talking about his job and how much he liked living on the east coast. Then his letter took a turn in a more serious vein as he mentioned how his father's health had declined and how difficult it was for his dad to keep up with the work the Lake Catherine home required. He further added since he lived out east, he and his father planned to put the cabin and property up for sale.

His next paragraph stunned me. The words still stick in my mind. He wrote:

> 'Hey…I want to bring something up to you. I think you might have some interest. My father and I have talked often how much you loved being at our lake cabin…and even your hope to one day own a place on the water. Well, my friend, here's your chance. We want to give you the first opportunity to buy it…or at least have the right of first refusal. We're not in any hurry to sell the place, but we'd like to know your response. We'd appreciate hearing from you as soon as you can…just so we know the possibility. If no interest, then we'll probably put the property up for sale later this spring. Let me know.'

He went on to suggest the price his father and he would be asking for the lake cabin. It was of course higher than I could afford. Beyond the price, there would be the other matters to consider…like moving…like finding another teaching job closer to Lake Catherine. The one factor that was not a problem was my second job as a representative with the Bloomington company. With that type of work, it didn't matter where I lived. I could travel to my accounts from any home base.

Still, the whole idea of buying the Hagan cabin was so outrageous. I summarily disregarded the thought before finishing the letter. Then it took less than an hour for me to be suddenly intoxicated with the possibility. I was ready to rob a bank to come up with the down payment. That emotion was then followed by me being sorry Johnny had even sent me the letter. His proposition only made me feel disillusioned over how my life had become so limiting. I was so opposed to risk. It had put me in a mindset where I might never be in a financial position to fulfill any kind of dream.

By the second day after receiving the letter, the inconveniences of changing jobs and moving were no longer problems. My entire focus was on how to buy the place. As creative as I was, my final and only plan was to lay the cards on the table and let Johnny and his father know what I could afford…and then ask if there was any way to arrange a purchase agreement over a longer period of time.

My counter offer was not so much an offer as an embarrassment. As enthused as I was at having the chance to take over the property, my letter was but a pathetic attempt to appeal to their sympathies. I suggested a much lower price and asked even then that they take but a 5% down payment. I of course did not admit to them that even that sum would deplete my savings down to barely enough money to cover a tank of gas and maybe a cup of coffee.

When I mailed that letter, I truthfully thought Johnny would not even respond to me. I ended the letter by thanking his father and him for giving me a chance to bid on a dream.

A few days later he called and agreed to everything I'd requested. He told me his father had insisted that Johnny do whatever he had to do to get the property into my hands. He said his father didn't want anyone he didn't trust to own his property. I was almost speechless as Johnny and I scheduled the next steps to the purchase.

The exhilaration and fear I felt after that phone call was the most emotion I'd ever felt. That one phone call changed the direction of my entire life. Now six years later, I'd never regretted for one second the purchase and all the work it took to replant my life at Lake Catherine.

When Johnny and his father accepted my offer, I still had ten more weeks of my teaching contract at Roseville. The very next day I began searching for teaching and coaching positions near Lake Catherine. I figured I couldn't expect anything better than a longer commute to whatever school I might be able to land a job. That didn't bother me. I had jumped into my dream and I was happy.

To save further money that spring I gave up my apartment and stayed at a friend's place near White Bear Lake until the school year was completed. From late March until Memorial Day I gradually moved my belongings to my new home while staying the weekends at Lake Catherine. Further luck arrived when a consolidated school system fifteen miles from my new home offered me the job of teaching as well as coaching basketball for the coming year. I was amazed how things seemed to fall into place...and showed me that taking a risk now and then was a good thing. The difference was that this move didn't feel like that big a risk. It was simply something I was going to do.

It was June, 1982, when I became a full-time resident at Lake Catherine. I remember being thrilled by everything about my new location...except for one thing. In the few short years since Ray Lindstrom's death, his peninsula had taken that downhill slide. The property was nothing like I'd remembered. At the lake's edge all around the peninsula the thick foliage mostly blocked the view of the Lindstrom house. In fact, I didn't really get my first real glimpse of the tired looking mansion until the leaves fell that autumn. Sadly, my knowing what it had looked like years before and comparing it to the present decrepit state could only be described as disheartening. It looked to me that the unkempt and scruffy look of the peninsula would likely be permanent until the land and mansion eventually got sold. Maybe another developer could build some nice lake homes on all sides of Ray's peninsula. Until then, it would always be a ghost of its former self.

During my third summer at the lake, there was one change at the Lindstrom property. A local man was hired to do some basic maintenance work on the landscape. His efforts that first summer brought the peninsula back to some level of acceptance. He even placed a few sections of the dock out on the water. They'd been stored in the two-story boathouse after Ray Lindstrom had died.

Unfortunately, the following summers the local man's efforts gradually waned. Most of his work centered on occasionally mowing the vast lawn and cutting back the brush, weeds and foliage. Half the problem seemed to be that no one was there to appreciate whatever work he was doing. As a result he put in lesser hours and allowed the brush and weeks to grow back up to full height once again. Somehow I doubted his pay decreased proportionally with his reduced effort.

Occasionally, while having morning coffee at the local general store, I'd hear that one or the other of Lindstrom daughters had stopped by their lake property. It happened once or twice each summer. I never saw either of them, not that I'd recognize them if I did. It was just as well. My irritation would have been too obvious for the way they were ignoring such a family treasure.

A distant rumble of thunder suddenly snapped my attention back to the present day. That distant weather bank had bubbled up into a more dramatic cloud system and was now pushing its way toward Lake Catherine. After years of living on the lake, this thunderstorm gave indications it would more likely skirt the opposite northern edge of the lake. However, there were other frontal systems predicted for later that Saturday and during the day on Sunday as well. For the present I felt safe. There would be time to take on some project around the house before the afternoon storms might hit.

Pulling my feet from the water, I was suddenly more energized. The vague image of the good-looking female who'd knocked at my cabin door that morning reappeared. I wished I'd gotten her name…where she lived. I did recall some things about her. She indicated she lived alone. That sounded good. She wasn't afraid to get dirty. She was an outdoors person. That also was good.

Wandering back up the hill to my cottage, I picked up some broken limbs and branches throwing them into a temporary pile. With another storm due later, that effort had no chance of holding my interest. That work could easily wait until after the next storm.

I again glanced over at my more vigorous neighbor cutting through another broken limb. While Dean Rutherford was entering another decade of his life, he looked in great shape. He made me feeling slightly ashamed. He and his wife were working vigorously on what had to be limited sleep time. It had taken me most of the morning just to fight back from the dead.

Watching my two neighbors tirelessly work next door, I suddenly got motivated to do something physical. Taking a jog seemed to be the answer. Less than a minute later I was stretching by my opened garage getting prepared for my run. The canoe the young lady had left leaning against the garage was unfortunately still there. I wondered how long it would remain until I either burn it up or dragged it to the dump. While more a relic than functional, I tried to visualize some use for it. It could be a planter placed at the back of the garage. If I was a gardener, it might be a good idea. Unfortunately, a green thumb was not one of my strengths. Any other creative thoughts ended right there. For certain, though, floating it in water didn't appear to be an option.

Thinking again of that female from the morning, I smirked. She must have looked at my place and thought it a dump ground…as if leaving the dilapidated canoe propped against the garage kind of fit my property's décor.

Peering into the garage, I yawned realizing all the projects I'd yet started. Earlier in the spring my plan was to repair the dock. Other things had taken priority…that is, anything else I could think of besides that project.

Moving over to the ratty looking canoe, I gazed at some initials etched in the side of the wasted vessel. The name 'Hagen' could barely be discerned. 'I'll be damned,' I thought, 'it was the original Hagen canoe.'

Grazing my hand over the rough exterior, the memory became quite clear how Johnny Hagen and I had prowled around the lake as kids in this now unusable craft. At other times we'd furtively paddled into the peninsula cove to cast a line or wishing we'd catch a glimpse of the Lindstrom daughters. As worn as the canoe looked, I found myself appreciating that I now had something from my past. 'Who knows,' I contemplated, 'maybe I could restore it.' I shook my head…another project to add to my list.

A minute later I was trotting down a side road connecting my property to the county road. It was the usual track I followed when jogging. Most times I ran along the south lake shore eastward where most cabins were located. That way if I saw someone I could rest and talk with them…and cut short my run.

That morning I decided to turn right and take the opposite quieter route on the county road up toward the peninsula. There was no reason other than I felt like running rather than talking with neighbors. I guess I felt obligated to punish myself for the previous night.

There was another reason for taking that direction. The longer route gave me a better view of the oncoming storm clouds. If they began turning more southward, I could turn around immediately.

I ran about two miles on the county road before turning onto an elongated gravel driveway. It led up towards the forgotten mansion on the peninsula. It was a path I rarely followed, since the shabby condition of Ray's peninsula was never a pleasant sight.

As I got closer to the opened main gate to the peninsula, I was surprised. The gate had previously been closed with an intimidating sign saying 'No Trespassing'. The sign had been discarded and the gate was open. I could even hear some activity ahead…like a lawnmower and some motorized equipment. I thought hopefully, 'Maybe that local maintenance guy was finally putting in some time.'

I continued up the long gravel driveway…something I'd never done… and saw in the distance two workmen scraping the sides of the house in preparation for painting. Then I saw two other men…one mowing and another stacking twigs and branches onto a mound that would soon be set afire.

'Wow,' I thought, 'someone is trying to make this property livable…or maybe saleable.' Either way I was bolstered. Slowing my jog to a walk, I stared for a time at the old house up on the hill. I shook my head thinking there was probably not enough time or money to bring that large dwelling back to its heyday of the 1960's and 1970's…though at least someone was trying.

At that moment I heard a rumble off to the north. The overhanging trees were blocking my view of the sky. It was likely the storm system had moved a bit south. I no longer could dally. I turned around and began picking up speed down the long gravel driveway back towards my home. Peripherally I caught sight of another worker down by the Lindstrom boathouse. On a closer look, I noticed the worker was a she. In fact she was dressed quite similarly to the attractive female who'd knocked on my door earlier.

I slowed down to a walk hoping to get a better angle so I might see her face. As she conversed with the other worker, I caught only a distant glimpse of her auburn hair…and her shape. She was definitely the same girl. Then again, she might only be part of the work crew.

Picking up my running pace again, I kept my head faced in her direction. It just didn't register that she could be one of the Lindstrom daughters. I couldn't imagine either daughter ever being that filthy and grimy. It went against every image I had of both females. I tried to recall what she'd said that morning besides bringing over the worn canoe. I had been too unconscious. I just couldn't remember.

Just then she began laughing with the other worker as she held up something looking like an old gas lantern. It reminded me how she'd said she'd borrowed a gas lamp from me the previous night. That had been the most bewildering part of our conversation. I'd never seen that gas lantern hanging on my deck ever. I didn't even own one! Still she claimed it glowed so brightly Friday night she could see it clearly from her storm-darkened house more than a mile away. That was why she'd come over to my house when she'd lost all her electricity. Now I wished I'd been home to help her out.

I chuckled thinking how I'd been so magnanimous. By God I hadn't been completely comatose. I didn't disclaim the lamp. By generously offering the gas lantern for her continued use, there'd be a good chance I'd see her again. I was kind of proud of myself for being such a quick thinker. My libido had still been intact despite my poor condition that morning.

Now certain it was her, I was tempted to jump over the barbed wire fence along the road and run across the hay field to the boathouse and strike up a conversation with her. Discretion told me to wait for another time. My pride had taken a beating that morning with her at the front door. Why take a chance on further humiliation by getting the crotch of my running shorts hung up in some dangling barbed wire.

The bubbly clouds in the distance reminded me again my more rational choice was to head back home. With one last glance toward the two people at the boathouse, I elevated my running speed once again along the graveled lakeside road. For a moment I thought one of those two workers waved at me…the one holding the gas lantern…but, I couldn't be certain. My peripheral vision was hardly twenty/twenty. It could have been she was just throwing more sticks and branches onto a garbage pile…or, maybe I just wished it was a wave.

Arriving home I was disappointed that no one had miraculously stopped by and cleaned the fallen branches off my lawn or repaired my dock. Dean Rutherford could have come over. What kind of rotten neighbor was he? He knew my penchant for procrastinating.

Scoffing at my folly, I could not list the times the Rutherfords had helped me and the numbers of lunches and dinners I'd had at their place. We had become fast friends having met the very day I moved into my cottage six years before.

I ate a couple over ripe bananas, a slightly dried blueberry muffin, and drank the last of my leftover coffee before finally venturing out onto my patio to check the weather. The massive cloud system now stretched across the northern part of the lake with some breathtaking lightning. Since my home was still in the sun, depending on the impulse of the winds, there was still a chance my side of the lake might miss the full brunt of the storm. This meant I certainly could start one of my outside projects and enjoy the view of the mighty thunderstorm while I worked.

I noticed some rotted wood on my outside sunroom window panels. It was yet another project. On a whim I decided to start that task. Taking down a couple of those window panels, I brought them to the garage for repair. The contrast of the bright sunlight beating down on me, the high humidity, and the blackness of the cloud cover across the lake made for a fanciful scene.

For twenty minutes I scraped the peeling paint from the panels. The next step was to paint them. Looking out from my garage, the dark sky to the north was just too picturesque to ignore. And, the calmness of the lake looked too inviting.

Putting down my work, I marched down to the dock. The water was still as death on my side of the lake. Stepping onto the dock, there was the usual wobble, but certainly not anything serious that required immediate repair. The dock project could definitely be prolonged…maybe until the next summer! Hearing a few boards crack as I walked to the end of the dock, I made a mental note to replace a few boards on the dock in the next few days, thereby possibly delaying the dock project for a couple years.

At the end of the dock, I stripped off my t-shirt and effortlessly dove into the peaceful water. The spring fed lake offered a slight shock to my system, but I was used to the coolness of the water. Rising out of the water, I could see Rutherford still sweating over another broken tree branch. He looked over at me and waved.

His envy was obvious. If his wife hadn't been working alongside him, he would have dove into the water and joined me.

I swam out into the lake until experience told me I should pay more consideration to the storm clouds. I'd always wondered if lightning hit the far end of the lake, would the electric current electrocute everyone in the water…even if I was on the opposite side of the huge lake. I'd never gotten a straight answer indicating I'd never actually asked the question or other people didn't know how to respond. Just the thought, however, persuaded me to return to my dock.

Pulling myself up to a sitting position on the dock, I put the t-shirt back on for warmth and continued watching the distant, active storm. Then I looked to the west towards the peninsula and was somewhat startled to see the blackened skies were extending much further south. The storm in fact was not going to pass along the north side of the lake. All indications now showed that the storm cloud was coming directly at me. I didn't have to seek cover just yet, but it looked more and more that the south side of the lake would get hit just as hard as the north side. The storm would give me good reason to paint those window panels inside the garage while the rain fell.

Fifteen minutes later I was still outside casually strolling along the shoreline tracking the slow moving storm and mindlessly picking up broken branches and stacking them on the sand. As yet, the water on my side of the lake was still undisturbed…smooth as glass. It brought forth the imagery that a person could run as fast as possible and maybe just maybe remain on top of the water for up to fifty yards before the glass would give way and the runner would plunge into the water. It was strange how I just couldn't leave the shoreline. I was hypnotized by the beauty of the approaching storm. Eventually I'd have to run up the hill to my cabin or garage, but I decided that wouldn't be necessary until the weather system had completely engulfed the peninsula. That would be my cue to get moving.

Looking the opposite way down the east side of the lake, there were a couple of boats pulling young water skiers intent on squeezing in every last minute of ski time. That was about the same time a huge blast of thunder and lightning exploded right over the peninsula. It shook the entire lake area.

In the next minute the lake was void of any boats. Distant, hurried voices echoed urgently to get everything under cover. Gradually even those voices became silent; only the distant rumbling in the sky and the slowly increasing air movement could be heard. Even the birds and squirrels began huddling up quietly in the cover of the trees. The lake continued to project a tranquil painting except for those periodic lightning bolts reflecting across the mirrored water.

My experience with storms told me there was still adequate time before the skies opened up. I stood on the shore mesmerized. The shear majesty of this particular oncoming storm was spellbinding. There I was on the south shoreline still in the sun and I was looking straight into the sweeping black rain clouds just over a mile away.

Ignoring the rumbling skies for a few minutes, I got interested in seeing exactly how many rotted boards I would need to replace on my dock. I'd made the count before but always forgotten the number demonstrating my interest in replacing the boards was not real. I can't explain why I was so casual with a storm so determinedly heading my way. Maybe it was because the sunlight was still cast upon me. I just wasn't paying attention to how fast that sunlight was disappearing.

Another explosion of lightning followed by a deafening blast of thunder over the peninsula made me lose my count again. Now it was time to seek cover. Leaving the dock, I grabbed some broken branches in the water and threw the pieces up onto the sandy shore. In the next moment the sounds of the increasing wind through the trees suddenly accelerated. The glass-like lake abruptly showed waves of water. More thunder and lightning combined to force me to pick up my gait as I marched up the hill.

To this day I don't know why I treated that gargantuan storm so nonchalantly. I kept picking up more loose branches as I climbed the hill. There was no reason I shouldn't have been more careful. Storms have always had such a strangely relaxing and calming impact on me. The beating of rain on the roof can put me to sleep faster than a sleeping pill. Furthermore, there was something about a fresh rainstorm…as if it was purging the surrounding area of all sins done by man and beast…. at least those evils done since the previous storm. Then, following this spectacular environmental cleansing by the thunderstorm, everything and everyone could begin afresh in any manner they wished…like a rebirth.

I stopped again on the way up the hill to take a huge broken branch off of a bird feeder. It was not the time to do such small tasks, but when I was in such a peaceful mood, it seemed as if I had the patience of Job. I had no urge to hurry. I just wanted to enjoy the beauty of the day and the splendor of the oncoming squall.

Again a flash appeared…this time directly overhead. I snickered over my far-fetched thoughts about a rain cleansing a person's inner self. There might be a question whether most people would even want to be 'reborn' anyway. The change might take too much effort and the new, improved model of their soul might not be to their liking.

I knew of no one else who got as inspired by a powerful act of nature as I did over a thunderstorm. Most people would already be huddled in a place of safety. They wouldn't be standing half way up the hill between their dock and their house watching the front edge of an approaching electrical storm. I began to ask myself what I hoped to prove…that I could coolly slip inside my cottage with a sheet of rain but ten feet behind me.

With a few drips of rain beginning to ripple the now wavy lake, it was time to hurry. Increasing my pace I glanced westward one last time. The sheets of rain now covered the Lindstrom peninsula. I no longer could even make out that piece of land.

Another strike of lightning hit low up the shoreline between the unseen peninsula and my property. The thunder immediately after told me the storm was moving incredibly fast. Huge drops began to fall. I had waited too long. Scampering up the remainder of the short hill, my profound thoughts were dissolving as quickly as the rain was soaking me. Another large flash of lightning with accompanying thunderclap made me duck…as if hugging the ground was going to do any good. I had seriously mistimed this storm. My heart pounded hard as a lightning bolt hit the ground near my neighbor's home to the west. I had often hustled in from on-coming storms from the end of my dock…in fact, numerous times… and made it to safety with only a slightly dampened shirt. This storm was like a bucket being poured over me.

Then, another jolt of thunder or lightning caused me to go down to one knee as if unconsciously my brain was forcing me to stoop. I got back up but as I moved one of my drenched shoes came off in some mud. I reached down to pick it up…and that was when things got hazy. The flash was unbelievable and instantaneous. I have tried to rematerialize that moment countless times during my life, but I have little recall of the ferocity.

My delay in making it up the hill to my cottage had been grossly misjudged and left me vulnerable. When that lightning flashed, it was as if I was being elevated off the pathway. I heard no thunder. I felt no pain, but I did feel an immediate fogginess and a tremendous jolt to my body.

I don't recall blacking out…only pumping my legs in an effort to reach my cabin. It was so strange. Despite churning my legs doggedly, I had a general languid feeling. I sensed my body was floating toward my screened porch. I had no memory of my feet touching the ground. Things were very bleary. The screen door flew open and suddenly it was dry and very quiet. Groggy and soaked, I sat down on my daybed and kept rubbing my head and eyes. I was conscious, but I wasn't certain about anything…as if my mind and body weren't in sync.

I laid my head back. I felt a chill as the wind and rain were blowing through the screens of the semi-opened windows. I opened my eyes and saw a mist floating across the small room. I kept popping in and out of consciousness. I couldn't believe how unstable I was. Unable or unwilling to close the window, I grabbed at a blanket and pulled it over me. Then things just went black.

I don't know how long it was, but I was surrounded by darkness when I finally regained some consciousness. My head was fuzzy, but I could tell it was much later. I looked outside and figured either the sky was overcast or I'd been sleeping for quite a few hours. The blackness made me question whether I was truly awake or dead. I lay there wondering if I was simply waiting to be transported to the here-after. It occurred to me that I should get up off the daybed and refuse to go? That was my first indication I was still among the living. I still had my sense of humor.

Shaking my head, my brains didn't seem to rattle any more than usual. Relieved I was still breathing, my vision was still impaired. I couldn't make out the time on the clock in the kitchen. All I had to do was get up off the daybed, walk into the kitchen, and get closer to the clock. The problem was that I just didn't feel like moving.

Suddenly there was a noisy sound coming from the outdoors. I sat up abruptly. It was so loud. Then I realized it was nothing more than the swishing of the wind through the trees. My senses were so intense. I could hear animals…squirrels jumping around in the outdoor leaves and brush…birds chirping very quietly but far into the forest across the road…even a fish jumping and making a small splashing sound in the lake. The smells coming in through the screen windows were so unbelievably fresh. There was no man-made smells of cooked meat from some party on down the shoreline, no stench of gas from an outside grill, no dank odor from the garage where so many projects waited my attention. There was only the smell of waterlogged foliage and the sweet smell of flowering plant life brought into the sunroom by the crisp, fresh breeze following the huge thunderstorm.

Still dazed, I struggled to stand and finally did. I staggered over to one of the open window screens. With the humidity, there was a moist nighttime fog hanging in the air. Other than my barely visible dock, I could see nothing else through the haze…no other lights…not the Rutherford's dock on down the shoreline…not even the broken branches I'd begun stacking down on the sand by the water. It was almost eerie.

Then my eyes returned to the faint appearance of my dock. Somehow it looked different, as if it had been newly built…or repaired. Maybe Dean Rutherford had come over and done a good neighborly deed after all. That thought was of course ridiculous. He'd been working hard on his own property. Still, my dock appeared somehow fuller and sturdier. As my vision adapted to the dark, I followed the outline of the dock and made out a small boat moored at the end of it. 'That was strange,' I thought, 'Someone's boat got blown over to my shoreline.'

I panned my eyes down the east shore past the Rutherford's lake home. What I saw through the mist didn't make any sense. Where was my neighbor's dock… or anyone else's dock further down the lake shore? Did the wind from the storm blow these docks up onto the shore? If so, why then was mine still standing? I wasn't located in any small cove to protect my cottage and dock from some high velocity wind. But, by God, there was my dock standing stalwartly in the water looking like it was built yesterday.

I decided to find out what was going on. Walking haltingly out my door, I maneuvered down the slippery slope of my lawn to the water's edge still feeling as foggy as the outdoors. The new stone walkway down to the dock that I'd toiled over the previous summer was completely gone. It sickened me to think that all my work had apparently been washed down the hill by the storm. But then, where were the bricks? Had they actually been washed into the lake? If so, then I'd slept through a doozy of a storm.

I stopped for a moment trying to clear out my brain. It was especially dark adding to my confusion. Maybe the walkway was on the other side of my lawn. Maybe….and then I stopped trying to think…nothing would compute.

Approaching what apparently was my dock, I immediately was filled with wonder and a new respect. My neighbors would have to rebuild their docks after finding them floating in pieces in the lake or broken up on shore. But, my dock survived the storm as if it was a mighty warship. I had thought it wobbled when I walked on it. How wrong I was. In fact, it was a pillar of strength.

I stood there straining to see anything familiar up and down both shorelines. There was only empty dark water along with an equally unlighted shoreline. I felt like the last living human being. I might have panicked had I not seen some lightning in the distant eastern sky. That proved the storm and come and gone. However, given the many hours I'd laid in my sunroom, maybe that departing storm was yet another tempest that had come and gone as I'd slept?

The air was now cooler, but oddly I was not chilled. I turned and looked down the opposite shoreline. It didn't surprise me I wasn't able to see my two neighbors' cabins to the immediate west. They were typically hidden in their own foliage even on an average night.

My eyes momentarily stared into the haze towards the peninsula and then directly across the lake to the village of Lake Catherine. Again I expected to see nothing… until I saw a glint…like a very faint light when a sea captain finally sees the first glimmer of a harbor light. I blinked again and again. I could see nothing else in the fog, but that pale gleam. It was not a stable light. It flickered… like a gas lantern. If it was an electric light, the beam would have been steady. The uneven sparkle seemed to be located in the vicinity of where the dock existed at the Lindstrom peninsula. But, that was not possible. That location was over a mile away! How was it that I could see that flickering light at the peninsula and I couldn't make out any lights down the more populated south shoreline closer to my property?

I stepped up onto my dock enraptured by the peculiarity. Half conscious or not, there was no doubt it was some kind of light. Thinking it some kind of mirage, I moved forward to the middle of the dock for a different view. There was no change…only blackness between my neighbors' homes between the peninsula and my place. In the hazy darkness, it was as if the two lake homes didn't exist.

I then looked back toward the peninsula. There it was again…that flickering light. I scratched my head. It was such an oddity to see that lonely glimmer.

I then finally moved to the end of the dock and glanced down at the vessel next to my dock. It hadn't just floated over to my property. It was actually tied to my dock. It was a very old style wood canoe but in usable condition…or, at least it was floating. I looked around wondering who might have brought the boat over to my place. Was there a person in my cabin having sought cover from the storm? I just couldn't figure why all these strange occurrences were happening.

My senses continued to be acute. I stood there on that dock now listening for any sounds of people's voices, distant car engines….anything. Normally there would be the croaking of frogs and toads…or the chirping of crickets. At that moment there were no typical nighttime sounds. But, in the far distance into the blackness of the night, I finally heard something. It was a voice…and even some laughter. Holding my breath so my respiration wouldn't interrupt the sound, I could discern the cackle was coming from the direction of that flickering light through the mist toward the peninsula. Apparently the sound was echoing beneath the fog cover.

While I didn't feel at full strength mentally, I felt very able physically. I drew in a deep breath and let out a yell. "Hey…can you hear me? Who's over there?"

Across the silent waters in the direction of the voice and laughter, my bellow must have startled someone. The voice and laughter stopped abruptly. The flicker of the light, however, remained.

A few moments later the voice rose again…this time a bit louder as if to find out who had responded to him. I couldn't make out the words. What possessed me then to get into that canoe, I can't explain. However, with nothing making sense, I figured it might help if I found out who was connected to that voice.

I paddled away from the dock close to shore but using that glimmer of light as a focal point. I felt no danger. The night was so serene. It reminded me of that time many years before during college when I paddled a canoe over to the peninsula thinking it would be my last night ever at Lake Catherine. Now my purpose was different. I just wanted to find someone to talk with…and maybe find out how serious the storm…or storms…had been.

As my oar sliced through the calm water, I felt like I was going faster than my strokes could support. The extreme still of the evening was disquieting, but I kept going with the bow of the canoe pointed directly toward that flickering light. I could hardly wait to see another human…just to make certain life as I knew it still existed. Besides, if I was truly injured, maybe that person hopefully located next to that flickering light could drive me to a local clinic.

As I neared that beacon of light, I slowed the canoe listening for that distinctive mixture of voice and laughter. There was only silence. I stopped paddling holding my oar across my lap. The only sound was a few droplets of water off that oar into the still lake. Then…there it was…that same voice…but much lower in volume. I was listening for a second voice but I could only make out one. A shudder went through my body. I recalled local stories of how Ray Lindstrom's voice could be heard reverberating across the lake late at night. Some said his voice and laughter could still be heard even years after his death, especially on hazy nights when sound could carry much further under the fog. But, those were folk tales. Old Ray had been gone a long time. Somebody staying at the mansion was obviously taking a page out of his legacy and doing a good job of impersonation. So good in fact that the tingle up and down my spine wouldn't go away.

I continued moving toward that vague blinking light, determined to find an answer. I was certain I was conscious. Though woozy, I figured I wouldn't have shuddered if I wasn't somewhat alert. My canoe glided into what I was certain was the bay by the peninsula. The low din of the man's voice was now more discernible. Nothing was going to keep me from talking with this person on the Lindstrom dock...whoever he was.

And then, as if by magic, there was a slight clearing in the air above the water. I could see the shape of the peninsula as clear as the night would allow. The dock was less than fifty yards away underneath the twenty foot ceiling of haze. Gradually a figure of a man sitting in an overstuffed chair putting some bait on a hook came into view. There was a lighted gas lantern at his feet. He was whistling...the very picture of a relaxed and contented human being. I leaned forward trying to make out the man's identity. Having lived at the lake for six years, maybe I'd know him.

I didn't want to startle the fellow, so I created some noise by softly hitting the side of the canoe with my paddle. As I did so, my eyes were fixed on the figure in the chair as if fearing the man might disappear.

I tried not to shout, but my voice came out fuller than intended. I roared, "Hey there...you catching anything?"

There was a delay and then a response in a surprised, low voice. "Who's that?"

Without responding to his question I moved closer to his dock and continued the innocent dialogue. "I'm just enjoying a quiet time on the lake in my canoe after a big storm. I saw your light. In fact, yours was the only illumination I could see anywhere on this side of the lake. Everyone else's lights and power must have been knocked out by the storm. I figured I'd just head this way."

The man with the fishing pole mumbled something about 'what other lights'.

I let that comment pass and continued adamantly forward not letting myself blink. If I was in a dream, I wanted to recall as much of this bizarre night as possible. My voice came out unnaturally shrill as I shouted, "Yes sir, I also wanted to ask your assistance. I think I got stunned by a bolt of lightning a few hours ago over at my cabin. I think I'm a bit dazed."

At first, there was no reaction. The man with the fishing pole didn't seem to understand that I was in some distress. In fact his hearing didn't seem to work so well. After a considerable delay, my words must have finally connected. He responded, "Well, paddle on over here. Let's see if you're all right."

I followed his order and paddled a bit faster. As I moved closer to the dock, I felt this overwhelming stab of pain whipping through my head...like I was someplace I wasn't supposed to be.

The image of that time when I'd stood up in the canoe at roughly this same location and knocked my head on an overhanging branch now came to me as clearly as if it were the day before. That night I had met Ray Lindstrom...and I had talked to him. I'd thought about that experience so often over the last twelve years. I recollected how unsteady I'd been, enough so that he remained with me until he figured I was in good enough shape to canoe back to the Hagen cabin.

Yet, there was one thing I couldn't remember from that time so long ago. Though I was on that dock talking with old Ray for quite a while, my thoughts and dreams of that night could not paint a memory of his face. I could recall he wore a hat with a brim that hung over his forehead. He had a grizzled beard with a toothpick hanging from his mouth. Even when I did look his way as he sat on his easy chair on the dock, the dancing flame from the gas lantern cast jittery shadows across his face preventing me from getting a real fix on his facial features.

Now so many years later I sensed I was living through the same experience... including the same dizzy feeling... but this time caused by my misadventure with the lightning bolt a few hours before. Floating up to the dock, I observed a scene that brought shivers up and down my spine. There was a man leaning forward on that same easy chair I'd seen on the dock so long ago. He wore a different hat, a fisherman's cap, but with the brim still worn low over his eyes. While I couldn't make out his face, I was conscious enough that I swore to myself I would do everything I could to get a full glimpse of his face before I left that dock.

The man suddenly got up from his chair and trudged toward me. At first I was skeptical until I heard his soothing voice. He sounded concerned. "Come on up to the dock, son" he said. "Let's check you out and see if you're O.K."

He offered his hand and I grabbed it. He had a glove on so I couldn't feel his skin. What immediately hit me, though, was the strange musty smell...like his clothing needed a good wash. The odor was somewhat balanced by the pipe tobacco he was smoking. I hadn't seen a man smoke a pipe in years.

As I got up on the dock, he observed my movement. "Well, young fella, you seem to be moving all right. Are you seeing spots?"

I shook my head. "No, but my brain seems to be working at half-pace."

Motioning for me to sit on the dock, he went back to his easy chair on the dock. Smiling he said, "Well, son, a lot of people around these parts would be satisfied to have their noggin working even halfway."

I couldn't help but laugh at his little joke. Seeing my reaction, he seemed less concerned about my condition. Grabbing his fishing pole beside his chair, he said, "Son, why don't we sit a spell and just talk? If you start acting goofy... well, we'll give old Doc Halverson a call. He's a good man. He'll come over even at this late hour. By the way, where did it happen...this lightning bolt that apparently got you?"

Disregarding his last question for the moment, I was perplexed by the name Doc Halverson. The musty smelling man talked of this doctor as if everyone should know the man. The only Halverson I'd known was a really old guy who played cribbage a couple mornings a week down at the General Store. He'd died five years before during the very next winter after I'd purchased the Hagen property. The coffee drinkers always referred to him as 'Doc'. My memory of him was that he seemed to have been retired from the doctoring game for a very long time.

I finally responded, "Oh yes…the lightning bolt…it happened a few hours ago. I live at the old Hagen place. I was scampering up the hill to beat the storm. It was too fast and overtook me. I just remember a huge boom. I guess I made it inside the cabin because I woke up but feeling foggy as the night. I went outside and saw nothing through the haze…except your light over here at the peninsula. In fact, the funniest thing…your flickering gas lantern was the only thing I could see in the darkness. I don't know how that was possible given the distance. It has to be at least a mile."

Not having an answer, the older man shrugged and said, "Well, it's good you saw me if you're not feeling so good. Why don't you take your shoes off and dip your bare feet in the cool water. Maybe that'll wake up your head."

I did what he said while he began baiting his hook. I didn't want to say it out loud, but fishing at that hour seemed a trifle weird to me. Feeling a bit odd, I was finding it difficult searching for something to say.

Finally he broke the silence. "Kinda late at night to go out canoeing, ain't it? Then again, you might be feeling the same thing about me out here fishin'."

The man was perceptive. I had to say that for him. Again not knowing what to reply, he thankfully continued talking. "For me, son, it's the time I find most relaxing…so silent and calm out here at this hour. But, that's my preference."

I snickered but stayed quiet still not believing my surroundings. He seemed content to refer to me as 'son' as if I was some kind of little league ball player. He never offered me his name as he continually cast his line out into the hazy darkness. I couldn't see it, but I could hear the bobber plop into the water.

Then he put his fishing pole down and reached around his chair. His voice brightened, "Son, you might want some of my coffee. It might give you a bit of a jolt and get you thinkin' straight again. Here…take some from my thermos."

He reached over and handed me the container with a plastic cup…like the ones used when I was a small boy at a picnic with my folks. His movement caused me to catch another whiff of the aged, mildewed smell of his clothing. Though distinct, it was not that bothersome.

I opened the thermos and the coffee was steaming. I was finally able to get a slight glimpse of his facial features under that low brim. His face was thin and ruddy with a couple days growth of grayish beard. His cheeks had deep creases, but his forehead was unlined…maybe a testimony to his preference for relaxing out on the dock. What I mostly noticed were his eyes. They were attentive and very alert as if trying not to show any concern over my malaise, yet observant if I showed any physical difficulty.

Until he leaned back into the darkness of his easy chair, I tried to memorize that face. I figured I'd eventually get his name, but I wanted to remember that face. For his kindness, I wanted to at least be able to recognize and greet him if I saw him again.

As I sipped the soothing drink, the old man appeared perfectly willing not to say a word while watching for a ripple in the area he was fishing. The water was surprisingly warm on my feet; the coffee was having the same effect on my insides. I began to feel much better, almost as if I could lay right down on that dock and sleep.

Instead, I remained determined. I wanted to find out who this old fellow was. He certainly reminded me of the long deceased Ray Lindstrom, even though I never saw his face that one night twelve years before. It was more in his mannerisms and voice that were faintly recognizable.

Trying to participate more in the conversation, I treaded lightly. "So, what makes you so content sitting alone out here at this late hour after a big storm?"

He grinned. "Oh, I don't know. It probably had a lot to do with my nature. I never took things too seriously. I appreciated the things that I accomplished. I tried not to think of too many sad times…like when people dear to me passed on. I mostly thought about the good times in my life…about the risks I took and how things turned out. Generally I'd have to say I enjoyed my life. Still, there were a couple things I wished I could have changed. But, I found out life was better if you could learn to accept your past, not dwell on the bad things that might have happened, and move on with hope and willingness to make things better."

As he chatted on, I noticed immediately how he talked in the past tense…as if the present was no longer part of his life. His comments were interesting. Not once did he refer to his current life…or what he was looking forward to doing. Tomorrow was not part of his thinking. Admittedly I was slightly unnerved.

Without ever giving so much as a hint as to who he was, this older gentleman just kept talking on. He related a story how he had won bids on two lakeside properties and how he'd made them very profitable investments. "It's what you make of what you get that counts." The fellow was full of sage sayings.

Then he was silent as he cast his line again far out into the darkened lake. The atmosphere was so relaxing. I was so afraid of nodding off only to wake up later with him gone and having to admit what I was experiencing was only a dream. But, it was not. I was there…on the dock…with a strange but friendly very old man.

I forced myself to keep asking trifling questions, so I'd stay awake and he wouldn't leave. I inquired, "So….you live here alone, do you?"

His answer skirted my question. He mumbled, "The property has been in the family name for a long time."

Hoping he'd say more I stayed silent. With one more cast, he spoke ignoring my question and making a reference to his family. "Yes, my wife and I instilled in our kids the importance of being responsible for their actions, to treat people as they wished to be treated, to enjoy life but not at the expense of others…and above all, to be honest. That's about it. Generally I'd say they've followed the advice."

There was a slight delay before he chuckled and expounded, "You know, son, that 'honest' thing can be difficult at times. In business that was easy. It was more trouble if you didn't deal in the truth. However, I wasn't always straight-forward with my wife and kids. He then grinned as if remembering times past. "Nothing serious mind you…like when my wife's weight fluctuated and she sought approval. I always said the right thing even though it might have been a damned lie. But, it made her feel better."

We both laughed at that rejoinder. It caused his body to move and that omnipresent musty smell to become stronger. He wasn't done philosophizing. Taking his pipe from his mouth, he said, "As for the kids, I often made up some stories just to make my point. When they were young, they never questioned whether my stories were true or not. As they got older, I think they knew the tales were a bit far-fetched, but they appreciated my efforts to help them."

We gabbed on into the night with him continuing to do most of the talking. I found his beliefs a bit too simple, but other times he made me think. All the time he was talking, I felt his eyes on me weighing my condition.

I reflected back to my own father…a small business owner in Faribault, Minnesota. He was respected in the community…a very good and generous man. I always felt he simply expected me to behave properly. He had confidence in me. I knew the difference between right and wrong and usually made the morally right decision. I certainly slipped up a few times. When I did, I did the best job of hiding those mistakes or misjudgments to keep him from being disappointed in me. Generally, though, I always thought he was proud of me.

Still, as I sat there with my feet in the water, I couldn't recall my own father ever talking as heartfelt to me as this man was as he sat there in his comfortable easychair on the dock. This guy was so sincere and simplistic in telling me about how he raised his offspring and how he influenced their attitudes on life. Despite my cloudy brain, I found myself nodding and even intrigued by his sharp perceptions.

I don't know how late it got to be. I must have had three cups of his coffee. He was constantly filling his own cup. I didn't think his thermos could hold that amount of coffee. The warmth of the drink kept me comfortable and probably awake. I recall the night being still as death except for his voice echoing under the fog. Even the breeze was nonexistent.

A fish leaped out of the water and made a slight splash. The splash was startling. The old guy blustered, "Damn, there's one I should have had."

He tossed his line in the direction of the ripple. He was silent again as he waited for a possible response from the fish.

Our conversation drifted to some other subjects including fishing…and the weather. I made another attempt to get this man to divulge who he was, but he would invariably dodge or ignore my question. In some ways I was afraid what he might say. It might prove that I had a brain injury after all.

I barged ahead anyway and asked, "Tell me…you mentioned your kids. No offense to your age, but they must be grown. If you're a normal parent, you have to be proud of them. Are you happy the way their lives are progressing? Are those values you've been talking about engrained in them?"

He seemed surprised by my curiosity. He lit his pipe before responding. His plaintive reply was much lower in volume. "You know, son, up to a few years ago, things seemed to be going well for them. Of course, I don't see as much of them anymore. They're married and don't get up here much."

'There he was,' I thought, 'talking in the past again.'

A few more puffs on his pipe and he continued, "I now only evaluate and hope for their happiness from a distance. I can't really worry about things I can't control."

I smiled at yet another of his bromides as he silently baited his hook again. I tried a different tact to keep the man talking. "So how often do you come out at this time of night? I've lived around here for quite a few years. I can't say I've seen you before?"

Showing a sly grin he said, "I'm out here as often as I can be, but usually later at night…and as long as the owner of the property doesn't mind. I like the solitude. There's nothing like the tranquility of the lake, the fish waiting gamely for me to tease them with my bait and line, and the strangely peaceful sounds of an evening thunderstorm approaching or departing."

The man was almost poetic. We both became silent once again. The fog still covered the lake area as if it would never dissipate. I couldn't even see the mansion up on the hill. Every now and again, I thought I saw an occasional light from the town through the mist, but I couldn't be certain. It might have been a reflection from the lone gas lantern light sitting beside the old guy on his easy chair.

The old man then stared at me as he stuffed his pipe with more tobacco. I was moving my head from side to side stretching my neck trying to get more blood flow to my head. Seeing this he sat back in his chair. He must have figured I wasn't ready yet to paddle back to my home.

Lighting up the pipe, the aroma immediately helped cover up more of the stale and stuffy smell of his clothing. As we talked, it occurred to me he took for granted I knew who he was. That made it more difficult to ask him his name. I didn't want to disappoint him. Besides, I figured he'd give away who he was eventually.

Then, with no prodding from me, he began talking about the owner of the property. I leaned toward him certain he was going to put more order to our conversation.

"Yep," he said, "I've been spending a lot of time on this here dock listening to a young lady talk about the challenges in her life. She has a job that keeps her very busy traveling. Her first marriage didn't take. She said her father never thought the guy was her caliber anyway. I guess a lot of fathers might feel that way…maybe until the son-in-law does something to prove himself. Apparently this guy never did. I guess a good thing was that they never had any kids. That made the divorce easier. She said he lives overseas someplace. They'll never get back together."

He shook his head in sympathy before snickering. "Lately when she's out here on the dock, her talk is not so much about her failed marriage as the enjoyable times she had while she was growing up here on this lake."

He stopped. It was the first time he'd talked in the present tense. That realization seemed to make him uncomfortable. However, I wouldn't let him leave the subject. I quickly asked, "So, where is she now? I'd like to meet her."

The older guy nodded. "Yeh, she's about. She's been getting up here more often in the recent weeks. She's been pondering whether to live here full time… or the other extreme…to sell the place outright. She's afraid living here she'll be too remote and won't be able to find the kind of work she wants to do. She sounds like she no longer wants to travel so heavily anymore. She seems to be looking for a change of pace. I have the feeling she'll make the best decision for herself. I've found her to be a real sharp gal."

He pulled his line quickly thinking he had a bite, but it didn't take. I heard him swear again under his breath before he interjected, "Yup, she's come up to the lake the last few Friday nights. She'll stay the weekend and just enjoy the place like she did so many years ago. Her talk is about a lot of things besides the peninsula. Lately she's been interested in chatting about taking risks. She wishes she knew more about what made her father take the gamble when he bought this property."

Then his voice again grew soft. "I know selling the property is heavy on her mind. It might not be a bad idea, but she just needs to talk it out. She's trying to weigh the possibilities in her own life right now. I believe she lost a bit of confidence about making decisions after her marriage failed."

The older fellow then sighed and mumbled something about "not being around anyway"…and then added, "While she's finding people around here she can trust, I'm glad she still seeks me out."

He paused to fill both our cups with more coffee and then said, "Just last weekend she was sitting just like you are with her feet dangling in the water. She looked more contented than I'd seen her in years. She began talking before I even sat down on my easy chair. She said, 'There's no way I'm going to sell the house or the land on the peninsula for now. It would be like selling a piece of my soul. I've made some money. I'm going to bring this place back to the condition it should be in…and maybe even try living here year round for a while.'

His mouth opened showing a smile with old teeth. There was then only silence before a slight burst of a northwesterly breeze made the leaves in the trees swish back and forth. It was the first real noise I'd heard since pulling up to the dock. After a thunderstorm it was not unusual for a weather system to blow through with cooler, dryer air. That wind was cool but it was also humid. The storms were not over at Lake Catherine.

That air movement brought me back to more consciousness and the old man seemed to realize it. He suddenly got up from his chair as if deciding at that moment to leave. He picked up his fishing pole and a small container holding some bait. Putting away his fishing gear, he silently grabbed the gas lantern and the coffee canister and began sauntering away from the chair toward the boathouse. He didn't even say 'good-by'. He just ambled away.

I didn't want him to leave and shouted out, "I'd like to stop back and talk with you some more after I get a good night's sleep. I'm feeling better. Are you going to be around?"

He chuckled, "Of course, son, just don't you mind if people around here begin thinking your nuts for coming over here so late into the night. They'll think you're talking to yourself!"

Then he laughed mirthfully as if he hadn't told a joke that funny for years. As he shuffled away, the effect on me was quite the opposite. His laugh caused a chill requiring me to pull my feet from the water.

Stiffly rising, I moved slowly down the dock not wanting the conversation to end. As he walked by the boathouse and began climbing the steps, I yelled out the first thing that crossed my mind. "By the way, what are the best areas to fish in this lake?" I figured no Minnesota fisherman could escape a question like that without offering an opinion.

Sure enough, he stopped on the second step. I could barely see him in the darkness. He turned taking a toothpick from his mouth and offered, "Son, if you got a fly rod, there are some great spots on both sides of this peninsula. Don't hesitate. Just come on over."

Urgently, I responded, "Great…I'll give it a try. In fact, I've been intending to buy a new rod. Mine is an old one left in the garage. It's in bad shape. I think it was Jim Hagen's fly rod."

I heard the old gentleman chuckle and then mumble, "Yeh, I remember that one. It was rusty years ago too."

I quickly asked, "What did you say?"

He waved his arm and shouted back, "Ah….nothing important."

Stopping once again, he yelled, "Tell you what. There's a fly rod in the boathouse that hardly has been used. Maybe if we talk again, I can let you take it home. I won't get a chance to use that new rod."

I thought, 'there he goes again saying things as if he wasn't in the present'. I decided to let the comment pass. His offer gave me hope for seeing him again."

I let him know my appreciation. "Yeh…that would be great. Thanks."

Then, he continued climbing the steps by the boathouse with the gas lantern moving to and fro until I no longer heard his feet clomping up the steps. He and the flickering gas lantern simply disappeared into the night.

That was when it hit me…about the fly rod. Ray Lindstrom had invited me to use his fly rod those many years ago. It was a parting offer from him…to lend it to me the next time I made it back to Lake Catherine. He must have assumed I'd be back…only much sooner than the dozen years since I'd last sat on his dock.

Another sharp pain attacked my temples. Who was this guy? How did he know about the fly rod in the boathouse? Furthermore, if it wasn't his to give, why would he make the offer?

I had to stop thinking. It was time to get back to the cabin. I was tired and it would take all my concentration to return and not get lost out in the middle of the lake. With the change in the temperature and the now prevalent breeze, it felt like rain could happen once again.

Pushing off from the dock and paddling the canoe closer to the shoreline, I made one last glance back toward the boathouse. I could barely make out the small building much less the dock or the easy chair where the old man was sitting. Though it was impossible, everything the man said and did reminded me of Ray Lindstrom. He certainly seemed to know the young woman who now owned the property very well.

I finally stopped thinking and just paddled. All the way back to my cottage, the air remained thick as pea soup. Usually a breeze might blow away the fog. That night the haze felt only heavy. Staying close to the shoreline, I was still unable to make out anything of my two neighbors' lake homes between the peninsula and my cabin as I passed. I began to wonder if their houses could have been seriously damaged by the afternoon's storm. Their docks were nowhere to be seen.

Thanks to the trailing wind, I made it back to my home in no time. I was exhausted beyond description. I wondered if I'd fallen asleep once or twice while paddling. The dock looked as sturdy as it had when I'd left it. Gazing up the hill, I was barely able to see my lake home. At least it was there. That seemed important at the time since nothing else familiar was detectable along my route.

Despite my exhaustion, I made certain to tie the canoe up to the mooring on the dock very securely. I wanted to see it there when I awoke the next morning. Staggering up the hill toward my cabin, I plowed through the screen door into my sunroom. I had no energy to go further. The daybed looked as inviting as my own bed. I didn't want to take another step…even to my bedroom down the hallway. Lying down, I snuggled under the quilted blanket. Sleep came immediately.

When I awoke Sunday morning, it felt like I'd slept for days. I was suffering no more ill effects from the Friday night party and my mind was clearing after the ordeal with the lightning flash the previous afternoon. I lay there pondering all that had happened since being stunned by the lightning. I recalled making it into the cabin and then waking up in the middle of the night. Vaguely I remembered seeing a flickering flame over at the peninsula, but seeing no other light, no other lake home, indeed, no other anything except a mysterious older fellow who talked a lot and was constantly casting his fishing line.

That man…his smell…who was he? I sat up abruptly, rubbed my eyes, and looked out the sunroom windows to a bright Sunday morning. All the haze and fog following the endless thunderstorm activity of the previous late afternoon and evening had evaporated into a beautiful day. I smelled my hands to sense if any odors from the fellow I'd met could still be noticed. It was vague, but I swore my hand had the aroma of coffee.

I lay back down hoping to re-run a few more clips of what I rationalized had been a very intense dream. My recollection was hardly warming up when I heard a soft, very pleasant voice calling my name from outside my sunroom door. It sounded faintly like that same female who'd dropped by the day before.

I was still wrapped in that quilted blanket. She was climbing the stairs to the door. Like a shot, I sprang from the daybed toward the bathroom. I'd be damned if I was going to reflect the same unkempt portrayal of the previous morning.

I felt better but I truly did not want to hear her fist pounding against the metal screen door. I greeted her with a stronger, firmer voice from the bathroom. "Good morning…I'll be right there."

Quickly throwing water on my face, I pulled on some clean pants and shirt. Throwing the towel over my shoulder to make her think I was getting cleaned up, I went to the back patio door.

There she was. She was cleaned up with freshly combed hair…a picture of loveliness. She was admiring the view of the lake from a different perspective than the one she had over at the peninsula.

Meeting her at the door, she gave me a once over as if trying to see the good side of me. Her only comment was very matter-of-fact, "You need a door bell…or a hearing aid. I decided not to pound on your front door considering you looked like death yesterday morning. I knew a light tap on your door gets no response, so I decided to come around to your sunroom on the hope I might find you. So…have you already died and come back to life from some other party you attended last night?"

I decided to stand there and laugh rather than to match her wit. Ignoring her impression that I partied every night, I responded, "So…I have a real comedian at my door testing out her stage act. What do I owe the pleasure of your company this fine morning?"

She seemed pleased that I could articulate and even be amusing. Her voice was very cheerful. "Anyway, I don't know if you remember me. I'm the one who brought over that canoe yesterday morning. I don't remember if you asked me, but my name is Abbie."

'Wow,' I thought to myself, 'I must have left a hell of an impression yesterday morning if she believed I was that far gone. And, she was right, I hadn't asked her name. Since first seeing her working at her property, I only thought of her as Lindstrom's daughter from the past. Of course she had a first name. Maybe I was that far gone after the Friday night party and then Saturday's episode after the lightning strike.

"Yes," I said, "you're the one bringing the junk around to people's homes. I'm the lucky one who got the canoe. By the way, I don't remember you asking my name either. It's Chris in case you ever have to introduce me to someone.

She openly laughed as if not believing more humor could be offered from someone who'd look so wasted only the morning before.

With my pride at stake, I opened the door and invited her in. She hesitated for just a moment and then entered changing the subject. "My God…that's two straight nights of thunderstorms. When does it stop around here?"

Hoping the question was rhetorical, I instead asked about something I'd remembered seeing sometime during the night. "So…did you lose your power again and found the need for that gas lantern last night?"

She smirked, "Actually yes, I needed it…but I couldn't find it. I couldn't remember where I'd left it. Turned out it was down by the boathouse. I'd left it there last evening. I'm afraid the rain got it. When I finally return it to you, it'll be so rusty, it'll never work again. But, don't worry…I'll get you another one."

I chuckled, "Don't worry about it. I can't remember the last time I needed it." I thought to myself, 'And that was the God's honest truth!'

Gazing out my sunroom windows, she turned and looked at me almost approvingly. "You look a lot better this morning than you did yesterday morning. Last night's party must have ended earlier."

She was certain she had me pegged as some kind of aging frat boy. I decided to end that impression. "Actually I slept long and very well last night. I must have looked pretty bad yesterday morning. Actually I didn't feel as badly as I apparently looked. Nonetheless, I'm apparently not mature enough to attend neighborhood birthday parties that go beyond 10:00 PM. I've already figured I can lay the blame for my condition on my next door neighbor. I'm taking the approach that it was his fault, not my fault that I died Friday night and barely came to life Saturday morning. I may never attend another of his parties again if he lets his guests eat too much and imbibe in similar fashion. I hope you see a new me this morning. I feel there's a good chance I'm well on the road to recovery."

She actually laughed again at my folly. It surprised me…and I liked it. Maybe the lightning bolt suddenly made me amusing. I gazed past her shoulder out my window to where that flash of nature had jarred me. Nothing had been very clear since that moment.

Still, it was Sunday morning and I was definitely alive with a beautiful female standing in the middle of my sunroom. That combination hadn't happened in a long time.

Realizing I was being somewhat unsociable, I rubbed my mussed hair with my towel and gave her my best early morning grin. "You want some coffee? I was just about to make some." It was a blatant lie, but she seemed to buy it.

I searched her face for her reaction. It appeared neutral…a better base with which to proceed than the preceding morning. At least she wasn't turned off completely by my early morning condition…and she seemed to appreciate I was far friendlier than her first impression.

Without committing, she pronounced, "I actually had a couple reasons for stopping by again. The afternoon storm was mild compared to last night's storm. I lost my electricity about 10:00. It's funny…through the sheets of rain I could make out your house and that same flickering light I'd seen last night at your place. But, I knew it couldn't be your gas lantern. I still had it here at my place… even though I couldn't locate it. It was the strangest thing. I was about to drive over and bother you again, but I figured you might think I was unable to fend for myself. It was late and all I was going to do was sleep anyway. I read by candlelight until I got tired. The power came back sometime during the night while I slept."

Then she paused looking perplexed. "There was something else. Sometime during the night I thought I heard some muffled noises down by my boathouse. I got up once and looked out my window. The fog was so thick I couldn't see past some trees in the front lawn. I figured I must have been dreaming. Anyway, I have somebody from the power company coming over later this morning. I'm getting tired of living in the 19th century. I need to get some dependable electrical power…and that's the reason I'm here. I was wondering if you had some spare freezer space so I could save some of my frozen meats. I'm here only on the weekends for a while. If the power goes off while I'm gone, the meat will spoil."

Then she kidded. "Besides, I figured you owed me a favor for bringing back your canoe."

"Yes," I replied, "and in such good condition as well."

Remembering the canoe I'd been in the night before, I glanced beyond her and out the sunroom windows to my dock. I was hoping to see a canoe firmly tied to a sturdy dock. To my great disappointment, the morning sun shined upon my actual dock looking as tired as it did the previous afternoon. To top it all, there was no canoe anywhere on the water…only the decaying one leaning out against my garage.

I shook my head trying to free the left-over cobwebs in my skull. My mind had been blurry last night, but not so vague that I couldn't remember tying up a canoe…in good condition…to the end of an equally strong dock. Something was askew. That canoe ride over and back to the peninsula had happened. It couldn't have been a dream. And, that old man…he was real…he smelled real… we'd had a long conversation even though I couldn't recall at that moment very much detail. Maybe I'd slept so soundly in the last hour of sleep. Wasn't that how dreams could more easily be recalled?

Befuddled, I had to tune back into the conversation. Trying not to reveal my exasperation, I muttered, "Yeh…that was some storm last night. I actually fell asleep during the downpour. I didn't know it went on all night."

She seemed surprised. "You must be a sound sleeper. It rained until maybe 9:00 and then this heavy fog moved in. Like I say, it was low and thick, but every now and again it would break up slightly. That was the only reason I could occasionally see along the lakeshore and pick out the light on your porch. It may not have been the gas lantern, but it flickered like one. Maybe it was your outside patio light."

Then as if needing someone to share my own weird story, I couldn't help but blurt out some parts of my own previous evening. I had to be careful. I didn't want her to think I was unstable or some kind of lunatic. I said to her, "You know, it's interesting what you said about the light you saw at my place. Sometime last night I got up and looked out my back windows. Like you said, the fog was thick as pea-soup, but for a short time coincidentally I could see a flickering light but in the opposite direction towards the peninsula. Isn't that the damndest thing?"

Seeing her eyebrows raise, I decided not to go further. If I told her about the canoe trip or talking with a very old and musty-smelling man, she'd probably start backing away towards the door.

Her only response was to finally shrug her shoulders. She had no more an answer to the mystery than I did. Breaking our momentary quiet, she said, "Well, if your offer of coffee is still good, I'll go out and transfer my frozen meat to your freezer in the garage. By the time the coffee's brewed I'll be back."

With nothing in my freezer, I nodded, "Please... load up my freezer with whatever food you have. I'm happy to help. If you forget about the frozen food, it'll be all right with me. I'll see that it gets eaten."

My attempt at humor sailed right by her as she was already out the door yelling 'thanks'. She had banked on the fact I would help her and likely had some open freezer space. I wondered if there was something about my lifestyle that gave her that assurance.

While she made the transfer, I quickly got the coffee brewing, shaved and combed my hair. It was easily the best I'd looked since Friday before the party.

I was about to go out to the garage and help her when she opened the back screen door. When she saw me, I could tell she was impressed. Of course if you cleaned up any person who looked like they lived in a coal mine, they'd look better as well. It was still nice to see the approval in her eyes.

"Thanks again," she exclaimed, "I didn't take up that much of your freezer space, but I'll come back and retrieve the food when I have the reassurance of steady electricity. I have to leave this afternoon, so you might have the food until next weekend if that's all right."

I nodded while looking her over. She also had cleaned up well. Her auburn hair had some light strokes of blond and it flowed well below her shoulders. The previous day she had the hair crushed under a baseball cap. I thought she was attractive then. Standing in my kitchen that Sunday morning, she was downright gorgeous.

Pouring her coffee, I pointed to a stool for her to sit at my kitchen bar. She probably sensed I was staring at her. I in turn sensed she was used to it.

Ignoring my eyes she fell right into conversation. "By the way...was that you running by my place yesterday?"

That one question confirmed once and for all she was a Lindstrom and the owner of...or at least the partial owner...of the peninsula property. Given her auburn hair, I also immediately ascertained I was having coffee with the older of the two daughters...the girl of Johnny Hagen's dream as a boy...and admittedly mine as well during those visits to Lake Catherine during my youth.

For further clarification, I responded with a question. "Was that you cleaning up the foliage with the others at the peninsula yesterday? I couldn't quite recognize you from that distance. But I recognized your shape...rather...um...let me just say you looked different than your workmen.

She smiled at my embarrassing slip of the tongue. "Yes, that was me. I've been coming up here the past few weekends and working on my property. I practically grew up on this lake and on that peninsula. My father owned and developed the land for many years. You might have heard about him from some of the locals. His name was Ray...Ray Lundstrom."

"Really" I replied rather lamely. Suddenly I was feeling uncomfortable. Practically anything I could ask about her life on the peninsula, I had a pretty good idea of the answers whether from her past or even the most current information about her life from my conversation with the old guy the night before. Nevertheless, to check if what the old guy had said was true, I made up a question. "So...are you cleaning up the property to eventually sell it?"

Pensively she looked again out my window at the peninsula in the distance. "Well, that was my intention about a month ago. When my father passed after I was out of college, my sister and I muddled over what we should do with the lake property. It's so distant from Minneapolis and from the kind of work I do. In my sister Emily's case, she lives even further away. We just don't have the time to enjoy or care for the house or the landscaping. No doubt the folks who've lived around here for many years have to be disappointed the way the property has deteriorated. Selling seemed like the best choice, but every time I came back here since he died...which hasn't been often...I'd have second thoughts. I'm considering a job change right now, so this is the first summer I've had the time to travel back here to Lake Catherine. I guess the frequency of my trips got me interested in reviving the house and land."

Looking wistful, she reflected. "Now with each weekend trip, I find myself questioning whether I really want to sell. It's not just the memories. I really like the place. It's relaxing. I even enjoy working with the landscape crew. And, at the end of the day, I seem to always migrate down to the dock, stare at the stars, and just contemplate my future. I find it so soothing. It's like I've fallen in love with this location all over again. It's a real dilemma whether I should recommend to my sister we sell the property or not."

Then she turned back toward me. "Funny about that old dock by the peninsula boathouse...my father loved to fish off that dock in the evenings. He had an easy chair he liked to sit on while casting his line. It's a big ugly thing with artificial leather. A couple weekends ago I moved it out onto the dock from the moldy place in the boathouse where it was being stored. It seems more at home out on the dock. I like to sit in the chair and remember the times he and I would talk back in college. It's silly, but it's like he's still there with me on the dock."

I nodded my head and remained quiet. I didn't know what to say. It was as if I knew what she was going to say next. How did I know about the easy chair? How did I know she'd been coming up to the lake for the last few weekends as she contemplated her future? How did I know she lived in the Twin Cities and was considering whether to sell the property or not? How could I know in advance those things on her mind?

And her statement about 'it's like he's still there with me' gave me a chill. I had half a notion to tell her what had happened to me the previous night. I might have if I wasn't concerned about scaring her away.

I grabbed the coffee pot and re-filled her cup and mine before making another pot. She didn't object. In fact, she seemed quite willing to continue our conversation.

And talk we did…for over an hour that Sunday morning. I determinedly stayed away from the subject of my midnight canoe excursion…and my meeting the old man on the dock. It was a great time getting to know her. We shared highlights of our lives and had more than a few laughs. I would have invited her out to dinner that night if she hadn't already stated she was returning to the Twin Cities later that afternoon. I had to put that invitation on hold.

As we conversed I found myself being delighted by her every gesture. Her eyes came to life when she spoke. She had an energy that added to her attractiveness. However, I was still distracted. I wasn't ready to tell her about my knowledge of her going back to when I was a young teenager visiting the Hagen's at the very cabin we were sitting in. I might eventually talk about that part of my life at a later time. Right then I just wanted to get to know her based on our present lives.

Engrossed into the mid-morning, we were interrupted by a distant rumble that had now become quite familiar. We both rolled our eyes knowing what we were hearing. The weather prognostications had been dead on accurate so far that weekend. It sounded like their next prediction of another thunderstorm that day was coming true. We walked out onto my deck to view the western skies. And there it was…another dramatic thunderhead to the northwest directly beyond the peninsula.

Her response was immediate but reluctant, "I'd better go. I've got workers coming and I don't want the rain to scare them away. If I'm there I'll find them other things to help me with in the boathouse.

I found myself irritated with Mother Nature. While accompanying her to her vehicle, I thought of all those times I'd chided Johnny Hagen about being so reticent and shy. That provided me the motivation to be more forward. I said to her, "If you'd like, we could pick up our conversation next weekend when you're back at the lake."

She brightened for an instant and then furrowed her eyebrow. "I'd like that. I'm just not certain I'll be back next weekend. Tomorrow I've got to catch a flight to Chicago to meet with the heads of my company. As I said, I'm in the process deciding whether I want to remain with them or not. I know they like me, so I kind of wonder what their response might be. I've been at their beck and call for the last couple years traveling on a moment's notice. The money has been good, but I'm tired. I've had enough of the constant travel and living in hotels. Whether I stay with them or not, it'll likely depend on whether I can see a better future with my present employer…and whether they're willing to pay me a lot more money. I feel I now have an alternative. I wouldn't mind living here at the lake for a while at least and maybe pursue some other career ambitions. Who knows what might happen in a completely new venue."

Then she caught herself as if she'd shared more information than she'd intended. I had to hide my exasperation. I knew so much about the anguish she was going through, yet I couldn't let on without creating some serious questions from her. The best I could do was shrug and weakly suggest, "Well, whether it's next weekend or the weekend after, let me take you out to dinner. Maybe I can open your eyes to some of the many advantages when living around here full-time."

It was a feeble invitation, but the best I could do. Her response gave me some hope. "Yes, I'd like that. It'd be fun."

I'd made the gamble and won thanks to being primed by the old man the night before. He sensed she really wanted to set up her life at the lake as long as she could visualize herself in some kind of worthwhile activity. I felt I was one move ahead of her. I had the advantage of offering her some thoughts and ideas as she sorted out what her future might be like if she lived at Lake Catherine.

As she got in her vehicle I called out to her, "Say, I've got an idea. I've just acquired a bunch of frozen meat and other food items…in fact, just this morning. They're in my freezer. If I knew you were coming back next Friday, I could have some of the steaks defrosted and on the grill by the time you made it up here."

Her laugh was infectious. The half-assed joke about the frozen food …her frozen food…had scored. As she pulled away, she leaned out the driver's side window and yelled back, "You know what…dinner next Friday sounds fine. I'll do whatever I can to make it. See you then."

Seconds later she was driving away on the county road. Suddenly, the air seemed sweeter and the sun on the south side of the lake seemed brighter… despite the ominous approaching storm on the opposite side of the lake. For the first time in a long, long time, I was taken…and by a girl I'd only met in the last twenty-four hours, yet I'd known of for over half my life.

As it turned out, the thunderhead that Sunday morning would move along the north of Lake Catherine. The south shore had but a few drops of rain. I could enjoy the wonderful spectacle of the cloud system moving eastward as I gathered up all the branches and debris from the previous storms. I figured to make a large stack and wait a few days for all the foliage to dry before setting it afire.

My motivation continued as I repaired and re-painted the remaining window panels on my sunroom. While I worked I would periodically glance toward the peninsula wishing Ray's daughter was available that afternoon. If she wasn't leaving to return to her home in the Twin Cities, I would have found some reason to boat over to her place.

Completing those tasks by early afternoon, I headed down to the water to take a dip. Seeing the rickety dock I was reminded again of the apparent dream I'd had the previous night. I guessed I must have some latent desire to own a more stable dock…and maybe even a wish to make that battered canoe leaning against my garage sea worthy once again.

Pulling off my shirt I ran to the end of the wobbly dock and dove into the quiet, cool water. I swam hard out toward the middle of the lake hoping that strange dream might vanish from my mind with more physical exertion. Approximately eighty yards from shore, I flipped over on my back to do some more restful backstrokes. That was when I noticed how wide the cloud system was to the west…something I couldn't entirely see from my dock. Lake Catherine including my side of the lake was going to get its third major storm in as many days.

The ensuing rumble in the distance ended my leisure. I switched back to my strong Australian crawl and was back at my dock in no time. I wasn't certain how fast moving was the approaching storm, but after my experience the day before, I was going to be in the safety of my cabin or garage before any lightning or rain started.

Drying off with my shirt, I headed for the garage. I hadn't been so highly charged since the previous winter's basketball season. I hadn't seen the back of my garage for at least a year or two. I was actually motivated to begin a general clean-up.

The rains arrived quite soon thereafter. While it rained, I began hauling out crap and discarded junk from the back of the garage. The massive system bringing the intermittent rain brought no thunder or lightning, but it gave me the time to actually sweep out the garage and create a pile of scrap I could take to the dump ground. The way I was working, I wondered if my altercation with that lightning bolt was the reason for my rejuvenation. Cleaning my garage was not even on my 'to do' list. I wasn't certain I liked the change in myself.

Seeing the garage freezer it reminded me of the frozen meat I was keeping for my new neighbor and how hungry I was. It was time to eat. Trotting through the light rain back to my cottage, I glanced toward the sky and was startled by flashes of lightning and rumbles of thunder moving towards my side of the lake. The weather system had no end and seemed like it was going to get worse.

Ten minutes later from the safety of the inside of my home, I watched the wind howl and the torrents of rain beat against my cottage. My own electricity jumped on and off…something that rarely happened. I thought about my new neighbor and the wise choice she'd made in leaving that afternoon for

Minneapolis. I edged over to the windows of my sunroom to watch the sheer power of the wind and rain. It was dark as night outside and it was only the late afternoon.

Giving a quick glance toward the peninsula, I wished the day could have materialized in a different way. I had just enough swagger to call her up and invite her over for dinner if there'd been any chance she was going to stay the night at Lake Catherine. But, she'd seemed determined to drive back to the Twin Cities.

Turning away from the back window, I suddenly jerked my eyes back outside. I thought I saw a light through the thick rain in the direction of the peninsula. I had a momentary shudder as if I was being drawn into that dream I'd had the night before. I pressed my nose against the window glass trying to either convince myself that light was there or admit my mind might be playing tricks on me.

And there it was again...a flickering light...like from a gas lantern. My eyes were now intensely focused on that one spot. I couldn't believe what I was seeing. It was intermittent, but it was definitely not my imagination. How was it possible for a gas lantern to be shining brightly enough for me to see it through the gray of the downpour?

My eyes tried to pierce the wet, darkened conditions to see if someone was out on that dock holding that lantern. It was just too far away. Besides, it was too dangerous for anyone to be standing out on that dock during an electrical storm.

The sky again lit up above the peninsula with streaks of lightning. A booming thunderclap followed indicating the center of the storm was right over the lake. The gas lantern in the direction of the peninsula dock still glimmered in the vapor of mist and rain. Lightning then hit the ground close by and my power went off...and then flicked on again. Another flash and my electrical power went off completely.

I stood there in the semi-darkness of my cottage considering my next steps. There was no reason to be too concerned. The generator in the garage would take over supplying power to my freezer if the electricity remained off for very long.

Torrents of water then made the haze even thicker. Still, I remained with my eyes glued on that one spot across the lake where I'd seen that small light. And, just like that, there it was again. It was like a mystical beacon of light for a wayfaring sailor hoping to find shelter.

I then became concerned as I was curious. That light had to be the gas lantern she'd borrowed from me. She might have left it on inadvertently before she left to return to the Twin Cities. If inside the boathouse, it could cause a fire if unattended.

Then I saw the lantern move from side to side...as if a signal. It was quite visible as the storm began to lighten. The fact that it was moving had to mean someone was on the dock carrying the light. Could it be the musty-smelling old man? If so, it was a chance to verify whether my conversation with him the previous night was real or not.

It was still raining when I ran out to my jeep. Starting the engine, I shoved the gear into first and left mud flying as I sped away from my home. I could drive only so fast because of the potholes full of water from the storm. The sky was still lighting up all around me as I drove.

Seven minutes later I was driving up the elongated driveway toward the mansion on the peninsula. The house was dark, like a grand hotel in some ghost story. There were no generators at this property so the darkness was magnified and more than a bit creepy. The rain was unceasing. Glancing down the hill toward the dock, I tried to make out whether the gas lantern was shining. I couldn't see a thing.

Ignoring the downpour, I got out of my jeep and descended the steps quickly. As I got to the bottom step and placed my foot on the dock, as if by magic the rain began to let up again. Looking down the dock my heart leaped seeing the easy chair with a cover lying beside it. Why wasn't the cover over the chair? Was someone actually sitting in it? Had I returned to that strange situation of the previous night? Was I about to smell the musty clothing or see an older man cast his line out onto the lake?

I made a subdued inquiry toward the chair. "Hey…is anyone there?!" I said it simultaneous to some distant thunder. There was no response, so I moved closer and repeated, "Hey…is anyone there?"

Again…there was no reply and no movement. I finally moved right alongside the easy chair and with some relief…and some disappointment…I found no one relaxing in it. Further, there was no gas lantern…lit or otherwise…anywhere on that dock.

I leaned against the chair and chuckled silently. I would have sworn a one month's teacher's salary that I just seen the flickering light through the storm only ten minutes before from my sunroom. Now there was nothing…no light… no lantern…no old man.

A breeze picked up and made me realize how chilly it was. With nothing more to see on the dock, I grabbed the cover and flipped it over the easy chair. It was time to leave and regain my senses.

As I turned back toward the boathouse, I almost fell backwards into the lake. There it was. The gas lantern was moving down the staircase by the boathouse as if floating in air. I was momentarily shaken until I thankfully made out the outline of a person. The figure was wearing a long plastic raincoat prevalent but never fashionable from the era of the 1960's or 1970's. The attached hood made the figure look like some New England fisherman out for a stroll.

I stood by the chair watching the figure step up onto the dock. I was just waiting for the words, "Well son, I see you made it back."

But, that was not to be. My disappointment would be short-lived. Pulling the hood from her already wet head was the lovely figure of Ray's daughter. She hadn't gone back to the Twin Cities that afternoon after all.

Relieved and frankly very glad, I smiled and called out to her. "A new raincoat I see…quite stylish. So…what are you doing here? I thought you'd left."

"I live here," she quipped not trying to be funny. "This used to be my father's raincoat. It didn't look very good on him fifteen years ago either."

Then she looked curiously at me and grinned, "Is it Friday already and time for our dinner? I've been under a cloud of rain so long I've lost track of time."

Bantering in return, I kidded, "No…I think it's only Tuesday or Wednesday. It took two or three days to clean my garage. My guess is that your boathouse might take longer."

Acknowledging that burdensome thought, she changed the subject. "So, let me ask the same question. What brought you over here on such foggy and rainy evening?"

Getting serious I responded, "Hey…I was looking at the peninsula from my cottage and I saw your gas lantern glimmering here on the dock or in your boathouse. The way it was raining so hard, I figured you might have left it burning in your rush to get back to Minneapolis. I came over here to shut it off and keep your boathouse from catching fire…unless of course that was your intention?"

Bemused, she replied, "That's odd… once the power went out I came down to the boathouse to find the gas lantern. I remembered I'd left it here. But, I never lit it until I brought it up to the house about an hour ago. I just came down here because I saw your jeep in my driveway.

I looked at her sharply wondering if she was kidding me once again. "You say you were up in the house with the gas lantern and not down here on the dock?"

"That's right," she said. Then she looked at me strangely. "You say you saw the light here at the dock?"

I answered her honestly. "Well, I saw it maybe fifteen minutes ago and frankly couldn't believe what I was seeing. Like I said, I only came over here to shut it off."

"That's really peculiar," she countered, "I actually looked on down the lake shore at your cottage during the rain. I swear I saw a flickering light similar to the one I saw Friday night on your deck. I knew you were home and almost drove over just to have someone to talk with rather than being alone on such a gloomy afternoon. With the thunderstorm I've put off leaving for Minneapolis. I wasn't particularly excited about driving for a couple hours accompanied by a major storm. It'll work just as well if I leave early tomorrow morning and switch my flight to Chicago until later in the day."

I was glad she was still home, but my mind was more focused on what she'd said about the flickering light she saw at my cabin being similar to the one she saw Friday night. The electricity had gone out in at my place as well. What light could she have been referring? Coincidentally that was about the same time I saw the light over at the peninsula. Something wasn't making sense…again.

Seeking shelter in the boathouse, we stood at the doorway as she waved the gas lantern light over the interior. It was four times bigger than my garage with easily that many times as much junk, scrap, and old equipment as I'd gotten rid of earlier that afternoon. Her boathouse was like a dark, dirty cave. Everything stored was filthy. There were countless useless, rusty empty five-gallon tanks for gasoline. Old fishing equipment and boating paraphernalia were lying around probably unsalvageable. Mostly there were construction materials and tools that looked too old to be useable. In fact, most everything inside that boathouse could be thrown or burned and she wouldn't lose much that had value.

I couldn't help offering my opinion exclaiming, "Abbie, maybe you should just throw the gas lantern into the middle and watch this place go up in flames."

She didn't take my comment personally. Her eyes did another general survey before nodding in agreement. "I believe I like your idea. Then I could cross this place off my list of things to do."

I found myself liking her even more. This girl had my knack for procrastination.

Then without missing a beat, her eyes shined as she said, "If you'd like, maybe we could go up to the house and find something to eat? We only have the lantern for light, but I still have gas power for my stove. I have a few food items I was going to take back to my apartment in the Cities. That could be our main course."

I wasn't about to debate whether we should just go back to my place where there was plenty of food. I had just been invited to be with her once again. I was not about to muddy the waters.

As we were leaving the boathouse, I knocked over a fly rod leaning just inside the door. It was as rusty and dirty as the rest of the junk in the boathouse. As I picked it up, I noticed a brownish-colored envelope wrapped around the handle. I wasn't sure why, but it got my attention.

I said to her, "If you don't mind I'd like to take this up to the house and look at it."

She shrugged not caring in the least. "Please…take whatever you want."

Climbing the stairs to the house, it did occur to me that I was on ground Johnny Hanson and I considered hallowed in our teen years. I smugly thought, 'if only he could see me now.'

Entering the side door to the kitchen, the gas lantern lit up the room with about half the normal illumination. The room was large with a wide island. An abundance of stools were placed around a curved eating area. At one time there were likely a lot of rear ends sitting on those stools…but, no more. There were enough cupboards to store dishes for a small army. Looking towards the adjoining family room, I could see the large windows giving a three-sided view of the lake. I'd only seen those windows from afar in all my years at Lake Catherine

Leaving the gas lantern in the kitchen, she grabbed her flashlight saying, "Let me get out of this old raincoat. I need to put on something dry. I'll be right back down."

With her out of the kitchen I inspected the fly rod as closely as I could in semi-darkness. It was definitely unusable despite having spent so many years in that mildewed boathouse interior. The envelope was taped tightly around the handle. After so many years, however, the tape disintegrated easily with help of my fingernail. The small envelope fell onto my lap. Opening the flap I pulled out the note. The print was almost obscured with time, but holding it close to the light from the lantern, I could see it was dated Saturday, June 13. The year was faded.

With overwhelming curiosity I held the note as closely as I could to the lantern. Immediately my mouth fell open. It read:

Jim,

I met the young man staying at your place. He was out in your canoe pretty late last night and ended up stopping by and talking with me down on my dock. He rapped his head on something…seemed a bit dazed. I didn't let him go back to your place until I was sure he was O.K. A nice kid…it'd be nice if my daughters meet someone like him down the road.

Anyway, I promised him I'd let him use this fly rod. See that he gets it. Tell him it'd be my pleasure if he just kept it. Stop on over. The fishing's been good off the dock. Bring your own damned bait for once, will you?

Ray

The spookiest chill shot through my body. That was the same date as that last Saturday night I'd been at Lake Catherine back during college. He had to be referring to me in that note. I was certain of it. He never got that fly rod in my hands because I never made it back to the Hagen cabin. Now that same fly rod was old, rusty, and possibly ruined. It had been sitting in the boathouse for twelve years.

Then the real macabre thought reverberated in my mind. The same offer of the fly rod had been brought up to me again…last night…by that old, musty-smelling man. That guy had to be Ray Lindstrom. How else did he know so much about the beautiful gal who now resided at the mansion? But, if he was Lindstrom, then the vision of him last night had to have been an apparition. After all, the man was deceased and had been for almost a decade.

At that moment my mind was so blown I didn't know what was real or fancy. There'd been so many odd occurrences since Friday night. Driving myself crazy with so many convoluted thoughts, I was rescued by the light from a flashlight shone on the staircase. She'd changed and was returning to the kitchen.

As she neared, her flashlight focused on me. I hoped she couldn't make out the ashen look on my face.

I enjoyed watching her movements as she opened her cooler from which she had sandwiches to be taken back to Minneapolis. She chuckled at the choices. "All I really have are sandwiches and some raw vegetables. So, how about a sandwich? I can offer you ham and cheese, ham and cheese…or ham and cheese."

I smiled at her and feigned excitement. "I'll try the ham and cheese."

As she busied herself with finding plates and glasses, I was drawn back to the fly rod now lying on the floor beside me. I grabbed the note and slipped it into my pocket not yet wanting her to see it. Then I asked her, "About this old fly rod…you know anything about it?"

She nodded, "Sure…that was my father's fishing rod. It obviously hasn't been used in years…and judging by it being stored in the grimy boathouse…it likely will never be used again. I can remember him talking about it."

Then she came over and examined it closer. "Yes…I remember him telling me he was going to give that rod to some young fellow he'd met, but he hadn't seen the guy ever again. He seemed disappointed. My Dad didn't take a liking to just anyone, especially guys in the same age group as my sister and me. He seemed to favor this guy for whatever reason. I actually think he wanted me to meet him. It was about the time I got engaged…almost as if he hoped I might meet someone else as an alternative to the man I eventually married. I guess he was right. My first marriage didn't last very long at all. My father never said I told you so, but I sensed it. But, that's all water over the dam. It was just another example of my father always looking out for me…as fathers tend to do."

I sat there nodding and not saying much. I pushed the note even deeper into my pocket. Things were strange enough that weekend without making any claim that I might have been that fellow.

Placing the sandwiches and some slightly chilled sodas on the island eating area, we both ate hungrily in the semi-darkness of the kitchen. We both seemed lost in our own thoughts. For a minute the only sound was the rain dribbling on the roof.

She finally broke the silence. "Chris, you mind if I tell you something?"

I was not about to say 'no'. I wasn't certain if my mind could take more confusion.

She didn't wait for my answer. "After my father's passing, as you probably can guess, neither my sister nor I have made it back very often to Lake Catherine. She lives overseas and rarely gets back to Minnesota. Since I at least have a home in Minneapolis, she's more or less left the responsibility of this place to me. For a while I was able to lean on Jim Hagen to hire people for landscaping and maintenance work here on the peninsula and the house. When his health declined, I had to hire and manage the peninsula as best I could from a distance."

She paused for a moment showing much disappointment. "I've had to put my trust in some landscape people who haven't done a very good job. It's been upsetting seeing this place get so run down. Each summer the place looks worse than the previous summer. Anyway, since cutting down on my travel and reevaluating my career in recent months, I've had the chance to take charge of the needed repair and maintenance and hire the right kind of people. I didn't expect by coming up here these past weekends that I would discover how much I missed this place. It's an entirely different life …and frankly one that I find inviting. I might even prefer it.

I also realized it might be helpful getting to know some people if I was going to consider living here at the lake. To be honest, that was why I came knocking on your door the past two mornings. Arriving Friday night and finding no electricity here at the house, my first thought was Mr. Hagen. He was always there to help us out. With him no longer here at the lake, I felt so alone.

Then I just kind of glanced in the direction of his home…your home…wishing he was still here. It was so foggy and rainy…even difficult to see my car parked outside. That was when I was so surprised to see a flickering light through the haze towards Hagen's old house…this house. Feeling kind of helpless in the dark, I guess I was drawn to your place for some assistance. That's when I drove over to your house and discovered the gas lantern hanging above your deck Friday night. It was so odd. I couldn't believe no one was home and a gas light was left burning. In fact I couldn't even understand how the lantern kept burning in such wet conditions. You know the rest. As I told you, I didn't think you'd need that gas lantern, so I borrowed it.

She paused looking a bit embarrassed, so I eased her guilt. "Hey…I'm amazed you came back a second time considering the shape I was in yesterday morning. This entire weekend so far has been quite extraordinary…in ways I won't even say. I can tell you it all seemed to start with me over-extending myself at my neighbor's party Friday night. What you saw Saturday morning when you stopped by was a person unfamiliar to me."

As she began chuckling, I added, "But, you have to admit I rallied. I was much better this morning when you again stopped by my place. I was actually neighborly…or, at least civil. With that kind of improvement, there's no telling how nice of a guy I'll be tomorrow."

Her hilarity seemed genuine. I liked making her smile and laugh. Then, our conversation simply continued from our talking in her kitchen that morning. Now, in her dimly lit kitchen for the next couple hours we hardly noticed the occasional flashes of lightning, the rolling thunder and the periodic downpours. We found we had more in common. Maybe it was because we were lake people however that term can be defined.

Eventually, I felt obligated to leave. We repeated our intentions of getting together for dinner upon her return to the lake the upcoming Friday. I drove back home with a spirited feeling I hadn't felt in a long, long time…if ever. I wondered if I'd ever not think of her during a thunderstorm at the lake.

Back at home with a lull in the rain, I ambled around the outside of my property to take another inventory of more broken limbs and branches on my lawn. According to the forecast, more rain was expected that night. The next day, however, the weather systems would clear and blue skies would return once again.

Then the droplets started again and I ran into my home. The power still hadn't turned back on, but I had plenty of flashlights and a few candles. I was tired. I figured I'd just catch up on my sleep and go to bed early. With one last gaze outside, I observed the omnipresent fog. Gazing reflectively across the lake toward the peninsula, to my surprise, there it was again. There was that light…that flicker of a flame. I initially took for granted the light was coming from the gas lantern in the Lindstrom kitchen. However, after standing in my sunroom for a couple minutes, the dancing light seemed to be located closer to the water's edge. It was a mystery how that intractable flame could be shining so determinedly on such a wet, hazy night.

When I'd left her home, Abbie's intention was to go to bed early with her alarm set for 5:30 AM. What would be her reason for going back down to the boathouse with that gas lantern during another downpour? It wasn't as if she'd forgotten anything of importance in the boathouse.

Finally, I just accepted this amazingly determined flickering light was just another piece to a thoroughly puzzling weekend. Pulling myself away from the window, I headed for my bedroom. It occurred to me a couple times before falling asleep that I might be going nuts. I still hadn't fully separated what was real and what was probably a dream in the past two days. My hope was that when I woke up the next morning, she would still be real. Whatever else might have happened, real or otherwise, didn't matter.

That following Monday morning I awoke to a bright day. The weekend full of thunderstorms had finally passed. I'd never experienced that constant ferocity of weather disturbances in all my days at Lake Catherine before or since. Understandably, I would always remember that weekend for more than just the weather. It was the weekend I finally cleaned my garage, apparently got struck by lightning, met an elderly, stale smelling fellow while inexplicably canoeing late at night in heavy fog, and I'd had the great pleasure of meeting and getting to know the older daughter of Ray Lindstrom. While I was still not clear about that Saturday night in the canoe and meeting the older man, there was no doubt she was real. I had the meat she'd brought over to put in my freezer to prove it.

The rest of that week was a blur. I was looking forward to seeing her the upcoming Friday night. As it turned out, that Friday dinner date never materialized. I knew it was a casual commitment since she wasn't certain she'd be back at Lake Catherine. Nonetheless, when her note arrived that Friday expressing her disappointment that we'd have to postpone our dinner date, I was disappointed more than I thought I'd be.

I held out hope that I'd see her the next weekend, but not having heard from her again, I deduced her trip to Chicago must have changed her mind and emotions about moving back to Lake Catherine. By the third week I wondered if she'd even remember my name. By the fourth week, I had trouble visualizing her face.

In the following weeks I took care of my yearbook and high school ring business. I traveled during the week days to various parts of the state staying overnight one or two nights in such places as Thief River Falls, Winona, and Worthington. Back home by Friday, my weekends were filled with my usual activities...golf, water skiing, dinners with friends around the lake, and some projects around my property. Unfortunately, repairing my dock was not one of them. More than once I'd look longingly over at the peninsula. There was no activity other than the landscapers investing a few hours on Saturday to maintain the improvements they'd been hired to do earlier in the summer.

As the hot, dry days of August moved towards Labor Day weekend, the school year was about to begin. It would be my seventh year at the consolidated high school. That unusual weekend back in late June had been memorable. I'd reconciled that a friendship with Ray Lundstrom's eldest daughter could only be fleeting. I'd enjoyed getting to know her...and that apparently was the best it could be. I surmised how she and her sister had so many guys interested in them during their younger years at the lake, maintaining contacts with those huge numbers of pursuers had to be difficult. That recollection must have stuck with her. Though it was years later, I had to have been just a continuation of that pattern from her life at Lake Catherine.

It was the Friday evening before Labor Day weekend that I heard a rapping at my front door. It was early evening and I was getting ready to meet some other co-workers. There was a dinner planned for the new teachers on the staff.

I'd just gotten out of the shower after an afternoon of golf. There was something about that knock that made my heart jump. I just didn't have that many visitors. I shouted out, "Just a minute...I'll be right there."

In less than thirty seconds I'd combed my hair, put on my cleanest slacks and golf shirt and hurried to the door. As I opened it, rain had just started falling. A very attractive female somewhat younger than me was leaning into my door trying to stay dry.

Immediately inviting her in, she brushed off and smiled at me. She was uncommonly comfortable in my presence for someone I'd never met. I studied the brunette hair and briefly the body shape. I had no memory of who she could be.

She stuck out her hand just stiffly enough to help me understand this was indeed our first meeting. Smiling, she said, "Hi...I feel that we've met. My sister speaks very highly of you. I hope you remember her from earlier this summer when she was coming up here almost every weekend. I'm Abbie Lindstrom's sister, Emily Christenson...that is, Emily Lindstrom Christenson. My husband and I are up here at the lake for the first time in years to check on the property my sister and I still own over at the peninsula. She says you seem to know the history of our place…and you know Jim Hagen who was such a good friend to my father."

My disappointment melted. I was quite taken that she would take the time to drop by my home. I implored, "Please….please sit down. Can I get you something to drink?"

She seemed almost apologetic for barging in, but I had a feeling there had to be some purpose for her visit. She nodded, "Yes, if you don't mind, a cold drink would be very helpful. My throat is kind of parched."

Searching my generally bare refrigerator for a soft drink, I suddenly had no problem recreating Abbie's image in my mind. Emily was pretty, but I could already notice some differences with her sister. Both sisters were attractive. Emily was not as calm and she was shorter. She had the same energy, especially in her speech pattern, as well as the most appealing smile. Her choice of wearing a skirt and blouse that evening, though, would keep me from ever mistaking her for a more casual lake person.

Taking the cold drink from me, she began to relax, although not totally. It seemed she was not quite ready to state the reason for stopping by my house. She commented, "It seems so unreal to come to this house and not see Jim Hagen. He was such a family friend over the years. I'm sorry to have lost contact with him as well as this area. Once I got married, my husband and I lived overseas. It's been so many years since I've last been to Lake Catherine. Now we're back in the states, but we'll be living too far away to enjoy this lake. In fact, there's little chance we'll ever be living near here again. I'm afraid that's the same story regarding Abbie. I know she was thinking seriously about moving to Lake Catherine. It seemed the moment she'd made that decision, she was offered a spectacular job by her company. They just didn't want to lose her.

She's now V.P. of International Marketing for her company and has been since July 1st. She's even given up her apartment in Minneapolis. She now primarily lives in Paris…when she's even there. It's been two months and she's been in countless cities in Western Europe introducing herself to her various clients. I'm actually sorry she made the decision. I thought I'd finally be able to see her more once my husband and I accepted positions at Northwestern University in Chicago. It's funny how things work out in life."

Emily's words suddenly became incoherent. While I tried to show interest, my attentiveness wandered. I hoped Emily didn't see the disappointment in my eyes. On the other hand, maybe she did as she suddenly got to the point of her visit.

She continued, "Anyway….Abbie mentioned she'd met you and talked constantly about how impressed she was with you. That got the two of us talking about a problem we have. You see we're still not ready to put the peninsula up for sale. It represents something very distinctive that our father accomplished. We don't want to lose that memory or the access to a place so important to us in our lives. We may sell it later, but for now we want to keep the property within our family."

Then she paused biting her lower lip. "Our problem is that we don't want the house or property to go to ruin like it unfortunately had done over the past few years since our father died. Abbie and I now have the money to keep the place in good condition but we have to find the right person to manage it. That's why she and I want to make you an offer...something we hope you'll consider even though Abbie said you were a very busy man."

My brow began to furrow sensing that whatever she had to say was not going to make me happy. I'd just learned that a far-out dream would never happen. Emily Lindstrom Christenson sitting on my sofa that night could never understand the disenchantment I felt at that moment. Abbie Lindstrom would apparently never know that disappointment either.

Unaware of my disillusionment, Emily obliviously talked on. "Abbie and I want you to consider managing our property...somewhat like Jim Hagen did for us before he sold his house to you and left Lake Catherine. Not only would we contract you to manage the peninsula and the house, Abbie and I would welcome any ideas you might have to produce some revenue off the property. Whatever your time might allow you, we'd be satisfied if you wanted to use the mansion for a bed & breakfast, a fishing resort, or just a weekend rental. The only prerequisite is that we want our attorney in Minneapolis to be involved in the details. As part of her job, we'd want her to make a personal visit to the peninsula at least once annually. All my sister and I want is the prerogative to gain back the property if we ever chose to do so. We'd give you up to a year's notice if that was our desire."

And then she was done. After her rather nervous, machine gun type of delivery, the sudden silence left me dumbfounded. The offer took me by complete surprise. I was still dealing with the letdown of her sister traveling around Europe with little chance of returning stateside. As disappointed as I was, there was still the growing realization that the proposal the two sisters were offering was very enticing and wouldn't take that much extra time.

I blankly asked Emily to congratulate her sister on her new job. Those words came out as if peanut butter was stuck to the roof of my mouth. Once that insincere comment was completed, I found myself actually considering the offer seriously. I responded maybe too quickly, "Yes...I am very busy, especially as the school year begins this fall. However, only because I've long admired your father ...and what he did with the peninsula...maybe we can work something out. However, I'd only be interested if the two of you are truly serious about accepting the expense in keeping the peninsula as grand...within reason...as it was when your father was living."

Then I sat there in silence while Emily couldn't contain her joy. After shaking my hand exuberantly...twice...we left it that she and I would meet again that weekend before her husband and she had to leave for their trip back to Chicago. In less than fifteen minutes she'd come and gone...and I'd just been offered a very intriguing responsibility if I wanted it.

The next afternoon it took Emily and me less than a half hour to agree on what I would be paid as well as an initial budget to maintain the peninsula. Both the salary and the budgeted amount were too much, but it gave me the added impetus to craft some ideas for generating some revenue at the mansion. From that day on, my dealing with the Lindstrom daughters ended. I only dealt through their attorney in Minneapolis.

Literally that Sunday of Labor Day weekend I took over managing the Lindstrom property. I'd been fascinated with the peninsula for as long as I could remember. Now I had the keys to the house, the boathouse and even the right to sit on that artificial leather easy chair on the dock if I chose. At some point if everything worked out, I knew I'd locate and call my boyhood friend, Johnny Hagen. Besides me, only he could appreciate the irony.

Within a week I'd hired three young men who lived at Lake Catherine to help me maintain the property. They happened to be members of my basketball team. They were excited about the weekend work and took their new job very seriously. After all, they didn't want to disappoint their basketball coach.

It's now been five years since I took on the management of 'Ray's Peninsula'. I've never seen either of the Lindstrom daughters during that span…only their attorney, a college friend of Abbie Lindstrom's named Samantha Alcott. Ms. Alcott had handled the legal work for Abbie and Emily on their father's estate and had continued to be their personal attorney. She'd begun carrying out her commitment to the Lindstrom daughters making the annual trip to Lake Catherine starting the very next June. By then, I'd already met her a couple times in the Twin Cities for dinner in order to discuss some ideas to build revenue at the peninsula and cover the operating expenses. By her first visit that June, Samantha and I were already friends.

We finalized our plans to make the mansion into a rental property with the goal of having the revenue cover her legal fees, the property expenses, and my management salary. With the approval of Abbie and Emily Lindstrom, the house was rented out a few times that first summer. By the second summer, there were very few weeks the mansion wasn't rented out to groups or large family gatherings. When the mansion did have guests, my neighbors, the Rutherfords, were employed along with those young fellows on my basketball squad to help support the small enterprise. Even Samantha, when larger groups rented the peninsula, journeyed to the lake to help out. The entire process worked well enough to break even after that second summer.

As for me, as the spring nights get warmer, I often relax on that easy chair on the peninsula dock. I find myself casting a line just like I saw Ray Lindstrom do so many years before. I inevitably stare at the stars and think about my life and how things happen the way they do. How fortunate it was that I grew so attracted to living at Lake Catherine. How lucky I'd been that my jobs allowed me to live at the lake year around.

Most certainly when alone, I reflect on that unforgettable weekend five years before when the storms seemed never to end at Lake Catherine…and how impaired I was both physically and mentally. I'd partied hard that Friday night and paid for it by feeling lousy the following day. I'd been struck by lightning… or at least accepted that I had. At the very least, that bolt had left me dazed.

Over time it has become more difficult in picturing what was real and what was imagined that weekend. Had I been in a trance as a result of being struck? Why else would I have taken off on a questionable voyage to the peninsula late at night in extremely foggy conditions? I had been in a canoe that looked compellingly like the one Johnny Hagen and I used to paddle around the lake during our youth? Where had that canoe come from? And what about old Ray Lindstrom…I'd met him that one time during my college years. Then, twelve years later on that Saturday night after arriving at the peninsula, I'd met an old man fishing on the dock. I never was sure he was old Ray Lindstrom, but he was eerily similar. Everything pointed to that fact, especially with his personal knowledge about Abbie Lindstrom and the challenges she was facing at that time. Even in my muddled mental condition, the conversation he and I had that night had been too real not to have happened. Yet, at the time he'd been gone for almost ten years.

Astoundingly, when Abbie Lindstrom and I talked that Sunday evening, she mentioned things I'd heard already from that mysterious, musty-smelling old man the night before. How would he have known her problems if he hadn't conversed with her? And, it was Abbie who said she felt her father's presence on those evenings when she sat alone on the dock pondering her life and the challenges she was facing.

How could that episode not have been real? On the other hand, it could just as well have been a dream.

At times while sitting alone in that easy chair on the peninsula dock, I'd question whether I'd ever really met Abbie Lindstrom at all. After all, that entire weekend had been just a blur of constant storms and fog…and me not thinking clearly. However, I'd eventually come out of that particular delusion and return to reality. It was no dream that she'd brought over to my house that Sunday morning her frozen food to be saved in my freezer in case her electricity shut down at the mansion. She'd never returned for that frozen food. I'd kept it in my freezer as much to preserve the memory of her as the food. That meat in the freezer would always provide the verification that I'd indeed met her that weekend.

It took me a long time to accept that she wouldn't return. While her memories of Lake Catherine had been re-ignited that spring, the flame was not robust enough to be sustained. My affection for where I lived was simply much stronger than hers. Her preference for where she wanted to live or what she wanted to do in her career didn't make her life better or worse than mine. She just required a different canvas to paint her future than what Lake Catherine, Minnesota...or even I... could offer her. Besides, while our meeting and our conversations that weekend were unforgettable, we just hadn't had enough time to really develop any real closeness. I would always believe it was both our losses. Then again that may have been more my ego talking.

It happened one day for no particular reason. I pulled out her freezer-burned and likely inedible meat from my freezer in the garage. Some of the steaks or hamburger had been in the bottom of my freezer for those five years. It took all of five minutes to toss the rock hard, freezer-burned frozen food into the trash can.

That very night something very bizarre occurred. For those years the meat stayed in my freezer, I had repeatedly seen during rainstorms and foggy conditions the sight of a flickering light across the lake at the peninsula. There were times I actually drove over to the peninsula during the rainstorm just to check out if there was a gas lantern burning on the dock. Each time I found nothing. It got so that I simply accepted that whenever it rained, the flickering light would predictably appear at the peninsula. I tried to ignore it, but it was there...always...as sure as I was breathing. Of course I never told anyone. Why cause people to think I was crazy?

When that freezer-burned meat was finally hauled away a couple days later by the county sanitation truck, there was a huge rainstorm that night. The fog was low over the lake. It was difficult to see the Rutherford's lake home next door much less anywhere else around the lake. But, when I happened to glance out my sunroom window in the direction of the peninsula... there it was...that beacon of light flickering through the thick haze. I recall just standing at that window trying to convince myself one more time that the light didn't exist...that it was too foggy to truly see across the lake.

What transpired then made my heart skip a beat. I observed something that had never happened regarding that dancing flame. The flickering beam seemed to dim. Then it began to move back and forth as if someone was carrying the gas lantern away. I watched as that flame retreated back toward the boathouse. I was so familiar with the dock area. I could visualize the light being carried up the stairs toward the mansion. Then abruptly, the flickering flame disappeared behind some trees.

I didn't think much about it the rest of that night. I went to bed and the incident didn't cross my mind until the next rainstorm a few days later. That evening when I stood by my back window and routinely glanced across the lake toward the peninsula, I was somewhat surprised. There was no dancing flame... only the hazy darkness. In fact, during all rainstorms from thereafter up to this very day I would never see again the flickering light at the peninsula nor the gas lantern ever again.

Letting Him Go

I should have been ready to let him go. My son was a young man. He'd been preparing for his new life. It wasn't as if I didn't see it. I just wasn't committed to the idea of him leaving. He was moving to another city and starting a new job. In addition, marriage was in the offing for him. How could I be anything but proud and thrilled for him?

Still, I wasn't ready to let him go even though it was very natural for a son to leave home at some point. Why couldn't I just give him a supportive wave, a satisfied smile, a pat on the back and tell him to call me when he arrived at his new location for his new job? It wasn't as if phoning or emailing wasn't part of our accepted communication process since he'd left home to go to college. And, it wasn't as if we wouldn't be seeing each other…periodically. Above all, this was not the first time a father said farewell to his son and watched him take the new road to his future. So, why was I so melancholy about his leaving?

I knew the answer. It was simple. I just couldn't get the vision out of my mind of the pleasure of raising him. There must have been some trying times as he grew up, but I could never recall them. My memory whenever I thought of him was his laughter, his curious mind, and his outward confidence. He was always such an entertaining kid. His brain was active, his sense of humor was ready to react to almost anything, and he was amazingly articulate for his age at any point in his young life.

My wife and I also enjoyed watching the marvelous relationship he had with his younger sister. That bond added so much pleasure to our family unit. And, starting in the third grade with the purchase of our household's first computer, he was the spearhead who led our family into the computer age. It was such a delight to observe the many traits he acquired from his mother combining with a few he acquired from me. His very presence…that was what would be missed.

Departing for college, my wife and I were so happy for him though our insides ached as we hugged our farewells. We knew this was part of the vicissitudes of life. Countless other parents had to do the same thing. They'd tear up as they were leaving their son or daughter as well. Somehow this kind of large group empathy didn't help. We were crushed with his leaving…and his school was only a half hour away!

Our one blessed consolation in this entire process was that our equally wonderful daughter was still at home and only a freshman in high school. She would help us take our minds off our son being gone from home. We no doubt had to be a large bother to her in those first few weeks. She must have thought her mother and I were slightly impaired as we kept inviting her to do things with us or just inventing ways the three of us could be together. It was as if we didn't want to miss a second of her life during the times she wasn't in school or sleeping… as if we lamented how much time we missed being with our son during the last years he was still living at home.

Thankfully she was patient with her parents as we gradually made that adaptation of our son living in another place. Eventually her life got back to normal, even though her mother and I continually tried to define the new normal in our lives.

As those initial college days whisked by, I rationalized that his being gone would be manageable since he wasn't that far away. Surely he wouldn't be gone so continuously from home. He'd want to return just to get a good meal, do some laundry, and fill us in on his new life.

That pervasive and determined thought was a nice cushion to my ache, but it generally proved false. Often when he stopped at home, I wasn't there. When I was, he was always on the run going to his next planned activity. I understood. It was natural for him to immerse himself in his college life. It was funny how those twinges in my stomach would jump around…so happy when I got to see him, so melancholy when he had to leave.

I recall as our son's college career began to unfold that first fall how my wife and I felt so lucky to have the modern communication advances available. We were certain they would provide a nearness to our son. She and I spoke often how our own college days seemed more distant from our families…and how this generation of parents and their college student son or daughter could be closer. Back then, both my wife and I made a ritual call home on Sunday nights just to stay connected. At that time the long distance rates were more costly. Interestingly, our parents didn't seem to mind that expense.

With long distance costs not a factor in the cell phone generation, we were contented, even overjoyed, that we could remain in contact with him at virtually any moment. Unfortunately, we would learn very quickly the convenience of a cell phone didn't guarantee contact. His cell phone seemed always to be busy or switched directly to voice mail. Even as email became so prevalent, responses from him seemed too delayed and certainly too short.

I wondered if my folks had the same lost feeling when trying to contact me when I was in college. Since I was also always on the go, or at least away from my room, calling my telephone was consistently unsuccessful. With no voice messaging, how exasperating that had to be for them. Yet as I thought about that inconvenience during my student days, I realized my parents likely did not have as much frustration as my wife and I were having contacting my son with all the latest tools of modern technology. My folks didn't expect to be able to contact me by telephone…at least very conveniently or very often. Their anticipation couldn't have been that high.

With that day's advances in communication, my wife's and my expectations were very high. Nonetheless, here it was a generation since my wife and I were in college and the communication problem persisted. We'd end up leaving a cell phone message asking him to call when he had time. Funny thing…that time would often end up being Sunday night.

Still we had that proximity advantage that neither my wife's nor my parents had during our college days. It was amazing how often the two of us found reason to shop, eat, or attend his college's events just so we could be near him…even if we couldn't see him on every visit. We would learn, however, a dinner offer at some restaurant was rarely declined.

When those summer breaks arrived, it was so special. Our family unit was together again. It took but seconds for that adaptation. While he still was gone so many nights until late, he had a summer job. He had to sleep which meant he ended most nights in his bed. For a short time things were back to normal. My wife and I knew it was temporary and always considered it a gift of time. I recall wishing those passing summer months would slow down. There was something comforting about having him sleeping in his room or hearing him clicking away on his computer through all hours of the night.

When August rolled around and he returned to school, that same melancholy when he first left home for college always returned. That down-hearted feeling mellowed a bit faster each fall, but never completely.

And then he graduated. His college years were suddenly over and his job searching was successful. Luckily for us he worked for a large company in the area for a year. For us it was like another extended year of his college life.

But, things had changed. He had a girlfriend…and that year she turned into his fiancé. At the end of that year, his life would take another thrilling turn. His fiancée's job and his job would relocate them to Chicago. Coupled with this move were their plans for marriage. Now he truly would be gone from the house. His bedroom in the house would become just a memory. He wouldn't even be stopping by to wash his clothes or have a quick meal with us.

We tried not to imagine not having his smile, his humor, his enthusiasm, and just himself so close to us. How do you say farewell to such a delightful kid…now delightful young man. He'd no longer would be part of our family's everyday life. At least when he was in school, we'd convinced ourselves that the twenty miles from his college did indeed keep him close. Now he really was going to be gone. It didn't seem real…or fair.

But, like it or not, that was another vicissitude. Other parents adapted. We'd do so as well. Besides, with email and that cell phone, we'd have more advantages of talking with him and remaining close to him. At least my wife and I were going to hang onto that belief with a stranglehold even though that assumption had never really lived up to the reality.

When the time came for our son to make that move, his enthusiasm and exhilaration knew no bounds. Why shouldn't he be excited about a new job and getting married? He asked that I help as he moved what furniture he had to Chicago. It was agreed. I'd drive his car; he'd drive the U-haul…and then I'd fly back home from Chicago.

We tried not to think about his leaving, only enjoying the days he was still around home before he left. We were still thrilled for him; we just wished his work would have kept him closer. But, it was not to be. So many parents often counted the months, days, or hours until their son or daughter finally left home. We couldn't relate to that feeling…not in the least.

When he made the request for my assistance, for an instant I wanted to selfishly say 'no'. It was an absurd momentary lapse. I of course nodded willingly. I always wanted to be there when he needed me. Those times would soon become so limited.

We talked often with our son about the best times for us to visit him in Chicago as well as looked ahead when he would be getting back home. He'd nod but we wondered if he realized how important his physical closeness was to us. However, we weren't fooling ourselves. The closeness with him would now mostly be emotional which of course was the most important.

While he wouldn't live close to us anymore, our wish was that we just wanted to remain a strong part of his life if that was still possible. His leaving home was supposed to happen. We were supposed to be prepared for his departure. We'd had years to have made the adjustment. We should have been ready. We just weren't.

When the small truck was packed for Chicago and his car was equally crammed with more of his personal items, we were ready to leave on that cold February day. I would follow his lead as he drove the U-haul truck. I could barely watch his mother saying farewell to him. She put up an appearance of joy for his sake; I wondered how long it took for her tears to dry after we left.

For me I had another gift being able to spend more time with my son before my final farewell. I kept cancelling that difficult scene from my mind as if it was not supposed to happen. Instead I'd call his cell phone as we traveled. We'd talk about anything in the world with him leading our two-vehicle caravan. As we drove, the weather was lousy. The snow was blowing across the open highway. The gusty wind at times jolted the car. But, the bad weather didn't bother me a bit. I didn't care if the travel time took forever. I found myself not wanting to arrive in his new city.

I recollect kidding him in one of those many cell phone conversations about driving what was left of his vehicle that had been new only four years before. It had definitely become his car complete with strewn tapes and CD's, loose papers, stained seats, dirty floor mats, miscellaneous candy wrappers, and innumerable boxes of breakable items for his new apartment that he thought would be safer traveling in his car with me. Truthfully, I figured the actual value of the contents in those boxes might be worth an expensive lunch. To him of course they were incalculable.

As we approached the outskirts of Chicago, the weather improved. The inevitable was going to happen. We'd unpack his stuff. I'd stay overnight at his new apartment and then fly back home the next day. Then it would be real. He would be living elsewhere working a new job as he waited for his upcoming marriage a few weeks away.

As we crossed into the city limits and into the 'loop' of Chicago, I was so happy for my son…and so selfishly glum. I couldn't believe what was happening. I was actually going to have to let him go… that little boy who I loved so much… and now that young man, so intelligent, so humorous, so unique, and so special.

We arrived at his apartment in the evening and began unloading immediately. The weather conditions were frigid. It didn't bother me since I was numb anyway. After four hours of going up and down an outside staircase in that miserably ice-cold weather…with more than a few essential rest breaks to warm our bodies… we finally finished the job. He kept asking me what I thought of his place, obviously seeking a favorable response. He was so enthused. How could I say anything but how impressed I was with his wonderful good fortune in finding this small apartment. He wanted me to be proud. He didn't have to be concerned. I'd never 'not' been proud of him.

The following day I was scheduled to fly back home from Chicago's O'Hare Airport. Home seemed a misnomer. Our daughter was now in college and we were going through the same emotions of missing her. She was at the same university where our son had been. We'd obviously learned something. Thirty minutes no longer seemed as far away. Maybe she had seen our angst when her brother had gone on to school and was more willing to come home promptly for anything. Maybe she shared some of that anxiety of him being gone from home and wanted to mollify our aches as much as she could. It would be like her to be that caring.

All that second day before I was to leave, I was hoping I would muster the fortitude to say farewell and not get choked up. Those hours before we were to depart for O'Hare airport were like a bad dream…only this one would never be forgotten.

As the time got closer to leaving, however, the weather began to deteriorate badly. We watched on his TV how a weather system was moving down from Wisconsin and Lake Michigan. It was already interrupting most forms of transportation. My son checked my flight and found that most flights including mine were grounded or cancelled… probably for the remainder of the afternoon and evening.

It was the best news I'd had since we'd left home. I'd have more time with my son. Being always resourceful, however, he got on the line to Union Station and found that the trains were moving. I could take the 'Zephyr' back home if I got down to the train station immediately. He thought he was doing me a favor. Now the best news had turned bad. I was going to leave him even earlier than I'd anticipated.

We were both quieter as he drove me down to the train station later that afternoon in cold, blizzard like conditions. I believe even he was recognizing my departure was a milestone for him…certainly an expected one for countless fathers and sons…but unique to us. Flashes of him were bouncing through my memory…the cute little boy with his match box cars…the young man who pitched a tennis ball against the garage more times than there were stars in the sky…the creator of infinite 'Legos' buildings and towns…the computer aficionado who constantly was helping his family members advance further into the computer age… the creative writer…and the kid who made us all in the family laugh constantly. He'd enriched our family so much…and now he would be on his own away from us.

As we plowed our way on East Adams toward Union Station, he began to chat animatedly about some plans with his apartment…about his upcoming life in his new job. He talked about going down to his office the next morning even though he wasn't supposed to begin work until the next Monday. I wanted to talk about other things, but my mind was blank. I was glad he was able to carry the conversation.

The traffic was heavy. The day was dreary. The sleet and snow pelted against the cracked windshield of his worn-out Mazda. He didn't notice any of the bleakness to the day. He was smiling. He was excited.

Finally even he became less talkative as we crossed the Chicago River and pulled up to the front of Union Station. I hated what was happening. The moment I hoped would never arrive had finally come. I was afraid he was just going to drop me off. At the last minute he decided to park the car and come into the station with me to wait for my departure time. Thank God. I just wasn't ready to let him go.

We marched through the wind and sleet toward the train station. At the corner of Des Plaines Street and West Jackson at the southwest corner of the terminal, a man with a loud voice was selling evening copies of the *Chicago Tribune*. We both wondered how he was able to keep his newspapers dry in such horrible conditions.

The weather had deteriorated even more since leaving my son's apartment. The blowing snow was blinding. It was also rush hour so cars were honking and driving too closely to one another trying to get an edge so they could make the next streetlight. Commuters were trudging through the snow, ice, wind and sleet with their heads down on their way to their parked cars, bus stop or commuter trains. They were ignoring normal safety procedures in their rush to get out of the bad conditions. Disregarding streetlights these impatient pedestrians took poorly thought-out chances by jaywalking across the busy, slippery streets. There was a statement on each of their faces how when they accepted whatever job they had in downtown Chicago, they did not mean to have signed up for such deplorable commuting conditions.

Competing with these impetuous pedestrians were taxis, cars, and buses trying to move forward in the difficult conditions. These vehicles would stretch the yellow on the street light to its limit. Buses were splattering curbside commuters with waves of built up icy water and snow on the street.

Despite the entire scene of mass pandemonium, that man selling the newspapers had five, maybe ten, of the latest afternoon copies under his armpit covered in plastic. He walked back and forth on the sidewalk at that busy intersection holding one plastic-covered newspaper in the air yelling above the din of the traffic for people to grab a late edition. A few people stopped momentarily and bought a newspaper. He thanked them, made change, handed people their newspaper, and kept walking and talking despite the horrible outside conditions.

What we noticed as we approached him was how he kept up his line of chatter even while making change. And much of what he was saying had nothing to do with selling newspapers. Instead, he was giving worried and incessant admonitions aimed at various pedestrians. His exceptional volume and energy transcended above the noise of the vehicles. His inflection was strong and steady, but had a curiously humorous tone to his cautionary intentions. Everyone walking by the man couldn't help but hear his concern and warnings.

He shouted, "Sir, you don't want to cross the street on that yellow light. No… No…No! You've got to get home to see your wife and kids in one piece"………..or, "Everybody's in a hurry. Hurry to work……Hurry going home……Hurry! Hurry! Hurry! My friends…please… please slow down and be more careful. You'll all get home soon enough"………or, "Be careful there, madam! Keep back on the curb there, sir. That light changes at the same rate during the winter as the summer. You waited in the hot weather…you can wait for it now. Come on, let's all be cautious!"

My son and I chuckled at the sincere warnings this man was shouting to all the commuters. He seemed to make eye contact with everyone even though the pedestrians with their heads faced downward to ward off the drizzle and snow rarely looked up to catch his attentive eyes.

As we marched by him, our heads were up. We waved in appreciation for his thoughtfulness and attentiveness to the single-minded commuters going home.

He caught our look and started smiling as he acknowledged our appreciation for his efforts. Then for some reason he looked closer at my son and me walking together as he kept up his non-stop admonitions to those around him. His eyes focused on me with my small suitcase and my son carrying nothing. Despite all the activity and monstrous weather around him he could see the forlorn look on my face and in my eyes.

That man then made the most startling observation. He yelled out in that wind and sleet with the most sympathetic tone in his voice, "On my…there's a man about to say good-by…and he looks so sad. You're the Dad aren't you… saying so long to your son. Isn't that right?"

My son and I stopped in our tracks and stared at the man in silent amazement. I didn't realize I was so visibly glum. I tried to think of something flippant to say, but the words weren't there. I just sullenly nodded my head. My son looked at me and gave the same kind of nod.

That corner newspaper man then followed up with a statement so caring and so empathic. I wonder to this day how he could have been so thoughtful. I've concluded it was just his nature. He called out through that wind and sleet with a voice showing so much understanding and kindness, "Well, don't worry, Dad, he'll be O.K.…and you will too."

My son laughed uncomfortably…and I followed suit. The man's observation had depth, consideration, and kindness beyond what anyone could have expected.

Recovering, my son and I both gave him another more enthusiastic wave and a heartfelt smile to let him know his remark was right on the money. He laughed, nodded his head, and yelled a final remark. It was aimed at me. "I've got a son too. Good-byes do hurt."

He then gave us a last wave as his attention abruptly turned toward another pedestrian. He bellowed, "Sir…..Sir…you don't want to jaywalk in this weather. Let's all calm down my friends. Some days we just have to be more cautious than other days. This is one of those days. Your families know you'll be delayed. You'll get home…don't worry."

We entered Union station with his voice still ringing in our ears. I purchased my reserved ticket on the train knowing the time was getting closer and closer that I'd have to let my son go. I tried to be talkative and up-beat, but I wasn't being very successful. He talked more about what Chicago had to offer…in better weather conditions. It was just idle talk. I didn't mind listening. I just wanted to hear his voice. I could see his face was showing a slightly sorrowful strain with my pending departure, but he willed his voice to be upbeat.

My train was scheduled to leave in twenty minutes. There was no reason for him to stay any longer. His parked car would only get more inundated with the falling snow and slush. I reached out and shook his hand which turned into a hug. I hurt so badly. I could barely speak.

We'd be seeing each other in less than a month at the wedding. That was my one consolation. He tore away from my hug and began walking away with that wonderful smile on his face and that final wave. I didn't move. I watched his every movement as he marched down the corridor. He was going to be gone from my life. He went out the front door without realizing I was still watching him. It took a minute, but I finally stopped staring at the revolving door that had just propelled him into his future away from me. I went over to a bench to recover.

My heart was heavy. My eyes were down before I finally lifted my chin letting my eyes check out the huge board giving the train arrival and departure times. At first the words didn't register. All over that electronic board were the words… DELAY! DELAY!! DELAY!!!

I wasn't thinking properly. I asked someone next to me if they heard how long the delay was going to be. The response was two hours…maybe three… for all trains!

Then like a streak of lightning, my brain finally understood. Three Hours!!! Was I going to sit in that chair being miserable and alone for the next three hours?

I reached for my cell phone to call my son. The signal was weak, but prayed the connection would go through. I waited for the ring tone, but there was none. There wasn't even a chance for me to leave him a voice message.

A shout echoed within my head, 'Damn!' He'd now drive through the treacherous blizzard back to his apartment not realizing I was stranded for the next few hours. All I could think of was what a waste of time when I had more time to be with him. If and when I finally got through to him on his phone, it would be too late and unwise for him to drive back through the dangerous snow and ice to the train station.

Suddenly my thoughts turned to which direction my son would walk once he exited those revolving doors. I shot out of my chair like a cannon ball and raced across the large train terminal to where he'd departed from the building just two minutes before. I had to catch him before he got in his car and drove away. I had to do everything I could do to stop him from leaving my life just then. I had a chance to squeeze a couple more hours of being with my son. I didn't have to let him go just yet. I had to have more time!

I ran with suitcase in hand down the one-way street toward where his car had been parked. It would be difficult to recognize with all cars being so snow covered.

And, in that instance I saw his car. He'd already started it and finished cleaning off his windows. He was pulling out of his parking spot trying to get into the traffic. The fruitless howl I made was like yelling into a jet engine. The noise of the wind and traffic muffled all other sound. I was almost abreast of his car but on the sidewalk when the traffic began to move again. He pulled away from my futile shouts and waving of hands without seeing me.

I couldn't believe it! He hadn't seen me! I continued to run on the slippery, pedestrian filled sidewalk toward the next intersection. I prayed that the light would be red. It was a half-block ahead. The light had just turned green. I couldn't believe my poor luck. Was fate going to keep me from taking advantage of one last time with my son before he and I would no longer be together?

I was crushed. I kept slogging along with suitcase in hand. My other hand was waving. My son was only looking ahead at the driving snow and the traffic problems he faced.

Then I heard that same piercing voice of the corner newspaper salesman. He was continuing his non-stop jabbering at passers-by making change for people buying a newspaper and simultaneously imploring people to be careful.

My son's car was now going faster than my awkward gait. I yelled out his name…again and again. Though his car was only twenty yards ahead of me, his head kept looking straight ahead…his concentration where it had to be. My efforts seemed pointless.

Then his car slowed for a moment giving me another bit of hope. I yelled his name louder and waved more determinedly. But his car lurched forward as the traffic pulled away. My heart sank again. It wasn't fair. Life wasn't fair. But, why was I being put through this torture?

Then, like a small miracle, something happened. That corner newspaper salesman saw the desperate look on my face. He heard me yelling and saw me waving at one of the cars in the street. Whether he recalled me or not, he saw which direction my eyes were focused and he heard me hollering my son's name. With not a second thought, that man split from his duties in an effort to help me. I'll never know why he did. And, I still don't know how he knew which car my insistent shouts were aimed. But, that blessed man took over. While still hugging his newspapers under his left armpit, he lit out down the sidewalk ahead of me. His voice was ten times louder than mine echoing my son's name he'd just heard. I watched in stunned hope as this man repeatedly called out my son's name to every car he passed.

Then, as if by magic, I could see the brake lights brighten as my son's car slowed. I saw the driver's side window lower. He stuck his head out the window in confusion. He couldn't believe someone was hollering his name. I could see the shocked look on his face as he realized an unknown African-American man was actually calling out his name and chasing down his car on a busy, snow-filled street in downtown Chicago. My son then completely rolled down his window and listened to what that saint of a man had to say. I could hear the man's words above the roar of the traffic. It was like a dream. "Your father is trying to catch up to you!!! Pull over!!! I'll stop the traffic!! He needs you!! Now you just wait for him, you hear?

And there I was choking to death not believing what this kind Samaritan had just done for me. The man had stopped my son from leaving my life too soon. That unbelievably benevolent corner newspaper salesman then waved his arms at the slow moving traffic signally for them to allow my son to maneuver his car over to the side of the street. That image of him controlling the traffic for those few seconds has never dulled in my mind. His actions were simply extraordinary.

In seconds of my son stopping his car I arrived at the scene. My disbelief was so thorough; my eyes were so ecstatically happy. I don't know how often I shouted 'thank you' to that wonderful fellow. I just remember him giving me the warmest smile while saying in a much lower volume, "Glad I could help out. Now I've got to get back to my post." There was a look of satisfaction on his face as he slogged away. He knew how much I treasured what he'd done for me. There was so much more I wanted to say to him, but he had already raised a plastic-covered newspaper offering the 'Final Edition' and warning people to be careful.

I swung the suitcase into the back seat of my son's car and told him to wait a moment. I just had to shake the man's hand for doing me such a favor.

I trudged determinedly on the slushy pavement back toward that newspaper salesman. He turned around and saw me coming. I don't know if he even recognized me right away. It had been less than thirty seconds since his magnanimous deed.

Looking him straight in the eye, I grabbed his hand and shook it vigorously. "Sir, I'll never forget what you did. You see…there was a delay… I just had to see my son once again before I left."

He had such a contented looked on his face completely the opposite look of each of those innumerable commuters plodding by us on the sidewalk.

Then he grinned. In a much more subdued voice, he leaned toward me and repeated, "I know how you feel. I've got a son too."

That was all that was said. We both looked each other in the eye and just smiled and laughed. Then he again turned and got back to business shouting in that miserable weather, "Newspaper! Get it here!"

I watched him trek back toward his corner. I didn't feel like I was done yet thanking him. And then he turned around and yelled back at me. "You'd have done the same for me! I can tell!"

He waved again and then turned his attention back to his chief concern. I heard his voluminous voice jawing at another pedestrian. "Sir…Sir…what are you doing!!! That's a red light! Don't walk across there. Your wife and kids can wait a couple extra minutes!"

Then another admonition…"Buddy, don't you even think about crossing that street before you see a green light. Come back to the curb! I've got to sell newspapers, not take you to the hospital!"

That pedestrian turned and smiled at him…then retreated back to the curb. I'd just had a selfless act given to me by a very decent human being. Now just a minute later, it was that commuter and the corner newspaper salesman having their own moment of humanity together.

That instance ended and the newspaperman's attention again turned to the busy intersection in front of him. He got back into his incessant cadence of comments to no one in particular. "Hurry…Hurry…Hurry!!! Everybody's got to rush someplace!"

He looked back in my direction one more time. I kept looking back at him not believing what he'd done for me. Now almost a half block away about to get into my son's car, I gave that man a huge wave in a final gesture of thanks. He pointed at me with a big smile while not losing the cadence of his warning cries to his customers and people filing by him

To a person lumbering by and seeing what he had done for me, his act of kindness toward me probably would have been forgotten minutes later. But to me, it was the most considerate and compassionate act I'd ever so generously received in my life.

I got into the car and told my son what that corner newspaper salesman had spontaneously done. He appreciated the story, but I could tell not as much as I who had seen the actual effort and been the beneficiary.

The rest of that evening would always be a blur. My son and I drove a few blocks, stopped at a restaurant, and had dinner until the re-scheduled time of departure. My principal thought during our meal was how I had cheated sadness. I was stealing extra time with my son…time that was not supposed to happen. And I loved every minute of that time I had stolen.

Over those next few hours, we both seemed so much more animated. I'd been so downhearted I hadn't truly been able to participate in our prior conversations. With the bonus minutes, we talked about everything. We talked about politics, sports, the stock market and even reminisced about previous winters when our family had lived in that very city. We just couldn't stop talking to each other.

Two and a half hours later when he dropped me off at the train gate, he parked and waited with me until we were certain the train would be departing at its new time. I was relieved he remained with me. I wanted to take advantage of every last possible moment before I had to leave.

When the call for boarding finally came, this time the farewell, although still subdued, was not as dreadful. I didn't have the large lump in my throat that I had three hours before. It was just a medium-sized one. At least I could still speak. That tightness in my throat would always be there whenever I had to say farewell to him. It would be the same with my daughter when it was her time to leave home as well.

My son and I had agreed on talking with each other by cell phone each day for the next couple days so I could hear how his adaptation to Chicago was progressing. He was glad I was so interested. I couldn't imagine not being so interested. I truly hoped the calls would somewhat lessen my pain of his being away.

It was still difficult to let him go but I gathered my small suitcase and made slow steps towards the gate with him beside me. When we hugged for the last time I was able to give him a forced smile. I blandly said, "See you in a couple weeks." I barely got the words out. It was the best I could do.

Passing through the gate, I turned and waved one final time. He waved back and gave me that confident smile. Then he turned and simply disappeared into the crowd of travelers. I stopped before stepping up onto the train staring for ten seconds at that space in time he had just occupied. That was it. Just like that he was gone.

I don't remember much about that train ride back home. I recall the snow beating against the windows of the train, the discomfort of the seat during the nighttime ride when sleep was so difficult, and the otherwise numbness I felt now that my son was going to be living in a different city. While I knew I'd be seeing him in the future…again and again…I wondered if I'd ever be able to bid him farewell and not have that knot in my throat.

Time has passed since I lived through that ordeal of finally letting my son go. I've adapted to him being so far away. That doesn't mean I like it. If he lived closer, we'd do more things together…maybe less things than I imagine, but certainly there'd be more opportunities to see each other.

But, that's no longer probable. The reality is that with the type of work he does, it would be unlikely we'd be very close geographically ever again. I would have to depend on visits, emails and the cell phone to stay close him…like so many other fathers and sons. That was the way the cards had been dealt.

Yet in the time since that difficult and sentimental farewell and the numerous calls and emails to stay close to him, I find myself often recalling that cold, snow-filled night outside the train depot on the corner of Des Plaines Street and West Jackson Street across the Chicago River from the Sears Tower. I can never forget that street newspaper vendor with a heart of gold. At any moment I can close my eyes and visualize him chasing down my son's slow moving car in a blizzard just so I could have some extra time with my son after that train delay. I just had not been ready to let my son go that night. Those extra hours meant the world to me.

I've always felt selling newspapers was only a small part of that man's life. His job only put him in a place where he could provide a higher level purpose. He had a gift for caring. He might not realize how his resonating voice cautioning people to be careful was all that important, but in further thoughts since then, I have to believe he did. He was a Good Samaritan who was just naturally observant and thoughtful.

For some unknown reason he'd seen the distress in my eyes and heard the pleading in my voice…and he'd answered my desperate need. How many others had he helped in different ways…even if all he'd done was cajole various pedestrians and commuters to slow down and be cautious so they'd make it home to their families safely?

People would walk away from him shaking their heads over his humorous and often brusque warnings to pedestrians…and they couldn't help but smile. How could you not appreciate his personality and his considerate warnings? Then seconds later those same people deep in their own thoughts would be moving on forgetting the man, but subliminally still heeding his warnings. There would never be any accounting of how many accidents or personal injuries were averted because of this man's constant chatter to pay attention and take caution. I want to believe there were many…and that is based only on seeing him implore preoccupied pedestrians on just that one cold February night with warnings like "Be careful there, ma'am, it's slippery!"…or, "Sir, please wait for the light. Your family needs you!"

I've thought many times about going back to that corner during one of my visits to Chicago and thanking that man for giving me those precious additional two-and-a-half hours with my son. However, it would probably be kind of trivial to him. There would be no reason he could ever recall such an unimportant incident, even though to me it was so special. For him, saying and doing considerate things every day for people was just part of his being. His act of benevolence for me was singularly extraordinary only to me.

Still, I have this dream where I wander by him as he's jawing at people while selling his newspapers. I'd be just another face, but I'd give him a hundred dollar bill for a newspaper and just walk away.

No doubt he would shout after me that he owed me change. I'd just turn, smile, and point at him saying, "No you don't!" Then I'd continue my stroll down the street waving an appreciative farewell. He'd look at me strangely not understanding my impulse.

Yet, I know the money would have no meaning to him. It would certainly be of some limited and temporary economic advantage, but that would be all. The question is how do you offer pay back for an unexpected and amazingly generous deed to someone who lives daily by such a benevolent code? Would the money, no matter the amount only cheapen the deed he did for me? I may as well give that man everything I own since his kindness shown towards me that snowy February evening outside the train station was priceless.

What Becomes of a 'Corporate Animal'

It might have been when Richard Fuller sent his last child off to college that his motivation to continue his long-time job seemed to have sprung a more serious leak. Actually, both situations had been in his mind for a long time… one was just inevitable…the other, leaving his place of employment, seemed both unwise and unreal.

When the Fuller's youngest daughter, MacKenzie, departed the Fuller home, that event had been experienced twice before. They had survived their older two children going off to school. Their son, David, had just graduated from the University of Minnesota. He was gainfully employed in a management program with General Mills, Inc. The high emotion of him leaving home had been tempered by him returning the very next week with two new friends. They needed a home-cooked meal. That need continued throughout his schooling much to the satisfaction of his parents.

The middle child, Laurie, was beginning her third year at the University. Her exit brought tears from both Fuller and his wife. They knew they wouldn't be seeing her as much. She'd always been more of a free spirit. However, that bit of sadness had been over-rated. Even she found reason to stop by the house at least once a week, but more often twice or three times ostensibly to do laundry or to find a quiet place to study in her room at home. She always seemed to arrive about supper time.

With the final blow, the Fullers knew the last of the brood was truly going to be missed. MacKenzie had always liked her life at home. Her bedroom was her own little domain. It was filled with things depicting her life more than the rooms of her older siblings. Though glum whenever Fuller and his wife walked by her now empty room, they had a silent hope she would find reasons to make it home as often as her sister and brother had.

That very evening after dropping MacKenzie off at school, Fuller sat in the family room with a football game on the television and an open *Time* magazine on his lap. He was paying little attention to either. While he thought about his daughter, his mind was also switching back and forth regarding his work. Things had not been going well…enough that he found himself pondering what might lie ahead if he left his company. Richard Fuller had been a corporate executive for a well-known Twin Cities based paper company for more that fifteen years. It had been a reasonably rewarding career with the St. Paul Paper Company, a privately held employee-owned organization. Only the employees could buy and sell company's stock. It was a profitable investment with the stock going up every year even prior to Fuller joining the company.

Fuller had risen fast within the company. As a sales representative he'd been a leader practically since the first few months on the job. Customers liked the way he made it easy to do business with St. Paul Paper Company. He was the top sales person for three years before being promoted into management. His upward movement continued until he was promoted to the Vice President slot at the relatively young age of thirty-six. Now forty-eight, he was still vigorous and had always carried much respect within the organization. With a national sales force of just over a hundred sales representatives, he'd led the organization to revenue increases every year since taking on the leadership role of the department.

He'd helped his company through numerous business changes. Finding new clients and creating new ideas for paper products was his hallmark as a senior level manager. Serving on the board of directors as well, his experience at St. Paul Paper had been fulfilling and personally profitable. With a nice home at Lake Johanna, life had been good for the Fuller family.

It had been only in the past two years that various changes in the business environment had brought on more and more challenges. There was even more of a need for modifications in the company products and the development of new ideas. Also, the advent of electronic information delivery meant that most of his company's long-term customers were looking to cut down on paper usage. This had all the earmarks that St. Paul Paper Company might be looking ahead to some leaner years. To Fuller it was all just part of business...just another hurdle the company would have to face. They'd overcome obstacles before. They'd do it again.

But, the monthly meeting of the board of directors was becoming more desperate, even before sales had begun to dip in the early part of the fiscal year in Fuller's twelfth year at the sales and marketing department helm. The general feeling in that board room was that a potential disaster was in the making. Fuller found with so many of the board members nearing retirement age, more dialogue was spent defining the problem than discussing possible answers to the future in their business. His ideas for acquiring other small companies or launching some non-paper products were generally met with disapproval. At present, the current year showed there would be a shortfall in revenue for the first time since Fuller joined the organization.

With the glory of success the previous years credited to him, the entire blame for the revenue deficit was falling upon Rich Fuller's shoulders. He'd continued to try and convince the board to authorize the development of non-paper products, but generally the board was hesitant about making such dramatic or drastic investments.

Fuller had been commenting to his wife more often about feeling like a professional sports coach after a few losses. He had heard some rumors about how he'd become soft, that he couldn't crack the whip anymore, and even that he didn't have the technical mind to lead the sales and marketing effort into the advancing electronic age.

It was convenient criticism even though he was the one pushing for change. When his proposal to the board to hire a separate technical group for product development was tabled until later, Fuller acted on his own within his department. He changed the compensation plan to emphasize sales representatives making more income based on finding new clients and new paper needs rather than just upselling the current customers. That measure had helped the first and second quarter business volume, but most everyone on the board gave more credit to the revenue increase to the company's annual price increases.

It was that fall when his youngest daughter went off to college that internal discussions in the company became more heated. The third quarter was almost completed and was lagging terribly. The board of directors continued to be indecisive and unwilling to take investment risks for the company's future.

It was a particularly frustrating time for Fuller. He was noticing something else. His sales group had been used to good times. When it took more aggressive maneuvering and a heartier sales effort to get new customers, he didn't have the sales managers or sales representatives who had the willingness or adaptive skills to change their sales methods.

Board meetings had become unbearable. There were complaints that the company's long held habit of promotion from within had finally caught up with the entire organization. It was suggested that there was no cross-pollination of ideas if more middle management had been hired from outside the ranks of St. Paul Paper Company. A few of the directors began advocating the need for outside consulting help. Fuller was lukewarm but generally favored the possibility only in the hope that the consulting group might stop the internal inertia.

The end of September arrived and the third quarter financials were even worse than expected. Fuller began to feel the very oxygen being sucked out of his lungs. The people he most counted on to discuss matters within the company seemed to flounder and be frustrated. They considered his views to turn things around either too radical or the wrong direction.

Even Gene Thomas, fellow board member and the Human Relations Director, had begun stopping by his office more frequently just to talk. He'd never done that before. Fuller was to learn later that Thomas was carrying out this duty by order of certain members of the board of directors. It was another way of building a case against any employee, including an upper level executive.

It was on October 20 that Fuller was not told but heard through the rumor mill that the CEO, Henry Miller, was interviewing someone for a new position called Vice President of Corporate Business Development. The person would be reporting to Miller. Where Fuller had no problem with the CEO doing what he wanted, the normal procedure would have been for Miller at least to have discussed the position…even having Fuller involved in the recruitment process. When he heard that the CEO had not only interviewed but hired a person in this new senior level position, Fuller had a queasy feeling in his stomach for the first time in his entire career.

It was 4:30 on the last Friday in October that Henry Miller called and asked Fuller to drop by his office before he left for home. What made the phone call so ominous sounding was the classic maxim that Friday's were the preferred day to terminate people. It was absurd to even think such a thing could happen. There was no direct clue or warning that Miller would go that far…especially with someone like Fuller who'd been such a proven asset to the company for so long.

Fuller's stomach was grinding as he walked to the adjoining building to meet with the CEO. First indications relaxed him. Miller's greeting was upbeat. He smiled as if the company was swimming in new revenue with only a rosy picture for the future. Still, the show of contentment seemed false. Fuller had no idea what to expect as Miller offered him a seat on one of the leather couches in his ample office.

As the company's CEO spoke, Fuller's concern became justified. Miller explained that he had been talking with his group of CEO's who met monthly at the Minneapolis Club. He made it sound as if those men were his personal consulting group. The explanation was only a preface for his reasoning behind creating the new Vice President of Corporate Business Development position. Miller stated that he'd found a uniquely qualified person to concentrate entirely on analyzing future business prospects. The man was a recommendation from a couple of his acquaintances at his club.

The CEO expressed hope the new addition to the company hierarchy, a man named Howard Jensen, had plenty of experience in the newly developing electronic industry. His hope was that Jensen could help carve out some new markets and suggest new products for St. Paul Paper Company…possibly even suggest a change in the company name to better reflect St. Paul Paper being more than just a paper company.

Fuller actually breathed a silent sigh of relief. It sounded like his position in the company was not being threatened, even though Fuller himself had taken great pains in the last year to do exactly what Jensen was being hired to do. The difference appeared to be that the company was more willing to give a new guy a chance with new ideas and proposals than with someone they had pigeon-holed as being a member of the 'old school' in the paper industry.

With the atmosphere in that office cooling down markedly, Miller and Fuller talked in a more relaxed tone…the way they typically communicated. The only red flag popping up was when the company leader casually mentioned Howard Jensen had been with five companies in the previous nine years. Fuller focused on the man he'd known for fifteen years and found himself perplexed after that comment. The

CEO abruptly cleared his throat sensing Fuller's surprise. He defended his decision by saying, "Rich, I believe the energy and experience supplied by this new man will be the type of outside perspective we need in our company. Furthermore, I've decided to put Jensen in charge of the marketing staff. It'll not only give you the freedom to concentrate on the sales group, but having the reins of the marketing support staff will give Howard more credence in his new position."

What could Fuller do but nod having had no opportunity to offer his opinion prior to the spontaneous decision? It meant that Fuller and Jensen had better be able to work together and support one another for the good of the entire sales and marketing staff as well as the company.

Fuller decided to be fair and say no more. Though he was astonished how the entire process had played out, he decided to trust the long relationship he had with Henry Miller. While Fuller was determined to deal with this Howard Jensen cordially, he did not like having to work closely with someone he'd never met. 'Then again,' he thought, 'it's likely this new guy might take some of the heat off my back.'

As he left Miller's office, Fuller hoped this new guy, Jensen, and he could feed off each other and team up to supply some improved leadership the company sorely needed that frankly the CEO had not been giving.

A lunch was set for the upcoming Tuesday to welcome Howard Jensen. Even though he wasn't yet on the payroll until the following Monday, he'd asked to come into the office just to get his office set up and to meet many of the people with whom he'd be working.

Before that Tuesday welcoming lunch, Fuller made efforts to uncover more background on the new senior level manager. He found additional detail about the five jobs in the previous nine years by this new man…and frankly found the history of Howard Jensen highly bothersome. It made Fuller seriously question the depth of Henry Miller's due diligence. How could anyone not question a career filled with so many short-term higher level jobs?

Nonetheless, the man was hired. It was a done deal. Fuller saw once again something he'd too often been concerned about when it came to Henry Miller. Anytime there was conflict, the CEO had generally shown discomposure followed by impulsiveness. At those times Miller didn't talk things over with people he should be able to trust. That had always been a burning question in Fuller's mind. How effective could Miller be when times really got tough?

Now, St. Paul Paper Company's very viability was at stake and the leader of the company was panicking. He was used to spending more time at his country club or downtown at the Minneapolis Club. Now his only reaction was to hire some unknown executive to save the company.

The Tuesday luncheon held in the company boardroom was set up primarily for the marketing staff to rub shoulders with Howard Jensen. The entire board of directors was also present at that luncheon. They were there to show support and smile with satisfaction for everyone to see over the new addition to the upper manager group.

Fuller stayed to the side with a pasted smile on his face watching various people get introduced to Jensen. The whole event seemed so contrived and hollow. In just ten painful minutes Fuller's discomfort grew as he observed Howard Jensen. Jensen was quite witty and sociable to those members of the board he saw. His behavior changed quite dramatically when he met people who would be on his staff or employees who were on a lower level. When he shook hands with the lady who was to be his Administrative Assistant, he looked through her as if she was a ghost. When she said something to try to connect with him, he smiled blankly as he looked past her and waved to Gene Thomas just entering the party from his Human Relations office. Thomas had been integral in arranging the move policy and the salary for Jensen. This man meant something to Jensen…as did the board members who would impact his ability to do his job. To everyone else he met, it was a shake of the hand, a plastic grin, and his eyes wandering around the room locating the truly important contacts.

Fuller was the last board member to get introduced to Howard Jensen. When that happened, Jensen's eyes locked on Fuller's eyes as if they were about to arm wrestle. Jensen gave Fuller a quick full smile that disappeared as fast as their handshake ended. He said nothing witty to Fuller as if to do so was a waste of time. His only words were, "Well, it looks like we'll be crossing paths."

Fuller thought it was a strange opening statement. 'Crossing paths' depicted conflict, not working together. It was a huge let down relative to what more positively could have been said. To Fuller, Jensen seemed to be looking at him as a relic…as an impediment to his plans…and someone he would be clashing.

Though hugely disappointed, Fuller gave the perfunctory 'welcome' and 'let's set up a meeting time after you get settled in your office'. Jensen hardly acknowledged the suggestion and then excused himself to go talk again with Henry Miller. Indeed he didn't even head toward CEO. He just wanted to get another glass of wine. In that one minute time lapse, Fuller knew that his relationship with this new vice president would be at best….strained.

Fuller went home that day sickened by what he'd seen and felt during that luncheon. He figured others certainly must have seen Jensen's insincerity. There was no question in Fuller's mind that St. Paul Paper Company would be yet another short term stop for Henry Jensen. The major question was how much damage the company would suffer while this new man established himself in a floundering company. Dealing with a difficult marketplace was challenging enough. It now looked to Fuller like this new transition was going to take precedent over everything else.

It was that very night Fuller again sat by the fireplace listening to a heavy rain splatter on the roof while contemplating his future and the direction of a company he'd invested so much of his career. He had a sports magazine in his lap…something that usually allowed him to separate his mind from business problems. However, it was not the case that night. For the way he had been feeling, St. Paul Paper Company was likely no longer the place for him to be working. The impulsive decision to bring some supposed fast change, hired gun in the name of Howard Jensen, was the final straw. Rashness…impetuousness…panic…these behaviors had never been part of the culture of his company. He'd lately learned that communication, decisiveness, and willingness to take worthwhile risks were also not part of the fiber of the company.

He poured himself some wine. He'd been doing that more and more that autumn. The question had become what else he might want to do for a living. The past year had injured his self-assurance. He kept asking himself if that was the way the business world was always going to be no matter where he worked. Would fellow workers' confidence drift away so dramatically when conditions got tough? He wondered if he'd still be able to give his complete 100% effort at another company. If staff members or employees on his staff…people he'd hired, mentored, and made to feel part of the team could become so disenchanted and unwilling to support change, was it worth the effort to build another team someplace else. At another company, he'd have a so-called 'honeymoon period.' However with no history with any new organization, that initial loyalty and confidence would be like a kite on a string…flying high as long as business was relatively smooth…but more easily eroded in times of difficulty.

Fuller knew that a lot of what he was thinking at that moment was typical relative to the circumstances he was experiencing. Employee ownership invited fellow employees to be very opinionated and sensitive to change. It was the type of company he'd chosen to be involved. He'd generally liked his choice of career and company except when the internal politics became too dominant and overwhelming. Now, with what he had observed in one short luncheon and being around Howard Jensen, he realized the word 'overwhelming' was likely going to be defined more specifically in the days and weeks ahead.

He raised his glass of wine as he stared into the dying blaze in his fireplace. It was a very sardonic toast to his future.

As if already written, everything in the coming weeks that Fuller feared came to pass. Howard Jensen was playing his game like the professional Machiavellian he was. Any idea presented to the board of directors by Jensen was considered sage…even if it was a duplicate of what Fuller had proposed months before. Outside the board room, anyone who disagreed with Jensen was given the plastic grin. Two product managers who reported to Jensen found themselves out the door after differing with their new boss. In one of their few exchanges, Jensen even asked Fuller why he'd kept the two product managers who were 'living in the past'.

Fuller was able to figure out Howard Jensen's strategy within weeks. Jensen's personal aim was to have lunch daily with a different member of the board of directors. That way he could figure out what was needed to win them over as well as note areas where they might disagree with him. He was a master of pitting one board member against another in order to overcome a contrary view. To Howard Jensen, his methods were perfectly clear. Anyone not supporting him was automatically an enemy.

Interestingly, Jensen never sought out Rich Fuller for one of those luncheons. In fact, Jensen and Fuller still hadn't had their initial meeting after two weeks of Jensen being in the office. Fuller made the effort of stopping by the man's office three times in that first week to try to gain audience. Jensen always had another meeting and promised to set a time in the near future. The cavern developing between the two men seemed to be what Jensen preferred.

It didn't take long for the hearsay to flow within the marketing department now under Jensen's control. In just those first few weeks, it was understood that Howard Jensen was the son Henry Miller never had. In many ways, his title in corporate business development was transpiring into that of assistant CEO.

It took no time for Jensen's underlings to understand his management style. In meetings, nothing about the company was right or worth keeping. His staff knew they'd better not be found to have spread any of his loud opinions and directives to any board members...or any other departmental employee. When he expressed his views, he made it sound like he was bringing them into his confidence....implying that the employee better remain loyal to him or he had his way of finding them out. Then he'd either terminate them or make their working life miserable until they resigned.

With Jensen literally running through the company like a tornado, Fuller began to recognize something else might be going on. Fuller began to believe there was a very real likelihood Jensen could be trying to bring St. Paul Paper Company 'down' rather than improve productivity and profitability. In this way, the company still very highly regarded in the business world, might become a take-over target. While its base of business had declined in the past few quarters, its image was still relatively positive.

Fuller didn't want to believe that Howard Jensen was an agent for someone to instigate this maneuver, but too many things were happening too fast to think otherwise. The difficulty for Fuller was having anyone to discuss his concerns... especially with Howard Jensen being Henry Miller's golden boy?

There was even another consideration. Henry Miller owned the most stock in the company. If the company sold out to another conglomerate, it wouldn't be that bad for Miller. He could retire an even wealthier man. Also, other longer term employees owning stock, including Fuller, would certainly profit from such a sale. But, most employees didn't own a large enough number of shares to retire.

Further, their jobs could be in jeopardy with another company taking over the assets of St. Paul Paper Company.

Fuller contemplated even a more devious plan. Howard Jensen might be so intrinsically involved in a potential takeover that he could be playing the card for his own promotion. With Henry Miller highly likely to be asked to step down after a takeover, Jensen could be named President, whether St. Paul Paper Company remained as a company…or a division of the corporation that bought out all the stock. Whatever the case, doubtlessly there would be a complete cleaning of the house under Jensen's new role.

As the end of the horrible year drew close, Jensen had been in his job for almost the entire fourth quarter. There were no 'new' ideas flowing from the 'technical' whiz hired in October. His staff was paralyzed with fear for their jobs.

There were days in early December that Fuller didn't even see Jensen in the office. He found out at one of his board member luncheons that the new vice president was traveling out east establishing some new contacts for increased business. Fuller knew that was crazy. Jensen had no more contacts in the industry and bona fide plans for the future of St. Paul Paper Company than his administrative assistant had.

Fuller thought to himself that if these travels were under the guise of 'business development', then his fellow board members were more superficial than he'd ever surmised. At the very least, Jensen should have talked with Fuller about any history with the companies he might be visiting. That course of action had predictably not been done.

When Fuller received a private call in mid-December from a competing eastern based paper company vice president, there became no question in Fuller's mind that Howard Jensen was marketing the company…not its products. That vice president confidentially wanted to know if St. Paul Paper Company was trying to take over his company! The man was just trying to plan ahead regarding his own employment.

Fuller of course declined knowing any such information. He covered for Jensen by saying that the new man was just attempting to learn more about the industry and the differences amongst the leaders of the paper business. What Fuller would never say was how St. Paul Paper Company was in no financial shape to take over a company the size of the eastern based company. If anything it was the other way around.

To Fuller, Jensen's motivations had become too obvious. He was dealing a company he'd been with less than two months. St. Paul Paper Company meant no more to him than if it was a card on a black jack table in Las Vegas. Not having actual proof of Jensen's motives, however, Fuller figured he had to wait until he had more evidence.

Fuller stayed the course regarding his national sales force. His message to them was an attempt to be positive for the coming year. He admitted to tough times, but urged the representatives to stay focused on the long term and remain close to their customer base. What else could he say or do with a new product and development executive not even lifting a finger to do his actual job. As for Howard Jensen's message to his home office staff as well as to the company's board members was to remain confident, that change took time before results were seen. It was the most glaring display of false marketing Fuller had ever witnessed.

By the end of the year, most of the employees reporting to Jensen had become especially skeptical about the future of the company, the leadership of their new boss, and the longevity of their jobs. Their morale and productivity was so low, it was affecting the outside field representatives as well. The efforts of the field managers tended to become daily baby-sitting duty for a very worried sales force.

Fuller found himself investing most of his time stemming the tide of negativity…even from the board members. So many of them, except for Henry Miller, were dumbfounded as to what was going on. Even Gene Thomas, hearing so many bad vibrations in his role as Human Resources Director was showing signs of strain. In luncheons with Fuller…luncheons he now asked for on his own account…Thomas kept inquiring how many employees might have to be laid off in the coming year because of reduced revenue and a difficult looking future. Yet, in almost the same breath, Thomas would express how fortunate the company was that they found such an able person as Howard Jensen to lead the company onto a new pathway in the future. After that statement, Fuller found other things to do than have lunch with such an easily deceived executive as Gene Thomas.

As the year came to a close…the worst year in the history of the company…. Fuller had to admit that his own concentration on his job was wavering. He'd been fighting an uphill battle seemingly alone. His interest in continuing with a company that had so long been his identity simply no longer held his interest. St. Paul Paper Company seemed to be completely off the tracks from the fresh, vibrant company he'd come to work for so many years before.

Some key middle management people had already left and found new jobs. Turnover in the sales force had not surprisingly increased. The CEO's leadership during the difficult times was hopelessly lax. The look in his eyes when he sat down with Fuller or during board meetings was that of a beaten man. It was as if he no longer had the energy or the ability to steer the ship. Fuller, especially in recent years, had privately felt the long-term success of the company had been accomplished despite Miller's leadership.

The holiday break at the end of December gave employees at all levels a chance to take a deep breath…and get ready for what would hopefully be a lot better coming year. There was no basis for that feeling, but it was a perspective people liked to hear.

Howard Jensen had not been around the office much in the last two weeks of December. The rumor was that he was investing a lot of time in finding a new home in the Twin Cities area. It was rumored he was looking in western suburbs of Minneapolis, even though the company was located in St. Paul. Word was that he thought St. Paul didn't measure up to the larger of the Twin Cities. Since most of the employees lived in St. Paul, including Henry Miller, that rumored comment would be comparable to a slap in the face to a bulk of Jensen's fellow workmates. Of course, if Jensen heard that his remark might have been spread outside the department, he'd invest in lunches with the board for the next month in order to refute the statement. Of course, to Miller and the board members, they would never believe such irreverence voiced against their capital city. To them, Jensen was still the second coming no matter where he wanted to live.

After a week's break over the Christmas holidays, Rich Fuller still held out some hope for his company. Jensen had actually become less of a factor in the department because of his absences in the past couple weeks. Nonetheless, the paralysis within his department was evident. His people were afraid to make any decision. It appeared only a question of time before more board members would realize the horrible mistake Henry Miller had made in hiring Howard Jensen. Fuller couldn't see Howard Jensen lasting through the first quarter.

Unfortunately Fuller could see right away in January his hopes were badly contrived. If anything, things at St. Paul Paper Company seemed to be getting even more out of control. Howard Jensen had hired two ladies within weeks of his arrival in October who had worked for him at the other companies where he'd been employed. Both ladies hadn't spent one moment trying to learn the names of people associated with them in St. Paul Paper Company…as if the very attempt would be a superfluous exercise. Howard Jensen, in their minds, was the CEO. No one else's needs were important. Their hateful stares at anyone who was in their boss's way or who might disagree with him were met with cold responses that made the January temperatures in Minnesota seem mid-tropic.

Fuller thought it interesting, though, that the two ladies never showed any animosity toward him. They just stayed clear of him. They called him 'Mr. Fuller' and wished him a good day. That was it. They wanted no other interchange with him at all. There was no doubt in Fuller's mind that if their man, Howard Jensen, took complete control, Fuller would be out the door the next day.

In the second week of the year, Fuller did try a new tact just to stir things up. He came into Jensen's office at the end of one of the days Jensen happened to be in his office and suggested they have lunch at least once a week…a way of talking things through, being on the same page when talking to the board members as well as the remainder of the employees, and giving the entire sales and marketing staff a vision of cohesiveness between the two of them.

Jensen appeared surprised, but shrugged his shoulders as though he had to think how the idea might be to his advantage. His response was anything but overwhelmingly supportive. He said, "Well, Rich, I'm awfully busy with travel and outside lunches as you probably know, but we could certainly give it a try…if you want. Fuller felt like a first year employee begging for an audience with some upper echelon snob in the company. Nonetheless, he swallowed his pride and reiterated that the luncheon could lead to better morale around the department.

Jensen told him to call one of his 'girls' and she'd arrange the luncheon times. To Fuller it would be his last effort to break through the hard, self-possessed core of this journeyman. In those immediate days ahead Fuller would attempt to set up some luncheons with Jensen through either one of the 'girls'. Most of the time he didn't get a return call. Other times one of the ladies would phone back and say simply that Howard was going to be out of town and wouldn't be available. Then, as if to stick the needle in further, they'd ask if there was anything they could do to help Fuller. There was no recognizance from them as to the true purpose of the lunch. The idea of the luncheons died with that last call.

In this environment each day at the office had become pure torture. There was no light at the end of the tunnel. For that matter, there was no sunshine. Even Fuller's normal competitive edge was frayed. He found himself getting mentally tired quickly at meetings…even looking at the clock wishing the work day would end. Contemplating where he was going to eat with his wife that evening became a nice break from the workday. With this unhealthy cynicism, he found any meeting of any length intolerable and his patience practically non-existent.

Howard Jensen, on the other hand, seemed to be the only one who had a tireless energy when he was in the office. His primary purpose seemed to be self-promotion through the lunches with the board members…and longer meetings with Henry Miller.

Fuller's intolerance finally reached a crescendo one day in February when he walked in late to a meeting with two of his field managers and the product managers who reported to Jensen. In attendance were both of Jensen's 'girls'. The group was arguing over the color of brochures. Fuller had no idea why he was even asked to attend such a routine and relatively unimportant meeting. He watched the bickering around the table in shocked disbelief.

They were immersed in what they considered the biggest problem the company had ever faced. Could more sales be gained from a blue or green background on the brochures? Jensen's 'girls' were singularly arguing for the green background. Others were in favor of the blue background. The 'girls' were obviously representing what Howard Jensen wanted. The very purpose of the meeting was ridiculous…a complete waste of time.

Fuller began laughing at the total folly of the behavior around the table. Those present saw no humor. He excused himself after five minutes. Later that day he approached the Human Resources Director about negotiating out of the company. Gene Thomas seemed not surprised. While Fuller never said anything negative about Howard Jensen, it was hard for Thomas not to acknowledge the obvious. Thomas did make one attempt to persuade Fuller to take a leave of absence or re-think his decision. Their discussion ended with Fuller communicating what he thought should be on the separation agreement. He wanted his full salary for a year-and-a-half to give himself a chance to reestablish himself in a new career, health insurance coverage, and the opportunity to maintain his stock in the company for five years if he so chose.

Thomas didn't blink an eye. This was the first time in his experience such a long term senior executive of the company wanted out of the organization. For what Fuller was requesting, it didn't sound like too much.

Thomas' shoulders were hunched when Fuller left his office. As for Fuller, he'd not had such a sense of relief and exhilaration for as long as he could remember. It was like he'd just survived surgery. He would no longer have to deal with the pain caused by the antics of a true corporate animal like Howard Jensen…or face the disrespect from his colleagues for singularly not leading the company out of this latest business dilemma. Some other scapegoat would have to be found in St. Paul Paper Company.

When he'd first intimated to Gwen his desire to leave the company, she was initially concerned. However, watching him suffer for so many months, she was more than ready for him to leave by the time he talked to Gene Thomas. When he got home that day, she seemed almost giddy in happiness that he'd finally decided to pull the plug. While he was somewhat concerned about their life style and what the future would bear, she was the one who showed the least worry. In fact, she showed excitement about their future. As she kept saying, "Life is too short to put up with the kind of strains you've been forced to endure."

When Fuller went into the office the next day, he felt like a new man. There was nothing of any urgency on his desk even though his inbox was filled. Within a half hour he was ready to leave for the day. His oblivious attitude was not lost on his administrative assistant, Laurie Schmitt. She walked hesitantly into his office and shut the door.

Without asking to sit down, she did. She said quietly, "Rich, where will I go within the company when you leave?"

It had happened that fast. Gene Thomas' secretary had spread the word. There was no point denying anything.

He said to her, "Laurie, as you well know, things have become pretty intolerable. But, don't you worry. As long as you want to work here, you'll have a job. Your reputation is very positive in this organization. If you want I'll ask Gene Thomas to consider you for opportunities in other departments. A change might be good for you as well, since you've been so closely associated to me."

She got up from the chair with a blank face. "Rich, is the company going to make it?"

Fuller tried to assure her. "Hey…nothing's guaranteed. But, we've been respected in our market for too many years for us to simply fold up our tent. Yes, we're going through some tough times, but we'll be all right."

Then as if she hadn't heard a word he'd said, she asked, "Rich, wherever you work next, could you keep me in mind?"

She got up from her chair and slowly strode from the office. She looked shell shocked.

Fuller scheduled himself to be out the next day. It was Friday so he would be away from the office for three days. Monday he planned on meeting again with Gene Thomas to finalize his leave package.

That Monday morning he took his time before driving to the office. The home phone rang while he was slowly reading the newspaper. It was his assistant. Laurie sounded very upset. She kept her voice as emotionless as she could. "Well Rich, they're wasting no time. They just named Howard Jensen as Vice President of Development. Sales & Marketing and Operations will be under him. Three of the six sales managers are being let go. Jensen has already announced a new pay plan for the sales force. He and Henry Miller must have been meeting the entire weekend to come up with all these changes."

Then she paused before realizing the obvious. "Rich, it was as if Jensen and Miller had all this planned out to begin the very day you decided to leave. They were planning on you negotiating out of the company."

She babbled on as if in a daze. "As for me, I'm going to be demoted to secretary for one of the product managers. Jensen's two 'girls' are being promoted to 'Corporate Administrative Managers'. I'll be reporting to one of them! My God, Rich, without the ink being dry on your severance agreement, major changes are being done all over the company. Jensen has scheduled a meeting tomorrow morning to go over the new organization plan. I suggest you not even come in this morning unless it's just to see Gene Thomas. Even he looks like most of the blood has drained from his body."

Fuller almost threw up. It was unbelievable how Howard Jensen had been able to position himself for so much power in such a short period of time. He would be drunk with it by the next day's morning meeting.

Fuller hung up the phone already picturing this anti-leader starting the meeting the next morning. Jensen would have a well-practiced, relaxed, effervescent smile as if everyone in the sales and marketing department should be sharing his joy as he reached this latest pinnacle in his career. What he would be unable to notice was that except for his 'girls', there would not be another smile in the entire meeting room.

He immediately called Gene Thomas to see that the exit agreement was ready and if Henry Miller had any problems with his departing requests. The response was so quick as to be disappointing. Without any sense of how unfortunate the situation truly was, Thomas responded matter-of-factly, "No…it's all good news,

Rich. Miller signed off on everything you wanted. All you have to do is come and sign it and we'll get the exit paper work processed. You and I can meet next week to discuss which search firm you might want to assist you in finding another position. We'll try to make this transition for you and your family as smooth as silk."

Thomas made the whole thing sound so rote. It was sickening to Fuller. He had contributed mightily to the success in the operation for over fifteen years. Now there seemed to be little disappointment for his leaving and no attempt to retain his services. All Fuller could gather was that Howard Jensen had done a beautiful hack job of undercutting Rich's value. It was done simply as part of Jensen's character and methods. Eliminating anyone…actual or perceived…in his path was a strategy as normal to Jensen as breathing.

Fuller sat there at his kitchen table stunned. As disgusted as he was about all that had unfolded in such a short period of time, he could only marvel at a master 'corporate animal' at work. Howard Jensen was one of those people solely in the business world for self-adulation and power. His motivation had little to do with improving the inner workings of a company or investing time or money into any long term improvements and increased revenue. He wouldn't be around long enough to lay claim to these types of successes…if any. And, certainly he wouldn't care to be around to repair or sweep up the damage he had created. His primary focus upon entering a company was to choose his pathway to the top. Lower and middle level people were pawns to be cast aside at his whim. The people at higher levels in his way were adversaries to be taken out as soon as possible. It had taken a fledgling company like St. Paul Paper Company to succumb to this villain's talents so quickly.

As a classic 'corporate animal', Jensen had recognized the key people who had to be his supporters and then worked them in whatever way he had to in order to preserve their backing. He would decide along the way which department heads and members of the board of directors were loyal to him…and undercut the less faithful in any way he could. He didn't need them all in his corner…just enough to know who would likely stay with him come hell or high water. He could then dismantle or make whatever changes he wanted to satisfy his power need…all in the name of progress and future profitability. Whatever the company sold or whatever reputation the company enjoyed in its marketplace was secondary or invisible to Jensen. The only thing important to a man like Jensen was his meteoric rise, so he could take that stature to a new and better opportunity.

In time other senior executives and board members might realize how they had been duped. Unfortunately, by the time these 'leaders' would become aware what was happening, the damage caused by the 'corporate animal' would be irreparable. Actions would be taken to deflate any impressions of naiveté and poor judgment on their part. First, they might quietly buy the 'animal' out… letting him leave with a favorable negotiated settlement. His leaving would often restore some morale within the company for at least a short period. Then it would be time for further self-preservation by those upper level executives or board members responsible for bringing this piece of human trash into their company. More change, more internal promotion for those people remaining in the company, a new pay plan, and maybe even the launch of a new product would happen to appease customers and employees alike.

While Fuller had the perspective that the days would be numbered for most any 'corporate animal', what he didn't know about Howard Jensen would have further shocked him. In Jensen's case, St. Paul Paper Company had been a dream opportunity for him to make another attempt at short-term corporate riches and power. It was a leading company in a fast changing business with long-term conservative leadership fearing the future of their products and growth. With his network of greedy headhunters always percolating and calling him weekly, he had a host of companies to consider for his own next selfish career move.

In previous years Jensen had joined a couple companies as a consultant to gain more inside information and ascertain whether the organization could be susceptible to his underhanded maneuvering. He'd taken these opportunities as far as he could. When he was no longer able to make inroads to the top people in the company he joined, he would simply move on and begin interviewing with other enterprises. That was why his resume reflected a twelve to twenty-four month work span with each of the previous companies he had been employed.

Jensen was a master in interviews. He could be charming. He was intelligent. He studied a company's background intensely. He was impressive the way he could display knowledge about an industry that he'd never worked.

When questioned about his short stints at previous companies, he had patented and well-practiced responses. For a small agricultural manufacturing company in the Midwest that ended up being sold within a year after Jensen joined it, he laid claim how it was just another example of how the many ideas he had instituted made the small company such an attractive takeover target. Yet another story he concocted was his decision to leave one of those recent companies on his own volition. He justified the action as predictable stating that if a company brought him in to initiate some helpful ideas, but were too conservative or fearful to support him, he was wasting their time and his time. He would therefore be insinuating to his interviewers that if they were of this breed, he would not be the type of person for their company. This proven bait was meant as a challenge. What company would ever admit they were too conservative or fearful to take risks? He'd found many of the interviewers became sensitive and used much of the interview time defending their company and giving examples how highly adaptable their organization was. Jensen liked those types of companies and interviews. It represented a possible better chance of gaining more control faster if hired.

Howard Jensen had played on the 'fear of the future' during his interviews with the St. Paul Paper Company leaders like CEO Henry Miller and Human

Relations Director Gene Thomas. He realized almost immediately in discussions with Miller that the CEO would put up little resistance to what Jensen represented as new ideas for growth and prosperity. Miller was desperately looking for someone bright and articulate who could exhibit ostensible courageous leadership. Very little due diligence was done on Howard Jensen. Even the headhunter representing Howard Jensen was surprised how readily Henry Miller was accepting the positive details about Jensen.

When Jensen was eventually offered a very attractive senior executive employment contract at St. Paul Paper Company, he was literally licking his lips in anticipation. Jensen already knew some people who might consider buying St. Paul Paper before he even started his first day on the job.

As a true 'corporate animal'…and if things went as anticipated in his new position with St. Paul Paper Company…Jensen hoped to have in a year's time the possibility of himself being put in charge of the company after it had been taken over. In another year he would hardly remember Miller or certainly the other board members. In terms of money, Jensen saw the opportunity as so bright, it was blinding.

He was also a seasoned and realistic gambler. If it didn't work out, he'd simply look for another vulnerable organization like St. Paul Paper Company and try again. In the meantime his negotiated contracts and severance packages kept him exceedingly comfortable financially.

Rich Fuller didn't go to the office at all that Monday. Instead he and Thomas met at an isolated restaurant two miles from the office. With the separation signed, Fuller and his wife impulsively took a week's trip to Florida just to relax and discuss the future. It was not as relaxing and peaceful as he hoped. Leaving working cohorts he'd known for so long was still sad.

Fuller was certain once it was learned that he'd left the company, there would be others who would leave. Furthermore, the rumors would increase about the company being a possible take-over target. He told his wife he wouldn't be surprised to hear of suitors vying for the rights to such a long-term established company as St. Paul Paper Company within the next couple weeks.

Returning from his trip, Fuller went to the office to for some final items he'd left behind and to say farewell to certain people in the company. He hoped these friendships would not end, but he wasn't certain.

The experience was worse than he anticipated. People he'd worked with for years found other hallways to walk. Many tried not to notice him. He said 'good morning' to a few whose responses were quiet nods or short greetings before moving on. Another few shook his hand and said they would miss him. He felt very much like a foreigner or someone with a catchy illness. It was as if these very people he'd worked with for so many years now no longer trusted him. They didn't want to get too close to him for fear of being seen with someone no longer loyal.

Laurie saw him and gave a weak wave. She looked like a truck dragged her to work. She was already at a different desk down the hall. Rich motioned for her to come into his office. She looked around as if hoping not to be spotted and then followed him. She left the office door open and stood at the entrance. Her voice was low. "Rich, Mr. Jensen wanted to arrange a farewell cocktail party for you sometime this week. He said just to call one of the 'girls' to set it up." She'd said the last sentence without even hiding her disgust.

Fuller shook his head. 'The cruelty of words,' he thought. He'd been with the company for over fifteen years and now a person with the company not five months thought there should be a celebratory party to commemorate the work he'd done…and to wish him well in his future endeavors.

"There will be no party," he mused, "This is not a time of happiness. Don't worry, things will tame down. People like Jensen don't stay for long. Just be patient. We'll stay in touch."

"Have you already got another job, Rich?" Laurie spoke hopefully and desperately.

He shook his head. "No, Laurie, I'm in no hurry to jump back into this type of game just now. As you well know, it's been rather unpleasant this past year… and especially the last few months."

Laurie nodded knowing exactly to what he was referring. Both could hear a meeting being run by Howard Jensen. Fuller thought about the poor souls who had to sit in that room. They must have felt worse than peons. How different the management style. If Fuller was running the meeting, there would be much discussion. In a Jensen run meeting, there would be only silence except for his voice. The people would support his methods, his ideas, and his insincerity…or they would no long be employed. Their opinions were unimportant..

Fuller got up to give Laurie a supportive hug knowing she had to retreat to her work station. "Well, Laurie, I just wanted to thank you for all the fine work you did for me. Once I gather some final items, I'll be gone for good."

Laurie nodded gravely and whispered, "Let me know where you land. I hope you'll consider me wherever you work next." Then she left with tears in her eyes.

As he walked down the hall out of the Sales & Marketing Department for the last time, he was glad there was a meeting going on. He didn't really want to face what was left of the internal sales and marketing staff who formerly worked so closely with him.

He still had some last things to discuss in Gene Thomas' office. When he walked into the Human Resource Department office, Denise, the assistant, got up immediately and came over and hugged Rich. She said simply, "We'll miss you."

It was touching. She was the first person who was handling his departure with some civility and empathy. Everyone else seemed so concerned about his or her own job.

Thomas came out looking tired and invited him into his office. There was still much planning to do with regards to Fuller's stock, his health insurance, the lump sum payment of his retirement plan, and the start date with the Career Counseling Firm. In thirty minutes, they'd completed their discussion. Thomas asked if he was going to stop by Henry Miller's office before leaving the complex.

Fuller's response was only, "Maybe."

With the packet of signed papers under his arm, Fuller rose to leave. Thomas offered a farewell handshake…as if a ritual. Fuller could see that Thomas was hardened to situations like this one, even to a long-term fellow board member. Besides, Fuller guessed there would be many other employees at various levels who would be following…and many not by choice. Gene Thomas would have to handle those sad situations as well…most as a result of one terrible human being.

As he headed for the company exit, people leaned over desks and gave him a cursory handshake and "good luck" while darting their eyes down the room to see if any senior staffer was watching them. Still others were silent. They just looked at Fuller not knowing what to think. They didn't know whether to be jealous, sorrowful, envious, or sickened by the spectacle of his leaving the company. Somehow they all knew it was not right the way the whole thing was happening…and the company was losing a good man.

Fuller did not stop by Henry Miller's office. In fact, he'd thought no more about it once he'd left Gene Thomas' office. He drove home and it was not yet lunch time. It was a strange drive. He was not in any hurry for the first time since….since grade school. Gwen would be concerned about his mental well-being despite the advantages they would gain out of Rich's negotiated separation. She wasn't particularly worried about their finances or about Rich finding another position…just his attitude. She was more concerned about how long the vile taste in his mouth would remain regarding corporate America.

It was a couple weeks later before he finally set up an appointment to work with a job search firm. The expense of the career counseling service was paid for by his former company. The entire process didn't interest him at the start, but over time his natural competitiveness and pride got him more involved. He'd done countless business strategies and marketing plans on his company's products and services in the past…but never on himself. He had hoped he could just spread his name to some friends in high level positions and doors might get opened, but that took time.

He learned immediately that the career counseling firm would do very little work for him except offer advice…which was still helpful. They didn't have a lot of patience for someone who wasn't committed to finding another job as soon as possible. Their primary purpose was to gain revenue from companies for displaced workers. It was up to the displaced worker to fit himself into the boiler plate activities of the counseling firm or that person would gain very little out of the relationship. If the worker found a job quickly, the counseling firm could claim success. The longer it took the worker to find a job, the more the firm would justify the delay as the person being an example of someone not determined in his efforts to follow the 'program'.

Fuller eventually began making more contacts on his own…including some meetings with former competitors in his industry. They wanted to talk with him if nothing else than to squeeze some competitive information from him. A couple struggling companies who at best were involved in guerrilla marketing tactics against St. Paul Paper Company offered a mid-management job to Fuller. However, they expressed concern more than once about whether his coming aboard with them would be effective given the loyalty he had to have had with St. Paul Paper. Fuller finally turned down their offer convinced that even if he could gain a new loyalty for a competing company, they would never truly believe it.

A larger company in Michigan, a competitor for twenty years with St. Paul Paper Company, interviewed Fuller twice…each time trying to check the level of bitterness he must have had against his former company. It was as if they were more interested in hearing Fuller echo their own distaste for St. Paul Paper. When he apparently didn't exhibit enough of a truculent attitude against his former company, no job offer came forward.

Fuller also explored opportunities in other industries. While his sales and marketing record was superb, he ran into upper management people in other industries who were convinced he could be of little help to them because of his weak knowledge of their industry. Again and again he heard this repeated…. whether it was a company selling yarn, diapers, a mechanical device, or medical supplies. He laughed to himself knowing so many of these companies hired truly young sales representatives who had no understanding of business to say nothing of the company products. Interesting that these same companies after offering a one or two-week training course felt these neophyte sales people could represent the company's products or services quite adequately. However, here he was, a proven senior executive, and ostensibly not qualified to join certain companies in a manager role because of his lack of knowledge about products or services that could take a couple weeks to learn.

As Fuller continued his job search, a few St. Paul Paper Company former cohorts remained in contact. Some had not been that close to him at work, but were now quite interested in the progress he was making in looking for a new opportunity. Other than these few people, he was truly disappointed to realize how many former workmates he'd thought were close to him at St. Paul Paper Company turned out to be fair weather friends. That was the hardest pill to swallow. It made him wonder if they were ever really friends.

One person who did call him once a week was his former Administrative Assistant, Laurie Schmitt. She talked about how dramatically the culture of the company seemed to be changing practically day to day. Howard Jensen had been given plenty of time to strut his wisdom and new ideas. His problem was that he was so deeply disliked, except by members of the board of directors. Even if some of his ideas were worthwhile, he didn't have a group of people who were willing to give their heart and soul to the company anymore. He had almost single-handedly destroyed whatever morale remained.

She intimated that some of the ill feelings toward Jensen were finally slipping between the cracks to the members of the board. However, these people practically to a man were not willing to believe the degree of distaste aimed at their new Vice President of Corporate Development. They were still certain Jensen was the 'savior'. While employees were made to understand that they either support the new man or leave the company, their jobs weren't worth that much to them anymore. Laurie reported that there were a surprising number of people taking sick days…that is, interviewing with other companies.

By the end of the first quarter more St. Paul Paper employees had been weaned out of the company. They did not gain near the measure of severance that Rich had negotiated. Remaining employees took on the work of these displaced workers. Many were now doing more to earn their same salary while putting in more hours to complete various tasks.

Jensen's reign of terror camouflaged to the upper management actually was given credit for some positive results on the balance sheet after that first quarter. Operating expenses were down. While revenue didn't increase, the profit picture was slightly better. But, with no investment in creating new products and no increase in sales cost to acquire more business, Jensen was leading the company nowhere. While the board of directors expressed some relief and communicated to the rest of the company that the corner towards better profitability had finally been reached, this leadership group was missing the real point. The abysmal morale and the noticeable loss of certain key members of the company at various levels could not be measured on the financial picture.

As the second quarter started in April, Laurie Schmitt intimated to Fuller in another phone call that Howard Jensen was strutting around the halls of the company like he was royalty. His factitious smile had become infamous to all staff members in the sales and marketing department. He was being imitated in the most contemptuous of fashions. Certain employees tried to hide from his view. Still others became physically ill when required to carry out some of his profound ideas for the good of the company. Laurie even kidded Fuller about his final words to her before leaving his office just a couple months before. "Rich," she said, "You said to be patient. Well, how long does it take for the powers to be in this company to recognize what a tyrant this man truly is?"

Then she said something that would stick in Fuller's mind for a long time. She sighed, "You know what's so tragic is that even when a horrible man like Howard Jensen finally leaves the company, he's free to prey on another company…and eventually make another group of people truly miserable. That's the really sad thing."

What happened a couple days later would cause Fuller to think back to that conversation with Laurie Schmitt again and again. He never asked her if she knew anything about the weird occurrence. It was just that her comment was so coincidental.

He heard that an incident occurred following a late afternoon meeting called by Howard Jensen. He spent an hour ranting to his sales and marketing management group about their inept work and that heads were going to roll unless he started seeing some more productivity amongst the sales force. He ordered the entire group to remain in the meeting room for as long as it took to devise some plans for increasing sales productivity. Jensen ordered Laurie Schmitt to remain and take notes of the ongoing meeting and have a draft on his desk by 8:00 the next morning. He wanted to know who was thinking and speaking… and who was just taking up space in the meeting.

When he stepped onto the elevator to leave for the day, some staff members still in the office at 6:00 mentioned they'd seen him depart with a smug smile on his face. To them he reflected a sense of power in ordering fourteen people to be sequestered…in effect, punished… in that meeting room forced to work very late that evening.

To a person each staff person and sales manager in that room offered the suggestion that Howard Jensen be fired or they would leave the company in bulk. She didn't document that message in her report, only that the group worked until 7:30 P.M. In fact they departed the meeting room after blowing off their steam only twenty minutes after Jensen had left the office. In her cursory notes she gave every one of the managers in attendance credit for many good ideas. She stated they wanted to share their ideas personally with Jensen rather than have Laurie take the responsibility.

The significance of this half-hearted meeting became quite an issue weeks later when Laurie Schmitt was questioned about her factitious notes. It became possible incriminating evidence because that evening when Howard Jensen stepped into the elevator, it would be the last time his body and image would ever be seen again at the St. Paul Paper Company offices. That night Howard Jensen would disappear…seemingly off the face of the earth.

The first hint that something could be wrong happened only the next morning. Each of Jensen's marketing team was in the office by 7:30 waiting for what they expected to be a tortuous meeting similar to the one Jensen had left the evening before. Each minute past 8:00 A.M. drew smirks from his 'team'. Where was Howard Jensen?

By 8:15, one of his 'girls' began to show some concern and placed a call to his apartment in Minneapolis. There was no answer. The weather had been clear the night before…followed by a truly sublime morning sun. Other than a car mishap, nothing should have kept him from at least calling into the office to advise everyone he was running late. But, there was no call. Also, no call was placed to his wife in St. Louis. His 'girls' knew he rarely talked with his distant spouse. Other than his estranged wife, there was no one else who had any close attachment to the guy.

Finally at 9:00 that morning, one of his girls drove over to his apartment. She was known for being extra close to her boss…close enough to own a second apartment key. When she arrived, she found nothing indicating malfeasance. It was just the same rather stoic temporary living space she'd seen any number of times.

Her call back to the office showed some concern. He always checked in with her no matter where he was. By late afternoon, still no one had heard from Jensen. His car was still parked in the company parking lot indicating he'd either never left the building…or he might have caught a cab to a restaurant…or had a friend pick him up after work. That last possibility ended as fast as it was suggested. When the police were contacted and questioned various employees, investigators found it interesting that staff members could name no friend…that is, one who might have picked him up after work.

The employees who had stayed late the night before had to do so again…this time at the request of the Ramsey County criminal investigators. Following the expected questioning, the police also combed Jensen's apartment. They found no clues to his disappearance. Hospitals around the five-state area were contacted to find if any unidentified victims had been brought into their facilities. There were two such victims…both dead…and they were both female.

Five days later a national search turned up no one who matched the description of Howard Jensen. The man had simply gotten on his office elevator…and vanished.

That week continued negotiations between lawyers for St. Paul Paper Company and the attorneys for a large eastern based information company about a possible takeover was put on hold. Jensen who had been secretly spearheading the entire transaction had to be present in many of those meetings to keep the fire burning over the possible transaction. By the next week with no Howard Jensen being found anywhere, the entire deal fell dead in the water. Both sides seemed to be relieved.

As the homicide division put extra people on the case, their findings were quite surprising. They'd never met such an uncaring group of people in any investigation…unless the murder victim happened to be a serial killer. Here was a corporate executive who was so universally hated…and not by just the people who reported to him at the St. Paul Paper Company. The same was true at almost all the former companies where he'd been employed. He was depicted as the devil reincarnated.

Except for his two 'girls', there was not one person on his staff who behaved even slightly upset that he was missing…even that he might be dead. Investigators began to privately joke that a stadium would be required to seat all the people who wished ill will on this man. Never did death for one person seem more earned... if indeed he was dead.

It was two weeks after the newspapers had reported Howard Jensen missing that Rich Fuller answered a phone call very late at night. He'd already been questioned by the police only days after Jensen disappeared. He could offer nothing in the way of help to the police. Again they noted that he was neither concerned nor saddened about the Jensen case.

Thinking that the questioning by police was done, Fuller was a bit irritated by the late call. Then again, he thought it might be a headhunter working late. He turned down the volume of the NBA game on the television and picked up the receiver.

It was a phone communication he would never forget. At the conclusion of the call, he couldn't have told anyone the teams competing or even the sport being played on the TV.

Taking the call in his study, the voice began before Fuller said "Good evening" It was a very low and muffled voice.

Succinctly it asked, "Is this Richard Fuller?"

He responded tersely, "Yes...who is this please?"

The voice continued on the same pitch. "Never mind who is speaking. I have some information for you regarding the disappearance of Howard Jensen. I was wondering if you might have some interest in hearing what I have to say."

Somewhat impatiently, Fuller tried to take some control. He repeated, "Who is this please?"

The voice hesitated for just a moment. "Mr. Fuller...do you need me to repeat my question one more time?"

Fuller took an immediate dislike to the no nonsense, domineering tone to the man's voice. If this man wanted to know the true answer to his question, Fuller would give him an abrupt and unequivocal 'No'!

However, he curbed his irritability towards the caller and his apathetic feelings for Jensen. He decided to exhibit some civility. "Look, whoever this is... whatever you have to say...should this not be said to the police? While I have some unease about Mr. Jensen's welfare, I am not the person you should be sharing whatever information you have."

There was a moment of silence on the phone. Then the barely audible voice repeated, "Mr. Fuller, I ask you again...do you have interest in what I have to say...or shall I hang up? I will not be speaking with the police."

Fuller was beginning to get a bit nervous...like he was getting into something completely foreign and out of his control. However there was something in the mysterious caller's tone and words that made him think he should take some responsibility for hearing what the low voice had to say.

Fuller sighed, "O.K...if you aren't going to the police, what makes you think I won't call the authorities the moment you hang up the phone? The way you are making this sound, the investigators should have a great interest in your comments."

The terse voice finally spoke. "All right...now that I have your interest, we can continue. I don't believe you'll be calling the police after you hear what I have to say."

Fuller, now echoing the droning tone of the caller, sat down at the desk in his study and resignedly replied, "O.K....go ahead."

The tenor of the voice on the phone did not change. "Mr. Howard Jensen is being held in a reasonably comfortable location far away from your city. He is going through a complete personality and character evaluation. If he is judged redeemable, he'll then start a process of re-indoctrination. The group I represent finds people like Mr. Jensen and we remove them from...shall we say...society. We closely select these individuals. Some we can't touch, because they are too visible to the public. Then we find other ways to limit their impact on other human beings. Those with family responsibilities, we find ways to ...shall we say...clip their wings...repeatedly...until they mollify their behavior and actions. Even then we continue to monitor them.

However, in the instance of a Mr. Jensen when the individual has no family obligations and he continues down his destructive path against high numbers of people, we remove people like him as soon as possible. In Howard Jensen's case, he was one of those individuals who had slipped by us. He should have been picked up long before he became employed at your former company. It was your leaving...who was it...your company's name again...yes, St. Paul Paper Company...that we finally took more serious notice. When a person of your caliber is so seriously impacted by a man like Jensen, that happening does not go unnoticed. In fact, we take it upon ourselves to assist that person. We help others in the same way...at various levels of employment.

So, part of this call is to let you know that you will find as good or better of a position...one that can be even more fulfilling than your previous job. We just suggest you keep doing your job search in the manner that you are accomplishing it. We will make certain that different opportunities will come your way. You will still need to be as effective as an interviewee as possible...and you will be totally responsible for choosing the opportunity you feel is best for you. Part of this call is just to say you are doing fine in your job search, to continue what you are doing...and don't get discouraged.

Fuller could not believe what he was hearing. The call started out sounding very ominous. Suddenly it was turning into a cheerleading and support call.

He interrupted, "Well, Mr........whoever you are....thank you for the pep talk, but it's a bit late. Unless you have something more I......"

The bland voice continued as if it hadn't listened to a word Fuller had just said. "When we see a character like Mr. Jensen, he qualifies for our program in

a number of ways. He is not close to his family, his friendships are few if any…
and at best superficial… he has a pathological need to be in charge…he has a
deep need to stir things up with no consciousness of any negative impact…and
most of all he has no sense of caring for another human being.

Fuller was looking to get off the phone and end this macabre phone call.
"Well, you know this man very well indeed. That kind of sums him…."

Again the cryptic tone continued, "A man like Mr. Jensen is surprisingly not
as materialistic as you might think. He has not much time for other things than
the mayhem he is causing. If he has a house or apartment, it is there just to store
his clothing and a place to do laundry and to sleep. He is constantly on the move
and totally focused on getting ahead."

Fuller was curious despite wanting to end the call. "Excuse me……are you
really telling me that you have this man imprisoned at some location for the
purpose of studying his quirks, motivations, and behavior patterns. What kind of
tortures are you perpetrating on this guy…and I might add, not that I really care?"

The pitch in the caller's voice for the first time changed slightly higher…
almost as if he was amused by Fuller's disrespect. "No…Mr. Fuller…we are not
torturing this man. We have just taken him out of circulation. He has a choice
of staying in our 'program'. However, we do not plan on letting this man return
to society until we've had an ample chance to institutionalize him. We consider
him mentally unstable…even mentally ill…one who has ruined an incredible
number of other peoples' lives.

I will tell you we have had a significant number of individuals in our
'program' who have been able to…..graduate. When we feel they can see their
way clear through reason and indoctrination we first test them in various roles for
periods of time. Most of these people under our guidance have eventually been
returned to society, but in quite an altered state from their previous behavior and
character…and certainly away from their positions in the work force. For certain
they are never again allowed to be involved in the corporate world in any major
decision making capacity or in charge of any people. I would offer they tend to
be placed in more altruistic endeavors and certainly lower level positions where
their work is focused more on assisting research, providing service to others, or
duties that tend to help mankind.

Fuller was not certain he hadn't blacked out and was only dreaming he was
having this phone conversation. His own tone changed to incredulous. "Are you
saying that Howard Jensen is going to come out of your program a completely
different man…likely one that will no longer be involved in destroying every
company, including my former company that he comes in contact?"

"Yes, Mr. Fuller, in simple terms that is exactly what is going to happen…
when and if he finally subscribes to our program."

Fuller quickly asked, "So…what happens when a person can't make the
change? You said 'most' people seem to buy into your program, but not all. What's

all that about? What happens to the people who don't pass your conscientious inspection?"

"Bluntly, Mr. Fuller, they don't leave here. We have gentlemen who have never left our re-indoctrination center in the twelve years of our existence. You wouldn't likely know their names, but they all have similar personal credentials as Howard Jensen. When these men disappeared, it was made to look like a horrible accident…the type where no remains could be found. I'll not get into the details. However, it was interesting how no one who had to work with any of them offered authorities any sense of pathos for their sudden departure. It has been the same case for Mr. Jensen. No one is truly sorry that this man is gone. There seems to be general relief that he is no longer able to impart his destructive will on others.

Many times our findings indicate the individual is simply irreparable. Initial testing and disclosures are that Mr. Jensen might be in this same category. These types of men are left to work in maintenance at our enclosed facility under close supervision. They are what we call permanent misanthropes. Mankind is evil to these unfortunate humans…except the perception of themselves.

Several of these so-called misanthropes have single-handedly caused the destruction of a number of companies, countless lost jobs, and immeasurable misery imparted on employees and staff members with whom they worked. One of these 'corporate animals' had a hand in causing five documented suicides by people working directly for him or with him before he was taken out of circulation. He was like a rabid dog roaming freely in the neighborhood…or in this case, the corporate world."

Fuller was speechless. He wondered how he should respond to such diatribe. Jensen had been kidnapped. He was part of what apparently was a 'human experiment'. He was alive, but he might never return to the world he knew. And if he did, there would be apparent consequences. Fuller didn't even want to approach that subject with the caller. Suddenly he wanted to end the call once and for all with this enigmatic, but not quite evil, sounding voice.

Irritably he retorted, "Again, Mr.….whoever you are…I don't know why you contacted me. You're right. I'll not go to the authorities because they'd put me in some hospital strapped to a gurney if I tried to relate this phone call to them. I'd have no proof of my statements. So…I guess the only thing to say…is good luck with Mr. Jensen. If he truly is under your 'care', I hope he comes out of your program with a certificate in botany or forestry….you know, something where the public never has to put up with his type ever again."

Then he caught himself. What the hell was he saying? His blustery outburst towards Howard Jensen was so bitter. He was not showing even an ounce of civility. For all he knew, Jensen was strapped to a bed in a windowless room kept in a drug induced coma all day. How long would this guy be incarcerated if everything this eerie caller said was true? Jensen was despicable, but not a proven murderer.

Fuller tried to correct his own reprehensible thoughts and words. He fumbled, "What I mean to say is…that is…what you are doing is obviously against the law. Just listening to you and realizing I'm not going to say anything to anyone about what is happening to Howard Jensen….well, it makes me feel like I'm now some kind of accomplice. My God! I am a law-abiding person. I won't report this conversation because it'll be more damaging than helpful. People will think I'm crazy. And, for someone who's trying to find a job, I don't exactly want my name bandied about in the news media claiming that Jensen was taken against his will and is somewhere undergoing unsolicited therapy. Frankly, I don't really want to participate any more in this discussion. I'm only getting more upset."

The voice went back to being bland. "We understand your dilemma, Mr. Fuller. Most normal people we contact want to end the conversation. However, I have just one more thing to cover. I'm calling you because you are the most recent highly ranked senior management person who literally had your reputation and business career seriously sullied by the likes of a person like Mr. Jensen. We're out to assist, if we can, in making alterations or modifications not only for you, but hopefully to others in your company who had their lives smeared by this human being. There are always limits in what we can do, but we might be able to correct some damages to the depreciated corporate image of St. Paul Paper Company. We already are working hourly with Mr. Jensen to un-do some of the unfair, cruel harm that he perpetrated against not only to your former company but even to previous companies where he was employed. Along the way we may be able to help clear up similar misconceptions he attached to various people he perceived as 'in his way'. In some cases it may be too late. After all, he was allowed to run freely and unrestrained in your former company for five months. A lot depends on the quality of leadership left over in the St. Paul Paper Company. The confidence they have with their customers and their employees can often times overcome the misdeeds performed by someone like Howard Jensen.

For the first time Fuller almost laughed. That type of leadership might never have existed at St. Paul Paper Company. Whatever this caller's organization could do to resurrect Fuller's former company, it would certainly be helpful. From Fuller's perspective, the company was internally in shambles. Clients likely didn't have any idea how bad it was. Orders were being made and processed. Revenue was still coming in, just at a lower level with no prospects for an increase.

The bland voice didn't stop. It had something else it apparently had to discuss. "Mr. Fuller, we sometimes can make quite a difference. We have a history of helping people and companies get back on their feet. We have enough information from countless interviews with Mr. Jensen about his actions in St. Paul Paper Company to initiate some corrective measures. This may even lead to you being asked to return to your company in your previous or better position with an increase in salary and some improved stock options. You may want to consider this choice along with other opportunities from other companies you will be receiving. In fact, I will repeat that. We can guarantee you will be offered some very fine choices for future employment. With your record of achievement…and our contacts…you will have some very complimentary and advantageous things said about you as companies do their due diligence on you. Nothing said will be dishonest, I assure you. Let's just say we can help a company realize you would be an excellent senior management hire. Again it will be up to you to make your choice."

Fuller was silent. What he'd just heard was difficult to comprehend. He had been quite surprised by his lack of worthwhile offers so far from other companies. It was as if he was getting sandbagged, possibly by individuals in his former company. He had to admit as he sat in his study after 11:00 at night with no real top level job opportunities or even networking meetings on the horizon, the statement just uttered by the mysterious voice on the line sounded both inviting and very helpful….but quite surreal as well.

There was silence for a moment between the two of them. Then the voice, sounding more relaxed said, "Mr. Fuller, our contact with you will be minimal if you wish. At times we would like to get some clarification over some things Mr. Jensen might be saying to our counselors. You need not feel obligated to help. On the other matter, you could be more helpful to us as kind of a confidential point man as my organization tries to improve the prospects for St. Paul Paper Company. We will make corrective actions for that company if it is possible. If we had your perspective, we'd feel better about going forward with some of those actions. If you rejoined your company, it might even make our job easier. Our only aim, as always, is to correct or undo as much damage as was created by a corporate animal. It doesn't guarantee the future of the company, but we've often been able to salvage the company's reputation while augmenting the morale of the employees as well."

He then added, "Mr. Fuller, our organization would like to hear from you in the next three to five business days whether you'd be willing to assist. I can only stress that time is important. The sooner my group can begin privately helping the image of St. Paul Paper Company, the better.

The low voice then showed some empathy. "I know I've thrown a lot at you this evening, Mr. Fuller. I've wanted to make it easy on you knowing a call like this one is very unique. I shall call you back in exactly three days at this same time. If you have interest in our helping us with your former company, then just state that fact upon picking up the receiver. If you decide my request is too unbelievable and what I've said makes you uncomfortable, just let the phone ring and don't answer it. We will understand and do the best job we can with the information gained from our constant dialogues with Howard Jensen. Be assured, though, as you continue your own efforts on resurrecting your career, do understand you won't be alone. We will be a very confidential career enhancement service for you. You will never know if or how we helped you. But, we will be doing whatever we can do…and legally with no obligations or cost from you or anyone else. That's simply the way we work."

With that last word, the measured voice ended the conversation curtly, but politely, by saying, "I'll be phoning you three days from this moment. Have a good evening, Mr. Fuller. Please sleep well." And then the phone line clicked.

Rich Fuller took almost a minute before he hung up his phone at his study desk. For the next hour he sat in the dark gazing outside at the street lights and pondering every sentence that was said to him in the most eccentric phone call he'd ever experienced. There was part of him yelling for him to call the police. Then there was a more rational brain wave that told him to not make any rash decisions. The story he would tell to the authorities would be just too incredible to believe. Besides, the last thing he wanted to do was to be involved in any way with the missing Howard Jensen mystery. It was an open invitation for him to become a key suspect in a possible murder. There was no better way to end his chance for a decent job opportunity than to become a suspect.

Just the thought of that word 'murder' made his skin crawl. It was something so far from his character. He'd not even gone squirrel hunting. He'd not killed anything bigger than a common garden snake at the golf course or pheasant with the front end of his automobile. Besides, if this organization….whoever they were…was actually taking steps to rehabilitate Howard Jensen, then they were performing a public service. Maybe in time they might publish a book or put on seminars aimed at human resource departments and boards of directors to take greater caution against hiring top executives with the nefarious nature and slick skills of a Howard Jensen.

Each time he contemplated what was 'apparently' happening to Howard Jensen, he shuddered. How could he morally accept what he'd just heard? On the other hand, what could he really do about it…even if it were all true? He also thought it odd how the 'voice' claimed their organization could often repair damage done by 'corporate animals' like Jensen. The 'voice' didn't guarantee a thing. The mysterious man simply stated that his group accumulated information and then decided how and if they could make corrections of the damage or negative impact from power hungry reprobates like Jensen. Now they were actually asking for confidential help from Fuller knowing he was in an awkward position where he wouldn't go directly to the authorities regarding the late night phone call. He couldn't imagine how this organization could do what the 'voice' said it could do. However, in the confident way the man made the claim, Fuller believed him.

It was well after midnight when Fuller finally went to the bedroom. He was exhausted. Gwen was already sleeping soundly. He admired her courage. She could have been crestfallen and negative in this watershed moment of his career. Instead, she just kept the home life moving along steadily. Her responses to him were always supportive and showed patience. She seemed even pleased to be seeing more of him. He felt lucky having her by his side.

He thought he'd sleep fitfully that night after the strange phone call, but he fell right asleep. In fact there was a look of contentment on his face as if he was dreaming there actually was an organization set up to counteract fiends like Howard Jensen…and even take them out of circulation.

The next morning Rich Fuller awoke early. He was surprisingly well rested even though the previous night's conversation seemed as if it was only minutes before. Taking a cup of coffee from the kitchen, he went to his study to call a few former cohorts at the St. Paul Paper Company about what they had heard about the Howard Jensen case. To a person they sounded more relieved than interested. None cared where Jensen was…just that he was gone from the company. It wasn't as if they hoped he was dead…only that he was never coming back to the company.

He found out from Laurie some temporary changes had been made in order to keep the sales and marketing department working as smoothly as it could. He learned that a woman he'd hired five years before as Administration Manager, Shirley Burkholtz, was asked to hold things together as a temporary department head until the Board figured where to find a permanent replacement for Jensen.

Fuller's former administrative assistant commented about the improved morale since Jensen turned up missing even though sales were still lackluster. In the quarter just completed, the revenue was down 30% over the previous year's gross income. After those results, Fuller knew true leadership was likely to flounder even worse.

Fuller gritted his teeth on how gullible too many top people, especially Henry Miller, had been taken in by this megalomaniac. He'd been periodically thinking about whether to consider returning to the company. Each time considering the present senior management team he'd have to reconstruct relationships, he found himself no longer interested. Why would he want to continue with the same company now that he saw how various key people…especially the CEO…reacted when the business cycle became extra challenging? Why would he want to work with individuals who proved to be so fickle, indecisive, and untrusting? In fact, he was thinking more seriously about liquidating his stock as soon as possible

It was just the next afternoon when Fuller got a call from none other than the stand-in Sales & Marketing Manager, Shirley Burkholtz. She claimed to just want to talk. Somehow, she had the idea Fuller might be willing to return to his former duties at the company. She said over and over again how everyone in the company now realized how much he had been submarined by Jensen…and how unsupportive Henry Miller and the Board had been to him as business became more challenging.

The more Shirley Burkholtz talked, the more he realized how over her head she was in her temporary position. She'd never even been on a sales call with a representative from the St. Paul Paper Company. During their conversation she lightly mentioned that she'd received a call from someone claiming to be a business consultant. He strongly suggested she contact the very man who had taken the brunt of the blows from the board of directors and Howard Jensen. She said the consultant suggested Fuller might want to return under certain improved conditions. She offered to take this possibility to certain members of the board if that were the case. She made it sound as if Fuller would be given a hero's welcome if he did return, since he was so often the calm voice of reason and motivation... qualities sorely missed in the company at that point.

Right then it occurred to Fuller that the mysterious caller from two nights before had already begun working on certain factors to improve the situations of both himself and St. Paul Paper Company. The call from Shirley Burkholtz and the stated intentions of that caller to help him were just too close together not to be coincidental. Fuller sat there mystified as Burkholtz continued to try to say the right things to massage her former boss' probable injured pride. Could that bland voice on the phone actually have either the clout or even the contacts to undo some of the destructive things a 'corporate animal' like Howard Jensen had done to his former company...and to Fuller himself? It was hard to believe, but as he listened to Burkholtz that was what she was trying to make happen.

As Fuller listened with half an ear to Shirley Burkholtz summarize the litany of problems that faced the company, he concluded the company likely didn't have the internal fortitude and know-how to fight its way out of their serious business downturn. This was the case whether Howard Jensen had joined the company or not.

In closing Fuller told Burkholtz he'd certainly think about her idea and that he appreciated the support he would have throughout the company if he returned. That was all he said. In fact, before he'd even hung up the receiver his decision had already been made that he would never return to his former company. There were too many brighter possibilities in his future. He could just feel it.

Fuller sat there contemplating the forty minute conversation with Shirley Burkholtz. With the skeleton now showing at St. Paul Paper Company, he had the most macabre thought. Though unintentional, Howard Jensen might have done him a favor by helping him decide to leave the company. If Jensen hadn't come and quickened the downward slide, he might be even more miserable wallowing his way through these crippling times at his former company. As a result of leaving St. Paul Paper Company with a stockpile of company stock besides another year-and-a-half salary and benefits, he was being given a second chance at a business life that could turn out far more positive than the distasteful previous two years. He decided to go play some golf...something he'd been doing more often since the spring weather had arrived. There was a bounce to his step and a spike of energy as he left the house. He actually felt lucky.

That evening he took his wife out to dinner. He never mentioned the strange caller two nights before, but he did share with her his feelings that he was fortunate he'd left St. Paul Paper Company when he had. He announced to her he was cashing in his entire accumulation of that company's stock as well. He wanted to be done with the company and most of the people who worked there.

The very next day he showed his excitement by concentrating his efforts completely on other companies in different industries. It was time for a fresh start…even at his age. He saw it as invigorating to enjoy a honeymoon period in his career again…..to be looked again as someone with the experience and know-how to lead a company's sales and marketing effort…and be working with other senior level managers who he could respect.

The call came as promised three evenings later after 11:00. Fuller wondered if the call would actually happen. There still was the chance the low, intense voice on the other end of the line had been someone's cruel joke. Whenever the phone rang…if it rang at that hour…he'd decided not to pick up the receiver. That was the agreement with the caller… if Fuller didn't want to be involved or was uncomfortable with the actions described by that mysterious caller…for whatever reason…the receiver would not be picked up.

Gwen was lying in bed watching TV when the phone began ringing. It was ten feet from where Fuller was reading a magazine on his leather chair in the study. He hadn't figured on his wife's involvement. She would find it odd if he didn't answer the phone. After all, it could be one of their kids needing help.

He shouted to the next room, "Sweetheart, I'll get it."

Fuller got up and dragged his feet toward the phone hoping it would quit ringing. It didn't. On the sixth ring, he finally and reluctantly picked up the receiver. He prayed it was one of his kids. It wasn't. At first there was silence on both ends of the line. Then the slow, deep voice of that same man who called him three nights prior spoke. He seemed not quite as intense. "Good evening, Mr. Fuller. I thought I'd misread you. I was about to give up. I figured you'd be too curious not to answer the phone. I'm certain you have questions…especially whether we really have taken Howard Jensen out of circulation…or for that matter to ascertain whether the man is even still alive. My assertions that my organization could help you reclaim your career had to also have piqued your interest…as well as the efforts already underway in trying to resurrect your former company. After talking with you, I sense you might be even willing to help us with this man even in a small way as distasteful as he is to you. Am I approaching some of your thoughts?"

Fuller had no other response other than to admit the caller was correct. "Yes…I guess those are most of the reasons I picked up the receiver. My primary curiosity seems to focus on how long do you expect to hold this man and do whatever you are doing to him?"

It was a fair question and mostly ignored by the caller. "Mr. Fuller, you need not be concerned about the health or welfare of Mr. Jensen. He is very much alive and in good hands…and as I said, out of circulation permanently as the Howard Jensen you remember."

Fuller felt his throat getting dry as the caller paused for only a second. "Now, as mentioned three nights ago, the important factor is to see where you stand on helping us do some repair work, as I call it, on what Mr. Jensen did to you, your career, to others in your former company and even to the reputation and future of the St. Paul Paper Company. If you have the interest, our organization will actively help you be re-instated back into your company. From what we've ascertained, your former company made a huge error in allowing you to leave. In fact, a consultant hired by us has already made contact with some of your former company's leadership about that very subject. That consultant has told four of the members of your board of directors in the last two days in no uncertain terms how big a loss it was when you left their organization. It is only with your permission and your desire to return that our consultant will turn up the heat. We believe Mr. Henry Miller could be making overtures your way within days if that is what you would like."

What Fuller was hearing went beyond belief. The caller's organization was already working on his behalf…and no doubt the company's behalf as well. The call from Shirley Burkholtz had not been coincidental. She was feeling him out for Miller and some of the board members regarding his possible interest. What the caller didn't know was Fuller's absolute disenchantment and disinterest in returning to St. Paul Paper Company.

He decided to remain quiet and instead probe for other information about this caller and his organization's motives. He asked politely but sharply, "Does your group have a name? For that matter, sir, do you have some kind of 'code' name that I can call you if you can't give me your real name? And, if indeed your organization feels they have a chance to restore my reputation and standing in my former company, you likely will need compensation. Your efforts on my behalf certainly cannot come without a price. I'd like to know the cost factor before I authorize any activity on your part. Finally, I'd also like to hear, in all due respect, your plan for assisting me."

The caller's voice became uneasy…as if he didn't expect such doubt from Fuller. "Yes, Mr. Fuller, we can go over some of the details. For now you need only to know that we have a business consultant who has already made contact with the CEO of St. Paul Paper Company. Our consultant's job is to look for every way possible to restore that company's good name and its position in its industry…at least as far as it might be possible. I will not mince words. Already he has discovered some glaring problems some of which you are most certainly well aware. The first problem is with Mr. Henry Miller himself. As CEO, he is a weak, out-of-touch leader. He should not be in that role. Also, the company's board of directors is indecisive and unproductive. Finally, Howard Jensen certainly did some noticeable damage that will take both time and investment to hopefully correct.

Our consultant found that the St. Paul Paper Company has been declining for some time. He uncovered things you tried to suggest that met with little support. In fact our consultant offered much praise for your efforts. But, our job is not to eliminate people from their jobs. We work, so to speak, with the deck of cards a company offers and then we do what we can to improve the direction and effectiveness of the company. I will say that Mr. Miller has been very content to listen to our consultant. Our highly experienced man will remain behind the scenes. He will be calling the plays; Mr. Miller will simply be voicing his instructions. We have others in our organization investing time to see where they can improve relations with your former company's key clients.

Mr. Miller will be given the credit for whatever improvements and restorations are accomplished to mend as much damage as possible that Howard Jensen has caused. I should add that our consultant is very concerned. He's done magic with many other companies. His worry is that St. Paul Paper Company might be too far gone for reclamation...at least to regain the industry leadership it once had in the upper Midwest. He noted a big help would be if you decided to return. You were an effective leader until you were chosen to be the scapegoat and your leadership was then compromised. He for one would gladly invite you back in your former role as well as being the de facto assistant CEO. He believes the company needs someone like you more than ever. He is in a position to make your return very lucrative; he would insist as much to Mr. Miller.

Fuller sat there again not believing what he was hearing. The 'voice' had ignored most of his questions and concentrated on the immediate needs for both Fuller and St. Paul Paper Company. He made it sound like a 'win-win' situation. Fuller knew it was not that easy even if he changed his mind and returned to his former company. With what he knew about Miller, the indecisive board of directors, the company's proven inability to compete in a changing marketplace, and even the still damaged morale of the employees, the risk didn't seem worth it. Furthermore, St. Paul Paper Company had become a takeover target. There was still some worth to the corporation. Certainly many other companies were sizing up the possibility of a 'friendly' or 'unfriendly' takeover bid. When and if that happened, Fuller would likely be out job searching once again.

Despite the caller saying things that seemed as if they were actually happening, Fuller didn't completely trust the 'voice'. He decided to be upfront and let his feelings about St. Paul Paper Company be known. "Well...sir...your organization seems to be making strides to help. I have to tell you that no doubt the offer for my return would be quite generous. However, I believe I'll pass on your offer. If anyone can improve the future of St. Paul Paper Company, it seems your consultant can perform some miracles as long as Henry Miller takes heed.

Furthermore, I believe my name and reputation has been seriously besmirched enough within the company that my return would be futile. If key people and other employees of St. Paul Paper Company were so easily persuaded by Howard

Jensen about my supposed frailties and ineffectiveness, I'm not interested in spending all my time trying to change that perception. I am certain there are many other more preferred paths I could seek that will be more positive and fulfilling. With that being my decision about my former company, my only final comment would be a request that your organization free Mr. Jensen. Your statement that he is 'alive but out of circulation' does not sound positive. As much as I dislike and disrespect him, I wish him no personal ill will.

There was a pause before the caller responded. He sounded dismayed. "Mr. Fuller, I don't think you understand. At no expense to you, we can assist in resurrecting or repair a good part of your image…something that was unjustifiably depreciated by Mr. Jensen. It would help you…and certainly our efforts…if you would consider coming back to St. Paul Paper Company.

The determination of the 'voice' made Fuller uneasy. Fuller repeated his wishes even more forcefully. "No, I have no interest. In addition, if my reputation was destroyed by Howard Jensen with such relative ease, then my worth and image had somehow depreciated anyway. It was time I leave. I'm done with St. Paul Paper Company."

Without letting the bland voice counter, Fuller matter-of-factly put a finish to the phone call. "So, with no need for us to converse any longer, I reiterate my concern for Mr. Jensen. In the remote possibility that an organization like what you are describing actually exists, I trust that you will allow Mr. Jensen another chance. If you have the experience to…as you say…re-indoctrinate someone like Howard Jensen, I only hope he will be placed in a location far from this area. While I don't want anything dreadful to happen to him, I would hope never to see him again. May I say thank you for your interest in my career, but I trust this will be the last time we talk."

Then not giving the caller any chance to respond, Fuller quietly hung up the phone. He hoped that call and the phone call three days before would be the end to the strangest communications he would ever receive again. Somehow, though, he doubted that would be the case.

To his great surprise, Fuller never heard from the deep 'voice' ever again. There were no more late night calls. There were no contacts from Shirley Burkholtz or anyone else from St. Paul Paper Company. He hoped a strong, competent consultant working behind the scenes could be the answer the company needed. From Fuller's perspective, that would be the only way left for the company to at least have a chance to survive. And, that was as far as Fuller wanted to think about the matter. He had neither the time nor the interest in keeping track of the progress, especially since he was about to liquidate his large stock holdings in St. Paul Paper Company.

In the weeks ahead, it was noted in the *Minneapolis Star* that the FBI and local law enforcement continued to keep Howard Jensen's name on the 'missing person's list'. Authorities were completely dumbfounded by the case. It was as if

Jensen had simply vanished into thin air. With family and friends lacking who might have insisted on a continued focus of the Howard Jensen case, the file folder evaporated into a cabinet of other disappearances or unsolved murder cases.

As for Rich Fuller within days following that last late night phone contact with the mystery caller, his efforts in his job searching began to pay off. He was called by five different headhunters and four companies, not in the paper industry, expressing interest in talking with him. In the next month he was flying around the country meeting and being interviewed by various interested parties.

These discussions helped him not only build an effective marketing plan for himself, but aided him in deciding whether he was willing to leave the Twin City area. Within weeks after all his travels…and turning down two job offers… he accepted a position with a large international transport company as their Vice President of Sales and Marketing. It never occurred to him why his path suddenly became smoother in his quest for worthwhile job opportunities. When it happened…and so quickly…he never put two and two together regarding the possible help offered by the late night caller. He figured it was all a question of time until his job search efforts would finally pay off.

It was four years later when Rich and Gwen Fuller left for a ten-day summer Alaskan cruise. Flying into Seattle, Washington, they boarded a large cruise ship in Vancouver, British Columbia a week after a Fourth of July family celebration at their home. That weekend they had said their farewells to their youngest daughter MacKenzie who had graduated from college a few weeks before. She had already taken off on a flight to Spain to begin graduate work in International Studies at the Universidad de Madrid. There were more tears displayed by Gwen and even some wet eyes from Fuller, but the two parents were happier for their daughter than sad for themselves. They'd adapted to her not living at home and were now more proud of the progress in Mackenzie's career.

Fuller was now a Senior Vice President with that same international transport company in Minneapolis. He'd taken the position six months after leaving the now defunct St. Paul Paper Company. A larger eastern based paper company had purchased the remaining assets of that company and now used the St. Paul office as a small Regional office. There were twelve people from the original company who had become employees of the new company.

That development hardly mattered to Rich Fuller. That didn't mean he forgot completely the former company that had been such an important part of his life. He had moved on both physically and mentally. He had heard from a few people after he'd taken his new job with the transport company…including Shirley Burkholtz. She was inquiring about a job. While he respected her and her conscientious efforts while working for him, he had nothing to offer her, but called another company's human resource department recommending her. Six weeks later he heard from her again thanking him for helping her land a job as an Administration Manager with a tool and die company in St. Paul.

As for his former Administrative Assistant, Laurie Schmitt, he found a job for her within his new company. After six months she was promoted to work directly for him. To both it was like old times with a loyalty that could not be erased.

As for Fuller, he had graduated into a new industry and into a growing international company. The business was lesser in terms of numbers of employees, but had three times the revenue. While he was pleased with his new organization, just as importantly, they seemed to appreciate his efforts. He was named to the Board of Directors before his first year was completed. It need not be said that he was making an income far superior to his best years at St. Paul Paper Company.

It was into the second day of the voyage toward Alaska after a brief stop at Port Hardy, British Columbia that the boat reached the open ocean. The weather kept most passengers if they chose to sit on deck huddled under a blanket with a hot cup of coffee or a brandy despite the sun shining brightly. Gwen was reading a book when Rich decided to get some exercise by taking the loop around the cruise ship top deck.

From the top perch he could enjoy the vast Pacific Ocean on one side and the lonely, but scenic Canadian seacoast on the other side. When he was at the bow, he noticed a couple maintenance people cleaning one of the social rooms. There were a few tables of bridge players. Off in the corner there were people drinking coffee and involved in a book discussion group.

Fuller tapped one of the maintenance people on the shoulder to ask what was going on at the far table. The man owned a longish beard, a complete head of gray hair, and a slightly ill-fitting uniform. He stood tall to respond and then deflated, turning away as if slightly intimidated by the presence of Fuller. His response was strange in that every other crew member from the Captain down to the lowest ranking uniformed person on board seemed to go out of their way to serve and be friendly with the paying public. The bearded man recovered and tried to be upbeat with his explanation. Continuing to face downward, he perfunctorily retorted, "That's a reading group, sir. You can sign up at the information center. The group meets daily at this time for about an hour. The reading list is on the bulletin board. You're welcome to come to one or all of the discussion groups."

All the time he was talking he never once made eye contact with Fuller. The bearded man then moved away busying himself with mopping the spotless floor. Staring at the back of the man, Fuller continued to find the behavior uniquely odd relative to the warm, amiable responses of the rest of the crew. As the man pushed his wheeled mop bucket further away, Fuller thought about how some employees he'd hired simply didn't have an ease with customer service. They didn't have it within their make-up to be amiable and helpful.

'Thank God,' he thought, 'there weren't many individuals like them.' Fuller shrugged his shoulders and wondered if the Captain of the cruise ship was aware of this particular glaring weakness of one of his hands. Maybe he was. Maybe that was why the employee was pushing a mop.

He continued his stroll on the top deck happy that he didn't have to be responsible for hiring and training maintenance crew for a cruise ship. Minutes later he was talking with another guest on the ship. The cold behavior of the crew member was out of sight and out of mind.

The relaxing voyage continued up the coast to Juneau. The next day the ship floated on past Cape Spencer toward the Malaspina Glacier. Visible from the decks was the highest peak in British Columbia, Mount Fairweather.

It was the next afternoon that the weather was quite warm and most of guests on board seemed to be outside enjoying the scenic beauty along the coastline from the multi-level decks of the ship. Fuller and his wife were leisurely walking when he caught sight of that same gray-bearded, silver-haired maintenance worker from the day before. The man was sweeping out the main dining room along with two other workers in preparation for that evening's dinner crowd.

Fuller couldn't keep his eyes off the man. He had a very distinctive look…a straighter back than the more common hunched over posture of an average maintenance man. There was also something about the man's eyes. He seemed more observant than the vacant look in the eyes of the men he was sharing clean-up duty. There was even something that made Fuller feel like he'd seen this man before. He briefly went through his mental filing cabinet of high school and college friends as best he could. Try as he might, he just could not place the guy. Nonetheless, he was certain there was some kind of tie between them.

Fuller strolled on with his wife talking constantly about the beauty of the landscape. He nodded his head blankly while periodically looking back at the maintenance guy. The bearded man continued his work unaware that anyone was looking at him. Fuller even tried to imagine the man without the gray beard… and even darker hair…but that was no help.

He finally asked Gwen, "Sweetheart, turn around and look at that maintenance guy in the dining room…the one with the mop in his hand…gray beard…silver hair. Have you ever seen him before? I swear to God I have, but I just can't place him."

She examined the worker from thirty yards away through a window. She shook her head. "No…….no, I don't recognize him at all. He could be someone who worked at our club back in Minnesota. Maybe you ought to just go up and introduce yourself and find out where he's from. That would end your little mystery.

Fuller nodded, "Yes…normally I'd do that. But, I talked to him yesterday and he was surprisingly cold in his reaction to me. I'm just surprised. Everyone else on board is so friendly and accommodating. Maybe that was what caught my attention. His behavior was so much the opposite of what it should be on a cruise ship. He was so distant …as if he shouldn't be working in a position where he has to deal with the public."

He paused and grinned at his wife. "Anyway, the hell with it, that's the Captain's problem. I don't need to have every maintenance guy like me.

Both of them were just about to turn away and walk on when that same man with the thick gray hair suddenly turned their way… as if having a sixth sense that someone was studying him. In that instance he caught both Fuller and his wife gazing at him. Instead of nodding like any other crew member might do, he looked down, gathered his mop and pail, and with some haste retreated to a side door. It was as if he was trained to just walk away if he felt someone was examining him.

That evening Fuller and his wife enjoyed dinner with four other couples they'd met on the cruise. It turned into a late night of drinking, dining, and dancing. When the evening was drawing to a close, the two of them decided to wear off some of the food and drink with a brisk walk around the deck. Back at their room, they got some warmer clothing and returned to the open air of the top deck. It was windy. Only a few other passengers were doing the same thing. The stroll was invigorating with the stars seeming to reach down to the very ocean level. It was beautiful.

At the bow of the boat, one of the crew members was standing alone, leaning on the rail and also enjoying the relaxed late evening scenery. He was smoking a cigarette and obviously taking a break from his duties.

Fuller kept walking slowly with his wife as they made a turnabout to walk back the opposite direction. At that moment, Gwen excused herself and moved toward the crew member. Fuller stayed back in the dark letting his wife ask whatever question was presently on her mind.

He could hear Gwen say, "Excuse me"…and then her voice was too inaudible to discern. The crew member turned toward her. He was the same bearded maintenance man. He doffed his hat and gave her a sincere smile. To Fuller's surprise, he was completely pleasant with Gwen. He even said something that made them both laugh as he pointed to something apparently on shore off in the darkness.

With time to further examine this bearded man, Fuller's curiosity was resurrected once again. There was something about his profile…his reserved smile…even the way he stood that made Fuller swear he'd seen the man before…. and more recently than college or even early in his business career.

He then heard Gwen say in parting, "Good evening and thank you for the information."

The crew member tipped his head and bid her a polite farewell. As she turned away and ambled back toward Fuller, he noticed the man's smile turned off like a light switch. The maintenance guy had been performing…just being polite because he was required…to yet another passenger on the cruise. Not seeing Fuller in the shadows, the bearded man then turned away and went on smoking his cigarette.

Gwen returned singing the praises of the crew member. "Rich, that crew member was so friendly…nothing like you described this afternoon. Interestingly, he spoke in a very educated, even cultured way. I asked him where we might see some Kodiak bears. He gave me a quick overview of when and where upon disembarking on the Alaskan Peninsula they might be seen. If this man is an example of the crew, this cruise ship has some very scholarly and articulate people in maintenance uniforms. I was going to ask if he does this work only in the summer months."

In the next couple days with stops in Anchorage and then again for a day trip on land through and around Kodiak Island, the Fuller's met more people and generally were enjoying the entire vacation. Thoughts of the maintenance man never entered Fuller's mind.

The cruise continued along the Aleutian Islands before heading back across the open sea toward Seattle. The trip had become far more social as more people became acquainted with one another. Even during one evening when the seas were a bit rough from a summer storm, the rocking boat didn't deter most of the vacationers from enjoying the evening dinner and entertainment. Still, that night about 9:00 Gwen told Fuller she was feeling a bit wobbly and needed to return to their room. Too much food and drink and the unstable boat had caught up to her. He escorted her back to the room. When she fell asleep, he decided to take a walk around the deck as the rain had subsided.

There were a larger number of passengers strolling at that earlier hour. Many had fallen in love with the night air and wouldn't miss taking their leisurely walk. Fuller recognized and greeted several couples as he approached the bow of the boat.

And there he was. The same maintenance worker was standing at the bow staring off in space and blowing smoke into the breeze with each deep drag from his cigarette. Fuller neared him to stand by the rail and greeted the bearded crew member. The man nodded and immediately turned away. There was no greeting…just a nod and silence.

The entire non-verbal response made Fuller a slight bit uncomfortable. He was about to say something to the man when he stared once again at the gray beard… the heavy silver hair…and tried to imagine the man with no beard and shorter hair.

His close scan was interrupted by a very straight-forward statement from the crew member. It was not a greeting. As soon as the man said a few words, the voice became familiar. It said, "I'm amazed. In a year's time since I've worked on this boat, I've recognized four different people on various cruises. They've all looked right by me…not aware who I was in the least. This growth of hair has been my best disguise. But, you…Rich Fuller…I believe you identified me right away."

Fuller was about to disagree when the man took an extra-long drag from his cigarette and seemed about ready to uncover the mystery. His eyes displayed a look indicating he was not thrilled to be talking with Fuller. He muttered, "So… Rich Fuller…it's been a while since our time together at the paper company. I trust your life must be going well given the money you had to pay for this ten-day cruise."

Just like that Fuller knew he was talking with the very man who had sabotaged his career a few years back...and won. Howard Jensen, with a camouflaged look no one could have recognized, had assumed Fuller did. His manner showed himself to be a changed man in other respects than just his physical looks. He no longer had a swagger. His eyes were still intense, but displayed a certain fear. His behavior showed him to be bitter...and quite wary. Even as he whispered those few words, his eyes were darting up and down the top deck deciding if anyone was watching them.

Jensen's words were spoken in a harsh tone as if not caring whether Fuller remained or immediately marched away in silence. Jensen expected no friendliness or respect. Fuller wanted to be impersonal and to show disgust, but the years had taken some of the edge of his revulsion toward the man.

Jensen continued talking in a low, emotionless voice. "I suppose I could thank you for saving my life, but you probably don't know that you did. So...I guess my words would be kind of empty."

Fuller finally responded, "Jensen, I'd have to say I'm relieved to see you alive. Everyone...and I mean everyone...thought your past had caught up to you...and you were...eliminated by someone from your past. That made the most sense to people, that is, those who cared."

Pausing for a moment as he recalled the hurt and evil this man perpetrated on him and others, Fuller's feelings suddenly boiled up. The words flowed so easily. "But, now that I see you living and breathing, I will tell you that I'd never known anyone people were so desperately glad to have out of their lives. The reasons for your disappearance became unimportant. You were gone. That was mostly what people all wished. If your body would have been found, there would have been few if any people sorry for your demise. I'm sorry to say I would have been one of those individuals."

Fuller suddenly realized he was in a position that an untold number of people injured or destroyed by Jensen would like to be. He felt himself in a unique situation. His career or reputation could no longer be hurt by this treacherous man. He felt a responsibility to carry out this opportunity as thoroughly and articulately as he was able. Standing on that deck next to such a disagreeable and dishonorable man gave him a feeling of opportunity and even 'power'.

He faced Jensen and in a low, measured voice let out more of his pent up furor. "Based on what I see, I'm very glad you appear to be in the type of work where you can no longer destroy people's lives. I don't know how you obtained this job, but it suits you as long as you never are in a managerial or supervising role again. I consider you a self-centered tyrant. Your goal was power. Your skills were used to do a hatchet job to any organization you joined and to do the same to people you deemed in your way. I feel my anger spilling over as I think of the hundreds of people's lives you depreciated just in my former company alone."

Fuller astonished himself how easy it was to so viciously excoriate this hideous individual. As unrelenting as Fuller was, he couldn't help but notice how his words seemed to glance off the man as if he was holding an invisible shield. The uniformed man remained quiet, listening but taking no offense to the harsh words being thrown at him. He calmly just took more drags of his cigarette.

Fuller was like a man possessed. "Jensen, I don't believe I've ever truly hated a man until I met you. I don't even know if I want to hear the reasons why you set your egotistical sights on me when you joined St. Paul Paper Company. You purposefully tried and succeeded in destroying me. It was like an act of murder… and I know I wasn't the only one in your career…your former career that is… that you assassinated.

Now seeing you in a maintenance job I stand here satisfied that you are alive, but just as important you apparently are no longer in a position to hurt people and corporate destruction is not at your treacherous fingertips. That mollifies some of my animosity. By your expression I get the feeling you've had to serve some kind of punishment…or re-indoctrination. As far as I'm concerned it seems your new path is going in the right direction. I would hazard a guess that 99% of people who have had to work with you would be relieved to see you in this role. As you might guess, many others would indeed wish you were dead."

Fuller finally took a deep breath and let his blood pressure settle. The only satisfaction he felt was the sense he had carried out his unassigned task of representing so many negative emotions from others damaged by this despicable man. He'd done the job. There was no reason to go on. The harm Jensen caused was in the past. It had been four years since St. Paul Paper Company basically had gone bankrupt and sold out. There was nothing that could be done about that situation. He realized it could be argued Howard Jensen was not completely the reason for St. Paul Paper Company to spiral downhill. Jensen simply sped up the process. However, there was no excuse for Jensen's utter disregard for people.

The bearded man continued standing there by the ship's rail seemingly not surprised by the tongue lashing he was hearing. The deep drags on his cigarette did seem to be more intense.

Fuller finally calmed down, but he was not done talking. Now he had questions…some having nothing to do with St. Paul Paper Company.

In a more controlled and quiet tone, he queried, "Jensen, would you please put some light on your disappearance. Within days or weeks, I received a couple very strange late evening phone calls relating to you. The person sounded very…. sinister…at first. Then he came across as trying to be helpful. I don't remember a bulk of the conversation, but he offered the services of some kind of organization. He said his group was there to assist people who had been harmed or discredited when dealing with people like you. It was unbelievable. He also claimed his organization's ability to repair a company's reputation and even prospects for continued business providing the damaged company's leadership could take advantage of his group's efforts to help them. He finally intimated that his organization was taking you 'out of circulation' for some undetermined time.

I didn't accept their services because I didn't trust the guy, but I will tell you in the following weeks after the two late night phone calls I received, my job searching began heading in a more positive direction. I had worthwhile interviews with companies interested in my background. The most difficult challenge was to decide which eventual offer was the best one. I thought it was all my personal marketing and effort paying off, but in retrospect I've often sensed that I had some unknown help. I heard from headhunters and companies I hadn't even sent resumes.

As far as your situation was concerned, the caller seemed to know I would not contact the police about this secretive organization causing your disappearance. He knew my story would sound rather bizarre to the authorities. He just suggested I forget about you...that if you were adaptable you would survive. He made it clear that you would never be allowed to be part of the corporate world again. So far, including even seeing you as a lowly mate on an Alaskan cruise, I have to admit the caller has been quite accurate. If you are willing, I'd like to ask you what happened. I won't repeat anything...just like I didn't four years ago after those two late night calls. I have a feeling your story would be rather unbelievable."

For the first time Jensen displayed some emotion. He smirked. Before he responded, he again showed caution glancing down the long deck. He seemed willing to talk, but only if he perceived the two of them were alone. He chose his words very carefully as he spoke. "What I can tell you will probably be quite satisfying to you. Because you talked with someone in the...ah....organization, and you kept your mouth shut, I'll share some of what happened. Yes, this operation definitely exists. I returned to the normal world almost two years ago, although I've been in a state of constant observation. This cruise is the first internship, as they call it, where I don't feel every move I make is being examined. I know there is someone on this boat assigned to keep track of my every action, but I've learned the difference between this job and a few others I've had. This job the scrutiny has been far less obvious. I know the observer is not you, because you would not be talking to me now. I'll never know the identity of the person or people tracking me until I get back to the operation's headquarters for my debriefing. I've had to earn this freedom. There were others like me who haven't fared as well. Between you and me, this is the best job I've had since being allowed back in the public eye.

He took another deep drag before continuing. "You've obviously put your business life back together. That's a relief to me. I can apologize for what I did to you, but as the program emphasized, it really doesn't matter if I'm sorry or not. The damage I created was so thorough and long-term that a single apology is like a rock dropping in the ocean. I was shown in no uncertain terms the resoundingly horrible impact I had on companies and the people in those companies. The organization drummed into me the effect my actions could be and probably are having on the very attitudes and lives of the off-spring of those people I destroyed or at least depreciated as well. The off-spring had to watch their parents live through the hell I created."

Fuller interrupted, "You say 'program. What do you mean?"

Jensen's eyes went wide showing actual fear....the kind of fear he caused in others at the St. Paul Paper Company. He said, "O.K., you can destroy me if the organization ever learned I said this, but I'll say it. It would be back to the compound...or worse."

Fuller was incredulous with Jensen's discomfort...such a far cry from the smug, deceitful businessman who flattered and ramrodded his way to the top of various businesses. He spoke in hushed tones as if he was talking politics in a public bar in a communist country.

Leaning in closer to Fuller, he whispered, "I'd be signing my own death warrant if I divulged where the organization is based and it was traced back to me. But, I will say this group does do what that late night caller claimed when he talked with you. They actually do help people and can often undo harm created by individuals...like me. It would be a safe bet they helped with your job search whether you offered to help them with me or your former company or not. They would still keep track of you until you were back on your feet. In fact that was their terminology...getting a company or individual 'back on their feet'. I was forced to assist in any way I could to help people I'd destroyed over the years. Because my actions slipped through the cracks...as they said to you four years ago...my list of people to help was mind-boggling in numbers.

I am aware you have brought yourself back to whole with your new job in Minneapolis. Still, don't doubt that they might have nudged certain headhunters to bring your name and background to the forefront even though it was you who won those job offers. They were hoping you might have wanted to rejoin St. Paul Paper Company. It would have made their behind-the-scenes efforts to save that company more possible.

When you showed no interest, they eventually saw the hopelessness. There really was no strong, resilient person left in that senior management team after you left the company. My selfish actions didn't help the company, but I was only their six months. The die had been cast even before I was hired. There was just a scarcity of effective managers and worthwhile experience at the level that was needed to save that company. It was the one time my efforts to find a buyer for St. Paul Paper Company that might have been for the best. The methods I practiced at the time would unfortunately have made a takeover highly unlikely. I was just not trusted by anyone...except most of those members on that unqualified board of directors at your former company.

The organization has a long record of bringing companies back from bad times. But, unfortunately they aren't successful all the time…as in the case of St. Paul Paper Company. I am relieved I didn't cause any suicides…at least that they are aware. That might have been the end for me.

Jensen took a long, nervous drag from his shrinking cigarette. "What they do with people like me is simple. They pull the individual out of the work force completely if they can. In my case it was easy. I had no real family or people who cared about me. If the person has family obligations, they arrange for that man's life to be ruined. If there are kids, the organization does a lot to help the guy's wife and kids in the way of financial support. Divorces are common. They help the spouse find worthwhile work. Once separated from his family, the man is pulled into the organization and put through what's called an 'indoctrination' program. Since individuals like me don't tend to be involved or effective parents, the loss of the man to his family would not be that significant.

In my case… my wife and I had been separated for many years. We had no kids. I was just pulled from life. I was incarcerated for months while I was studied and asked questions about my misdeeds. It took a long time. There would be understandable belligerence initially amongst each new 'inmate'. That was how we were referred…as 'inmates'. Eventually we were made to understand that our attitude towards people in general had better change or we'd just disappear. An 'inmate' not able to adjust would cease to exist. It was that cut and dried. This group is expert at dealing with unruly 'inmates'.

Following my initial battery of interviews and tests, I found out later I was on the probable list of inmates who would vanish forever. However, the contact they had with you saved my life. Your response of not requiring or desiring any help whatsoever in finding a new opportunity in your life and your concern for my welfare though I had done so many incredibly terrible things to you had a noticeable impact. I was given some higher level consideration by the 'stewards' operating the program.

Within days of them realizing you were serious in your wish to be left alone as well as not to return to your company, the committee sat me down and told me they would give me a chance. They didn't sound hopeful, but they said they'd work with me for a short time on all aspects of my character even though they considered me irreparable. If I kept passing various tests and they could see progress over a period of time, then they would give me a chance. They kept one carrot out there for me. I could be saved if I showed the willingness and adaptability to make mandatory character changes. I would literally be allowed to go on breathing if my signs of redemption proved sincere. Then further re-training would continue. They said it might be years, but that I'd have a chance to return to society in some menial tasks just to evaluate if I was truly adapting. Still they never offered me much hope. They weren't there to boost my spirits… only to provide a chance as long as they thought a positive result was possible.

The first two years I just existed. I changed without really knowing it. I was told one day that I had become eligible for an 'internship' slot on the outside. Depending on how it went and how I conducted myself, I was told other 'internships' might be in my future. In no uncertain terms, however, I was told I would never be allowed to be a principal or owner or manager of any organization…or have any supervisory responsibilities. I was never to be allowed to have even one person report to me. They said I might return to the work force in time, but I would be carefully watched and examined in each job I was involved. If I ever showed any tendencies of returning to my former business behavior patterns, I would be returned to the compound. It was called 'one strike and you're out'…indicating that I would likely vanish for good.

So, Mr. Richard Fuller, while you look at this maintenance job on this cruise ship as a kind of a punishment…or me getting my due… I look at this as a gift. I actually have a chance to thank you. Without you showing some humanity towards me with that caller four years ago, I wouldn't be here. You can rant on as you wish about my behavior and morals from years ago, but that is past tense. I'll do whatever humble tasks are available in any of the internships just to remain in society."

Fuller then began to look down the long deck now realizing he might be putting Jensen in possible jeopardy just by being seen with him. He whispered one last question. "Jensen, how were you found out? There are people like you in every organization…individuals who are interested only in the power and caring little about the company or people in general. How were you chosen to be taken from the human race?"

Jensen nodded as if anticipating the question. "I had the same question the very day I was brought before the tribunal. The simple answer…I was on their radar screen, so to speak, from my actions at previous companies. I had already been monitored and labeled a 'misanthrope' by the organization, but some internal flaws in their procedures had let me run free for too long. It was the speed with which I devastated the internal workings of St. Paul Paper Company and the overall misery I created with so many employees that finally caught their attention.

The circumstances were so bad at your former company. On the night the organization removed me, as they term it, from 'circulation', they created a scenario that my disappearance was a possible murder. They were very expert at causing people to vanish. Generally when they make their move, they often concoct a realistic story of suicide. It was a bit difficult in my situation. I was so headstrong, over-confident and powerful within the St. Paul Paper Company, there was no cause for me to be suicidal. But, they felt they couldn't delay. They had to let my disappearance continue on the books as an unsolved crime. It will be that way forever.

My name, Howard Jensen, now no longer exists. The only way I have returned to civilization is that I've gone through and completely accepted an entire new character. I had no choice if I want to continue breathing. And, if my former identity ever has the least chance of becoming known again, I will be pulled from civilization once again for an undetermined amount of time. If you happen to divulge that you and I met on a cruise boat and that Howard Jensen is alive, I will have to be re-indoctrinated...if they feel I even deserve a second programming.

Since we've now met, I actually have two choices. I can let the organization know of our inadvertent meeting...or stay mum. I frankly don't want to say anything. I would be returned to the program and forced to cover every syllable of our conversation. You might even be contacted to see if you were inclined to go to the authorities with what we just now discussed. I have the feeling you won't do that if for the only reason that you don't want to get mixed up explaining to a lot of people this very unlikely and unbelievable story. Besides, your own sanity would be in question. Nobody needs that kind of albatross on their back.

If I am asked if I saw you, I will probably affirm it, but I'll say you never recognized me. I'll just say we talked about the cruise and the beauty of the Alaskan coast...and then you went back to your cabin. I might suggest that should be your story as well...for both our sakes.

Fuller nodded in understanding unconsciously putting one of his fingers over his lips trying to give the former Howard Jensen some reassurance. The bearded man gave a slight shrug and then looked away from Fuller. He stared out into the black night as another couple strolled by on their late evening walk. Jensen then lit another cigarette, turned slightly and tipped his hat in greeting them without saying anything. Fuller just looked out to sea as if lost in his own thoughts.

As the couple got out of listening range, Jensen perused once again down the deck to see if there were other passengers approaching. When the darkened deck was clear once again of any other passenger, Jensen threw his cigarette out into the dark ocean. Fuller sensed the man was ready to end the conversation.

Through his thick beard, Fuller could barely see the man's lips move as he whispered barely audibly, "Rich Fuller...I know I was unable to give our business relationship a chance...and back then I did what I could do to destroy you...but I'm glad you appear to be all right. In over five months working on this vessel, I've seen a few people from my past life. With my increased weight, gray hair and heavy beard, they didn't recognize me. You apparently saw right through my masquerade. That tells me my image must still be very clear in your mind. It tells me there might be others who could identify me and I need to put more effort into disguising myself further.

Since you happened to have made this cruise and they have your name in their files, please be aware they may make some kind of follow up contact with you just to see if you did recognize me. If you say you did, they will appreciate your honesty. Since you've talked to them before by phone four years ago... and you kept your mouth shut over that conversation...they know you won't be intimidated by the call. They'll want to know if we talked. I deserve nothing from you, but again, it would help if you confirmed that we talked about the cruise ship and the Alaskan coast.

There was a silence only interrupted by the strong breeze blowing over the bow. Fuller wasn't ready to end the conversation. He wasn't quite certain why he felt some compassion for this raggedy-haired man, but he did. It was an odd emotion since up to that moment he loathed the very thought of Howard Jensen. Now that Howard Jensen no longer existed.

Not looking at the bearded man, he asked, "If you choose to say we had this chance meeting, what's really going to happen to you?"

Jensen didn't move as he answered. "I'll be transferred to a more remote type of work…like the ones I first held when the organization allowed me out of the compound almost two years ago. They incorporate you back into civilization very gradually. My previous assignments allowed me little or no human contact. I was a forest ranger in the Yukon Territory for a year. Then I lived at a lighthouse at the very edge of the Western Aleutians for a period of time. Apparently I must have passed that test since I was moved to this position after only a few months from that isolated location. I'm under strict orders to do whatever maintenance work is assigned…and to only enter into conversation if necessary. When I started this job, I immediately thought they were making a mistake. I've had more human contact in this maintenance job than I expected. However, I've come to realize this assignment has been for that very reason. They want to test the legitimacy of their re-indoctrination and training with me and my sincerity in accepting my new life. The fact that I've been on this boat for almost a half year gives me reason to believe I'm fulfilling their wishes…at least so far. But, I never let my guard down."

Fuller stood there nervously…for Jensen, not for himself. He would not have believed a word of what Jensen had to say if he hadn't had those two late night calls from that 'bland-voice' four years before.

Jensen began to move away. "Rich Fuller, don't take it wrong if I don't acknowledge you for the rest of this voyage other than to tip my hat if we happened to pass each other. It's best that way. After all, it's not as if we're going to be friends anyway. In fact, the tribunal doesn't allow me to have any close friends…only workmates and a few acquaintances. Chances are you will never see me again. For that matter, that would probably be the best for both of us. I bid you a good evening…and a good life."

Fuller watched as the virtual unidentifiable Howard Jensen slowly meandered away and down the deck. As he evaporated into the slight fog enveloping the ship, Fuller half expected the man to vault the railing and plunge into the sea ending whatever life he had remaining. Then again his survival instinct had to be strong. He didn't want to simply replicate what his 'organization' would do to him at their whim if he showed the slightest bit of recalcitrance.

For a moment Fuller contemplated whether Jensen could be lying…that he had been threatened years before and found it best just to disappear. If so, he'd made a miraculous change in character by himself. Fuller doubted that was possible with Jensen's phenomenal ego along with his cold, calculating character... at least up to four years ago. Then Fuller immediately cancelled that notion. He'd heard the bland, emotionless voice of someone from the 'organization' twice on the phone. It was the kind of tone Fuller felt relieved he was on the right side of the caller's intentions.

Jensen, being definitely on the other side, showed every sign of being motivated by fear. He'd perpetrated a similar fear and unhappiness in too many other men and women throughout his career. Now the group that had taken over his life was inflicting the same thing on Jensen. The difference was the employees rocked by Jensen's antics and disrespect could quit and hopefully find another job. In Jensen's case, he didn't have that choice. He faced the unrelenting pressure from the organization daily. There was no option for him or other re-programmed corporate animals to 'quit' unless they no longer cared about breathing.

The voyage ended two days later in the port of Seattle. Fuller never saw Jensen anywhere on the boat over those last forty-eight hours. He wondered which choice Jensen would make...whether to let the organization know about his chance meeting with a former work colleague or to keep the entire episode secret. If Jensen did divulge the coincidence, Fuller might expect a clandestine late night call wanting to know the extent of Fuller's recognizance of Jensen.

As Gwen and he strolled down the gang plank to a van that would take them to a Puget Sound hotel for the night, Fuller made one last glance back at the cruise ship from bow to stern. He noticed one man standing alone on the bow on the top deck wearing the familiar crew uniform. He focused his eyes and saw that it was Jensen...with his longish gray hair and beard flopping in the breeze. He had a mop in his hand, but had stopped his work for a moment to watch the vacationers de-board the boat.

At that moment Jensen stopped panning the scene at the dock and let his eyes distantly meet Fuller's eyes. A lone bead of sweat ran down Fuller's back giving him a momentary chill...a strange reaction since he had no fear of this man. He immediately realized it had to be a fleeting reaction of the extreme and excessive unpleasantness caused by this individual...and how it still lingered in his memory. The physical response ended as quickly as it happened. Fuller was satisfied this hated man would no longer have such an impact on others again.

Taking his wife's arm at the bottom of the gang plank, Fuller took one last look up to the top deck. He watched as the bearded man slowly put his finger to his hat in a gesture of farewell. Fuller did not return the acknowledgement.

In the next instance someone stood beside Jensen and began saying something to him. The man was not part of the crew nor could Fuller recognize the man as one of the vacationers on board during the ten-day cruise. Jensen never said a word in reply; his head simply lowered...and then nodded.

Watching this brief scene, Fuller hardly blinked…and the serious looking man along with Jensen then disappeared from sight.

Fuller and his wife strolled toward the hotel van as he repeatedly glanced back towards the top deck of the large boat. He thought he might have seen the top of Jensen's hat moving slowing along that top deck, but he wasn't certain.

Gwen kept marveling and pointing at the 'Needle' saying she'd like to elevator up to the top of that structure before their plane returned them to Minneapolis the next day. Seeing nothing more where Jensen had been standing, Fuller finally gave his wife his full attention. With a supportive nod he replied, "Yes, that's a good idea. In fact, let's make reservations and have dinner up there yet this evening."

Within a half hour they had checked into their hotel in downtown Seattle. Their luggage was delivered to their room within the hour. Nothing was missing. Going to the 'Needle' restaurant for dinner, the Fullers completed a memorable final evening in that city. Although the view of the Puget Sound shoreline was intermittently beautiful and then unseen as it clouded over, Fuller found himself studying the people in the restaurant as if someone was looking at him. After a couple glasses of wine, he lost interest in that possibility.

Upon returning to the hotel, there was a message for him. It was a phone number with no name attached. He was unfamiliar with the number and at that late hour had little interest in returning the call. By the time they boarded the airplane back to Minneapolis the next morning, he'd all but forgotten about the previous night's message. If someone wanted to talk with him, they could call him at his office when he got back to work.

In the weeks and months that followed, Fuller occasionally wondered if that message at the hotel in Seattle had been a follow-up call about Howard Jensen from that bland-voiced late night caller of four years before. It was a question that never got answered. Richard Fuller would never receive any such call ever again.

The Mismatched Foursome At Lake Lindsay

A sudden burst of applause from the crowd around the first tee box thirty yards away gradually brought me back to reality. I'd been off in some kind of dream world a million miles from the golf tournament that Saturday morning. As I stood by mindlessly chipping a few golf balls onto the practice putting surface, I had to think for a moment where I was.

I looked around and didn't see anything that surprised me. It was a typical golf event. Off in the distance was a huge lake...so large the opposite shoreline could not be seen though the golf course was high on a bluff. The lake was unrecognizable. I was certain I'd never traveled in the area previously.

Still, everything else was so familiar. There was the one-story, rectangular clubhouse overflowing with tournament golfers and volunteers, the parking lot filled to capacity with more vehicles haphazardly parked up and down the roadway outside the golf course entrance, the tent covering the huge blank scoreboard in case it rained, the volunteer announcer enjoying his day in the shade under that same tent, the spectators roaming around with nothing to do until the competitors finally teed off, the smells of coffee, bacon and sausage seeping out the screened windows from the clubhouse kitchen, and of course the nervous contenders....a huge assortment of them...anxiously waiting for their foursome to be called. These so-called competitors were occupying their time by practice putting, nervously chatting with friends, or simply standing alone hoping whatever work they'd done the previous week on their game would pay off with a respectable round of golf by day's end.

Slowly the realization of where I was began to get clearer. I was so unfocused. The last week I'd been particularly tired. I'd been pushing myself through an inspiring but tiring previous couple months and just lately I hadn't been able to re-start my engines as quickly as I had in all prior weeks.

Then I saw the sign above the clubhouse entrance saying 'Lake Lindsay Golf Club'. That logo along with the large throng of spectators clapping for yet another player being introduced at the first tee box finally lifted the fog from my brain. I was seeing the same picture around me that I'd seen every weekend since the first week of June. Since returning home from my first year of college, I'd come to expect this scene each Saturday morning. The gallery was welcoming the group of golfers who would be playing in front of my foursome. I was but ten minutes from teeing off on the first nine holes of the annual two-day Lake Lindsay 54-hole golf tournament.

As planned, this was my ninth straight weekend of competing in a golf tournament. So far it had been a great summer. I'd played and competed better than I had reason to expect. I'd not only enjoyed the challenge of competing against the best golfers in the area, but I'd been finishing in the top five each weekend with a tie for first three weeks before. In the process I'd met a lot of nice people and was proving to myself that goals and hard work can pay off in various other ways than just competing.

This tournament, though, was different. I wasn't feeling right. In fact, I was wondering why I was even standing on the Lake Lindsay golf course. A week before I hadn't even heard of the place much less knew there was a golf event scheduled.

But, there I was with a golf club in my hand breathing in the fresh morning air and unfortunately being in kind of a stupor. I was not feeling the usual excited anticipation. I'd felt the lethargy even as I'd driven the two-and-a half hours to the tournament location the prior night. There was a point about half way to Lake Lindsay that I questioned whether I should just turn around and return home. I felt no eagerness…no enthusiasm about playing in the event…only a desire to take a break from my single-minded routine.

But, I'd continued on even though this golf event at Lake Lindsay bore no real significance. I just had this deep need…this obligation to see how good I could be as a competitive golfer each weekend. I could only be tested in tournament competition. To not participate would be turning my back on the commitment I'd made to myself at the start of the summer.

The drive had been long. I'd fought sleep the entire way. Upon arrival at the golf course Friday night, I had less than an hour to get a feel for the course and practice before sundown. I'd ended up eating a good supper about 10:00 at a lakeside restaurant. Then I parked my car back at a secluded area near the golf course, unpacked my sleeping bag and fell asleep in my mobile motel…my station wagon…the moment my head hit the pillow. It was before 11:00. What followed was a good nine hours of sleep.

I awoke rested but still void of energy. It crossed my mind that I was ill. The tiredness I'd been feeling from my previous two months schedule was not going away. Typically my week ended with me arriving home very late Sunday night after a golf tournament and then rising very early the next five mornings to work my summer job. I was aware I might get worn down. Up to the previous week, I'd always survived and regained my zeal at least by Tuesday. After all, I was young and used to late nights with little sleep.

However, that typical recovery by the Tuesday before the Lake Lindsay golf tournament didn't happen. I'd never felt fully rested. It was a different form of fatigue…more apathy than drowsiness. Even my evening practice sessions at the local golf club were done half-heartedly. Physically I felt all right; mentally I was not concentrating well.

I didn't want to admit it, but possibly my vigorous daily schedule for the past nine weeks had finally caught up to me. I didn't have the resolve or the freshness I'd had at the beginning of the June. It wasn't as if I hadn't been warned. A couple friends cautioned me about taking a break. I'd just ignored them. That morning, however, the way I was feeling was proving them right.

I thought back to May. What started out as an innocent sort of personal challenge just weeks before completing my final college tests had turned into what best could be described as an obsession. The only real obligation I had was to work a forty-hour summer job to earn additional money for college expenses. I'd calculated there were one hundred twenty-eight hours a week remaining to do as I pleased. While I had to apportion some of those hours to eating and sleeping, it weighed on me that I could waste that additional time or maybe I could be more productive.

The idea just kind of percolated throughout that spring. Prior to entering college, I had displayed some noticeable and proven golf talent as a high school player. Mostly, though, I considered myself a nonentity...an unknown as a competitive amateur tournament golfer. Since starting school the previous fall, I'd rarely picked up a golf club. Over the winter while adapting to college life, golf wasn't even on the radar. That spring, however, what had been natural for the eight previous years seemed to be calling out to me. Competing in golf had brought me some mild success; now I missed that part of my life.

In early May I found myself drifting out to the college golf course a few times just to hit some practice balls. However, with no real goal, the practice sessions held no real purpose.

As the summer break drew closer, the notion to resurrect whatever skills I might still have in my dormant golf game became a daily preoccupation. It ate at me that I shouldn't let something I'd shown some talent simply fade away.

Eventually that thought wave became a fixation. What transpired was not just to answer some whimsical need to play the game, but a personal challenge requiring even more effort and commitment. I wanted a purpose...something that could be done in conjunction with my weekday summer job. When I was not working...and eating or sleeping, I wanted to focus every evening on unflinching practice in order to raise my skill level.

I wasn't certain I'd be able to continuously treat the challenge seriously. I figured the first couple weeks would dictate how important the challenge was to me. It was during those last two weeks of May that I saw a calendar of golf tournaments around the state. There were a number of events each weekend in various parts of Minnesota from the first of June through the end of September. Entering some of those tournaments would give me more purpose and help me assess whether the work on my game was paying off.

When my final tests were completed in late May, my motivation was high. I could think of no reason not to support my impulse. The timing for such a commitment was ideal. I had no other responsibilities except those forty hours per week obligated to a summer job. I had no girlfriend to turn my head. I had a local golf course just down the road from my folk's home available to me for practice. Pre-set one or two-day amateur weekend tournaments could be scheduled every week near enough to where I would be living that summer.

As I planned out my weekend venues for June and July, the tournament schedule fell into place with but one minor glitch. There was no weekend event being held within a reasonable distance of my home on the last weekend of July. Then August would continue giving me more choices of weekend tournaments to enter closer to my home town.

At first I was bothered by not having an end of July event. A voice in the back of my mind, though, suggested that after nine straight weekends maybe a break in the middle of the summer would be warranted. That free weekend might give me a breather I might need especially with some bigger golf tournaments coming up in August right through Labor Day weekend.

Still, that voice didn't convince me altogether. My aim over the three summer months was as much a challenge to stick to a well laid out plan as it was to improve my golfing skills and my ability to compete. I wanted it to be a rigorous and repetitive daily effort…the summer job during the day, practicing each evening, and competing each and every weekend. Work, practice, and competition… work, practice, and competition…and so on. I expected there would be times I might feel fatigued from the vigorous day-to-day program, but that was part of the challenge. I wanted to observe how I handled any kind of obstacle.

To some, my actions looked and sounded not only obsessive, but even tedious. At the start of June, I had my doubts as well. Could I hold this commitment through September?

Initially, just practicing gave me hope. I still had remnants of a decent golf game. Luckily, there would be little boosts along the way that would keep me motivated. I didn't have a goal or belief that I could win any of the golf events I entered over those three months. All I hoped for was the chance to see some noticeable improvement in my game.

Through the month of June I adhered to my blueprint for the summer as if it was a mandate on my future. No doubt the key to following my self-inscribed summer challenge was the fun I was having. I enjoyed every minute of the evening practice sessions and the preparation for those weekend tournaments. I did not have the same constructive feelings about the summer job. It was monotonous. However, that daytime work was of course integral to the whole challenge. Whether I enjoyed the day time job or not didn't matter. It was part of the deal.

So, what started out as a lark…just something to do that summer with some purpose…turned into a pre-occupation. In looking back on that period in my life,

I can't exactly explain why I so resolutely abided by that day-to-day itinerary…but I did. Had I not achieved some noticeable results could my resolve have wavered? That question has always been moot. After the first week of practice and that first weekend golf event, any doubt never came to mind.

I still look back on that time period with great appreciation. I learned how a good work ethic combined with passion can produce some amazing results. Passion might not always be there with every endeavor even if a strong work ethic is. I was just fortunate to have had both ingredients that summer.

Frankly I was stunned what I'd been able to achieve during June. That I'd beaten anyone in the Championship flight that first weekend came as a nice surprise. By the end of June after tying for first in a weekend tournament in Windom, Minnesota, I truly valued the results of my incessant practicing and weekend competitions.

Though I'd lost in a playoff on the last weekend of June, my confidence was bolstered. If anything my obsession became maniacal as I adamantly continued my weekly schedule of 'work, practice, compete…work, practice, compete'. For a guy who thought his competitive golfing days were over once he went to college, I was experiencing something I hadn't thought possible.

In early July, my weekend tournament results continued to be gratifying. In those first three July weekend tournaments, I came close to winning in all three including another tie for first. I just hadn't risen over the hump of actually winning. I looked ahead to that 'free' weekend in late July with more anguish. I so wanted another chance to compete and carve out a win.

Acquaintances at work and my friends at the local golf club kept kidding me about my fanaticism. They compared me to a robot…or a machine that never got tired. I could see the humor, but I wasn't about to change. Going back to school in the fall would come soon enough. That would end my fanatical routine anyway. I just kept on repeating what had been working for me…the daytime job, followed by playing golf and practicing every evening, and then traveling to a tournament on Friday night not to return home until later Sunday night. I countered their jesting by challenging them to join me. I didn't get any takers.

I never took the idea seriously that I could actually get tired…mentally tired… until I was driving home the second to the last weekend in July. That was the tournament I'd lost in another playoff. I was disgusted. I was also fighting sleep all the way home over the one hundred eighty mile return trip. So fixated had I become I couldn't accept that exhaustion could interrupt something I so thoroughly enjoyed.

That was why once I'd learned of that heretofore unknown golf tournament in Lake Lindsay only a week before the event, I knew I would be there. I'd committed to competing every weekend. I wouldn't feel right stopping the process. Though it was outside my acceptable travel radius, not competing would be disrespecting the very plan I'd laid out for the summer. I had a couple days to decide, but by Tuesday I'd made the decision. Wednesday morning I called. The

Lake Lindsay golf tournament had two openings remaining. I immediately took one of them. My obsession had taken over my sanity.

Now Saturday morning my insatiable thirst to compete was not spurring me onward in the least. I was just going through the motions of warming up. I wasn't used to being so unmotivated…especially moments before tee-off. I was so far from home. No one knew me. Whether I scored well or not hardly mattered. I was just another name trying to win a relatively obscure golf tournament. It would likely be a very long ride home Sunday night. Without my usual motivation, I'd be irritated for my lackluster play. I'd be angered that I'd let golfers with less ability but more spunk beat me. There I stood…disgusted… and I hadn't even hit my first shot in the tournament.

A hollow-sounding public address system interrupted my negative thoughts and announced my name along with three other players whose names I was unfamiliar to check in at the registration table near the tee box. There I would learn of any peculiarities or special rules pertaining to the golf course. Again this was standard. I'd experienced the exact same thing for nine straight weekends. Even the voice on the microphone sounded the same. It would be within minutes after shaking hands with my fellow competitors in my foursome that we would be individually introduced to the sparse gallery before embarking on a fifty-four hole marathon over two days.

In all previous tournaments that announcement would have been an automatic spark to get any player's competitive juices flowing. If there was no feeling of some nervousness or excitement upon hearing one's name being called, there should be a question why the player even showed up for the tournament. That question was hitting me squarely in the face.

I knew every other golfer approaching that first shot off the tee box would have some level of anxiety. That morning I didn't share that feeling. A golfer's unease would invariably be related to how confident he was about his game. Some players unraveled having to display their lack of golfing talent in front of so many people.

In my case after nine straight weeks of uninterrupted evening practice and tournament competition, my efforts and results had earned me some self-assurance about the quality of my game. My nervousness in the first tournaments of the summer had given way to a resolve to shoot well and an impatience to get play underway.

Picking up my golf bag, my only wish was that I'd gain some mysterious shot of adrenalin that might suddenly spur my interest in this out-of-the-way golf tournament. As I ambled over to the registration table by the first tee box, my daydreaming continued. The entire scene was so familiar and repetitive. I kept taking note of the common threads from this event to all previous tournament venues. So prevalent were the numbers of stone-faced golfers deep in thought worried about the health of their golf game and silently praying to play their best. Even the followers of these golfers showed some level of angst. Either they remained deathly quiet or they were constantly offering reassurances to their favorite player. I felt I was in a newsreel depicting all past golf events I'd attended.

I looked over and saw a man steeped in self-importance holding a clipboard. Without a second thought, I knew he was the tournament chairman just by the way he imperiously acted and the way various volunteers surrounded him. He had concern written all over his face that something might go wrong. Yet, he loved every minute of being in charge.

I then noted the announcer sitting in front of his microphone with his wide posterior overlapping the folding chair. I swore it was the same guy announcing at all previous events. There were the seemingly same women volunteers offering sweet rolls and coffee for the early morning competitors. The players were exchanging kidding remarks with the ladies to show their coolness before facing the battle that day. I rolled my eyes watching these same players wolf down the ideal food and drink items to make them even jumpier before teeing off.

I smiled knowing that the fellow with the wild shorts had to be one of the bankers in town. It had been explained to me in one of my previous tournaments how a banker was the only man in town with the money to buy the shorts and the guts to wear them in public.

Two nervous local kids wearing their local high school colors were standing with some of their buddies. Every tournament had a couple fresh-faced, inexperienced 'youngsters' likely having been on the high school golf team and now just graduated. For the first time they were eligible to compete in their hometown annual golf tournament. They'd played their home course thousands of times, but this would be the round they'd remember forever. They tried to look cool, but their eyes deceived them.

Yet another very serious thirtyish-looking skinny fellow remained off by himself trying not to let anything or anyone bother him while he prepared to tee-off. His limited tournament experience had told him this was the only way to prepare. And yet a few other competitors attempted to ward off their own nerves by talking about the condition of the golf course with each other...as if that factor might keep them from scoring well. I'd seen all these players so many times in past tournaments.

My eyes then panned over to the many spectators waiting for play to begin at the first tee box. They were also so recognizable. Wives or girlfriends of players would show different levels of interest. Some would stand close to their favorite player. Others would be sitting on the patio of the clubhouse either too nervous or too bored to be near their mate. Still others were at the golf course for their own good time. It was a place to see other women friends and have coffee together. The tournament was just a different setting other than the downtown coffee shop or at one another's home.

Except for my uncommon listlessness about the tournament, I found myself chuckling over the entire scene around me. Why was I seeing so many of the same individuals at this faraway weekend golf tournament? It was as if these people had all caught the same bus to Lake Lindsay from the other golf events I'd participated. Their shapes…their antics…their wardrobe…their behaviors… were all the same. The only thing different was their faces.

Working my way through the crowd around the first tee box, I could only hope my pride would compel me to concentrate. I'd never played half-heartedly in any tournament and I was upset how this could be the first time. The atmosphere around me was more spirited. I held out hope that I might catch some of the liveliness before I teed off. In all likelihood, I could sense I was in for a long, disappointing weekend.

Standing there not paying attention to the foursome in front of my group being introduced, I searched for anything that might provide me some motivation, even something that may never have inspired me in the past. One obscure thought momentarily piqued my thoughts. Maybe this event could be used as another kind of test. Certainly there'd be other times in my life whether on a golf course or not where I might not be enthused about taking on a challenge or an obligation. This could be a trial to see whether I had the mental fortitude to overcome my indifference. I allowed that faraway impulse to bounce around in my mind in order to see if it was worthy of some consideration. I had an immediate sense I was really stretching to find any real purpose for my being at Lake Lindsay.

I was desperate. I had to have some kind of impetus or I doubted I could hold my game together that day. Something had to provoke me or supply me the shot of energy I needed to at least care about my score. If I could get over that hurdle and finish the first day with a competitive score, the second and last day of the tournament would take care of itself. If I was within a few shots of the lead, how could I not be spurred to play well on the final day of the event on Sunday?

The logic was sensible. What was going to stimulate my interest was not at all clear, especially with seemingly everything but golf catching my attention that Saturday morning. My eyes were darting from one non-golf related thought to another. I found myself staring unceasingly at the dazzling view of the lake looming below the bluffs of the golf course. Also, I was more cognizant of the birds chirping, the squirrels scrambling from tree to tree, the butterflies landing on the pretty flowers alongside the tee box, and the familiar antics of the people surrounding the tee box. Usually I'd be standing there stretching my neck and upper body in anticipation of teeing off. I'd be taking note of any kind of wind as I prepared to play. Instead I was feeling the beauty of the lake breeze churning up those bluffs, closing my eyes as I listened to the wind swishing through the oaks, elms, and pine trees on the slope. The smells were so robust…so fresh… and so peaceful. I sensed I could either be a very attentive spectator that day…or I could lay under one of those trees and sleep for the next four hours.

The crowd applauding one of the player's tee shots startled me. I shook my head not believing how disinterested I was. In all past tournaments I might have noticed the lake view for a few seconds, but my focus would be on my golf game. I wouldn't be hearing the birds chirping or watching any squirrels skittering about. As for the breeze, I'd ordinarily consider it a warning sign of higher winds arriving later from the Dakota plains and how that would impact the golf course as the day progressed.

Again the staccato blare of the speakers rang out. The oversized man at the microphone introduced another player in the group that would be playing in front of my foursome. To me, his voice was only a minor interruption…an insignificant noise. Turning my attention to the golfers teeing off, they also were similar. Each one reminded me of other players in another part of Minnesota who I'd competed against in previous tournaments. Those observations then cued something that I normally didn't think about until well after the tournament got underway…or even later after the Saturday round of golf was completed. With the competition out of the way for that day, my mind would drift and I'd find myself observing people. My observations had created a little game. Watching various golfers and local people, I found myself categorizing them by the way they behaved or dressed…or even by their golf swing. I wasn't doing it maliciously; it was just that I recognized so many similarities in local people and players from town to town. It was just an innocent mental exercise to lull away the slower times in any tournament.

At times I even took these observations onto the golf course. I liked to spot certain types of golfers by the way they swung the golf club, how they conducted themselves, and how they played in the local tournament. That summer I'd come up with some very descriptive logos for various distinctive golfers. It was fun. I was amazed how often the names I'd placed on some of these players or local citizens were descriptions that proved surprisingly accurate from town to town, tournament to tournament.

What was disconcerting at that moment was that I was already playing my little people and player observation game…and the day had just begun. It only showed how disinterested I was in playing a golf tournament that morning.

The foursome playing in front of my group was just leaving the tee box and I focused on each of them. Quickly forming an impression of each one… the way they dressed, the way they walked, even their behavior as they trudged forward down the fairway…showed me nothing noteworthy. In this group, no mannerisms or quirks really stood out. None of them typified the labels I'd categorized certain golfers I'd seen in the past. They were all just very ordinary golfers who would likely be very nice people to play golf with at any time.

My mind flashed back to some of the types of golfers I'd characterized in past tournaments. There were some distinctive individuals who were so easy to spot. Every tournament had at least one golfer with the ability to be a contender, but alcohol had eroded his skills. There were plenty of boozed up golfers with little ability, but it was that former champion type of competitor who I found interesting to watch when alcohol could be used either as an excuse or crutch. This golfer likely no longer worked very hard on his game and he knew there was a good chance he'd only embarrass himself out on the links. Some of this variety of golfer would become inebriated as the tournament ensued based on the quality of his play that weekend. I titled this kind of player as logically 'The Drunk'. I sought side bets with him whenever I could, since he would fold up like a well-used accordion when the going got tough. He'd likely be carrying a beer in his bag in anticipation of his predictable downfall sometime during the heat of the round.

Another golfer routinely playing each week at the town's annual tournament was the 'Starry-eyed Kid'. He was the local young star who was playing in his town's yearly golf tournament for the first time. This kid could be recognized at any club because the local members would be whispering too loudly how this young man was the next golfer to replace Jack Nicklaus. As a result this unfortunate kid felt the pressure of the community on his shoulders. The tournament was supposed to be the place he would show his true abilities. It was the most important time of his life up to that point, possibly including his birth The self-imposed pressure he placed on himself was tantamount to self-suffocation. Feeling nerves he'd never felt before, the 'Starry-eyed Kid's' chances of playing golf anywhere near his capability was implausible. With this building stress, his demise in the tournament could often happen as early as his first shot of the tournament when his opening tee shot would go so far out of bounds a collective gasp would echo across the entire golf course.

Another stereotype I saw at each town was the peevish, petulant local golfer. I called him 'Father Grim'. He never smiled on the golf course and he watched for rule infractions as if he'd written the book. It was truly unlucky to be paired with this guy. He was unfriendly, obnoxious, and rarely shot well in a tournament. He was so busy concentrating on everyone else's actions for possible rules violations that he had little time to pay attention to his own game. I always thought this guy's idea of winning a golf tournament was to be the only competitor left standing after everyone else had been disqualified for possible breach of the rules.

The golfer I was always seeking out in each town where I competed was the local hero. There was always one and sometimes two or three of this example. He might be the natural golfer who simply didn't have time to play or practice, but somehow did well. That local hero was rare. Most common was the local hero who was expected to do well by his friends, neighbors and fellow club members. He was used to the local acclaim and generally performed well in men's day matches and local club events. In the big annual town tournament with so many good golfers entered from other golf clubs, too often the local hero would eventually succumb to the pressure.

Yet another type of player showing up at every weekend tournament was the well-dressed and unfortunately often egotistical golfer from the private country club from the big city…in this case, usually the Twin Cities. He would be playing in the local tournament because he had a friend who lived in the town and invited him to play or his wife grew up in the town and the two of them were ostensibly visiting family. Whatever brought him to that tournament, he had a built in disdain for the relatively rough terrain of the local nine-hole golf course compared to the manicured links of his private country club. For this particular private club player, the one trait that seemed to be common was his constant complaining. Since the rural golf course could never measure up to his private club standards, this player would be frustrated and angry most of the weekend.

Finally, one other player I invariably saw each weekend was the complete opposite of that supercilious private country club golfer. This person was the grizzled veteran who had played in these weekly golf tournaments in the area since the beginning of time. His lesser golf ability did not give him much of a chance to win, but his compulsive interest in the game kept him signing up wherever the next weekend golf tournament was to be held. His aim at each event was not to win, but to play in a flight of golfers composed of poorer players like him. That way he had a greater chance of driving home on Sunday night with some kind of prize. I glanced back toward the practice green filled with golfers. I had no doubt there were a couple of these battered soldiers standing on that green getting ready to tee off when their names were called.

The announcer's voice calling my foursome to the tee box ended my trance. I could evaluate local players later and place them in categories if I wished. Right then I had to answer the call whether I was keen on playing golf that morning or not.

I absent-mindedly slipped through the crowd to make my presence known as a member of the upcoming group. Stepping onto the slightly elevated tee box where no one but the golfers and the starter were allowed, I felt the crowd's stare. It was more a glower. In all past tournaments I'd gotten to know so many people whether golfer or spectator. I'd normally acknowledge them with a wave or nod. These were people I'd be seeing later in the bar, sharing some laughs, and having dinner with in the evening.

At this Lake Lindsay tournament, it was as if I was in a foreign land. I knew no one. There were a lot of disapproving faces since I was such an unknown. When my name and hometown were eventually announced, their scrutiny was even more intense. My town was located far enough away that the crowd generally exhibited a countenance that I shouldn't be trusted. So, having never competed in that part of the state, there was no doubt I was the 'foreigner'.

It was then that the three other golfers in my group presented themselves on the first tee box. I'd of course never heard of them much less seen them before. Immediately, however, I noticed something about each of them. I couldn't put my finger on it. Maybe I had seen one…or two…of them somewhere else. But, I couldn't imagine where that might have been.

Suddenly I had a funny feeling. I found myself not able to take my eyes off of them. I became preoccupied with their actions and mannerisms…even their facial movements. I kept thrashing through my mental filing cabinet trying to re-construct where I might have played with each of them in the past. There was something about their behaviors…their style of clothing…that had me transfixed.

I tried to look away in an attempt to focus on my own game, but their antics continued to grab my attention. They were so distinctive. One of the players was blatantly narcissistic. It was the perfection in how he dressed himself that morning plus his grandiloquent movements in front of the crowd that made me snicker. He was prancing around the first tee box as if he was a movie star. His attire all matched perfectly down to his golf shoes. Even his golf bag and head covers coordinated with his clothing ensemble. He knew all eyes were on him…and he loved it. His only disappointment had to be that there were not more people in the gallery…or, that he didn't have a full length mirror to admire himself. I sighed resigning myself to the reality that I was going to have to put up with this man's ego the entire day. I had an inclination this player was a classic

Switching my eyes over to another member of my foursome, I studied him with more curiosity. He was silent and serious as a monk. Distinctive about this individual was his size. He looked like a giant compared to the folks around him. With the large entourage of people pressing close to feel his aura, it didn't take much imagination to realize this man had to be a local Lake Lindsay favorite. In that close-knit group of people around him had to be loyal family, friends and sycophants.

Again I just shook my head. There was no doubt this man was a local 'hero'. It would likely take me a few holes to watch him play before I could define what type of local star this guy might be. I'd played with or seen local 'heroes' with their over-excited support group every weekend. The commonality with all these local stars was that they were in their glory for at least a while. They weren't just nervous; they were tense. The circumstances and often their egos would make it difficult for them to interact with the other players in their foursome…at least until that local star figured if he was having a good day or bad day on the golf course. Gazing at this particular silent but strong-looking local hero, I was certain of one thing. If he said one word to me the entire day, I'd be surprised.

Finally my eyes jumped over to the third and final player in my foursome. He was hunched over smoking a cigarette almost camouflaged by the oak tree he was leaning against. He was dressed in dark, ill-fitting clothing with stained brown golf shoes. His sullen, discomfited look exhibited a man seemingly beaten by life but having nothing better to do than play golf.

It was logical his unsociable nature would make him ill-at-ease with the large crowd surrounding the first tee box. His only response to this temporarily uncomfortable situation was to stay as far away both mentally and physically from the tee box, concentrate on inhaling his cigarette as deeply as possible, and stare morosely down the fairway as if facing a firing squad.

I'd seen this type of golfer too many times to count. They weren't all the same in behavior…sometimes they were so quiet few words were spoken throughout the entire round of golf. More often, though, once out on the golf course, this prototype could camouflage his nervousness by talking constantly, oblivious to the cares or preferences of the other players in his group. He'd know all the hackneyed lines golfers spewed and would constantly repeat them in hopes his fellow golfers would find him witty. As I examined this scrawny man in his drab, unfitting clothing, I couldn't imagine him being verbal much less amusing. He appeared to have the personality consistent with the tree he was leaning against.

The spectacle of playing with three such obvious character types left me bemused and feeling not just unmotivated, but unlucky. After traveling so many miles and having little interest in playing, I was being rewarded with what looked like a very long, unpleasant day on the golf course. Conversation with my self-absorbed and predictable playing partners would be minimal. I scoffed and looked at the ground. I'd met so many fine people over the summer at the many towns. I surmised that good fortune was going to average out. I was due to play in a group composed of two duds and a local hero immersed in the glory perpetuated by his devoted followers.

Shaking my head, I turned away. I hoped my initial appraisal of my golfing mates was wholly inaccurate. However, it didn't look promising. I made a silent prayer that I might get an emergency call allowing me to escape from this golf day in hell. After all, I was still tired. I was still listless. Mostly, I was already impatient just to get the day over.

The starter then made his presence on the tee box for the purpose of bringing my foursome together for some rudimentary rule explanations and to give us a chance to introduce ourselves to each other. He first walked to the front of the tee box to wait for the foursome down the fairway to complete their second shots before turning back expecting my foursome to be gathered for his little speech. The delay was especially long giving me another chance to peruse the characters I'd be playing with that day. I was imploring the Almighty to make my initial impressions incorrect. Every second I looked at any of the three of them, though, I realized I was wasting a prayer.

The obvious local hero had his enormous group continuing to stand close as if he supplied the very oxygen they breathed. This large man with the huge shoulders and jutting jaw now reminded me of the picture of George Washington crossing the Delaware River. He had the same unblinking, icy look as he gazed solemnly down the first fairway. He paid no attention to the noise and activity surrounding him. He was in his competitive mode.

I spotted his caddy with little trouble. Experience told me the straggly-haired kid nervously wiping off one of the hometown favorite's golf clubs had one of the more important jobs on the golf course that day. A closer look indicated a slight similarity in facial structure between the teen-ager and the 'hero'. It ended there however. The kid had a string-bean build and was dressed sloppily. Nonetheless, the longing way he looked at the huge golfer next to him left no question that I was looking at the son of this probable hometown legend.

An average caddy would be shy and quiet in front of a man of such stature, but not when the kid was the golfer's son. He kept talking to his father to make the huge throng understand how imperative he was to his father's success that day. The big man showed patience with his off-spring…nodding his head but not listening. He wanted some space to be left alone, but the son being on stage with his father just couldn't read his father's non-verbal preference. There was such a difference between the two of them. The father was cool. The son was jumpy as if scared this one tournament could be the first time his father might not measure up to the heroics of his past. I had no doubt the faithful son would swallow golf balls whole if it meant his father would do well in this golf tournament.

Watching the entire scene unfolding around this player, I still had the same question I had every weekend when I saw a hometown hero. What was the true caliber of this player? This huge man looked like the real thing…that is, a golfer of some merit and skill. As mentioned, however, local heroes were so similar at the start of an event…and then they changed as the tournament progressed. All of them were edgy before teeing off, but desperately trying to look cool. Local heroes knew their hometown golf course better than any other tract of land except their lawn back at their house. Generally they could play the home course blindfolded and still score well. They were expected to do well…and that expectation was what made so many of these local stars overwrought. The town's invitational tournament would be, if not the biggest, then certainly the most important contest many of these local top golfers would play in all summer…and they would have to perform in front of all the folks in their community who thought them superlative. If that wasn't nerve-wracking enough, it was the one time that year they had to prove to themselves and their fellow club members they still had that old magic to win against strong out-of-town competition.

All eyes of the local community would be on these local golfing stars. As a result, the annual tournament had the potential to be the worst weekend of their summer. They lived in fear and apprehension of that one summer when they knew their former golfing skills were nowhere near what they once were. Time invested in their business life and their family responsibilities would understandably erode some of their prowess. Sensing this common eventuality, many local stars would eventually choose not to play in their home club's annual weekend tournament. They would be gone that weekend claiming a wedding or a family get-together had to take priority. The tournament had become something hostile…too much stress for something that was supposed to be enjoyable. They were expected to win; if not, they failed. Even winning second or third place might not be enough in the eyes of the locals.

For the local family-oriented stars who continued to play in the annual tournament, they faced the local hero challenge with some trepidation, but knew their family would love them no matter what they scored. They often could be picked out by the way they dressed. The young son often unfamiliar with golf would be there to pull his Dad's two-wheel golf cart and looking bewildered as to what he was supposed to do. The father with the ultra-white legs sticking out of his new plaid walking shorts the wife and kids had gotten him for Father's Day, would be taking smooth, athletic golf swings at leaves on the ground hoping something miraculous would help him find his game. This hero was no longer a serious competitor as he once was and it hardly mattered to him most days except during the weekend of the annual golf tournament. He knew in his heart a decent golf score was highly improbable. He just didn't want to humiliate himself too badly. It wouldn't be unexpected if he parked his car at the end of the parking lot just so he could quietly slip away from the club after a less than stellar day on the golf course. As far as his son caddying for him, the young man would still make his dollar for pulling his Dad's cart. This tournament was of no real importance to the young man.

But, there were other hometown stars who didn't want to face the potential misery knowing their skill level had declined. They preferred to blame it on something else. That was when the previously mentioned alcohol consumption idea could be conveniently utilized as a ready excuse for some poor scoring. Depending on the level of anxiety the local low-handicapper might choose to drink himself into unconsciousness the night before the tournament thereby later being congratulated that he scored as well as he did given his condition.

At times, however, getting plastered backfired on this type of local hero…at least for a while. I'd witnessed a few times the local star showing up the morning of the tournament so pickled from the previous night's drinking marathon he was actually numb. He felt too lousy to be nervous. He didn't expect to shoot a good score and had his ever ready excuse obvious for all to observe. However, as bedraggled as he might look, this type of local hero might experience one his luckiest rounds of golf ever. Putts would keep rolling in or close to the hole even though he couldn't see straight enough to line them up properly. Trees would spit his wild tee shots back onto the fairway. A water hazard would take on the characteristics of a street of asphalt causing the golf ball to skip back onto the fairway or onto the green. When those first nine holes ended, the hung-over local idol would wonder how anyone could think the game of golf was so difficult.

Unfortunately, there would be another nine holes to play after lunch that Saturday. During this short rest the adrenaline would drain from his system like a plug was pulled. As the golfer returned to consciousness, his world was suddenly a different place. His temples would throb so badly he didn't want to move for fear his head might fall off his neck. His energy level would drop precipitously. Any movement, including blinking, would make his eyes water and then blur.

Every sound echoed. Even the club head striking the golf ball made an annoying noise…like a jackhammer on pavement. The rotten taste in his mouth wouldn't go away. He swore something had died on the back of his tongue. This sensation would completely take away his appetite.

With little or no lunch, his condition would go from bad to worse. He would begin to sweat profusely no matter the temperature. On an extremely hot day this particular local 'hero' often would not be able to complete the second nine holes. For those hung-over heroes who were able to play the final nine holes of the day, the minutes on the course would seem like hours. The sensation of wanting to throw up would become so overpowering, he was afraid of losing his innards when reaching down to tee up his golf ball. Constantly parched, water would not quench his thirst. Fainting seemed to be a threat with each step.

In his afternoon round of golf, he would have his small entourage following him…not to cheer, but to be the emergency unit. There would be some husky men to pick the hero up if he keeled over. Three or four pot-bellied gentlemen were assigned to block this hero's view of the beer stand, and his wife or lady friend would be driving a cart holding a couple cases of ice for his head. Too often this golfer would heroically crawl off the last green of that second nine-hole round with a score resembling one of his first outings on a golf course as a kid. Still, as bad as that score was, when combined with his incredibly lucky first nine-hole score, the total was inspirational considering his condition. Though missing the championship flight cut and instead being in the lower satellite flight the next day, there would be no cause to change his strategy. He could drink himself into the ground that night at the clubhouse party…or not drink as much, recover and shoot a respectable round the next day when there was little pressure on him to perform. If that was the case, his local 'hero' status, though slightly tarnished, may even be maintained for another year.

And then there was a third type of hometown hero…the one who truly deserved the title and wore it with pride. The large man on that first tee box that Saturday morning had the look of a champion…a local legend of the highest standard. I suspected he'd been a tremendous athlete in his day and now with age and a family, golf was one of the few athletic endeavors left where he could show his competitive fervor. Frankly, the type of local 'hero' I was observing on the tee box looked like he could score the next touchdown even though it might have been fifteen or twenty years since he'd hung up his pads and cleats. The crowd around him kept using hackneyed phrases like "Go get 'em, Big Dave"… or "No one can touch you, Big Guy".

I guessed everyone around the clubhouse would be abuzz whenever this hero showed up at the golf course to play…even if it was to play nine holes with his wife on Tuesday night. If he was like other legitimate stars, the attention caused by this annual invitational golf tournament might get a bit onerous even for this man. I could imagine with each passing year he would consider not participating in the event for no other reason than to lower people's expectations. He knew the level of his game was not what it used to be, but on any given day he could play with the best of them, even though his best competitive golf was behind him.

However…deep down…a hero of this ilk really wanted to play in the tournament…but only if he could perform to the high standard he'd always achieved in the past. As each year followed, the aches and pains…and the practice required to maintain his skill level…would eat at him. With each birthday, not only would he have some doubts about his proficiency, but uncertainty would also creep into the heads of his ever faithful local fans. They wouldn't say it, but they'd nervously shiver while thinking 'Is he still good enough to win?'

If he could win…or at least gain second place…the weekend tournament would have served its purpose. He would re-establish his athletic competency and place himself on the local 'best athlete' pedestal for another year. In the short time I had to evaluate this man that Saturday morning, everything pointed to 'Big Dave' being the best example of a hometown hero.

I turned away from the local star to unfortunately cast my eyes once again on the obnoxious showman. I'd had the label on this category of golfer from long ago. He could be spotted in seconds. All big city golfers weren't like this man, but there were enough of them to earn a not so flattering description. I branded this variety of golfer the 'City Slicker'.

This particular golfer was nattily dressed with a bright apricot sweater, matching pants and golf shoes. He also maintained a theatrically ferocious, even comical, look of superiority on his face. He continued to saunter around the tee box as if modeling his attire. He stopped for a moment by his extra-large golf bag to grab a cigarette. After lighting it, he then stood up tall, his only movement being his right hand taking his cigarette out of his mouth…very slowly. He gave the first green over three hundred yards away his most intimidating stare. Snapping the ash of his cigarette onto the fresh grass, he slowly exercised his head and neck. He gauged that everyone in the crowd around the tee box that morning wished they were him.

This fellow was hardly a challenge to recognize. I knew his sense of superiority would keep him from looking me in the face…especially someone of my age. I was not at his level…culturally, socially, athletically…nothing. To him, I was a speck of dust. He wouldn't remember my name until the end of the afternoon and then only if I shot well.

I remembered so well this type of golfer when I was a kid caddying in my hometown annual golf tournament. The 'City Slicker', even then, had always been the term my friends and I used to refer to this kind of golfer. It wasn't complimentary then, and the intent of my definition hadn't changed. That Saturday morning, central casting could not have sent over a better prototype. He would undoubtedly have little patience for anything less than perfect conditions. Otherwise, his ability to play well would be seriously compromised.

I wondered how soon it would take this 'City Slicker' to begin complaining about the condition of the Lake Lindsay golf course. Rural area golf courses usually had a few holes that were a bit trickier that only local knowledge would understand where the bounce or roll might take their golf shot. That local knowledge of these country golf courses could be worth a one or two shots per nine holes. Also, the golf course could not be kept up to the costly standards of an expensive private club in the city. The rural greens were always just a bit smaller and slower. Balls rolled inconsistently. Fescue rough was unevenly mowed. The sand in traps might be at inconsistent depths.

As a result of these factors, unlucky breaks could happen to anyone, but especially to this very sensitive type of player. At the first bad bounce, the 'Slicker' would begin mumbling how the golf course was in no condition to have a tournament. If misfortune continued, his frustration would become more vocal. He could be heard saying how he would never return to the rinky-dink small town golf course again. Most locals nodded their heads hoping he'd live up to that threat.

Experience had told me that this player could easily be baited for a side bet. If I suggested a small wager...like $5.00 for nine holes for the afternoon round, I knew his ego would prevent him from not taking the bet. The situation was totally to my advantage. His predictably poor behavior would put him at a decided disadvantage. I looked at the money I won from these city slickers as a donation. I was good, but coupled with their expected anger and frustration ... well...it was like taking candy from a baby.

The sun poked out from behind a cloud brightening up the entire landscape as my attention moved again over to that last member of my foursome, that is, the man who was camouflaged by the tree truck. I really wasn't certain if he was a player or just a sullen caddy. He seemed so gloomy...and truly uncomfortable being around so many people. He'd blended so well against the backdrop of tree bark. Finally moving away from the large tree next to the first tee box, I could see he held an old driver in his hand. He was definitely a player in our foursome.

Immediately I felt sorry for the guy. Just the way he carried himself, I knew he had neither the game nor the confidence to play very well...and certainly not skilled enough to be a true competitor in this tournament. As he fumbled for a cigarette in the chest pocket of his worn golf shirt, there was no doubt I was seeing yet a third designation of weekend tournament player. In fact, except for this faraway tournament, I'd seen the same guy with the same attire at each previous tournament. This guy was only unfamiliar because he had a slightly different face. Why had I been uncertain? I'd seen this type of golfer not only through the summer, but for years before as a kid while caddying. This man profiled everything I never wanted to be. He was the fidgety sort...smoking his cigarette like it was his last one...his eyes jumping around like he was about to shop lift a candy bar. Being near him was discomfiting.

On that radiant summer day he was dressed in a drab, unfitting, and clashing dark green shirt and greenish-tan pants…like the ones you buy at the farm supply store for outdoor yard work. It could be one-hundred degrees and this man would be wearing that outfit including the dog-eared hat with the worn decal of some obscure golf club in the area or of a brand of crop fertilizer.

Yes sir…I was familiar with this player profile. He was one of those grizzled veterans. His summer life for decades had revolved around these weekly golf events. What he did on the weekends during the winter months was anyone's guess. He probably just thought about golf.

In getting to know various golfers of this kind, I often admired how so many of them…though unskilled…held an unspoken feeling that victory…someday and somehow…was possible. Truthfully, it would have to be one of those days when God was looking the wrong way. That golfer simply hoped to be playing in a tournament when that miracle might occur and God was preoccupied with something more important.

Despite playing in so many weekend tournaments, this ageless sportsman still displayed the pre-tournament nervousness before teeing off despite sensing no miracle was in the offing that weekend. He'd faced this reality so often that it wasn't a huge disappointment. He would automatically reconcile that his best shot at winning some kind of prize that weekend was missing the cut in the championship flight. The next day he'd be competing in the loser's bracket where there was no pressure and he would be contending with others of similar lower level talent. True veterans like this man would have a record of winning the secondary or 'satellite' flight at these events a number of times.

My friends and I while caddying back in our boyhood days sarcastically called this variety of golfer the 'weekend warrior'. That nickname had stuck in my mind and had become a weekly observance. The profile of this player offered quite a contrast…as in a Jekyll or a Hyde. I'd met warriors who were the nicest people. On the other hand, they could be irascible and classless. My boyhood friends and I had little respect for the latter type of 'warrior'. He usually had a poorly manufactured golf swing that would break down in any kind of stressful situation. Mostly, though, this ornery type of weekend warrior just seemed to dislike kids. He called us all 'son' as if we were too low in social class to have a name. We'd never caddy for a bastard like him unless desperate for some spending money.

That Saturday morning, I unfortunately calculated which type of tournament veteran I was facing without so much as another consideration. Just by his surly, self-doubting expression and bearing, I had him pegged. My only consolation was that I wouldn't be playing with this fellow the next day. He would not be qualifying for the Championship Flight by the end of Saturday. His very posture told me he was an also-ran. He'd be teeing off early the next morning in the 'satellite flight' with the other golfers who'd made the worst scores after the first day of the tournament.

Nonetheless, I had my assigned group. That day I would have to play with this sullen 'Weekend Warrior'…along with the ego-maniacal 'City Slicker'…and the cold, dedicated and silent 'Hometown Hero'. I looked skyward wondering what I had done wrong in the last week to deserve such misfortune.

My negative thoughts were mercifully interrupted when the tournament chairman and starter asked the four of us to gather around him on the tee box. He was ready for us to begin. After welcoming us to the Lake Lindsay golf course, he quickly related some of the unique rules pertinent to their local golf course. Then, as customary in the gentlemen's game, the four of us were expected to give each other a cursory handshake and even a routine comment like 'good luck' or 'play well'.

As I shook hands with each of them, even that perfunctory action was foreseeable.

This Hometown Hero shook my hand firmly with no emotion showing on his face. His eyes glared at me as if sizing me up in less than two seconds for what level of competitor I might be. He mumbled something that sounded like 'play well' but I wasn't certain. Then his gaze returned to the challenge in front of him. There was something about him that I neither liked nor disliked…but I found myself respecting him. In no way was I intimidated, but I felt a burn inside me like a gas flame on a stove waiting to be lit. I wasn't going to let this guy and his partisan followers simply ignore my very existence.

The City Slicker had a quick, insincere handshake. He said nothing and his eyes never met mine. He held his hand out apparently to be shaken or kissed. I chose the former and wished him 'good luck'. He didn't hear me because he'd already begun moving back to re-establish his own staging area away from all of us. He seemed bothered that the introductions had caused the gallery's eyes to temporarily move away from him and his apricot ensemble. He got his wish as he stood to the side of the tee box alone so all eyes from the gallery could again return to his royal visage.

His every movement was followed with both dislike and awe. He held his chin high letting the wind blow through his perfectly coffered jet black hair. That flame inside me now burned more steadily. My only thought was that I'd be damned if I was going to let this obnoxious son of a bitch beat me.

As for meeting the Weekend Warrior, his handshake was like holding onto a recently expired eel. It was weak, slimy, and made me want to wash my hand off. His eyes met mine only briefly, but the glance was both diffident and spiteful. He mumbled something incoherent and then his eyes dropped to the ground. I'd met more confident people in kindergarten. One thing for certain, he didn't like anything about me. I obviously represented the youth he no longer had with the skill he'd likely kill to own. It was not daunting to me in the least since I'd run into the likes of him too often. My mode was to ignore him as best I could until the eighteen holes were completed.

While I didn't take notice right away, the one thing those introductions did accomplish was how my indifference had suddenly dissipated. My observations of my golfing mates that day created a smoldering in my stomach. Those looks and handshakes from all three of my playing partners had turned that burn into a flame. The irritation I felt being placed in the company of three such predictably unsocial and unpleasant characters was intense.

As I walked back to my golf bag to ready myself for play, I was no longer tired or disinterested. It was not unusual to play with one of these types of golfer in a tournament. To do so didn't bother me one way or another. I had my own game requiring my total concentration. However, this was the first tournament... and hopefully the last one...where I was being placed with three golfers who dramatically epitomized three of the more disagreeable and unfriendly categories of players I could define. As unpleasant as that entire prospect was, I'd just received a triple dose of motivation. I was not about to surrender to exhaustion or indifference.

I steeled myself as I got ready to be called to the tee box by the announcer. As I waited I could tell I was in a completely different mood than ever before in a competition. I was angry. I had no nervousness. Even the momentary 'butterflies in the stomach' were not in flight. My usual pleasant bearing was non-existent. If I had to be stern and unsmiling throughout the day with these jerks, then I'd survive the ordeal in that manner. Whether the annoying Weekend Warrior, the aggravating City Slicker, or the taciturn Hometown Hero and his large, biased following, they all would learn very quickly it wasn't easy to disregard me. I'd dealt with all three types of golfers too often to count...just not all at once.

The first man to lead off our group was logically the Hometown Hero. He actually had a name. It was Dave Lewis. But, I found that no one referred to him in such a common way. To the locals he was simply 'Big Dave'.

I would learn later this Hometown Hero was truly the real thing as my initial impressions had dictated. Like so many other local stars in other towns, 'Big Dave' owned a local business, a bulk oil business. Other local heroes I'd met in other towns typically owned businesses like a farm equipment repair business, a construction company, a dental practice, or an insurance agency. The independence these vocations offered gave some of them time to practice or play golf when they wished. Naturally more confident, they could become quite good, especially on their home turf.

I watched as 'Big Dave' made some minor comment to his close friends and relatives standing so close. They all dutifully laughed. His comment, whatever it was, was said as a ruse to make certain there was no question he had everything in hand. He also wanted to show them that in the off chance this could be one of those one-in-a-million days where his golf game was not at Grade A level, his joking around might help these followers realize that he had more important things in his life than playing in this golf tournament. The flaw in that allusion was that no one including this hero could name one other more important thing at that moment! This tournament represented a continuation of his local lore. No one wanted to witness, least of all this Hometown Hero, his dethroning. He really did not want his image as a local god to end unceremoniously on this golf course on this particular weekend at his tender age of thirty-nine.

I would find throughout that weekend folks talked of him as if Paul Bunyan was his little brother. 'Big Dave' looked like he could pick up the town's water tower and take a drink. Locals spoke of him with awe. He had been a star athlete at the community's high school many years before…and everyone guaranteed he would have done the same with the University of Minnesota football team save for a knee injury that cut short his potential star studded career.

He played every sport well. Rumor was that he took up golf and mastered the game after playing three times. He was purported to be the longest driver of the golf ball in the entire state. There was no way of authenticating either claim, but few people argued the point. This Hometown Hero was awarded the 'longest hitter' title simply because of his size. As I would learn that weekend…he could truly hit the ball a long way!

He carried himself with a pride and confidence that he had earned. Those that catered to his legend were always given a nod or slight wave of his hand. Otherwise, you were a piece a dust on his well-worn, off-white golf shirt with his local oil company logo displayed on the sleeve. Added to his calm, cool nature and his experience in knowing how to win, I was well aware of some additional factors that gave him an edge. He knew every bounce on the golf course and the speed and break of each green. There was no question this guy would be one of those I'd have to beat if I was to win this particular tournament.

As 'Big Dave' stretched one more time before taking the tee, I couldn't help but again appreciate his sizable entourage. The caddy…his son…tried to carry the highly confident look of his father, but his mien lacked his dad's depth and believability. I hoped the kid had other skills from his mother's side of the gene pool. It occurred to me how a hometown hero type of person would naturally have married the prettiest and sweetest girl in his high school class. She would have a kind, thoughtful disposition completely different from her dogged and determined husband. As nature took its course, the resultant offspring might have some of their father's athletic ability, but not necessarily his tenacious spirit and natural talent. In short, the son was just not the tiger his father was.

I'd seen these sons of hometown heroes often in my life on the golf course. 'Big Dave's' son was almost too predictable. Where his father wore his hair short completely ignoring the longer hairstyle of the time, the son had to show some individuality with the longer, completely unkempt locks. His attempt at sideburns and a beard were hilarious. The sideburns were composed of his hair growing long at the side of his head where his ears stuck out. The scraggily attempt at a beard or moustache represented about six months of not shaving. Whiskers were only visible when standing close to him. True to form, the kid wore cutoff jeans, a T-shirt with a cartoon figure emblazoned on the front, and a cap so dirty and worn, it looked older than the kid himself.

Whatever his differences with his father, that weekend the son envisioned his dad as a Greek god. The kid knew his father was about to unleash his natural ability, though the son was still nervous knowing a good score was not guaranteed. While he tried hard to ignore the possibility his dad might fail, just in case, the son showed an animosity toward any other player who might challenge his father. I was naturally in his vision. The son's glance over towards me was one of absolute enmity.

Then there were the key followers of this Hometown Hero. These bootlickers could have been high school friends or perhaps they worked for 'Big Dave'. In either case, they personified the words 'fanatical' and 'loyal'. It didn't seem many of them even knew the game of golf, but they were there to see their hero win.

There were two of these zealots who were most notable. One of them wore a very used farmer's cap with a battered decal of a type of corn seed. The guy looked like he slept in the hat. He gazed at the 'Hero' as if he'd take a bullet for the large man. This fellow was neither a golfer nor was he at ease at such a grand event. His eyes danced around like he was observing a different culture…and he didn't like anything he saw. He was only there to protect 'Big Dave' if any assassin tried to take the life of this Hometown Hero. The fixated and frenzied look on that man's face never altered. He was a bit scary.

The other very noticeable character was the sycophant in the more standard mode. If the Hero said something…anything…this guy laughed as if turned on and off like a light switch. He was quick to nod at anything his star said and gave the impression he perpetually needed to urinate. Everything the Hero said was witty. The bootlicker was half the size of the Hero and was as nervous and excitable as the big man was unruffled. If some dust particles from this Hero's successes blew his way, the twitchy guy's life would be fulfilled. The only difference this small man had over the others in the support group was that 'Big Dave' seemed to appreciate having this disheveled fellow worship his every move.

That summer I had been paired with various hometown heroes. In fact I felt I was playing with these types of fellows an inordinate percentage of the time. I had plenty of experience being disliked immediately by the followers whether the hero was the over-the-hill type, the drunk, or the legitimate competitor. Generally, that antipathy would fade as the weekend progressed; however, knowing no one at Lake Lindsay, I did wonder if the initial hostility towards me would ever wane.

At least considering my irascible mood, those cold stares from those folks surrounding 'Big Dave' hardly fazed me. I rationalized how much more of a threat to the local star I must be perceived since I was such an unknown factor. That I exhibited no concern or fear had to be especially galling.

There was one other dynamic that morning that also worked in my favor as far as the partisan crowd was concerned. I was not the only one in the group receiving the frosty glares from the gallery. With the unlikable City Slicker calling so much attention to himself, he would share some of the revulsion. This guy was particularly insufferable. I wasn't certain if the crowd would ever warm to this character.

As the Hero readied himself, all eyes turned toward him. In other cases, some local stars looked and felt totally exposed with so many people studying their every move. They could feel as naked as a sheared sheep. Their long-term reputation as a winning competitor was at stake. Some heroes would admit later they doubted they could have squeezed a guitar string out of their butt before they hit that first shot of the day.

But, this Hometown Hero showed no such apprehension. I could see he was special. As he bent over to tee his ball up, his joking had long subsided. He was slightly flushed. His followers around him showed signs of serious gas pains… many wishing they had some glue to hold their cheeks together. Their spectator game faces were as serious as their hero's expression. This was a very important day for them. They absolutely did not want to see their local champion fail.

As the large man addressed his golf ball, his entourage's icy stares continued back and forth between their Hometown Hero…and the other three opponents in the group. I watched as the muscles in his calves and arms became taut as he paused before taking the club back. Then the neck muscle bulged as he forcefully started his backswing. What ensued was a demonstration of controlled power I'd not seen often on the links. His downswing was not so much a whipping sound as it was a powerful wind causing an explosion when his clubhead made contact with the ball. The golf ball took off on a high, impressive trajectory that would more accurately be described as a 'launch'. As the ball shot its way into the crisp blue sky, it was startling to see a ball travel so majestically. There was both disbelieving laughter and silent awe in the crowd around the tee box after having just witnessed such a stroke. The response was similar from his fellow players…as the ball sailed straight and true…and so long! Respect for this man's game was immediate. 'Big Dave' calmly returned to his bag handing his driver to his caddy with no change of facial expression. Yes, this Hometown Hero was the real thing all right.

The City Slicker was introduced next…slightly bothered by the attention the Hometown Hero had pulled away from him. But, the Slicker was able to return the gallery's eyes back to himself almost immediately. His outfit had now become the talk of the crowd…just like he'd hoped. His perfectly pressed matching elastic waist-banded golf pants made him appear that he'd just stepped out of a magazine advertisement. He looked exquisite…and he knew it. What he took as wondrous stares, though, were also many disapproving reactions. Gallery members murmured to each other with pursed lips about his attire…as if he was wearing a swimming suit to church. They couldn't imagine being caught dead in such a flashy outfit much less buying it.

As I watched the Slicker pose on the tee box, I was really not looking forward to sharing the day with this particular stereotype. I could already hear his irritable and snappish comments about the golf course. At times this type of golfer could be quite entertaining given the colorful language he'd choose in making his points. However, this guy seemed so full of himself that I doubted he'd have much of a sense of humor.

I estimated it would be by the second or third hole upon failing to get his approach shot onto the green that he might begin to unravel. Because of slower greens on these rural courses compared to his private club greens, his chip or pitch shot would then invariably be short of the flag. Then his putt would also be short of the cup for the same reason. It would be the slower speed of the greens that would get him fuming. The next few holes he would try to make up for that bogie by attempting to overpower the rural golf course. That would further his undoing and add fuel to his wrath. He would swing harder, make more low percentage shots, and generally frustrate himself beyond repair.

At that point his disgust would be discerned by anyone within hearing distance of his angered shouts. This stereotype would unsparingly offer his repertoire of swear words against the golf course's greenskeeper…further decreasing his popularity amongst the locals.

I always marveled how a slicker's bad luck would solely and personally be caused by the ostensible horrible condition of the golf course. No other player, of course, had it tougher than the poor city slicker.

After his introduction, this City Slicker puffed out his chest, flicked his cigarette nonchalantly to the side, and finally teed up his glistening new golf ball. I would hear later of a remark by a volunteer that this Slicker had seen the winner's trophy in the clubhouse and inquired how much money he…as the winner of the tournament…got to spend in the clubhouse golf shop for being the champion. I should have given him credit for brash confidence, but that comment only made me want to beat him all the more.

As he slowly took his backswing, in no way was he going to unleash the power of the Hero's drive. Nonetheless, his swing was grooved with the numerous lessons he'd taken at his private club. He hit a respectable drive right down the middle of the fairway posing at his finish in case people had cameras. Quite frankly, I was impressed with the City Slicker's swing and his opening drive considering his interest appeared to be more that of a fashion plate than a golfer.

Ending his pose, his tee had flown forward about five yards as the ball had careened into the cloudless blue sky. The Slicker looked only momentarily at the tee now on the ground…and then scoffed at it. He lifted his head and paused as if giving himself a grade on the length and accuracy of his drive. As for the tee, it was beneath him to pick it up…even if the color of the tee did match his pants. Let it be a souvenir for someone in the gallery. He walked back to his golf bag and shoved his driver into his bag with a slight vengeance just to display to everyone what a tenacious competitor he was. It was all showmanship. For the moment his caddy looked at him with a reverence. That impression would fade as the young man got to know the personality and behavior of this City Slicker.

It was an unpleasant job caddying for any city slicker. The caddy would have to decide how desperate he was for money. An extra $1.00 per nine holes might be possible if the caddy could put up with the slicker's constant carping. After a day of listening to a 'slicker' whine about the golf course, the way the tournament was run, and the unfair conditions on each hole, another day for the caddy with this fellow would be tortuous. The caddy not returning for the final day of the tournament to face another day with this bore would not be a surprise.

My eyes slipped over to the third and last member of our group as he was about to be introduced. Even the name of the Weekend Warrior exemplified so perfectly his banal personality. His last name was 'Jones'…or 'Brown'…something forgettable. His first name was 'Harvey'. I tried to imagine Mr. and Mrs. 'Jones' or 'Brown' sitting down and deciding to name their new baby 'Harvey'. He had to have been one God awful looking baby to warrant a name like that on the day of his birth.

As that weekend progressed, I would find out that my generalizations about this man were so accurate it was spooky. He worked in city maintenance for a small town sixty miles up the road from Lake Lindsay. He had a wife but no children. If his wife ever showed up at one of these golf events, it was usually once a summer and only when the weekend tournament was scheduled at their community's public golf course. If she was like many warrior wives, she had little knowledge or appreciation for golf and little interest in learning anything about the sport. She'd competed and lost so often to her husband's preference for golf that people thought she was a widow. With little attention from her husband until the fall when the summer golf tournament schedule was completed, she hardly knew how to act or dress when she ventured out to the home golf club at their big annual tournament. But, she could be readily recognized for her bone white skin, her beehive hairdo, and her high heels.

It was a certainty that all weekend warriors disliked intensely having to play with a young guy like me. They would have their firm beliefs that youthful, 'whippy-wristed' golfers had no responsibilities and could play golf whenever they wanted. Younger golfers therefore had a decided advantage over the hard-working, five-day work week veterans. These warriors would show irritation to any young player who could beat him, at times even sneering at the young golfer's shots or playing little mental games to work on the youth's psyche…calling him 'Long Ball' or 'Big Hitter'.

These silly mental games were so obvious and so ineffective. Using the term "whippy-wristed" or calling the young golfer "the longest hitter he'd ever seen" hoping to induce the young golfer to swing even harder were generally met with disgusted looks from other golfers in the foursome no matter their age. It was such a classless and usually vain attempt to rattle the young competitor. Later in the bar the warrior would typically blame their inability to make the Championship flight cutoff by lamenting, "Yup...the kids who get to practice all the time beat up on the old guy again today."

I knew this particular Weekend Warrior was going to live up to my impression of him seconds after shaking that limp hand and noting the malevolent look in his squinty eyes. As I pulled my hand from his, I could sense he was already formulating some derisive comments to aim my way at the appropriate time. I had no regard for individuals like him. He didn't know anything about me other than I was young. It didn't matter if my normal golfing skill was hitting the ball long and crooked or short and straight...or what my past record was as a golfer. He just categorized me as someone he could psyche into disrupting the typical rhythm of my swing. If he could throw off my timing...by causing me to swing harder...and score poorer, then he'd be satisfied.

I tried to wipe away the smirk on my face as I turned away from him, but it was difficult. I felt contempt for him and we'd just met. I wondered if in the hundreds of these tournaments this 'Warrior' had played, had he ever gotten a charge out of just playing some really competitive golf, rather than focusing on ways to bother his fellow competitors. Did he ever enter a tournament anymore for that one time in his lusterless amateur golf career where he could play with the leaders...where he would not complain about his own lack of practice time and just enjoy being in the hunt for the top prize? I doubted it. If his game was what I thought it would be, his swing would not stand up to any kind of tournament pressure.

When the starter announced the Weekend Warrior as the next player on the tee, this veteran of many tournaments showed surprising discomfort...possibly because he had to follow two such visible and prominent players. He'd never experienced nor did he expect any support from the gallery.

Watching him tee up his ball and take a stiff practice swing, I calculated his average Saturday eighteen-hole score would be in the 80's. This would allow him to comfortably miss the Championship cutoff, yet easily be one of the leaders in the 'satellite' flight the next morning.

He held the cigarette in his mouth as he got ready to address the ball. Then he stepped away, inhaled deeply and threw the cigarette on the ground. He didn't even take a drag of the cigarette with as much class as the City Slicker. It wasn't part of his nature. Everything about this Warrior exhibited a lower stratum. There was no color to his personality...perfectly matching his dull wardrobe. His golf shoes were the hush-puppy type that looked better on the shelf than they did on. Shoes of this type were cheap and looked used after five minutes of wear.

Since his golf shoes had been through the tournament wars, they now looked more appropriate as old garage work shoes. As I took in his entire ensemble and image, I could only surmise this was how he desired his dreary life to be…never to stand out in any crowd. And, if that was his goal, he had to be very content.

Before describing the first shot of this Weekend Warrior at the Lake Lindsay Golf Tournament, a portrayal of the first fairway would be an important prelude. Each golfer faced a tight out-of-bounds along the left side of the fairway producing a host of emotions depending on the skill level of the player. The opposite side… the right side of the fairway… was wide open. Strangely for a lot of golfers, their first shot would surprisingly come very close to the penalty stakes on the left despite their determined aim to the far right side of the fairway. Nervousness can do odd things to a golf swing.

True to form, after flicking away his cigarette, this Weekend Warrior targeted his drive so far right away from the tight out-of-bounds on the left that golfers completing their putts on the seventh green located almost laterally to the right a hundred yards away actually started to duck thinking he was aiming at them. They needn't have gone to the trouble.

I could see the strain in the eyes of the Warrior as he started his uncontrolled backswing. Knowing he was aimed too far right, the Warrior tried to make a correction at the top of his backswing before accelerating his downswing. The saying in golf is that he went 'over the top' meaning he looped his swing bringing the club down in a way that caused the golf ball to fly to the left. The consolation is that these shots would usually curve back to the right. The net result is that the ball doesn't go very far, but at least it generally lands in play.

This Warrior tried to recover his balance on his downswing, but by then recovery was impossible. He performed a move I'd rarely seen. He not only came over the top, but he closed the face of his club on the downswing and sent the ball curving wildly to the left. If he had aimed down the middle of the fairway and swung the way he did, his ball would have flown the parking lot on the left and possibly the pond even further left of the parking lot.

Through the history of the Lake Lindsay golf course there had never been a ball hit into this pond to the left of the parking lot from the first tee box. The Weekend Warrior could have had his name emblazoned dubiously in the local lore. But, thanks to his aim being so far to the right, his disastrous swing had produced a shot that ended up just a couple yards from the out-of-bounds stake on the left side of the fairway. To the gallery watching the flight of his ball, they simply applauded believing that this man meant to hit his ball in that direction.

As for the Warrior, he was noticeably shaken. He'd never experienced a swing like he'd just applied. He realized he was lucky he hadn't whiffed. It had been a very close call. As he watched his golf ball fly, his ashen-faced reaction spoke volumes. Seeing the ball come to a stop only yards from the parking lot, he couldn't believe what had just happened. Hitching his baggy work pants he'd bought the previous

January on a clearance sale rack at a farm and garden store in his hometown, he retreated unsteadily back to his golf bag. He'd made that purchase when he was twelve pounds heavier after a dessert and beer filled Christmas season. No longer carrying those extra pounds, he had the added pressure of possibly having his pants around his ankles at the finish of his golf swing.

He tried to keep a poker face, but that one shot had emptied him of whatever confidence he had. He grabbed another cigarette in an attempt to calm his nerves. He had just pulled his opening drive over one hundred twenty yards and doubtfully netted much more in actual distance. His caddy likewise was stunned. The kid didn't know whether to laugh or cry.

I suddenly had the feeling this particular Warrior was not going to be as bothersome to me personally as I'd anticipated. After just that one shot I guessed his only goal was to survive the day without posting the highest score of his career. This was only the first shot of many he would be making during the day. It was obvious whatever swing he had, it had completely deserted him. He had no idea what his next swing was going to produce.

As the Warrior tried to quiet his gurgling stomach, my name was then introduced over the loudspeaker. When the announcer included where I was from, people in the gallery looked at each other as if they'd never heard of the town…to say nothing of me. I had the feeling they thought I was from either another state or possibly another planet.

With my renewed resolve, I was devoid of nervousness or even excitement. The irritation, even the vehemence I felt, for having to play with the three bothersome prototypes in my foursome was strong. I'd felt anger on the golf course after a poor shot or missed putt. However, I'd never had the particular rage prior to my first shot of a tournament.

Taking a deep breath, I slowed my backswing and then powered through the ball. The golf ball took off into the sky with the familiar slight hook as it drew back to the middle of the fairway. With a big kick it rolled past the City Slicker's ball and ended up on the right center of the fairway. It was long, but probably thirty yards short of the prodigious drive gunned down the fairway by the Hometown Hero.

I admired my drive maybe a bit too long. I didn't mean to pose at the end of my swing. It was just that I'd never played the golf course before. I didn't have any perspective where my shot would land. As I returned to my golf bag, I felt the eyes of my fellow competitors and the gallery studying me. My drive indicated that I could play. My 'pose' at the end of my shot hinted I might have too much of an ego. That didn't please my fellow competitors or the gallery. No one said, "good shot." Everyone faced forward and started marching down the fairway in silence.

Trailing my fellow players and the parade following the Hero, the cold reception I got on the first tee box made me wonder how my three competitors might be profiling me…like I'd already done with them. I had to smile knowing they might consider me a type of player I'd seen at various other tournaments…a description I called the 'Young Gun'. That portrayal was not admirable. A young gun would often be a college player who thought he was pretty hot stuff. He'd be self-centered and petulant. He'd show impatience if another golfer delayed or interrupted the routine of the round of golf. Hunting for another player's lost ball or unwanted conversation could set off this arrogant young golfer. He couldn't be bothered by a 'common' man…and would only show interest in talking to the friend or college golfer who accompanied him on the trip to the tournament.

Just by the galleries initial reaction to me, I figured I had to be considered this category of player. I was actually tempted to act the part of a conceited young gun just to agitate my fellow competitors. After all, I might be good pay back since all three of my playing partners were likely going to be aggravating me the entire day.

But, that ridiculous thought passed. I wanted my wrath to be channeled more towards my true focus…that was, to bury these three fellows in my foursome.

So, the four of us were off on our eighteen-hole first day adventure. The Lake Lindsay Golf Tournament followed a format that was similar to most weekend tournaments at that time. Eighteen holes would be played on the nine-hole golf course on Saturday. That was the qualifying round. A player usually had to be in the top twenty scores at the end of the first day of competition to qualify for the Sunday's Championship Flight. The Championship Flight then played either eighteen or twenty-seven holes on Sunday with both days' scores counting toward the over-all low score medalist. In this tournament twenty-seven holes were scheduled for Sunday. This automatically meant I'd be getting back home extremely late Sunday night…easily two hours later than any tournament I'd played in previously. Getting up for my summer job the next morning would be brutal.

With the Saturday qualifying round, there was always a certain tension throughout the day. A golfer desperately wanted to play well enough to make the 'cut'…as if his very masculinity rested on this result. Making that final group of twenty always created many entertaining stories later shared at the bar of survival and catastrophe. Empathic friendships often sprouted at those times.

Those players missing the cut would then play in that previously mentioned 'satellite' flight on Sunday. I never understood where the word 'satellite' was derived. I only knew it was a better designation than calling the flight something more embarrassing like the 'choker's' flight…or the 'loser's' flight.

Like everyone I could feel some strain of making the cut on Saturdays until I found some rhythm usually within the first couple holes. I had made every Championship Flight cut so far that summer. I expected no less of myself that weekend. Except for the Weekend Warrior, it was apparent the other two players in my group had every intention of making the low twenty scores as well.

On this day through the first few holes, each of my playing partners I'd profiled were living up to their definitions with remarkable accuracy. The City Slicker became ill-tempered after his first bogie on the third hole. He was enraged over a lousy bounce when his shot flew to the right of the green. He voiced his irritation how his shots were getting all the bad bounces. He commented that if the local maintenance crew had done a better job of manicuring the golf course, he wouldn't be getting the luckless bounces. That led into his voicing disgust over the slowness of the greens. He said something about the putting surfaces being as slow as shag carpeting. By then even his caddy had to roll his eyes.

By the fifth hole following his second bogie, the City Slicker was ready to hire an assassin to find the golf course greenskeeper. On that hole there had also been a dead branch that bothered his backswing. He claimed the branch should have been trimmed. The poor man….everything was against him.

As for the Hometown Hero he was playing golf like there were no other humans on the golf course. He was in his own world…and playing well. He was so deathly quiet I began to wonder if he had an injured larynx. His only forms of communication through the fifth hole were periodic nods or shakes of his head. Even those were subtle.

It was not until the last three holes of the first round did I sense a change in the City Slicker's outlook. It was all because of what happened on the seventh hole. This querulous and undeserving golfer had a downhill putt of twenty feet for a birdie. He gunned his putt way too hard and actually began swearing a blue streak as the ball was only halfway to the cup. The fast moving ball somehow hit the back rim of the cup and miraculously shot straight up in the air before settling in the hole. It was likely the luckiest putt of the summer for this player.

From that moment on the behavior pattern of the Slicker changed… with just that one piece of good fortune. The now jubilant golfer danced around the green in celebration. He triumphantly held his fist in the air and smugly accepted the polite applause of four of the forty people following our group. Now, one-over par on the day after seven holes, the Slicker had recovered some of his swagger and again was ready to make minced meat out of the rest of the field. He wanted to conquer the world. He even tried to become engaging by asking the Weekend Warrior and me on the eighth tee box to repeat our names.

On that hole he stroked in another twenty-foot sidehill putt for his second consecutive birdie. You'd have thought he'd been elected senator with no opposition. His behavior now changed once again. He portrayed himself in the demeanor of the serious Ben Hogan. His feelings of superiority once again returned. He was truly a man with many faces and numerous moods. I was amazed how dropping two lengthy putts could transform this man from being a self-absorbed bore to a temporarily fun-loving sportsman to a solemn contender.

If he made one more putt of any length, there was no telling where his arrogance could take him.

It was difficult to take this City Slicker seriously. His temperament was so volatile. I could hardly wait for him to inevitably make another bogie. I was certain he'd unravel once again.

But, this particular City Slicker throughout the tournament would prove me wrong. For that matter some of my other generalizations about the other two players would prove inaccurate as well. The Slicker that Saturday would actually add one more birdie in the afternoon and finished with a very strong 71 qualifying round, one off the medalist for all the Saturday qualifiers.

Even then, I still did not consider him a threat to continue his superior play the next day. He just didn't have the mental strength to control his temper and maintain his concentration. A couple bad holes on Sunday early in the round and he'd have a beer. That would be his undoing. I loved it when my competitors had a nice cold beer on a hot sticky Sunday afternoon. Their shot making would invariably depreciate. He could say later in the clubhouse bar, "I just didn't get the breaks this weekend."

As for the Weekend Warrior, there was not a person on that golf course that day who would believe his score after his opening tee shot. I would learn later that evening this 'Warrior' had actually made one Championship Flight in Fergus Falls earlier that summer. He had finished dead last the next day. The next week he had missed the cut and ended up winning the non-qualifier's flight. He was just a perpetual consolation flight player. That didn't mean all was bad. He would still win money to spend in the pro shop…and he would feel fulfilled receiving the handshakes and pats on the back for winning the 'satellite' flight.

After that frighteningly poor opening tee shot by the Warrior on the first hole, something happened on his second shot that all of us …players as well as caddies and spectators, would remember as the start of that something. He proceeded to top his second shot from alongside the parking lot. It was hit so badly yet it had a strong over-spin as it rolled forward. Unbelievably it continued rolling down a hill and then up another incline to the green. It settled about fifteen feet from the hole. The Warrior hitched up his loose-fitting trousers, stuck his chin forward as he marched toward the green, and pretended the shot was exactly the way he meant to play it. While he missed that birdie putt, he still made par…just like his playing partners with their prodigious drives.

The Warrior walked toward the second tee-off with his chin held high… anyway, what could be seen of that chin. He acted as if slapping a ground ball onto the first green was his preferred shot. But, his inner-self, as shallow as it was, knew that something was askew. His swing felt so foreign he wondered if he'd ever played the game before.

The shock to him was that he'd participated in what seemed like one million small town Saturday/Sunday tournaments… and played poorly in almost all them.

He was used to his swing being loose and unpredictable. He couldn't understand why it was so much worse than normal. At forty-five years of age, he only knew summer weekends as golf days. He had all but forgotten why they called Sunday the Sabbath. The closest he'd ever been to being at church on a Sunday was five years before when he hit a ball onto the property owned by the Church of the Nazarene at a town thirty miles east of Lake Lindsay. The 'Warrior' had let go with one of his unholy cuss words when he found his ball out-of-bounds. The minister was outside watering the one bush in front of the church that Sunday afternoon when he heard the Warrior irreverently scream, "Why in the God-damn hell does a dang church have to be located so near the fifth green!" The minister was horrified over the dismissive words of blasphemy slandering his humble house of worship. With a voice still warm from that morning's sermon, that man of the cloth told the Weekend Warrior in less than sermon-like verbiage to take his wayward golf ball and get his unholy ass off the church's hallowed ground.

Even when his weekly tournament schedule ended in late September, most weekend 'Weekend Warriors' never accepted Sunday as what it was intended. This type of golfer would generally either change his interests to fishing or hunting…or begin his seasonal weekend job…like at the bowling alley or the local pool hall. In the weeks ahead he'd also be on-call as part of the county road crew keeping the machines ready for snow plowing as the upcoming hard, cold winter would only be weeks away. Of course the wife of a 'warrior' would always attend church each week and put in a good word for her husband if she didn't consider the false testimony sacrilegious or a waste of time.

As for this Weekend Warrior, he was embarking on a journey that July morning he would not soon forget. His fellow players and gallery members following our foursome would likewise always remember his play that weekend. It was a level of golf he'd never encountered…that is, a new 'low' level. After two unexplainable shots, he'd almost made birdie on the first hole. While that experience was positive, the swing he'd brought to the golf course that day was unfamiliar. He remained in a daze as he tripped along the path to the next tee-off.

After the rest of us hit our drives, he stood on that second tee-off in shocked silence having no sense of where his next shot might go. The second hole was a 500-yard par-five where longer hitting golfers had a chance to hit their second shots onto the green. The Warrior did not have that kind of length to his shots… not that day, not any day. He would need two full wood shots and a short iron third shot to reach the green…that is, if he was hitting the ball well. Unfortunately, whatever golf skill he might have owned earlier that week, the feeling was so distant in his mind, he was actually hesitant in teeing up his golf ball.

Since the second hole was a dogleg left, the Warrior hoped to duplicate his previous drive and somehow pull hook the ball so it might follow a lucky path down the middle of the fairway. As he did on his first drive, he duplicated his strategy aiming so far to the right we wondered if he knew the actual fairway curved left. I could see the contemptible, smart-mouthed City Slicker wanted to say something snide but for once he decided to stay quiet. He must have figured the Warrior knew what he was doing.

In truth, the grizzled veteran of weekend tournaments had not a clue. His swing was noticeably different from his swing on first hole. This time the ball started out further right than he was aimed…in fact, incredibly right. As we were waiting for the ball to possibly curve left in order to have any chance of landing close to our fairway, the ball suddenly curled dramatically further right. There was not supposed to be an out-of-bounds on the right because it was supposed to be virtually impossible to hit a golf ball so dramatically in that direction. Fellow players, caddies, and spectators collectively gasped as the Warrior's ball flight took a course so catastrophically inaccurate that its final resting place would certainly have been deemed unattainable by the golf course designer.

The City Slicker couldn't stay quiet. He remarked sarcastically, "Partner, I believe you're further away from the green out there than where you're standing right now!" The rest of us tried not to laugh at the quip, but the Slicker had a point. As the ball disappeared into the far woods on the right, there was a serious question whether the ball could even be found.

But, have no doubt of the Weekend Warrior's good fortune that day; the ball was not only found, but there was an opening in the woods for him to advance his ball to the fairway. Under ordinary conditions that ball shouldn't have been located until the next glacier moved the ball closer to the golf course.

With this good fortune, the Warrior then tried to hit his ball over some trees and advance it further up the fairway. The attempt was sincere but feeble. Again, he mishit the ball. It started out three feet off the ground…and never got higher. A wall of trees loomed so thick a mosquito would have difficulty finding a straight line through those branches. Somehow the ball made it through those trees and squirted out to the edge of the right side of the fairway. The Warrior could try another hundred shots from that same position and he couldn't have ended up with a better result.

Unfortunately, the Warrior remained over three hundred yards from the green after that second shot. Adamantly he flailed away for the third time. This time the ball headed toward the out-of-bounds on the left side of the fairway… when it abruptly hit a fence post and dropped straight down only yards from the penalty stakes. He had advanced his ball another one-hundred ten yards. From one-hundred ninety yards away for his fourth shot, he bladed this attempt…the ball clipping the tops of the blades of grass. Mercifully the ball headed straight for the green. It rolled…and it rolled…finally hopping onto the green some thirty feet from the hole. He had hit approximately one thousand yards worth of golf shots on the second hole in various directions and had arrived on the green with a putt for par. Naturally his putt had eyes. He drained the putt for a par five. We all stood there dumbfounded. The three of us ended up missing short length putts for a birdie. Our scores on that hole were the exact same as the score of the Warrior.

Golf was never intended to be fair.

Those first two holes turned out to be a forerunner for the rest of that day. The Weekend Warrior played as if he'd never seen the game. Rarely hitting a shot squarely, he was in shock most of the day. The Hometown Hero, the City Slicker, and I looked away rather than watch him hit the ball. Of course, we saw very little of him since he seldom hit from the fairway. When his first nine-hole round was completed, we thought the Warrior must have shot a score close to 50. However, his scorecard indicated he'd recorded an even par 36. He had putted like a magician with ten total putts on nine holes. It was easily the hardest working 36 I'd ever witnessed in my life.

After a short break for lunch, even the taciturn Hometown Hero commented whether the Warrior's heart could handle the strain of another wild and uncontrolled round of golf. We wondered if our 'fourth' would even show up for the final nine holes of the day. But, sure enough, there he was at the first tee box waiting for us and looking like he'd just been flogged. He was sweating so badly, even his ever present cigarette sagged soggily from his thin lips.

He was last to tee off and started his next round with a similar drive to the one he'd launched that morning. This time his ball went a bit further, but it was curving madly to the left. The tree branch stopping his ball from bounding across the out-of-bounds parking lot could not have been more than two inches in diameter. The Hero, the Slicker and I just looked at each other not believing what we were seeing. As for the Warrior he behaved as if all this unbelievable good fortune was just standard.

I swear I saw his knees almost buckle as he staggered off the first tee box. Sure enough, he escaped with another par on the first hole for a second time. He continued slapping the golf ball all over the county for the next five holes as he continued to make scores of par. The rest of us were playing our own game and didn't really take notice until the 17th hole that the Weekend Warrior was hanging onto a very nice score for the day. If he made par on those last two holes of the day, he'd shoot an even-par 72. He'd easily make the top twenty cut for the Championship Flight play on Sunday. Anyone watching him hit the ball that day would never believe he could have scored better than a 120!

Then as if all his good fortune had caught up to him, his ugly, curving five-iron buried in a greenside sand bunker on the par-3 hole. By then we were all kind of pulling for him. We hung our heads in sympathy for the inevitable disaster that was about to happen. At best he might be able to hack the ball out of the sand sideways and somehow chip and putt for his bogie. Likely though, it was probably an unplayable lie in the trap.

Upon inspecting his possibilities, only the slice mark on the top of his soft-covered Wilson golf ball showed above the level of the sand. The Warrior didn't say a word. In fact, he'd said very little all day. He just silently hopped into that sand trap to face his next challenge. Taking little time he ferociously applied a chopping swing unleashing a truck load of sand onto the green. Yet, in that storm of sand a white golf ball could be seen as if in slow motion rising and then floating without spin only inches above the embankment to the green. The ball landed surprisingly softly onto the putting surface and immediately began rolling…..and rolling…way too fast. It looked like it was going to run across the green to the sandtrap on the other side.

That's when the golf ball crashed against the flag stick. It took not a millisecond from there for the gashed ball to dive into the cup like a terrified baby gopher. The man had scored an improbable birdie two from an impossible position in the sand. Every person around that green…including his competitors raised our fists in vicarious triumph and sheer delight for this man's unbelievable luck. We all knew what was happening. He was now one-under par with one hole to play.

You'd have thought he was playing the British Open with a one shot lead going into the last hole as the Warrior unsteadily trudged over to the eighteenth tee box. No one was talking to him so as not to take him out of the zone he was in. Word had spread that our group was playing rather well, so there were maybe a hundred more people who'd come out to follow us. With the best score so far posted in the clubhouse as a 74, the Weekend Warrior had a chance for first day medalist honors…an achievement no one would believe if they'd seen him play.

But, the Warrior was not the only one in our foursome scoring well. While his scoring was remarkable relative to his poor shot making, our entire foursome had a chance for best first day scores. We just weren't paying as much attention to our own scoring because the Warrior's spectacular putting display was making us pull for his success.

On that last tee-box for the day, his hands shook so badly we all prayed his caddy would not have to perform the indignity of placing the ball on his tee for him. The twitch on his face as he drew the club back coupled with his trembling hands and wobbly legs gave him the look of an addict entering re-hab.

How he made contact with the golf ball on that eighteenth tee box was beyond explanation. His swing was short and loose. The shot while certainly not great may have been the finest shot he hit that entire day. It carried only two hundred yards but it landed on the fairway. The Hometown Hero and I applauded him and gave him a supportive pat on his shoulder. Even the City Slicker controlled his own self-absorption long enough to smile and shake his head in disbelief over the score this man was accomplishing.

The eighteenth hole was a relatively easy par-4 finishing hole. There was a small creek in front of the green. Longer hitters had to lay up so they wouldn't hit in the water off the tee box. From there a short wedge shot over the creek onto the green gave most golfers a shot at a birdie. Even facing a gale wind, a competitive golfer felt he should birdie this hole more often than making par.

This was far from the thought waves of the Warrior. That man just wanted to finish his eighteen holes without injuring anyone…himself included. His drive ended up a good forty yards behind the rest of us. He had roughly one-hundred fifty yards remaining to the green. His second shot would have to fly over that small creek in front of the green. The way he'd been hitting the golf ball, this was no routine shot.

Sure enough…the six-iron he scuffed was hit so perfectly in the middle of the ball that he'd cut the ball down to the very core. At best the golf ball reached its pinnacle of height at no more than eight feet off the ground. Our shoulders all hunched as we expected the ball to disappear into the creek, thereby earning him a penalty stroke. At best a double bogey six was likely.

The ball actually landed short of the creek so poorly had it been hit. But, with the luck on his side all day, the golf ball bounced over the creek clearing the water by inches and then amazingly kept rolling. In fact, it bounded just up to the fringe of the green about twenty-five feet below the cup. It was so inexplicably lucky we all swore the Warrior would have to change his pants before putting.

Now all of us…even the impudent City Slicker …were clapping our hands and yelling some positive words of encouragement towards him…laughing and shaking our heads as we did so. This man was just two putts from shooting a one-under par 71.

However, he wasn't done yet. That twenty-five foot putt was no easy shot. There was a five-foot break to the right and the green's surface had become very hard and fast with all the foot traffic that day. He could easily three-putt.

When the Warrior set up to address his twenty-five footer, there was a special feeling in the air. I remember looking at the City Slicker while the Warrior was about to address his putt. I nodded my head indicating I thought the Warrior was going to make the putt. The Slicker caught my nod and smiled back at me. He nodded as well. We knew that putt was going in the hole before our struggling playing partner stroked the putt.

As hopeless as the Weekend Warrior was on the links that day, he was calm and collected over all his putts. That stroke was no exception. The ball started out even further to the left than any of us would have played it. As it slowed down it broke more dramatically to the right and began slowing down. The last two inches seemed to last five minutes. The ball just kept trickling until it disappeared into the cup for a closing birdie and a final eighteen-hole score of two-under par 70. None of us figured we'd ever see anyone score that well while hitting the worst collection of golf shots any of us could recall. We were happy for him…and a little in awe.

The Weekend Warrior had achieved medalist honors that day and would be in the leader group in the Championship flight the next morning. He would be playing with the City Slicker who played better than I believed possible while scoring a one-under 71. The local Hometown Hero played very well on the last nine holes and scored a two-under 34 for a total score of even par 72. The fourth member of our foursome was not to be outdone. By the end of the day I had little memory how I'd felt that morning. I was no longer exhausted or disinterested; in fact, I would have preferred to continue playing. I had played consistently, but unspectacularly. I had left a lot of birdie attempts on the edge of the cup while scoring a par 72 over the eighteen holes. It was a round that could easily have been three or four shots better.

My play had spurred my competitive zeal. I was excited about competing the next day. I even found my playing partners not to be as boorish as these types of players so often were. The Hometown Hero, though abnormally quiet, had an impressive game with tremendous height and length on his shots. He actually talked a few times during the second nine holes of play. The City Slicker had not been as intolerable, although that might have been because he was paying more attention to the implausible adventures of the fourth member of our foursome. As for the Weekend Warrior, he was not nearly the curmudgeon he could have been. Truly, how could he have been? It was his day to be operating in a kind of twilight zone. It had taken all his concentration just to survive.

Incredibly, our foursome had the top four scores in that Saturday qualifying round out of all one hundred and fourteen players on that golf course. I'd never experienced that coincidence before or since. We'd be playing in the very same group the next day. Little could we fathom how this happenstance would set the stage for an unforgettable Sunday. At the end of Saturday's qualifying round, those that made the championship flight cared little about who they were paired with the next day. There was only the satisfaction that each of us was in such good position to potentially win the next day.

All, that is, except the Weekend Warrior. I'd never seen a golfer more exhausted upon the completion of a round of golf. The day had taken a lot out of him. If he hadn't been putting well, he might have scored the highest...not the lowest...of any competitor in the field. However, this day he was the medalist, supposedly the best golfer on the golf course that day. The probability of his maintaining that status the next day was something far beyond reality. There was no point in even discussing the subject further...and, no one did who saw him play that day.

After the Saturday qualifying round at these weekend tournaments, the remainder of the day and that evening were filled with conversations at the bar about anything related to golf or that particular tournament in which we were playing. A dinner would begin at 7:00 and turn into a party that would go very late for some. The local golfers playing in the tournament would go to their homes after the golf and get cleaned up. The rest of us would either shower at the club or at the only motel in the town. I chose the clubhouse since I didn't have a shower or sink in the back of my station wagon where I slept when on the road.

The Saturday evening gathering was always part of the tournament fun. Every weekend I would try not to eat too heavily for fear of feeling stuffed and languid the next day. However, after lasting the day on a ham sandwich or hot dog, I would always fail in my attempt to eat with some reserve. I was usually the first one at the buffet table…and I returned multiple times.

Given the special nature of the evening, many local folks dressed their best for what was often the biggest social occasion of the year in that community. If the day was bright and sunny, many of the golfers got sunburned. With just adequate lighting, the entire inside of the clubhouse eating area was blinding from all the reflections off the red faces and bald heads.

The similarities at this festivity were also quite predictable relative to other annual town golf events. It was the local banker who inevitably wore his mustard or lime-colored sport coat with a flowery shirt. Spouses arrived in their best hair-dos and most colorful dresses. Other local participants in the tournament wore suits that hadn't seen the light of day since the previous year's tournament.

The Hometown Hero showed up wearing what I gathered was his only business suit. He looked befittingly uncomfortable, obviously having been forced to wear the choice of clothing by his wife who looked matronly but sweet. His son still wearing the same sloppy outfit he'd worn all day caddying for his Dad would show up with that insipid cap on his head and his timid girlfriend as well. Attending her first 'adult' party, she was especially overwhelmed.

The City Slicker competed with the local banker for the loudest sportcoat. He was thinner and in better shape, so he could pull off the audacious look. People were milling around him like he was some kind of celebrity. His ego was able to handle the adoration with ease.

The Weekend Warrior wore anything that would help him blend into the wall color. His very uncharacteristic position of being the first day medalist left him completely ill-at-ease. His brown pants and dark tan shirt would normally have camouflaged him nicely against the walnut colored bar. However, this night everyone was slapping him on the back and congratulating him for his apparent superlative score. He was not comfortable having to be so friendly. Accepting compliments was entirely unsettling for him. Making excuses and laughing about other players' misfortunes on the golf course was more his usual scene. The plain fact was that he was living through his fifteen minutes of glory and disliking every minute. So unaccustomed was he to such positive feedback, he would eat and leave the club early that Saturday evening, believing this was what first day leaders were supposed to do. Normally he'd be one of the last ones to leave the party and his role as an observer.

After dinner the evening's final event began with little fanfare. The Championship Flight qualifiers would be auctioned off to the highest bidder. It was called a 'Calcutta'. Only the golfers' Sunday scores would count for the win, place or show pay-off to the gamblers. If the small town was a county seat, the local county sheriff and the county attorney were always unexplainably absent that night…since gambling was illegal. The county attorney and county sheriff knew that if they wanted to be re-elected, they needed to keep their constituents happy. This one-time gambling exception was considered socially if not legally acceptable.

It was always a rowdy affair at these local golf clubs. Each player would be introduced and the gamblers including the players themselves would enter into a back and forth bidding competition to get the player or 'horse' who they thought would score the best the next day. The owners of the top four golfers after Sunday's competition would gain a portion of the "pot" on a 40-30-20-10 percentage split. The club would first take 10% off the top of the entire money bet for their profit which everyone didn't really mind. It was understood the golf club was entitled to make some profit from their invitational tournament.

My interest was on a completely different level. As a 'horse' my take would be usually 10% of whatever my buyer or buyers won. With this as a guarantee there was no reason I should buy even a portion of myself…especially since I didn't have any extra money to gamble with anyway. If I finished in the top four, I'd get a piece of the winnings. If I didn't do well, I was out nothing.

The total pot could be as little as $3000 or as much as $10,000 in these small town affairs. It depended how well the farmers were doing that particular year. That's right….even in this unimportant little golf event, the farming economy of Minnesota dictated whether players sold for a lot or a little.

This 10% under the table payment to the golfer was a tremendous incentive for me. Depending on the tournament and how I finished on Sunday's round of golf, I could drive home with more under the table cash than what I would make in two weeks at my summer job. I was not about to question the definition of 'amateur' golf.

By the end of the evening's Calcutta everyone had smoked at least a pack of cigarettes including the non-smokers. The room was so thick with the hovering haze, it was difficult to see across the room. The air-conditioner invariably would become ineffective with the outside doors to the deck left open. Most people had overeaten and over imbibed. I left the fanfare after I was introduced and then sold at the Calcutta to a couple guys I'd never seen before. They came over and introduced themselves trying not to say anything that might rile me. They wanted me at my best the next day. From my perspective I wanted to know them so I could seek them out to get my 10% if I finished with one of the four best scores the next day.

When the betting was finally completed, most people departed. However, every weekend there would be too many stalwarts remaining at the clubhouse trying to squeeze the last bit of enjoyment from the party. Lake Lindsay golf club was no exception. As for me, I was not part of that crowd. I was better off getting some sleep. I would leave by 10:00, drive around town for a while, get some ice cream, and then park my station wagon/sleeping quarters in the quiet back corner of the golf club property. I would hear the wild noise from the clubhouse party until I fell asleep. I knew the next morning there would be stories circulating about the late night rowdiness. With too many people trying too hard to have a good time, the juvenile mayhem among some adults would overflow on these late Saturday night parties. There would be inebriated local folks of various ages who would think it a good idea to play some night golf for a lot of money or have unlighted golf cart races for the same kind of money. It sounded like so much fun at 1:00 in the morning when the late-night party-goers were all 'shit-faced'. Rarely would this fanciful competition last very long into the night. When the adolescent fun ended, not all participants would be accounted for as the dipsomaniacs crawled back at different times to the relative comfort of the clubhouse. At times the greenskeeper on Sunday morning would be hauling back one or two party-goers who had passed out on the golf course the previous night.

There would also be stories of guys falling asleep in the clubhouse for the night and then retreating back to their home before 6:00 in the morning hoping their wives kept the front door unlocked. I don't know how all these stories would become so public within the first hour of registration on Sunday morning, but I had to consider some of the stories were from previous tournaments. Nonetheless, watching some of the early morning golfers stagger to the first tee box made you wince with sympathy.

On that Sunday morning at the Lake Lindsay Golf Club, I awoke very early. The serenity was quite a contrast to the atmosphere the previous night. The vast lake down the bluff from the golf course had just a hint of fog hovering over the glassy smoothness. The sky was bright. The birds were chirping. The only other sound was the mowers preparing the greens and fairways for that day's play. I was invigorated…also quite a contrast in this case to how I'd felt the previous morning.

My group's tee-off time was scheduled for 9:00 AM. We would be playing twenty-seven holes that day. The tournament would not be completed until 6:00 if there were no interruptions. My Sunday morning habit was to leave my golf clubs in my car, stroll down to the men's locker room to wash up, and then eat breakfast at the clubhouse. Invariably I'd hear the stories circulating about the previous night's party. An hour before being called to the first tee box, I'd leisurely warm up and then invest some well spent time on the practice green.

As I was completing my routine, there would be the non-championship flight golfers arriving for their early morning tee time. This parade of inept golfers had no routine other than to show up at the tee box minutes before their tee time. With only a cup of coffee as a warm up, those players many of whom had chosen to party late into the night had the added challenge of trying to maintain their balance while hitting their first shot. Most of these red-eyed golfers silently begged just to get their golf ball airborne. If the ball flew wildly left or right that would be all right…just so the ball ended up someplace close to the golf course. They might show theatrical negative reactions as if they expected a better result, but generally this level of golfer, considering how they felt that morning, were just relieved to have made contact with the golf ball.

Of course, there were always a few party-goers who were not able to answer the bell for their Sunday morning tee time. They were probably better off. I witnessed too many times a few golfers who should have stayed in bed. The Lake Lindsay tournament offered a typical example of one of these men. I would hear his story weeks down the road at another golf tournament. His name was Walt. He was the local hardware store owner.

Walt didn't have many days during the year where he had the time or the inclination to enjoy the golf club nightlife. The Saturday 'Calcutta' party was one of the few nights in the year Walt would let himself go. He allowed himself to get blindly drunk with the confidence that a friend would get him home. Unfortunately that Saturday night his friend was in no condition to carry out that responsibility.

It turned out the only reason Walt showed up at the golf course on Sunday morning was that his car never left the clubhouse parking lot from the previous night. When his body clock woke him up at 7:00 he was just minutes away from his third flight tee time. Since he was already at the parking lot and his car was only twenty yards from the first tee, he figured he could play. While seated in his car, he pulled off his dress pants and put on the still sweaty walking shorts he had worn the previous day. He also took off his dress shirt and tie he'd worn at Saturday night's party leaving him with a no-sleeved T-shirt. He cut quite a contrast to the City Slicker's attire as he slowly and carefully tip-toed from his car to the first tee box hoping people wouldn't take notice of his condition.

With the severity of his hangover, Walt had many characteristics of a cadaver on that Sunday morning. Only the ability to breathe and stand separated him from being a corpse. He was in bad shape. While he didn't have those walking shorts on backwards, that was just luck. With some assistance from a friend, he was directed toward the first tee box. He whispered to one of his playing partners that he had a headache that only death itself could cure. Then he stood there miserably hoping that statement would happen soon.

When the announcer blurted out his name to tee off, he almost passed out from the concussion of the airwaves. He proceeded forward to tee up his golf ball when he realized he still had his last evenings dress shoes on. With his multi-colored walking shorts with undone zipper and that no-sleeved t-shirt, it was fortunate many of his neighbors and friends hadn't arrived at the clubhouse that early.

There was one other minor point. Walt had not a clue where his golf clubs were located.

The hardware store owner then grabbed a wood from one of his playing partner's golf bags as well as a golf ball so as not to appear unprepared. As he attempted to bend over to tee his golf ball up, his eye balls temporarily disappeared into his forehead. He stopped and gathered himself before bending over again.

One of his playing partners could see a tragedy about to happen and tried to grab Walt before he bent over for the second attempt to tee his ball into the ground. The playing partner didn't arrive in time.

Had Walt simply keeled over and then unceremoniously been dragged off the first tee box by tournament volunteers, the embarrassment would have been noteworthy but eventually forgiven if not forgotten. Unfortunately the first tee area was elevated with a gulley directly in front of the tee box. The intrepid hardware hack had already begun to pass out in the midst of bending over that second time. The last thing most of the people around that tee box saw of old Walt was his feet as he went into an involuntary dive over the front of the tee box. He then simply disappeared down into the weeds in the gulley below.

One of his playing partners walked over to the front of the tee box and waited a couple seconds until the body had apparently stopped its bumpy journey down the slope. He paused yet a few more seconds to note whether the body still had movement. The wait was uncomfortably long before suddenly he put his thumb in the air indicating Walt was still among the living. Not two seconds later, the announcer, as if nothing out of the ordinary had happened, said, "Next on the tee from Starbuck, Minnesota, Craig Johnson." The tournament had to go on. A passed out competitor could not hold up something as important as the local invitational golf tournament. That morning, Craig Johnson's fourseome had but a threesome.

Twenty minutes went by and two more foursomes teed off before a group of local volunteers ventured over the crest of the tee box to descend to the depths of the valley in search of one very inebriated member of their community. Another group teed off as those volunteers were below finally finding a very wet, grass-stained, and unrecognizable human being in some long brush, weeds and grass. They at first weren't certain because until one of them recognized the dress shoe on Walt's right foot, the general feeling was that they'd stumbled upon a dead deer. His left shoe had been lost on his descent into the valley. It would be found later that week when one of the maintenance people mowed over Walt's lost dress shoe.

Having slept for about a half hour in the weeds at the bottom of the gulley before being carried up the hill, Walt still showed some life after the volunteers deposited him back at his car. In fact, the disheveled hardware store owner had become downright feisty when the volunteers leaned him against his car and began walking away thinking they had convinced him to get some coffee and go home

But no! He still wanted to play golf. It now took more folks to convince old Walt not to play. One charitable soul suggested he go home, change clothes, and when he returned he could meet his group for the second nine holes. That sounded respectable. He allowed one of the volunteers to drive him home. He was not seen for the rest of that Sunday.

I would learn from one participant at that tournament two summers later that the infamous 'Walt' was not seen again at his local golf club for another couple weeks…and that was only to clean out his locker. By then he had heard most of the only slightly exaggerated stories regarding his antics that Sunday morning. He didn't play golf again that summer.

Apparently the next summer, Walt planned a fishing trip that coincided with the weekend annual golf tournament. While he wasn't at the tournament, his legend lingered. The mower mangled dress shoe was a permanent fixture on display in the pro shop hung on the wall. Walt never played in that annual event again.

When my foursome's names were called that Sunday morning to make our appearance on the first tee box, there was tightness on each of our faces. We had wanted to earn the right to play in the leading group on that last day of the tournament. We'd accomplished that first goal…or, at least three of us had. The Weekend Warrior had no such dream. For him being in a foursome of the leaders was akin to a bad nightmare.

Each of us had taken care of ourselves the previous evening. There had been some overeating, but no overdrinking amongst our group. We all therefore should have felt reasonably healthy and rested.

Unfortunately, the exception was again, the Weekend Warrior. As the previous day's medalist, he'd had his back slapped and hand shaken so many times at the Saturday night clubhouse party, he felt like he was running for office. He had never left a clubhouse on Saturday evening that early in his life. Usually closing down the bar at tournaments on Saturday night, he was completely out of whatever routine he practiced at all previous tournaments he'd ever participated.

He had gone to bed by 11:00. The pressure of being the first day leader weighed so heavily on the Warrior's mind that sleep at best had been intermittent. Also, he'd had such a continuous and incessant looseness from his extremely nervous stomach, he lived in fear of losing one of his organs if he used the bathroom one more time.

On that first tee, the Weekend Warrior looked completely out of sorts. Being the leading qualifier in the Championship flight on that Sunday morning was as foreign to him as going to church. He looked bewildered and beaten before he took a club out of his bag. Any betting man paying attention to this outwardly nervous man would put a lot of cash on the table that the Warrior would be lucky to break 90 on the first eighteen holes of play on that beautiful, but windy day.

The City Slicker with his qualifying 71 and one stroke behind the Warrior was again strutting around like a movie star. He had his game face on. There would be no interviews from the media…no photo shoots with any advertisers… no autographs until play was completed…and only a few words to his caddy before he teed off. After all, this is how Arnold Palmer would behave if he were in this important career enhancing amateur golf tournament at Lake Lindsay. It would take a couple holes before the Slicker could come back down from his elevated dream world. Until then, he was on his favorite tee box showing off his new matching lavender golf pant, shirt, and sweater ensemble.

The Hometown Hero had arrived at the golf course with half the town following his every step. He didn't recognize anyone. He was in his own zone. Even his wife and son got no feedback nor did they expect any. His concentration was unflinching. He had made it through qualifying with flying colors only two strokes off the lead. It was a perfect position for him to aggressively attack the golf course and roll over every competitor only allowing them to fight for second place. It was evident this man would be the player to beat if I wanted to win.

As the fourth member of this group, I had none of the emotions of indifference and exhaustion I'd felt the previous morning. I was in the hunt with the confidence and skill and now the golf course knowledge to be a serious challenger. This was another benefit of my summer long obsession. I was glad I made the long trip to Lake Lindsay.

Being in the leading foursome on the final day of the tournament meant that whatever gallery there was, they would be following our leading group. I craved being in these competitive situations. I had no doubt I could do well with just a modicum of luck.

Of course there were sixteen other golfers who had qualified for the Championship flight besides our group of four. Invariably when you were playing in the leading group, the other golfers went unnoticed until later in the day when some of them might play themselves back into contention. With twenty-seven holes to play that day, there would be a regrouping at the end of the first eighteen holes late Sunday afternoon so the top scorers could play together the final nine holes. I loved that entire atmosphere. The gallery would be at its largest for the leading foursome. The clapping and cheering would be more enthused and the gamblers from the Calcutta of the previous night would be anxiously watching their 'horse' perform. My goal was to always be in that final group later in the day. That would be the ultimate test of whatever skill and confidence I had gained from the past weeks while performing in front of a large group of spectators.

On the opening hole, the Hometown Hero and I were the first of our group to tee off. We both powered our shots right down the middle of the fairway with my ball coming to rest only ten yards behind his shot. He had a look of satisfaction that he had proved his manhood once again by outdriving my shot. It's amazing how a ten-yard difference can boost the ego of even a championship golfer.

The City Slicker hit his drive quite far but to the right in some rough. The slightly errant shot caused his forehead to furrow, a melodramatic pose he'd likely practiced. He held his facial contortion just in case the local sports photographer wanted a picture for the hometown newspaper article on the tournament.

When the announcer finally introduced the Weekend Warrior as the previous day's medalist, I believe I wasn't the only person praying for the Warrior to get off the tee without filling his pants first. He had told his caddy he had such a gas build-up in his nervous stomach he was scared to bend over to tee his ball up. He did it but it was an obvious strain. His face was pale but relieved when he stood back up.

Addressing his golf ball, the shear difference in style between the Warrior and the City Slicker was never more evident. The Warrior had chosen a startling multi-colored dark shirt that looked more appropriate for the upcoming bowling season in the fall and winter. It had a decal for some brand of motor oil on the lapel. The short sleeves hung below his elbows. Apparently he'd bought the shirt thinking it would shrink when washed and dried. It obvious hadn't yet been laundered.

His black pants hung low and were held up by a belt down to the last hole. Given his digestive tract problems, he appeared to be about twenty pounds lighter than the previous day. In fact, it was difficult to even see him inside his clothing. The shirt and pants appeared to be at least four sizes too large. With his floppy fishing hat adding to his unique look, his face would have been undetectable had it not been for the omnipresent cigarette in his mouth.

It was not apparent to many new members of the gallery how jumpy he really was. But, to those of us who'd witnessed his golfing nightmare on Saturday, let there be no mistake. The Warrior was more panicked than the day he relinquished part of his freedom and surrendered to his girlfriend's demands that they get married…something she had to have found to be one of her biggest regrets.

He of course tried to sustain some semblance of looking cool. With his ball teed up and the color somewhat back in his face, all he had to do was make decent contact with the golf ball and not embarrass himself so completely in front of the large crowd. The Hometown Hero looked away not wanting to watch while the City Slicker observed the scene with an insolent grin as he waited for this medalist to provide another moment to remember. I was holding my breath. I truly didn't expect the Warrior to score anywhere near as well as he did on Saturday. He just happened to shoot the round of his life. Duplicating that effort the following day for any golfer no matter how skilled would be infinitely more difficult. I just wanted him to hit a reasonable drive down the middle of the fairway before he died of a heart attack.

Gazing down the first fairway with visions of his two errant drives the previous day, he had to be wondering why he'd even signed up for this tournament. He had no faith he would be able to hit the ball squarely. To him, the fairway must have looked tighter than a hallway. His eyes tried not to focus on the looming out-of-bounds in the parking lot on his left, but he was losing that battle. Taking a waggle to loosen up his paralyzed muscles, he took another look at the parking lot only to see his pick-up truck in the very area where a poorly hit drive might land. He looked momentarily disgusted as he tried to recall why he parked there.

Now there was something additional for him to be concerned. He then took the strategy he'd followed the day before and aimed far, far to the right. Some of the gallery on that side of the tee box moved away wondering why he was aiming his shot so severely to the right. Having played with him the previous day, our group simply shrugged our shoulders, winced, and now stared down at the ground not wanting to witness another of his frightening attempts at hitting the golf ball.

With a few more practice swings to steady his nerves, the Weekend Warrior was ready to launch his drive. Watching his every move I could see by his address he was going to employ yet another different swing concept. On Saturday, he seemed to invent a new swing thought whether on his backswing or his downswing with every shot. As bad as that was, this new swing attempt Sunday morning looked ill-begotten from the very beginning. As he took the club back, I unconsciously grimaced expecting the worst.

Luckily, as it turned out, the worst did not happen....but, it was very close. It should be understood that when a club head enters deeply into the turf while attempting to make contact with a tiny golf ball, a couple things happen. First, it's a foregone conclusion the ball is not going to go very far. The next concern is whether the ball is going to go anywhere at all. The final fear is that the mud and grass flung up from the club gorging into the ground might go further than the ball.

With much relief to everyone, the ball did leave the tee box. There was a deep gulley in front of the tee box, the same one that had swallowed Walt, the local hardware store owner, two hours before. A thirty-yard carry was required for the golf ball to make it over that deep valley. The Warrior's club did indeed imbed itself so deeply into the sod that the golf ball never really met the face of the club. With some hesitation the golf ball suddenly was seen floating as if in slow motion over that gulley and landing softly...and safely... on the other side of that gulley like a light leaf falling to earth on a peaceful fall afternoon. It didn't get much roll as a result of how it had been hit, so the total yardage on his first tee shot was about thirty-five yards. You could have buried a small animal in the trough he had dug with his golf club on that first tee box.

The Warrior was of course mortified. The sweat pouring from his brow was flowing as he tracked the abbreviated flight of his golf ball. While he was relieved he didn't have to do the ultimate embarrassment of climbing down the gulley to retrieve his ball, his thirty-five yard opening tee shot was almost as humiliating.

He pulled his cap further down his head. If it weren't for his pointed chin the cap would have engulfed his entire head. As it was, while lumbering on to his next shot, he was slouching so badly, his cap appeared to be resting only on the top of his neck. The opening hole was not starting out propitiously for our Weekend Warrior.

His second shot approximately three hundred yards from the green was topped and mercifully rolled up to the drives of the Hometown Hero and my own first shot. It brought some ray of hope and comfort that he was back with the big boys although laying two when everyone else laid one. While the Warrior was able to save bogey on that first hole, he already had hints that his day would be a continuance of the struggle he'd experienced from tee to green the previous day.

The other two competitors and I, however, could not let the Warrior's despair interrupt our concentration. The three of us struck wedge shots right at the flag. My shot was the furthest away from the cup leaving a putt of only twelve feet for a birdie. The other two gentlemen were within five feet of the pin. My ball rolled lazily down the speedy slope and disappeared into the cup for a birdie to the muted cheers from the crowd. The other two players made birdie as well. The Weekend Warrior' dragged himself to the next tee having lost whatever lead he had to all three of his playing partners.

The remaining holes of that opening first round were competitive. Except for the Warrior, the three of us matched marvelous shots into the greens. Unfortunately we just could not make any birdie putts. The only time we did make a clutch putt, it was for a par.

The City Slicker was maintaining a very strong performance at this tournament. I personally couldn't believe it. I was just waiting for him to blow up after a poor shot and place the blame on the condition of the golf course. So far he hadn't had much of any bad breaks…only missed putts. With no one else making any putts, he seemed to be taking his misses with relative calm. It was not like a City Slicker to be that patient.

The Hometown Hero continued to plow along with consistent but not brilliant looking shots. He did bogie the par-3 eighth hole. When his four-foot par putt failed to go in, his evil stare caused even the gallery to step back. The absolute silent shock amongst his entourage after he missed that putt was spooky. The look of rage on the Hero's face as he marched to the next tee box could have made a marine blink.

Going into the last hole of the first nine holes, we faced that short par-4 three hundred and fifty yard ninth hole. The only difficulty was the second shot over a small creek by the green. At that point in the tournament, the City Slicker actually had a one-shot lead over me and a two-shot lead over the Hometown Hero. Both the Slicker and I were under par for the tournament. All four of our drives on the last hole were lay-ups landing at various yardages well short of the creek. Even the Weekend Warrior finally made a decent drive including a second shot finishing some thirty feet from the hole. Like the previous day, he was still putting well despite his atrocious play. Now with his first birdie attempt of the day, it seemed natural that he promptly rolled it in. We had no idea what he'd shot for the round, but we figured he'd shot his way out of the tournament.

The best approach to the green on that last hole was the Hometown Hero's sand wedge from sixty yards out. He ended up a tap-in away from the flag. After his shot, the local folks went nuts. They were still cheering when I hit my sand wedge shot from fifty yards out over the flag and backed the ball up to within two feet of the flag. I closed with a birdie and a nine-hole score of 34.

The City Slicker didn't have quite as good of an approach shot. He too rolled his putt of ten feet into the cup for a similar closing birdie.

All four of us had birdied the last hole. Gallery members were especially loud appreciating the quality of play from our foursome. The Slicker and I had scored identical two-under nine-hole totals of 34 keeping me one shot behind the arrogant guy from the Twin Cities. The Hometown Hero finished one-under par with a 35. He was two shots behind the lead. We were surprised to learn that the Weekend Warrior had actually scored a 41. We hadn't expected his score to be that good. Walking off the ninth hole the 'Warrior' actually looked relieved. He was back in his more comfortable role of obscurity. He was now six shots behind the leader and completely forgotten as a possible competitor.

We had to wait another hour and a half to begin our second nine holes with the golf course filled to capacity with the lower flight golfers. It gave us a chance to relax and eat before continuing with our middle nine-hole round of golf. There was one other score of note. The local high school golf coach had shot a 33 on Sunday morning's first nine holes. With a 75 the previous day his score left him only three shots behind the over-all lead. There was a possibility this young golf coach might just join our group for the final nine holes since the Weekend Warrior no doubt was no longer going to be amongst the leaders.

With the excitement going on at the golf tournament, none of us had been paying much attention to the hazy overcast moving from the Dakotas toward Lake Lindsay. As we ate in the clubhouse, someone began chatting about the apparent tornado warning for the western part of the state that afternoon and possibly lasting until early evening. This new development caused some consternation. In such a 'significant' competition like the one we were involved, an interruption like a thunderstorm or tornado seemed almost unholy…especially considering it was Sunday. It was a day all of us on that golf course were supposed to be allowed to escape all the trials and tribulations of our regular lives. Petty disruptions like thunderstorms were just not supposed to happen.

But, the reality of Mother Nature interrupting our lives became quite evident as each of us wandered to the clubhouse picture window and observed the western skies getting darker. After lunch each golfer milled around the scoring tent with one eye on the scoreboard and one eye on the cloud system.

The speed and size of this storm was awe-inspiring. It wasn't just an impressive thunderhead. This weather system simply made noontime look like dusk across the entire western sky. I still marvel at how the tournament organizers pretended the storm didn't exist or that it would somehow skirt by our location. There was no Weather Channel at the time so they had only a slight idea how wide or fast the storm cell was moving. The foursomes for the various lower flights just kept teeing off as if the menacing black cloud rising over the huge lake was only backdrop to a stage production.

When it was the Championship Flight's time to tee off, there was visible anxiety on every golfer's face. The officials, desperate to continue the tournament with no delays, kept repeating there was nothing to worry about since they were prepared to have golf carts come out to retrieve us if the impossible did happen.

We should have known better. Why would the Lake Lindsay tournament be any different? No golf cart would make its way out onto the golf course during a howling thunderstorm.

We had just teed off and were walking very slowly down the first fairway when a piece of lightning practically incinerated the flag pole on the distant county courthouse. That would usually be a mild indicator that all hell was going to break loose, but not to this group of tournament organizers.

The Weekend Warrior was unimpressed. He had been to Hell and back just a couple of hours previous on the first tee box. A minor electrical storm with accompanying tornadoes seemed like a grade school picnic compared to the trauma he'd been facing so far that weekend. He may have been hoping if that day's play was scratched because of the weather, they might award the winner's trophy to the prior day's medalist. And if he was struck by lightning, he might still get the trophy posthumously. What a way to go…in a blaze of glory.

I'll always remember the Warrior's shot into the first green on the first hole of the second nine holes of play. It was easily the best shot he'd hit the entire weekend. He had scraped a drive of two hundred ten yards down the middle. He was fifty yards behind the rest of us but he could at least hold his head high. His drive was like a work of art compared to his previous 'prodigious' thirty-five yard opening drive of the morning round. Now he was marching along as if he could get right back into the tournament lead with just a slight bit of improved shot making. It's interesting to see spasms of optimism appear when they have no right to emerge.

The Warrior's five-iron shot from one hundred sixty yards pierced the darkening skies as more lightning rippled across the lake. The ball flew straight and true at the green. It stood out like a marshmallow against a blackboard in a darkened room. It was beautiful. It landed almost on top of the flag and stopped about three feet on the other side of the cup. The Warrior let out a roar like he had just bowled two straight strikes in the tenth frame to break 200. He was ready to play through a tornado, a blizzard, or a world war…which ever was more harrowing.

The Slicker, the Hometown Hero and I walked onward another fifty yards to our drives. There was little reason to walk any further. The storm was moving across the lake with purpose. We could see golfers on the far end of the golf course begin running toward one of the shelters. It was getting frightful. None of us even wanted to take a club out of our golf bag for fear it would act as a lightning rod.

The Hometown Hero stood alone in front of us like a general perusing his battlefield position. He turned around showing no emotion and blandly stated, "My son and I are going to walk in. I believe it's going to rain on us shortly."

The serenity with which he spoke those words was in direct conflict with my general feelings. I said nothing. I began running back to the clubhouse with my golf bag slung awkwardly over my shoulders. I couldn't believe I had let myself get out onto this golf course with such impending inclement weather. I had been caught in one too many storms to allow this to happen to me once again.

The City Slicker handled his retreat to the clubhouse in his typical fashion. He let his young caddy carry his bag of 'lightning rods' back to the club while he high-tailed it toward the safety of the clubhouse ahead of everyone else. His self-centered, selfish nature remained consistent in all facets of his life.

We all left our golf balls out on the fairway. As I ran back to the clubhouse, large raindrops began to pelt the ground and the wind picked up dramatically. A couple golf carts actually appeared and picked up the Hometown Hero and his son, the caddy. Another golf cart coming in from the second hole picked up the Warrior. He didn't want to leave the course but was only convinced when another deafening clap of thunder and lightning bolt lit up the entire western half of the state.

Strangely no one noticed me. I was just someone from out of town. I had to fend for myself. If I was struck and killed by lightning, someone would drag my body off the golf course so I wouldn't be in the way when play resumed. Once at the morgue the hope would be someone someday from the foreign land where I lived would claim my remains.

A hundred yards from the first tee box, the rain began to fall in buckets as I continued sloshing toward the clubhouse. I was running as best I could with my golf bag over my shoulder, but I felt like I was moving in quick sand. I looked over at one of the shelters by the seventh hole and had to laugh. There were ten people huddled under the bent tin roof. The shelter was made for two people... and even then they had to be closely related. Those ten people tried to become one under that hopelessly inadequate shelter. The water flowing off the bent roof funneled down first one person's shirt then the next person's shirt as they all jockeyed for better position.

I finally made it to the clubhouse and walked into what seemed like a Red Cross station. People were milling about trying to find towels. The Hometown Hero was peering with chin thrust forward out the window as if daring the storm to interrupt his championship run. I looked like a drenched rat as I shook myself off in the entry of the clubhouse. I half-heartedly waved to the Hometown Hero. He didn't even recognize me. As for the City Slicker, he'd barely gotten wet since he'd parlayed a ride back to the clubhouse. His twelve-year old caddy was still walking in from the storm. The Slicker looked disgusted and continually commented that his equipment was getting soaked. He was worried that his golf grips were going to be slippery from the rain.

The Weekend Warrior was sucking on a cigarette trying to look like the heroic sportsman he now envisioned himself to be after his second shot into the green on the first hole. He was talking and trying to make people within earshot share his joy that he'd finally found the answer. He'd hit one good shot on the first hole and suddenly he felt as if he was the man to beat......another case of golfer insanity.

The storm lasted about an hour before the sky began to lighten to the west. Once the light appeared it didn't take long for the rain to stop. There were puddles all over the place and temporary lakes where fairways formerly winded through the trees. The tournament officials said the event would continue as soon as the golfers could all get out to their respective holes. They didn't want to lose the entry fee money by having to cancel the tournament. It looked hopeless that play could continue, but within another hour the water had drained surprisingly well off the fairways with only a few small puddles on the fairways, greens and sand traps where a golfer would have to take a free drop. These minor inconveniences would be dealt with by calling the entire golf course a temporary water hazard. With this ruling golfers could walk their ball to the nearest dry area no closer to the pin and take their next shot.

When the tournament re-started, all golfers were stiff from the long layover. No one expected there to be any more sterling play or scoring, especially with the golf course soaked and playing longer. Everyone just wanted to finish their rounds and complete the tournament.

The problems began showing up almost immediately as play was resumed. First, the air behind the weather system was breezy and cool. It seemed impossible to stay loose and maintain a fluid swing.

There was only one man who seemed comfortable in the dire conditions. It was the same man who had ventured back from a meeting with the Devil himself only that morning. The Weekend Warrior could give himself a perfect lie and there was suddenly no pressure on him to perform well. A score of 41 on the first nine holes would normally have eliminated him from contention. However, he had found a sweatshirt under his tool kit in the back of his truck. It kept him warm. Caring little about the grease spot all across the shoulders of that worn piece of clothing, he was comfortable for the first time that weekend and literally enjoyed watching all other players struggle to stay warm.

The Warrior returned to the first green to face his three-foot birdie putt. He promptly stroked it in the hole. The Slicker made a bogie and the Hometown Hero and I barely made our pars. We were cold and truly not enjoying ourselves. The hope was that the sun might reappear and give some warmth to the remainder of the day.

It did not get much better. The ground was drenched leading to a lot of mishits in our group with the golf ball rolling only a few feet after it landed. The air remained chilly. By the eighth hole of that middle round of nine holes, I was hanging onto a three-over par score. The Slicker was four-over par and moaning louder and louder about the horrible conditions, as if he was the only one who had to deal with them. The Hometown Hero was holding his game together and was only two-over after eight holes.

As for the Weekend Warrior, he was back to enjoying some wonderful luck. After that opening birdie, he had reeled off six straight pars without hitting one green in regulation. On the seventeenth hole, he chipped in from the other side of a sand trap. He again had changed a bogie into a birdie. He was actually scoring two-under on the first eight of those middle nine holes. The Warrior had made up almost all the shots he had lost during his opening nine holes of play that morning. He was no longer bothered by his atrocious play from tee to green. He was used to playing scramble golf. And, once he got on or near the green, he was a different man. His chipping and putting were phenomenal.

Our foursome hadn't figured it out at the time but all four of us were tied for the lead going into the eighteenth hole of the day. Because of the long delay, it seemed like a day ago that we had all birdied the ninth hole during our morning round.

The Warrior teed off first and hit a horrible drive so far left we just shook our heads. The rest of us hit mediocre shots that tunneled into the soaked turf down by the creek in front of the green. The Warrior again went his own way only to meet up with us again on the green. This was typical of the way he was playing his game...we rarely saw him until he reached the green. On that final hole he would chip out of some weeds and then hit an eight-iron onto the green from one hundred twenty-five yards out. His side hill par putt from fifteen feet was as true as the word of the Pope.

The Weekend Warrior had scored a miraculous and improbable 34 on the middle nine holes in golf course conditions that were difficult if not impossible. His eighteen-hole score of 75 left him one-over par for the thirty-six holes he had played that Saturday and Sunday, and tied with three other golfers for the lead. Those golfers just happened to be the other members of his foursome. The City Slicker, the Hometown Hero, and I had scored 40, 38 and 39 respectively on the very demanding middle nine holes. After thirty-six holes of playing together and being tied, the coincidence would continue with the four of us playing together those last nine holes. I'd never experienced such a happening through all the tournaments I'd ever played in or caddied. The only person close to our total scores was that local golf coach who had fought his way to a 39 in his middle nine holes. He was two strokes behind the four of us.

The third and last nine holes on the Sunday of these rural, small town golf tournaments were always lots of fun. Most of the gallery would be following our foursome. There would be cheers or groans with every shot from the crowd. Considering this would be one of the larger gatherings of people in this town except for the local high school football or basketball games, the number of spectators attending the golf event was impressive.

The owners of players from the Calcutta would be slogging their golf carts around the golf course trying to calculate if their 'horse' purchased from the previous night's gambling event was still in the race for the pot of gold. A new cup would be placed in each green so the nine-hole golf course might play slightly different the last nine holes.

Because of the Sunday early afternoon storm, play had been delayed for two hours. We did not begin our final nine holes until 6:30 that evening. As long as there was no weather disturbance, we would finish before the sun went down…that is, if we didn't have to invest too much time finding the Weekend Warrior's golf ball. There was a slight concern if there was a tie for first place after the twenty-seven holes played on that Sunday, darkness would be a problem. A sudden death play-off would be required.

Though the golf course had dried considerably, there was now an evening haze that made it feel later than it actually was. The temperature had gone up only a few degrees and the wind had changed to a northwesterly direction. It was surprisingly strong. The four of us had changed to wear the warmest clothing we had brought along.

The Warrior was first. The Hometown Hero, the City Slicker and I had now watched this bundle of nerves tee off on this first hole four times with some of the most hilarious shots we'd ever witnessed. In fact, those previous four drives were easily the worst series of drives ever accomplished by a person leading a golf tournament.

Yet, on this fifth attempt by the Warrior' he showed a completely different personality. He seemed no longer bothered about his consistently poor shot-making. It mattered no longer. No one expected him to hit the golf ball squarely. He'd been able to fall back on some wizardry on the greens that was unmatched by any human that weekend. All he had to do was get his ball somehow onto the putting surface and he'd make the putt.

With a short choppy swing, his drive was by far the best he'd hit off the first tee. Of course that wasn't saying much. He hit the ball on the heel of his driver and it headed toward the parking lot as if a magnet was drawing it there. However, this time the ball sliced back to the fairway. It was all of 215 yards and left everyone shaking their heads trying to figure out how this guy could be competing in this tournament with a golf game that looked like he should take up another sport.

The City Slicker was next to play. He had purchased a new sweater…. the most expensive one in the golf shop. He walked around the tee box as if to evaluate the wind. He was really just displaying his new sweater. He also wanted to check out if there were any pretty girls in the gallery since the crowd had increased to about three hundred people. He theatrically teed his ball up very slowly and calmly finished with an elegant practice swing before addressing his golf ball. He hit the ball off the toe but it hooked back to the middle of the fairway. It traveled about two hundred forty yards but actually rolled twenty more yards thanks to a rather strong trailing wind. To the unknowing public, the shot looked exceptional, especially compared to the sick looking drive of the Weekend Warrior.

The Hometown Hero, looking formidable as ever, was next to hit. He would raise his head and push his chin forward as he walked up onto the tee box. He had a disapproving frown as if disgusted he'd allowed any golfer to be within ten shots of his score. He looked like he really wanted to just drive for the basketball hoop or run through the middle of the offensive line for a touchdown. Unfortunately, he was in a non-contact sport where he had to confine his natural aggressiveness and show his talent for hitting a little white ball. As he addressed the ball, he paused while each part of his body began readying his muscles for the launch of the next missile. You could just feel the power emanating from this athlete's body. Everyone around that tee box knew this ball was going to fly a long distance.

It was this combination of the Hometown Hero's concentration of power and a breeze that had turned into a gale that produced the most monumental of drives. Hole #1 was a relatively easy hole that after two hundred seventy yards went downhill into a slight valley and then uphill to an elevated green. It measured only three hundred forty yards. The Hero's ball started out right and began hooking back to the center of the fairway as if tracking the green. Of course driving this green had rarely if ever been done so that thought never entered anyone's mind…probably including the mind of this local star. We were all waiting for it to hit the flat part of the fairway and then possibly roll over and down the hill resting twenty or thirty yards short of the green…certainly an enormous drive in its own right.

What surprised everyone was how the ball did not land on the flat ground before the down-slope but actually flew long enough to career off the down-slope. All of us players and spectators alike watched with transfixed stares as the ball bounded down the hill in front of the green before lazily rolling up onto the green. The gallery erupted into a cheer that could be heard across town. The ball kept rolling to the top of the green until a slight back slope made the ball roll backwards toward the cup. Though wind aided, it was still a drive that long would be remembered. The Hero had a fifteen-foot eagle putt on the par-4 first hole. It took a couple minutes for the crowd to settle down. The Hometown Hero had definitely added another chapter to his reputation.

Announcing my name was anticlimactic. The gallery at this point did not understand why the last nine holes would even have to be played. The Hometown Hero had proven with one prodigious shot how no man could compete with him when he was on his game. I remember smiling thinking that the pressure was really on this guy to perform. He would be over-swinging the rest of the day after that impressive drive.

I've rarely had the feeling I had on that elevated tee box that breezy evening. The wind off that enormous lake swirling up the bluffs behind me gave me a sense of power. I was capable of hitting the golf ball a long way…just not as far as this local superman. My game was not based on length. A significant part of my practice time was invested more in shots around the green and putting. But, that weekend I'd been swinging rather well and hitting the ball seemingly longer than normal. My timing had been outstanding.

When I addressed the ball, I felt very strong. There was a silence around the tee box, even though so many people were hovering close. When I hit the ball I knew I'd hit it flush. The breeze behind me seemed to add another level of height to my drive. It started slightly right of center and began curving back. I was pleased. I figured it would hit the flats and roll over the hill leaving me very close to the first green.

However, something strange happened. It did not hit the flat area. Like the shot hit by the Hometown Hero, my ball landed on that same down-slope and bounded forward similar to the route of his golf ball. I could see the ball begin to roll up by the green. Then as if by magic, the ball calmly rolled onto the green. The crowd erupted once again. Amazingly, my golf ball ventured to the top of the green, stopped momentarily, and then rolled back toward the cup, similarly to the Hero's ball movement moments before. The local star and I had pulled off the most perfectly duplicative and prodigious shots ever seen at this golf course… certainly with help from the wind. My ball came to rest next to his ball. We both had fifteen-foot eagle putts. I would now become part of that local lore the Hometown Hero had hoped to enjoy alone.

From that point forward it was really a match between him and me. We both barely missed our eagle putts and settled for birdies. The Weekend 'Warrior scraped his way to the green and missed a five-foot par putt. The look of shock on his face was almost heart-breaking. His bogie seemed like a score of ten on the first hole compared to the scores made by the Hero and me. The Slicker hung in there but soon realized his new sweater was not going to attract the attention away from the Hero and myself. His shot-making was not holding up and he again began blaming the golf course as early as the second hole. He would have his first beer by the fifth hole when he realized he was in all probability playing for third place.

If there was any doubt that the Hometown Hero and I were going head to head and no one else was in our league that day, it occurred on the par-5 third hole. It was five hundred yards in length with some definite wind advantage. Much to the Hero's chagrin, I out-drove him by a couple yards. I was literally over-swinging barely maintaining my balance and timing…but I was in a groove. We both hit six-irons for our second shots into the green because of the favorable wind. His ball ended up five feet from the hole giving him a putt for an eagle for the second time in three holes. I decided on the same club. It was another duplicate. In fact he had to putt first. We both made our eagle putts. We were three-under par on the first three holes of the last nine holes of the tournament and seemingly threatening to lap the field.

We finally came back down to earth and bogied the fifth hole against a much cooler and bothersome wind. It played entirely differently against the wind than it did earlier in the day. After that bogie, the Hometown Hero and I were still tied and four strokes ahead of our nearest competitor.

We remained tied as we approached the seventh tee box and the twenty-fifth hole of the day. The Hero now had his friends and family in a total frenzy with each shot he played. I was looked upon as a nemesis who they wished would just go away. But, they had faith. They believed sincerely it was just a matter of time before their star competitor would chop me into little pieces. But, we had only three holes left if he was going to make me into minced meat.

I remember seeing how important this competition was to the home folks. Even the Hometown Hero was now showing some strain. A victory would ensure him another year or more of hero worship from his local community. He normally could intimidate his opponents with his length, course knowledge, and athletic coolness. He was bothered that his formidable countenance wasn't working on me. This tournament win was more important to him than he wanted to admit...and to his followers as well.

Two things struck me. One was that I couldn't believe this small town tournament was so important to so many people. The Hero's followers were jittery and yelled vociferously after each of his shots. My shots were greeted with either silence or very light applause.

The second thing that occurred to me was that I'd probably get my tires slashed if I beat this guy.

The day was now losing its light very rapidly. The evening haze was becoming twilight as a distant large cloud system in the northwestern sky began shortening the day even more. There was some concern that we might not finish the final couple holes with enough light to see our shots.

Nonetheless, the Hometown Hero and I were only paying attention to our shots. We were competing. Our eyes would adjust. The seventh hole was a dogleg left directly into what remained of a determined strong gale. There was a major valley to the left of the fairway that could swallow up a good round of golf with just one bad swing. The Hero knew how to play the hole in this type of wind. He drove his ball far right and safe. I thought he chickened out. I, of course, wouldn't have said that to his face. I was young, but not stupid.

From my perspective, I figured to cut a low driver right over the valley. The result could be that I would be within chipping range...maybe twenty to thirty yards from the green. I was confident. My shot was strong, but higher than I intended. The wind began to take control of the golf ball. Mother Nature had the edge. Landing short of the flat part of the fairway, my ball bounced feebly into the valley. I was lucky there was a gallery or the ball would not have been found. Even then I was surprised the ball was located given so many fans of the Hometown Hero were in the crowd. But, it showed that the local folk wanted their man to win fair and square.

I had a second shot that was like hitting over the Great Wall of China from forty yards away against a substantial wind. I was fortunate to advance my ball to the top of the hill just short of the green. Bottom line, I made a bogie to the Hero's safe par on that hole. He was one shot up with two holes to play. I still figured I could catch him. As far as I was concerned, the pressure was all on the Hero.

The eighth hole, the second to the last hole of the day, we tied with par. We both had difficulty seeing our shots land on the short par-3 green because of the advancing darkness.

Now the last hole would be played in three-quarter darkness. The players in my group could only rely on the folks down the fairway to find our drives and then guess the yardage to the green for our second shots. I had played the last hole twice before that day. However, the Hometown Hero had played the hole one million times in his life.

Not to forget our two other members of the foursome. There had been another competition that had developed between the City Slicker and the Weekend Warrior. They were cumulatively tied with three-over par scores. That circumstance and to be particularly galling to the Slicker. How could he believe the Warrior could be within ten shots of him the way the latter was hitting the ball. Incredibly, he was. The Warrior had continued making some remarkable putts while the Slicker had missed a few short putts. On the last hole they were playing for third place.

I knew I had to make birdie on the last hole to force a playoff with the Hometown Hero. I relished the challenge. I wanted to know how the local tournament committee would handle a tie for first in their event given we'd be in mostly darkness at the finish. Pistols at ten paces might not even work with the pitch black night upon us.

The gale wind persevered as we played the last hole. No longer would we be hitting pitching wedges into the final green. As the cool of the day descended on us and the wind determinedly shut down the flight of our golf balls, I found myself one hundred forty yards against the wind with the pin on the back of the green. I chose a six-iron and choked up on it for more control. After overpowering the golf course all day, my last shot of the day would have to be a low finesse shot designed to fight the dominant wind.

Ahead there were numerous trucks and cars with their headlights shining on the green and down the fairway. Frankly as I looked at the green, the lights were blinding me. I noticed the Hero was shading his own eyes as well from the welcomed but bothersome man-made lighting.

I was first to hit. I kept my head down so I wouldn't get a direct blast of headlights in my eyes. It also assured me that the ball would come off very low to the ground. I caught that six-iron as pure as I've ever hit an iron in my life. The twenty people standing behind me could follow the initial flight of the ball. There was a collective "ah-h-h-h-h" from those folks as my shot pierced through the wind and darkness.

The golf ball was heading in the exact direction of the flag pole on the green. I barely saw the ball land but I knew it was close. Hitting the green, the ball bounced once forward toward the flag before seeming to stop. The crowd by the green yelled loudly not knowing who hit the shot, but appreciating the result nonetheless. Then I heard a groan as the ball gradually rolled backwards because of the slope of the green to about twelve feet below the cup. Immodestly, it was a masterful shot pulled off without any thought of possible failure. Picking up my golf bag and marching forward, I sensed that all the practicing I'd done had given me those expectations and the ability to carry out that one shot under pressure.

The Hero gave me a sportsmanlike nod and then promptly ripped an impressive iron shot of his own onto the green. The result was not as good as mine, but under similar pressure, he'd pulled off a competitive shot…about thirty feet left of the hole now showcased by a panoply of automotive head lights. All he had to do was two-putt and make a par on the final hole. If he accomplished that feat, I'd have to roll in my uphill twelve-foot putt to tie him.

On the other match the City Slicker hit his second shot short of the green just over the creek. His chip to within seven feet of the cup was giving him an edge over his unimpressive opponent, the erstwhile and never say die Weekend Warrior. The Warrior had scraped his drive along the ground. He didn't have a long enough club in his bag to get over the creek so he had to play his second short of the creek. His third shot was supposed to be a high wedge, but it looked more the height of a three-iron as it rolled past the cup above the hole about twenty-five feet from the hole. The Warrior would be lucky if he didn't three-putt that speedy downhill putt. The Slicker could feel the third place prize already in his pocket.

A couple more cars drove close to the green to add more light as the four of us concentrated on our respective putts. The Warrior was the first to putt. He and the Slicker wanted to hole out and let the Hometown Hero and I have the stage. In itself, that had to be quite a sacrifice for the vain man from the Twin Cities who preferred the limelight.

The end came quickly for these first two competitors. The Warrior had to be careful with his fast downhill putt. If he two-putted for a bogie and the Slicker missed his seven-foot par putt, they would still tie for third. It would be the highest individual finish ever for the 'Warrior'. He had achieved last place in more Championship flight competitions than he cared to remember. Even fourth place would be his top finish…ever!

What can't be forgotten was that the Warrior was in such a zone with his putting, he could probably putt a basketball into a thimble…on that day anyway. Yet, this was no time to get overconfident. He took some extra time and an extra practice stroke. I thought that additional time might destroy his rhythm. He tapped his twenty-five-foot downhill par putt with a confidence only he owned that weekend. At first I thought it was hard enough to roll off the green and into the creek. It likely would have gone that far had not one thing happened…the hole got in the way. The ball hit the back of the cup and leaped straight in the air as if it had seen a ghost. The ball then disappeared into the cup as if suffering from stage fright. It was the last hole of the day and one final 'routine' but improbable par for the Weekend Warrior. The crowd around the green roared their approval for the unlikely brave putt and the phenomenal result. The Warrior now had a lock on being tied for third place. Still, the Slicker had to make his putt to maintain the tie.

The Slicker was still gazing at the Warrior with the most indescribable look of shock…and disbelief…when that twenty-five foot putt was pulled from the bottom of the cup. He now realized how important his putt had become after taking for granted he had a lock on third place. Now, the Slicker's seven-foot par putt looked longer than the twenty-five foot bomb the Warrior had just drained.

The Slicker had more birdie putts during any of the previous nine-hole rounds at this tournament than the 'Warrior' had for the entire fifty-four holes. Losing to this country bumpkin could not be allowed to happen…not if he was going to preserve his celebrity. I could see the haughty character of the Slicker slowly drain as he stood over his short putt. With his confidence sifting away, I wished I had bets with every person on that golf course who thought he would calmly knock that putt in the cup. I could have paid for that fall's tuition, room and board.

I sensed that with a couple beers in his system and the pressure of having to make the putt, the Slicker was facing too big of an obstacle…and I was right. When he stroked his golf ball toward the cup, it didn't even graze the hole. He made a bogie on the last hole. He finished in fourth place losing third place by one shot to someone he thought of as an aged 'Tom Sawyer'.

The 'golfing gods' were hovering over Lake Lindsay Golf Course that evening and they had made their point. The City Slicker had been put in his place.

As for the Weekend Warrior, he was in shock. He had never putted that well in any tournament. He would never putt that well again. He also would never hit the ball as poorly as he did in that particular tournament. And, third place was as high as he would ever achieve individually in any weekend golf tournament. The next week he would get fourth place in the satellite flight at the Sauk Centre Golf Tournament.

The championship was now down to two competitors waiting to putt on the final green. The Hometown Hero had to carefully stroke his thirty-foot birdie putt close enough to the hole so he could at least make a routine par. A three-putt bogie would be unthinkable. It was not the time to be aggressive. I had a twelve-foot putt to tie the Hero…or, to conceivably win the tournament if he three-putted.

Every gallery member surrounding that final green figured I would nail my uphill twelve-foot putt after hitting such a quality shot into the green. It was anticipated that the Hero and I would tie with scores of 33 on the back nine under some difficult wind and golf course conditions. People were already talking about the playoff having to be played in semi-darkness. There was no other choice. Before we putted I heard some tournament officials whispering that a playoff would begin back at the par-3 eighth hole. More vehicles were being requested to supply that short one hundred sixty-yard hole with as much artificial light as possible.

The Hometown Hero was first to putt on that last hole. With the pressure squarely on his shoulders, he did his job...as everyone watching expected he would...including me. He rolled his ball across the green kicking up some evening dew that would slow the putt. The slope brought the ball down to within two feet of the hole. He decided to finish immediately and drilled the two-foot putt into the back of the cup to complete his score of 33 on the final nine holes and three-under par for the tournament leading score.

It was my turn next. I had to make my putt to tie the local favorite. While staring at my competitor finishing his last putt, I had a brief thought about all the amazing things I had seen during this particular tournament. I had observed the predictable places and people in this small town. I would be going to another similar community the next week...and the week after that...and the week after that. Those communities would each have their own hometown hero...just maybe not as talented as this particular competitor. I would not see this local hero again unless I chose to enter the Lake Lindsay golf tournament the next summer. This was the only weekend tournament of the summer he ever entered.

The following weekend, the Weekend Warrior would no doubt be at some tournament...maybe the one I chose to enter or another one a hundred miles further up the highway in another sector of the state. But, I'd see other weekend warriors at my upcoming tournaments if not him. That would be assured.

There would also be some new city slicker, maybe even a couple of them, showing up at the next weekend event. They would have their noses in the air wondering if any of the local sods could beat someone of their private club quality. And, as certain as the day meets night, those city slickers would begin complaining immediately upon their first poor shot and lament how the rural golf course was just not up to the big city golf course standards.

I smiled and collected my thoughts. I loved this situation. That's why I played tournament golf. I wanted to compete...test my skills...and win.

My twelve-foot putt was straight up hill. The wind still blew but had weakened slightly. The increasing amount of dew on the green would have to be taken into account. My putt was not difficult. I just had to stroke it on a line at the right edge of the cup...and hit it hard enough to get to the cup.

I took one practice stroke. I relished these moments. The murmuring in the background as I was addressing my putt quieted. Another mumble was hushed with an impatient shush from one of the tournament officials. The dew on the grass was becoming more of a factor with each passing moment. I could feel a momentary breeze against the side of my head as I stood motionless over the ball. Stroking the putt true and directly at the inside right of the middle of the cup, I was satisfied. I couldn't have hit a better putt.

It was only forty-five minutes later that I was packing my car with the merchandise I'd won for placing second in the tournament… as well as the 10% share of the Calcutta money I had won for those three local fellows who bought me as their 'horse' at the previous night's auction. I'd never seen or met them before. I also collected some personal bets with some people I'd gotten to know that weekend. But, those wagers were few. In other tournaments where I knew more competitors, it was easier to find betting opportunities.

I gazed through the darkness toward the ninth green one more time. I was a bit wistful about my last putt. The ball had bounced and hit the side of the cup and literally rolled around the cup right back at me. That dreaded "horseshoe roll" had been the final result of that putt. The ball remained stationary at the front edge of the cup with a third of the ball hovering over that front edge. That was it. The golf ball was not going to roll uphill into the cup. A convenient and sudden earthquake would be the only thing that could budge that ball. My last shot of the tournament was a putt from less than a tenth of an inch…but it counted for a full shot. I finished with a par, a score of 34 on the last nine holes, and lost by one shot to the Hometown Hero.

There were cheers…but mostly groans. The entire gallery had immediately become my friend with that one missed putt. They gave me a bigger cheer when the prizes were awarded fifteen minutes later than when the Hometown Hero stepped forward to receive his trophy and first place prizes.

Don't get me wrong. The hometown folks were thrilled their local hero had won. But they were very happy that he had to work very hard for the victory. As I was packing my golf clubs in the car for the long ride home, I had various local people saunter up to me and politely congratulate me for my play. I modestly said thanks to each person and complimented each one for their golf course being in such good shape and for running such a first class golf tournament. I figured it never hurt to make people feel good.

I was cleaning my golf shoes when the City Slicker slowed down and stopped by my car while exiting the parking lot. He leaned out the window as he was gunning his Dodge Charger for his long drive back to the Twin Cities.

He sounded surprisingly gracious. I decided to give him the benefit of the doubt. He seemed to be taking his fourth place finish better than I would have anticipated. He yelled above the motor, "Nice going, Long Ball! You gave him a hell of a run! I was pulling for you to beat him!"

Those were strange words coming out of the mouth of someone who was so self-absorbed. It amazed me he would think to be so cordial. But, amazingly, he was. He seemed to appreciate that I stopped with my packing to go over to his vehicle to thank him and shake his hand one last time. I added, "You know, this was a special tournament…one that the four of us will never forget."

He thoughtfully agreed. With nothing more to say, he gave a final wave and peeled out of the gravel parking lot. This particular City Slicker and I would see each other at a few other tournaments in the future. Arrogance was just a style he preferred when meeting new people. I was no longer 'new' people. He would consider me a friend. I actually got so I liked the guy. Whenever he saw me, even years later, he had a kind of brotherly look when he greeted me. His handshake would be sincere and the look in his eyes was one of respect. He and I would have a lifelong memory of one another. When together we would reminisce and entertain folks with stories of the Lake Lindsay Invitational Golf Tournament. That unique event was about the only thing he and I had in common, but it was enough to maintain that periodic and distant friendship.

As players and people in the gallery continued to clear out of the parking lot, I felt another presence as I was about to get in my car for the long ride back to my folk's home town. It was the Weekend Warrior. He had come over to offer me his congratulations as well. I was actually touched. Someone like him didn't like individuals in my age group. But, we'd gotten to know each other over the two days. I gave him the warmest of handshakes and congratulated him very sincerely for his competitive play. There was something about him. I knew he rarely received words of praise.

He put his hand on my shoulder and looked down at the ground as he spoke. His words were emotional for a guy who didn't like to show much if any sentiment. He was practically apologetic as he murmured, "I really appreciate you putting up with my poor play. We both know I'm not as accomplished of a player as you guys who play in the Championship Flight. But, I putted better than any human being could hope to putt and I finished higher than I could ever have believed, much less deserved. It will be an experience I won't forget. And…I felt like you were pulling for me. You never showed me any disrespect no matter how badly I played. Along with that, you played very well and almost beat the home town guy. But, as well as you played, I'll always remember you more for your gracious support and friendly manner. I just wanted to thank you."

And, then he walked away saying, "I'll probably see you next weekend at the tournament in Sauk Centre, if you're going to be there."

This particular Weekend Warrior and I would see each other occasionally during the summers ahead when we happened to be playing the same tournaments. We indeed did become friends. I no longer thought of him as a weekend warrior. He became a regular person to me after the Lake Lindsay Golf Tournament… someone to share a lot of golf stories and laughs. Although, he and I also had nothing really in common besides golf, that was enough. That weekend gave us a special bond. I often called him 'Magic' referring to his phenomenal putting that weekend. He was the only one who knew why I called him that nickname… and he seemed to appreciate the reference as well as the memory.

There were now only a few vehicles remaining in the parking lot. I backed up and was about to drive away when another vehicle sidled up beside me. It was the pickup truck driven by none other than the Hometown Hero. His business name was on the side of the truck. His son was sitting in the passenger side holding the first place trophy and a bunch of golf shop merchandise his father had won. Disliking me so earnestly during the tournament, the son now gave me a smile and a wave. He was just being an expected loyal son to his father.

The Hometown Hero at first didn't say a thing. He just gave me his own quiet and respectful smile including a thumbs-up signal. He was a man who let his physical skills and athletic ability do his talking. His sign language was his most sincere symbol of respect. I returned his thumbs-up sign. He smiled and finally remarked, "Enjoyed it."

I knew he would remember our head-to-head match with as much appreciation as satisfaction. He added sincerely, "You have a safe trip home."

Then he took off. Truly a man of few words, but we had gained some level of admiration for each other.

His mind was already past the tournament. His wish that I drive safely knowing that I had a brutishly long nighttime trip ahead of me after a long tiring day on the golf course proved again that this man's mind was not dominated by his golf game. His concern was genuine. He knew how exhausted I was. He felt the same way.

In his case he had a five-minute drive home. I had at least two and a half hours ahead of travel ahead of me at a high rate of speed. The Hometown Hero would shower, eat a good meal, and watch the 10:00 news before falling asleep by 10:30. He wouldn't admit to anyone how tired he was and that he felt more relieved than jubilant about his victory that day on the golf course. He would be at his work the next morning at the regular time of 7:00. His win mattered little in his successful bulk oil business or to his many customers. However, there would be happiness and contentment from those who knew anything about golf around the community for the remainder of that summer and fall golf season. The image of this hometown 'Paul Bunyan', that larger than life woodsman of Minnesota, would live for another year in that area of the state.

I would find out later that it was the ninth straight year he'd won the Lake Lindsay Invitational Golf Tournament…and he truly played in no other small town weekend tournaments during the summer. His previous victories were won by as many nine shots and an average of six shots per event. I had taken the Hometown Hero to his closest win in almost a decade. Fortunately, because he had won, the world would continue spinning on its axis in its fashionable way. I had not caused any unsettling emotional trauma in the community of Lake Lindsay by defeating the heroic local figure.

It was almost 10:00 Sunday evening when I drove down the bluff and proceeded south out of town. It was like a ghost town. Folks were apparently settled in for the night except for a few teen-agers shuffling down the street. I would stop at a drive-in hamburger place before it closed and grab something to eat before attacking my long journey back to home.

It would be a lonely ride down Hwy. #75 along the Minnesota-South Dakota border, especially after being so spoiled with the attention and applause from the gallery during and immediately after the tournament. There would be few towns along the way and almost no lights by the highway except the outside yard fixtures at various distant farm houses. The overcast skies made the night seem even darker making me welcome the occasional late night driver flashing his headlights as he met me on the opposite lane.

Halfway through the ride home, I would begin fighting sleep. My body ached to just lie back and close my eyes. But, I couldn't stop. I had to be up by 6:30 the next morning to go to work. Surviving the excursion back home was just part of the weekend adventure. This condition was a repeat of every Sunday night with the only difference being this passage home would be my longest ever that summer.

To continue my battle against sleep I would have the radio dialed into the 50,000 watt AM station out of Oklahoma City, only eight hundred miles to the south of my lonely location on Hwy. #75. The rock-n-roll music would keep me singing at the top of my lungs in order to stay awake. This activity while driving too fast down some highway very late on a Sunday night had also become ritual.

An hour from my folk's home, the cloudiness began to dissipate and the stars became resplendent in the vast clear darkness of the sky. It was beautiful, but only made me more relaxed. Increasing the volume on the music, I rolled down my window and let the cool wind whistle through the interior of the car to create more noise and keep me awake.

I would make it home by 1:00 AM remembering very little about the drive the next morning. I'd arrive at work bleary-eyed but promptly at 7:00 the next morning. It would be one of those days I would truly appreciate how fortunate I was in having a summer job where I could be semi-conscious and still perform the work. Periodically that Monday I would recall the weekend but mostly how I'd challenged the late night exhaustion and made it home safely from yet another weekend.

It would take me until Wednesday to feel somewhat rested and regain my usual energy. By then I had thought more and more how I'd experienced a very unique couple days up at Lake Lindsay.

That July weekend would be the last time I would ever venture to Lake Lindsay and play in their annual tournament. The next two summers another more convenient tournament happened to be scheduled on the same weekend. I would never again see the embodiment of the true Hometown Hero as depicted by Big Dave Lewis. He would stick to his preference of rarely traveling to another tournament site besides his home golf course. He didn't live to test his skills against other golfers. He was satisfied just to take on all competitors at his local golf club each summer and let them see if they could beat him. He knew someday he'd get beat, but until then he had nothing to prove. Besides, with his business and family, he had other interests and successes to appreciate.

Despite his lack of interest to test his golf talent at other golf events, I never had a doubt about 'Big Dave'. He defined the label I'd created. I would meet other 'hometown heroes' literally at all future weekend tournaments. Yet, never again would I meet someone of the stature, power, and skill of that Hometown Hero.

It has now been years…decades…since that memorable golf tournament. Much of what I did that particular summer so long ago would no longer hold my concentration from week to week. I have more interests…more responsibilities. Even that next summer prior to my third year of college, a change took place in my scope. That summer I had a different job…not quite so mind-numbing. I had to think…and deal with people. It was more fulfilling and enjoyable work. Also, every waking hour outside of that summer job was not spent on the golf course. It had something to do with preferring some time with a beautiful girl who would eventually become my wife. I still practiced golf…a lot…and competed most weekends…but I no longer was as obsessive as that one unique summer. Despite not being as fixated, I still managed to compete and even gain some wins during those following two summers.

When I look back on those nomadic days on the golf tournament trail for all three summers during college, that distinctive Lake Lindsay tournament weekend has always maintained its conspicuous prominence. From stereotyping those players in my group, to the steadfast folks who followed their hometown star in the gallery, to the excitement of the competition, to the smell of the freshly cut grass, to the magnificent thunderstorm that Sunday afternoon, to the view from the bluff overlooking that huge lake, to the pressure golf shots I'd played, to the warm farewells I'd received just before leaving that golf course, and finally to the long tiring drive home…they all combined to make that one event the epitome of all the weekend tournaments I'd ever played or participated in since. Even the familiarity of the townsfolk seemed to most perfectly personify the similarities I'd seen in my travels to other communities that summer.

However, what makes that whole weekend so curious and brings forth a grin on my face to this day is that it occurred at all. It has always been interesting how that golf event at Lake Lindsay had never been in my plans until just days before the tournament. I hadn't even heard of the golf course prior to that time. Furthermore, I'd not been enthused to compete until just minutes before I was to tee off. And most of all, for all the memories that tournament created, it was one I didn't even win!

The Girl on the Hill

From that summer day so long ago when Toby Robinson raced his new Mercury Cougar into the parking lot of my hometown municipal golf course, how could I have ever guessed the impact this one man would have on me from that day forth. Others like my parents, some teachers, maybe a few people I worked with have certainly taught me things or left me with positive memories, but this man…this one man…affected me quite dramatically in ways that have stayed with me over the many years of my life.

There were a few peculiarities that made this statement especially curious. First, it was only a whim that he and I even met. Secondly, we were together only one day in our entire lives…and that was for less than two hours. Thirdly, the two of us never saw each other again after that one time. In fact, had the two of us passed each other on the street even a few years later, I doubt he'd recall our meeting.

While likely Toby would not remember me, I'd always believed I'd recognize him whether a few years or even a few decades later. Though the pounds might be added to his tall, athletic frame and as his hairline might have receded or turned gray, there was just something about his entire countenance that was unforgettable…things others might not see because they hadn't seen him in a highly emotional state as I had. My memory has filed away his strong, confident manner and his quick smile. Yet, it was the intensity in his eyes when he was lost in his thoughts that day. And, how could I not recall his kindness towards me though his mind was on another matter.

I was just a kid when I met him that one time. I was impressed with the guy's style and confidence the moment he stepped out of that red Cougar. If I should ever meet him again, I probably would not share with him the odd but remarkable impact he'd had on my life. He might be complimented. Then again he might find the story I would tell him rather odd. Instead I'd kid with him lightly about my memory of his speeding into the gravel parking lot at the local golf course kicking up pebbles and rocks until he came to a screeching stop by the first tee box. I'd tell him about how I talked him into letting me caddy for him, even though he might have preferred to go out onto the golf course alone carrying his own bag.

It would come as no surprise if he looked blankly at me not recollecting anything that I'd said until I mentioned it was the time when he was back in town to attend his tenth high school reunion. Then his image would get quite clear as I continued telling him how I caddied for him for only three holes until something happened causing him to lose complete interest in finishing his round of golf. I wouldn't have to remind him about the reason… or that we both walked briskly back to the clubhouse. I'd like to think his eyes would begin shining with that wonderful memory and he'd shake my hand again with more purpose and delight. Frankly, I couldn't image Toby Robinson reacting any other way.

That trim, athletic, dark-haired guy of twenty-eight back in 1967 would now be almost sixty as I tell this story in 1996. That young kid who met him that day is now past forty and seeing some gray at the temples of my still full head of hair. My hope now and always is that Toby as unrecognizable as he'd probably be would be in good health and swinging the golf club as smoothly as ever… and that his life has been happy and fulfilling. For the impact he'd had on me, without him possibly realizing it, those good wishes are the least I could feel. It still leaves me in wonder how this man could have had such an impact on me. How could that short time together on a golf course of all places have been so unforgettable? And, would my life have been far different if I'd never met him?

The answers lie in this story. Interestingly, in addition this Toby Robinson would have an impact on some others as well. Those people and I would become intertwined in a web triggered by that fluke meeting so many years ago on that very ordinary hot, humid day in August, 1967.

That summer I had just become a teenager and was enjoying what I considered absolute freedom at the local public golf course. I had finished playing twenty-seven holes of golf. It was the middle of the afternoon. I was deciding whether to play another nine-hole round or simply ride my bike home. While mindlessly practicing on the putting green, my friend Glen was waiting my decision as he rested against a tree drinking a bottle of Black Cherry pop. He was staring off in space thinking about whatever a thirteen year old thinks about when there was nothing else to do. He glanced at me a few times. I could tell he really wasn't up for more golf, especially since the two of us would likely play at least another twenty-seven holes the next day. Besides, he'd lost most of his two dollars he'd come out to the golf course with that morning. If he hadn't won a bet in the preceding round of golf from an older guy named Clint who often played with us, he would have been leaning against that tree with no soft drink in his hand.

There was no question, I was the decision maker. If I wanted to play more golf, he'd be there with me. He liked to play and the competition as much as I did. If he lost, we'd stop by his house on our way home. He'd raid his coin collection or borrow from his mom to get the money he owed me. We never ended a day without balancing our debt. Thankfully, it was usually his debt.

Truth be told, I wasn't excited about playing another round of golf, but I didn't really want to go home too early either. My mother had a way of finding me something less preferred to do to cover my free time until supper. But, there was now a more wrenching factor. The start of school was only two weeks away. Golf would abruptly end on the weekdays and be limited to the weekends until the weather turned too cold to play. With no summer and no golf, it was as if a vast emptiness had cast its net over my life. My preferred and more interesting life would suddenly disappear for the fall and winter. Spring would return, the grass would green and school would end. The next summer would bring back my more favored life.

That's not to say there wouldn't be the stimulation school and its many activities, but as the summer was rolling to a close it was more the disappointment of no longer being in control of my own time. Teachers, coaches, and parents would again take charge of my life. I didn't like my loss of independence.

By that tender age of thirteen I'd learned the advantages of being so free… at least I had that sentiment when I was at the local golf course. My perspective was so immature, but I had the feeling I was in control of my entire life. Living each day on the local links made me sense I had graduated to a higher level than just being another kid. I had a reputation as a good player. I knew how to behave with adults and they seemed to enjoy playing golf with me. They treated me as if I was older and therefore I felt older and more accepted.

When away from the golf course that sensation would lessen; when in school it was back to being regarded as just a kid. As a result, with less than two weeks before the school bell rang, it didn't take much to understand why I wanted to live every waking moment at the golf course.

Nonetheless, Glen and I were tired that afternoon. It felt just as good to let my friend sit by that tree and let me hit putts on the practice green. Sometimes we talked; other times we just stayed quiet with our own thoughts. No decision to play or not to play was that urgent.

I had another vague reason to stick around the golf course. As it got later in the afternoon, members came out to the golf course to play a quick round of golf before dinner. I could make as much as $1.25 caddying for those nine holes, though my normal wage was $1.00…$.75 when the cheap county judge came to the course and needed a caddy.

This occupation had been rather dependable in the previous couple summers, but that summer the opportunities had waned. Times were changing. With the advent of the motorized cart, there were lesser numbers of players who hired caddies. This could be termed another sad tale of machines winning over man, but frankly I was no longer bothered. Caddying was not my chief source of income anymore. I'd elevated myself to a higher level of earning money that summer. My age and perceived maturity along with my dramatically improved skills on the golf course had given me a nice alternative for making money. I didn't just learn various gambling games on the links, I learned how to win…and it didn't always have to do with how good I could play the game. It had more to do with effective negotiating and knowing my competition.

Everyone gambled on the golf course no matter one's age…and that included my friends and me. In my case I not only made…and won…wagers against players my own age, but with adults as well. My advantage on those rare occasions I lost against an adult was that he'd feel so guilty he wouldn't want to accept payment. However, it was imperative that I did…or else he might not be open to make a wager next time we played together. Sometimes I had to reason with the guy to let me pay him if I'd somehow lost a match. I'd remind him the small amount of money I'd just lost to him was inconsequential compared to the wad of money I'd won from him in the past. I'd tell him it was only a 'loan'…and I'd get him next time. I can't remember losing twice in a row.

That situation…that is, my losing…didn't happen that often. There were enough 'fish' in the pond that I rarely went home after a day on the golf course with less money than I arrived with that morning. As a result, while caddying was still viable, it would be my last summer as an everyday available caddy.

Glancing periodically at Glen, he showed no interest in helping me decide whether to play another round of golf or not. Sitting idly against that tree, he seemed perfectly happy to sit there for the rest of the afternoon. He'd had an average day with twenty-seven holes of golf and losing $1.15 cents to me. I had a feeling after all the junk food and pop he'd consumed that day, he didn't have much money left in his pocket. If I was going to bike straight home and not stopping by his house, playing again and taking him for more money seemed fruitless. Even though I saw him every day, I'd learned not to wait until the next day to get paid. Glen had a poor memory when it came to paying off debts especially when the sum got into some real money…like a dollar…or sometimes even more!

It was during that little break while my friend was finishing his drink and I was putting on the practice green that a sharp-looking 1967 Mercury Cougar sped into the mostly vacant golf course parking lot. The noise and dust kicked up by the vehicle even got the attention of my lethargic friend. As for me, my mind was already working. I stopped practice putting immediately. I was already prospecting. Someone who could afford such a cool car, likely had some money left over to afford a first rate caddy.

Emerging from the car was a tall lean fellow already wearing his black golf shoes. His lanky frame was further accented by his long legs stretching out of his black bermuda shorts. The yellow collared golf shirt, black visor, and sunglasses gave me a hint that this guy had some class. I was used to seeing various golf club members showing up on the first tee box in their yard work clothes and golf shoes that hadn't seen polish in years. This guy looked like yard work was the last thing on his mind.

As he opened his trunk to get his golf clubs, he couldn't stop gazing out onto the golf course. He had the most contented look on his face. He was seeing memories out on that landscape. Being a betting 'man', I would have wagered all ninety cents I still had in my pocket that this guy and this golf course had something in common. He was looking at the golf course with the same appreciation I did every day. I could tell there was no other place he'd prefer to be at that moment.

His eyes finally flickered and he looked over towards the first tee off and the practice green where I was standing. He gave me a nod and then leaned into his trunk to pull out his golf clubs. In my case caddy opportunities have to be recognized quickly or the chance might disappear. Without saying anything to my friend, I began moving toward the Mercury Cougar as naturally as it would be to bend and pick up a dime on the sidewalk. I had reached a confidence and experience level where I had no qualms or hesitations about approaching any adult golfer offering my services as a caddy…especially to an out-of-town visitor.

As he pulled his golf clubs from the small trunk of his vehicle, he saw me approach him out of the corner of his eye. There was a slight smile on his face. That was a good sign. I believe he knew what was on my mind.

I had a gift for sizing up prospects very quickly. The initial bad sign was that he was younger than I'd realized as I neared his car. He had the strength and energy to carry his own clubs. Still, there was hope. He was alone. He might get bored playing by himself. I quickly decided to lean on that factor until another possible hook could be found to win me the job. I'd certainly played that card often in the past to persuade some indecisive adult to hire me.

My sense as I kept moving toward this fellow was that I had an above average chance at winning the opportunity to make a dollar. One had to stay positive when asking for a caddy job and be ready to handle possible objections. I was used to being refused the first time. Hearing people's initial negative response rolled off my back like water over a dam. It bothered me not in the least.

As far as I was concerned the real negotiation didn't start until the adult first declined my generous offer to be their caddy. It was the way they said 'no' that dictated how determined I got from that point forward. Depending on the manner of his initial negative retort, I would decide in an instant whether pressing the issue would be worthwhile…and of course how I planned to move forward as well. If I felt there was a glimmer of hope, I would use my well-practiced intuition to persuade the adult of the benefits of my offer. If it was especially hot, I would remind him of the heat. If there were very few people on the golf course…like it was that particular day…I might remind him that it was no fun just to play alone…even though, often times it was. If the adult wasn't biting on my altruistic approach, I might use humor…like pleading poverty. It was my least favorite approach, but if it worked once it was worthwhile to keep that idea on file. I'd mentioned to my prospect that it would be my third straight supper of potatoes and water if I didn't get a caddy job. If I made him laugh, I stuck with humor to win the prospect over.

On the other hand, if an adult responded in a particularly irritable way, I would usually make an instantaneous decision to say no more and just walk away. I wasn't out to make my own life miserable. Life was too short. Having to put up with some peevish adult for the next couple hours was hardly worth the money. The hell with him!

Or, if the guy answered me in a condescending manner…like the use of the term 'son', as in "No son, not today"…that would be a dead giveaway this man enjoyed being around kids about as much as I liked to eat beets. I hated beets. I wasn't that poverty stricken. I would typically turn around without saying a word and leave the man alone with no further comment…and silently hoping his wife would serve him beets that night as part of his supper. Money from that kind of adult wasn't that important to me.

Only a few yards from the Mercury Cougar, another twinge of hope presented itself. As he leaned his golf bag up against his car, the latest model of Wilson woods and irons shined in his golf bag. There was no question he could afford me. It was a dollar to caddy for nine holes, but I saw greater potential… maybe he was a $1.25 man for nine holes.

Then…another setback…I noted the size of his golf bag. 'Damn,' I thought, 'That monster golf bag and the oppressive heat!' It was large enough to contain his lunch, dirty laundry, thirty golf balls, and probably some rain gear. Lugging that thing around for nine holes was not something I relished…even for $1.25.

Still, I thirsted for the chance to caddy. I figured to win the job first; then resolve the weight of the bag issue after he committed. Could this be my first $1.50 job?

Then doubt entered my mind again. I couldn't get greedy. I had to be careful. I didn't want to price myself out of consideration. Oh the problems of a young businessman!

Nonetheless, I was committed. I had to organize my approach…and quickly. Closing the trunk, our eyes met. Without delay I looked him straight in the eye and inquired, "Sir…do you want a caddy? I know the golf course…and while you play, I can be quiet…or I can talk…whatever you prefer."

The lines on the younger man's face immediately softened as he sized me up. That was a good sign. He gave me a surprisingly patient grin and responded, "Well, I guess that might be a good idea. I don't feel like playing alone. How much you charge for nine holes?"

I could have been blown over by a breeze. He was so friendly…and his voice indicated he was even younger than I'd thought. What were the chances that a man this young would want a caddy? My statement about just walking with him and keeping him company must have worked. I had a live one…a serious bite. It felt good.

I took a wistful look at that golf bag leaning against his car and replied maybe a bit hastily, "I charge a dollar and a quarter to carry for nine holes." Then I lost my courage and added. "…but, I can do it for a dollar if you can lighten that big bag."

He responded with a chuckle and made me like him even more by saying, "Sure…that's no problem. I can lighten my bag. But, I don't want to pay you just a buck. I want your best effort. I'll pay you the dollar and a quarter…and buy you a pop when we're done. How would that be?"

I was back to being a kid, not a businessman. I had found a small nugget of gold on an obscure weekday afternoon. My enthusiasm spilled over as I gave him a huge smile. "You got yourself a caddy. My name is Ben. What's yours?

He grinned. "Toby Robinson"….and he held out his hand. "Why don't you just call me 'Toby'?"

He then eyed me and looked at his bag. "Tell you what, I'll rent one of those pull carts so you don't have to carry my big bag. How would that be?"

I nodded appreciatively. By God, I had hit the jackpot with this guy.

He then went into the clubhouse to pay his green fee as I gathered my own bag full of golf clubs and took them into the clubhouse where they would be safe for the next two hours. Glen didn't need any further explanation. He knew commerce when he saw it. He just got up from the bench and proceeded to his bicycle saying with a yawn, "See you tomorrow."

His comment wasn't even needed. Of course we'd see each other the next day bright and early ready to play some golf.

On the first tee Toby stretched and swung fifteen or twenty times before completing his warm-up. Then he hit three balls off the first tee box. Normally golfers just hit one ball and if they hit it off into the woods or over the embankment on the left down into the river, then they'd hit another shot…a mulligan. In Toby's case he hit the first one down the middle of the fairway. He then asked me to throw him another ball. He hit that one down the middle. When he asked for a third ball, I began to wonder if he was going to play golf or just hit practice balls. That third ball rocketed down the middle as well, this time a bit longer.

He said to me, "Yeh…that's better. It takes me a few shots to loosen up."

Walking down the first fairway, I answered all the questions adults typically ask a kid… my age, about my family, and what I liked best in school. I had well practiced, short responses to those basic questions so we could graduate to a more interesting level of conversation.

I was able to ask him a few questions as well. Toby divulged he was in town for his tenth high school reunion. He said he hadn't been back to town in years and one of his primary aims was to play the golf course that afternoon. He intimated that was as much his priority as actually attending the reunion events that night and Saturday evening. He said he'd driven quite a few miles that Friday, August 18, to fulfill his need.

That was when he suddenly stopped talking. His face turned wistful and he thoughtfully looked off in the distance…his mind a million miles away as we strolled down the first fairway. The silence was kind of uncomfortable, so I brought him back to earth by telling him about the changes on the golf course in the last couple years. Those comments succeeded. He seemed to wake up again from his dream. He asked questions about the alterations. We then just discussed the golf swing. It had hardly taken any time at all for us to converse as if we were longtime friends.

Somewhere in our conversation, he asked how good I was at golf. I decided to be only semi-modest. I had a certain confidence in my game and I saw no reason to be shy. I responded, "Well, I'm good enough to beat most members at this golf course."

Then smiling, I countered, "Of course, that isn't saying too much. But, I do practice more than anyone else out here."

With a gleam in my eye, I added, "Most importantly, I know how to bet with most of the local golfers. I know their weaknesses."

That brought a guffaw out of Toby. He snickered, "So kid, how good are you?" He paused for a moment and then asked, "Could you beat me?"

I knew when to be confident and when to be humble. I'd only seen him hit a few shots, but I hadn't seen many golfers better than Toby. I figured he asked the question half in jest, so I maintained the humorous track of our conversation and gave him a comical look. "Well, I don't know yet. I've only seen you hit a couple shots. Give me a few more holes to watch you play, and maybe then I might figure out a game where I could come out on top."

Then I paused with my eyes shining, "But, since I'm just a kid, you'd have to give me some strokes anyway."

We both laughed over my gamesmanship. He could tell at that very moment he wasn't with a novice at golf or in games of chance.

He played two balls into that first green…and then hit a few practice putts to get the feel of the speed of the greens. As we marched over to the second tee box, I noticed his eyes kept focusing on a spot ahead and away from the golf course. I couldn't figure out what he was looking for…nor was I close enough to him as a friend that I might ask him what the hell he was trying to see.

On the second hole he hit only two balls. He proceeded to make one ball for a birdie and two-putted the other for a par. No question about it, the guy could play. I was having a hard time figuring if there was any game I could create that would give me any chance of beating him.

Caught up in my own personal thoughts about a possible match, I didn't realize how subdued Toby had suddenly become as we both strolled down a slight hill to the third tee box. Since the third hole was the most difficult test on the golf course, I was used to any golfer being reticent as he cast his eyes on the sheer extended beauty of this extended golf hole as well as the challenge it presented.

From tee off to the far off green was 565 yards running parallel to a river on the left side of the fairway and a high hill of dense rough, brush, and tall grass on the right. God meant for this piece of ground to be on a golf course.

If a golfer hit his golf shot to either side of the fairway, the ball often ended up lost thereby causing additional penalty strokes. The fact that the river and the high hill of rough paralleled the fairway all the way to the green meant that some golfers were intimidated the entire hole. A golfer could easily lose more than one golf ball. Therefore, the result could be expensive as well as accumulating a lot of penalty strokes.

As a golfer and caddy I'd seen so-called golfers walk feebly off the third green literally shaken from their adventure on what the locals referred to as the 'river hole'. Witnessing scores of ten and twelve were not uncommon. I'd seen a lady make a seventeen…and she cheated to keep her score below twenty. Many players simply gave up after losing two or three balls. To me, the river hole was a true test of golf…and an abundant source of stories and laughs.

With this as a background, I was waiting for Toby to say something about this beautiful golf hole…whether how daunting it was or possibly some experiences he'd had on the hole during his youth. However, something strange was going on with him. His eyes showed neither stress nor even appreciation for the tranquil charm of this scene. Oddly, instead of teeing his ball up, he began looking through the trees and shrubbery behind the tee box…the opposite way of the fairway. He seemed frustrated with the umbrella of greenery completely blocking any vision.

I was about to inquire what he was doing, when he finally gave up. Without further delay, he teed up his ball. He then swung and drilled the ball right down the middle. Generally this drive from the third tee-box was the most nerve-racking shot on the entire golf course. Undaunted Toby had swung away as if he'd hit that shot a hundred times…or like he didn't really care where the ball went. I realized Mr. Toby Robinson had more 'game' than I had surmised. He could play well even when his mind was a thousand miles away.

He took out a second ball and without hesitation ripped it just as far down the left side of the fairway. However, this time he pulled the ball more than he'd intended. Depending on the bounce, the ball might just go over the edge of the fairway into the tall grass by the river. I heard a quiet 'damn' emitting from his lips. I'd heard that word so often on this hole by other golfers…but usually louder…and with 'God' in front of it. Often times, more creative profanity developed as that golfer continued playing the hole.

Sure enough, on the second bounce the ball did disappear over the embankment toward the river. I'd seen that same result hundreds of times. The ball was going fast enough to possibly bounce into the river. It looked like even a guy with a good game like Toby Robinson played would be earning a penalty on the treacherous river hole.

I put his driver back in the bag and we walked down the path from the tee box to the fairway below with him ahead of me by twenty yards. He was walking faster having not said a word to me since arriving at the tee box. For whatever reason, he obviously wanted to be alone.

As we both ambled along the edge of the fairway along the river, I noted how his gaze was not so much looking for his golf ball as it was staring back toward the tee box. I went down by the river and began kicking through the tall grass trying to find the second ball he'd hit. I took for granted he was going to assist in the search, but there he stood, still back up on the fairway. He hadn't moved...and he was now facing back towards the tee box as if expecting to see something or someone.

I continued to kick around the grass and weeds looking for his ball, but his strange behavior never changed. It was then that I moved back toward the fairway to see what was catching his attention. Immediately I realized he was not staring back toward the third tee-off; he was instead fixated on something else. I couldn't imagine what was attracting his attention. Past the third tee box was the community park. Through the thick trees and picnic areas of the park there was then the same twisting river that eventually flowed right by where we were standing. Beyond the river the only thing left to see was an impressive hill of which the summit was framed with high grass, trees and bushes. What made the view even more distinctive was a single tree...like a small oak or maybe an elm tree...located right at the edge of a remarkably precarious cliff. The tree itself seemed to be located so precariously that a good wind could topple it over and have it plummet down the abrupt rock face to the river below.

Usually I gave that image only a brief look. I'd seen it so often it was like a snapshot filed in my brain. With the western skies beyond that cliff, the entire site was more like a painting. Except for the clouds, this particular scene never changed. Despite it being quite picturesque, I rarely looked at the hill except if the threat of bad weather was moving toward the golf course.

Still, every now and then I'd wonder while glancing momentarily back at that vista what it would be like to climb that steep cliff...just once...so I could appreciate the opposite view down onto the golf course. Not only would I see the fairway along the river looking like a long airport landing strip, but I'd be able to see certain landmarks as I looked beyond toward town. I was certain it would be a great vision seeing the numerous church steeples, the water tower, and maybe the drive-in theatre on the other end of town. Yet, that curiosity would be so fleeting. As soon as I finished playing the long third hole, the motivation to scale that high hill would disappear as fast as it took me to get ready for my next shot on the fourth tee box. That cliff would not be part of my thought pattern again until I strode down the third fairway once again and just happened to glance back toward that precipice.

Toby Robinson continued to be lost in his thoughts as he gaped in the direction of that far hill with the din of the river rapids flowing beside us. His mind was so engrossed…as if he was waiting for that high hill or that single tree to shout out a greeting to him.

I remained quiet not wanting to barge into this man's own deep thoughts. Yet, as a good caddy I wanted to be somewhat mindful of maintaining an acceptable speed of play. With no players behind us waiting to hit their shots, however, there was no reason to be concerned other than I didn't feel like spending the night on that third fairway. Finally he shook his head. He lowered his eyes and shuffled up to his first ball in the middle of the fairway. He had the most melancholy look and it had nothing to do with his second ball having been lost in the river.

Then he asked me something strange. He said, "Ben, this is the 18th of August, is it not?"

I had to think. I knew it was two more weeks before school started…summer would end…my life would be out of my control…the weather would deteriorate further. Golf would be over until spring. I sighed thinking what an insensitive question to ask a kid when I was about to lose my summer and my independence.

Unenthusiastically I responded, "Yeh, I think it's the 18th." Then I moved away from him not wanting to continue that line of conversation.

There was more silence as he stood there with only the noise of the flowing water bouncing against the rocks in the river. With one more glance back at that hill, he addressed his golf ball. Again he ripped the ball down the middle…and then chose not to hit a second or third ball. Without saying anything more, he trudged slowly down the fairway while I strode along the river bank to see if I could find another ball to replace the one he'd just lost. It was something good caddies did.

All the way down the fairway I saw him periodically look at his watch and then turn his head back craning to see something in the direction of that hill. When he finally reached the green and putted his ball into the cup for a par five, he seemed totally disinterested. He handed me his putter without saying a word. I'd seen that look of disappointment quite often, but usually stemming from the exasperation or anger caused by a high score. Toby had played the hole well.

He then slowly began to shuffle off the green all the while staring far back at that hill now even further away. I was already heading for the shortcut path to the fourth tee box when I realized he was lagging. I couldn't understand what was keeping him from leaving the river hole.

Then as if a magnet was pulling him back down the third fairway, I noticed a complete change in his composure. His entire face was lit up… like a kid on Christmas morning. The emotion in his eyes had changed from melancholy to the most elated happiness. It was as if the sun came out from behind a dark cloud. The change was spellbinding. I stopped walking and turned to look back down the fairway in the direction he was gazing.

Shading my eyes, I saw nothing on the fairway…no one was playing behind us. I followed his eyes and gazed past the golf course to the city park…and then to that high hill beyond the third tee box and that single tree.

I didn't expect anything other than the usual landscape, yet as I focused I realized there was something quite distinctively different. There was a person standing a few yards away from that lone tree on the edge of that cliff. As I squinted to see better, that person was wearing some kind of long, casual dress. Her clothing plus her long hair were blowing in the breeze…and there was a dog standing by her side. The distance was so far away…maybe another thousand yards on the opposite side of the third tee box. It was impossible to see her face, but there was no doubt she was slender and my hope, of course, was that she was good-looking. Something new had been painted into that unchanging framed picture of the hill.

There was no movement other than her hair and dress flowing in the wind… her arms just hanging from her sides. For certain, though, all indications showed that she was staring down the river hole at the two of us.

I looked over at Toby and I swear he had a tear in his eye. I didn't know what to say or do. I was not used to seeing any man showing even a subtle degree of that kind of emotion. That female…whoever she was…obviously meant a great deal to Toby Robinson.

As if in a trance, he began walking slowly back down the fairway toward her. She was so far away. He began waving, first slowly…then more vigorously. He truly wanted that girl on the hill to somehow recognize him. Feeling kind of a brotherhood with Toby, I put his golf bag down and began waving my own arms over my head in support of him toward that distant figure on the hill. I even took the towel off his golf bag and flapped it like a flag over my head. Getting her attention seemed crucial to him. I would have felt badly if she didn't see him signaling to her.

And then it happened. At first it appeared she was raising her arm to shield her eyes from the sun. But, she moved…as forward as she could next to the edge of that embankment right in front of her. Her arm went straight up as if giving a trial acknowledgment. Then seeing his desperate wave…as well as mine… she returned the motion…first slowly as if she still wasn't confident it was him. Then her wave became more animated…almost frantic. Toby stood there just captivated at the lingering sight of her. His smile was now stretched almost unnaturally across his face. I of course couldn't tell if she was smiling, but there was joy in her actions.

Even in my relative youth I could see there was something exceptional between these two people. I put my arms down and retreated backwards very slowly feeling like I was now interfering in a private affair. It didn't take me long to figure out these two people had somehow agreed both would be within view of each other at that approximate time on August 18th. Apparently that hill, that precipice, was a location uniquely special to both of them.

Why they had this unique agreement was far beyond my imagination…and none of it my business. Still, how could I not be curious? If I was so inclined to see a girl…which at my age I was not… I might have gone over to her house. But, the shear secrecy of this clandestine meeting was obviously not that simple. My thoughts went even beyond what I thought I was capable. This was the time of a tenth high school reunion. Could that girl on the hill be an old flame from that singular time only ten years before?

I watched as he finally slowed his waving and put his arm down to his side. Off in the distance she followed suit. Then they just stood there, she beside that single tree on the edge of the high hill and he standing twenty yards back down the middle of the fairway himself looking like a slender tree in the middle of a grassy meadow. They were so far from each other, but by the look in his eye they were right next to each other.

Then she gave him one final wave and faded back behind the tree apparently walking away with her dog jumping happily beside her. Toby stared at that hill until she disappeared. Then he slowly turned. As he strolled toward the same short-cut path I was on, he had the most satisfied smile on his face.

I was waiting for him on the fourth tee box as he slowly approached. His head was down, but his face was immeasurably more relaxed. Suddenly he was more talkative…and acting as if he was the only one who had experienced the previous ten minutes. As if I were deaf, dumb, and blind, he said to me, "Ben, it looks like something's come up. I've got to rush back to my motel room and get cleaned up. I have to go see ……someone."

His speech was halted by not finding the right word. I was young, but not completely dense regarding matters of the heart. He was obviously smitten by the prospects of seeing that girl on the hill.

I gave him a matter-of-fact nod. I was truly disappointed. I'd just lost my caddy job, my $1.25, and my bottle of pop…all apparently in the name of 'romance'. At my young age, I'd never seen any advantage to having a girlfriend. This was just another example supporting my belief.

Without delay, we began the long walk back to the clubhouse. There was no mention of the girl on the hill. Instead he seemed more interested in continuing our lesser provocative conversation about the changes he was noticing on the golf course since last he was in town.

Arriving at the parking lot, I didn't expect much of anything in payment for my caddy services. He had played exactly three holes of golf. I had to caddy nine holes to earn my dollar and a quarter. I hoped he might remember his offer to buy me a bottle of pop.

Then he pulled a wad of dollar bills from his pocket. My hand wasn't out to receive any payment. He seemed to understand my hesitancy. He grinned, "Hey, Ben, we made a deal. You did a good job. It was my choice for having to quit so early in the round." Then he grabbed my hand and placed a dollar bill in it… then a quarter from his pocket change.

As he plopped his clubs into his trunk, I held out my right hand to shake his hand in thanks for hiring me. He seemed pleased with my politeness. I didn't let go of his hand until I told him that I would look forward to either playing or caddying for him in the future. He smiled and nodded. "Yes, I'd like that. Maybe we can make that happen before I leave town."

Our extended conversation gave me the chance to make a brief comment about the female we'd seen on the ridge above the river hole. I tried to be nonchalant. "Hey...that was amazing the way you recognized that girl on the hill. I could barely see her."

His grin was surprisingly innocent for a guy I considered an adult. He glanced back out onto the golf course and surprisingly shared part of the story. "Yeh....I recognized her all right. She and I used to meet up on that hill quite often during the last two summers of our high school years. It was kind of our own private meeting place. It was a great location to see the town and miles beyond while she and I just sat and talked. I honestly thought I'd be married to that girl by this time. In fact, it was this very day ten years ago that we promised to stay in contact after we went to college. But, it didn't happen. That day was the last time I ever saw her. We exchanged a few letters, but it wasn't the same. The distance of where we went to school was too far and our lives were changing."

He paused with a look of melancholy before remarking, "With this tenth reunion coming up this year coincidentally on August 18, she got in contact with me. I guess she got my new address from the class reunion committee. I'd always wondered if she ever thought of me after all these years. I guess she had.

In her letter to me, she said she wasn't certain if she could make it back to town, but suggested if it happened we meet back up on that hill behind the third tee box...at our usual time when we used to meet there....about 3:00...and ten years to the day on August 18. I guess I was surprised and kind of touched she remembered that time in our lives.

Well, this morning I hesitated. I wasn't certain if I wanted to meet up with her. While it would be nice to see her again, we could just as well wait and see each other at the reunion activities. Besides, it made me kind of ponder whether I'd done much with my life since I'd last seen her. I didn't want to disappoint her.

This afternoon I was curious. I wasn't even certain she'd made it back to town for our reunion. I decided to see if she'd be up on that hill today. Rather than go to that old meeting spot, I chose to be at a location where I could see her if she was there about 3:00. I timed my golf today to be playing the third hole about that time. If I didn't see her atop that hill then I'd see that she didn't make it home. At least I'd be playing golf on my old home golf course, so I wouldn't be completely disappointed.

He smiled looking back out on the golf course. "Well Ben, you saw the whole thing. She was there. And now I'm going to drive out there to see her...ten years to the day since our last personal good-by. I have no idea if she's married, has kids, or where she lives...but it doesn't matter. She was my girlfriend at one time in my life...and I still think about her often. It'll be good to see her again."

Not knowing what else to say, I gave him a silent nod. Though my understanding was limited, I finally drudged up a decent comment...one that surprised even me for its empathy. I shrugged and said, "Well, Toby, good luck. I hope whatever happens is what you want."

He seemed to appreciate my attempt at compassion. I waved and began walking away. I had a dollar and a quarter more in my pocket...and hadn't taken much time to earn it. I would have preferred to have been his caddy the entire nine holes. It had been fun being out on the golf course with the guy. He was a pleasant fellow and an impressive golfer.

Suddenly before he got his car, he yelled over to me, "Hey Ben, I forgot. I owe you a pop!"

He flipped me a quarter from twenty feet away. I caught it in the air and gave him a big smile and another wave in thanks. That last small deed would forever cement the positive image I had of Toby Robinson. He got into his Mercury Cougar and in the next few seconds drove away in a cloud of dust. I stood there even in my raw youth hoping that the day would end very well for Mr. Toby Robinson. He just seemed like the type of fellow I hoped I'd be when I reached the advanced age of twenty-eight.

Even though it was not to be, I also lived with the hope that this man would come out and play more golf the next day or the day after once his reunion activities ended.

I recall keeping my eyes on the parking lot every time I finished playing nine holes the next day...and the next day...in hopes of seeing that Cougar parked in the golf course parking lot. I stayed later both Saturday and Sunday just in case he returned. But, the result was the same...no car...and no Toby Robinson.

By the third day Toby's tenth reunion had come and gone. His classmates had their fun reminiscing with each other, showing pictures of their kids, and otherwise trying to make their lives seem worthwhile compared to their fun-filled, irresponsible high school days. He was likely already back at his home, wherever he lived. There would be no reason for him to come back to his old home town for a long time...possibly many years...maybe not until his twentieth reunion.

The memory of that August 18th afternoon would stick with me like it was burned into my very soul. I'd seen something very emotional...something I wasn't used to experiencing...and I didn't even know the final result. For that reason alone I'd be constantly tantalized when I recalled the short time I'd spent with Toby Robinson.

Whenever I did think of that day and his eventual meeting with his high school flame, I'd always arrive at the same conclusion. It seemed like their situation didn't have much chance of a satisfying ending. At twenty-eight years of age, she likely was married, with kids, even living in a faraway place. As for Toby, the only thing I knew about him was from his license plate. He lived someplace in Minnesota. Then again, was that a rental car? He might well live out-of-state...even out of the country.

In those next two weeks before school started, I found myself while playing the river hole as often as four times a day gazing back past the third tee box and up to the top of that hill. It was as if some strange force would remind me to imagine that girl with the flowing dress and wind-blown hair with her dog standing next to her and that lone tree right at the cliff's edge.

When finishing the river hole and walking up the short-cut trail to the fourth tee box, I couldn't help but relive the scene with Toby looking so remarkably happy…and wondering if that happiness continued once he'd met up with that girl on the hill. It made little sense why I pondered that question so often. After all, I'd only known Toby Robinson for less than two hours.

But, time moved on. When school started and golf ended for the summer, my own self-interests took over. Fall moved into winter and thoughts of my previous summer dulled with the gray of November and the inundation of snow and cold over the winter. I would not think again about Toby Robinson…and that girl on the hill for a long time.

As my adolescent years in high school continued at a snail's pace, the recollection of Toby Robinson and that incident with the girl on the hill faded, but never completely disappeared. There would be occasions each summer while I played the river hole that his expressive face would sprout once more in my memory. If it happened, I was probably playing alone thinking of nothing and everything. Something would cue me and I'd look back at that lone tree standing like a monument having survived another winter. I'd half-close my eyes remembering the pure joy on Toby's face when seeing that girl on top of that ridge standing there with her hair blowing in the breeze and her dog alongside her. I'd then open my eyes fully. Of course she wouldn't be there…only that scruffy-looking tree. But, the memory of seeing her was always unblemished.

Life moved on to college life away from my hometown. When I returned home those first couple summers, I worked a summer job for the county. After work I typically headed straight to the golf course. Then it was as if time had stood still. I was changing…maturing…but nothing around me out on the links was altered all that much.

It was during those college summers that I found myself paying even more attention to that singular tree atop the cliff when walking down the river hole. I still remembered Toby Robinson. I'd try to draw up his image, but it wasn't as clear as it once was. I could see that Mercury Cougar…his black bermuda shorts….and black golf shoes…and his fluid golf swing. But, the imageries didn't last as long.

He'd be thirty-five years old…not old by any stretch of the imagination, but possibly a hint of gray along the temples in his jet black hair. While I was still certain I could recognize him, I doubted strongly whether he could identify me. At twenty years of age I'd filled out. I was just over six feet tall. My hair was longer. Furthermore, I wondered if he'd even recall that warm August day when I caddied for him as a kid.

While I would likely be very inconsequential in his life, it was still curious how much his image and his behavior that day had impacted my thought waves… especially when it came to girls I was dating…and even choices I made in my day-to-day life. The intensity and sheer happiness exploding on his face when he saw that girl…it made me feel that unless I had that same passion toward a female or even a job, why continue it? If I felt no real excitement or satisfaction, then move on. I promised myself to try and concentrate on those things that better satisfied me.

It was a simple approach that seemed to keep my life more fulfilling. When I wavered from that tact, life was more frustrating and certainly less satisfying. With girls I dated, I would inevitably think back to Toby Robinson and the zeal he felt toward that girl back on that hill. Unless I had those same feelings, dating the girl seemed like a waste of time. The result was that I seemed to have a lot of relationships that ended after a few dates.

It was after my third year of college that I didn't return to my hometown for the summer choosing instead to take some classes overseas. With my senior year approaching followed by graduation and then work obligations, I figured it would be my last summer to do something out of the ordinary.

I was back home for only a week in early September before having to return to school for my fall semester. With six days off, I played my hometown golf course as if each day would be my last. Morning to night I was playing golf with old friends…mostly adults I'd known…but just as often playing by myself. Each time I played the river hole, I found myself staring back at that distinctive hill… just like Toby Robinson did so many Augusts before. I didn't expect to see some female standing there with her long hair blowing in the breeze, but I distinctly saw that lonely tree. It still lived atop that hill and looked no worse for wear.

I thought a lot about Toby Robinson and the girl on the hill that week. When I walked up the short-cut trail to the 4th tee box, I focused on the exact spot where he was waving his arms wildly at her. It was astounding to me how a relationship could stay lit for ten years despite not seeing each other. Now older it made me appreciate how unique that spectacle really was. In fact, I began thinking the emotion Toby Robinson showed that day was an impossible benchmark for me unless I gave a relationship a bit more of a chance to succeed.

Beginning the very next week after classes started again, I began dating some coeds with the idea that Toby Robinson's standard shouldn't necessarily be my standard. I was just different than him. I had to accept that my emotions were obviously not as deep and robust as his.

There were no sparks that fall with any of those girls I dated, but unconsciously I was molding my mind about the kind of girl I might prefer. I no longer expected Toby's level of exhilaration. By the spring I'd met the girl who seemed to match those preferences. Her name was Katherine Thomas. She was good-looking and intelligent. We had common interests with travel and outdoor activities. Most importantly we seemed to enjoy being together. That seemed to be comforting for both of us.

By the time I graduated from the University of Minnesota in 1976, Katherine and I were talking engagement and marriage. With my father and mother having moved the previous winter from our small community in Minnesota to Arizona, I had no real family living in Minnesota any more.

Landing a job as an engineer at KSTP-TV in the Twin Cities, that also added to my feelings that my life was headed on the right track. The job was a job… no real excitement for me…yet, it provided me income and experience to move on with my future. With the engagement and the new job, everything seemed to follow a certain logic.

It all happened so fast. Katherine and I got married the next January after we both earned our degrees. She worked full-time, but odd hours at the University of Minnesota Hospitals. I worked even odder hours as a sound engineer at that large television station. With her working some extraordinary number of weekend hours and me working later into the evenings, in a short time we became like two ships passing in the night. It seemed not long at all before the logic of our bonding turned hazy.

It took only into the second year for our both of us to realize our experiment in being married was just not working. She got bigger…and not because she was pregnant. I figured it was lack of stimulation on her job, not caring about her looks or nutrition, and obviously, the two of us not seeing each other. I was no exception. I ate a lot of the wrong kinds of food. I didn't exercise much except for playing golf on the weekends when the weather cooperated. My weight gain was thirty-five pounds in the year after we were married.

With my free time on the weekend, I certainly could have returned periodically to my hometown golf course. Though my folks no longer lived there, I could have stayed one night in the local fleabag motel and played golf both Saturday and Sunday. The town was only two hours away.

The plain fact was that I just wasn't interested. I guess I didn't want to go back and compare my life as a youth to my present life in the working world.

In our second year of marriage, she got better hours and we saw more of each other. By then, it was just too late. Even with the time in our schedules to be together, it was like talking with someone I hardly knew. I looked at her and wondered what I had ever seen or felt that made me want to be with her for life. By her words and the look in her eyes, I could see she was having the same thoughts. We seemed to have no shared interests and whatever spark we did have while dating during college had long been defused.

It was shortly after our third anniversary in January that we separated. By then I was disillusioned about everything in my life. I was forty pounds overweight, unimpressed with the institution of marriage and working in a dead-end job. I blamed the entire debacle on our decision to get married.

Our separation was almost too simple. We rarely talked once we moved away from each other. It was no different than when we were married. The final divorce was done with little conflict. We had no kids. Our townhouse had been rented. She took over the full rent while I found another place to live. We didn't even have a dog or cat to negotiate for visitation rights. After signing the document, we never saw each other again. We didn't even send each other a Christmas card or call on each other's birthdays. We didn't hate each other. We just had no interest in reminding ourselves of the tremendous mistake we both had made in getting married. Exchanging vows had been too convenient. We both had jobs and were making money. Those combined incomes made our life together seem so logical…so economical…so normal…so business-like…and turned out so wrong.

During that time of separation and then divorce, I often reflected on that image of Toby Robinson gazing so yearningly and nostalgically at that girl on the hill. I'd never had that feeling with my wife. There just had been so little emotional investment in our marriage.

Hardly a week had gone by after our parting that I began a new regiment to completely change the course of my life. I went at it fanatically as if I wanted the extra poundage and the burdensome weight of a bad marriage to disappear as soon as possible. I found a temporary upstairs living quarters at an older lady's home on Long Lake, west of the Twin Cities. Mrs. Ogden, a retired teacher, provided me more nutritious meals in exchange for doing some basic maintenance around her place. Working out daily and eating right, I shed twenty-five of those extra forty pounds by the start of spring. With a renewed interest in golf, those remaining pounds were worn away by the end of June. Feeling so much better, I even decided in the second week of June to travel the two hours out to my old home town to play the golf course. I hadn't been there in a couple years.

That weekend turned out to be a catharsis. I stayed overnight at the local motel and played golf all day Sunday. The golf course was as green and lush as I hoped it would be. The smell of the freshly mowed grass, the budding of flowers and shrubs, the trees fully leaved, and the 'who….who' mourn of the doves all brought back some really nice memories. I met up with some old friends and played golf with them. I was twenty-five and alive again after feeling numb and rudderless for so long.

Arriving at the river hole for the last time that weekend, I'd been so absorbed in conversation with my friends I hadn't glanced back even once at that picturesque hill behind the third tee box nor had I reflected about Toby Robinson, that single tree, or the girl with the flowing hair standing beside her dog.

Pulling my tee ball toward the river, I split off from my group to look quickly for my ball. Jumping down a small embankment toward the river, I was suddenly cast into that quiet little world with no other sound but the flow of the water and some birds chirping. It was so peaceful. As I looked for my golf ball, I unconsciously turned and faced back toward that distinctive hill. The bright afternoon sun was shone onto the steep dirt laden cliff highlighting that lone tree. I stood there staring and feeling surprisingly nostalgic. The recollection of Toby Robinson and that girl with the flowing hair rolled through my mind as if it had happened yesterday. The fervent and demonstrative waves of joy I'd see the two of them share that day so long ago actually made my throat tighten. It was an emotion I'd never experienced. It had been twelve years since that episode. The entire thought left me slightly depressed.

Luckily I was jarred out of my pall when my friends yelled at me to admit defeat. The ball was lost. They jokingly offered to buy me a new golf ball to replace the one I'd just lost. It was good-natured kidding and I joined their laughter, but while doing so I kept glancing back at that hill all the way down the fairway. Later when driving back to Long Lake that Sunday evening, I couldn't get that scene and what it had always represented to me out of my mind.

The annulment turned out to be a real turning point in my life. Within that same year I'd quit my tedious job as an engineer at KSTP-TV. I wanted to take my career in a different direction. That would include earning an advanced degree in business, which would take two or three years depending on the number of classes I could fit in while working full-time. That summer I pursued and landed employment as a business/mathematics teacher at a private high school in St. Paul the coming fall. I'd like to say I became a teacher out of altruism, but the truth was that I preferred the schedule with the summers free while I earned my MBA.

For the next few summers, the kid in me wanted the summers off. It meant that I'd be extremely busy in the colder months of the year teaching high school along with taking my evening graduate classes. This new schedule also worked out well regarding my folks. They'd missed the more comfortable weather in Minnesota from June through August as well as their family and friends. They stayed those months at the lake home of my Uncle Alex on the north side of Green Lake near Spicer, Minnesota.

Following my first year of teaching, I followed their lead and moved the next summer into a spare room over the boathouse at my uncle's place. Uncle Alex was a widower and welcomed the energy my folks and I brought to his summertime life. He paid his mortgage and taxes, and we paid for other expenses. In addition, I took over all the maintenance work.

Living in that boathouse was therapeutic. Besides being around family, I was intoxicated by the quiet atmosphere...the smell of the lake in the morning...and in the evening. It was heavenly. I wondered how I had allowed my life to get so off center relative to the things I really enjoyed.

By the second summer, I had completed two-thirds of my MBA while teaching in that same private school. I enjoyed the challenge during the fall, winter, and spring of teaching during the day and being a student in the evening.

Admittedly, the true enjoyment was my knowing once I had that advance business degree, I would be pursuing other interests. That was my true motivation.

It was the beginning of that third summer as I again moved into that boathouse bedroom at my Uncle Alex's lake home that a letter was forwarded to me from my Twin Cities address. It was an invitation to my upcoming tenth high school reunion scheduled for Friday and Saturday evenings, August 20-21. My only reaction as I threw the invitation in the garbage was that there must be some mistake. Ten years since high school seemed too soon.

A few weeks later I received another reminder asking if I was going to attend. That notice got thrown away for no other reason than indifference. At best I thought I'd drive down to my old home town one of those nights to say 'hello' to a few people, share a few drinks, and then return to Green Lake. My former hometown was only an hour away. While I felt better about myself, I still wasn't interested in comparing my life with others in my high school class. I hadn't done anything to boast about as yet.

As those August dates got closer, I got one big surprise. A couple of my high school friends in separate letters wanted to know if I'd be up for golf on both those days of the reunion since the main events were in the evening. They even followed up and called me to secure the golf plans. Just like that I was suddenly going to attend my tenth year class reunion.

On the Wednesday before that tenth reunion, I decided to drive down to my hometown and stay an extra night or two at the local motel. My feelings had changed over the summer. Besides seeing people at the reunion, there were old friends I hadn't seen for many years. My hope was to see some of them on Thursday and maybe coax them to play some golf or go out to dinner. My plan would also give me the chance to practice a bit and then lie to my classmates on Friday how I hadn't played golf for a couple weeks. Of course, being single and free, I'd had plenty of time to play golf over the summer. However, I knew my old high school buddies. They'd be working on their golf games before our play on Friday. They'd claim the same lack of practice time.

Checking into the small motel on the edge of town with a swimming pool, I observed the property still looked as tattered as it did when I was a kid. Still, the pool made it more inviting. In another town I might not have stayed in such a rag-tag motel. But, having grown up a couple blocks away, the facility seemed perfectly fine.

I didn't make it out to the golf course that Wednesday until after lunch. Typical of a middle of August weekday, the golf course was empty save for a maintenance guy noisily filling the garbage cans collected from the wild Men's night the previous evening. The scowl on his face and his permanently stooped shoulders indicated his life had not turned out as he might have preferred. I gave him a longer than usual look of empathy realizing he'd likely never experienced passion and true happiness at any juncture of his life.

The nostalgic beauty of the golf course brought my mind around to more satisfying thoughts. I'd always felt contented at this location. A grumpy maintenance guy couldn't depreciate my feelings.

When I walked toward the clubhouse, I also noticed a couple kids sitting by the practice green just talking and hitting some putts. It brought back another memory from half my life ago.

Entering the clubhouse to pay the green fee, I was met by a bored high school age girl behind the counter. She was more interested in her teen magazine. Without looking at me, she took my money, told me I could tee off anytime I wanted, and then faded back into her magazine. I couldn't relate to her tedium. I could only recall how much I loved the atmosphere of this small town golf club.

As I strolled over to the tee box stretching and readying myself for my first swing, I glanced over at the practice green. The two young kids were studying me. Out of the corner of my eye one of the kids put his club down by his golf bag and approached me with an air of adventure.

I didn't feel that old at twenty-eight, but the young man obviously didn't agree. He asked pensively, "Hey Mister, you need a caddy?"

A remembrance of my youth flowed through my body like a wave. I had been that very kid roughly fifteen years before. Even the clothing style hadn't changed that much. He was wearing cut-off jeans and a Minnesota Twins T-shirt. What I mostly appreciated was his entire approach. Just like me at his age, he showed no nervousness. He was going to ask me a simple question about my possible need for a caddy. From my initial response, he'd further size me up as a prospect or not. Certainly he expected a negative response since that was the usual answer… just like I'd always expected. It was from that point forward how the kid handled the first objection would dictate whether the sale could be make or not.

I didn't really want a caddy, but thinking back to my younger days softened my reply. I decided to give the kid some hope. I replied, "So…how much do you charge?"

He still wasn't certain about me as a prospect, but his response was automatic. "Usually a buck and a half for nine holes…but I'll do it for a buck and a quarter today."

Except for a slight increase in the rate, where had I heard that line before? By offering to cut his price, he sounded as desperate as I would have been.

I was about to say 'why not' and accept his offer when I decided to take a different tact. I didn't really feel like playing golf alone that afternoon. Seeing his clubs by the practice green, I said to the young man, "How about this…if you and your friend over there want to play along with me, I'll buy you both a pop when we finish the nine holes. How would that be?"

The young man's face brightened up and he shook my hand like we were old friends. "Sure…that'd be great. My name is Steve. My friend over there is Scott."

His eyes were excited. Like me at his age, he preferred to play over caddying.

Steve yelled over to his friend, "Scott, this guy said we can play along with him….let's go!"

My young friend didn't even bother to mention anything about the pop at the end of the round. It was more important that he and Scott had a chance to play golf with someone besides themselves.

I also guessed that depending on how I played, this young kid was a hustler just like I'd been. I could sense him already contemplating some kind of 'game of chance' for the three of us to play. However, I was certain I wouldn't hear a peep about any wager until he saw the quality of my game. The longer it took him to suggest a 'fair' bet, the more he would be impressed with my golfing skills. It therefore would take him longer to devise a game that he could twist to his advantage. I'd barely met this kid and I had him figured out.

As his friend lazily got up and grabbed his clubs, young Steve whispered to me, "Don't worry, we won't hold you up. We play pretty fast."

Then he giggled as he looked at his friend. "This is great. I'll get another chance to win some more money off Scott."

The kid was already starting…letting me know that he was well suited to play for money on the golf course…even with me.

The three of us got up onto the first tee box. Scott didn't look me in the eye like Steve did. He hadn't learned the social skills of shaking hands and introducing himself. That told me a lot about both boys. Steve was obviously more comfortable and confident around adults. It might take a few holes for his friend to relax.

What proceeded was just another ritual of golf. It didn't matter if those kids were eleven or forty-one. The three of us played our game to whatever ability or skill we had and talked golf from the moment we left the first tee box. Steve was definitely the better player of the two kids and was two strokes ahead of his friend after two holes.

Approaching the third tee box I was again taken by the beauty of the long river hole. The sounds of the rapids flowing along the fairway was only interrupted by the two kids trying to negotiate another bet since young Scott was well on his way to losing the first wager. Their voices were almost inaudible as a host of memories swirled through my head. And then like a switch turning on, the memory of Toby Robinson clicked into my brain. Here it was, fifteen years since I'd met that man much the way these kids had just met me.

My eyes switched in the direction of the high hill behind the tee box. The thick brush and overhanging branches on the tee box made it impossible to see the ridge until I got down on the fairway and had a look back from the river.

A flood of thoughts surged through my mind. It had been quite some time since I'd thought about that one day…the girl with the flowing hair and long dress up on that hill and the way Toby Robinson reacted to seeing her in the distance. That image had been so etched in my mind. Over the years if I hadn't responded that way to the females I'd dated, my interest would soon wane. The only time I ignored the importance of that kind of reaction, I'd made a huge mistake. My short-term marriage to Katherine Thomas was the prime example. Experience had told me that reaching the heights of the emotion Toby felt that day was not simple and very exceptional. Based on that premise I expected to remain a bachelor for a very long time. Still, it was exciting to anticipate the unforgettable picture that would solidify that memory of Toby and that girl on the hill once I got down on the fairway by the river and looked back.

After hitting our tee shots, the two kids continued to debate their second bet as we descended the trail from the tee box. Both young kids paid no attention to my silence. They were bickering about that second wager.

We headed across the fairway toward the river's edge where young Scott had hit his ball. I looked back and there it was…the ascending hill to that same cliff… and that lone single tree in full bloom atop the ridge. Nothing had changed on that canvas. That visage gave me the warmest feeling.

I walked along with my eyes riveted to that hill closing them slightly to imagine that girl standing atop the hill with her hair flowing in the breeze, her skirt swishing in the wind, and her dog jumping around beside her. And then I looked down at the other end of the fairway where I'd witnessed the animated look in Toby Robinson's eyes as he gazed back at her so distantly in the western horizon. I wondered after so many years what had become of those two people. Both would still be relatively young…only in their early forties. I pondered whether……and then I stopped.

Steve was looking over at me as if something was wrong with me while his inattentive friend aimlessly kicked at the long tall grass looking for his golf ball. Steve was no longer helping his friend. He was staring at me in wonder as I gaped at the high hill in the distance.

That was when he asked the most remarkable question. As if in some kind of fog, he said to me hesitantly, "Are you him?"

I blinked and looked at him strangely. "I don't know what you mean? Who do you think I am?"

He said it again as if in a trance. "Are you him?"

Slightly annoyed, I repeated, "Steve, what are you talking about?"

He then shook his head and turned away ignoring my questions? As he did he murmured, "I guess not."

Now I was the one staring at him. As he pleaded for his friend to throw another ball out on the fairway, he felt my stare. Finally he shrugged and replied, "Oh….it's nothing. It had to do with a story I'd heard when I first started coming out to this golf club. I hadn't thought about it for a couple years. It was like you were dreaming as you looked back at that hill. I guess I wondered if you were him."

He turned away again hoping he didn't have to go into any detail, but I wouldn't let him off the hook. I said a little too urgently, "So….tell me…what's the story?"

He shrugged again, but seemed willing to talk. "Well, apparently there's some guy who comes back here to this golf course every year. Nobody really knows him. He just kind of shows up…pays his green fee…and goes out usually alone to play golf. I don't know the exact date, but I remember hearing that he doesn't finish the complete nine holes. I've heard someone say that he plays through the river hole and then quits and takes the long walk back to the clubhouse. He gets in his car, drives away, and no one ever sees him again until sometime the next summer. He doesn't even get his green fees worth by playing nine holes!"

Steve then paused but seeing my interest he went on. "I guess there's something special that happens to him when he gets to this hole. I once asked Herbie, the maintenance guy back up at the clubhouse, about this visitor. He thinks he's seen this fellow once or twice over the years. Herbie is kind of a creep, so I don't know if he's just pulling my leg, but the way you were behaving just now and looking back at that far hill on the other side of the community park… well, it just reminded me of that story. And, if you say you're not that guy and you quit after this hole, then I know you're lying."

Steve looked at me as if still waiting for me to express my innocence. I was tempted to pull his leg, but I didn't. I smiled at him as well as his shy friend now looking inquisitively at me. "Steve, I hope this will answer your question. I came here to play golf. I plan on finishing the nine holes this afternoon. So…no…I'm not that fellow."

Steve seemed to accept my response. As far as he was concerned, the matter was over. He and Scott moved away from the river and toward their next shots. I followed them trying not to look back at that bluff too often. Yet, my mind was continuously rotating that memory of Toby Robinson along with that girl with the wind blown hair and long dress. Could it be that Toby actually had come back in recent years during August for another tryst with that girl on the hill? Was that really possible? It had been fifteen years. It was too unbelievable to consider.

I absent-mindedly played my ball up the fairway wandering by myself while Steve and Scott were jabbering away on the other side of the fairway. When Scott hit another errant shot up into the woods, I listened to Steve giving his young friend some specious support. In a voice that sounded more delighted than concerned, Steve called out, "Don't worry. I've got it spotted…but I think it'll be unplayable."

There was silence between the two of them before Steve said matter-of-factly, "We might as well start a new game on the next tee box. You've already lost two bets. You've got to do something to win your money back."

I smiled at the innocent hustle. Scott nodded his head as if he had no choice. I was going to yell over to Scott that the best idea was to quit playing for money until his game improved, but there would have been no point. Scott really believed he had a chance, though Steve was more talented both in the game of golf as well as making wagers that sounded fair.

A smile came on my face as I recalled my days when I was in Steve's shoes. I said the same thing to my friends who didn't stand a chance against me.

Once we left the river hole, my mind came back to my golf game. I let Steve talk me into a little wager for the remaining six holes. I made certain the bet would require a miracle for me to win so the two kids wouldn't owe me any money. I bought each of them a bottle of pop and watched Scott pay Steve the last coins in his pocket from their five bets they'd made in the nine holes. Steve looked pleased with the $1.50 he'd made from winning all the bets including a quarter from me, but he also showed some concern. He had to keep his friend hoping. With renewed sincerity he added seriously, "Don't worry, Scotty boy, you'll probably win back some of this money tomorrow when we play."

Scott nodded as if he believed the possibility might happen. Steve smiled at the reaction knowing the odds were against it.

I bid both kids good-by and told them I'd probably be seeing them the next two days since some of my classmates were going to join me for some golf as it was our tenth high school reunion. I told them of our 11:00 tee time on Friday in case one of my friends wanted a caddy.

Steve's response was exactly what mine would have been. He said quite contentedly, "Ben, Scott and I will be here whether you guys show up or not. This is where we live during the summer."

As I placed my clubs in my car, both kids sat over by the practice green enjoying their pop. It was quiet and slow at the golf course. I figured to take a swim at the motel, eat some food, and then return to the golf course for some evening golf.

I was about to get into my car when another vehicle drove up and parked several parking spots away from my car. He was a younger fellow. I nodded a silent greeting as he walked by my car with his golf bag slung over his shoulder. He returned the nod and headed for the first tee box. He hit with hardly a warm up swing and was off on his round of golf. While changing into my street shoes, another man drove up and quickly grabbed his clubs from his trunk. He seemed in kind of a hurry as well. I didn't get a good look at the man, but he was older than me.

I believe it was only that moment I realized the day was August 18. I'd not even thought about the coincidence of my being at my home golf course on that particular date. Now the vision of Toby Robinson readily bounced around in my head. With him now being in his forties and likely have added some salt and pepper to his hair color, I wondered how time might have changed him. He'd be more defined by middle age. This second fellow looked to be in the right age group. He walked with a slight hunch and wore his golf visor practically down over his eyes. Could it be possible?

Then I heard young Steve call out to the man. "Hi, Doctor Overton...you look in a rush. Gonna try to get in a quick nine holes?"

The guy who apparently was some kind of local doctor grinned quickly at the boy and replied, "That's right, Stevie. I've only got a little time to play before I've got to get home. Karen and I have a dinner engagement tonight. I can't be late or she'll kill me."

Both boys scoffed. Steve was the joker. He countered, "Somehow I don't think you'll die of the wounds. It'd be kind of bad advertising for your clinic."

The doctor and the two boys had a good laugh. The little interchange was another reminder how bantering on a golf course was ageless.

My whim about the doctor being Toby Robinson was obviously fanciful. I couldn't believe how the golf course and that river hole had me so mesmerized. I gave the two kids another wave, got in my car, and drove over to the motel. I ended up lying by the small swimming pool and chatting with a couple passing through town from Oklahoma. They'd been married thirty years…longer than I'd been alive.

I never made it back to the golf course that day. Instead I went to a popular local restaurant hoping to see some friends or former classmates already in town. Not only did that not happen, but I didn't recognize anyone in the entire eating establishment. My old home town was no longer my town.

The following day I drove around town repeatedly trying to get reconnected to my boyhood community. That Thursday I mostly visited old neighbors and friends. I played eighteen holes of golf and again ended the day flopping in that pool and talking with some other out-of-town guests at that motel. It was the kind of day a single teacher with the summer off and low expenses could really enjoy.

Friday was even better. As planned, golf with my former classmates was delightful. We were talking, reminiscing, and laughing so much I don't even remember taking one momentary glance back at the high hill while playing the river hole. Our golf on one day later on Saturday continued right up to an hour before the main reunion event was to begin conveniently right there at the golf club. I found myself unhurried as if I didn't really want to attend the gala. Nothing had changed since I got that first invitation. I didn't have that much to brag about in my life. I lazed around in the motel pool until some rain convinced me to get dressed and make my way back to the party.

Arriving late, the guys I'd played golf with that afternoon waved me over to the bar. It took me ten minutes to get there with the greetings I got from various other former classmates. Over the next hour I was pleased to see that after ten years most of the guys still had their hair. A few girls looked radically different, but name tags helped. A lot of my classmates were heavier, but their basic personalities were unveiled as they got talking. Only a few wouldn't leave the bar.

The one girl who my golfing classmates said was single and suggested I meet up with again was my prom date from our junior year of high school. Her name was Janet Patterson. My three golfing classmates had been looking for her to enter the party even though they were all married. Having not arrived yet, it proved to me she was as unsure and casual about attending the function as I had been.

The word on her was that she'd gone through a divorce in the past year. I hated to think that was the primary thing we had in common. I also learned that she was far ahead of me in a number of other ways. Not only was her career going very well, but she had a five-year old daughter. Hearing she was being considered for partnership with her accounting firm, I was impressed how she was keeping her life very much on focus. I figured our eventual conversation would be mostly about her since my record was nowhere near as inspiring as hers.

When Janet finally walked into the festivities, I was surprised at my reaction. I thought she looked even more eye catching than she had been in high school. The years had added depth to her eyes and confidence in her bearing. I knew at that moment I'd be spending some time with her that evening. I also had a feeling that even if I wanted to get to know her better, her schedule just might limit that interest. Somehow that gave me a sense of relief.

Watching her slowly make it through the crowd of greeters and former classmates, the reality of how badly I had misread my former wife flashed across my mind. I had assumed so much about Katherine…and I'd been dead wrong. Now here I was doing the same thing with Janet Patterson…basing everything on how she looked and greeted people. The only difference was that I at least had some adolescent years I shared with her. Scoffing silently to myself I thought, 'God, what a great judge of character am I.'

Momentarily my mind went back to Toby Robinson and that girl on the hill. At least Toby had a chance to communicate with his former high school girl friend before he met her again on their tenth high school reunion. I looked at Janet and tried to visualize her on top of that hill. That picture wouldn't print.

I nonetheless approached her after one more drink at the bar. Jostling my way through the crowd of classmates smiling and giving certain girls hugs in greeting, I moved closer toward my junior year prom date. I truly wanted to see if she was generally the same person despite her unsuccessful marriage.

I was about to tap Janet on the shoulder when I got intercepted by another female classmate. I recalled how she had thrown up on a table in kindergarten. Some memories don't go away. She talked about her kids and showed me a picture of the three of them under a Christmas tree. It took my breath away how disagreeable that whole scene looked. None of those kids were cute. She wasn't either, but she was more attractive than her kids. I gave a silent prayer hoping I wouldn't have to meet her husband that night. He'd have to be the ugliest guy in the room.

When she finally stopped for a breath, I flashed my empty glass at her and pointed to the bar. Telling her I'd be right back, I pretended to be intercepted by the group that included Janet. When she saw me she brightened up and leaned across the group to give me a hug. It was a lingering hug. I thought she must have been relieved seeing me. At least I was relatively the same size as I'd been in high school. My deep tan generated from living at Green Lake probably didn't hurt. Either way, it was nice getting that kind of response from her.

We separated from the group and caught up for almost ten minutes before we were all called for dinner. I told her my story in less than two minutes…and she told me hers in about the same amount of time. We seemed conscious of not boring each other…as well as not showing too much interest.

I was as impressed with her as I thought I'd be. Not only was she on that partner track at her accounting firm in Coon Rapids and bringing up her daughter alone, but she was completing her Masters of Accounting program in the evenings in the same way I was finishing my advanced business degree during the school year. She didn't look harried, but her eyes showed some tiredness and distrust not necessarily toward me, but toward life in general. I wondered if my eyes showed the same thing.

Some of our former female classmates suddenly appeared. I got the idea they might have arrived to rescue Janet from me. I figured my story had to have been spread around the room from the mouths of my golfing friends. That was confirmed when one of the females standing near me commented how I must be on the prowl again. It was an unkind remark that needed only silence for a response. To end the awkwardness, I again showed an empty glass.

Nodding at Janet, I moved along toward the bar hoping we might talk later. I thought I saw her nod and her stare linger.

At the bar I initiated a conversation with Dale Jensen who'd just downed his third bourbon and water. It was the first time I'd ever started a discussion with him…and he'd been a classmate since the third grade. He had a great sense of humor as he made some snide remembrances of some of our classmates. He made me sorry I hadn't gotten to know him better back in high school.

As the night progressed I ended up sitting at the table with the classmates I'd played golf with earlier that afternoon. With dinner over, I was already thinking of leaving. People were drinking a bit too heavily and I'd run out of things I wanted to hear from them. Jumping in the pool back at the motel sounded more entertaining.

Then as if she was reading my thoughts, Janet came up and apologized for what that one female classmate had said…and tried to make me understand she really didn't want to get rescued. This led to us sitting out on the deck of the clubhouse away from the remaining crowd. She seemed appreciative having the chance to converse about her life with a male rather than just another female. It was a deeper conversation than I would have preferred. When I mentioned how I was generally satisfied in my single life, she didn't seem to be of the same mind. Being a parent she was obviously not as free-wheeling as I was able to be.

By the end of the evening I had her phone number and she had mine. We might have done the exchange just to be polite. Nevertheless, the door was opened if either she or I wanted to take another fling at a relationship. After all, if we went out, it would not be as if we were on a first date.

As I drove back to my motel room that night…alone…I realized I had no intention of calling Janet Patterson. It was certainly nice to see her again. She was attractive. And, frankly I was happy for her that she was moving ahead so positively. The problem I had was simple. I couldn't visualize her up on that ridge waving at me with the same genuine excitement that girl on the hill seemed to have for Toby Robinson. I also didn't have the same enthusiasm I saw in Toby's eyes when he returned the wave.

The thought caused me to burst out laughing. I apparently would always be influenced by that scene from fifteen years before. It got me further thinking. I'd always taken for granted he and that female had gotten together and had spent many blissful years together. However, the story I'd heard at the golf club from that young kid, Steve, pointed toward a different conclusion. His description was a stranger who just showed up at the golf course each August, headed for the river hole, and, as the story was circulated, often didn't complete his round of golf.

That story was too coincidental not to be about Toby Robinson. Yet if Toby was returning each year, then it meant his relationship with that girl had not evolved. Something hadn't worked out.

It was a disappointing thought. If those two people never got together, then life truly wasn't fair. Yet, they somehow remained motivated to return home every summer to see each other. The whole thing seemed so inconceivable. What had stood in there way? Or, why hadn't they faced the reality that they weren't going to get together?

I went to sleep that night with a growing disillusionment. I'd based every potential relationship on whether I had that same high level emotion Toby Robinson had towards that girl on the hill. It was a bit disconcerting. If the two of them hadn't been able to combine their lives with the passion I saw in Toby's eyes, then where did that leave me? It made me reason that I was not the type of person who could get that intensely emotional about anything or anyone.

By Sunday morning, I was awake and ready to leave my hometown before 7:00. I was suddenly anxious to get back to Green Lake and take pleasure in the life I'd developed for myself. A bunch of Uncle Alex's neighbors were going water skiing that afternoon. There'd be a big party later. It was the kind of life I'd come to love.

In the months ahead I returned to my regular non-summer schedule teaching at the private high school in the Twin Cities and completing the last year of evening business courses at the University of Minnesota. Occasionally I'd had the inclination to call Janet Patterson. I imagined she might feel complimented with my call, even if she was dating someone else. Something in my psyche kept me from picking up the phone. I knew the reason. It had to do with seeing that hill again the previous summer at my boyhood golf course.

Those final two semesters to complete my advanced business degree opened my eyes to many opportunities outside of teaching. While I enjoyed teaching and coaching, I knew that year would be my swan song as far as working in the field of education. My final year in my twenties was upon me. I wanted something different...even if it meant giving up my free summers.

By the springtime I was right on schedule to complete my MBA degree. There was no question I'd aggressively go on the interview trail...or as the saying goes, 'take my new degree for a spin' and see what new career path I might follow.

However, with the end of my teaching job and the coming of the warmer months of summer, I found myself procrastinating. So much for my claim of growing up and moving on...that upcoming summer was just too enticing not to return to my Uncle Alex's place and be close to my folks again. After living the past four summers in that small room above my uncle's boathouse, I was not ready to give up that simple and relaxing life just yet.

Knowing that the upcoming summer might be my last with him, Uncle Alex showed a renewed urgency to influence my future. He kept trying to fix me up with some local gals in the Spicer area. He kidded that the small apartment above his boathouse could be used for something besides sleeping. I had no intentions of becoming a monk, but I still didn't trust having any kind of serious relationship. I dated a few more times than average that summer but it all seemed so unimportant. I didn't want to get involved. Changing careers meant that I could be anywhere by the coming winter.

Twice that summer I did return to my old hometown golf course. I had the passing thought that I might be moving away from Minnesota. Both times I played, I found myself glancing back at the single tree atop the hill as I walked along the river hole. That tree had become as much a symbol to me as the vague vision of that girl on the hill...of a possible relationship that I'd never found...or fought finding. With too much of its root system protruding out of the cliff, it showed vulnerability yet a sturdiness and ruggedness alone atop that hill. Despite the harshness of winter, or the deluge of wind and rain in the spring, or even the hot blazing sun during the summer, that 'single' tree budded every spring and looked just as strong and healthy one year after another. I saw it metaphorically depicting my life...being alone, but determined to forge on. I figured as long as that tree could survive the seasons, so could I.

Halfway through the summer, I hadn't done a thing to market myself with my newly earned MBA. It became clear I was not going to make any effort until I was back in Minneapolis that fall. I'd have to do something to take up the slack in time that I no longer would have to attend evening classes. I did decide to let my private school employer know I'd be willing to work to the end of the calendar year. I was relieved when I received word I'd be welcomed back. That bit of news relieved any pressure I felt to get aggressive with my new career search.

I'd get more purposeful as I faced unemployment in January forcing me to give my advanced degree the ride it deserved.

It was just two weeks before I was to return to the Twin Cities that I visited my hometown golf course that second time. It was a Thursday and my folks and Uncle Alex decided to go to the Twin Cities given rain was in the forecast. There was a wedding at Lake Minnetonka. They wanted to get there early to enjoy friends they hadn't seen for a long time. That meant I'd be alone for a couple days since I didn't particularly want to watch two people…for good or bad… venture off into their new life.

When the three of them left that morning for the wedding, the skies were overcast… the perfect kind of day to feel even more morose. I whimsically made a choice to drive across South Dakota to the Black Hills and Mt. Rushmore… eight hours out and eight hours back…and return on Sunday. At that moment, it sounded kind of adventuresome.

After they departed I left Green Lake for a little road trip that I hoped would enliven my spirit a bit. Passing through my old hometown and feeling hungry, I decided to stop downtown at a café I'd frequented often as a kid. There I watched the day change to brightness as the cloud cover moved away. With the food and the sunlight, I felt refreshed. I no longer had the desire to travel across South Dakota just to get away. Being less than a mile from my hometown golf course, I'd traveled as far as I needed. A day of golf, maybe meeting up with some old friends at the golf course, and maybe even an overnight at that local, inexpensive motel with the swimming pool sounded more inviting.

Arriving at the golf course, it was not surprising to see such a vacant parking lot. A weekday in August…people's interest wavered away from golf. With little interruption, I hoped to golf until at least the mid-afternoon before some rain was forecast in the area. If it did rain, I would simply return to Green Lake and take in a movie in Willmar.

I looked around and felt the strong sensation of time standing still. The clubhouse hadn't changed since I was a kid. There was a foursome finishing up their nine holes. I could hear the maintenance guy in back of the clubhouse filling the garbage cans. Young Steve and Scott were not there, but a couple other kids were sitting by the practice green. All these were timeless scenes.

The morning was still cool, but with clear skies it promised to be a great day until the rain arrived in the afternoon. Taking my time and hitting multiple practice shots on the first two holes, I finally arrived at the picturesque river hole.

Hitting two drives off the tee box, I strolled along the left side of the fairway mesmerized more by the shear quietness of the day than any thoughts of that lone tree back up on the hill, or the girl with the flowing hair, or even of Toby Robinson. Finally completing play on the hole, I picked up my golf bag and stared back at the high hill that still laid there like a painting while slowly walking toward the fourth tee box.. There was that singular tree still steadfastly standing

on the edge of that ridge. That vision again gave me a kind of spark. That tree…
and I…were still surviving quite well. Whatever had been bothering me in recent
days had gradually drifted away. I found myself glad I'd come to my senses and
not driven across South Dakota. I had an antidote for melancholy right there on
my old hometown golf course.

When I completed the nine holes, I stopped for lunch before teeing off again.
By the time I'd finished that round of golf and the food, it was mid-afternoon. As
predicted, some rain clouds were moving over the golf course. Just sensing I wouldn't
be playing the golf course for a long time, I wasn't ready to leave town. I really
wanted to play one more round. Sitting in the clubhouse watching the slow drip of
rain, I decided it was not so much of a downpour that I couldn't at least try to play.

The young high school girl sitting behind the counter taking green fees and
reading her magazine was the same one from the previous year. In a year's time,
however, she'd learned to smile.

Pouring me some coffee, she said, "Well, if it weren't for you and one other
player, I doubt we'd even have the clubhouse opened right now. The forecast
scared people away."

My eyes brightened. "Oh…there's another player on the golf course?"

She nodded looking out at the light rain. "It's not really that bad outside. Of
course it could be a heavier rain and that other golfer would still be out on the
golf course. He told me this was an afternoon he had to play…even if it snowed
in August." Her comment caught my attention. I asked her, "Do you know the
guy who's out there playing in the rain?"

She shook her head. "Nah, he's a local member, but I really don't know him
well. He doesn't play golf that often."

Her response was peculiar. Why would a golfer who didn't play much
decide to play during such foul weather? I was curious enough to keep up our
conversation. "So, you said he doesn't play very often, but here he is playing in
the rain. That's kind of strange, isn't it?

She hadn't given her statement much thought but shrugged, "Yeh…I guess
it doesn't make a lot of sense. He also said he was running a bit late today and
had to hurry. I don't think he even played the first hole. He just walked quickly
over to the second tee box."

Her little story was fascinating, especially when I glanced at her calendar
behind the bar and saw the day was August 18. What a coincidence. Still, I
certainly didn't expect the man out on the golf course to be Toby Robinson.
She'd just said the guy lived locally.

With my curiosity having risen and nothing better to do that afternoon, I
found myself wanting to see this local fellow. Downing what was left of the coffee
and hamburger, I proceeded out into the dribble of rain and teed off on the first
hole. Watching me from the clubhouse window, I could see the young girl was
mystified over trying to understand the mentality of an apparent golf fanatic.

I played the first two holes rapidly looking over the rest of the golf course to spot the other golfer. Seeing nothing I proceeded to the more secluded third tee box. Staring far down the river hole, I blinked in surprise. There was the only other player on the golf course. He was approximately five hundred yards away; recognizing his face was impossible. I couldn't tell from that distance if the man was older or younger. He was just completing putting on the wet green.

There was still no question in my mind the golfer couldn't be Toby Robinson…until what happened next. It made my heart leap. I watched as he picked up his golf bag to move on toward the fourth tee box. Suddenly he stopped and placed his golf bag back down on the ground. He then began walking a few steps towards me…and began waving wildly. His motion startled me. How could he recognize me? Who the hell was he? Feeling obligated, I began to raise my hand to wave back…but then stopped myself. There was no reason for him to be waving at me?

Then I realized the fanfare was not intended for me….but someone behind me. Standing on the river hole tee box, I tried to look through the heavy brush and trees, but I couldn't see through the screen of foliage. Hitting my ball quickly, I hurried down the inclined path to the fairway desperately looking back toward the hill behind me.

First thing I saw was that tree…that single tree rising determinedly from the top of the hill. And then…as if in a dream…I saw her! It was as if a ghost from the past had just decided for no particular reason to return to that special place on the hill. This time I was nearer her than so many years before when I stood at the other end of the long fairway close to Toby Robinson.

Amazingly she still looked quite young. If she was twenty-eight years old when I had first seen her while with Toby Robinson, she now had to be in her early forties. I'd seen plenty of women in their forties and while still attractive, they generally didn't maintain the hairstyle of a young girl. But, there she was… her long hair blowing in the breeze. And, she was so lithe in the way she moved her arm and body. She reminded me of a girl who could be half her current age.

I turned and looked back down the fairway toward the golfer. He was still standing there apparently in his own little world just waving toward that girl so far away on that hill. My eyes went back and forth as if I was watching a tennis match. Standing between two people completely absorbed in one another made me feel as if I was intruding. The entire spectacle was so unreal…and after all these years.

I was now more puzzled than happy for the two of them. It made no sense. Why would two people continue to meet each other in this way? Maybe their wave was a kind of signal to meet some place later. I certainly hoped so. Yet, this furtive communication meant they still hadn't gotten together after all this time. My God!! It had been fifteen…now sixteen years…since I'd first seen them wave at each other from afar. What had happened?

Then as fast as the greeting took place, the man down by the green picked up his golf bag and with one final wave disappeared up the path to the next tee box. In turn she just melted back into the forest behind that lone tree. Suddenly I was just standing there alone on the side of that fairway not certain what I'd just witnessed.

Desiring some kind of answer, I played the river hole quickly. I wanted to catch up with the golfer. What if he was Toby Robinson? But, the girl in the clubhouse said he was a local guy. What would a local guy be doing waving back to that young female up on the hill?

My mind went back and forth as I breathlessly arrived at the fourth tee box. I'd hoped that I might see the golfer walking down the fairway and get some answers. Instead I saw nothing. Whoever the fellow was, it appeared he'd chosen to walk back to the clubhouse just as Toby Robinson had done years ago.

It began to drip more steadily and I remained in a shelter at the fourth tee box. I could have run through the rain trying to catch up to the man, but something no longer seemed right. That ideal relationship between Toby Robinson and that mysterious girl on the hill had been tainted. Whether that golfer was Toby Robinson or not, the whole situation was not only peculiar, it was sad.

When the rain finally subsided, I played the remaining holes, got in my car, and drove the seventy miles back to my Uncle Alex's lake home. That night I sat quietly on a lawn chair on the porch watching an electrical storm edge across the sky line many miles to the south. The thunderstorm gradually moved east away from my vision. I remained on that porch until there were no more distant lightning flashes. The cloud cover had given way to a starry sky. All the while I thought about what I'd seen that afternoon at my home town golf course. I never considered myself a romantic. I'd just held onto an innocent dream from my boyhood about Toby Robinson and that girl with the flowing hair up on that hill. It had caused me to always strive for the ideal in a relationship. The question I kept asking myself was how did I define 'ideal'? How unfair was I being?

That night I contemplated what I might have missed by following that delusion so determinedly.

Ten days later I returned to my apartment in the Twin Cities. Before leaving Uncle Alex's lake property, I had worked especially hard to complete some maintenance and repair needs. I had the feeling I wouldn't be coming back to Green Lake that fall or for certain anymore summers except for maybe a short visit. With my new emphasis on using my free time more productively that fall and continuing my teaching contract through December, there would be no reason to delay taking that MBA degree for a 'spin' and prepare myself for a new direction in my life. At almost thirty years of age, it was over the time to get on with it.

It was years later...nine to be exact... before my life brought me back to Minnesota on a more permanent basis. It was May 1992, a great season to be back in my home state. It brought back the memory of the autumn in 1983 when I was teaching my final semester of high school while simultaneously working on a career change. That fall I began marketing myself in the same way I'd been taught in many of my business courses...as if I was a product or service.

Now thirty-eight years old, I didn't feel as if I was closing out another decade of my life even though the calendar confirmed it. With some free time before beginning a new assignment, I had returned to the Business Department at the University of Minnesota to greet some former instructors. There were still a few who remembered me.

Later as I sat alone in a coffee shop along University Avenue I couldn't help but reminisce about that fall nine years before. By November I'd had three job offers including one that required me to move out of state. That opportunity came from a large, local company on the east side of St. Paul called 3-M Corporation. The job required me to move to Dallas, Texas. That offer had caught me in the right frame of mind. I felt like spreading my wings. I considered the 3-M job offer as good pay and no risk. I'd be traveling. If things went badly, I could always come back to Minnesota and teach.

Happily, the new task not only didn't go 'badly', it went quite well. Over the next nine years, my willingness to be mobile and the results I was achieving in various jobs provided me promotions which offered me the chance to live in four different cities, including one assignment in Germany. It was that European job that brought me right back to the main 3-M headquarters in St. Paul. I was named head of a marketing division for one product line. The promotion gave me every indication I would be staying in Minnesota for the foreseeable future as long as I remained with 3-M Corporation.

My return was an exciting time. Monetarily I was on an entirely different level than the one I lived while teaching at that private school. Now I was seriously considering one of two homes to purchase...one in North Oaks on the golf course north of St. Paul...and the other along the St. Croix River north of Stillwater. It was pretty heady stuff for a guy still single...and one who wouldn't admit to anyone that he would still prefer taking the summers off as I did when I was a teacher. But then again, don't a lot of people have that dream about the summers...especially in Minnesota?

It was shortly after I moved into my home choice...the house along the St. Croix River... that I received a letter from one of my high school classmates about the upcoming August being the date for our twentieth high school reunion. I was impressed she'd found my new address. The reunion was scheduled to be at one of the new rages in Minnesota...a gambling casino located only a few miles from my hometown. I didn't think much about the event and threw away the invitation.

It was July when I got another reminder about the reunion. The dates were Friday night and Saturday, August 21-22. Nothing was cued in my mind about that date other than the thought that if I did attend, I might drive down the day before and play my old home town golf course. It had been nine years since I'd played it. That sounded as exciting as the reunion itself.

Through all this time with 3-M, thoughts of Toby Robinson and that girl on the hill had all but vanished. There had been a couple instances where the image of him and that lone tree on the hill would pop into my head...coincidentally after dating some female more than a few times. The vision awakened me as if I'd been jolted out of a coma. As strongly as I thought about these women, I simply did not hold an intense feeling for either one of them. I sensed they had the same lackluster feelings about me as well. I was a fun date with money. That was as far as it went.

When the reunion week finally arrived, I'd made up my mind to attend. I looked forward to taking Friday off and drive early back to my hometown for a day of golf. I had made a reservation, though I didn't need one, at that same inexpensive motel with the swimming pool. There was just something comforting about that thought.

Then my schedule had to change. Some important clients would be in the Twin Cities on Friday. There was even some chance that these fellows might want to stay over Friday night and play some golf on Saturday. It then looked as if I might have to skip the reunion completely. I actually felt worse about missing the chance to play golf at my old home course.

Then I got a notion. Thursday, August 18, appeared to be a slower than normal day. I made a quick decision to drive down to my home town Thursday morning, play some golf, and then return to the Twin Cities yet that evening. If I still felt like it and my clients left town on Friday, then I could still drive back to town Friday night for the reunion...and some golf with my high school buddies on Saturday.

And, that was what I did. Even then, business kept me at the office until late morning. I didn't arrive at my old home town until 1:00. I drove around town to note the changes that certainly must have happened over the nine years since I'd last driven into the town limits. It was as if time had stood still. Physical changes were minimal.

It was past 2:00 when I drove into the parking lot of the golf course. Like a typical late summer weekday afternoon, golf was not on everyone's plate as August continued into autumn. It looked like I'd be playing alone. Stopping in the clubhouse to pay a green fee, a skinny, bespeckled young high school aged gal yawned, took my money, and told me the tee was open. She wasn't the same girl from nine years ago, because that teenager had to have aged. Similar to one of her predecessors, she never made eye contact and seemed slightly bothered to have been pulled away from her magazine. Maybe it was the same girl after all.

I hit a couple balls from that first tee box just to get loosened up and took my time playing the first two holes. Playing alone I examined every aspect of the place I'd lived as a kid. There were not that many changes. Some new trees offered different barriers. Mostly the golf course had the same feel. It helped me rediscover my old golf swing…as if I could just put my swing on automatic pilot from so many years of having lived on that very ground.

Arriving at the third tee box, a host of thoughts began resonating through my head. I heard the slow moving stream below running parallel to the fairway. The sun was shining, but the northwest breeze kept the air temperate. I still had no thoughts about Toby Robinson…only the many recollections of shots I'd hit or seen on this intimidating river hole.

Though still relatively young at thirty-eight, I was pleased to see I hit the ball just as far as I did twenty years before…just not as accurately. Playing on my hometown course gave me a sense of comparison.

Teeing my ball up on that tee box, I stood over my golf ball at address when a crazy thought flashed through my brain. What day was it? I relaxed my stance and just stood there for a moment. Could it be? I ran through my meeting schedule. Wednesday had been August 17. We'd had some folks in from one of our international divisions. As if by magic I realized I was about to play the river hole on of all days, August 18…and it was the middle of the afternoon. It was the oddest sensation of déjà vu.

I turned to look in back of the tee box, but of course could not see the high hill behind the thick foliage and overhanging trees…just like always. Now my concentration was shattered. I stepped up and mishit my tee ball down the middle of the fairway about two-thirds of the distance I usually hit the ball. It didn't matter how far the ball went. My mind was no longer on the shot anyway. My only thought was the anticipation over what I might see…or not see. Quickly walking down the now paved path to the fairway along the river, I was more interested in seeing the top of that ridge behind me than hitting my second shot.

Finally on the fairway, my eyes became riveted. It was as if I was still a boy… looking at the same landscape…the same painting. Mother Nature had not changed a thing. In this instance, time really had stood still. Pangs of nostalgia dripped from my heart thinking about all that had happened in my life in the quarter of a century since I'd seen Toby Robinson fawn over that girl on the hill. And, for me, the most remembered part of the vision now was that single tree. And, there it was…still looking like it should fall off the edge of the cliff, but still standing alone and strong at the crest of that hill.

My only differing observation was that the hill didn't seem as high. The tree didn't seem as impressive. The cliff didn't seem as far away. But, it all didn't matter. The scene was still picturesque as ever.

Then that other memory came to mind…the one of that girl on the hill. My eyes studied that lone tree looking for any movement. It was silly to think she might be standing up on the top of that ridge, but I couldn't help wishing she was. Now she would be a woman past fifty...long past the adolescent time of a high school crush.

But, I knew it had been more than a crush...by the urgency of her wave...and by the ardent look in the eye of Toby Robinson. Through the passage of time there now would be no reason to expect that same scene to ever happen again. Still, my unique perspective of that day twenty-five years before...the coincidence of what day it was...and the rush of my personal memories on that river hole.... they all caused me to continue staring back at that tree atop the hill.

It took some kids on inner-tubes shouting as they floated down the river for me to come out of my trance. I realized I'd have to keep moving if I was going to finish eighteen holes and drive back to the Twin Cities before it got too late.

I gave one more fleeting glance back at the hill and then tried to concentrate on hitting that next shot. I took an indifferent practice swing...and then turned back toward that scene up on the hill once again. I was anything but a hopeless romantic, but I was so curious about what had happened to those two people... Toby Robinson...and that female with her long hair waving in the breeze.

I addressed my golf ball not caring where it flew when I suddenly got an inspiration. It hit me like a wave. I'd had many chances in my life to climb that very hill, but not a lot of reasons to do so in my younger years. Now here it was twenty years since high school and I was finding myself with the strongest urge to actually hike up that hill. It was some distance away, but the thought was overwhelming. I'd always seen this image from the perspective of a golfer...of Toby Robinson... from down on the fairway looking up. As important as this memory had been in my life, I now desired to witness this entire scene from atop that ridge looking backwards down toward the river hole.

Though never having made the climb, from what I remembered about the city park between the third fairway and the high hill, it didn't seem that demanding. Walking toward the city park, I dropped my golf bag by some bushes below the tee box where they would be safe, I was trance-like marching through the woods to the river flowing right below the cliff. With the river flowing lower at that time of year, I expected crossing the water from rock to rock would be easy...and that part of my trek offered no problem. There were plenty of rocks jutting out of the low stream.

On the other side of the embankment, there was a miniscule path that looked as if it might be the way leading upward to the crest of the hill. How good the path was didn't matter. I was already visualizing myself standing next to that lonely tree that had been so metaphoric in my life.

Ten minutes later I was halfway up the hill. I wasn't fifteen anymore. The path was steeper than I'd imagined. I had new respect for the height of the cliff. Adding to the climb on the winding trail were overhanging tree branches and poison ivy. At times it seemed jungle-like. I couldn't really see much beyond the river flowing directly below. My heart was beating rapidly as much for the harder than expected journey as the inspiration for having taken on the challenge.

The path then became less conspicuous. I was forced to push my way through some thick brush. Not many people apparently made this climb or there was a better route. It had become a bit more of a test than I'd figured.

Finally coming to a slight clearing, I found myself directly below the apex still fifty yards from the top. I gulped. It looked like a straight up climb on a barely discernible path that hugged the edge of the cliff. I was now staring down into a pit of gravel, stone, and weeds at the bottom of the cliff followed by another straight drop off to the rocky stream below. One slip and I was going to miss more than golf and meeting with some clients the next day to say nothing of the reunion.

I cautiously kept climbing. To add to the adventure recent rains had made the path slippery in places. My breathing became heavy. I was working up a good sweat. Deciding I needed a rest, I sat down hanging my legs over the edge and looked up at my goal. I was close…high enough to now enjoy the view of the river flowing along the golf course as well as to observe some of the higher prominent buildings and church steeples in the town beyond.

Catching my breath, I plodded onward and upward warily completing my ascent by holding onto tree limbs. It was exhilarating. When I reached the top it would be like stepping into the frame of the picture I'd seen since boyhood.

And then the path just vanished as I stepped into a flowing meadow of grass leading up the last small incline to the top of the hill. The grass was about a foot high. The background of trees ahead was much closer to the edge of the cliff than I'd visualized. Beyond the trees was just a vast, flat field of corn stalks now showing signs of dryness, but still looking like a green sheet had been placed over the landscape. Straight out across the corn field I could see an old barn far off in the distance. It looked to be at least a mile away and mostly obsolete. This location was as secluded as I'd pictured…as if the farmer planted seed as close to this grove of trees and grassy meadow as possible…and then didn't return until harvest time.

I panned to my right and there was the tree…the object of my focus every time I looked up the hill. At first glance the size was almost disappointing. I could see some of its protruding roots sticking out of the cliff below the precipice. It was any wonder that tree made it through the tough northern winters with part of its root system open to the elements. My displeasure with the size of the tree was minor as I'd already had tremendous respect for its ability to survive.

At the peak, I finally turned toward the golf course and town and inhaled the beauty. I now could see more of the taller buildings in town. I momentarily wondered why there were so many church steeples since each one, except for the Catholic Church, obviously depicted yet another Protestant religion. The number of churches supposedly professing the same beliefs seemed kind of excessive. Beyond the town and the golf course was a continued sea of greenery. I could make out the new water tower and even some Harvester Storage units and windmills on some farms far off in the distance. I also caught sight of a small plane landing at the local airport two miles east of town near the now defunct drive-in theatre.

I don't know how long I sat there. I hadn't expected anything miraculous to happen and nothing had. Nonetheless, I still had the thrill of being inside the landscape photo. I sat there for five minutes with my legs dangling over the cliff's edge until a little voice reminded me that time was indeed moving on. I had to get back and finish my round of golf. There was no reason to remain. I had fulfilled a quirk and I'd now never forget the view from the picture frame outward. I looked wistfully down at the river far below wishing there was an easier exit.

I was about to get up from my perch and leave when I realized I'd given Toby Robinson and the girl on the hill no thought at all. If this was their meeting place twenty-five years before…and apparently many times since…I imagined there had to be a road from the cornfield side of the ridge. I slumped back resting on my elbows with my legs hanging over the rim thinking about their times at that exact location. The memory clicked in from nine years before…the last time I'd played golf at my home golf course…when I'd actually seen the girl on the hill as well as that someone who could have been but was probably not Toby Robinson. I had left the golf course that day saddened that things had not worked out for those two people. Life had dealt them the wrong cards.

Continuing to lay back and just gazing at the sky, I was content to just sit there thinking about those two people. I knew once I left the edge of that cliff, I'd likely never again sit in that one spot again or would I visual the top of that hill in the same way ever again. In fact, I doubted I'd ever think of Toby Robinson and the girl on the hill ever again. Why remember something that would never be a happy memory.

I was about to get up and begin what I hoped would be an easier downward passage back to the golf course when the silence was broken. There was a humming sound coming from the other side of the woods. The noise was sweet-sounding, but didn't seem real. I saw the flash of some clothing through the thick trees. I hadn't expected anyone else to be entering this picture frame. Not moving a muscle, I waited for the person to emerge from the woods.

And just like that, out from the depths of that forest came of all things…a woman. She wasn't a young girl…neither was she as old as what the 'girl on the hill' had to be now twenty-five years later. In fact the young lady looked to be in her late twenties…maybe early thirties.

She was wearing a long sundress and hat. She was looking at the flowers at the side of the meadow and noticing nothing else. She was obviously quite comfortable expecting no intrusions. She had not a clue I was resting in the grass at the far end of the ridge. What I immediately noticed was her longish hair under her hat. As she approached the tree, she removed her hat and let the breeze blow through her brunette hair. She was quite striking.

Then she held her arms across her chest and just stared down at the golf course as anyone might do when first arriving at that promontory. After appreciating the beautiful site, she stopped her humming and called out, "Jigs come here boy. Jigs!"

And then I saw a dog come bounding through the woods toward her. I was so shocked I realized I had no saliva. Still resting back in the tall grass along the edge of the cliff, I wanted to greet her without frightening her, but I couldn't find a word to say. She certainly wouldn't expect another person to be sharing the top of the hill with her.

Finally I just got up while waving to her. In a dry voice I called out to her, "Hey there…I don't mean to scare you. I just wanted to say 'hello' and let you know I was here."

She was understandably startled.

I tried to keep her calm by taking my eyes off of her and concentrating on the view while continuing to talk. "I was captured by this hill. I just climbed up the trail from the river below to see the sights. I was about to start my descent when I saw you coming."

She didn't say anything and luckily showed no particular fear. Her dog growled sensing his owner's mild discomfort.

I remained still not stopping my gaze at the beautiful landscape. Now more quietly, I said, "You know…it's as spectacular as I thought it would be."

My words and behavior seemed to relax her. Her dog stood beside her as she scratched his neck. She finally responded, "Yes. It truly is gorgeous. I guess I've never seen another person up here, so pardon my surprise."

We talked for a few moments about the locations and buildings in town. She became more at ease with each passing minute. I made some inane comment about the loss of the cupola on the courthouse proving to her I must have some past tie-in to the town. Then I moved over toward her and stuck out my hand in friendship to introduce myself. She followed showing no hesitation. Anne Nelson was a common name for the area, but she turned out not to know or be related to the many Nelsons I was acquainted from my time living in the town.

I shared with her some of my past history on the golf course below. "Since I was a boy…twenty-five years ago… I've seen this high hill and never bothered to climb it. Now, for some reason, I'm in town and just had the urge to make the hike. I left my golf clubs down at the river hole."

She nodded as she glanced down at the long fairway below. "Yes, I don't play much golf, but I'm very familiar with that part of the golf course."

As she got more comfortable, I decided to push my luck and see what she was doing up on the hill on this coincidental time and day. "Well, Anne, do you come up here often? You obviously know the preferred trail to the one I chose." I pointed to the precarious path along the cliff's edge that I had just scaled.

For the first time she chuckled. It was refreshing. She nodded, "Yes, I definitely take a different route. My mother lives through the woods about a mile away. I've come up to this beautiful place often…at least when I used to live here. Now I only come back for a few weeks every summer to see her. I'm a graduate assistant at the University of Wisconsin. It's nice to have the free time in the summer to come back home."

The lady was describing my preference exactly. We had something in common already. As we talked I found myself not caring whether I finished my round of golf or not. I returned to my sitting position with my legs hanging over the cliff as she continued talking. "I like to come up here because it's as if life has stood still. It reminds me of some good times. Nothing has really changed in the landscape of the town. Maybe a few more houses can be seen on the far horizon than a few years ago…but generally the same vision…the same river… the same golf course view."

I broke in. "I sense the same thing but from the opposite perspective…the same hill…the same single tree…the same sky behind the hill. I basically grew up on that golf course down there. It's a great memory. When I think of this golf course and my boyhood, I think of that river hole. It's like a painting in my mind. Now for the first time I get to sit right here within the frame of that picture. It's quite a unique perspective."

I stopped not intending to have gotten that profound. She nodded but her attention had suddenly been reverted to something else. I turned and saw her abruptly move toward the very edge of the cliff. It concerned me at first. I didn't know what she was planning to do. Then I saw that her eyes were trance-like… looking far off. She was gazing intently down at the river hole below.

Then as if I wasn't even there, she put her hands through her hair causing it to blow wildly in the breeze. Her eyes were unblinking as she stared below at the river hold. I just sat there all but obscured by the tall grass and partially blocked from seeing the entire fairway by some tree branches. I stretched to see where she was focused. That was when I got my second surprise of the afternoon. Someone was standing in the middle of the third fairway. He was facing back and looking toward her at the top of the hill. I leaned back further so I wouldn't be seen.

Then as if on cue, they both began waving at one another…first slowly… then with more energy…almost desperately as if either one might not see the other. Anne's face was resplendent with a radiant smile…her hair and dress wildly flailing in the wind. I couldn't see his face down below, but the vigor of his wave indicated he was smiling as well.

I felt like I was imposing. I slid back even further to make certain I could not be seen. Within a few minutes their waves finally slowed and they just stood in place for a minute before their actions ceased altogether. She finally put her hand down and stepped back toward the tree and out of his vision.

I stretched to see what the man down on the fairway was doing. He had already turned and had continued strolling down the fairway. She watched him unseen through the branches of that single tree. I maintained my invisibility, but observed him until he was on the green at the far end of the fairway. At that point he turned toward her one last time and gave a final wave. She stepped forward one last time as well and reciprocated. Then she moved back behind the single tree again watching his every step as he moved toward the short-cut path up to the next tee box. Finally he no longer could be seen.

I didn't know what to say. I just lay there stupefied as she continued standing there hidden behind those tree branches. However, I was not so befuddled that I was going to let this little scene pass without saying something. As she stood there looking both content and somewhat somber, I finally broke the silence. "Anne, you obviously know that man. I don't know how you could recognize him. My eyes aren't that good."

She put her sun hat back on and pulled her hair into a pony tail to keep her hair from blowing in her face. I was expecting some kind of explanation…but not the one I was about to hear.

She sat down with her own legs dangling over the cliff's edge about five yards away from me as her dog lay down on the other side of her. She looked over at me with a hopeful stare and then commented, "Ben, I was carrying out a kind of responsibility. It's difficult to explain…and for that matter, I shouldn't even talk about it with you or anyone else.

I shrugged trying not to be too meddlesome, but I was not going to let the incident just pass by. In fact, if I had to tell her about the incident I witnessed twenty-five years before to get her to open up, then I would do so.

I carefully prodded her. "Well, if it's that personal, then I respect your silence. I was just impressed with your certainty that the golfer down there on the fairway was the fellow you wanted to apparently make some kind of connection."

She chuckled over my last few words and then hesitantly spoke. "Actually I don't know who that man is who waved back at me. He has repeated this action every year…rain or shine…about this time…3:00…every eighteenth of August. I've been coming up to this site as a favor to someone for years. My acquaintance and the man down there on the fairway have had some kind of long-term relationship…one that could never be imagined. I don't know the entire story but apparently his business reputation, his marriage, even the respect he has within his large family would be seriously defamed if it was found he was still obsessed and possibly having an affair with a girl he'd loved since high school. His life would be ruined.

Looking at me for some kind of reaction, I could only shake my head and show my confusion. She continued, "I do know that years ago they almost shucked everything and ran away together, but they luckily recovered their senses and didn't let it happen. She would have faced the same purgatory in her own life. But, they made a pact that if anything changed in either of their lives that might allow them to be together, they would choose this particular August date every year to communicate that possibility…or, if nothing had changed, then to simply see one another and hopefully re-commit once again to their long held feelings for one another.

The agreement was that if there was no change in their lives, but they wanted to maintain the possibility of eventually getting together, she would be on this hill and he would be down there on that golf course. If all they could do was wave it would indicate the flame was still there even if it wasn't safe or advisable for them to meet. It was apparently just too big a risk for either of them to be seen together. If either one didn't show up, their yearly effort would end and that flame would end."

I had to believe the story was incomplete, so I remained silent. Sure enough she volunteered more. "I mentioned this female was an acquaintance, but I've actually never met her. She was a classmate of my mother's. I've tried to put this whole story together over the years, but my mother is not very forthcoming with many details. All I know is that this annual episode, as strange as it may sound, has been going on for a long time…maybe a couple decades. It's my understanding… or at least my best guess…that the man down there on the fairway is not only married, but his very livelihood and personal life depends on him being absolutely clean of any wrongdoing or immorality. My mind jumps around to someone who might be a very visible politician or corporate leader to even a well-known national religious leader. I might be over-reacting, but for this situation to last as long as it has, that man down there on the fairway is being very protective of his life and his loved ones while wanting desperately to cling to one nostalgic memory of his youth. He obviously doesn't want that remembrance to disappear.

As far as my mother is concerned, she is extremely protective of her friend. She has never divulged anything else. But one thing is for certain, whatever that relationship was many years ago, that friend of my mother's and that well-known man who stealthily comes into town every August 18 …well, they refuse to let their feelings for one another fade. They want that chance to be together if ever things happen in their lives that might make it possible. However long it has been, he's down there renewing his fantasy of being with her every year with his wave."

I had no doubt the story Anne was telling me was the actual truth at least in her mind. She had only to point to the man down on the river hole to corroborate it. I carefully asked her, "So…why are you here and not the original lady?"

Anne nodded hoping her trust was not misplaced. I must have made her comfortable because she responded as if her own need to share this story with someone had become important to her. "As I said, she was a friend of my mother's. There was a time quite a few years ago where that woman couldn't make it back to Minnesota on this particular date. She actually asked my mother to stand-in for her. This girl…this woman…this friend of my mother's didn't want to lose this special relationship she had with the gentleman down there on the fairway.

My mother was hesitant, but eventually agreed. She replicated everything the woman asked her to do. She let her hair blow in the breeze…she had our dog by her side…at approximately 3:00 on August 18 and waited at the top of this hill in the hope that this man would begin to wave at her from the golf course below. That first year she felt so guilty when it actually happened. She told me it was heart-wrenching to see through the man's body language and wave how anxious he seemed. She imagined the effort he'd taken to arrive on time on that day in order to maintain a memory that was so precious to him…and he could only assume her feelings were mutual for her to be up there on the hill.

She found herself quite moved by the spectacle. As he waved from that far distance, she found herself waving back just as vigorously.

Curiously, she thought her favor as a stand-in for her friend would only be that one time, but she was asked to substitute one more time the next August as he friend had another complication getting to town on that August date. This time my mother did it as much for the man down there on the fairway as for her friend. That next August 18 there he was again waving as enthusiastically as the previous year and she reciprocating with the same energy. She told me her heart strings were pulled watching him finish playing the river hole and then giving one last long wave toward her before disappearing into the woods on his way to the next tee box.

It was that third year that my mother and her friend lost communication. It might have been over this issue with the man down on the fairway. Anyway, her friend apparently moved overseas. They never spoke again.

When August came around, my mother wasn't going to keep the dream alive until just an hour before 3:00 on the that August date. She was so much younger then. She put on the same long dress she'd worn the year before, tramped through the woods letting her hair flow in the wind and arrived on this very hill just as she saw the man waving at her from so far away. She just didn't have the heart to take something away from a man who valued a relationship so dearly from his youth.

The long and the short of it… I honestly don't how many years she planned her time so she'd be at the top of this hill on that time and date. He was down there on the fairway at the agreed upon time as faithfully as the sun rose in the morning. I recall her often in tears when she returned to our farmhouse from a mile away atop the hill. I know she felt a sense of happiness towards the ardently loyal man waving back at her…but, she also felt guilt for maintaining the delusion."

Anne finally stopped with her story. I found myself feeling sorry for Toby Robinson. He'd been carried along all these years believing that the girl on the hill was still that special person who wanted to maintain a contact with him as much as he did with her. However, for so many of those years, it was make-believe carried on by Anne's mother. The actual relationship had ceased for years.

I asked the obvious next question to Anne. "Clearly you've become a replacement for your mother in maintaining this….charade. When did this happen?"

Anne got a forlorn look in her eye. "It was eight or nine years ago that my Mother was seriously injured in a car accident. In August she was unable to walk yet. Her angst over not being able to meet her obligation for this man down there on the golf course was taking an emotional toll on her. I think she'd become obsessed with the illusion. He represented the sentient male she'd always wished she had in a husband. My father and she had been divorced for years. He never knew she was a stand-in for her high school friend. Truthfully, I've always wondered if my mother's fascination with this unknown man down there on that golf course had something to do with her disillusionment in her own marriage.

Anyway, to ease her mind during her recovery, I volunteered to substitute for her.

When I completed that stand-in episode waving at that man on the river hole, it relieved my mother noticeably. I tried not to make any big deal out of what I'd done for her, but I have to admit I had a tear in my eye for that man down on the fairway. I wondered what kind of life he'd had that an obsession with a high school flame was so important. I found myself feeling sorry for him. I also began to feel the same way that my mother felt. If this man was making the secret trip every August to see that girl of his dreams…even at a distance… why should I suddenly burst his fantasy?

The next year my mother had put on a lot of weight from being immobile as a result of that accident. Still, that August obligation was still very much on her mind. The bottom line is that I've schedule vacation back here in my hometown to see my mother around the week that included August 18. I've carried on that man's dream, for my mother's sake, since my college years. Truthfully, I've gotten tremendous satisfaction from performing this romantic little deed. I smile for days after knowing I've kept alive a dream."

I sat there stunned. Her story would have been too unbelievable if I hadn't seen the eyes of Toby Robinson so many years before. I finally blustered, "Has that man ever done anything but wave? Has he never been up here on the top of the hill at 3:00 on August 18 hoping he could take the relationship with the girl of his dreams a step further?"

She shrugged, "Never. Apparently the importance of his keeping this strange liaison absolutely hush-hush is as important as ever. My mother and I have never sought out who he is. We don't want to be the cause of his business or personal demise in case this story ever got discovered."

I sat there staring down at the golf course not believing that the Toby Robinson I'd met and been with for less than two hours twenty-five years before had been hoodwinked for most of the years he returned to that spot on the golf course. Though it was the girl of his dreams who, in effect, broke off their agreement without telling him, it was that girl's friendship with Anne's mother that continued the charade. Then, it turned into both the mother and her daughter who didn't want the illusion to stop for the man's sake….and they didn't even know him.

There was a part of me that wanted to tell Anne about meeting the man down there on the fairway a quarter of a century before. But, there was no point.

The entire affair was none of my business. Leaving her with the thought that I was a visitor who had just climbed the hill on a whim was the way I wanted her to remember me.

I'd been brought up-to-date on a story that had affected my life for longer than I cared to admit. I glanced at my watch trying to figure out how to end the conversation with the young lady. A part of me wanted to stay and talk with her. She seemed so appreciative finally sharing the story with someone….someone she believed had no connection to the community any longer and therefore had no reason to destroy the confidentiality. I felt complimented she had that kind of trust…or maybe, she was just ready for the entire spectacle to come to an end.

To give her some confidence that I was going to keep her secret, I said soothingly, "Well, Anne, you are a very generous person. It sounds like you are going to be right here next August 18 and the one after that…and so on…just for the sake of that man down there on the golf course as long as he keeps arriving at that river hole at the appointed time?"

She answered me as honestly as she could. "Who knows where any of us will be tomorrow much less next August 18? Maybe next year that man down there on the golf course will decide not to return. I'll not see him and I in turn will not stroll up this path the following August 18 or any future August after that. Then the fairy tale will end and I will never know why this devotion to a relationship suddenly ended after all these years…nor should I care. It's really none of my business."

I blankly nodded, but then assured her, "Well, I'm not going to be responsible for bursting the bubble either. It's a heartfelt tale…kind of energizes my own feelings about how some relationships, as unrequited as they might be, can be sustained for so long. How can anyone not feel at least a little bit moved by that man's loyalty and emotions toward a long lost love in his life."

We sat there nodding silently until I finally I stood up and brushed myself off. "Well, Anne, I've seen this hill at various times through most of my life and I've never climbed it until today. I guess if I knew someone like you was up here, I would have made the climb much sooner. You're delightful. Thanks for making this an unforgettable day."

I wanted my departing words to make her feel good…even radiant. I gave her a final wave and headed for my precarious path downward. A minute later I looked back. The girl on the hill and her dog had already disappeared back into the forest from where she had emerged.

It took me much less time to get back to the golf course. Retracing my exact route downhill was much easier. I retrieved my golf clubs still hidden in those bushes and continued playing the third hole. As I strode down the fairway I gazed back at that hill at the lone tree…again and again. Now it wasn't the tree that stood out in my mind. I finally had a face that would be permanently stamped in my mind of the girl on the hill. I also could visualize myself sitting by that tree with my legs hanging over the cliff talking with her. I had a new regard for that entire scene. I had become part of the picture within the frame.

Completing play on the river hole, I gave one last long distance look at the faraway hill and then plodded up the shortcut to the fourth tee box. I thought about Toby Robinson. He was now fifty-three. The jet black hair was probably more gray than dark…that is, whatever hair he still had. He was no longer that thin young man. I questioned how he could be still so fervent about the image of that girl he knew so many years before.

Then something occurred to me. It hadn't been that long since the man waving up at Anne Nelson was playing the river hole. Whether that golfer was Toby Robinson or not, the day was so beautiful there might be a good chance he continued playing golf rather than walk directly back to the clubhouse. It had been less than forty minutes atop that hill since I'd seen Anne Nelson wave to him and her telling me her unbelievable story. It had taken me twenty minutes to come down the hill and make it back onto the golf course. I looked at my watch. If that golfer was still playing, he might be on holes eight or nine. If I walked toward the Number ninth tee box I might just see him. If he was Toby Robinson, it would be a thrill to see the man after all these years.

My golf clubs were clanking in the bag as I rushed over to the ninth tee box while panning my eyes over the golf course looking for the man who'd waved from the river hole. I realized there would be no reason he would remember me after all these years. That didn't matter anymore. In fact, I had to be concerned what I might say to him if we did talk about that day so long ago. I couldn't betray the trust I'd just promised to Anne Nelson. Besides, I wouldn't want to destroy his dream either.

Breathing heavily with the bag of clubs bouncing on my shoulders, I stopped to rest on the ninth tee box. From there I could see down the eighth fairway. There was no golfer there or anywhere else on the golf course.

Getting up to walk back to the fourth hole and complete my round of golf, I shot one last pensive look down the eighth fairway. It was then, as if a ghost was appearing, a man suddenly strolled out of the trees on the eighth hole striding forward toward the green. Hardly blinking, I watched the guy address his shot into the eighth green. He was still thin. That made me smile. He was over fifty, but he'd kept himself in good shape. He wore a golf hat. I couldn't make out if he had black hair or not. After hitting his shot, the golfer strolled ahead with the brim of his hat resting very low over his face.

I moved back slowly over to the bench alongside the ninth tee box still not believing what I might be seeing. There was no question I was going to wait… and suggest we play the ninth hole together. I was certain he wouldn't mind playing the last hole with the kid who'd caddied for him a quarter of a century before…on this very date!

I studied him as he got closer. He seemed so youthful relative to his age. In fact, I was finding him too young in his movements. It couldn't be Toby Robinson. Disappointedly, I had to finally admit there must have been another golfer on the golf course who I hadn't seen before.

I stood up focusing on the remainder of the golf course trying to locate if there were any other golfers in view. There were none. We were the only ones playing golf on the entire course. This guy had to be the person who waved at Anne from the river hole. But, why did he do it? He was definitely not Toby Robinson.

I still waited for him. Whoever he was, I wanted to play the last hole with him and possibly raise the question about his strange behavior on the river hole.

When he had putted out and approached the ninth tee box, he gave me a very friendly smile. We agreed to finish the last hole together. After hitting our drives down the middle, we exchanged names and where we lived. His name was indeed not Toby Robinson, but Dan Thornton, a local dentist. He was easily twenty years younger than Toby Robinson's current age.

Nonetheless, I had to satisfy my curiosity. I finally came right out and asked him, "Dan, by chance were you down on the third fairway….and….you waved to a woman up on that hill back beyond the third tee box. I was close by and noticed her waving to some guy. Was that you by chance?"

He seemed unwilling to respond at first, but finally nodded as if embarrassed. "Yeh….that was me."

He paused. "And to be honest, I have no idea who that girl is atop the hill… or what she looks like…other than she has long hair that blows in the breeze. I guess there're plenty of girls who have that hair length. But, she's there once a year…on this date and approximate time…just as sure as we're standing here."

His voice got shallow and his words came out almost in a whisper. "I just don't get it…you know…why she's always there….waving from on top of that hill…on this date….August 18 …every blessed summer."

Dan Thornton then walked on toward the ninth green, of course having no idea the depth of my own understanding. Then he stopped and looked in the direction of that high hill that was then only partially in view. With a sheepish grin he said, "You know, I've never told this story to anyone before, but since I'll be moving out of town in a couple months to join another dental practice in Rochester, I guess I just feel like telling someone since the whole thing ends right here. I'll no longer be part of it."

He looked reflectively at me and asked, "You have time to hear a rather unusual tale?

I nodded trying not to show my eagerness. We went into the clubhouse, ordered two beers, and sat down in the far corner of the barroom. He seemed like he wanted to get a load off his chest. I'd become a very willing listener.

He started out in very low, measured tones so the young lady behind the cash register couldn't hear. "It was quite a few years ago…like maybe eleven or twelve years ago … when I met this visitor…a former resident…on the first tee of this golf course. That's right it was on this very date in 1980. I remember because I was just about to open my new dental practice the next Monday. Anyway, this fellow somewhat hesitantly agreed to play a round of golf with me. His name was Toby… Toby Robinson. He claimed he was back for a high school reunion, but I found out later he was not. Apparently he used it as a convenient excuse. He was a nice fellow… turned out he was not only from out of town…but from out-of-state. In fact he said he spent most of his current working life overseas. I recall him being quiet and very preoccupied those first two holes. When we arrived at the river hole, he became particularly anxious. He kept looking back toward that high hill beyond the third tee box. I'll bet he looked back there twenty times until we putted out on the third green.

He really looked dejected as we picked up our golf bags to walk to the fourth tee box. He was lagging behind. Then I didn't see him. From the short cut path I looked down on the river hole and there he was with a completely different expression on his face. The glow and happiness on his face made him look like a completely different man. I looked through the branches in the direction he was gazing and damned if I didn't see what appeared to be a female standing on that distant hill next to that scraggily tree that's been there forever.

She was waving for all her worth. It was as if he was in another world as he returned her wave very energetically. I have to tell you, it was quite a tender sight. I didn't know the circumstances, but you had to have a heart of stone not to be moved by that little scene. These two people obviously had a great feeling for one another.

I'll bet they waved for two minutes at each other…him with the biggest, most ecstatic smile on his face. Given the vigor of her wave, she had to have shared the same feeling. I remember how they slowly put their arms down and then just stood there…almost a mile from each other…and just stared at one another. They were lost in their own private thoughts. Then she drifted back toward the tree and disappeared into the woods. He gave one final wave, blinked, and then trudged on up the pathway to the fourth tee box without saying a word. Once there, he sat down on a bench and seemed unable or uninterested in continuing our round of golf.

I tried to make the man feel better by making some off-hand comment. It was something like, "Wow…I couldn't even see the lady. You apparently could recognize her with no problem. The two of you obviously must look forward to seeing each other."

He didn't respond at first as he leaned back on that bench. His anguish was very evident. Finally, he hesitantly just started sharing with me part of his story. His voice was soft and contemplative as he murmured, "Yes, that girl you saw back there on the hill has always been someone special…going back to our high school days. Back then, we'd meet up on that hill. We always thought we'd be together, but it hasn't worked out that way so far. We just haven't given up yet that there might still be a chance."

Toby looked to be about forty years old with some salt and pepper gray in his hair and a slight paunch. I didn't want to say anything, but it looked like the two of them had been waiting a long, long time for their chance to have something happen. He must have sensed my wonder because he then began to bring more details into his story.

He described a typical tale...when college entered the picture, the two of them eventually lost contact......not a big surprise. They married others. They lived on opposite sides of the Atlantic Ocean. As it turned out, their unions were unfortunately not happy. For reasons he didn't detail, divorce was out of the question for both for the time being.

It was a month prior to their tenth high school reunion in 1967 they communicated for the first time. For old time's sake, they decided to meet up on that same hill if both could make the reunion. It was not lost upon either of them that the day they planned to meet was August 18, 1967, exactly ten years after they'd last seen each other.

Apparently their meeting together brought back fond memories and mutual wishes for the future. It had to have been a hell of a weekend for them even without their tenth reunion. Anyway, they committed to seeing each other each year back at their old home town and up on that hill as long as they both felt there was a chance for them to eventually be together. But, they both agreed being discreet was absolutely necessary. Neither of them wanted to create any embarrassment within their respective families. They knew they'd just have to be patient. Dissolution of both marriages seemed imminent.

It was then thirteen years later as Toby Robinson sat on that bench on the fourth tee box...and he had a dilemma. Everything up to that summer of 1980 had worked out with the exception that annulments had not occurred. They'd nonetheless kept meeting secretly on that same day in August all those years. It was something they valued and they made the effort to sustain a distant but very involved... bond.

She had a readymade excuse in coming back to town each August to visit her mother and some local friends. In his case, since he traveled more, his pretext would be simply that he enjoyed a once a year escape to play some golf back at his old hometown golf course.

Every year she'd be up on the hill around 3:00 and he'd time his return to the golf course to be on the river hole about that time on August 18. The signal would be her standing there by that lone tree waving at him. He'd then leave the golf course and promptly make his way to that hill. He claimed their yearly meetings were something neither of them wanted to surrender. They always held out some kind of fantastic hope they might eventually be together.

Then he explained how their time together had changed in the last two years. The two of them would not be seeing each other that afternoon. There had become too many problems with him returning to the small town every August. People in his organization, his family, and even a few individuals at the local golf course had become highly suspicious. Even the two of them meeting elsewhere would be impractical. The best they could do until something changed in both of their lives was to offer that wave to each other each August 18. It was their personal signal that they didn't want the possibility of their being together eventually to stop.

He ended by saying in the last two years since not being able to reach out to her personally, he'd become very disconsolate and frustrated. With nothing changing at least in her marital situation, he wasn't certain if he could continue just seeing her each August from afar. Then he apologized for being so emotional. What could I say but I was impressed how long they'd maintained contact and hoped things would work out for the best.

We finished playing golf. In the parking lot of the golf course as we were leaving, we shook hands. He thanked me for listening and asked me if I would please keep his story just between the two of us. There was no question in my mind that I would. Being new in town, I didn't want to do anything that might put me in the middle of any controversy. I strongly assured him his story was safe with me. I repeated my hope that his future would be bright. He wished me well in my new dental practice. We shook hands and departed. That was it. I figured I'd never see him again."

Thornton then looked at me as if wondering whether I believed a word he was saying. To help him relax so he might continue, I interjected, "Based on you being down there on the river hole now twelve years later waving at that girl on the hill, I have a feeling there's more."

Thorton grinned slightly. "Yes…there's a lot more. It was six years later in 1986 that something else happened. By then, I'd pretty much forgotten about that weird tale told to me by Toby Robinson. I hadn't seen him again. I assumed his self-professed gloom and frustration back in 1980 would have caused him to end their very heartfelt relationship.

I just happened to be at the golf course on August 18 during the middle of the afternoon. Believe me, it was coincidence. The date meant nothing to me. By then I was married with a kid on the way. It was a slow Monday. I'd taken the afternoon off to play golf knowing once the baby was born, my golf time might be limited. I saw a man walking down the first fairway just ahead of me. I'd never seen him before, but decided to hit my ball and see if I could play with him. Well, he was playing so fast I wasn't able to catch him…until the river hole. That was when I saw something unbelievable. This man was standing far down the fairway by the green. He was facing back toward me and waving for all his worth. I knew better than to think the wave was for me. His actions created a surge of memory…about that guy I'd met years before and that girl…the one on the hill.

He completed his greeting then slowly began walking up the hill towards the fourth tee box giving some final farewells. By then I was down on the fairway. Sure enough, as I looked back toward that hill far in the distance, there was that girl with her hair flailing in the breeze just standing there giving that fellow in front of me some final waves. I didn't know what was going on, other than I knew this guy playing golf in front of me was not the same golfer I'd met six years before. When their greetings were done, he vanished up the hill and she drifted back into the woods. That was it.

I sensed this fellow was not going to rush away from the golf course, since he was not the Toby Robinson I'd met a few years back. With that in mind, I hustled ahead and finally caught up with him on the fifth tee box. In fact, we finished the round of golf together. His name was Greg…Gregory Sanders…and he was from St. Cloud.

It took only until we played the next few holes together when I began asking him about that girl on the hill when he was playing the river hole. He was reticent at first until I told him I'd seen another golfer do the same thing…and I'd never shared the story with anyone. I told him I was just curious who the popular girl was on that hill.

With that, Sanders felt comfortable in opening up to me. He said he had no idea who the female was on that distant hill, but that he taking care of a commitment he had to a guy he'd met five years prior in 1981. Sure enough, Sanders told me the same tale I'd heard from Toby Robinson the year before. The difference with Sanders' story was that Toby seemed even more exasperated. He doubted he'd be able to return to his old home town the next summer. He hated most of all that a relationship so important to him and that girl up on the hill would likely have to end.

Sanders must have shown a real soft spot about Robinson's story because Toby actually approached the subject whether Sanders might 'stand-in' for him the next August in 1982…just to keep the dream alive for the female's sake. There was no commitment from Sanders that afternoon, but the idea was introduced."

Thorton stopped for a moment to take a drink of his beer. I could suddenly see where this story was going. I interrupted by saying, "Dan, is that what happened. This Sanders guy actually agreed to, as you say, to 'stand-in' for Toby Robinson."

Thorton nodded. "Toby Robinson actually got a hold of Sanders a couple weeks before the next August 18, 1982. Sanders said the man was extremely persuasive offering him money to cover costs just so the dream could live on. Robinson was so distraught about disappointing the female up on the hill, Sanders finally acquiesced. All he had to do was wave to her from the fairway and that would keep the deception going until the next August when Robinson assured Sanders he would return.

Sanders agreed but really didn't think he could pull off the ploy. Astonishingly, the whole ruse worked like a charm. Furthermore, he said fulfilling the favor didn't take that much extra time and made him feel really good for taking a vacation day from his work. He thought the matter was done and he'd never hear from Toby Robinson again.

It was two weeks prior to August 18 the next summer of 1983 when Sanders got a note with $500 included in the envelope. The message simply requested that Sanders substitute for Robinson once again. There was no explanation and no return address, but the letter was mailed from overseas. The salutary simply asked him if he would keep 'her' dream alive. With no return address, Sanders this time felt obligated. Again he fulfilled the favor. And, he continued to do so for four more years until I met him in 1986. By then it had been three years since the last time Toby Robinson had pleaded by letter for Sanders to help him out once again. By 1983 Toby had given up on the long-term relationship. The frustration had gotten too much for him to manage.

As Greg Sanders and I talked that day, we became like two conspirators agreeing to keep the lid on this very personal and unique relationship for the sake of that loyal and spirited female waving from atop the hill. We exchanged business cards. I even invited Sanders to call me if he was going to be in town and wanted to play some golf...adding that it certainly didn't have to be on August 18. He seemed appreciative of my offer.

Over the next couple years, I didn't hear from him. Mostly the entire matter was forgotten. I figured it would become too inconvenient for Sanders to drive all the way from St. Cloud to continue keeping a fantasy alive as wholehearted of a gesture as it was. I was certain the dream was over...that is, until I got a call from him two years later just a few days before August 18. He proceeded to tell me he'd continued to arrange his schedule to drop by the local golf course each August 18 even though he'd lost complete contact with Toby Robinson. He'd done it for the sake of the girl on the hill. He said there was something about her loyalty to a very old relationship...and that urgent, desirous wave that made him not want to disappoint her.

I kidded him about being a real sentimentalist and he laughingly agreed. Still, I had great respect that he would take the effort for a woman he'd never met and for Robinson who no longer had reason to sustain the fantasy for himself. We agreed to play that August 18. I could sense a real friendship since we both had determinedly kept this 'girl on the hill' secret from everyone else.

On the day before we were to play, I got another call from him at my dental office. This time his voice sounded hesitant and very emotional. He said, "Dan, I'm not going to be able to make our golf date. I've got a family emergency."

I could sense what he was going to ask me to do. Sure enough, that's what happened. Sanders pleaded with me to carry out this act of kindness just that once. He said, "Dan, it takes no more time than just being at the river hole around 3:00. If she's on that hill, then wave. If she's not there, then it's likely this distant relationship has finally played itself out. There's just something quite special about this story. I think you agree as well."

I didn't know what to say. It was not an inconvenient request. I'd planned to play golf with him that afternoon anyway. But, I could sense myself getting into something that was none of my business. I agreed to fill in for him but got assurance from him he would take back the responsibility the next summer. I told him otherwise I wouldn't feel comfortable with the deception.

His voice sounded pained as he responded, "Dan, of course returning next August would be my intention. It just makes me feel good to make someone feel wanted. We probably all want to feel that way.

And that was it. I did it. I went out to the golf course that afternoon of August 18 to substitute for Greg Sanders who I'd met once in my life and who had been standing in for Toby Robinson for the previous six summers.

Golfing alone, I arrived at the river hole that afternoon feeling a bit nervous, but exhilarated. It was quite an unbelievable situation. I was temporarily involved…or at least I thought it would be temporary…in a private little deed so important to at least one person…maybe two people…maybe more. Whatever the case, I was doing something both generous and a bit irrational. The funny thing was that it made me feel good.

As I walked down that fairway looking back every other second until I could get a clear view of that lone tree up on the hill, I wondered if she'd really be there. It took until I was almost at the end of the river hole before I saw her emerge and stand by that lone tree. At first she stood there like a statue. I was only there as a substitute, but I was now a central point of an emotional current. I stopped walking, turned, and began enthusiastically waving at her. With no response, I wondered if she was able to see me. Maybe I had to move further back down the open fairway. Maybe she had to wait until she was certain it was the man she hoped I would be. I was now waving my right arm even more urgently.

Then her motionless body took notice. Her waving was gradual, but then she began to wave with the fervor of a girl who'd been waiting a year to let the person below on that fairway know that she still cared. I continued waving back with equal zeal. With just those urgent arm movements, the relationship had been completed for yet another year.

I finished the hole still looking behind and seeing her standing by that tree. That vision has always been so vivid…of her standing by that lone tree with her hair blowing in the breeze…the dog jumping at her side…and of her staring at me no matter the long distance. Admittedly, I thought I'd feel guilty for deceiving her, but my feeling was quite the opposite. Instead I felt fortunate to have continued this long term bond between two people I knew so little about. Not many people would have done what Greg Sanders had done for those few years. For that matter, not many people would have done what I had agreed to do that afternoon.

Then I gave her one last wave and marched up the path to the fourth tee box while watching her drift back into the trees behind that single tree. I had done the favor Sanders had asked me to do…and I felt a warm glow in accomplishing the request. And that was it.

In the weeks and months ahead I never heard from him. There was no note of thanks or phone call asking how it went. Frankly I was surprised. But, I also figured he'd live up to what he said and take over the responsibility, if he so chose, the following August. If not, the saga would end.

I never heard from Greg Sanders again. I was curious enough that I found his business card he'd given me. I actually called him the next summer a week before that August date. The number was no longer in use. He'd moved.

I recall the empty feeling I had. Now I, Dan Thornton, the second stand-in, was going to have to be the one to keep this fabrication alive if I thought it important enough to do. As those days went by leading up to the August 18 and realizing Sanders was out of the picture, I accepted that the deception was over as well. It was too bad that heart-warming story had to finally come to an end. That gal on the hill would have to deal with another of life's disappointments like so many other people had to do.

Yet, the closer it got to August 18 I knew what I was going to do. Though I was two guys removed from that man named Robinson, it simply was not that difficult to arrange my schedule. If it kept a dream alive for that girl on the hill, then why not help out one more time…and make me feel good for what I was doing for her.

So, at 3:00 on the designated day, I was on that river hole….and there she was again up on the hill with her hair flailing in the breeze standing with her arms folded waiting for that special person from her younger days to appear. I felt a warm glow all over as I stopped dead in my tracks two-thirds the way down that fairway, turned, and held my arm up as high as it would stretch. It was as if a shock wave from my hand was immediately shot back to her so far away. Suddenly her arm reached skyward and she began a slow wave…and then continued with more vigor. My own wave matched her intensity. I was so moved how this female wanted this long term hope to live for another year. I'll admit to you I had a tear in my eye when I finally finished playing the river hole that day. Maybe it was because I couldn't believe a person could feel so strongly about someone as she did towards Toby Robinson.

I believe I realized on that very afternoon that as the second stand-in I was going to continue making that dream live on for that girl as long as she was waiting up on that hill and as long as I lived in the community. I never tried to find out who she was. I only figured she likely had to travel every year maybe a great distance to get the renewal of that special relationship. I was not going to be the one who caused her any disappointment.

And, now here it is 1992…five summers of waving to that girl on the hill. The story will have to come to an end next August. Moving to Rochester is going to change my availability. It's no longer going to be convenient to simply schedule some golf in the middle of the afternoon on any future August 18."

We both were silent as we gulped down the last of our beers. I ended up repeating similar words to the well-meaning dentist that I'd said less than two hours before to Anne Nelson. I mumbled, "Dan, certainly this story will conclude sometime in the future, but something tells me you won't be the cause of it. I think you're going to find some way to help this fantasy continue."

He only nodded as we threw some money on the table and walked out of the clubhouse. I wished him well on his move to Rochester. I had no sense what he was going to do regarding that special date in August the next summer. My only thought was how Anne Nelson would be so disappointed the following summer when no one would be down at the river hole waving up to her on the hill on August 18. The dream she carried for her mother and her mother's friend would no longer exist.

Driving back to the Twin Cities that Thursday evening, I had no other thoughts than the stories told to me by Anne Nelson and Dan Thorton…and how I'd been a part of the story so much longer than the two of them in a much different way. Theirs was a generous act of giving of their time to preserve a long-term relationship and youthful dream. My connection went back twenty-five years to a much younger Toby Robinson. He demonstrated such an enthusiastic response to that girl on the hill and that response had affected me throughout my formative and adult years when it came to females I'd dated.

That night I drove back to my home in the Twin Cities already reminiscing about the extraordinary day. The next day on Friday, my clients and I played eighteen holes of golf at North Oaks Country Club. I offered dinner but they were anxious to return to their home cities. There would be no golf on Saturday with them. Having already thought that I would simply miss my twentieth reunion, I made a quick decision to drive the two hours back to my home town and attend the affair after all.

Packing in five minutes, I had my clients at Minneapolis-St. Paul International Airport by 5:00 Friday afternoon. I then just continued on through Bloomington and Eden Prairie towards my hometown to stay at the same inexpensive motel Friday night. Despite the reunion, there were plenty of rooms available. I was tired. I lazed in the motel pool for an hour before heading back to my room. I wanted to be rested and ready for a day of golf on Saturday morning with the same group of former classmates I'd played with ten years before. Saturday night would be the main occasion…the reunion dinner at the Indian Reservation casino.

The golf was as good if not better than it had been the last time my three classmates and I had played together. The joking and kibitzing started with the first handshake on the first tee box and didn't stop until we ended our play later that afternoon. It was as if we'd golfed together every weekend.

That night at the twentieth reunion party, the atmosphere was entertaining and fun. Classmates were more established in their lives. There were not as many baby pictures being shown. However, compared to the tenth reunion, this time some of my female classmates were completely unrecognizable. As for many of my male classmates, there was less hair. Too many of my male classmates expressed how fortunate I was being single and independent. I didn't want to shatter their hallucinations and inform them that I had some responsibilities as well. I just stayed quiet and let them contrive whatever daydreams they wanted about my life.

The gathering began slowing around 11:00, so I sauntered out to the main gambling area of the casino. Some of my former classmates had already split from the reunion bash. We waved at each other knowing our lives and preferences went far beyond the little get-together that night.

Interestingly, Janet Patterson never showed up for the reunion. I counted that as fortunate. I didn't have a polite prepared answer as to why I hadn't called her, even though it had been ten years since we'd exchanged phone numbers.

Trying to get motivated to try my luck at the blackjack table or go back to my motel, I took notice of a female at one of the tables. She looked peculiarly familiar for someone who hadn't been at the reunion party. And, I knew very few people in my home town, especially at her younger age. She sat there with some girlfriends discussing whether to take another card or not.

It must have been the way her long hair moved when she turned her head… or her disarming smile. I kept racking my brain trying to recall where we'd met. Her friends around her…all women…appeared to be unescorted, so my effort to remember seemed worthwhile.

Finally her laugh tipped me off. I realized she was Anne Nelson…the girl on the hill…or at least the third girl on the hill. She was dressed quite differently from two days before when she was wearing a long sundress and hat with her hair streaming in the breeze. This night she had her hair in a pony-tail with the tail sticking out of a baseball cap. She looked like she had come from some sporting event. She was quite striking in either mode of dress and I made a quick decision to stick around the casino for a while.

Feeling no hesitation to greet her, I sat down at her blackjack table and placed a $5.00 bet. I was hoping she wouldn't have the same difficulty recognizing me. I hadn't changed hairstyles like she had. More importantly, we now had a brief history. We'd shared a little secret up on that hill on Thursday afternoon.

She finally glanced in my direction. I could tell she was quickly trying to make the same recall I had just done. It didn't take her long.

She greeted me with a genuine smile. "Oh… hello. What a nice surprise to see you again."

There was no outward appearance of disinterest, but she didn't say my name. Not leaving anything to chance, I greeted her in return. "Hello to you, Anne. If you remember, I'm Ben. You may recall we shared a hill together recently."

She chuckled, "Ben, I haven't had that much to drink tonight nor did I get a concussion in my softball game earlier this evening. How could I not remember our conversation? In fact, I shouldn't admit it, but I've thought a lot about our meeting on Thursday. You seemed like the person I hoped that man would be down on the river hole waving up at me."

Her statement momentarily embarrassed her so she quickly turned her attention to her friends surrounding her and introduced them to me. Letting them know I was attending a class reunion on down the hallway of the casino, her friends immediately warmed toward me since I'd been a local resident at one time. Then, as if sensing something, they politely drifted away one by one as Anne and I continued to talk.

After losing $10 apiece in the next fifteen minutes, we'd satisfied our gambling urges and moved toward the exit. As we walked together, I couldn't help but bring up the subject of her being on that hill. In no way was I going to share with her the story I got from Dan Thornton, but I just wanted to say something nice to her. To me people like Dan Thornton and her were exceptional…that they would be so unstinting with their time…and not expect anything in return.

I said to her, "Anne, I don't know how long you'll be able to keep up your kindheartedness…both for that fellow down on the golf course as well as for your mother and her friend. But, I'll tell you I'm impressed with your selfless effort."

She leaned towards me while whispering, "Like I told you…it just makes me feel good. As long as that man keeps coming every year on the same date and time, I want to be there to preserve his personal dream. And maybe it's important to me as well. It keeps my own dream alive that such devotion can still survive in a relationship…even one that has had to be so distant."

I nodded blankly. If she only knew the man to whom she was referring had not been down on the river hole for well over ten years.…well before she began substituting for her own mother up on that hill. But, she had a dream in this matter as well. And now, based on what I'd learned from Dan Thorton, he'd shared in that dream that gave him the same type of pleasure.…giving of himself for another person's fantasy. Now, however, the next August the illusion would be shattered with him moving out of the community. It would be a personal disappointment to her. I had a feeling he'd feel the same kind of sadness when he wouldn't be showing up on that next August 18.

Instead, I repeated my accolades to her. "Well, it's a wonderful thing you're doing. It'll end sometime in the future but for now the memory of a past relationship lives on thanks to you. It's just marvelous how thoughtful you've been for your mother, her friend, and this gentlemen who shows up on the river hole every August."

She shrugged her shoulders as if she couldn't contemplate not doing what she'd done. Not wanting our conversation to end, the best I could come up with was asking her if she'd like some coffee before going home. She responded without hesitation. "Yes, that would be nice. There's a late night café back in town. Maybe we could get a coffee-to-go and you'd like to see the road that takes you to the top of the hill. It's really beautiful out there at night. I know the road since my mother's home is so close. You can follow me."

After arriving in two cars at her mother's home in the country, we trekked along a worn path through some woods towards the edge of the cliff on the hill. Her pathway to the top of the hill even at night was far easier than my way up the side of the cliff during the day. The star filled night as well as her flashlight had us standing by that lone tree on the edge of the ridge in twenty minutes. It seemed strange to see that tree in the dark. It was certainly no prop. It remained as stable and motionless at night as it did during daylight hours.

For the next hour-and-a half we sat along the cliff's edge enjoying the view and just talking into the night. It had been years since I'd stayed out that late. There'd been no reason before. The panorama of the town's lights, the sporadic farm light's in the countryside beyond, and the clear, star-studded sky made the picture atop that hill even more memorable.

It was past 1:30 in the morning when we strolled back down the hill to her mother's home where Anne was staying. We eventually said good night but not before I invited her out to lunch the next day prior to heading back to the Twin Cities. Again she nodded readily to the invitation. It was nice to sense her comfort with me.

Sunday we sat and ate at a local restaurant that up until that time had never offered any special recollection. Since my formative years living in the town, it had been nothing but a local café. It now provided a very positive reminiscence.

That weekend was the beginning of a relationship that grew despite her living in Madison, Wisconsin and me in the Twin Cities. In the months ahead we would be wearing out a lot of tire rubber between St. Paul and Madison. By the next summer she and I took up residence at my riverside home along the St. Croix River near Stillwater.

While we had a great summer, the most unforgettable day was a year since I'd first met Anne. It was August 18 and I sat out of view under that single tree up on the hill while she fulfilled yet another annual deed in waving to Toby Robinson…or at least his surrogate… down on the fairway of the river hole. I was worried for her since Dan Thorton had moved from town. I had concluded the deception would end that afternoon and she'd be upset.

But, something happened that afternoon that thrilled me as much as it did Anne. There was the stand-in for Toby Robinson loyally and exuberantly waving back to her from far down the fairway at the river hole. In her mind nothing had changed. She had sustained the man's dream… and her mother's similar dream for her friend yet another year.

From behind that lonely tree, I stared down at that man waving back at Anne. I didn't know if that person was Dan Thornton or someone he'd talked into replacing him. It occurred to me he might have just driven back from Rochester just to keep some long-term special relationship alive for another year. Either way he had contributed his part again to maintaining a long-term loyalty to a bond where the original members had long ago been out of the picture.

Anne's happiness in fulfilling her mother's wishes was so genuine. For that reason alone I confirmed in my own mind how I would never reveal to her that the man down on the golf course was possibly the third stand-in for the original Toby Robinson. If she ever found out, it would be through someone else. Her continuing act of wholeheartedness just made her that much more attractive to me. We were married that fall.

In the four years since we first met during the week of my twentieth high school reunion, she and I still make it back to our former hometown on August 18 and walk up to that spot by the single tree atop that hill…only this time with our young one either cradled in my arms or as he got older playing with him in the grass meadow away from being seen from the river hole. I stay out of sight sitting by the tree while she waits for 'Toby Robinson' to present himself down on the fairway below. She's always so excited about defending the relationship her mother's friend and then her mother believed in so deeply and now my wife also wanting to continue that dream that has been so precious to the man down on the river hole fairway….and frankly to all three ladies. I now share that same exhilaration.

However, it does intrigue me who that man waving back to my wife might be. Dan Thorton was long gone. There'd be little reason for him to be returning to the former town he lived in every August 18. The inconvenience and the unrequited personal satisfaction had to have worn thin.

Yet, there he was…or at least his substitute was there. The man down on the river hole was waving as energetically as I'd witnessed Toby Robinson doing almost thirty years before when I was a kid. It did occur to me that given the silence that surrounded this tale, would Anne ever think of finding a stand-in for herself. That time would certainly come at some point. It would mean this story of a long held dream and devotion between Toby Robinson and the girl on the hill could be recycled…conceivably forever.

I still ponder that entire scene…many times…during the year, especially when I realize how lucky it was that I found Anne. I am awed that a man I'd only met and talked with as a kid for less than two hours could have affected my life so dramatically. Even now I can picture that look in Toby Robinson's eyes as he looked back at that girl on the hill. Life never allowed the two of them to come together, but that didn't matter anymore to me. I had established in my own mind how I wanted that same feeling…and to have my eyes warmed to that same kind of vision. I'd accepted that if I never felt that same kind of urge and excitement Toby exhibited that day so many years ago with that girl up on the hill, then that female simply wasn't out there for me.

I was almost convinced she didn't exist until that one August 18 just before my twentieth high school reunion when I vaulted up to the crest of that ridge on a whim and found my own girl on the hill.

Uncle Joe's Secret Life

He was a man shrouded in mystery. I've met other people who were private…or maintained a level of confidentiality, but none of them… and I mean 'none of them' came close to the clandestine life of my Uncle Joe. From the time I first remember talking with him…and that goes back to grade school…it seemed I had a sixth sense about understanding his nature. Though it was only limited times that I did see him during those elementary school years, that would change as I passed into my teen years.

Uncle Joe along with his wife, Jane, was the only direct relative who lived outside my home state of Minnesota. They lived in South Carolina…Charleston specifically…where Aunt Jane was a native. Uncle Joe was my mother's brother. He was named my 'godfather' almost in the same breath as when I was given my name…Peter Michaels.

In a Presbyterian upbringing, the moniker of 'godfather' many times isn't that important. But, to my great fortune, Uncle Joe took the role very seriously. He and my Aunt Jane never had any children, so I benefited from them carrying a special place in their hearts for me. In my younger years the two of them never missed sending me gifts for birthdays, Sunday school or regular school graduations, Christmas, or notes congratulating me on something I had accomplished. I learned during those years that my mother kept Uncle Joe and Aunt Jane up-to-date with my life no matter how mundane it was.

There was probably another convenient oddity that brought Uncle Joe and I closer together despite the distance between my home and his home. My mother was the first to comment how similar I was to Uncle Joe not only in temperament, but in looks as well. As his little sister, she had plenty of first-hand experience to make the comparison. As I grew older, the entire family commented on our resemblance. I had the same square jaw line, a similar build, the same quiet nature, yet the same attention to detail and desire to make people laugh. Upon hearing these comparisons, I felt more and more biologically fortunate. I enjoyed hearing about our likenesses.

My family lived in a northeast town that barely qualified as a suburb of Minneapolis-St. Paul. Uncle Joe graduated from Stillwater high school, but left for good when he went into the military in the latter stages of the second World

War. Following the war he remained in the military for years being stationed in Washington D.C. where he went to college. After graduation he was assigned to a base in Charleston, South Carolina. That was where he met my Aunt Jane. If there was any hope that he'd ever return to his old home state, it ended when he married her.

As it turned out, the Christmas holidays were the one time when they'd venture back to Minnesota. I recall that first time she visited. I felt fortunate they stayed at my house. It gave me a chance to witness family members in both Minnesota and Wisconsin stream into my home to greet Uncle Joe and his new wife. It was not just that she was from the south, but she was from South Carolina as well. Their marriage had created quite a stir. Here was a northern Navy guy having pursued and won the hand of a southern belle. Even with my sparse knowledge of Charleston, I wondered how Uncle Joe got along with Deep South folks even though he'd lived in that state for over five years. After all, he was still a Yankee. Most of my family took for granted that my uncle couldn't very well be treated in a friendly manner. I heard a couple of my Minnesota uncles make the statement that at least he was a 'Minnesota' Yankee apparently hoping that those 'radical Confederates' in Charleston wouldn't hold too much against him.

When asked, my Uncle Joe handled the concern with his typical aplomb and humor. He kidded that most Charlestonians he'd met wondered if Minnesota was even part of the U.S. While that comment caused a lot of laughter, even from Aunt Jane, I would soon learn upon my first visit to Charleston how true that statement had been. Upon mentioning my home state to some friends of my aunt and uncle, I sensed those folks actually felt sorry for me having to live so close to the Arctic Circle! There were two other friends of Uncle Joe who questioned me whether Minnesota was a province of Canada. I honestly couldn't tell if they were serious or joking.

As for Uncle Joe and Aunt Jane, they lived on a beautiful piece of land along the Ashley River throughout their marriage. Occasionally while visiting in Minnesota at Christmas, they would allude to the additions they were building onto their house. Not often, but sometimes they brought a few pictures mostly of the inside of the house or of the additions. They included in the photo album numerous photos of downtown Charleston and the bay. Their intent was not to create envy; it was more that they wanted the family back in Minnesota to realize the beauty of the historic South Carolina city.

Each Christmas I still recall the excitement when Uncle Joe and Aunt Jane arrived at my house. They brought gifts and happiness. The warmth of their spirit during the dull, bitter cold of Minnesota was like a refreshing boost of energy for the entire family. Their stay was always too short. They would return to South Carolina after a couple days claiming they had to thaw out before returning to their work. More honestly Jane would intimate that Uncle Joe had to get back to his responsibilities…whatever they were.

Regarding Uncle Joe's job, that became a much discussed family question. I always thought Uncle Joe could have taken the extreme curiosity out of the matter by just informing the family what he did for a living. I speculated that he should have simply lied about his vocation just to appease everyone. Instead, he chose to be vague. I still don't know why he handled the subject that way. Over the years I eventually rationalized that because he lived so far away and only saw the family once a year, he simply didn't know how hot the topic was.

As a result, when he did arrive for Christmas in Minnesota, various family members tried everything to get him to talk about his job. Sometimes the questions were subtle; too often they became more blatant as time grew short before Uncle Joe and Aunt Jane had to leave.

His typical answer was that he was simply a government worker carrying out some boring work. It was the kind of answer that created more questions than it answered…especially when Jane showed pictures of their house.

But that was all Uncle Joe had to say about his work. I witnessed again and again him changing the subject without family members realizing it. He'd gradually alter the conversation by suddenly talking about Aunt Jane and her family and what they did back in Charleston. He'd go on and on about the art store her family owned. It was located on some place called the 'Battery' which made no sense to family members least of all me. He'd boast that her folks lived in a big anti-bellum home along Charleston Bay…and they were the sweetest, kindest people anyone could ever meet.

From a story like this one, family members eventually reasoned that Uncle Joe had married into wealth and really didn't have to work. It would be on my first visit to Charleston that I would learn how this story about Aunt Jane's family was as farcical as a fairy tale. I met her family. They certainly were very nice. They lived over in Mt. Pleasant along the harbor. Out their living room window was a perfect view of Ft. Sumter…at least what was left of it after a century of little care. Her father owned a small restaurant on the wrong side of the Cooper River and her mother was a school teacher. Again, why my uncle made up that tale about his in-laws owning an art store and lived in Charleston is anybody's guess.

As for my mother and father, they just considered Uncle Joe a busy man with a kind heart and married to a wonderful woman. They didn't care what he did, as long as the geographic distance didn't estrange my Uncle Joe and Aunt Jane from the rest of his Minnesota relatives. I would learn it was my mother who had some idea what her brother did for a living. While she never said a word to the rest of the family, she knew Uncle Joe traveled a lot on assignments for the government. Whether it was the occasional postcards from Jane who at times traveled with my Uncle Joe or his surprising knowledge of cities, countries, and their governments around the world, she never divulged what she knew nor did she speculate what he did during his overseas travel.

It was the winter of my sixth grade year that I was especially interested when Uncle Joe and Aunt Jane came back home for Christmas. I'd been studying world geography in school and I wanted to hear my uncle talk more about his travels… that is, if I could get him to open up. That Christmas I hung around my uncle every waking moment. I'd watch his manner, his speech, his attentive eyes and his uncanny ability to change the subject whenever a question got too sensitive regarding his work.

He seemed in control of every situation. Nothing got by him. He was aware of everything going on around him and seemed to judge how far he wanted to go when talking about his and Aunt Jane's life. And, when he did talk about places he'd been, he made it sound as if his experiences were part of a vacation he and Aunt Jane had taken.

Sometimes I felt like I was the only one who surmised that his travels were more work than play. The rest of the family would just get lost in some of his humorous tales…entertaining ones like being caught in a rain storm on the top of the Eiffel Tower, asking for directions in a busload of overly helpful people in Milan, meeting the very short Francisco Franco in Spain, or being given the royal treatment in Cairo until he finally convinced them he wasn't the famous military general they thought he was. All his stories were amusing…and they always seemed to end too soon….as if he had to limit how far he could talk about a particular trip.

My questions were why was he in Paris or Milan…how did he happened to meet Francisco Franco…or how could he have possibly been mistaken for a military leader? Occasionally I'd try. Then I'd fall victim to his suave manner as he switched the subject so smoothly. Too often it was an abrupt question about the whereabouts of some other relatives or former friends in Minnesota. Family members would begin looking at each other and discussing back and forth the whereabouts of these people. Uncle Joe would then just sit there with a satisfied smile on his face knowing he'd successfully taken the attention off himself. He would only misfire with me. He'd look over at me sitting closely on the floor just staring at him. He knew I was onto his methods. He didn't seem to mind. He'd just smile at me and give me an almost indiscernible shrug and a wink.

It was only the next spring as I was looking forward to leaving elementary school and joining the ranks of junior high school that my life took a major change for the better. I was taller than average and therefore probably seemed a bit older than I really was. I could tell Uncle Joe was impressed the previous Christmas by my interest in world geography and my incessant questions about the places he and Aunt Jane had been.

It might also have been that Christmas visit even he could see the unbelievable resemblance I had to him when he was my age…especially when Aunt Jane would repeatedly comment about the similarity. She also remarked how my quiet but determined personality mirrored my uncle even though I was but twelve years old at the time.

Whatever it was that happened, my Uncle Joe showed an interest in taking his 'godfather' responsibilities…whatever he thought they were… even more seriously. I found out that Uncle Joe and Aunt Jane had asked my folks over Christmas whether it would be all right if I visited them in New York and Washington D.C. over my Easter break. Uncle Joe said that he had some meetings to attend, but had enough free time for Aunt Jane and him to show me some sights.

It would be the first trip on my own. My folks hesitated for no other reason than they wondered if I would be a burden. But, seeing my enthusiasm and hearing Uncle Joe's continued urgings, they eventually gave in.

I believe my mother was excited about my trip as well because I might be able to provide a further link in keeping the family closer. With all my non-traveling relatives living in Minnesota, Uncle Joe and Aunt Jane could just as well be living in a foreign country. No one including my own family ever thought about making a trip to the southeast.

As it turned out in those seven days in New York and Washington D.C. with my aunt and uncle, I visited places and saw things that regular tourists would have a hard time fitting into their schedules…mainly because of the many contacts my uncle had. Who else could have arranged a private boat to go down the Potomac to see Mt. Vernon with a friend who happened to be a five-star general? Who else could have lunch in the United Nations building with the Secretary General, a long-time personal friend of my Uncle Joe? Who else got a private flight on a helicopter to Gettysburg and then south to Fredericksburg, Virginia, to tour those famous Civil War battle sites with the elderly great grandson of one of the generals who fought there? That was the kind of trip I had. Having to go back home was painful. I didn't want my adventure to end.

That little Easter break trip set the stage for a number of invitations in the months and years ahead. I don't know what it was, but my aunt and uncle seemed to take pleasure in my time with them. They commented constantly about my youthful curiosity and enthusiasm. The next Christmas when they visited Minnesota, we began discussing my coming down to Charleston for the next Easter break. It turned into five days in Boston and then five more days back at their home in South Carolina. This time Uncle Joe actually had some business to conduct. I didn't see him for two days. That just meant that Aunt Jane and I toured the Boston area very thoroughly without him.

She said he had to fly some place. She never mentioned where.

It was in June after my fifteenth birthday that a one week visit turned into two weeks. My folks thought I would be in Charleston or Washington D.C. the entire time and Uncle Joe said there were some special events he wanted me to attend…including a Yankee baseball game. The truth of it…I actually spent only three days in Charleston…the remaining time I was in London, the Netherlands, northern Germany, and Spain. I never did get to Yankee stadium.

When my uncle was busy with meetings in those countries, Aunt Jane knew enough about the geography and history of those areas that she and I again went off on excursions of our own. I was seeing and experiencing places that my friends in Minnesota had no idea existed. It was just as well. At times, Uncle Joe indicated to me that it would be best if I didn't let anyone know about certain places that we'd visited. That type of intrigue made those trips even more fascinating for a young Midwestern kid.

It would be no surprise that I never wanted my time with Uncle Joe and Aunt Jane to end. With the melancholy they showed when I had to return home, I sensed my feelings were shared. At the conclusion of each visit, Aunt Jane was a softy. She'd hug me while shedding a tear or two and then just hold a handkerchief over her nose. She would then wait in the terminal while my Uncle Joe walked with me down the corridor to the waiting airplane back to Minneapolis. He'd be talking already about some ideas for our next excursions. At the gate he'd give me a handshake followed by a big hug. Then he'd slowly walk away as I moved toward the gate entrance. I would look his way because I knew he would stop and stare at me for what seemed like an inordinately long time. Then he'd give me a big smile, a wave, and disappear down the corridor.

By the time I was a junior in high school I was making two trips a year to see them…once for ten days over Easter break and then again in the summer for at least two weeks. And those trips didn't end with some tearful farewells until the next excursion. We stayed in contact. I talked with them a couple times a month. The first call would be as soon as I returned home. They of course wanted to know that I arrived safely…and to tell my folks how delightful it was to have me with them.

Those phone calls obviously served another purpose. They maintained my connection with my aunt and uncle. Uncle Joe would check in with me from the darnedest places. At times I wondered if he was really where he said he was. Sometimes I could hear the roar of an airplane or locomotive in the background. I remember thinking since there were no telephones on the commercial airlines…at least in the 1970's…he had to be on some sort of private plane or special transport.

Other times his calls seemed to be from half way around the world. His voice would echo on the phone line. Later I would find out he was indeed on the other side of the globe. He was always quite vague as to where he was. He'd eventually steer our phone call around to my activities, our next planned trip, the coming Christmas visit in Minnesota, or simply recalling some of the good times we'd had on previous trips. In all from 1972 to 1978 from my twelfth to my eighteenth year, I made fifteen different extended trips with my Uncle Joe and Aunt Jane including some quick four or five day journeys just to Charleston to play golf and get filled with more local history. To say those experiences became exciting highlights and memories of my formative years would be an understatement. I never admitted to the places I'd been overseas during all those six years of high school while traveling with Uncle Joe and Aunt Jane unless my uncle gave me the O.K.

It was during my freshman year of college at the University of Minnesota when I received news that would have a major impact on our entire family, but mostly on my Uncle Joe. Aunt Jane had come down with a serious illness. I recall thinking there must be some mistake. I had just been with her and Uncle Joe earlier that summer for almost three weeks in Europe. She seemed often tired, but generally in fine spirits. Her being ill…it wasn't right! It wasn't fair!

Her death in November hit me like a hammer. It made no sense. As usual I had talked with her and my Uncle Joe in July and August…and most recently a couple weeks after I started school in September. Neither of them discussed her health in any great depth. In that last call Uncle Joe mentioned she was not feeling well and sleeping which was the reason she was not part of our phone conversation. I guess I was subscribing to youthful ignorance thereby not letting myself suspect anything dour. I simply had expected her to recover.

When I got word that she had passed, I seemed to be the only one in the family who didn't understand the inevitable nature of her illness. Nothing could have been done. That fact was never shared with me. I reacted angrily as if my rage would matter. Of course, it didn't.

That fall I made an unscheduled trip to Charleston for my dear Aunt's funeral in early November. Uncle Joe and Aunt Jane would not be making it to Minnesota together for the Christmas holidays ever again.

With her death, my Uncle Joe was understandably disconsolate. It was the only time I'd ever seen him completely lost and uncaring. They'd been as close as a couple could be in all the things they did together. I left Charleston worried about my uncle. I couldn't see him living without her.

When I returned to my first year studies at the University of Minnesota, I had a hard time concentrating. It was the first time in six years he and I had not discussed some kind of future trip. It would have been of course unconscionable to bring up such a selfish topic while at the funeral. The one thing I thought of often was that Aunt Jane's passing could well be the end of my travels to South Carolina…and points beyond. It was like the three of us were a private trio sharing a secret regarding all our special travels. With Aunt Jane's death, we were no more.

As that winter turned into the spring, no one including me had much contact with Uncle Joe. My folks had received a single postcard from New Delhi, India saying he'd been on the road for six straight weeks and sorry he'd been out of circulation. I was relieved when he added on the card, 'Say hi to Pete. I'll try and give him a call.'

In the months ahead I never got that call, but I did get some postcards and short letters. Those notes were fine. It was just that they were no replacement for the travels we'd done together. Even more, I definitely did miss those many phone calls I had from Aunt Jane and him. Nonetheless, I kept writing him…a routine every two or three weeks that wouldn't stop. I sent them to Charleston where I figured he'd eventually receive them.

The summer after my freshman year of college was the first time in the previous six years I didn't find myself somewhere on foreign soil. Life had changed for me, but then again so had it for Uncle Joe. His many postcards and letters sent to my family indicated he was traveling more than ever. The envelopes never had a Charleston, South Carolina postmark. It was not difficult to reason that his work had become his therapy.

As for me, that summer before my second year of college, I took a job at Dellwood Country Club near White Bear Lake. With no travel in my future, my day-to-day activity centered on working in the golf pro shop, golfing in my spare time, and winning some dates with some member's daughters. It was a fun summer…but nothing like portions of my previous six summers.

In the following two summers during college, nothing changed except my part-time jobs. In 1980 more than three years had passed since my Aunt Jane's death and those many trips with my uncle and aunt had become a great memory of my youth. I still got many short letters and postcards from Uncle Joe, but rarely a phone call.

Completing my college years and working a part-time job at WCCO-TV in downtown Minneapolis while going to school seemed to be my only quest. Nothing really exciting was happening in my life until my senior year when I was accepted into graduate school in political science at Georgetown University in Washington D.C. I would have never applied there if I didn't know the city so well. I'd been there often with Uncle Joe and Aunt Jane…sometimes just passing through for a day and other times longer as in that first one where I toured the sites for three days. I'd even been there once with my own folks. They were impressed how much I knew about the city…and that was when I was but fourteen years old.

Within a week of graduating from the University of Minnesota, I moved to Washington D.C. where I began a summer job as an intern on the hill for a Minnesota congressman. During my interviews for that job I remember how impressed the congressman's staff was of my knowledge of foreign geography and international politics. To them I admitted I'd traveled thoroughly and often around Western Europe and the Middle East. I never mentioned a thing about traveling with my uncle and aunt. I still never talked about Uncle Joe's business…whatever it was. After I won the internship I appreciated once again how much my travels with Uncle Joe and Aunt Jane had such a bearing on my life…including the confidence and maturity far beyond so many people in my age group.

I recall that a graduation card was waiting for me at the D.C. office the first day I reported for work. It was from Uncle Joe and postmarked from Athens, Greece. The contents included congratulations on my summer job and my acceptance at Georgetown University...and an open-ended round trip airline ticket to Europe. It was a hell of a present, but I had neither the funds nor the desire to travel by myself. After all, I'd been at countless cities in Europe and the Middle East with the best guides offered...my aunt and uncle.

Over that summer I got even more cards and letters from my Uncle Joe. I wished he'd call instead, but the now more frequent communications had a way of keeping us closer in touch. He kept reminding me to send any letters I wrote to his Charleston address since he'd usually be there for a day or two every other week. He never told me what he was doing or why he was so busy...and I didn't ask. I knew better. But, I could tell from the energy transmitted in his communications he'd finally gotten back to being himself...not completely, but so much better than the two years after Aunt Jane had passed on.

That first year of graduate school was energizing. If a person wasn't invigorated living in Washington D.C., it was his or her own fault. There was so much going on. Though I no longer had that internship on the hill, I'd made enough friends to have plenty to do.

For the first time since June, I ventured home for the Christmas holidays. I half hoped Uncle Joe might just show up for the family Christmas. As it turned out, my mother received gifts for the family from him and a phone call telling her it just wasn't in the cards for him to make it back to Minnesota that holiday. However, just the fact that he'd called and sounded disappointed that he couldn't be with the family brought a sense of relief to family members, especially to my mother.

My Christmas break was almost four weeks in length that year. After one week I was ready to return to D.C. I'd already looked up and gone out with many of my high school and undergraduate college friends. Each night I returned home late, at times after too much drink and a cloudy mind. It took only days to develop some poor sleeping habits as I got up later and later each morning. I really wasn't looking forward to following that pattern for the following three weeks, but I wasn't finding many other alternatives.

That was when fortune came my way. The phone call from Uncle Joe came totally out of the blue. For the second time in my life I got a call that would change my life. He and Aunt Jane had impacted my life so many years before... and so many times up to her death. But, this phone call was from my Uncle Joe... alone. It had been so long since I'd heard his voice sound so excited.

The phone rang about 11:00 at night a couple days before Christmas. I had just returned home from sitting at a bar in downtown St. Paul with three high school friends. I didn't want to drink the night away, so I'd bid them farewell figuring I'd see them at the same bar or at some party in the next few days anyway.

I was watching the 'Tonight Show' when I picked up the phone after one ring so it wouldn't wake up my folks. The voice on the other end of the line was distant. It had that same echo I'd heard many times in the past. His words that night still make my throat tight for their impact. It was so refreshing to hear his voice.

He yelled into the phone line. "Pete, you got to be going stare crazy being in the Twin Cities after your fall semester at Georgetown. How's about using that ticket I gave you last summer and come on down to Charleston for a couple days after Christmas. I don't want to take you away from your folks, but you've probably brought them up to date with your entire semester by now. What do you say?"

I couldn't believe what he was saying. A very important person was back in my life with just one simple phone call. I was ecstatic. And, I was exuberant to sense I was going to be part of my uncle's life once again. Though the pain of his loss would always be there, Uncle Joe had recovered enough to get on with his life.

The conversation was short because the phone line quality was so poor. It lasted long enough that we agreed I would fly to Charleston on December 26 and stay for a week. I'd then return to the Twin Cities for a couple days before traveling back to D.C. for the start of my second semester of graduate school. The scheduling sounded marvelous.

I hadn't even thought of checking with my folks. After our conversation ended, my mother came out to the kitchen. She'd heard the late night ringing of the phone. With a smile, she said, "When are you going to Joe's place?"

I chuckled. He'd already called her to see if it was all right to steal me away after Christmas. She knew I would jump at the chance to once again enjoy some days with my uncle.

Suddenly my world seemed to be flying on a different level. Christmas was special once again. The day after Christmas couldn't come fast enough. I had some pangs of concern whether my trip to Charleston might bring back some memories to my uncle about Aunt Jane, but I had to figure he'd somehow come to terms with that probability. Frankly, it was me who might get more emotional and nostalgic than my uncle.

I traveled to the historic South Carolina city truly believing I was going to unpack my bags and have a leisurely stay. It had been four years since I'd been in Charleston and I was looking forward to my return. I loved the city. I marveled how Minnesotans typically knew very little about South Carolina other than it was that radical southern state first to secede from the union back in 1860. And, of course with Ft. Johnson along Charleston Harbor being the place where the first shot was fired at Ft. Sumter to begin the civil conflict between the North and the South, why wouldn't any uninformed patriotic Minnesotan look askance at anything or anybody who had something to do with South Carolina.

With that Civil War legacy plus the race issue being such a powder keg in the South, each time I traveled to Charleston during my early high school years, my ignorant friends and relatives would worry about me. They'd ask if I was going to carry a gun or hide out on some golf course to keep from getting shot. If they only knew what they were missing.

Uncle Joe picked me up at the Charleston Airport on a cloudy and cool December afternoon. In the years since I'd seen him, other than being slightly grayer, he looked in excellent shape. We had plans to play golf that very afternoon at Patriot's Point over in Mt. Pleasant.

His greeting was as enthusiastic as ever. He was genuinely glad to see me. I was relieved. We picked right up from our previous week's phone call. He looked me over. "Pete, you're looking good. I'm so glad you could make it down to play a little golf with your old uncle."

That statement right there proved he was back. Already he was deceiving me about my general shape and his supposed decrepit condition just so he could get a few more strokes from me on the golf course. Given my study schedule in the fall and my recent week of too much food and drink while at home, I knew damned well I was not in the peak of condition. But, I was young. My energy would propel me.

As for him, he looked like he could run one leg of an 880 relay and still have something left to play a round of golf. It was not in vogue then to jog and lift weights. But, I surmised right then that whatever Uncle Joe did for a living, it required him to keep himself physically fit.

He started talking about the plans for the week while we were waiting for luggage and my golf clubs. He was actually more animated than normal. I figured he was just nervous or excited that I was visiting him. As we left the airport, the top was down on his Mercedes-Benz 450 SL convertible. The air was cool as we passed through the low country back toward the city. Not a mile away from the airport we were talking as if we'd been conversing weekly for the past two years.

We had just turned onto Hwy. #61, a short-cut to his place along the Ashley River when he looked at his watch and reversed his plans. He yelled out while the wind whistled around us, "Pete, tell you what, I've got an errand to run on the way home and then we'll stop by the house before we head on out to play some golf. We may not get in eighteen holes today, but we've got tee times set up for every morning...and maybe some fishing in the bay if we feel like that activity instead. We also have to get you back to some of our restaurants. I know you like ocean fish. We'll be eating out nightly." He sounded like he was looking forward to the upcoming days as much as I was. There was little complaint from me if golf and food were in the plans.

The temperature was just above sixty degrees as we entered downtown Charleston. There were still all the Christmas decorations remaining along the streets and in the windows of stores proving again that snow and cold weather were not obligatory to properly celebrate the holidays as so many Northerners presumed. It always amazed me that despite my northern background I felt so comfortable in this famous southern city. Of course, if I lived with the flair of Uncle Joe, I could probably live and feel comfortable anywhere.

We stopped at a law firm on Broad Street just down the street from St. Michael's Episcopal Church. There had been other times he'd have to time out for some business when I was traveling with him. I knew the drill. I would wait at the nearest bar or restaurant or museum until he completed his meeting. This particular time he said it wouldn't be long so he suggested I cross the street to a small café and order the sea bass and she crab soup. As he said, "Pete, you might as well get started with the culinary delights down here. I'll be along shortly. I've just got to find out what's brewing with my real estate attorney. He's on retainer, so it must be important."

In the past I might have let that comment slip by. Now it caused me to smile. What person keeps a real estate attorney on retainer?

I sat by the window of that restaurant on Broad Street and actually saw my uncle enter the real estate attorney's office. There were numerous real estate attorney offices on that street. I wondered how he'd chosen that particular one. Further, it appeared to be the only law firm office opened given it was the day after Christmas.

I watched through that street side window as the attorney greeted him and motioned for my uncle to sit down in his office. Neither man handled anything that looked like a contract for real estate or any other legal agreement. They just talked…and very seriously.

I saw Uncle Joe shake his head in a very disappointed way. I thought, 'It must be a hell of a difficult real estate deal for the two men to be so grim.

They were in that office for about ten minutes. Uncle Joe had a manila envelope under his arm when he left the law office. It reminded me of how often I'd seen him carrying a briefcase or manila envelope, his face intense with concentration as he strolled off to some meeting in some far off city. Watching him stride across the street reminded me again of my often thought description of my Uncle Joe being such a the man of mystery.'

Uncle Joe was no longer in a hurry when he joined me at the café. His face showed no emotion from that disappointed look he exhibited at the real estate office. He renewed more questions about the family back in Minnesota. In moments I'd forgotten about his reaction while at the attorney's office. We both had the sea bass and then got back in his Mercedes-Benz. I could have downed a second course.

We left downtown heading southwest across the Ashley River Bridge towards his home on James Island. My uncle was back in good spirits behaving like a travel guide pointing to and commenting on everything historical. His enthusiasm was unbridled. I couldn't help but get caught up in his zeal. Certainly no one I knew from anywhere in Minnesota talked with as much gusto about his community like my Uncle Joe did about Charleston.

A short distance after we crossed onto James Island, we turned a sharp right onto a private road. Some gates opened and we drove into a small estate. The gateway caught my immediate attention. To me, a gated community represented both money and safety. Uncle Joe had moved from living in the historic district on Queens Street since the last time I was in Charleston…and he apparently had moved up as well. As we began driving up the tree-lined driveway with overhanging Spanish moss, the Ashley River was just ahead across a large lawn that looked more like a golf course fairway. I thought I might be going into a development but I couldn't see any other homes. In fact, there were no other inhabitants. Wherever Uncle Joe's new home was located, his house was the only one needing those security gates. I looked at him with some awe. He smiled. He knew I'd be surprised.

Finally, a rather large stately home came into view as we drove along the Magnolia lined driveway. The house had pillars at the front like so many notable southern mansions. It was beautifully positioned at the curve of the Ashley River so the water view of both the river and Charleston Bay could be seen. Trying to keep my eyes from bulging, I looked at Uncle Joe while holding back a gasp.

Trying to play it down, he modestly nodded. "It's just a house. Your Aunt Jane and I had some good fortune. I sold our previous home for a surprising profit two years ago. I had to stick the money back into another house or face some crippling tax consequences. This home came on the market and I bought it. I've added a new addition to it recently."

We stopped in front of the house as Uncle Joe got out and nonchalantly strolled up to the front door. It was a double door of rich-looking, reddish mahogany. Holding the manila envelope under his arm, Uncle Joe called over to me, "Pete, make yourself at home. I've got to make a few phone calls. Help yourself to anything you want. I'll see you in about thirty minutes in the kitchen. I'm certain you'll be able to find the refrigerator. There's a small practice range in back. Hit some golf balls. You're probably a bit rusty after being up north these last couple months."

I just nodded. I was numbed by the spectacle of his magnificent property. In the next ten minutes I walked through the main floor of the house that held the kitchen, the dining room, and a huge library with windows displaying a huge grassy area with the peaceful Ashley River flowing by at the end of the property. In the remaining portion of the first floor was a huge master suite with more windows that opened up to a pond. I couldn't imagine what was on the second floor. As far as I was concerned, that upstairs square footage wasn't needed… especially now for my uncle.

The place was so large I figured to use the kitchen as a focal point. That way I knew I wouldn't starve if I got lost. In the adjoining library, there were displays of pictures showing Uncle Joe and Aunt Jane with some prominent looking people. None of them were recognizable to me, but those pictured were either in military garb or in obvious foreign type of apparel. My aunt and uncle actually looked out of place in the photos with their American style clothing.

There were a few other pictures showing him having dinner with some high level military individuals based on the number of stars on the uniforms. Again,

Uncle Joe was the only one with non-military attire. My mother had told me a few years before that he was doing government work in a non-military capacity. I surmised by the picture that her explanation was not entirely accurate.

I'd not thought about what my uncle's actual occupation was for a long time, but now in just an hour since landing in Charleston my curiosity was renewed. It brought back memories of the times while I was visiting my aunt and uncle that even their local friends always seemed puzzled. Since I was family, many of them would sidle toward me at a restaurant or dinner at someone's house and inquire, "So Pete, you've got to be really proud of your uncle. We know he's doing something important. He has a habit of just suddenly leaving Charleston and being gone for a couple of weeks. No one ever knows where he goes. He and Jane never talk about his trips. Do you know where he goes?"

As promised to my uncle, I would shrug my shoulders and respond, "Uncle Joe's just a busy guy. All I care is that he gets home safely so I can keep coming back to visit the two of them."

That reply was never adequate to the questioner, but it was satisfying to me to be involved in my uncle's confidentiality…especially since I was in the dark as much as anyone.

It did get humorous. I'd overhear some folks in Charleston talk about 'Joe' being on the PGA Board of Directors because of his love for golf and his penchant for showing up at the various golf tournaments around the country. Still others thought he was a part owner of some privately held conglomerate based overseas. Still others, including members in my own family, thought he was semi-retired and enjoying the good life in South Carolina. They thought his travels had to be generally of a personal nature and more for enjoyment. All these conjectures were so ill-conceived. Of course, I had the first-hand knowledge that no one else had except for my aunt. When I accompanied Uncle Joe and Aunt Jane on a few of their international trips, the travel was certainly fun, but there was also business related matters for my uncle to attend. At times Uncle Joe would be away from Aunt Jane and me for as long as a day or two. I could see by the strain on his face, some of those side trips for him had not been pleasure voyages.

I recalled telling my uncle once how inquisitive people were. I hoped my statement might coerce some additional information from him. It seemed each time he'd ignore my concern and deftly launch our conversation in another direction, in particular the wine industry. It was as if my angst automatically cued him to discuss wines. Even while still in high school, he emphasized being educated about fine wines and how that information might help me in the future. He allowed me to always taste each wine so I could understand the differences in port. There was one day that he did choose to ease my mind about being incessantly questioned by various people about his occupation. His response was brief, but complimentary. He said, "If I could tell you more I would. Just keep handling the nosiness the way you've always handled it. You're doing just fine."

That was it. He again moved back to talking about wines.

I did have one other time I tried to press him on what he did for a living. It was the summer before Aunt Jane had become seriously ill. I'd arrived in Charleston for a planned ten-day visit knowing that I'd be on a plane heading for Rome, Italy the next morning. Uncle Joe showed strain and a need for sleep when he picked me up at the airport. Certainly his mind had to be on Aunt Jane and her condition. On our trip to his house, I absent-mindedly asked him where we going in Italy.

His patience remained, but he looked at me and said quite seriously, "Pete, it's better that you don't know. I know you have an idea I do some kind of work with our government as well as some other countries around the world. Much of my work has to be highly confidential. So, let's just do what we always do. The less you know, the easier it will be to ward off questions about my work from anyone who asks."

I nodded that I understood…which I didn't. However, I did take note that he said 'other countries' confirming his work was sensitive, high level international work…at least that was what I chose to believe.

I remember back then on that particular trip being quiet as we continued driving toward his home. I felt badly that I'd overstepped my bounds. As we arrived at their house, he noticed my silence and grinned, "Pete, don't stop asking questions. Just because I don't talk about some things, it doesn't mean you can't ask. Your Aunt Jane and I have always had the goal of extending your education beyond your regular schooling."

While Uncle Joe was finishing his business on the phone, I continued my perusal of the house always gravitating back to the kitchen and the refrigerator. He and Aunt Jane had always filled the refrigerator with foods I favored… unlike my folk's refrigerator.

I was not disappointed. Uncle Joe had stocked the refrigerator with choices reflecting the nephew he used to know. As a kid I lived on pizza and ice cream. Now in graduate school, my palate was more sophisticated, but my interest in pizza hadn't changed. There were at least ten frozen pizzas in his freezer section. He had also purchased gourmet sausages and pre-made hamburgers. The ice cream bars were a bit youthful, but that didn't stop me from grabbing two of them. A case of Dr. Pepper was in the bottom compartment of the fridge as well. The man just didn't forget.

Taking the ice cream bars out onto the patio, I was impressed how a long green lawn was part of a golf practice area allowing short irons to be hit. At the end of the practice area was the back property line by the river. There was a dock with a large boat covered by a protective canvas. It looked unused.

Conveniently, I noticed some golf clubs placed under a storage roof connected to the pool area. Showing my true interest, I took the clubs and commenced trying to find my golf swing that had not been tested since the previous August in Minnesota.

It was about fifteen minutes later that I heard him yell out to me from the second floor deck. "Pete, I'm ready. Let's get going so we can get in some golf before it gets dark!"

Just hearing his enthusiastic voice echoing words I'd heard in the past bolstered me. I put down the club and trotted back to the incredibly large house. My secretive uncle had always been well off. But from what I was observing, he had raised his level a couple notches. Now my questions were plentiful, but unstated. I wanted to know what had caused his higher financial status. How did he gain this phenomenal home? Who was that Broad Street lawyer and what were the contents of that manila envelope my uncle carried in his hand with a death grip? Who were all the foreigners in the pictures on his desk and wall? I smirked wondering if he could be some kind of international spy. It was a ridiculous thought... but there had to be some answer.

Once back at the kitchen, Uncle Joe seemed preoccupied as he looked at some notes pulled from that manila envelope.

I reacted. "Is everything all right, Uncle Joe?"

He looked at me and smiled. "Yeh.....everything's fine. I do have to talk to you about a few things. Some of my plans have had to change, but you'll be part of whatever happens, so don't be concerned."

Momentarily he looked disappointed. Then, in the next instant, his eyes started to shine. "Let's get rolling. We've got enough daylight for eighteen holes at Patriot's Point if we hurry. Then I've got this new restaurant down on East Bay Street that's been restored since you were last in Charleston. There will be a few of my friends there as well. You'll probably recall some of them."

And that was what we did. The wind off Charleston Harbor was strong enough that both of us had trouble scoring, but we had fun. Like in the past, we kidded around and played for a few bucks. Following the golf we went back across the Cooper River Bridge to the historic district and that eating establishment Uncle Joe had referred. Always thinking ahead, he brought along a couple blazers for us to wear over our golf shirts. He always preferred to eat in style.

Entering that restaurant was as if he'd arrived home. So many people greeted him and shook his hand. His eyes sparkled with pride as he introduced me to everyone. I found myself unconsciously copying his energy. A couple people remembering me from my past trips remarked how much I had grown. I thought it more likely I needed a shave. Additionally, it was nice to hear comments once again on how my uncle and I looked so much alike.

I did notice one thing that had changed in light of the passing of my Aunt Jane. He was getting a lot of attention from almost every lady in the bar area...no matter their age. Then in his fifties, Mother Nature had been very kind to my uncle. His tan, lantern jaw and ready smile captivated so many women. Females sauntered over to him at the bar and gave him a hug or a kiss on the cheek. It was pretty easy to see Uncle Joe could be back in circulation as much as he might want to be.

Later he told me he'd only taken a few women out socially…and all of them were at functions overseas. In Charleston he claimed no interest in asking local women out.

He chuckled, "I tell you, Pete, taking one local lady out for dinner would cause stifling rumors. Besides, I could never be certain if the lady would be more interested in me or my house." He tried to say that last line kiddingly, but I knew he was at least half-serious.

When he was finished greeting all the people he knew, we finally sat and ordered a bottle of wine. An hour later we were still talking at the table and finishing our second bottle along with a full meal. It was then he introduced our schedule change. I'll never forget how casually he launched into the 'slight' alteration of our plans. It was something I'd learned to expect.

Coolly he said, "Pete, how would you like to take a few side trips in the days ahead? It may interrupt some of our planned golf, but the rest of the adventure should balance the disruption."

There was only a moment of disappointment about the golf, but I knew the alternative would be adventurous. I was certain not many people would be experiencing what I would no doubt see in the days ahead. I tried to be casual but my response gave away my excited anticipation. "Sure, Uncle Joe, I'm game. It's not like I have to re-pack. So, where're we going?"

He studied me as if he'd forgotten how enthusiastic I'd always been in our travels. Then in that inimitably calm voice he whispered, "We'll be leaving tonight, but there are a couple things we have to discuss. You are going to quite a few places in the next couple days and our sleep hours will be on an airplane. This should be no surprise to you, but everywhere we go has to be highly confidential."

I gave him a look and a shrug, as if saying, 'why tell me something I already knew?'

He then added, "You're of course not going to be in any danger, but when you get back home, let's always just talk about the golf we played and the restaurants we frequented here in Charleston. And, not to worry, my intention is to have you back in Minneapolis to be with your folks for a couple days before you head back to Georgetown. Is that O.K.?"

I raised my wine glass in affirmation. The image of Uncle Joe, Aunt Jane, and I going sky-diving in the Alps outside of Interlaken in Switzerland a few years before shined in my mind. I never told my folks. Nor did I tell any family members about the three of us helicoptering above Victoria Falls, crawling along the perilous cliffs of Mesa Verde National Park, zooming along in a speed boat at over a hundred miles an hour on a lake along the French-Swiss border or being caught in blinding sandstorm in central Egypt. To have told anyone about these or other travels with Uncle Joe would have meant explaining that I hadn't been in Charleston after all. It was easier just to say I was in South Carolina all the time.

The next few hours were a whirlwind. Within two hours of leaving the restaurant we were back at the Charleston Airport delivered by a limousine.

Uncle Joe was lining up our flight plans while in transit. He still had not offered me even a hint as to our first destination. I didn't know if we were going to fly commercial or private jet. In the past it had been both.

The answer came immediately. There was a small private jet awaiting us. The inside of the plane was like a family room. There were no aisles or normal airline seats. Instead there was an L-shaped leather sofa with small table. A music system and television were built into a mahogany shelf. There was a small refrigerator that caught my attention. The entire plane was like a flying hotel room. Towards the rear of the plane was a small office with adjoining bathroom.

My role just like in the past was to get on board and stay out of the way. As the plane's motor revved up, I marveled at how my life changed whenever I was with my uncle. The small information piece on a side table advertised that the jet was capable of an air speed of four hundred miles per hour. Uncle Joe walked by and gave me a cursory smile and told me to get comfortable. "We're about to take off. I've got some work to do. I'll see you later in the flight."

He slipped to the back of the plane and into his small office. My nose was pressed against the window of the plane as we took off into the now darkened evening. As we gained altitude, I observed the Atlantic coast line. The lights along the coastal waters were intermittent then solid while flying toward Myrtle Beach, then Wilmington, North Carolina, and then Norfolk, Virginia. Finally the cloud cover thickened causing me to lose any sense of direction.

The day had already been full and I was exhausted. That morning I'd gotten up early in my Minnesota bedroom before being rushed to the Minneapolis-St. Paul International Airport. Now I was on another plane at the end of the day likely crossing the Atlantic Ocean to another continent.

With the whir of the plane, I lay back on the couch and enjoying the feel of privilege. There were current news and sports magazines. I tapped the refrigerator for a snack of fruit and a soft drink. For the thousandth time I thought about my uncle's occupation. There were no hints anywhere on the plane. However, by simply being on this private jet hinted strongly that he was paid well for whatever he did.

I don't remember falling asleep, but I do recall Uncle Joe throwing a blanket over me sometime during the night. I awoke once and noticed he was sound asleep on a pull-out bed. I rolled over and went back asleep with the drone of the jet engine in the background.

The sun was peeking through the airplane window as I awoke. I looked at my watch. I'd slept for five hours. It was 2:30 AM on my watch...the actual time much later relative to the number of time zones we had crossed. I could hear my Uncle's muffled voice on the phone in the other room. With the glow of morning, I guessed we were across the Atlantic given where the sun was in the sky. Pressing my nose to the window I saw only intermittent clouds and the shoreline. The ocean was on the west side of the shore verifying we'd definitely crossed the Atlantic Ocean.

Still groggy, I was finally awoken for good when one of the two pilots quietly shuffled by saying, "Good morning." He spoke English with a heavy northern European accent. I was well-traveled enough that I should have deciphered what country, but I was out of practice. He was friendly as he offered something to eat. "We've got some coffee if you want as well. We'll be on the ground shortly. Then you can get some real food."

I hadn't even met the pilots when we boarded. Uncle Joe and I had just climbed on board the plane. The cockpit was closed. The outside door slammed shut. And we had taken off. The whole trip was adding up to even more mystery than in the past. Uncle Joe was obviously on a tight schedule.

I could feel the plane beginning a descent as my ears adjusted to the air pressure. I got up and folded the blanket. A map had been placed on the table in front of me. That was my first hint that we were descending into Paris. Uncle Joe had subtle ways of ending some of the mysteries.

I'd been to Paris several times with him in the past. The map gave me a good reminder of the layout of the city. With the coast behind us, I looked ahead trying to locate the River Seine. Once I could locate that geographic landmark, I would find the key landmark for me of Paris…the Eiffel Tower.

Uncle Joe's voice startled me as he came out of his office. "Pete, I believe if you look out the right window you'll see the Eiffel Tower off in the distance. It's beautiful in the mist of the morning. It's also where we're going to have either a late breakfast or an early lunch.

He chuckled at my surprised look. "Anyway, the Eiffel Tower would be the first place I'd be looking when flying into Paris." Uncle Joe had a way of bringing himself down to my level.

We landed at a minor airport closer to the city. I had just been in the air for eight hours, sleeping most of the time. I thought back to Charles Lindbergh landing at night in the middle of Paris at an airfield lit by automobile lights after traversing the Atlantic and the English Channel in a small aircraft. It was over fifty years later but I could now relate to Lindbergh, except in my case I was better rested. His trip took thirty-three hours; our travel time was substantially less.

It was a late breakfast, but true to Uncle Joe's word, we got a table on the second level restaurant of the 984-foot tower after an electrifying taxi ride through the streets of Paris. The break neck speed of the ride seemed silly, but Uncle Joe wasn't bothered. He was browsing the newspaper. I was pointing at places of interest as we rode. He patiently nodded while reading. When we arrived at the Champ De Mars where the impressive tower hovered, he wasted no time in walking toward the huge erector set.

We took the elevator to that mid-level area of the tower. The city of Paris stretched out to the horizons on all sides. Uncle Joe was looking around the eating area while reminding me of the history of the tower and pointing out several other landmarks of the city. The Arch De Triumph was below us on the left. As my eye followed the Seine, there was the majestic Cathedral of Notre Dame. He also pointed out some impressive buildings between Notre Dame and our perch. He told me he hoped the two of us would have time to stop by the Louvre Art Museum. He seemed engrossed in something but pleased that I was with him.

As for me, I kept thinking about awakening in my own bedroom just the day before excited about flying to Charleston. In the duration of the twenty-four hours I'd played a round of golf, flown to Paris, and now was having a late breakfast halfway up the Eiffel Tower with my uncle.

Finishing breakfast, he stood up staring at his watch. I'd seen the look before. He had somewhere to go…someone to see. He said, "Pete, I'm going to leave you for a couple hours. Here's five hundred francs for you to get around until we meet in front of the Grand Palais on the Avenue Des Champs Elysees a few blocks up from the Louvre Museum. Let's meet at 3:30, have some wine, and then go over to the museum from there."

As he handed me the francs, he also gave me a plain envelope about a half inch thick. He added, "In about fifteen minutes, why don't you make your way over to the Arch de Triumphe. I want you to meet a gentleman and give him this envelope. His name is Alex Gustave. Believe it or not, he'll be wearing a Minnesota Twins baseball cap. He went to school in the United States and he likes baseball. I got him the cap last year. He'll take you to a couple of places I pointed out on the tower. He knows more than I do about the history surrounding Paris. But, don't forget to give him this envelope. He'll drop you off at the Grand Palais. See you later this afternoon."

Among the many things special about my Uncle Joe was his trust and confidence in my ability to follow his directions. Here I was alone in Paris being asked to find a person who needed the contents of the envelope I was now carrying. It had to be something important. I just couldn't imagine how vital the contents were. I laughed. There were times years before when my folks were nervous leaving me being alone in downtown Minneapolis. Now I was being left at the Eiffel Tower with a large amount of francs in my pocket and a vague description of who I was to meet shortly at the Arch de Triumphe.

Five minutes later I hailed a taxi and he made the short trip to yet another coffee shop adjacent to the busy traffic circle that surrounded the Arch. I waited with the other pedestrians until the French chan darme allowed us to cross the street. He finally frowned and with a disdainful wave directed us to cross the busy circle.

I recognized Alex Gustave right away. He was reading a French paper and sitting on a small bench. The Twins baseball cap was resting unnaturally on his head. As soon as I arrived he took the cap off and put it in his small bag. He was about forty years old, three inches shorter than me, and not quite twice my weight. He greeted me with a very genuine smile and only a slight accent. I immediately gave him the envelope as my uncle had requested. The shape of the envelope felt like it contained some money, but I also knew that my imagination might be working overtime. Anyway, Gustave stuffed the envelope into his coat pocket and that was the last time I gave it any thought.

His first words were familiar. "You look like your uncle, do you know that?"

I nodded. It had been only the previous evening I'd heard that statement in that Charleston restaurant. Again I enjoyed the comparison.

I finally spoke. "Senor Gustave, my uncle said you might have time to drag me around to a few sites. If you're too busy, I'll certainly understand."

Gustave ignored my attempt at being polite. He seemed to have little time for wasted politeness. He chuckled, "Call me Alex and I'll call you Pete." Now, let's get moving, we got a lot to see in a short time."

Alex knew the ropes. He had hailed a taxi in moving traffic circling the Arch. He got a sharp whistle from the arrogant chan darme, but it didn't faze Alex at all. Alex was grinning and giggling using a not very complimentary French slang word for the officer as he and I dove into the cab. I found myself liking the guy's irreverence.

We were moving down the Avenue Des Champs Elysees after meeting only two minutes before and he was already displaying his fountain of knowledge. He would ask me questions to better understand my level of knowledge about French history. When he found out I was a political science graduate student, he seemed impressed. When he learned of my sparse knowledge of French history, the shine in his eyes was slightly reduced. Still he remained considerate and showed no disgust. He simply pared back his monologue to the level of my historical background.

We drove by the Grand Palais and the Louvre Museum before arriving at Ille de la Cite. The Cathedral of Notre Dame loomed before us. Alex was without a peer both in information and energy. He kept buying me coffee from street venders to fight my jet lag. Despite sleeping on the plane, I was still struggling. The cool air kept me yawning, but the caffeine kept me reasonably attentive.

Touring Notre Dame, he had a street vendor pour me another large coffee before taking me through only two small rooms of 17th Century French and Flemish paintings at the Louvre Museum. Despite telling Alex that my uncle and I were going to tour the place that afternoon, he smiled patiently and said, "I suppose you can tour Minneapolis in an afternoon, but we're talking about the 'Louvre'. You never have enough time to enjoy the entire Louvre. Shall we proceed?"

He made his point but after forty minutes I was showing unrelenting signs of mental exhaustion. The time zone difference had simply caught up with me. Towards 3:15 Alex and I had been talking, walking, and drinking coffee since late morning. He showed little wear while I had deteriorated down to a mumble. Finally we grabbed a taxi and went the short distance to the Grand Palais for my scheduled meeting time with Uncle Joe.

Alex and I were about to say farewell when I realized how little I knew about the man…though I'd asked. He had Uncle Joe's gift of turning the conversation around to anything but him. Usually I'd have picked up on that action, but my senses were dulled from the time zone change. But, it was very clear he'd been very generous with his time. I figured he must have owed my uncle a huge favor to be saddled with me for those many hours. As he departed, he gave me a warm handshake and slap on the shoulder. "Pete, you're a fine young man. Of course, any relative of your Uncle Joe's, I would expect as much. Come back to Paris when we can spend more time."

Dulled by my weariness, I shook his hand and thanked him. He pointed to the front entrance of the Grand Palais where my uncle was leaning against a rod iron fence outside the front entrance to the palace. I waved to him expecting Alex to follow and greet Uncle Joe. Instead, he was gone, having just drifted into the crowd of pedestrians.

Uncle Joe was reading the paper as I approached. It didn't seem to surprise him that Alex hadn't joined us. I unconsciously yawned while saying to him, "Uncle Joe, I must say I am far worldlier than I was earlier in the day. Does it show?"

He gave me a refreshing smile. "Well, you look a little worse for wear, but I'm glad you enjoyed the tour. Alex is a knowledgeable guy and a good friend."

As he spoke, he was looking around as if trying to see if anyone was following either him or Alex. I found that mannerism slightly strange. It was as if he was concerned about being recognized in Paris…and it was quite the opposite at his favorite East Bay Street restaurant in Charleston.

Then he interjected, "I'm not entirely certain right now the time we'll be leaving Paris, but it will be this evening. You'll probably be ready for a little nap anyway once we get on the plane."

Then as if a firecracker went off beside him, there was that snap to his posture. He didn't like wasting time. He suddenly started moving while saying, "Come on, Pete, instead of going to the museum, how about we explore the Grand Palais. I know someone here who can give us a personal tour. First, let's get you some more caffeine and some food."

We ate at a coffee shop along the Avenue des Champs Elysees. I ate some very tasty chicken wrapped in a soufflé with cream sauce in it. I kept examining my Uncle Joe. I was dying from exhaustion and gulfing down the food like it was my last meal. He was more composed leaning back in his chair browsing a newspaper that was neither English nor French. While I devoured the food, he scanned yet another newspaper in yet another language. He seemed in no hurry so I rested my head back to rest until my blood sugar level had been revamped.

It seemed a minute later when the smell of yet another cup of thick coffee was thrust in front of my nose by some uncaring waiter. Uncle Joe was about ten meters away busily talking on a street phone. It was almost 4:30. I had caught a forty-five minute catnap.

Uncle Joe smiled at me and motioned for me to take some swigs of the coffee while he was talking on the phone. Then he hung up and came back to the table saying, "That little nap and the coffee should recharge your battery. We still have time to tour the Grand Palais."

He seemed more enthused than I about going into the palace. However, I gathered myself knowing I was about to go on a special tour. The man never ceased to amaze me what he could set up in such a short period of time.

The tour guide turned out to be my uncle. I couldn't believe anyone else could be as entertaining. We had a group of sixteen people who eventually followed us around the palace as Uncle Joe told little vignettes about various rooms and furniture in the rooms. He had people laughing telling stories about the many self-important looking monarchs who appeared on tapestries and paintings.

After an hour even Uncle Joe was finally slowing down. We grabbed a couple of sandwiches from a street vendor and hailed a taxi. It was time for our return to the airport.

He sat back and relaxed. "Pete, like I said, we'll be leaving Paris shortly. But, tell me, have you been to Switzerland recently?"

He and I both chuckled with that bit of nonsense. I played along. "Not recently, Uncle Joe. Just during the war years. I was hiding out in the neutral zone of Switzerland, so I wouldn't get my rear end shot off."

That got a laugh out of my uncle. It was good seeing flashes of the old Uncle Joe. I guessed with Aunt Jane being gone, he likely didn't have the same opportunities to play off a traveling companion like Jane. I could tell he was now relishing the camaraderie of our long-term relationship.

As we got in the taxi to the airport, I finally asked him about Alex Gustave and how it was odd the way the man had just disappeared into the crowd on the busy street.

My uncle seemed unprepared for what I thought was an obvious question. He lamely responded, "Oh, he's just a friend. We've known each other and done business together for almost twenty years. He's the son of the right hand man to General De Gaulle for the French Resistance during World War II."

That was it. I couldn't believe my ears. My uncle was so nonchalant. I was being toured around Paris by a man from a very prominent family. If I had only known, I would have asked about his father's life of which Gustave most certainly would have been proud. It embarrassed me that I'd been so dull-witted not to have taken more initiative.

In that next moment I decided to be more forward. "So, Uncle Joe, why and where are we headed to in Switzerland?"

While staring out the window in the taxi, he ignored the 'why' and without thinking responded to the 'where'. "We're going to a beautiful city in the Swiss Alps named Lucerne. It's just north of Italy. I have someone I need to meet. We'll stay the night and day in Lucerne. From there we may be going onto Naples, however, that might not be a sure thing." His voice then tailed off.

We boarded the plane and he nodded off to sleep even though the private jet hadn't started its engines. I read some of the news magazines and just watched the activity at the airport until the plane's engines revved up. That was like a lullaby. I was asleep before we took off.

It was night time when I awoke again. The engines were barely whining indicating we were at full speed somewhere above what I guessed would be the Alps. I could hear my Uncle Joe's voice in the adjoining room on the plane…very deep in conversation. I couldn't understand what type of business would require a man to be on the phone at all hours.

Falling back asleep, it was still dark when I could sense the plane was descending. I took for granted we were arriving in Lucerne, but we could have been anywhere for all I knew. I dozed off and didn't wake until the plane was on the ground. One of the pilots was doing some logging in the cockpit, and Uncle Joe had deplaned already.

Still pre-dawn I went to the cockpit to greet the pilots. The one not doing the logging spoke straightforwardly. "Good morning…Joe said to let you sleep. He'll be back shortly. It's almost daybreak. Your uncle said he's got a great place for the two of you to have breakfast."

"Are we in Lucerne?"

"That's right. We've been here for a while. Apparently we're not moving on until sometime tonight or tomorrow."

I found it curious that the pilot never introduced himself to me. He knew who I was and that was enough. Nonetheless, I marveled at the excitement of not knowing where I was going or what the day was going to offer. It wasn't my preferred pattern of life, but with my uncle, it all seemed expected.

I used the miniature bathroom to clean up. Minutes later Uncle Joe drove up to the plane in a shiny new Mercedes Benz. He looked refreshed, almost as if he'd had a shower someplace. Galloping up the steps into the fuselage, he greeted me. "Come on, Pete. Time's a wasting. Let's eat. I've got some business to conduct with a gentleman waiting in the car. I'll introduce the two of you, but then I'll be mostly be talking to him in another language. So don't feel badly if you feel ignored."

I nodded. Frankly I felt relieved my presence wasn't going to cause any inconvenience. Even more, I was pleased Uncle Joe remembered my adaptability.

In the back seat of the car, Uncle Joe introduced me to a very dapper European…a guy named Valde Waldstatter. The man spoke mostly German, but greeted me in English. Our conversation was limited from that point forward. There was no reason to believe we were going to become close friends anyway. With Mr. Waldstatter and Uncle Joe engrossed in their business while talking German, we drove alongside Lake Lucerne into the city. I let the scenery occupy my thoughts.

The traffic had already started that morning. For a beautiful Swiss city the traffic was not only fast, but surprisingly loud. People were sitting at outside cafes drinking their morning coffee within a couple feet of speeding vehicles zooming by. It made you wonder how many Lucerne commuters and pedestrians didn't make it to or from their work alive.

We arrived alongside a boat at the main marina on Lake Lucerne. It was a tourist boat. The name of the boat was spelled like Mr. Waldstatter's name sounded. I didn't ask if it was his tour boat company. It didn't matter. When we boarded, I was introduced to two more of Uncle Joe's associates…a man who barely glanced at me and another man who studied me. I'd seen the look many times. He was curious if I was Uncle Joe's son.

Neither man spoke English apparently very well. They had their minds on something else. Nonetheless, I held onto the handshake of the man who was ignoring me to force him to acknowledge my presence. He finally grudgingly did so but showed his discomfort. Uncle Joe chuckled understanding how I wouldn't let this unsocial fellow show me any disrespect. My uncle had no problem with my methods.

Moving away from that small group, I headed for the boat's café where the view of the surrounding mountains from an outside table was stunning. I knew no one and I figured to be sitting there alone on that boat for a couple hours. I had no complaints. In fact, thinking about the alternative of being back in the Twin Cities probably waiting for some friends at some St. Paul bar, I was thankful and thrilled as to where I was sitting at that moment.

While I paged through a French magazine looking at the pictures, I saw my uncle and the three other men off in the corner of the boat's café talking very seriously. It occurred to me of all the times I'd thought my uncle might be doing something clandestine; all those wild thoughts of mine were suddenly becoming quite real as I noted the postures and intense discussion going on among the four of them.

Not wanting to be seen, I moved to the adjacent lounge and began talking to an older couple on holiday. I remained at a perfect angle to where I could pay attention to Uncle Joe and the three other men while pretending to look at the older couple. Mr. and Mrs. Newton White of Cork, England just chattered away as if I was absolutely engrossed in the story of their lost luggage. All the while I nodded but really was more absorbed in the body language at my uncle's table inside the cafe. It did not look like the talk among the four men was going well. One of the men…the man who didn't look me in the eye when Uncle Joe introduced him to me… was looking down at his shoes with his arms folded across his chest wearing a deep frown. His behavior alone showed me that there would be problems stemming from their conversation whatever they all thought they'd agreed to when their meeting ended.

Mrs. White suddenly stopped her wringing story of bad luck and with her inimitable high-pitched English accented voice asked me, "So, Peter, what brings you to Lucerne and this particular excursion?"

I didn't expect any questions and had to fight to think of a quick response. A swig of coffee and my lie was formulated. Uncle Joe would have been pleased with my answer. I actually spoke the truth. I said, "Oh…yes…Mrs. White, I'm just an American graduate student enjoying a holiday with my relatives before I go back to the states. We'll be taking off later on today."

Mr. White took the pipe out of his mouth and commented, "Well, I hope you needn't get to the airport too soon. This is a rather long excursion. We'll be boating across the lake and stopping at a small village with a tram station. The tram will take us to the top of the tallest peak surrounding Lake Lucerne for lunch."

Sure enough, whether Uncle Joe wanted to be on this cruise or not, we were going across the large Lake Lucerne to some unknown destination…at least a place new to me.

We arrived at a small alpine village that seemed as if it hadn't changed in centuries. Many quaint little homes had thatched roofs. It was like a painting with no movement of people…just smoke coming out of an occasional chimney.

The two gentlemen meeting with my uncle and Mr. Waldstatter departed at the tram station. The shaking of hands was curt. One of them walked to a waiting car and took off down a slender winding road back in the direction of Lucerne. Another strolled across the street to what looked like the only café in the small hamlet. Mr. Waldstatter stayed on the boat.

Uncle Joe appeared to be done with his part of the morning meeting. His eyes hid anything unpleasant as he approached me. He went from the serious businessman back to tourist in the flash of a moment as he commented, "Well Pete, thanks for putting up with the interruptions. I had some important things to discuss with those fellows. Let's walk over to the tram station and go up the mountain. There's a great little hotel and restaurant up at the top."

It amazed me once again where this man had been. He'd already been at this out-of-the-way hotel at the top of the mountain sometime in his past.

With a couple of tickets purchased, we entered the tram. The seats were positioned so passengers all hunched forward before the engine and three cars started up the steep incline. Folks looked a bit uncomfortable. I asked Uncle Joe why the tram seats were constructed in this way.

He winked and said, 'Just sit down…you'll see."

When the tram began its ascent, my question was answered. All of us leaning forward at the station were now seated comfortably facing only slightly upward. Otherwise by now, we would be lying on our backs as the tram car was inclining at more than forty-five degrees in some areas

Every breathtaking second of the journey was a panoramic view of Lake Lucerne. We eventually approached that quaint hotel just below the peak of the mountain. Once outside the tram, the temperature had declined noticeably as we strolled toward the hotel entry. Uncle Joe and I were greeted by a waiter at the hotel café and were directed to an outside table at my uncle's request. There was snow all around us, yet the sun was shining. With the wall of snow providing a windbreak, the eating area provided a strange mixture of temperate comfort.

After lunch he had to make a call. He didn't want me to miss a thing and pointed towards the back of the hotel. He said to me, "Pete, I'll be disposed for five or ten minutes on the phone. I suggest you walk out the back exit and up the path to the peak of the mountain. It's only a short walk, but spellbinding once you get there."

I nodded and then trekked up the path to literally the sharp edge of that particular mountain peak. It provided a dramatic sight in every direction of the entire wavy range of the Alps as far as the eye could see. The wind was fierce. Far below was the city of Lucerne so small it seemed as if it could be covered with a small plate.

Suddenly cold, I stepped away from the surprisingly feeble looking safety fence and began walking back to the hotel. Immediately I saw Uncle Joe talking not on the telephone but personally with a peculiar looking fellow. The smaller, stocky looking individual was of very dark, ruddy coloring relative to most of the pale looking people visiting the small mountain retreat. Again, both Uncle Joe and this guy were in deep conversation. It ended with my uncle handing the short fellow an envelope. They shook hands and the darker man retreated to a hallway and then disappeared from view. As my uncle turned to face me, I simultaneously turned away. I didn't want him to think I was spying on him.

Strolling towards my uncle, I couldn't get over how Uncle Joe's clandestine work just seemed to materialize everywhere. This trip I was seeing too much making it more difficult to be play dumb or be discreet. One thing for certain, it was not entirely the fault of my relatives back in Minnesota that they were not close to Uncle Joe. How could they understand any of what I had witnessed in the past or even the few episodes I'd seen since the previous day in Paris?

He met me at the exit. He decided he wanted to stand on that mountain precipice to see the view before we left. The wind was whistling over the peak and blowing against our faces. It was bitterly cold but Uncle Joe didn't seem to mind. He began to describe some Swiss history including the background on the picturesque city of Lucerne. I figured he was giving that stocky fellow a chance to exit the hotel so the two of us wouldn't accidentally run into him.

Walking back from the peak, he revealed our next stop. "Pete, my business is done here, but I have another destination. Afraid it's going to be another overnight flight. I have a Tuesday meeting on the western African continent. Have you been there recently?"

There he went... again trying to defray my curiosity with a joke. I just chuckled. I hadn't even looked at any of the last ten years' worth of National Geographic magazines that centered on some country in Africa.

Trying to stay casual, I responded the only way I knew. I kidded, "No...I haven't been to Africa in quite a spell...with school and all taking my time."

He chuckled ignoring my lighthearted comment. "I've got to see someone in Tangier, Morocco. We'll take an alternative route rather than fly straight to

Morocco. We'll fly into Malaga in southern Spain tonight and then drive down the Mediterranean coast to Gibraltar in the morning. We'll take a "boat" across the Straits of Gibraltar. I think you'll enjoy the trip."

I didn't doubt the man's words for a minute. Five minutes later we were descending the mountain in time to catch a boat on Lake Lucerne back to the city. After an early fond du dinner, we returned to the airport. I hadn't actually had a shower since leaving Minneapolis and I'd spent my nights sleeping on a jet-powered airplane. Uncle Joe said we wouldn't be staying in a hotel until Malaga. It would be another sink bath on the plane that evening.

The private jet was ready at the Lucerne airport. There was an open map on the table inside the fuselage. It was Uncle Joe's way of inviting me to query him on anything relating to geography, history, or politics relative to our destination. The only thing I knew better than to ask was the purpose of our travel.

We took off into the darkness of the Swiss mountains as the lights of Lucerne disappeared behind in the clouds. I was asleep within ten minutes.

Hours later the plane was resting on the runway in Malaga, Spain. This time I hadn't even felt the landing. I was actually getting used to sleeping on that plane. Out the window, it was barely dawn, but yet another vehicle was waiting for us...this time with no driver.

Uncle Joe took the wheel as we traveled the 130 kilometers down the coastal highway to Gibraltar. It was during a lull in our history conversation that I probed more than usual about North Africa being our next stop. I worded my inquisitiveness very carefully. "Uncle Joe, you have to understand our travel together is always exciting, but you have to also realize I'm curious as hell as to the reasons for some of these purposes of all these stopovers. A couple years ago you said it was best that I didn't know. Is that still the way it is?"

His eyes danced. "I've been waiting to see how you were going to ask me that question. You've always been observant. I didn't think a little jet lag would squelch that attribute for very long.

He paused and then asked directly, "Tell me, what do you suppose I do for a living?"

I fumbled around before responding, "Well, it's apparently quite important, whatever it is. I've seen you talk with some people who have been very quiet and sometimes highly nervous. You seem to relax them with the possible exception of that unfriendly gentleman on the boat we were on this morning on Lake Lucerne. You also seem to be passing or exchanging envelopes with various people. At times, you've had to leave me or ask me to leave so you could conduct your business. It's difficult to believe it's not something highly secretive and sensitive."

He nodded approvingly. "Very good, Pete...while you haven't lost your powers of observation, I might say your imagination might have got the better of you."

He leaned back in the driver's seat and said, "Let me tell you a few things." My business is oil. I negotiate prices for certain oil companies in the U.S. In

Paris and Lucerne I met with various people from Middle East Oil producing countries. We talk politics, economics, and eventually price per barrel of oil. I have been doing this work since shortly after I got out of the Navy. I have to be ready to travel at a moment's notice. That's what happened last Friday after you arrived in Charleston. I tried to delay the trip, but then decided to go since I figured I could make it another great experience for you. Anyway, I hope that's what our few days of travel are turning out to be for you."

I nodded quite sincerely.

He continued, "Of course, like always, I have to ask you to keep our travels under wraps. Don't say where we've been to anyone…even your folks. For a lot of reasons I want to keep my work private. I'm telling you only because you've proven you can keep our talk and travels confidential. But, I've always wanted to give you an idea what your old uncle does for a living."

I was impressed….and flattered. I was also relieved. In the back of my mind I had been concerned Uncle Joe was involved in some underworld activity that not only was illegal, but highly dangerous as well. Divulging that he negotiated oil prices meant that he was performing some laudable work for some American oil companies. Furthermore, I didn't know enough about business…especially the oil business…to ask any follow up questions.

To show him I was more than appeased, I changed the subject to asking about the history of Gibraltar. He seemed relieved.

Arriving in Gibraltar we bordered an "airboat" to traverse the Straits of Gibraltar. We went through the border patrol with little problem. Uncle Joe said we were just on holiday. He mentioned nothing else as to why we were going to Tangiers.

Uncle Joe seemed to know the timing and the routes as if he lived locally. The trip across the Straits was exciting. The hull of the boat actually left the surface of the water while some arm-like wings barely touched the water. Passengers had the sensation of flying just above the sea. As we got closer to the African coast, the weather worsened. The seas were choppier and the "airboat" definitely was no longer 'floating' over the water. People with weak stomachs were losing their lunch right and left. The sensation of seasickness was broadly introduced to my stomach a few times, but I managed to control the desire to toss my fish lunch.

Through all this Uncle Joe was relaxing in a chair reading a newspaper he bought. It was in Spanish. The bumpiness in the boat hardly fazed him. He just poured over the newspaper like he was reading the sports page on the back patio of his house.

Our trip by taxi to the outskirts of Tangier was not as exciting. There were so many people walking at the side of the road…and they were miles away from the capital city. Closer to the main city, I watched tourists getting out of their taxis and immediately being swarmed by countless street vendors or beggars. Those poor souls were desperate to sell their goods or in lieu of any sale, simply be given money. There was nothing like this in the U.S.......except at maybe a car dealership on a Saturday morning during an end of the month sale.

Thankfully Uncle Joe had us dropped off at a prominent hotel by the water front. He told me he'd meet me in the lobby in two hours. Given the circumstances in the streets, he suggested that I stay around the hotel or walk out on the Atlantic beach. He got no argument from me.

He shoved some French francs in my hand again and told me to get something more to eat since we'd be traveling again that night. He took an elevator to his meeting and I headed for a small shop. Three days before I'd been innocently getting on a Minneapolis flight to Charleston via Atlanta. I doubted anyone in the world had just completed three days like I'd just experienced.

I thought of going out to the beaches and admiring the female form, but an English worded newspaper, the *London Times* caught my eye. I don't know how much I paid for the newspaper, a tepid bottle of water, and some kind of bakery item packed in a plastic bag, but the teller greedily took one of my bills and gave me some worthless coins as change. He went back to reading his own paper with a very satisfied smile on his face.

I was hungry for news from the U.S. but got little from the London paper. I browsed through the paper in the lobby cafe while observing the intense and weirdly dressed native people walking by the restaurant. It was a hot day and dust seemed to be simply part of the environment. It was not a clean country. I had no appetite to eat any Moroccan food. Life just seemed hard and harsh.

In time, though, food was required. I finally ordered some kind of fish and rice dish to keep the waiter from getting more perturbed. He thought I was loitering in the hotel restaurant... as if he owned the place. Finally getting him off my back, I was able to focus more on the newspaper.

While browsing the newspaper, a particular news item caught my eye. In the corner of page ten there was a story of an oil executive from a Middle Eastern country who had been a target for a possible assassination attempt at a cartel meeting in Paris. The article said the assailant was killed in his efforts to escape. In the same article it said two other oil executives who were traveling to that cartel meeting in Paris were first reported missing, but had been waylaid somewhere in Switzerland. Two other assailants were intercepted and gunned down Monday morning in Geneva, Switzerland.

It did not get by me that Uncle Joe and I had been in both Paris and Switzerland in the past three days. There was no way I would have even heard of these murders if I hadn't sat down and picked up that British newspaper. I doubted either of these stories would have been covered in the American press other than a *New York Times* story buried on page twenty.

Now I was more than curious. In fact I was more than slightly unnerved. I wanted to see Uncle Joe's reaction when I showed him the article. I guess most of all I was concerned for his safety.

In the time before meeting Uncle Joe, I ate the leisurely lunch and did make it out to the beach to walk barefoot and look 'west' across the Atlantic Ocean. At the appointed time I returned to the lobby of the hotel to await Uncle Joe. He didn't see me when he walked off the elevator. Exiting that same elevator was one of the men I saw in Switzerland. It was the same stocky, darker skinned man who Uncle Joe had momentarily talked with at the mountain hotel overlooking Lake Lucerne. There was something sinister about the guy. He looked as evil on the cold mountaintop in Switzerland as he did in the lobby of this hot, dusty hotel in Morocco. Neither of the two men said farewell. They just walked out of the elevator as if they didn't know each other.

Uncle Joe finally saw me and strolled over to where I was sitting as if he didn't have a care in the world. "Pete, we are done here. What do you say we take an excursion across the Straits over to the Rock of Gibraltar? We have to go through Morocco's border patrol on this continent before boating over to Gibraltar on the Iberian coast. It's just the way it's done. At least it's a great day for sightseeing."

I wasted no time. I didn't move from the straw chair I was sitting and pointed to the newspaper article about the assaults and killings in France and Switzerland. I said blandly, "Uncle Joe, I didn't know if you saw this article. I figured you might know these people."

I stared at him to see if there was any reaction. There was none. I figured he knew the oil industry executives. I hoped he didn't know the deceased assailants. Showing no emotion, I was disappointed. I couldn't believe his heart was made of stone.

He finally said something after he seemed to collect his thoughts. "Yeh, I heard about this situation."

Then he shook his head…and that was it. I was expecting more of a response. Instead he simply added, "We'd better get going."

The side excursion ride over to the Rock of Gibraltar took the remainder of the day. Returning to the African mainland we caught another airboat across the Straits of Gibraltar for the return to Spain. In all, I crossed that thin section of the Mediterranean four times that day.

I was still upset about what I'd read. Uncle Joe tried to ignore my preoccupation, but I was just too quiet and not my normal self. Finally trying to break through my anxiety, he responded. "Pete, I can see you're upset about that article in the *London Times*. Let me guess…you're concerned I might be in some kind of danger?"

I nodded. The two events were just too coincidental.

He leaned in close so only his voice could be heard. He whispered, "Pete, let me share some additional information just so you don't have to worry. I can't tell you everything, but while I represent a couple oil companies in negotiating prices on oil, I also work for the U.S. Government. I'm not a spy. It's not that romantic. I do have a lot of friends in the oil business. I've just spent the last couple of days not only working for one of my oil company clients, but I've worked in trying to keep some oil industry executives alive. The price of oil has such an impact on business around the globe. It raises a lot of emotions from all borders.

My colleagues in the U.S. let me know that a partisan group from Saudi Arabia had earmarked the death of three oil industry executives after last week's meeting of the Mid-East Oil Cartel in Cairo. The partisan group thought the Cartel was being blackmailed into keeping the price of oil lower than it should be. This group believes that various oil producing countries in the Middle East are being taken advantage of by the oil companies. This weird faction wants to send some kind of message…in blood…to the oil companies. Their belief is that the economies of key oil producing nations, especially Saudi Arabia, are being held back by these oil company executives.

There was another cartel meeting in Paris over the weekend. Pete, I was called upon to assist in saving the lives of those three oil company senior executives. That's why we were in Paris. One of the men was a Frenchman and we had to use him for just a short time to get the assassin out of his protected cover. You now know that French businessman quite well. Alex Gustave was a marked man. By Alex taking you on that little tour, he was unexpectedly away from the cartel meeting. The announcement simply said he was feeling under the weather with flu symptoms and he was resting in his room right there at the hotel where the meeting was taking place.

Investigators hoped that either the partisan group's infiltrator in that cartel meeting or the would-be assassin might become unnerved or at least show some frustration over Gustave's absence. After that announcement, anyone who left that meeting was followed. Three people left within fifteen minutes…one to the rest room, one to his hotel room, and one to the front of the hotel to hail a cab. The man leaving the hotel was ordered to stop as he left the hotel. He pulled out a weapon and I'll not go into any other details. You read about his last minutes in the *London Times*. His attaché case when opened proved he was after Gustave.

Just so you know, Alex Gustave really is a very good friend of mine. He is a top executive for the British Petroleum Company. We didn't even want him near that meeting or the hotel since we didn't know how many people were after him. We snuck him out of the hotel and he became your tour guide for a couple hours.

As for those two would be murderers in Geneva that was part of the same partisan group. Those two assassins were hired to eliminate the two men you briefly saw on the P.S. Waldstetter on Lake Lucerne. I had called a meeting of these two gentlemen of the Mideast Oil Cartel to meet Waldstetter and me in Lucerne. They were told it was a small conference to ostensibly iron out a pricing problem that had developed. In fact there was no problem. We just needed to get them to drop whatever they were doing and divert their travel schedule away from Geneva.

While they were on the boat, I informed them a couple oil cartel private investigators were waiting at the Geneva hotel for the two partisan assassins assigned to kill them. Those were the two men you met. They were perfectly safe as long as they were with my friend, Senor Waldstetter, and me. As you read, those assassins met a similar conclusion to the assailant in Paris.

This was a big hit against that Saudi Arabian partisan group. They now realize their organization has been infiltrated. Our action won't curtail all threats toward various people in the oil industry, but it gives us a better idea of the type of fervent and obsessive people and their followers that we are dealing with in our current world."

Uncle Joe paused and examined my face. "Are you feeling better…or worse… about your innocent uncle from Charleston, South Carolina?"

I smiled and nodded my head only somewhat reassured. I felt compelled to ask another question…something he hadn't covered. "Uncle Joe, who then was that rather serious looking man that you met on the mountain resort in Switzerland and then again a couple hours ago at the hotel in Tangier. He walked away from you like he wasn't supposed to know you.

Uncle Joe's forehead showed a couple wrinkles. "Oh, so you saw Andre."

I nodded my head. Andre Mandello works with me on another project. He is a director of twelve private schools around the Mediterranean area. He lives in Naples, but he travels quite a bit. The recent problems with oil industry executives and their families being either harassed or facing possible bodily harm could have an impact on our enrollments in the private schools. Andre is highly upset by the recent developments. We've talked twice in the last couple of days. He has relaxed only slightly since he's found out how the oil companies are more effectively managing various threats on their people through much assistance from hired private investigators.

We met today because he was visiting our school in Tangier. We have one in Lucerne. We have two in Paris. We even have one in Malaga, Spain. That's why I know these cities so well. I travel to them quite often. The oil companies I represent finance many of the schools since so many children of the executives attend. Naturally the parents want to be assured of safety for their children besides them getting a good education. Andre and I have been working together for fifteen years. Your Aunt Jane lived with his family in Italy one year during college. She's stayed close to that family ever since. That's how I got to know him. He has always been like an Italian brother to her. He's a very quiet and intense man, but he's got a big heart. We're hoping to open up a few more schools and are negotiating to do so in Cairo and in Kuwait."

I was blown away. I should have had more confidence in my uncle. I was frankly embarrassed over what I'd been thinking. In no way would he ever know that fact. I now understood and fully accepted while his oil company representation was his main job, he also supported a private educational project for families of oil company employees working in foreign countries.

It was Tuesday night when we returned from our tour of Gibraltar to Malaga. I had been on a whirlwind four-day tour that had brought me to France, Switzerland, Spain, and Morocco. Uncle Joe and I decided it would be all right to tell everyone when I returned to Minnesota that he and I had visited Paris for a couple days. However, he repeated that the remainder of our travels should not be discussed.

I was to fly back to Minneapolis from Charleston on Friday. It was only Wednesday morning over breakfast in Malaga that I kidded Uncle Joe, "So where do we go for the next two days?"

I remember Uncle Joe scratching his jaw. By the twinkle in his eye, I knew he'd already been thinking about that subject. The result…my trip back to Minnesota was actually delayed a couple more days. Uncle Joe dropped me off in his private jet at the Minneapolis International Airport on Monday, a day before my flight back to school in Washington D.C. was to depart on Wednesday. He had called my folks and told them of the two-day delay because of the trip to Paris. They were thrilled I had the chance to be in Paris. They confirmed they'd be meeting my plane Monday night in Minneapolis.

I thought it interesting that the telephone call was made from 22,000 feet in the air somewhere in transit to Tokyo, Japan. On the way there we had five days of stop and go travel in various cities I'd only read about or seen in films or newsreels. While we visited only a couple key sights in each city, we took the time to enjoy the cuisine at each stop as well.

Uncle Joe and I finally arrived in Minneapolis via Anchorage late Monday night, just over a week since I'd flown to South Carolina. Uncle Joe could only hug my Mom and Dad hello and good bye before having to take off for a meeting the next day. He said he had to get back to Charleston to pack for his trip. He never said where he was going.

As for me, I had Tuesday to wash clothes, pack, talk with my folks, and mull over the previous nine days. I'd literally been around the world.

Saying farewell to Uncle Joe after that secretive trip was difficult. I didn't want to leave our adventure. I hugged him hard whispering to him that I wish I'd had a few more days in Charleston since our golf had been interrupted."

He chuckled and nodded. "You're right. What do you say I look at my schedule in late May after you finish your next semester? I'm certain we can find four or five days that you can come down to Charleston. Then he winked, "…..unless there's another interruption!"

My mother and father and I bid him farewell and watched him walk down the corridor. We moved the opposite way towards baggage. Before taking the escalator I turned to look back down the long corridor. There was Uncle Joe. He had been staring at me as I left. There was a look of pride in his eyes. Then he waved and disappeared into the busy crowd marching toward their appointed flights.

Driving back home my folks asked me about Paris and Charleston. I talked about everything that encompassed approximately two whole days of my nine-day outing. It must have sounded like Uncle Joe and I had spent three or four days in both cities. They had no idea I'd been staying on a 'flying hotel' and had never spent one night in Charleston or Paris.

Since taking off from Malaga, Spain the previous Wednesday, Uncle Joe and I had made stops in Athens, Istanbul, New Delhi, flown over the Himalayas to Hong Kong and then onto Japan. It would be our secret round-the-world trip for the rest of our lives…just part of my Christmas break from my first year of graduate school.

I believe I truly didn't come back down to earth until well into that second semester. Class work and studies barely kept my interest compared to the more fascinating reading I was doing regarding the political and economic history of all those countries I'd visited.

It was not until many years later that I learned from him the impact I had on his life during that Christmas 'break' years before. He brought it up once in the spring of 1990 when we met for dinner at a restaurant on the wharf of San Francisco Bay. We both had business on the West Coast and worked out our schedules to meet for an afternoon and evening. I was a history professor and making a guest lecture for a professor friend at Stanford University. As was typical, I had no idea what Uncle Joe was doing out west.

We were reminiscing about our many trips together…and planning another one…when he said to me, "You know, Pete, that first trip we traveled together after Jane passed away when you were in graduate school turned out to be quite an experience for me as well. I know we've traveled a lot over the years, but do you remember that one?

I nodded as if wondering why there was a question. "Yes…like it was yesterday. Why do you ask?

He had a satisfied grin on his face. "I can't tell you how much that helped having you with me again. I had been really down and out for those couple years after Jane left us. I wasn't as careful in the jobs I was doing or the places I was going. I was involved in some…well…at times dangerous activities. I hadn't been thinking sharply. I was taking risks that in retrospect weren't very advisable.

Your youthful spirit just energized me so much during that trip. I was so interested in keeping you safe as well as making the trip worth your visit that it got me back to thinking there were other people quite dear to me including yourself. Truth be told, I never should have brought you along on that trip. There was some danger in Paris. That was when I felt so guilty. I could have inadvertently put you in harm's way. If anything would have happened to you… well, I don't even want to think about it. After Paris I made certain you were safe before I went ahead with my mission. Frankly it was just good for me to care about someone again and not take some of the chances I'd been taking."

His reference to our trip as a 'mission' caught my attention. Then he said something else that struck me as odd. He must have thought I knew more than

I really did. He took a sip of wine and looked out on the bay before saying, "My God…that first stop in Paris! Those couple hours you were with my friend, Alex Gustave, I was able to weed out the undercover assassin at that oil company cartel meeting. If I wasn't back at the Grand Palais by 3:30 that afternoon, Alex was to take you on more touring until you dropped from exhaustion, then take you to the plane to rest until I returned."

Then catching himself, he exhaled, "But everything worked out smoothly. I was able to stop that assailant and Alex was able to return to that cartel meeting where he was one of the main speakers. I only made it back to the Grand Palais within minutes of our meeting time that afternoon."

Then he paused for another sip. The rest of the trip…it was a good time for us, wasn't it?" He was already beginning to change the subject.

I nodded about the good time we had as the waiter opened a second bottle of chardonnay. As Uncle Joe conversed with the waiter about the bottle of wine, it gave me time to think. I'd periodically thought over the years about the strange and coincidental happenings of those killings that occurred the same time Uncle Joe and I were in Paris and Switzerland. I had so innocently accepted his quick explanations.

Now years later he was slipping up and telling me what he thought I knew since we were so familiar on most other things. We'd had quite a track record together. But, just the word 'mission' and the phrase 'I was able to stop the assailant' cued my brain. I had always been under the impression Alex Gustave was a high executive for British Petroleum. Whether he was or wasn't, he obviously worked closely and had the trust of my uncle. For the first time it became clear that it was my uncle who had eliminated the assassin in Paris. It caused me to question who my Uncle Joe truthfully worked for…maybe he and possibly Alex Gustave were those cartel special investigators paid to find the assassins. That would certainly make more sense.

I peered over my wine glass and wondered for the first time in ten years since that incident what my uncle had really been doing for his living back then…or even at present. I wondered if even Aunt Jane had a total understanding before she died.

That old feeling I once had about my Uncle Joe being such a man of mystery suddenly returned as if the flood gates had opened. This man had been pulling the wool over my eyes since I first started traveling with him and my aunt. He was 'taking care of business' on every one of those trips while he was joined by his wife and often times his nephew for an apparent pleasure voyage. At that moment, I knew that I didn't want to know any more than what I already knew about my uncle's work.

As he continued to talk with the waiter about the wine being served to us, I watched his mannerisms. He paid such close attention to details around him. When the waiter also spoke of the desserts for that evening, Uncle Joe's eyes moved around the room just giving the waiter enough attention to understand the offerings.

I admired that as we aged, he and I still had many facial and body features very similar to each other, except his hair was completely gray…and mine was jet black and longer. We were the same height and weight. However, I reasoned that our similarities probably ended with those physical resemblances. I figured I could never really be like my uncle. Based on his life, who could be? Who would want to carry on a clandestine life that very likely included him not only protecting top level corporate or political leaders, but also being paid to kill any perpetrators as well?

I watched him order one of the desserts in that impeccable and debonair mode. I observed how Uncle Joe didn't just order the dessert; he focused on the waiter's eyes, examined the man's conduct, yet made the server comfortable in their dialogue. The only people he didn't necessarily scan or study so thoroughly were the people he was absolutely confident he could trust…like me.

Yes, my uncle was smooth as silk…and I had only that evening in San Francisco to fully realize he was a very well paid international agent. I marveled how after almost twenty years since I first went to New York and Washington D.C. with Aunt Jane and him, I couldn't believe how little anyone in my family really knew about him. He was just Uncle Joe…still showing up for most Christmas holidays with the family. And I realized, even as his closest relative and a person he at times confided, I had but an overview.

Then the image of that short stocky man crossed through my mind…the one my Uncle Joe had met on top of the mountain in Switzerland after protecting the lives of those two Middle East oil executives on that boat on Lake Lucerne. I fought to remember the man's name, because I saw him get off the elevator with my uncle a day later in Tangiers. The two of them had walked the opposite way as if they didn't know each other. That was not typical behavior for a school administrator and his benefactor. That man could well have worked with my uncle…but probably not in the position my uncle described.

I thought hard. Yes…Andre….Andre Mandello…that was the man's name! Uncle Joe had told me this guy was a director of the series of private schools my uncle had set up in various countries in Europe and the Middle East? That intense dark-skinned Arab looked and behaved no more like a 'director of a school' than I looked like a nineteenth century Colorado blacksmith…me with the soft hands of a college instructor as well as my long lanky body with shoulders and arms looking anything but powerful.

Shrugging my shoulders, I resolved that it didn't matter anymore. Whatever danger my uncle was involved in then was now all water under the bridge. Now he was older…certainly close to retirement age…and I hoped not as involved in the intrigue that so dominated his life ten, fifteen, even twenty years before. He still traveled a lot, but I had hoped the trips were primarily for pleasure….like the ones he and I still took once or twice a year overseas. Those travels to the British Isles and Western Europe in the previous five years included mostly golf when we were in places like Scotland, Britain, France, and Sweden. There was little chance he was conducting any 'business' during those kinds of excursions... or at least that was what I kept forcing myself to believe. And for a fact, I knew he couldn't have conducted too much business whenever I flew down to Charleston for some long weekends of golf. Oh yes, he was on the phone a lot, but he didn't leave the city until the day I returned home.

I grinned into my glass of wine and took another long gaze at my uncle while thinking, '...or has he slowed down?' Then I'd shake my head. I had to believe my uncle was done with such messy, pressurized work. It was just a fact that this man, my Uncle Joe, sitting across from me in that California restaurant, would always be shrouded in mystery.

When that dinner ended, he needed to be dropped off at San Francisco International Airport. I had a rental car, so I drove him to the airport. He told me he had a meeting the next day in Washington D.C. We talked about the next time our paths might cross before our upcoming summer trip to Sweden and Norway. He mentioned South America as an alternative in June. He was priceless the way he introduced the idea. He said, "I've got to see a couple people...but that won't take long. There are some great golf courses in Rio de Janeiro and Buenos Aires."

That was my Uncle Joe. Just by the way he spoke and the way his mind was buzzing, I realized he was no more looking at retirement than I was. I parked and walked with him to his gate. I noticed it was an overseas flight. He had said he was going to Washington D.C. Last time I'd looked at a map, D.C. was on the continent. Maybe he was going to end his trip in Washington D.C. I mentally gave him a break.

We shook hands at the gate, then hugged as we always did when we greeted or said farewell. Then I retreated back down the corridor. As was also my habit, halfway down the hallway, I turned around to see if he was staring at me. Sure enough...there he was gazing at me with both a happy and a sad look in his eye. He'd had that same look every time I departed since I was a teen-ager on my first trip with Aunt Jane and him.

I laughed and pointed at him. He returned the laugh and waved back. I could tell he was proud of me. Then we both turned away simultaneous and moved on with our respective lives.

I wondered how long he was going to maintain his active and busy schedule. He wasn't old looking or acting, but he was in a younger man's business...at least to the extent I imagined it.

We did that trip to South America the next June and played golf for three days. However, we had to take a side trip over to Tangiers on the Moroccan coast for a night. Then we headed to southern Spain where we played golf for two days in Malaga before heading back to Charleston. I never questioned anything. Why should I? I was used to it!

Now many years later, I often think of my Uncle Joe around certain times of the year...semester break...spring break...the early summer. He had been found out on the lawn of his Ashley River property five years after that dinner we had in San Francisco. He'd been hitting golf balls and simply sat down and didn't hit anymore...on earth anyway. And, how I still miss those phone calls and our travel adventures. No matter what time of year, he'd remind me to schedule in some time in December between semesters to visit him in Charleston. He'd say, "You know, it'll do your soul good to play a little golf around Christmas time... unless we have to time out for a little travel. And, if we do, we'll still play golf someplace."

Folks in my family still mention how much I remind them of him. It's a compliment I'll always relish. Until he passed, we talked with each other a couple times a month no matter where either of us was located. Sometimes his voice echoed on the phone line indicating he was some place on the other side of the planet. If I didn't call, he would. He'd start talking about some other ideas for our next trip and question me as to how much time I'd be able to spare in my next visit to see him. I'd say four or five days. He'd say, "Better plan for at least a week, Pete, just in case."

And, I always did.

The Encounter on the Lake

The motorboat on White Bear Lake was peeling along at full throttle sounding like it was attempting a water speed record. I really couldn't estimate the actual speed since I couldn't see it. However, comparing my own speedboat and the sound of my motor, I knew that engine had to be going full out. What bothered me was that the boat was going so fast and it was past midnight. Even during the daytime that speed might be bordering on negligence depending on how many other boats were in the water in the vicinity. But, at night it was just plain thoughtless and irresponsible. If the boat hit anything or anybody unseen, the driver would be arrested for a number of unforgiving charges, i.e. recklessness, various rules against boat safety, maybe attempted murder, and not surprisingly drunkenness. However, given his speed, those considerations couldn't on the boater's mind.

There was one other significant factor about this particular boat. It had no light…or, at least it couldn't be seen. It added to an already potentially dangerous situation.

Coincidentally at that very hour, a small sailboat was also out on the lake. The boat was moving smoothly through the water with only an occasional wave that bounced up onto the thin deck. The sailor was not speeding nor was he inebriated. He was just enjoying his own bit of nighttime excitement being out on the large lake with nothing to think about but the air and spray against his skin. I knew that fellow well since I was that intrepid sailor.

I often took my fifteen-foot sailboat out at night if the breeze was inviting. Late night sailing was so relaxing…and a bit different. There rarely was another boat moving on the lake at that late hour. I always felt like it was my own time with nothing or no one to bother me. Nonetheless I still carried a small flashlight in case I heard another boat nearby.

That night the resonance of that wide open engine made for a different feel. I wasn't relaxed upon hearing the high-pitch of the on-coming motorboat. I felt strangely vulnerable. Other than throwing a sweatshirt and jeans on, I had not really prepared myself properly for a post-midnight sail. I hadn't even thrown a life preserver in my sailboat. During the day that would have never happened. It was habit to wear the life jacket. But, when I went sailing in the nighttime breeze, I always did it on a whim usually while standing on my dock and feeling enough wind to make the attempt at sailing worthwhile. I never went far and usually sailed closer to shore. I guess in the back of my mind knowing that I was a strong swimmer I never felt I was putting myself in any real peril. What did concern me that night was the remaining power on my flashlight batteries. The flashlight was stored in a small compartment in the boat. I'd been meaning to check the strength of the light, but had failed to do so each time I'd recently taken the boat out for a sail. It wasn't that I was being cavalier. I just usually sailed during the daylight hours.

That evening it had been a spur of the moment thing like always. In past summers I'd taken my boat out as late as 3:00 in the morning when I wasn't sleepy. All those nights the sky had been generally clear with some noticeable moonlight. That night the sky was not as distinct as it should have been. There was some cloud cover, but it seemed to be moving with the strong breeze. I expected to be seeing the stars within the hour.

The hum of the motorboat's engine seemed so far away. My eyes strained to see any hint of a moving light on the lake, but I saw nothing. The sound made me uncomfortable enough to consider returning to shore. Then again, I had to believe that any boater going that fast had to know where he was going and his trip would be a short one…like from one lake home to another…maybe across the faraway south end of the lake. If it was much longer, I'd have to wonder what was wrong with this late evening boater. It would be irritating that someone could be so callous.

I was only out on the water less than ten minutes when I realized I was straying further from the shoreline. More haze was not helping me navigate. I could still see back to shore where my cabin was located. 'What the hell,' I thought, 'I'll keep sailing.'

My thoughts were only the slight concern of seeing ahead with the growing fog than having my little sailboat and that irresponsible driver of the speedboat ever coming near one another. The lake was just so huge. I was convinced even if we got close, we'd certainly see each other despite the darkness. We'd have time to veer away from one another.

I sailed another five minutes and solitude of the boat cutting through the water was just so relaxing. However, that distant din of that motorboat would not go away. What troubled me was that the sound of that high-powered motorboat was actually a bit clearer than it had been just a few minutes before. Once again I strained my eyes into the darkened night air for the sight of anything. Still, I could see nothing, not even a small light on the motorboat.

My good senses told me I should reverse course and head for shore, but my need that night for some adventure and my difficulty in sleeping convinced me to sail on. It was a difficult business project that had become more expensive and troublesome. That's what had gotten me out of bed in the first place. With a cool wind whispering through the trees and blowing through my screened window in the bedroom, I figured I'd pull the blanket up over my shoulders and I'd be asleep in minutes. That night the breeze only kept my eyes opened.

Finally in frustration I had gotten up, pulled on the jeans and a sweatshirt, and meandered out onto my patio. The late evening was quite humid despite the chill. There were intermittent low lying clouds that were moving quite fast under a general overcast. Despite the periodic haze, I could see half way across the lake from my patio. That wind invited me to whimsically consider taking that nighttime sail.

With visibility being adequate, I strolled down to my dock to further consider going out on the water at that hour. My sleeplessness and the soft gale coaxed me to ignore the fast moving clouds and just go.

I promised myself it would be swift…maybe half to three-quarters the way across the lake and then return. That would be enough effort to get me tired. If the weather happened to get ugly, I'd just take the extra time to tack my way back to shore. I'd sleep well into the morning in either case.

I'm anything but impulsive; however I disprove that statement repeatedly… as I did that night. I untied the ropes of the sailboat and took off from the dock with not a second thought. My sailboat was a small one; only two, maybe three, people could sit comfortably under the lone sail. Within seconds that one sail was in full volume. Moments later I was moving steadily along the shore and then because of the wind I could go faster if I made a heading toward the middle of one of the larger lakes in the Twin Cities area. I'd been sailing less than ten minutes when I realized that slight mist had gotten a bit thicker on White Bear Lake, but the breeze was so invigorating and the boat was sailing so smoothly. I didn't mind having that the slight moisture hitting me in the face.

So, there I was…peacefully sailing in the middle of a dark night enjoying the shear tranquility. Nothing could really be heard but my boat swishing through the water….and of course that distant hum of a speeding motorboat.

I kept waiting for the wind to blow away the haze over the water. I could look up and see the low flying clouds racing with the strong breeze. I was indeed a strange weather night, but in no way did I feel threatened or uncomfortable.

Then I sailed through some even thicker fog. That was the first time I completely lost sight of the shoreline. I was waiting to see some lights from lake homes, but there was no opening. All I could see was gray fog surrounding me. I slowed the sailboat trying to recover my bearings, but the discomforting result was that the distant high-powered motorboat now seemed louder…and closer. The sound was augmented underneath the low cloud cover.

Why I didn't just stop my sailboat entirely at that moment, I can't explain. I didn't feel like I was being reckless. I just kept sailing expecting to come out of that fog at any second so I could then get my bearings and head for the shore.

Then the mist turned into light rain. It was not hard just persistent. I looked up hoping to see some open sky. Instead, if anything the cloud cover seemed denser. The night now had gotten darker. I had truly misread the weather conditions and had lost my sense of direction. A reasonable guess was that the wind was generally from the west, but it could be from the northwest or the southwest. My growing anxiety now made me slow the boat. That only seemed to make my situation more stressful. Without the noise of the wind against the single sail and the boat cutting through the water, the sound of the loud growl of the distant boat engine had become louder. The boat was heading in my direction.

Stopping my sailboat entirely, I sat there entombed by the fog. My hearing became my only dependable human sense. I listened…and listened…but I could get no awareness of where that high-powered might be coming from. It was in an open-air surround sound with no controls to regulate the volume or the tracking.

I still had no fear. All I could do was keep scrutinizing the darkness for any kind of light. Despite the unease of that approaching motorboat engine, it just required patience to remain still until the fog and haze dissipated.

It continued to drone on. I could even tell by the sound what type of motorboat engine it was. It had the familiar high-pitch of my Evinrude engine on my own powerboat. Regrettably, it gave me no comfort.

Sitting there on the calm water motionless with a fresh breeze made seconds seem like minutes. I could tell I was getting more fidgety as that distracting sound grew in volume. The noise was so pervasive…and potentially threatening. For the first time fear finally entered my brain. If I could just discern the direction of the high-powered boat, I'd turn my boat with what little wind there was in order to hopefully turn from harm's way.

I sat there with my hands over my eyes calling for my sense of hearing to rise up to a never before level of performance. But, my ears were only so good. The stereophonic nature of the blare under the low cloud cover made the direction of the motorboat impossible to gauge.

Finally I decided I couldn't just sit there. I had to do something else. Letting the sail completely out to take advantage of whatever air movement there was, I was betting if that motorboat did come close, the driver might have more of a chance of seeing me. The thought of a collision was still distant from my mind. There were so many other options before that tragic result might happen.

As my boat began skirting slowly through the water somewhere in the middle of White Bear Lake, the din of the motorboat was lessened with the more immediate noise of the sail flapping and the water splashing quietly against my boat's hull. My thoughts changed to the frame of mind of the driver. What in the world was he thinking? Was he really so upset or so intoxicated that he could completely discard the safety of others regardless of himself? I could visualize him either staring madly ahead into the soupy mist or arrogantly steering with a beer in one hand and maybe his arm around his girlfriend with the other. She'd have to be equally drunk to let him put her life in such danger. Whatever the circumstances, the driver of that speeding boat could only be paying partial attention to what he was doing to be driving that wide open in pitch darkness and pea soup fog.

Thinking even further, I just couldn't imagine two people in that speeding boat allowing such irrational thinking. One of the two people would logically have some sense to insist the boat be slowed. Certainly that had to be the case. With that reasoning I concluded there could only be one very troubled person who also was likely inebriated.

I, on the other hand, was quite sober. I wasn't angry...or unbalanced. So, how had I made such a rash and ill-advised decision to be out on the lake in a small sailboat? If I was the driver of that motorboat, inebriated or not, the last thing I might think of encountering was any kind of a boat in the middle of a lake...especially a sailboat in the present conditions and the lateness of the hour.

My whim to be out on the water had now put me in a rather ridiculous and even embarrassing situation. The absolute tranquil night had lulled me into being completely unprepared for any emergency. I thought I'd been awake, but I must have been half-asleep to have been so spontaneous. And that business project... why was that keeping me awake? Was it really that serious that I couldn't relax on a Saturday night? 'For God's sake,' I thought, 'that's pretty sad'.

I then spent the next minute mentally kicking myself as the steady, grating sound of that motor provided additional emotional punishment. Swearing out loud, I wondered how people, including me, could be such idiots.

In that dark, foggy night, I of course had time to rationalize and countered by telling myself if one didn't take some risks now and then, life would be pretty dull. Strangely, thought, I never considered taking my sailboat out after midnight to be much of a risk. What I had done was so simple. I merely wanted to take a leisurely sail, enjoy the tranquil night, return to my dock, and go back to bed. That wasn't a risk; it was an innocent whim.

The engine of the motorboat continued to increase in volume. It was without question moving toward my location on the lake. I looked up again hoping there might be a break in the clouds. Maybe I could spot some stars and retrace my route back to my lake home. It was wishful thinking. If anything the air was even murkier. There would be no way the motorboat could see my sail until he was on top of me. Shouting would be fruitless. Nothing would pierce the clamor of the rampaging motor. If the motorboat did collide with my sailboat, the vision of a bug against a windshield came to mind.

My heart started to race as I frantically tried to muster up more options. First, my sailboat was so small. What were the real chances of our two boats crashing into one another? It would be smart just to stay alert and try to sail to either side of the oncoming thunderous noise. When the speedboat was practically on top of me, wouldn't I have just enough time to maneuver my boat to one side? Wouldn't he have the same opportunity?

I conjured up another alternative. I could dive off my sailboat and swim away from it. If the speedboat came at me, I'd dive under the water. I could perform that stunt very quickly if I saw the boat in time. Yet, if my boat was hit and destroyed, I was out in the middle of White Bear Lake without a swim vest. How strong of a swimmer was I…especially when I didn't know the direction to the nearest shoreline? I hoped that option wouldn't be required.

Thirdly……..well, I didn't have a third idea other than to stare circumspectly into the gloomy darkness. There was a reasonable chance I could escape unscathed if I could just ascertain the direction or the path of the murderous, approaching boat. I was surprised the sound being kept at lake level with the low clouds and fog would give me such a problem discerning the boat's direction.

The noise now was just so omnipresent. The compressed sound volume had been increased many decibels. I was paralyzed in my little sailboat not knowing which direction to even look. The blare was now so prevalent it felt like the speedboat was going to overtake me at any moment. I couldn't tell if the moisture on my brow was from the mist…or my own sweat. I started praying for the speedboat to motor by me no matter how close…whether by half a football field or by inches. Accept for some bouncy waves from the wake at least I would survive. I tried not to think of the other more deadly alternative, but my tightened stomach was already anticipating that result.

I stopped the boat completely allowing my ears and eyes to take over the predicament unimpeded. The blare of the motorboat had now become all encompassing. The fog was so thick, it was apparent my ears were the only dependable sense I had. But, they weren't. I couldn't understand why! Where was that damned motorboat? The echo of that engine under the cloud cover was all around me. It was bizarre. The only thing for certain, the noise was growing more strident by the second and coming straight at me.

Sitting in that boat like a wounded deer waiting for a lumbering lioness to suddenly attack and put me into permanent blackness, I wondered why I wasn't panicking. I had no control of the situation and few ideas to secure my safety. I thought my life would flash before my eyes, but that was not happening. I was ready for anything, but focused on what I considered my one chance… that is, to dive in the water at the last minute just before the front sharp hull of the motorboat would tear my boat and my body into pieces.

Each second crawled along as I sat on my lone little fifteen feet of temporary safety. A flash through my mind occurred again about the condition and personality of that driver. I wondered if I had a gun, would I shoot the man just to stop him. After all, he was literally driving a speeding bullet right at me. What could make him so furious that he would be so inexcusably uncaring? Did a girlfriend really mean that much to him that he didn't care to live without her? That stuff was in books and movies, not to be played out in the middle of White Bear Lake.

And what would make him so angry that he wouldn't consider the lives of others. It was sheer madness!

My mind repeated the other side of the coin again. Nobody sailed at night in these conditions. So, why was I questioning the driver's sanity when most other people would be questioning mine in the same breath? I had put myself into this predicament. If I was taking a risk, unperceived as it was, by sailing after midnight with no preparation, why hadn't I considered the consequences?

I answered my own question. There had never been any concern any other night because the night sky had been clear.

The roar was really close now. I wondered how my being cut into pieces by a speeding motorboat would be reported in the newspapers. I could see my neighbors reading in a couple days, 'Missing local resident was found dead lying face down in the lake with pieces of his sailboat floating around his severely injured and lifeless body. The accident was believed to have occurred after midnight.'

And, that would be it. What else would there be to report. What would be the explanation for my being out on the lake in the middle of the night? The only thought would be that I was as unstable as the motorboat driver.

I thought about my folks. They would be so upset. Deep down they would wonder what kind of problems I had causing me to be so careless. The sheer lunacy of this worthless action precipitating my death was something I found quite disgusting. The repulsion made me peer even harder into the dark mist for some hint of that approaching motorboat.

The growl of the motorboat's engine was now loud enough to know that if the boat missed my sailboat it would not be my much. My eyes were penetrating into the pitch black night. With my conviction that my only chance of survival was to wait until the last possible second before diving away from the mortal blow of the motorboat's hull as it slammed against my little sailboat.... and my body...I took a position on the stern like a one hundred yard sprinter waiting to take off at the blocks.

Surprisingly, I still was not panicked. My senses were on full alert. I was ready and strangely calm. I was determined to take my one chance to survive and make the best of it. I crouched on the edge of my sailboat waiting to make the quickest dive in the history of water sports.

I've thought about the next few moments of that night often.... and for many years since. It was so quick and so final. It was nothing what I expected... absolutely nothing. In fact, the whole thing was like a slow-motion film. At the height of the noise from the high-powered engine, not one but two out-of-control speeding motorboats collided with such force that they literally disintegrated and exploded in a ball of fire. I felt like I could have put my hand in the explosion it was so close. Not twenty yards from my eyes, a ball of fire rose up in the air so high and so sudden, I had trouble figuring out if I should inhale or exhale. I was literally blown to the deck of my sailboat and then the force of the explosion tipped my sailboat and threw me into the water. I actually had the awareness to hold my breath and go slightly deeper underwater as a safety measure from the pieces of the boats being strewn around me. While under water, I could see those parts of both boats hitting the water all around me.

With my lungs screaming for air, I finally came to the surface hoping that no more large fragments from the boats were still landing in the water. My adrenalin was pumping so hard. I could barely catch my breath. I didn't lose consciousness, but I was in such shock that I just held onto the side of my sailboat and stared in awe at the tragedy unfolding around me. Who could ever believe that two human beings would be in the frame of mind to career across a lake so fearlessly? The thought would never even enter my mind. It was crazy!

The crashing boats burst apart so completely that some pieces were still descending in the air. Some were still on fire…and then sizzled as they hit the lake water. A piece of a canvas cover landed a few feet away from me still burning. The lake water put it out with a hiss and some momentary smoke rising.

Seeing the wreckage around me, I then had the answer why I couldn't place the direction of the full-throttled engine noise. The cacophonous echo was caused by not one but two motorboats reeling heedlessly across White Bear Lake from different directions. No wonder I couldn't get a reading. There was not one maniac out on the lake speeding that night, but two. The motor noise had been so intense. Neither driver could have picked up the vociferous sound of the other boat's engine.

I went from shock to disbelief. Motorboats do not speed in pitch darkness across lakes, especially in foggy, hazy conditions. And then they do not collide so perfectly. It was as if the two drivers were being directed to their deaths. I kept thinking, 'what were the chances?' It required two highly irresponsible and angry males to accomplish this horrible feat. The probability of them having this fate had to be infinitesimal. And, both drivers had to be oblivious to the possibility of any possible danger looming in front of them so late at night, especially if their judgments were dulled by booze. Either person would have not believed there could not be another uncontrolled and thoughtless idiot like themselves doing the same thing at the same time.

And then it hit me. I was alive. I was spared. It had nothing to do with being sober or more deserved of life than them. I had learned long before that it didn't work that way. For me, it was just plain luck. I was saved by one or both boats intercepting the other one only seconds before one or both were going to collide and tear apart my little sailboat…and possibly the limbs from my body.

My arms began to sting as I held onto my still floating sailboat. I realized then that I had been hit by either some flaming pieces of the boat or I simply got burned from the exploding flames. I let go of my boat putting my arms and face in the water to relieve some of the pain. The cool water helped. My injuries as far as I knew were minor, although my face still felt hot in places. I looked around while treading water. What became immediately astounding to me was that my little sailing vessel was still floating amongst the debris. Even the limp sail seemed all right.

There were still some small fires on the larger remaining sections of the two boats. The burning pieces radiated a slight glow that gave me enough light to inspect my own boat for any gashes or damage. Seeing nothing serious, I crawled up on the deck with some difficulty. I couldn't decide whether I had other injuries besides the minor burns on my arms and face. I didn't feel much pain. If I had cuts on my face, I couldn't really tell. Finally I did see traces of some blood from a cut on my right shoulder. I also realized that the shock from the explosion and the concussion likely caused my body to be whiplashed as I was thrown into the water. I was certain I'd feel that pain in the next few hours after my adrenalin level lowered.

That thought got my mind working again. I had to see if there were any survivors. From the deck of my sailboat I brushed off pieces of boat…at least I hoped that's all they were. Then I paddled and pushed my boat toward the largest piece of remains from one of the speedboats. My sail flapped loosely in the night air as if to say, 'let's go sailing'. That seemed unbelievable as I perused the complete demolition of the two motorboats.

I could feel the heat of something burning as I finally made it to one of the larger pieces of one of the damaged vessels. I yelled out hoping to hear something from one of the boaters. There was no response. I grabbed a piece of fiberglass floating on the water and used it as an oar. I could move faster. I saw a piece of steering wheel, more hull fiberglass pieces, and some plastic seat cushions. Then I smelled the telltale stench of beer and the common additional smell of gasoline that seemed to hover around any motorboat whether docked or out on the water.

The small fires began to extinguish as both the mist and the lake water doused any final flames. Floating pieces of both boats continued clunking against the hull of my sailboat. I repeated my yells to implore if anyone was still alive. I heard only silence.

Almost as suddenly as the conflagration, the entire scene quickly began to return to the dark, deafening quiet that I had expected to hear when I'd originally decided to go out for a late night sail.

I was certain the explosion had to have been heard if not seen from the shoreline. People would certainly rise, go to their windows, and try to scan through the fog for any signs of an accident. Some would hurry out to their docks in order to see better or listen for any cries of help. Maybe a couple residents might have gotten a glimpse of the explosion if they were still up that late at night. But, the dark night combined with the low hanging clouds and mist had made the scene from the crashing boats subside as quickly as it had happened.

I knew my lake neighbors would eventually do the right thing and call the authorities. Then they would contact one another and momentarily debate whether they should rush out into the foggy lake to see what had happened. On that particular foggy night they would not go out on the water. It was safer and easier to let the safety personnel do their job and earn their salaries for what they'd been trained to do.

I would of course not know it at the time, but within five minutes of the collision there would be ten calls to the local law enforcement offices from all directions on the lake. No one could pinpoint the location of the tragedy. Within fifteen minutes, patrol boats were cautiously motoring out into the middle of the foggy lake. The county helicopter pilot was given a late night call for assistance as well, but his job was more difficult given the conditions in the air.

Meanwhile, I was still floating among the remains of both boats. After five minutes, I had not yet heard one peep or sound from any emergency person or vehicle. I kept looking and listening for any boats that might be traveling out to assist. I pondered whether I should wait for the shore patrol. I couldn't direct them to this spot, but they would no doubt gradually spot some debris. It would be rather obvious what happened the moment they arrived. Since I wasn't in any urgent need of any medical attention, I wasn't going to be of much help.

In the next couple seconds my mind was made up. There floating face down in the water was the obviously dead body of one of the boat's inhabitants. I could see that he was wearing a gray t-shirt and he had a scruffy beard. I began to row my sailboat closer to the body when I abruptly stopped. A wave of nausea made my eyes roll up into the eyelids. It was very apparent the body was not whole. That ended my interest in finding a further way to help. My responsibility was not to salvage body parts…only to save anyone who could still be saved. The incredible crash and subsequent explosion had done its deed to at least one human being. I frankly didn't have the stomach to look for the other silent victim.

Finally I heard some faint sounds of a siren as the shore patrol motorboat began advancing across the lake. They would have large spotlights to give them some vision on an otherwise still foggy night. I could see nothing. The approaching hum of the shore patrol's motor was like a repeat of what I had just experienced. With the sound getting closer, I got more and more uncomfortable. Also, the unmistakable thumping of a helicopter droned in the mist. I expected to see a huge spot light beaming down from above momentarily.

I decided I just wanted to leave. There was still part of me that was embarrassed for having put myself out in the middle of the lake at such a late night hour. I didn't want to have to explain myself or to be thought of as the possible cause of this boating accident. Without a second thought, I let my sail fill with the cool night breeze. It still amazed me that the sail was not damaged. Immediately I began creating a wave as I floated away from the deathly carnage with the patrol boats within minutes of discovering the scene.

As I sailed away, it must have been instinctive. It just felt like I was going the right direction toward my cabin. That instinct seemed to be the only thing working on my body. My head ached. My shoulder was sore making it difficult to hold the sail. And, my stomach was in knots over the scene of destruction and death I had just witnessed.

As my boat maintained a steady speed, I found myself swearing relentlessly under my breath. I was so angered at the two drivers of those motorboats. They were so reckless, thoughtless, macho, and ignorant…besides probably drunk. Their lives ended that late night as the result of the convergence of two egregious acts of stupidity. I threw up over the side of my sailboat thinking about why these two idiots had to pay the supreme price.

I was but five minutes from the scene when I detected the dull glow in the haze of the helicopter spotlight. I had retreated far enough that my boat could not be seen. I just stared at the picture behind me. It was like watching a lighted boxing ring from the top balcony seat of the Superdome in New Orleans. I was too far away to see much, but I could vaguely make out the patrol boats as they slowed to a stop as they came upon the sickening sight of the larger pieces of the wreckage. They'd soon discover at least the one partial body and their minds would forever have to file that horrible scene.

As for me, they wouldn't be looking for another boat. They'd be concentrating on the horror in front of them. It was a thankless job the shore patrol had to do. I was quite satisfied not to have their job that night.

Within ten minutes, I finally made out some lights at the shoreline. As the houses became more visible, I discovered that I was down the shore about a quarter mile from where I lived. It took me another half hour of tacking back and forth before I made it through the misty fog to my boat dock. I realized it was better that way. Not many people would have remained out on their patios or decks if there was nothing to see out on the lake. It meant that they would not see me float into shore…and I wouldn't have to hear a lot of questions I was in no mood to answer.

However, I wasn't completely lucky. As I secured my boat to the main post on the dock, I was startled to see my neighbor, Stan Wright and his wife Rachel scrambling out onto my dock to talk to me. They were old friends who knew my love of sailing.

I waved to them, but Stan interrupted my wave with a shout, "Thank God, you're O.K. We know you like to do some late night sailing."

I was surprised they knew. I thought I was being stealthy. My arm was bleeding and I didn't realize I had some facial lacerations until I looked in the mirror later that night. It was curious Stan and Rachel hadn't noticed my injuries. But, again, the night was very dark.

Stan quickly continued, "When we heard the explosion out on the lake. We were scared you had been part of the accident. Rachel and I worry about you if we see your sailboat gone at night."

I eased their concern with false bravado and an immediate lie by saying, "Yeh, I'm fine. It was a heck of an explosion. I was just sailing by the shoreline, but I couldn't help but hear that collision. I've only been out on the water for a short few minutes. It had to have been a ghastly scene."

Stan was excited. "I've been listening to the police reports on my short wave radio. I heard the shore patrol at the scene say that apparently two motorboats were going full blast across the lake. They couldn't see each other with all the fog and maybe the noise of their own engines. Then, bang. It was the ultimate of bad luck!"

I scoffed, "Or, stupidity. I'll bet they'll find alcohol was a key ingredient over bad luck."

What could he do but nod? He'd seen or heard of many booze related water accidents over the years. People didn't need to be licensed to drive a boat.

Feeling an urgency to not create any more curiosity from my neighbors, I began moving toward my home. My arm hurt as I raised it to wave. Saying 'good night', I tried to walk as comfortable as possible. Truthfully, my leg hurt like hell and my neck was stiffing up.

Stan was still on the dock looking out toward the blurred spotlights on the lake, when he suddenly shouted after me, "Hey, you want your life preserver brought up to the house or do you want to leave it in the sailboat?"

I thought he was kidding me about my lack of heeding proper safety precautions since I forgotten to take one when I went sailing. Then I saw him pick it up out of my boat. It wasn't mine, but it was definitely a life preserver. How could….then I stopped.

Evidently a life preserver had been catapulted over to my boat during the explosion from one of the ill-fated motorboats. The projectile had landed conveniently in the small open seating area in the front of my sailboat. It had been too dark to notice it when I sailed away from the tragedy.

There were many ways I could have died that night. But, I didn't. If my sailboat had been damaged or made immobile, as luck would have it, I might have discovered that life preserver…even if I'd been more severely injured. Bottom line, I was just apparently not scheduled to die that particular evening.

I'd like to think I learned something from that ordeal. I can't say that I did. It's mostly a night I try to forget. I did call the police and tell them I was out on my boat lounging in the late hours when I witnessed the 'sound' of collision from afar. When I said, "afar" to the officer on the phone, I felt badly for lying. If he'd seen me in person, he would have known I was closer than I was letting on. In fact, once in the house I discovered more cuts on my arms, face, and legs from the splinters of the exploding boats. I even had some body hair singed off of my legs and burn marks on my face and arms. I wore long sleeved shirts and long pants for the next week until the abrasions showed signs of healing.

The police officer thanked me for calling in, but told me the investigation was fairly routine and quite apparent. Two drunken college-aged kids had been very unlucky and very foolish that night. He asked me for my number in case they had any more questions. I gave it to him. I was never called.

Friends of the two deceased boaters were interviewed by a newspaper reporter. They divulged that both young men had been drinking heavily earlier that evening. None of their friends had any idea either of them was going to jump into their speedboat and take off pell mell across White Bear Lake. Both young men had been at different parties and had been delivered home by friends. The decision to go out on a high-speed boat ride after midnight was each one's own quirk. There were no other dead bodies. The fact that it ended in their deaths was unconscionable to each person quizzed by the reporter. As stated in his article, 'young people are supposed to be untouchable and not suffer this kind of result.' The simultaneous actions by these two youths would forever be part of the local lore.

In the weeks and months ahead, I too often relived that tragic collision not only in my dreams but in my daily thoughts. It was probably a blessing I didn't know either young man so I didn't have to have their faces pictured in my mind.

I only went out sailing one other night since witnessing that terrible disaster… maybe to make certain I could still do it. There was not a cloud in the sky and the moon was full. The breeze was steady, just right for a quick hour long sail into the night to get my mind off whatever problems I had that day. I brought along my biggest spotlight and a couple flashlights and wore a life preserver. I even carried an extra one for no particular reason.

Having pushed off from the dock, the sail immediately rose to its fullness and I was on my way. Almost immediately I heard a whining sound from across the lake. Through the crystal clear night, I could see a motorboat from far off down by the south shore rapidly moving across the water. I just sat in my sailboat not moving transfixed by the speed of the boat. It was fully lighted and careening diagonally across the lake from my right to left at full throttle.

I must have sat there almost motionless for fifteen minutes just staring at the traveling light as it crossed the wide lake. The boat never got close to my side of the shoreline. Still, all I could think of was how it made no sense for that boat to be going that fast even on a clear, star-filled night.

I found myself perspiring despite the cool breeze. I kept my sailboat very close to the shoreline. My heart rate raced throughout that boater's trip across the lake. There was no accident. There was no other boater out in the middle of the lake at that hour. Had there been other boats, the drivers would have had ample time to see one another's warning lights.

I was out on the lake for no more than a half hour that night. Then, I returned to my dock. That was long enough. Night time sailing had lost its pleasure. The business and personal problems or whatever kept me awake didn't seem as severe any longer. Leaving the dock, I walked toward my cabin feeling tired. I'd go sailing in the morning.

For a long time my mind was constantly on alert during the night whenever awakened by the hum of any motorboat on the lake. If I had not gone to bed yet, I'd go to the window and look to the sky hoping the night was clear. If I was sleeping, the buzz of the nighttime speedboat would awaken me. I'd not go back to sleep until the noise from the motor passed by and disappeared into the night.

The Confrontation with Professor Grant

I still wonder about that class…that time in my life…and how it happened. It was just a college class…and an elective at that. I registered for Intellectual History 301 because I'd heard there wasn't much coursework required… and I enjoyed previous history courses. I thought I might take a class just for the joy of learning. The only real on-going effort that history course would necessitate was me getting my body across campus twice a week in the dead of winter by 9:45 AM. When registering for classes, a lot of things had to be considered. The classroom building was only six blocks from where I lived but I'd be walking against the typical north wind. Still, I was a native Minnesotan. That inconvenience didn't seem too taxing or unreasonable.

I'd heard rumors that as a student in that class one didn't even have to attend class. No role was taken. An end-of-the-quarter term paper was all that was required to complete the course. Talk about an ideal elective course. This history class would allow me to concentrate and put more effort into other classes that related more to my major in Business Administration. Of course believing I'd actually invest extra study time in my business coursework was delusional, but the rationale was sound. I guess the true inspiration about this elective course was that I'd even found it in the vast array of course choices. You had to be a veteran student who knew the ropes in college class registration to find a prize like this one.

The bottom line was this class was simply on my agenda for the credit hours. It was intended to be one of the least significant classes I would ever attend. Completing this three-credit course would keep me on pace for the right number of credits required for eventual graduation. That was it…little work, little effort, and a good chance for a good grade. How interesting life can be when good planning can pay off.

In truth that Intellectual History 301 class would turn out to be a complete waste of time. It would etch itself deeply in the time line of my college experience, not because of work involved in the class, but something completely unique and different in my college experience. As far as its value, it still was the most insignificant class during my college career…although Geology was a close second.

Unfortunately the memory of that class…the vivid remembrance…is that something happened…something I believe to be quite rare…at least in a classroom environment. There was an occurrence…a situation…that caused me to have a confrontation with of all people, a professor. It happened during the winter session of my sophomore year. To this day I still wonder what possessed me to get involved in such an incident. After all, squabbles in college were usually with one's age group and typically forgotten about as fast as they materialized. Most of these disagreements were minor…just part of growing up in a competitive world.

This altercation was far different. It was with a man with a doctorate of History, therefore a supposed respected scholar…and me, a relative non-entity amongst the many thousands of students attending that university. As time as moved forward, the question of why I reacted the way I did has become even more of a mystery than even back then. Even when I consider the circumstances now, I can't fathom that I reacted the way I did. If I were an ornery, irascible, competitive type of student, that conflict still would have been unimaginable. The odd thing was that I wasn't even close to being that type of person. I liked to compete, but not in a war of words with a person who makes his living through his own supposedly effective use of the English language. The incident was so out of character for me. I wasn't even interested in debating various questions of that era. It wasn't as if I'd never stood up for what I believed. I just didn't make a habit of it. I had enough depth to know that most of my thoughts were shallow. I figured that was why I was in college…to add some meat to my thoughts. What opinions I did have, my ability to communicate them was generally suspect anyway. The combination of these shortcomings meant that I didn't get into a lot of verbal spats nor did I think it important that I force my thoughts on others. My primary aim was to get a college degree and move on with life.

So….back to this so-called confrontation…why did it happen? Why was this any different than any other tiff? Since I didn't take a lot of things very seriously, why did this particular incident reach such intense proportions? How close did it come to a nose-to-nose hostility? If the turmoil had reached such a hostile stage, how bad was the predictable exchange of sharp words? Was name-calling involved? What was the result of the conflict? What possibly could have been the circumstances that brought a tenured professor to lose his cool as well? And, as much as I don't want to consider myself average then or even now, how could a supposedly ordinary college sophomore reach such a point of anger? What kind of disagreement could it have been for me at that age to leave the comfort of my 'give a damn' way of living life? And now, why has that altercation remained so vivid after so many years?

Even now when I think about that situation, my heart beats just a bit faster…. the picture becomes more focused….and the emotion builds. The staging of the entire scene is still so unblemished after all these years. Nonetheless, I always end up shaking my head not believing the incident really occurred. Yet, it did… and I'm glad it did.

So, why it occurred? Given it was during my college years, an obvious guess for the outburst might be that it was about a poor or unjustified grade. It would be a logical guess, but completely wrong. I had not even yet received a grade from this instructor…and would not until the end of the quarter.

Another wishful conjecture would be that I was provoked by the professor's fiery lecture causing a kind of break-out in my educational experience. Maybe someone had finally jolted me out of my mild demeanor and proclaimed something contrary to my upbringing or my value system. Could that have been it?

Sadly…no. Either of those reasons could have been so much more understandable…maybe even praiseworthy. Unfortunately it was nothing so personal.

As I've looked back it does make me appreciate how the set of circumstances had become so amazingly aligned and so quickly. The small flame of discontent flared up within me moments upon his entry into the classroom that first day of the session and remained simmering. With each of his classes I attended, the scene became more combustible with my growing disgruntlement. Therefore, I'd have to place most of the reason for the outburst on me, but there would have been no eruption without the unique traits of the professor supplying the fuel. He was the epitome, at least in my eyes, of the most despicable type of instructor. Not only did I burn inside for having selected the class, but I was absolutely disgusted that such a man could have reached his station in life. How could he be a tenured professor at this large university? He had years of experience to exhibit his ineptness as a teacher. But, he had gained tenure nonetheless.

When I happened into his class in my sophomore year, he was in the glory days of his professorial career. For some instructors, like this man, the self-acknowledged grandeur of his brilliance translated into an ego so large it was a wonder his head could fit through the door of the classroom. This tenured professor was heaped in so much self-importance that he had acquired an insatiable appetite to feed on his own exaggerated view of himself. Any clash with a student…especially an undergraduate… would have been unimaginable to an instructor, at least in his own eyes, of his elevated magnificence. He was on his home turf…in the safety of his academic environment. He was above having a fray with a student. He held student's lives and minds in his palm. He was in a powerful situation. And he knew it. And he loved it. And, I didn't like that an oaf like him could have this supremacy over anyone…least of all a bunch of impressionable students… when it was so undeserved.

My eyes became slits of disapproval with every action this man took. My teeth gritted with every supercilious attitude he displayed. I'd had a few people in my life who affected me this way. My eyes could roll and my jaw could tighten with wrath, but nobody made my blood curdle and made me react so adversely as this man. This so-called instructor…this purported expert in his field…this tenured professor…this pompous ass…he brought out every negative emotion in me in a way even I thought could not be possible.

So, this little divergence was not trivial in the scope of both our lives. While there was no question who started this verbal clash, it has to be pointed out that he incited the conflagration. It was remarkable was how this arrogant professor allowed himself to be brought down to the level of exchanging harsh words with an insignificant undergraduate. That says something right there to the man's feeling of superiority. He couldn't tolerate something happening that was unplanned or wasn't going his way. He had to best me. That was where his enormous ego only increased the heat of the exchange and kept me from backing down.

Since I was the one who actually jumped out onto the battlefield first...as I readily admit...there were certainly reasons why I behaved so out of character in that classroom. Prior to that day I would certainly have described myself as a respectful person. Even after that day, the description would have been valid. People generally liked me. I held doors for the elderly and for most females. My folks loved me. I was kind to children. I had a good heart. I was not cruel to animals. I enjoyed telling stories. I appreciated the witty joke whether off-colored or not. I preferred to smile, laugh, and seek an enjoyable life. I considered myself intelligent...certainly, at times that could be disproved. I was spontaneous and some say, quick-witted...but I was careful not to overuse that trait at the expense of someone's pride. I operated under the principle that if I kidded someone too much, I might hurt them...and that was rarely my intent.

With this as my general character, it might be hard to reconcile my behavior at that confrontation. Then again, it should be understood there were other factors contributing to that outburst than simply to evaluate my personality...and not just that it was the cold, miserable weather of the middle quarter of school when being ornery was justified. Consideration could also be given to me being a male when my entire college career was simultaneous with those tumultuous years of the Vietnam War conflict. Male college students lived through a time when guys our own age not in school were serving in a very unpopular war. Fellows were getting killed, seriously wounded, or mentally injured as a result of having served in Southeast Asia. The tragedy to my age group at the time, male or female, was a sense that America was not fighting for its safety and freedom... not when the military action was an undeclared war on the other side of the globe.

As a result, most males going to college tended to be very militant.....about trying to stay alive by 'not' going to Vietnam. Draft eligible male college students did anything to stay in school and maintain their student deferment. Once that student deferment was gone due to low grades or graduation, that student on many draft boards went to the top of the list of male eligible draftees. The entire matter reeked of inequity and waste.

As a typical college student I was certainly caught up in the feelings of my peers and shared the accompanying frustrations. I didn't like the thought as a freshman that if I didn't have a 'C' average after my first quarter of college classes, my butt would be in basic training at Ft. Bragg before the next session's mid-quarter examinations. The draft was like a preying monster just drooling for new meat. The new male college student knew he'd better adapt quickly to campus life or he'd be gobbled up by this drooling dragon in the form of a county draft board before the exit door of the college slammed shut.

Did that time period and the outside pressure of Vietnam partially contribute to my flare-up with the professor? I remember that stress so vividly having seen many of my fellow students fall prey to getting drafted after not adjusting well or fast enough to classes and college life.

Most certainly, though, there were other reasons contributing to my sudden behavioral change that day. They went right back to my freshman year, even though I was a sophomore when I registered for that history class. As a first year student, there were so many radical and subtle changes throughout the freshman year. Being mostly independent and living away from home, college students had choices on how they wanted to live their freer life. Some first year students had goals; most seemed to be just trying to adapt and survive. However, no matter how one lived through that first year of school, each student exhaled a sigh of relief upon its completion. They'd figured out the ropes and proved they could handle college life. In most instances they could smugly leave campus for the summer and regroup ready to attack their sophomore year with a bit more self-righteousness and confidence.

That sophomore year was so refreshingly different. We didn't have to put on an act. We were more comfortable with ourselves. We looked ruefully at the wide-eyed new freshman mixing the end of their high school frivolousness with their newly found freedom as a college student. You hated to believe you had been like that only a year before.

Traits of a sophomore became very apparent. Doing things the easiest way was the measure of success and pride. For example, registering for a class close to your dorm or bus stop…with the classroom on the first floor of a building instead of the third floor and within short walking distance of your next class were factors worth bragging about…….repeatedly.

As cool as we sophomores thought we were, it became more important to establish the direction of one's course of study. The sooner that was done, the sooner that sophomore could feel even more assured that the degree was within his or her grasp. Dreams might begin to formulate, but the biggest aim was just to graduate. It was a time when we pondered how our college experience might help us venture into the outside world and survive with a measure of our family life style we had upon entering college.

As a sophomore, we began to tacitly face the realism of our plight. We got into the flow of school quickly upon arrival back at school in the fall. Now we cherished our independent life. Besides going to class and making grades, we had become cognizant we'd never have such little responsibility in our lives again. Furthermore, we now had the understanding how much time we had to invest in various types of classes to achieve the grade we needed. As a result, practically from day one of that second year of school, the college experience became more enjoyable. Could being more relaxed in my college atmosphere have spurred me to react so outwardly as I did against that professor? It probably contributed.

I recall another vague but pertinent factor that added to my confidence was a decision about a major. The motivation stemming from that choice was one of the most motivating experiences for me. Just like that I could plan my remaining two and a half years of classes and begin to see the light at the end of the tunnel. It was exciting to contemplate how better to use the next two summers in order to possibly bring more value to my resume upon graduation. From that point on, my grades improved measurably. I enjoyed being a more motivated student. I've always thought that dynamic …of being more inspired and confident…brought me to the stage where it probably had become less daunting facing up to a college professor.

The major factor, though, in leading up to the confrontation with the professor, had to be my actual decision to take the class in the first place. It wasn't until the end of that fall quarter of my second year that the circumstance even surfaced. In planning for the winter quarter, I still had some elective courses I was expected to complete. I sought elective course choices based on some obvious factors. I wanted a class I might enjoy where a good grade could be gained… truthfully…with little extended work.

It was in this investigation of the vast numbers of classes at the University that I happened upon some history classes that would answer my needs. I liked history. The classes didn't require a lot of work. There was usually a mid-quarter examination and a final test. Maybe there would be an essay requirement. But, class attendance might not be essential. During the cold of winter, that would be a huge plus as well.

Not being in the age of computers where students could readily read bios of possible professors or teaching assistants, a student during my time depended on word of mouth to find out about the quality of a class or the reputation of a particular instructor. There were many good instructors, and you'd make note of them. The weird, ineffective, or egotistical professors…you made note of them as well. Steering clear of that type of instructor, especially in an elective course, was preferred. A student had to deal with the quirks of some professors in their major. No reason to make matters worse by having to deal with an odd instructor in your electives.

By November it was time to register for the winter quarter. I was still questioning which elective course to take. I had my parameters defined. With nothing much else to do but study during that cold winter quarter, I wanted to take eighteen credit hours to give me a cushion for graduating two years hence in the spring. I was seeking an elective class where attendance would not be mandatory. Reading the text would be the primary method of preparing for the mid-quarter and final exams versus class notes. I hoped also to find an entertaining and knowledgeable lecturer who might make me want to attend his class. That didn't seem like too much to expect.

By word of mouth a new consideration into my elective choices was brought forward to me only one day before I was to register. It was a history course taught by a tenured professor with classes only on Tuesday and Thursday. That sounded favorable. I had planned on taking either an American History course covering the Nineteenth Century or a History of Journalism class. These latter classes had professors who were known to be good, but classes were Monday, Wednesday, and Friday, my busiest days for my more important classes.

A friend finally persuaded me to take the Tuesday-Thursday class. It was entitled "Intellectual History of the United States". The professor required students to submit a paper which would be due at the end of the quarter. There would be no final exam…no mid-quarter exam…and no roll call would be taken. There wasn't even a required textbook. The professor had a few recommended paperbacks, but that was voluntary reading. With eighteen credits that winter quarter, 'voluntary' reading was not a top priority. Truth be told, if I had only twelve credits that quarter, 'voluntary' reading would not have made my list of priorities.

The instructor was a full professor in the History Department. His name was Professor Winfield E. Grant. Everything sounded fine…a potentially interesting class with little work. When I finally made that instructor and his course as my elective selection, I did so with the notion of actually going to his lectures. I loved this class before I even set foot in the classroom. It was an opportunity to enjoy a course purely for the pleasure of learning. No work…..just a paper. If I had to miss a few of his classes, so what. I was congratulating myself for having found this course. I had achieved the ultimate as a second year student in the art of registration.

Final tests and Christmas break came and went. Within days after recovering from various New Year's Eve parties, college students returned to the hallowed halls to buckle down for the long winter quarter at the University.

During those first days of winter quarter, there was no doubt it was January in Minnesota. Different from the pleasant September days of the start of fall quarter or the cool fresh days of early spring quarter, the initial days of winter quarter were simply brutal. Nonetheless, as harsh as the first days of class were, every student adapted quickly to the elements and inconveniences. College buses were filled to the brim the first couple of days of class. These buses took inordinately long between stops as riders were trying to stay warm while juggling their class schedule and figuring the best routes to their classroom buildings. Hardier college students would march across campus with the cold, hard wind biting into their faces.

For native Minnesotans, they would recall how cavalier they were in high school. They dressed lightly while taking the short trip by car or school bus. It was an act to show how tough they were.

With no one to impress and a spread out campus, a University student was fighting his or her way to class with thousands of other students. There was no reason to be heroic. College students couldn't find enough warm clothing to wear. In class the floor looked like the end of the day after a major sale in a department store clothing section. Scarves, jackets, parkas, gloves, stocking hats, etc. were strewn on the floor where students had stripped in the overheated classrooms. After class, each room full of students became like a uni-sex locker room with students getting re-dressed to embark on their journey to the next classroom.

On my second day of classes, I bundled up for my five-block walk to my first lecture with Professor Winfield E. Grant. I was looking forward to the class. No pressure. I had even articulated to a few friends this noble idea of registering for a course for the pleasure of learning. They had given me a blank stare not knowing how to respond.

My face was frozen by the time I arrived at an old medical building where Grant's class was held. The class was in a dated amphitheater presumably used for medical students to look down on a doctor performing some kind of medical procedure on a patient, or worse yet, a cadaver.

When I walked into the small auditorium, I was midway up into the amphitheater. I gazed down several rows of seats to a small podium on top of a circled stage no more than eight feet in diameter. The entire emphasis of this unique classroom was on that small stage. I wasn't certain if I had the right building and classroom. If I saw a cadaver being wheeled in, I figured to make a very curt exit. I checked my registration slip again and verified again that it was the right location.

I walked up a few steps until I was two-thirds of the small auditorium up from the stage. It gave me a sense of power to be looking down at the podium. I liked the distance from the arena. I felt like I was on top of a tornado vortex looking down into the funnel.

I sat down taking off my coat, scarf, gloves, stocking cap and sweater since the heat was rising in this tubular classroom. Locating my pen and notebook stuffed in the sleeve of my coat, I settled in to enjoy the first class about ten minutes before the 9:45 class was to begin. While I would never arrive that early again, I had no doubt the honorable Professor Grant was such a veteran that he wouldn't make his presence until seconds before the class starting time. It was all part of the typical professorial act. I understood the pretense. After all, I was an experienced college student in my own rite. I knew the ropes.

Within nine minutes, I was sweating like a road construction worker in July. The heat in that cone-shaped room was still rising. If the overheating continued, I'd have to move down closer to the stage if I wanted to cool off. That change in seating was unacceptable since I'd lose the freedom to walk out of the classroom when and if I wanted.

As time grew near for the professor to make his entrance, I took note that of the two hundred seats in the small auditorium, there were only forty students sitting haphazardly around the classroom. All the bottom three rows of seats surrounding the podium were vacant. It was very intimate setting with only about eight seats in a semi-circle next to the stage in each of those three rows. Obviously my fellow classmates had the same idea I did. We wanted no part of intimacy in this elective class. We just wanted the grade. Still it bothered me that so few students had enrolled in this class. I expected at least the first day of class to be standing room only given the lack of work required for the class.

About a minute before the class was to begin, I heard some shuffling at the stage level door below. I guessed it was Professor Winfield E. Grant about to make his entrance. The door by the podium opened up gradually and a flood of twelve to fifteen students entered with all their eyes on the gentleman in the middle of their conclave. This man had a hat in the style that my father wore. It looked so out of place. Students wouldn't be caught dead in that fedora style of hat. Not letting anything get by my observation, I correctly deduced that under the hat had to be the professor.

The students surrounding him seemed to be older. I guessed them to be graduate students or fourth year history majors. My first reaction to this parade was negative. I didn't want my one paper to earn a decent course grade to be in competition with a bunch of older history majors working to obtain their advanced degree. I didn't sign up for this class to get anything worse than a B+.

These twelve to fifteen students had been all looking back at the professor as they entered the lectern area. It was a wonder they didn't trip over each other. There was a mumble from the man under the hat and all the students laughed dutifully. I let my mind change. I thought, 'Maybe I lucked out. He's got them laughing. This Professor Grant must be an absolute spellbinder if he's got these older students eating out of his hand.'

I looked around the room as this entourage took the closest seats to the podium. I noticed all eyes from the 'peanut gallery', that is, the other forty students in the room, were also fixed on that man under the fedora. My fellow students were anxious to see, as I was, whether this tenured professor was more in the style of Walter Cronkite, John F. Kennedy, or if more entertaining, maybe Bob Hope or Johnny Carson.

As the graduate students finally settled in their chairs, their eyes were still riveted on their preeminent professor. These history majors didn't even take time to remove their coats. They just sat on the edge of their chairs waiting for the performance to begin. Apparently they did not want to miss any of the choice words Professor Grant was about to share with them. Frankly their excited anticipation got me eager to hear the man as well.

With the last of two students still milling around the podium getting the last of Professor Grant's choice comments, they finally broke the umbilical cord to the professor and took the nearest seats now in the third row. Those two students looked distressed they couldn't be closer to the podium.

Professor Winfield E. Grant was now alone, on display, and ready to perform. He took off his out-of-style hat. Then he removed his overcoat with a theatrical flair. He offered a furtive glance to his surroundings above the third row. He seemed neither pleased nor displeased with the sight. He delicately placed his coat, scarf, and gloves neatly over a stool conveniently placed on the small stage. It occurred to me that he might have practiced this act before an ample mirror in his office.

He then bent down to take one sheet of paper from a worn, thin briefcase. If that was his outline for his hour and fifteen minute class, I was impressed. He stood up behind the podium and again made one cursory glance at the upper rows of the small auditorium before lowering his eyes and smiling at his minions in the first three rows.

I now had the full view of this academician. He was a balding, round, bespeckled man of approximately 5'8" in height. He reminded me of what Napoleon Bonaparte might have looked like with another hundred pounds around his middle. The look on Professor Grant's face was one of royalty. He smiled just to show that he could smile, yet that smile was inauthentic and could be turned off with a blink of an eye.

I began to slowly shake my head. There were growing hints that I was about to witness my first mistake of the New Year. I kept staring at him praying that I was wrong. He had not articulated a word as yet, but his body language spoke volumes. He kept inhaling bringing his belly to his chest unsuccessfully as he glanced at his one page outline of his lecture. He made it look like he hadn't taken it out of his brief case since the previous September when he had last given this opening lecture. If that was true, I again held out hope that he was just building up to a crescendo before launching into his well-practiced lecture. I was not ready yet to give up on him, but things were not looking favorable. I just kept telling myself that he couldn't be as vainglorious and arrogant as he appeared. After all, didn't my friend recommend this class... and the instructor?

The students, graduate level or fourth-year history majors, who had accompanied him, were waiting with baited breath in the first three rows for his first words. He cleared his throat a couple times and then appeared ready to speak. A quiet smirk emanated from his mouth. I could see it from two-thirds up into the auditorium. His students began to twitter and giggle. They were expecting something special to come out of his mouth. The other forty students in the small auditorium leaned forward to greet his introductory remarks as well.

Finally he spoke. "Ah......Ah......." The students in the front row began to laugh.....not smile.....but actually laugh.

Professor Grant continued, "Ah........Ah........" Then he began to laugh. The rest of his sycophants joined the laughter. The remaining forty students in the upper rows leaned further forward thinking they had missed something. What was the inside joke?

The professor stuck his chin to the sky and then added words to his masterful beginning. "I….ah……..guess……this is……ah …..that….ah…. Intellectual History…….um …..class that …..undergraduates take……..ah……to…….ah ………. to fulfill……ah …….their……….ah……..ahhhhh…….electives."

He then scoffed with his chin pointing upward toward the forty undergraduates in attendance. They could readily see the disgust and distain on his face no matter how high they sat in the auditorium.

The bootlicker students in the first three rows shook their heads side to side with a spurious attempt at showing their own repulsion. They were not about to turn around and see the faces of such low grade and hopeless undergraduate students.

Professor Grant then took the one page he had relieved from his briefcase. Without saying anything he gave it to one of his sycophants. It held no outline. It was a blank sheet of paper. His minions then began to write their names. The professor either was taking role or needed a repeat of the names of his graduate students. Anyway the paper stopped with the names of the students in the first three rows and was returned to him.

Looking back up at the forty students splattered around the auditorium, he held the paper above his head and then said without looking up, "At… ah…the…end…of class…ah…I…ah……need……ah …your…ah…name… ah…..on this…….ah…paper… returned……ah ……..ah………ah for those of ……..you……wanting……..ah ……..to …….take …….this ……class. Ah…… except……for………ah ………ah …… the term paper……..at….ah …..the….. ah end of the …..ah ……ah …..quarter,…….ah…….. I ……ah……won't……. need…….anything…..else…ah…from……you.

There was a pause of one second.

"James Madison………ah…….the…….ah ……..fourth President ……… ah …….of…….the……um……..United …….ah………ah………….ah……… States……once said………"

There was some laughter from some of his entourage apparently loving the way he could stomach no longer talking to the undergraduates in the classroom and simply accelerated into his lecture.

Professor Grant's voice then trailed off in my mind. The "ah's" were beyond anything I had ever heard, including that unfortunate girl in high school who would break up three syllable words with "ah's" when she was speaking in front of the class.

I examined this Doctor of History in both shock and awe. I could not follow a thing he was saying. His constant interruptions with his "ah's" made the memory of fingernails on a blackboard sound melodic. I didn't know whether he had a speech impediment, he was nervous, he was unprepared, he was actually searching for the right words, or he was unaware of his slovenly delivery. But, to the fawning three rows of graduate students in front of him, you'd have thought the Messiah had arrived.

As the Professor got warmed up, he was in his own little zone. He showed no interest to his audience above the first three rows and frankly not a lot of attention toward those graduate students either. They were just staging….and had learned to laugh on cue. Occasionally his voice would rise as he put a smirk on his face as he effused a cute academic word apparently to show his intellectual depth. When his chosen erudite word was spoken………finally……his followers in the first three rows would teeter from their chairs in mirth. They were so loyal. They were so sickening.

A half hour went by. His cadence had picked up. He no longer said "ah's" to the extent that he did when he was getting warmed up. However, if he ever wanted to find the right word or emphasize something, he could repeat the interjection "ah" up to four times before mercifully giving his numbed students his choice word.

After forty-five minutes, I looked at my notes. I'm no artist and the hieroglyphics on my note page had many strange drawings proving my artistic ineptitude. Professor Grant was speaking only to the walls of the small auditorium. He was enthralled with the things he was thinking, the way he was saying them, and how he looked when he said them. His voice only rose when he was making what he thought was a robust and cogent point and hinting to those first three rows of students how they should be ready to laugh. All I could hear were the "ah's".

Of the forty people in the rows above the first three rows, there were only about ten students remaining when the tortuous class ended. I stuck out to the end of the class just so I could go down to the podium and add my name to the list of registrants to his class. I found out later it wasn't necessary. As for the twelve to fifteen graduate students or history majors, they had hung on every word of the professor. I marveled at their attention, allegiance, and determination to stay awake. I couldn't believe anyone least of all these experienced students would give this guy the time of day with his haughty behavior and unbelievably murderous speaking style.

As for me, I had a headache that made my eyes water. I had spent most of the class looking through my registration book trying to find any replacement course. Unfortunately this Intellectual History class was the only one that really worked with my current schedule.

For the last twenty minutes of the class, all I could think about was how my friend could possibly have recommended this class and this professor. He should be shot for giving out such misleading information. Easily, Professor Grant was the most haughtily contemptible and vain professor I had ever witnessed. Added to this arrogance was his own apparent feeling that he was an extraordinarily funny wordsmith, ala Mark Twain or Will Rogers. I was simply shocked that my University which was held in such high esteem could permit such an embarrassingly inept egotist to hold classes on this campus. I was hugely disappointed.

I trotted down the steps towards the front of the classroom to locate that sheet of paper to sign my name onto the class roster. Professor Grant was practically being carried off the podium by his graduate sycophants. I kept wondering what I was missing. What had this man done to deserve such a following? Certainly those graduate students could not be sincere.

After signing my name I remained watching this pompous man receive the flowery congratulations on the mind-killing lecture he had just given. I figured I was witnessing one of the worst cases of misdirected deification in the history of education. It made no sense why these graduate students were placating this man by behaving so obsequiously. He had nothing special going for him i.e. looks, speaking ability, content of lecture. The only thing he had to his advantage.......and it was a big factor....was his power over the future of these students. That was my only explanation.

Grant eyed a couple of coeds amongst his small group of followers. He helped one of the girls with her coat. The other followers acted as if they had reached the high point of their own academic existence. When this prominent professor who apparently had invented 'history' would stoop to assisting a girl with her rap, then they certainly must be in the midst of greatness.

The professor said something in a low voice to the young lady. She blushed. The others around who heard what he had said laughed loudly to possibly cover up their embarrassment.

I stood there dumbfounded. How could such a repulsive human being think himself so intelligent, so humorous, so avant-garde, so witty, so suave, so superior, so........ 'ah'.....special. If there was ever a time that I thought the world was not a fair place was standing in that amphitheater watching this annoying spectacle. Whatever level of cynicism I practiced as a sophomore at the University paled in comparison to the increased level of scorn and skepticism I felt when I departed that classroom of Professor Winfield E. Grant.

I left the old medical building with my gloves in my pocket and my stocking hat stuffed in the same place. It was bitterly cold outside. I didn't even notice the temperature. I watched Grant's entourage move like a centipede down the street, no doubt staying together until he reached his office. There he could close his office and allow only those he wanted to entertain with his wit and humor. No doubt the young co-ed whose coat he touched would be in that invited ensemble.

A cold blast of wind woke me up. While in Grant's class, I had determined it would be necessary to change to another elective. Yet, after trudging back to my fraternity house, I had changed my mind again. I had to remind myself how I never meant "Intellectual History" to be a class I was going to invest a lot of time. Except for the huge disappointment of watching this poor excuse for a professor, that damnable 'Intellectual History' class expediently fit my schedule and my preference for a limited work effort for an elective course perfectly. Besides, if his lectures got too bad, I had the choice of not attending his class. I would just do the paper at the end of the quarter, pray I would be given a fair shake on the grade, and move on with life.

My next class was not until that afternoon…..a 2:00 Geology class. That was supposed to be my boring class! It fulfilled a science requirement. Now coupled with this 'Intellectual History' class, Tuesdays and Thursdays showed signs of being cripplingly tedious. I was disenchanted beyond what a seasoned sophomore who knew the ropes was supposed to be. I hadn't come to this university to be saddled with classes like Geology and a professor like Grant. But, despite all my planning, it had happened.

By the next 'Intellectual History' class on Thursday, I had attended all my other classes. Given the expected workload of those classes, the die had been cast. Professor Winfield E. Grant's class on Tuesdays and Thursdays fit too conveniently for me to cancel. I had the ability to write a decent paper. I saw no reason why I couldn't achieve an 'A' whether I attended his class or not.

Since I had that lunch scheduled with a friend at the nurse's cafeteria after Grant's class, I figured to show up for his class twice a week and remain as long as I could before I was repulsed by his egotistical antics or his rapid fire "ah's". At that point I could just leave and read the newspaper at the cafeteria until my friend arrived.

And that's what I did. I had made it to the start of his class religiously for four weeks. I lasted as long as thirty minutes and as short as fifteen minutes in each of his classes before shuffling out through the mid-auditorium exit door. He never noticed me or the other underclassmen as we paraded out early. He really didn't seem to care.

By the end of January, the temperature hadn't gotten above freezing in three weeks. People were grumpy. For a native Minnesotan, this type of weather was even intolerable. I usually didn't succumb to irascible behavior caused by the weather, but trudging to his class on one of those last days of January, maybe I did yield a bit to the bitter icy cold temperatures. I kept asking myself why I was walking across the campus in such blatantly cold conditions, just to see how long I could stand listening to Professor Winfield E. Grant.

It was during the fifth week of his class…the first days of February that the incident happened. I didn't see it coming at all. There was no reason to presume something out of the ordinary would transpire on that dull, overcast cold Tuesday morning. But, something was different. It wasn't quite as cold…or overcast. The worst of winter had come and now it had passed. Those students still walking to class…including myself…had survived. Since the start of the quarter, I had trudged. I had plodded. I had slogged. I had made the struggle to attend that Intellectual History class twice a week. The professor simply made my effort a waste of time…for that my brain was slightly heated every time I walked into that old medical building auditorium.

That morning the sub-freezing temperatures had broken…and I strolled. The temperature had finally risen above thirty-two degrees Fahrenheit the previous weekend. There were a few more smiles on people's faces as I passed them. It was as if spring was in the air, even though it was still two months before warmer temperatures would begin the budding process in April. There was a sense of hope that more tolerable weather could be expected.

I walked into his class barely one minute before he did. I now sat next to the exit door because it saved time when exiting his lectures after fifteen minutes. I watched for the fifth straight week as his followers practically carried him onto the stage. The whole scene turned my stomach. I kept repeating the same question…how could an oaf like him become such a highly-regarded professor? What was I missing? Maybe that's why I was attending his class. I might find out why these graduate students and fourth year history students were fawning over his every breath.

This day he pulled out a hat and put it on before the lecture began. His followers behaved like they were about to be given a special homily by the Pope. The hat was in the style of that worn by someone in the colonial era. With no syllabus to the course, I had no idea what his lectures were supposed to mean or what he would be trying to teach his class.

He left the hat on as he prepared to perform causing the most insufferable and contagious twitter amongst his followers. They seemed awed by his creative imagery.

When he began that lecture with a series of "AH's", my brain began to pass into a timeless sleep. It was torture beyond what I considered human as this egomaniac smirked and stumbled his way through his discourse. There was not even a suggestion that he was actually teaching anything. Mostly he was demeaning some American colonial hero.

I sat there wondering what other type of work he was capable of doing. It certainly was not teaching or public speaking.

Of course the last time that he even looked beyond the first three rows of that auditorium was back to the first day of the class. He was mindless that there were any other bodies beyond his sycophants. Actually, by that fifth week, he was correct. Those forty students at the beginning of the quarter had dwindled to about eight. And, why any of those eight students showed up was anybody's guess. Most of these eight underclassmen, like me, exited within thirty minutes, or as soon as they had finished reading the morning newspaper.

That Tuesday morning for the first time in my life, I fell soundly asleep in a classroom. I don't know for how long. I didn't own a watch that worked. I awoke to the explosion of his followers all laughing at once over something Grant had eventually said. When I woke, it was with a jolt. No one paid me any mind, least of all the graduate and history majors sitting ten rows below me. I tried once again to listen to this egocentric slob, but within a minute, it was hopeless. The subject of his lecture didn't exist. I heard his voice rise as it did when his bootlickers were being warned that they should get ready to laugh. When he "ah'd" his way through whatever punch line to his story, most of his small group of followers laughed submissively. I did notice that some of the students sitting in the third row smiled but did not give him the mirthful action as they had four weeks before. There was some hope for those graduate students after all.

For me, enough was enough. For the fifth straight week, I began packing my stuff. I had already stayed a half hour longer than I normally did...and that was because I had fallen asleep. There was still a torturous thirty minutes left in the class.

As I was about to get up to leave, I glanced down at the professor and noticed he had put on another hat. It looked like the type Ben Franklin might have worn. For a moment I wanted to admire the creativity and energy that Grant was trying to put into his lectures, but I began to realize he was putting on a comedy skit that had little to do with learning anything about Ben Franklin. His efforts were aimed specifically at lampooning Ben Franklin, not using the character to teach anything.

It was at that point my constant burn became enflamed. My patience had long departed. It was not that I wanted to stand up for Ben Franklin. I hadn't read enough about the old gentleman to know his positives or his idiosyncrasies beyond his inventions. I did know enough that he was a respected colonial era character who contributed much to the formulation of our country. However, Professor Grant seemed to delight in trying to show disregard for Ben Franklin. He presented many not so funny mug shots depicting an ignorant and promiscuous Franklin. Franklin may have liked the ladies for all I knew, but it didn't necessarily make him a licentious and wanton fool.

It struck me again about the purpose of this lecture. Why was he investing so much time in downgrading Franklin? Was he trying to elevate himself against a man he couldn't compete with in any way?

I began to wonder why this course was even being offered. For that matter, what was this goof trying to accomplish in any of his lectures? What were his students supposed to glean...that Franklin or people of his generation were ignorant and the sex fiends of their time?

Professor Grant then said as he doffed his hat in exaggerated politeness of the Franklin time, "Ah.....good evening.......ah....madam......ah ......are you going to honor me with your presence.........ah...when ...the ......ah...... party......ah ......is .....over?"

His sycophants squealed with delight over his promiscuous slant aimed at Franklin. Imagine this elderly statesman propositioning a young lady at a party........gee, was that the first time that had happened in the history of mankind? Not likely. Was that depiction of Franklin really supposed to be creative?

I sat there on the edge of my chair staring at this quack trying to be a teacher on his little stage. He obviously considered himself the gift of historic parody.

At that moment I found myself getting up, but leaving my coat at my seat. I stepped slowly down the stairs and shuffled into the seventh row. I centered myself right in front of the podium. I was now only slightly elevated above his stage but no more than sixty feet from Professor Grant. No one else was seated in the fourth….fifth….sixth ….or seventh rows. All other undergraduates were in the fourteenth row or higher.

He was into his "ah's" searching for the word or the extraordinary humorous phrase to add to his slander. But, under his three-edged hat prop, he had noticed me shuffling my way to the center of the seventh row. I had broken his concentration. I could see he was irritated. I had broken the mood of what he considered one of his finer performances.

I sat there and just stared at him. While his followers were laughing dutifully, there was no emotion coming from my body language or face.

He tried to ignore my minor interruption and gushed forward with another attempt at wit and sarcasm. The sycophants strained to laugh. A few of them made a noise more like a grunting animal with a spurious smile pasted on their faces. Being closer to these graduate or history major students made me appreciate the effort it took for them to coddle to this enormous buffoon.

My eyes never left his eyes. I had destroyed his temperament…his artistic mood…and I had gained some satisfaction that I had.

He was saying even more "ah's" as he tried desperately to recover. I was amazed how truly bothered he was by my interruption. I was waiting for him to stop and make some deprecating comment towards me.

But, I didn't give him a chance. I had lost it.

I heard a voice echoing in the small confines of that amphitheater. The voice said, "Is this supposed to be educational…….or funny….or what is the purpose?"

There was a sudden silence at the podium. The self-loving professor stopped immediately. He looked around and said, "Did someone have a question?" He knew damn well who had interrupted his tortuous diatribe.

That voice interrupting the professor shockingly was mine. It was a calm voice, but there was a tone of desperate curiosity mixed in with disappointment and controlled anger. While I had done something very much out of the ordinary, I was very comfortable in what I'd just asked. Nonetheless, I sat up fully prepared for an onslaught of enraged words from this so-called teacher.

I spoke again. "I said…sir…what is it that you are saying or doing that is educational? What are we supposed to be learning…..that Ben Franklin was an imbecile?"

The professor's eyes began to bug out unwilling to even recognize that there could be another voice in that auditorium. Finally, not wanting to respond to me, he just gave me an imperious stare as if that was supposed to end the brief interruption to his purposeless performance.

I remained seated just glaring back at him. I thought I had spoken my feelings with some measure of restraint. I had expressed myself with sincerity even though I knew he would consider my statements an outburst. I now waited for his response in a room where not the slightest breath could be heard.

He composed himself reapplying that supercilious grin on his face, while looking at his loyal followers in the first three rows. Then he gave me a momentary glance and spoke condescendingly while trying not to look at me. "I guess.... ah......some of our undergraduates....ah........ don't have a sense of....ah...... humor.......nor the.........depth to ....ah.....understand."

He began to laugh. Some of his followers attempted a chuckle.......at least the one's in the first row. In row three, the four people among his disciples just sat there frozen. I wondered if they had been waiting for something like this to happen.

With baited breath these graduate students in the third row as well as the few undergraduates left in the auditorium waited for the next volley of words. For those graduate students I sensed this spectacle was already making up for the many miserable hours of coddling to this worthless excuse for a teacher.

The professor began to roll his head with his big haughty sneer. I could tell he was thinking of the best put down applicable to this situation. But, his mind worked too slowly.

I was surprisingly calm as I responded, "Sir, I have a very good sense of humor. I didn't know I signed up for bad comedy when I registered for your class. I believe I'm supposed to gain more depth and understanding of American History from classes like yours. But, your class is more about glorifying yourself with your hanger's on than teaching anything. My question remains...what am I supposed to be learning while attending your class...or, specifically in your lecture today?"

Calmed for the moment, he shot back indignantly, "Well...ah...... young man...ah...if you attended every class.......ah.......you would get a .....ah... ah......picture.....of how I look at ....ah.........society over the two hundred plus years...ah...... we've been a...ah....ah...republic. But, maybe....ah...you ......had........ah a....few.....puffs......on ......the .....WEED...BEFORE ... ah......CLASS."

I watched his delight in his attempt to berate me. I wondered if his entourage had become sickened by the way he would raise his voice when he was about to deliver his punch line. Still, it was the first time I'd ever heard him utter a sentence with so few "ah's". Strangely I was not derailed by his weak attempt to demean me. It just hadn't worked. Even the first two rows of his followers had trouble laughing since I sounded more calm than he did.

I ignored his attempt at humiliation. "Mr. Grant," I said, refusing to offer the more respectful 'Professor' or 'Doctor' title, "First of all, I have attended every one of your so-called classes since the beginning of the term. However, you have driven me out of your class before the allotted time with your excessive ego display, your extremely weak delivery, and your purposeless content."

I was surprised how smoothly these words rolled off my tongue. Of course, I had said these words a million times in my mind, so I couldn't give myself credit for spontaneity. Unfortunately for him, my words were even more forceful and effective because of the directness of my cadence. I had not said "ah" one time.

The redness around his jowls could be seen. He was trying desperately to handle this young upstart and critic in the most light-hearted way. His problem was that it had been so long since he'd been apparently questioned by anyone. He was used to having followers. He might have been waiting for them to turn around and attack me verbally and possibly physically. The trouble was I did not sound like a nut case. I had asked him a couple simple questions that related to why he and his course even existed at this university. He was trying to overcome the seriousness of the question by denigrating my words to a wild slur about me being some drug-influenced student.

He then took the parental approach. "Ah…..young man …….ah…..I'm doing a……ah…… lecture for my……..ah……. students. If you have a problem……. ah…… maybe you….ah…….. need to see me after……ah……. class."

Then to dismiss me, he said, "Now…….ah……ah……. maybe we can……. ah…… get on with the……ah……. lecture."

I was not to be denied. I realized I had probably already crossed the line, but his condescending response to say nothing of ignoring my direct question had kept my fuse lit. He was trying to make me into the culprit when it was he who was perpetrating the wrong. I was not going to stand for it. He was wasting student's time, parent's money, the university's reputation……and all for the purpose of fondling his own ego.

"Mr. Grant," I said again, "Ask any of your disciples or followers…..whatever you call these people who pamper your ego. What have they learned other than to try and laugh at your so-called humor?'

One young lady particularly agitated over my impolite remarks, spoke up in his defense. Unfortunately her tone was so snotty that her comments sounded even more obsequious.

She declared with eyebrows raised, "Well, if you'd be quiet and listen, you'd hear some very interesting points from Dr. Grant."

I had to laugh. It was not a respectful laugh. I looked at her and said, "Name one,"

She couldn't. She just sat there with her mouth agape holding the most hated look I'd ever seen on someone's face. It was filled with discomfort and embarrassment.

Professor Grant dismissed her attempt at defending him with a disgusting look in her direction. He had apparently expected more from her.

His voice rose. "Young man….ah…….. whatever your name is,……ah……. maybe you should just leave. If you're not getting anything……ah…….ah…. out of my class ……then you shouldn't………ah…….be…….ah …here. Just turn in your paper........ah...... get your grade.........ah......ah....... and move on in your ......ah........ah........questionable college career."

He just couldn't help but put me down. To him I should be dismissed as just a lowly student. His attitude infuriated me. I thought I was done, but his disrespect caused me to continue.

"Mr. Grant, my college education has been going along very well thank you...but, back to my question if you don't mind. I heard rumors that purposeless classes like yours could exist. You've rationalized that your self-professed brilliance is all you need to earn your salary. You don't even try to reach other students in your class. Apparently, you also want everyone to come out of your class with a cynicism towards everything including our country's history. Is that what I'm supposed to be learning? I wonder if you've ever enjoyed or respected anything in your life......besides yourself.

I had gone too far. He was now understandably riled.

His voice boomed, "O. K. ....ah.......that's enough!!!" He pointed to the door. "Out of my class.....ah........ah......out of my class!"

I had definitely crossed the line. His students in the first three rows were now staring at their books or feet. They wished they were anywhere but in that small auditorium. I sensed they knew I was on point, but couldn't admit it...at least not in that classroom.

I got up and marched up the stairs to my original seat. Only the fan from the heating system interrupted the silence in the room. I grabbed my coat and headed for the side exit with Professor Grant staring at me with fire in his eyes and still pointing regally at the door. He was trying to look commanding. Instead he just reminded me of a clown.

Just his posture kept me simmering. It irritated me that he could not respond to my questions about his course. Obviously no one had ever talked that way to him. He was above being questioned or criticized by a student. Now he was speechless. The trouble was that I was anything but wordless. His disrespect towards me as the only way he could defend himself only fueled my contempt towards him. I could feel I wasn't done.

Halfway to the exit, he tried to get the last word. "Young man.....ah....... it's lucky.....ah..... I don't know ......ah.....your name. You could save.....ah..... the time it would take.......ah...... to write a paper."

He was indicating I would flunk his class if he knew my name. Now he had crossed the line! I stopped in my tracks and then went down a couple steps staring directly at him. His eyes got bigger wondering what I was going to say or do next. I was close enough that he could see a renewed fire in my eyes. I'm certain the burn caused my face to flush. I was ready to continue the verbal warfare if Grant wanted it that way.

I panned my eyes to his entourage and then to the few undergraduate students sitting in the upper seats. I bellowed, "Did you hear what he just said? He said he would flunk me if he knew my name. Just because I questioned him about the purpose of his course and the intent of today's lecture, he pulls a power play."

Looking directly at the graduate students and the fourth year history majors with their heads staring blankly down or straight ahead, I added, "Is this the kind of professor you need to coddle in order to get ahead. That's really sad. Good luck to you all."

The last line was said very sarcastically.

Since my last statements weren't directed specifically at the professor, he stood there blubbering trying to find more words to shame me. I went back up the stairs to the side exit and then turned around for my final curtain call. I couldn't resist. He had spoken so condescendingly toward me. I figured it was only fair that I give him a final return volley. I hadn't intended to bring this subject up, but he had shown his arrogance once too much. I was now going to offer him some advice.

As I opened the door to leave, the words I chose came out as smoothly as if I'd practiced them. I said simply, "Oh yes, Mr. Grant, one other thing. I suggest you look into taking a beginners Toastmasters course. My folks did. It might help you like it helped them."

Then I walked out with the door slamming louder than I'd anticipated. 'Fat chance in hell that he even knew of 'Toastmasters' I thought to myself as I marched out of the building.

So…there it was! Game…..Set……Match!! I had not intended to stand up to the professor like I had. But I had done so. And, I was no worse for wear. I had not let that fat oaf intimidate me or dismiss me as a heckler…and I had scored points…in fact, multiple points…but, for what type of contest, I was not certain.

When I walked down the steps of that building towards the nurse's cafeteria, I was exhilarated, but I was also shaking. I was striding along the walkway much faster than normal. The above freezing temperature felt warm after so many weeks of bitter weather. Some sweat was running down the inside of my sweater, but the cooler breeze seemed to balance the heat inside my clothing.

I was so deep in thought I marched right by the cafeteria and continued the five blocks to the house where I lived. I was not overly proud of what I'd just done, but still very contented. Although I thought of a hundred more things I could have said, I was generally satisfied I had handled the confrontation effectively.

Then my mind turned to the possible repercussions I might face. I wondered if he would be able to find out my name. If that were possible, he would undoubtedly flunk me. I was convinced of that. A man with his power base could do that.

I also accepted there was no point in returning to any of his future classes. I could do so to prove how courageous I was. The truth was I wasn't that brave. Besides, I was in his element. He had the advantage. I had caught him during a moment of weakness. It had taken me weeks of frustration to build up my own unexpected explosion. It wasn't something I could turn on and turn off like a light switch. Next time I saw him…if there was a next time…I wouldn't have the same rancor or resentment toward him. I frankly felt general sorrow for those graduate students and those fourth year history students who had to deal with the man day to day. I felt nothing but disrespect for this man who was supposed to be a teacher. Except for an end of the quarter term paper, I was done with the man…forever as far as I was concerned

In the days following that incident in the classroom, I found myself still bothered by the confrontation. It made me neither happy nor sad. However, by the next week after missing the next three of his classes, the trauma of the word battle eased. I found it interesting how so totally inept he was at standing up for himself. He certainly had debated various historical factors throughout his career. I guessed the difference with my combative posture was that my statements had nothing to do with his beliefs or opinions on history. My questions related directly to him personally…the purposes of his class and that day's lecture…and then flowing into what could be interpreted in no other way than my criticism of his overblown ego and his own ghastly delivery getting in the way of his ability to teach anything. I figured with his exaggerated view of his self-worth, even his wife, if he had one, probably wouldn't approach the personal side of his chosen vocation.

I had not returned to Grant's class for five weeks and the end of the quarter was but a week and a half away. It was the middle of March; the wind was cool, but not bitter. The hope of spring was in the air. Jackets were being worn, not parkas, stocking caps, gloves, and scarves. The snow was gone, but one last burst of snow was always being threatened by the local weathermen.

I'd been concentrating on my other five subjects and given little thought to 'Intellectual History'. But, now it was time. I had to complete the damned term paper for Professor Grant's class. Somehow I had to get the assignment. I had to have some idea what to write. I recalled someone who had attended the first two lectures way back in January. I'd seen him before. He was a fellow who'd lived down the hall in my dormitory when we were freshmen. His name was Freddie something. I had no way of contacting him without his last name.

I finally found another dormitory mate back in my freshman year and he helped me with Freddie's last name. It was Browning…not that difficult, but obviously the fellow hadn't left that much of an impression on me. I found his number in the student directory and called him.

When I called, Freddie was apparently studying, but when his roommate shouted my name, he came very promptly to the phone. He seemed surprised but pleased to hear from me. There was a certain excitement in his voice when I inquired about the Intellectual History class and whether he'd been to the class to get the final term paper assignment.

Freddie repeated my question as if trying to remember something so insignificant. He said, "Let's see…have I been to Grant's class recently? Well…. yes, I was there last week…for a while. What a God damned waste of time. I read the morning paper and a portion of another book until that blowhard finally finished his senseless lecture. At the end of the class, he finally gave us the final exam assignment. He said he wanted at least three pages from everyone about how society improved during the fifty years between 1850 and 1900. The final paper is due by Monday of finals week and can be dropped off at the old fart's office. Can you imagine…a three-page paper for a final grade? What a lazy son-of-a-bitch."

I took a deep breath of relief. I could spit out a three-page paper in an hour or two. Even better, I could slip the paper under the door to Grant's office after hours and never have to even come in contact with the man.

I was about to thank Freddie when he came out with a question of his own. "By the way, have you been to his class recently?"

"No," I said. "I couldn't waste the time." I was being truthful. Yet, I knew Freddie brought up the question for a reason. I inquired, "So…why do you ask?"

He seemed pleased that I was curious. "Well, I heard there was some guy who acted up in the peanut gallery…as Grant derisively refers to any rows above eye level in that eerie little auditorium. You had to have attended a few of his classes to have seen how he doesn't even acknowledge the existence of students above that third row elevation. Anyway, from what I heard, some undergrad in that peanut gallery began to give Grant some heat about the purpose of his class… among other things. Grant tried to dismiss the comments, but the kid kept coming at him. Grant got really flustered. It was as if the kid wasn't altogether wrong, but the professor's own arrogance couldn't allow himself to respond appropriately. Instead, he tried to berate the kid insinuating the student was some kind of disruptive pothead. Unfortunately for Grant, the kid was anything but high. He was calm and nailed Grant again and again about what the purpose was of his class and his lecture that day. Grant got so mad he ordered the kid to leave the classroom…and inferred he'd flunk the kid if he ever found out his name. That brought out some more wrath from the student. I tell you, it was a masterpiece of a confrontation….from what I heard."

I didn't let on that I knew anything about what he was talking about, but I couldn't help but show some interest in what transpired. I played dumb and asked, "Freddie, so what became of the kid? Did they drag him out with a police escort?"

"Oh man….hold up, I'm not done. This is the best part. The kid got in a parting shot after Grant blew his lid over the kid's comments. The kid told this University professor he should take a basic Toastmasters public speaking class. Can you believe someone having the testicles to say something like that?"

He was now being reduced to laughter and tears on the other end of the phone. I couldn't help but laugh along with him. For someone who wasn't in attendance that day, he seemed to have gotten the story fairly straight.

As we both recovered, I inquired somewhat nervously, "Freddie, does anyone know who the kid was? Did he ever come back to class?"

Freddie loudly coughed up some mucous trying to get his voice back. He finally spat out, "No, that's another interesting point. The kid was speaking above the main lighting. All the graduate students in the first few rows were sitting with their backs to the kid. None of them turned around. There were only a few other students in the rest of that strange little auditorium. Basically, no one really got a good look at the kid. When he was done with Grant he disappeared out the side exit. He's never been back to that class. I don't blame him. Talk about a guaranteed "F" if Grant ever finds out his name."

I felt my stomach gurgle as I responded, "That's sad that Grant has the power to flunk the kid when that student only asked him to account for the class and the subject of his lecture. That doesn't seem right, does it?"

Freddie only mumbled, "I guess not. But, there's nothing much we can do about it...not with the control of the grade in the hands of that bastard. We can only hope that kid cancelled the class if for no other reason than to preserve his grade point average.

The two of us talked a bit longer, caught up on other people we knew from the previous year's dormitory hall, and finally discussed how we were going to attack the three-page term paper assignment to complete Grant's class.

Upon hanging up with Freddie, I felt better about the aftermath of my confrontation with the professor. The incident was being interpreted accurately for now. However, if the story maintained some life, there would certainly be hyperbole. I was relieved that up until that conversation with Freddie, I had heard nothing about a student's skirmish with Professor Grant. My assumption was that the affair likely died a quick death. Only the few people in that small auditorium had witnessed the fracas and most of them were the graduate students or those fourth year history majors. They weren't about to say a word. They had to stay on the good side of Professor Grant.

I finished the paper over the weekend. Monday was the last day it could be turned in and had to be done so by 5:00 at Grant's office. I had another final that afternoon, so I planned to turn the paper in before I went to my Math final. That time period also coincided with him not having office hours. In no way did I want to have a chance meeting with this man. Still, it was an abnormal week with finals replacing the regular class schedule. He could be in his office grading the term papers already turned into him. That thought bothered me enough that I changed my plans and decided to go over early to his office building Monday morning and just slip the paper in a manila envelope under his office door. I didn't like the cowardly approach, but at that point I just wanted my Intellectual

History class to be over. I had put no real effort into the class, other than the altercation and the two-hour investment of time to complete what I thought was a fairly good three-page term paper.

I was studying Sunday night when one of my roommates answered a surprisingly late phone call. He shouted up the stairs that I had a caller. I ran downstairs hoping it wasn't some kind of emergency. The caller turned out to be Freddie.

His voice was too lively for 11:00 at night. He didn't even say 'hello', but just assumed I'd recognize his voice by his question. "So, you finish your three-pager yet?"

I wasn't trying to be impolite, but my mind was on a business course final for Tuesday. A bit impatiently I answered, "Yeh…is that the only reason you're calling?"

"When you gonna turn it in?"

"I don't know…I was thinking about tomorrow morning…maybe just before my Math final. Why do you ask?"

"I've got some things to do. I was hoping you could turn my paper in to Grant's office at the same time."

I rolled my eyes. Dropping a paper off at some professor's office was not that big a chore. Nonetheless, I patiently nodded, "Sure, Freddie. You drop your paper off at my place and I'll deliver it with mine. How does that sound?"

His voice was strange. He countered, "Nah, I'll give it to you over some coffee. What do you say we meet for coffee tomorrow morning? You've studied enough for whatever test you have coming up. Come on…take a small break. I'll buy the coffee for you delivering my paper."

It sounded like a halfway good idea. I'd need some caffeine anyway in the morning. Nodding I said, "Sure, Freddie, let's meet at MacDonald's down the street from where I live. But I can't spend a lot of time. I can't study enough for this Math final."

Freddie's voice indicated he didn't give two hoots about my Math final. He just answered quickly "O.K., see you tomorrow morning at 8:00 at MacDonald's."

Then he abruptly hung up.

At precisely 8:00 the next morning Freddie came waltzing into MacDonald's. He had a different look…like he had something on his mind. Nonetheless, we jabbered about other things than the three-page papers we were turning in for our quarter grade in the history class. We talked about finals and the NCAA basketball tournament. We conversed about the classes we were taking in the spring quarter. He started talking about some girl he was taking out until I began looking at my watch.

Then there was a slight pause. He looked kind of sheepish as he said, "Hey man, it looks like I have time to drop by that old windbag's office after all. I've got to meet this girl right down the block from Grant's office. We're going to study a bit and hopefully fool around a bit before she has to go to work on campus about noon. I might as well take your paper and turn it in with mine. You can use the extra time to cram a bit more for that final you have this afternoon."

It seemed strange that he was making this offer. It meant we had to walk two blocks back down University Avenue to my house to get my term paper. Frankly, though, I appreciated his idea. Now there would be no chance I'd run into Professor Grant. It was cowardly on my part, but I liked the extra time.

We walked the two blocks back to where I lived near campus. I was relieved. In some ways I felt like I had been in hiding for the past six weeks. Since that classroom clash, I hadn't even walked by the medical building where Grant conducted his so-called class…although I continued having my morning coffee at the nurse's cafeteria a block away.

Freddie took my paper and with no further delay put it in his folder and left. Realizing I was putting a lot of trust in a guy I barely knew, I called after him, "Hey Freddie, call me for Christ's sake so I know you turned in my paper. I just want the assurance."

He responded, "Yeh…yeh…yeh…I'll give you call. Don't worry. I'll take care of everything."

With that pledge, I relaxed. The rest of the day went well. The Math final was difficult as expected, but I was relieved it was over. I then could concentrate on my next big Statistics test where I was pushing an 'A'. The only final test remaining after that was Geology II. I hadn't given a damn about that class and my grade showed it. I had to do reasonably well on the final just to save a 'B'. Once that class was completed I'd have my science requirement out of the way and winter quarter would finally be completed.

That evening I got that call from Freddie as promised. There's always a slight doubt when depending on someone else to do what you should have done yourself…even if it was just delivering a paper to a professor's office.

His first words were, "Guess what…I saw Professor Grant when I handed in our term papers earlier today. I stopped by during his office hours!"

It was the last thing I really wanted to hear. I was immediately exasperated. "You did what!?"

I heard some muffled laughter on the other end of the phone as if he expected my reaction.

I gritted my teeth trying to maintain some patience. "Freddie, why didn't you just put the essays under his door when he wasn't there?"

I was rolling my eyes wishing I had not trusted Freddie. I now expected the worst. I was incensed more than I should have been. "So, tell me what happened."

Freddie became serious…quite out of character. "I'll tell you, man, I did it for a reason. I wanted to see that son-of-a-bitch. He made me mad the way he talked to you that day."

I was suddenly incredulous. My voice turned into a disbelieving whisper. "Freddie, were you really there…in that auditorium that day?

Now his response was more like Freddie. He excitedly replied, "You're damn right I was in that class when you and Grant went at it nose-to-nose. I was sitting behind you up a couple rows. I arrived about fifteen minutes late for the class….as if that mattered. You were working a crossword puzzle. You had no idea I was there when you stood up and took on that fat bastard. Hey man, that was a beautiful sight. I'm proud to know you. It's the best thing I've witnessed since the invention of education. Except for those brown noses sitting down by Grant, there were only seven other people up in that audience who witnessed your performance. You said some things to him that every one of us wished we had the guts to say."

As shocked as I was that Freddie had seen Grant and me go at each other in class, I was more concerned about what Freddie said to the professor earlier that day. I asked him directly, "Freddie, tell me straight up…does he now know my name?"

I heard an evil laugh on the other end of the phone. "Not unless you called him up and introduced yourself."

I wasn't following him. "What do you mean?"

"Well, the seven of us undergraduates up in that audience were enjoying your little battle until we heard him threaten to flunk you for making him come off his high and mighty pedestal. That pissed us off as much as it did you. We got talking and formed a pact a few weeks ago and decided to give you some support for what you said. I volunteered to go face-to-face with that big ass while turning in as many term papers in bulk as we could get a hold of from our fellow undergraduates in that class. That's why I tricked you into letting me turn your paper in along with mine and the others. We didn't want you to have to take the chance of being identified. He could have had one of his graduate student puppets hang around his office hoping to recognize you when you turned in your paper. I wouldn't put it past that old shit to do something like that."

I began to relax. "So Freddie, let me get this straight. You handed Grant your paper, my paper, and six other students' papers…and then beat it on out of there without saying another word. Please tell me that's what happened.

Freddie chuckled again. "Well…no…not exactly. We got a hold of the class roster from the registration office and called as many of our fellow students signed up for that class as possible. They of course had not seen your classroom performance, but more than a few of them had heard about it…and were delighted by it I might add. Anyway, in all I handed in over thirty final papers…but not before I had my say with that old windbag.

I again got kind of uncomfortable. "Freddie, what do you mean, 'you had your say with that man'?

He seemed anxious to respond. "I tell you when I plopped those papers down on his desk I was very prepared…just like you seemed to be when you had it out with Winnie. And, I wanted to be well organized because I was going to be talking on behalf of the ignored undergraduates in that class. I felt responsible to do a good job.

Anyway, Professor Grant looked kind of surprised at my loud entrance and holding a stack of papers in my arms. In an aggravated voice, he said, "Ah….. What's this?"

I looked him as calmly in the eye as you did six weeks ago and said, "These are the final term papers from thirty of the forty undergraduates in your Intellectual History class…you know, the ones you didn't give a shit about throughout the quarter…and the same ones you bored half to death until we didn't come to your class anymore."

Freddie then started to cackle like he'd pulled off something that had gone better than he expected. "Man, I didn't stop there. I told him we all supported every word our fellow undergraduate said to him back in February. Grant then gave me a dark look that only pissed me off more. I told him…and good luck in finding out who I am or who that kid was that stood up to you six weeks ago."

Freddie stopped for a minute to catch his breath. I couldn't believe what I was hearing.

Then he chortled, "I'm not done yet. Wait'll I tell you what I said next. I could see he was turning red and about to explode. I think you've experienced seeing that look. As far as I was concerned he had no right to get so angry. It was his students who were the ones who had the right to be mad as hell. He was about to say something but I snapped. I told him…just for the record, sir, you should be fired. You have no business teaching when you care so little about your students."

Freddie began to hoot as my eyes bugged out. Despite myself, I couldn't help but start chuckling. I finally gasped, "For Christ's sake, Freddie, what was his response?"

Freddie was enjoying drawing out his story. His voice got calm as he replied, "Well, he stood up as if to come at me when I made a step towards him as well. I'll be damned if I was going to let that bastard try to intimidate me. He stopped immediately.

Then I delivered the big blow…the key point I wanted to make. I was prepared. He wasn't. I said to him, 'One additional thing, Mr. Grant, if you grade these papers any differently than you would normally grade other final assignments, I want you to know that three of these thirty students have fathers who are lawyers. Another one has a mother who is a county judge. If you think of getting even with these thirty students by giving us lower grades, you will be served with a defamation suit that we as undergraduates will take to the student newspaper until we can bring your ass to the courtroom or you get dismissed from this University.'

I then turned around ready to exit. I thought I'd said enough. But, I had one more zinger that went back to one of your comments to him. I just couldn't help myself. I said to him…kind of like you did that day in class…'Mr. Grant, ah…. you …..ah …could really use a basic….ah…Toastmaster's class.'

I then walked out. I don't remember him getting in a word."

There was a momentary silence on the phone until we both began to howl. Freddie's giggle turned into an explosion of laughter. We laughed until we were balling. I actually felt badly I hadn't gotten to know Freddie better back at the dormitory. Suddenly I no longer cared what grade I got for 'Intellectual History'. Knowing I had other unknown people in my corner supporting what I had said gave me a great sense of satisfaction and relief. It would be the kind of thing I'd never forget. At least I could say I gained something from that God forsaken class.

When I recovered, I asked Freddie who the lawyers were who would be contacted if we all were flunked or given a grade of "D" by Professor Grant.

Freddie broke up again before saying, "What lawyers? We don't know any lawyers. Who'd have the money to pay them anyway? We also don't know any woman judge. I just said that stuff to rattle his cage. I wanted to see how good a poker player he was. Man, I could clean his wallet in an hour with just average cards."

My laughter was again so hard my side hurt. What Freddie and his band of "Intellectual History" undergraduates had executed was a feat that would stay with them...and me... long after the day we graduated. They had formed a conspiracy to protect me from Grant. They were also putting themselves on the line and making a statement against a truly reprehensible instructor at a much respected university. For him to now carry out a vendetta against me...even if he knew my name...and my other classmates would not be worth the possible controversy or threatened lawsuit...as bogus as that warning by Freddie was.

We talked on for a few minutes promising to get together the next quarter. We would do so that quarter and every quarter until we graduated. Freddie Browning and I indeed became good friends. Before hanging up I thanked him and asked him to express my appreciation to the others in that 'Intellectual History' class....when and if he ever saw them again. That aspect had to be said since fellow students in classes that were electives might not recognize or run by each other at a large university. The other reality was that it had been six weeks since my confrontation with Professor Grant. Most of my fellow undergraduates who were present that day in that class wouldn't necessarily recognize me anymore.

It was a week later that I got my grades. As much as I was hoping for that 'A' in the Math class, I couldn't help but look first for the grade in "Intellectual History". My finger went quickly down the list of six classes. I saw no 'D's'....or any 'C's'...not that I expected any. I saw an 'A-' in Math. I gave a roar over that achievement. Then I saw another 'A'...then another 'A'. It was actually an 'A-' and it was in Intellectual History. I lowered my head in relief. I had been graded fairly by Professor Grant......whether he knew me or not. I thought about the term paper. It had been well written. The paper deserved a good grade. I had stated my points and backed them up with some readings from a text of an AP history course I had taken in high school. I hadn't even bought the voluntary paperback readings for Grant's class. He never referred to them anyway as far as I knew.

The grade did not reduce my disgust for the man. I was still convinced he would have given me a poorer grade had he found out who I was. But, my identity had been protected thanks to Freddie and his wild threat of exposure about Grant's incompetence. The professor must have decided "discretion was the better part of valor" and graded the papers fairly…and maybe even too fairly.

Then again, he may not have been intimidated in the least. Maybe he just did his job and graded the papers impartially as he always supposedly had done. Somehow that latter thought never stayed with me for very long.

The crucial factor on how he had decided to deal with the situation was to let it die. He really didn't have to care what I said or what Freddie had laid on him. Grant had his tenure. Why let a bunch of wild-eyed undergraduates destroy his gravy train. It was nothing to give all those undergraduates a higher grade and be done with them.

If that was his attitude…and it probably was…then he would be right. There would be no follow-up about his ineptness in the classroom. Unfortunately as far as I was concerned, the circumstances no longer interested me. It was out of sight and out of mind. I had escaped Professor Winfield E. Grant's class with an outburst and an 'A-'. Nothing more was going to be done.

Had the story ended right there… in the last days of winter quarter of my sophomore year…it would still have been memorable and a tale to tell often after leaving my college life. The truth is that there was yet another chapter to this tale. In fact the memory of that confrontation lived on not only with me, but I would find out with Professor Grant as well.

I went home at the end of winter quarter with a 3.6 grade point average for my quarterly average. It was my best quarter ever in school…college or high school. I had also gained a girlfriend. I met her at the nurse's cafeteria two weeks after my verbal battle with the professor. Maybe my new found courage had given me more self-confidence. Or, it was just that I had time to talk with her since I wasn't attending Grant's class anymore. All in all, life was good.

Spring quarter would come a week-and-a-half later. It was a far different atmosphere on campus with the warmer spring weather bringing new energy to everyone's college life. I had no classes near that medical building with the cone-shaped auditorium, so I was rarely reminded of the verbal skirmish. I still thought about it though. But, there were other things that took my time including that girlfriend. I finished that quarter with more gangbuster grades. I'd finally figured out how to study in order to make good grades in college.

I returned to school that next fall. Memories of Professor Grant's class for the most part had faded. I had more important thoughts with my upcoming classes and that same girlfriend.

I was now in my third year of college and half way to my undergraduate degree. College life agreed with me. I was in my element. There was nothing that daunted me regarding my scholastic endeavors. The only thing that periodically nagged at me was the realization that I'd be out of school in less than two years. What were my career goals? That year I was generally able to douse that pesky thought with simple procrastination. I had my entire senior year to face that challenge once I saw my business degree as kind of that light at the end of the tunnel.

By happenstance that fall, I had a class one block away from that old medical building where I had taken Intellectual History the previous winter quarter. I was reminded each time I walked to my accounting class of that confrontation with Professor Winfield E. Grant.

With those constant reminders, I couldn't help but be curious about him. Had anything changed? Was he still boring people half to death with his pointless lectures and mind-bending delivery? Did he actually believe he was educating his students? Did it matter to him?

I guess most of all I wondered if he remembered that confrontation he'd had with that certain undergraduate nine months before. Had my comments had any effect on him? Each time I thought about that question, I scoffed at myself. Did I really believe I could influence a tenured teacher who had an ego the size of the football stadium?

It was a Tuesday in late October, about halfway through the fall quarter when I was again walking by the medical building. I'd had a meeting with a professor in one of my business courses. It was not the usual time I would pass by that building. It was about 10:30. I began to think.........the timing would be about midway through one of Grant's lectures if his class was still being held in that same small auditorium.

It was totally unplanned, but I found myself strolling down the hall of that old university building. I wasn't certain why I was heading toward that classroom. I do know that I had a very deep-seeded inquisitiveness.

The entrance to the small auditorium was straight ahead. I recalled the door was halfway up the amphitheater. It was the perfect inconspicuous exit for students to slip out of the class without interrupting the instructor.

For the hell of it, I decided to go into the class. Grant wouldn't be noticing any interruption that high up in the cone-shaped auditorium anyway. I figured there would be plenty of seats. As I opened the door, I felt like I was stepping into the past. Not surprisingly I had the sensation of that moment not necessarily being one that I wanted to revisit. But, I entered the theatre-type classroom anyway.

It was truly strange striding into that unique little auditorium. It was smaller than I'd remembered. Furthermore, it just didn't feel that long ago that I'd been in his class. In fact the last time I had set foot in the building…in fact that very classroom… was the very day of my confrontation with Professor Grant nine months before.

I walked in and looked down toward the podium below. I couldn't believe it. Class was in session and there was Professor Grant. It truly was as if time had stood still. He was wearing some ridiculous hat. I rolled my eyes thinking he was apparently lampooning some respected historic leader. The classroom make up was the same. There were the graduate students hanging onto his every word sitting in those seats closest to the podium. They could have been the same graduate students, but for their sake, I hoped they weren't.

There were about thirty or forty other students spread around the remaining two hundred seats in that auditorium. It occurred to me that in my class, there had been only seven or eight students who continued to come to Grant's class after the second week. I was surprised by the turn out that day.

As for the professor, he was in some pioneer person's character pontificating about something. His speech seemed to be smoother, but still blanketed with a number of "ah's". Breaking that habit at his age would probably never happen…….. unless he would take the time to care and improve his diction.

I shouldn't have done it, but I wanted to remind him that he should care. I quietly walked down to the seventh row.….the very row where I sat when we began our shouting match. I went over specifically to the center seat and silently sat down. No one noticed me…except for one person. That person was Professor Grant. He kept his little performance going, but I could tell he was eyeing me… as if he was reliving a nightmare. Lightning was never supposed to strike in the same place, but it was happening to him.

I sat there quietly and tried to be innocuous, but I could sense he remembered me as much as he probably didn't want that memory. Also, on that day in that classroom, I wasn't one of his students. He had no power over me. He had to ask himself why I was there. The flashback had to be making him very uncomfortable.

But, to his credit he continued his performance. In those next minutes, he kept glancing at me unsure if I was that same student. He probably couldn't remember my face anyway. The way I wore my baseball cap so low over my face also made it difficult. Nonetheless, the fact that I was sitting in that same chair in the seventh row, I knew he was inclined to think I was that same undergraduate. I guess that was what I wanted him to believe.

I was about to leave, when he stopped and looked up into the amphitheater at the thirty or forty undergraduate students and left his memorized script. He said to them, "Now, young heads, remember….ah…. when I parody Abraham Lincoln…ah…I am simply giving you the thoughts of the opposing political party…ah…ah… as well as the…ah…state's rights people in the South at the time. When you…ah…read about his administration and…ah… what he had to do to keep our…ah… government afloat while the country was…ah… split…..you'll appreciate the leadership this…ah… man had to display…..though highly questionable…ah…. in some of the actions he…ah…employed…ah…during his administration. In your first of …ah…two assignments….ah… this quarter, I'll want you to write…ah….on whether you agree or not with his methods…ah… as President from 1861 to 1865. Please…ah…drop the three…ah…ah… or four page paper off…ah… at my office…ah… by Thursday of next week."

There were some barely discernible moans coming from the students. They had not wanted to get an assignment. Their reactions were highly expected.

Professor Grant then went ahead with the remainder of his lecture. I got up as noiselessly as I could to leave. I noted that little assignment was given to the undergraduate part of his class right in the middle of his lecture, not at the end of the hour and fifteen minute class as would be more typical. This professor had actually instituted a change in his class that fall quarter and required a mid-term paper as well as an end of the quarter final term paper.

I tried to remain modest, but he'd felt compelled to hand out that assignment right at that point in time, while I was sitting there. I actually felt complimented that I might have caused some small change in the methods of a very headstrong instructor. It was probably just my imagination, but he'd never acknowledged the undergraduates in the classroom after the first day of class when I was his student. I was impressed with his use of the phrase 'young heads'. That didn't come across as condescending or pejorative. In fact, his tone was more endearing. He had no sneer on his face when he looked up the semi-circled rows at them. That was the real change.

I silently climbed the few steps to the exit so as not to disturb the hesitant cadence of the Professor's drone. His speaking style would always be a problem for me, but at least he was showing that he cared about his teaching responsibilities by bringing the undergraduates into the fold of the class. The assignment and the lecture, as far as I could deduce, seemed to have more purpose. He didn't have such a pompous delivery expecting guffaws with his every sentence. Those in attendance would learn something if they invested some attention, as difficult as it was to listen to him…along with some extra reading and study time on the course. When I had confronted him, my frustration level had been so high. All I was seeking was a worthwhile class where I might learn something. Tragically, I had not learned a thing. It seemed as if his changes in that fall quarter class gave his students some chance of learning.

Before leaving the small auditorium, I turned at the exit door and looked back at him. He kept right on speaking in his unique style. Yet, something happened that further surprised me. I swore I saw him give me a slight wave as I left. It was not dismissive. It actually looked and felt like he had offered it as a friendly gesture. I was shocked. I hesitated…and then I subtly returned the wave. A couple undergraduates looked at me like they wondered what I was doing entering and exiting the class so quickly. They had seen the almost imperceptible exchange between the professor and me. They must have thought I might be a friend of Professor Grant.

I then exited quietly and strolled down the hall to the outside doors. It was a beautiful autumn morning on the University campus. My faith was slightly restored. A professor was showing me he'd given some thought to the gist of our classroom confrontation....maybe more than once.....and he'd made some adjustments. Had I not seen the wave, I might have felt I was flattering myself. I honestly felt like I'd seen some change...some purpose to his class. The fact that there were more students attending his class halfway through the quarter gave further credence. Whether our confrontation had broken through his egotistical wall, that possibility would never be something I could evaluate....nor did I have any desire to do so. But, I knew this... by acknowledging his undergraduates in that classroom, that action alone showed him to have more consideration for all the students in that small auditorium.

My curiosity never ceased. I found myself going into his class midway through the next quarter...as well as the final four quarters of my college career. I entered his old medical building amphitheater only once each quarter, usually in the middle of the term precisely in the middle of his scheduled lecture. Each time I quietly slipped into the seat in the seventh row in front of the podium. Within minutes, he would notice me. Over time he might have recognized the low brimmed baseball cap. I wore it that way purposefully each time, so he wouldn't get an easy fix on my face.

I found that within five minutes of my entering his lecture hall, he'd declare the purpose or repeat the key points of his lecture up to that moment. One time he stopped his lecture to discuss educational benefits of the written assignments he had given his undergraduates the week before. Another time he repeated something he must have told his undergraduates during a previous class. Some of the undergraduates looked at each other like "why is the Professor saying this again?"

Each time I only stayed for no more than ten minutes. Then I quietly...always quietly...slipped out of my seat to exit. Each time I stopped and looked back at him before leaving. Now the acknowledgement was no longer subtle. He would give me a short wave and a nod. With some budding respect, I would return the wave and nod. Then I would exit quietly the small auditorium while he continued his work. We never saw each other on campus other than those few times in his class.

After I graduated I rarely got on campus other than to occasionally attend sporting events or cultural functions. I never saw him again. But, to be sure, whenever the matter of my college days entered my mind, the first thing I thought about was my unexpected confrontation with Professor Winfield E. Grant. Again, I might be deluding myself, but based on what I saw each quarter when I stopped by one of his classes, I sensed he remembered with great clarity our verbal altercation.

The last of his classes I visited was in the last quarter of my senior year...
over two years since we'd clashed. No longer were there seven or eight bored
undergraduates. I counted as many as seventy additional students in that
amphitheater besides those graduate students who still occupied the first three
rows around the podium. I have to admit I felt good...for him. Word must have
spread that his course had some worth.

As the years drifted along and I was entrenched in my own career, I had occasion
to meet some recent University graduates at various functions my firm supported.
I'd invariably ask them if they knew of or attended Professor Winfield E. Grant's
Intellectual History class. Some actually had. I invariably asked them a leading
question about the class size fully expecting them to describe how the class size
declined as the weeks progressed through the quarter.

Actually that response never materialized. Those former students failed
to pick up on what I was implying. One young person commented, 'Oh yes,
Professor Grant had a strange speaking style, but you always felt part of his class.
He invited students in the upper tier of the small auditorium to come closer to
the podium so they could be more involved in his lecture and any discussion.
He had this group of graduate students sitting down in the first few rows close
to his podium, but they never said too much. He seemed to get more delight
whenever the undergraduates came closer and raised their hands with questions
or thoughts. He often asked students to raise their hands 'yay' or 'nay' on some
controversial issue he was covering. Then he'd ask students why they thought as
they did. His class was kind of fun. I remember many subjects he covered in that
class to this day. Frankly, I don't believe I missed many of his classes. Besides,
it was important to attend his classes. The final 'test' covered the subjects we
discussed during his lectures."

I recall some twelve years since my own undergraduate years that I learned
from yet another recent University graduate that Professor Grant's Intellectual
History class had become quite popular. In fact, I was told his classes had become
a preferred elective and began to close early during registration.

Admittedly, I found myself feeling good for the professor. He'd made some
changes and created more energy and learning in that small amphitheater. His
class had obviously improved far beyond the atmosphere that had caused our
little battle scene so many years before. Whether I was a possible catalyst or
Freddie and my other classmates taking the stand they did against him, he must
have had some kind of epiphany to transform his entire attitude about how he
approached his job. He had to be feeling the same displeasure in his classroom
his students generally felt. And, something caused the inspiration for him to
change his teaching methods.

I have to admit I do feel I was part of his makeover. I felt gratified any time I heard some young former students describe how this man seemed to truly enjoy his classes and the discussion points from some of his 'young heads' in his classes.

It was some twenty years after my college experience had ended that I learned Professor Winfield Grant had retired. That word came from a client's son I saw during intermission during a concert at Orchestra Hall in downtown Minneapolis. I remember returning to my seat and thinking about the professor. I closed my eyes imagining Grant down on that small stage in that old medical building theatre delivering one of his lectures wearing one of his weird hats depicting some historical figure. I wondered if he would find himself ever staring at the center seat in the seventh row.......... about midway through the quarter......... and remembering that altercation he had with that young undergraduate. Then later would he remember a visitor once each quarter who stopped by his class... with a baseball cap on...and who sat for only a few minutes during his lecture. Would that remind him how he would invariably interrupt his own lecture and refer to some ideas that might help his undergraduates with an assignment he'd given them or clarify a point he was trying to make in his lecture.

I chuckled as I remembered the sound of the predictable moans from those undergraduates when he referred to the assignment. Despite that reaction, Professor Grant had to have felt a better sense of gratification for bringing more purpose to his class. At least, I wanted to think he did.

As the patrons in Orchestra Hall slid by my seat in anticipation of the curtain opening once again, I slid back into my dream visualizing Grant behind that podium with his graduate students surrounding him during his lecture. Now, however, I envisioned the many undergraduates now seated closer to the podium in anticipation of some of the thought-provoking interchanges he was going to have with all his students. I imagined as he exited the amphitheater behind the stage after a particularly good class he would at times gaze back toward the seats and look almost mystically up into the small auditorium. Would he see the ghost of a former dissatisfied student standing alone in the seventh row now politely applauding his effort that day?

It should be said that he wasn't the only one who took something away from that skirmish we had so many years before. I'd learned from it. Youthful ideals and impatience had made me blow up at that time. I never publicly did anything like that again...even if tempted. I had thought through that situation and determined that in my business career I'd strived to handle my frustrations more professionally. If I have a bone to pick with someone, the image of that scene in Grant's classroom simmers me down. Then I handle that disagreement or dissatisfaction later in private with that individual.

Still, back then I didn't have the experience or credibility...or the intestinal fortitude to approach the professor privately. If I had, it would not have worked. I've always believed my abrupt action was the only way I could have gotten through the core of Grant's enormous ego. My outburst, though unwise, was effective at that one time and place. The same could probably be said for Freddie's actions along with the support of our classmates at the end of that winter quarter as well.

I have never boasted of my confrontation with the professor. There would be no point. I couldn't really prove the result of my agitated eruption was the primary reason for the changes he imparted in his lectures, his classroom management, or even his own attitude as a teacher. But, deep down, I just believed.....and still do....... that I had some impact.

It has been many years since his retirement and I still think about that incident. I envision how I wished I had taken one Tuesday or Thursday morning off from work and driven over to my former university during the last quarter that Professor Grant would lead that class on Intellectual History. Oh how nostalgic that would have been to drop by that old medical building at approximately 10:30 and attend his class in that ancient small, cone-shaped auditorium.

The classroom would be still vivid in my mind. There would be more undergraduates in the class and they'd be taking up more seats closer to the podium. Professor Grant would be wearing some kind of hat of a person in the era pertaining to his lecture. Students would be sitting forward listening closely in case he asked for their thoughts. I would walk into that small auditorium in my business suit no longer sporting the baseball cap I so favored during my college years. He wouldn't notice me at first because I could no longer step down to the seventh row and slip unnoticed into a center seat. That row and the many rows above it would be occupied. Instead I would seek the center seat in the more open twelfth row. I would quietly slip by two irritated students on either side wondering why this businessman was interrupting their concentration.

Then he would see me. He would look slightly older with his hair more gray and his glasses no longer a prop for one of his characters. And, he would recognize me despite no baseball cap and in my business suit. A slight smile would form as he continued talking. The memory of our confrontation so many years before would be recalled in both of our minds at that moment.

In the next minute he would interrupt his lecture just to clarify to his class the purpose of that day's lecture.....or to repeat the purpose of the term paper assigned to the undergraduates. Mention of the assignment would produce that expected sigh amongst the undergraduate students. They hadn't wanted to be reminded of that task.

I would listen to his lecture for a short time; then as unobtrusively as possible I'd get up to leave by the side door. Before exiting, I'd stop and turn toward the podium. He'd already be waving and smiling...not even subtly... while continuing to speak to his class. While leaving, I would smile... respectfully... and wave respectfully back at him.

Sammy's Last Golf Ball

It was a Monday in the middle of the summer…typically the slowest, dullest day of the long hot week yet to come. I was still a kid…thirteen years old… but already thinking I was smarter than most adults…not all, but most… in my small, rural community. It was the third straight summer where the local municipal golf course was my home away from home. It often seemed like I was further from my house at that golf course than I really was giving me a true feeling of independence. The golf course was on the north end of town in a valley with a river flowing along it that eventually would flow into the more primary Minnesota River. To me that place was heavenly…but the scenery wasn't the reason I invested so much of my youth there.

I was drawn to the local golf course for a number of factors. The most conclusive ones tended to be the opportunity to enjoy a sense of freedom, to learn how to deal in the adult world, and to appreciate the results of working determinedly on my golf game. It was also where I made my spending money. In fact, that golf course would continue to be a kind of training ground for life until I left town for college. And, I loved every day of it…even those slow, dull Mondays.

To most people it might seem each day would have been too repetitive. Funny how that thought or feeling never entered my mind. For me each day offered a new blank scorecard. Whether I won or lost the previous day, I had the opportunity to compete and face challenges all over again the very next day. I couldn't rest on my laurels nor could I remain too angry if I'd played too poorly. I loved the competition against my friends…and even adults who had become friends. In fact, I played golf often with adults, especially on the weekends. Age simply didn't matter as long as a kid knew the rules and showed proper behavior on the golf course.

Regarding the money making opportunities, there were the normal caddy jobs that guaranteed a dollar for nine holes. However, it was the games of chance out on the golf course playing with friends that offered the most enjoyment and a better payout. Caddying slipped to a weak second place as my golf game improved each summer. My friends and I gambled with dimes and quarters from the time we first started playing golf and graduated to dollars by our last years of high school. Many adults were initially skittish about playing a kid for money. I found the more I won, the more willing they were to wager since they rationalized they would only be retrieving back some of their past losses…if, of course, they could beat me.

Still, I'd have to admit there were similarities to certain days at the golf course…particularly Mondays. After a busy weekend, the golf course was usually under some kind of repair that day. Adults were back at work. The sprinklers were watering the fairways. The greens were being cut. The sand traps had to be re-raked and smoothed. The only real players that day would be junior golfers… many of which were there because it was proclaimed junior day. Too many young golfers were out there because they could find nothing better to do. It was an attitude to which I couldn't relate.

It was already hot and humid about 8:30 that Monday morning as I was biking to the golf course. The accelerated heat would mean the golf course would be devoid of those young non-committed golfers…especially that late in the summer golf season. The number of those hypothetical young golfers had declined noticeably by late July. They complained about getting sunburned or being too tired on Monday to play.

By August the only youths really playing golf were my immediate friends and me. We would have the golf course to ourselves for most of the day until a few adults showed up in the late afternoon. If ever there was a day at my hometown golf course where I would have bet nothing special might happen it would have been on a slow Monday.

As for me, I always looked forward to that first day of the week. Every Monday morning, I had my regular group…just like so many men did on Friday afternoons or Saturday mornings. There were four of us who always played golf together on Monday come rain or shine…and only interrupted by the start of the school year in the fall.

Two of the guys didn't play every day like my friend Sammy Wright and I did. Apparently they had other facets to their lives that maintained their interest. Or, they just liked to sleep in on the other weekdays. As for Sammy and me, we played golf together on each Monday morning…and Tuesday morning…and Wednesday morning…and so on…unless we had a Little League baseball game. That took precedent even over golf and really only delayed our tee time. If we couldn't make it out to the golf course until noon, it didn't ruin our day.

On the weekends it was still the two of us sitting around the practice green both mornings waiting to find an adult who didn't mind playing with two kids… or caddy if the opportunity arose.

That Monday morning Carl Sanford and Duane 'Dewey' Brown could always be counted on to join us for what we all understood would be at least thirty-six holes of golf. However, we never limited ourselves to only that number of holes. As for the other weekdays, sometimes Carl and Dewey would join us for golf and other times we wouldn't see them. What either of them did the other mornings didn't seem important and was rarely discussed. Sammy and I just couldn't believe Carl and Dewey had other past times that limited their exposure to our beautiful little nine-hole municipal golf course.

As Sammy said, "It's their loss."

As for Sammy, he and I had been friends for a long time…since we were nine years old. By kid's standards that was a long time…almost 25% of our lives. I don't know why we didn't know each other prior to that age. He lived a couple blocks away. I guess our paths didn't cross much until we got out of the fourth grade and found that we both really liked to play sports, especially golf.

In looking back it was kind of surprising how we were attracted to that particular sport at such a young age. We liked baseball, basketball, and football as well. However, in golf we didn't have to round up a bunch of other kids to play. We just grabbed our golf bags and rode our bikes to the golf course a mile away and teed off. Rarely were there any interruptions with other golfers on the weekday mornings. Even the afternoons weren't that busy…except for Wednesday's men's day and Thursday's ladies day. All other times, we just golfed. No tee time was needed.

We started playing the game at the same time. It took until Carl and Dewey were eleven years old before they joined Sammy and me a couple days a week on the links. The four of us always competed…always for money…even if it was just for a dime on nine holes. In those younger years we may have been on a team that beat the other one in some another sport, but once on the golf course that other victory or defeat was forgotten. The golf course seemed to be the only true one-on-one test where the result could prove who was the better player…at least until we teed it up for the next round of golf. As the years passed, possibly more than any other activity or sport we participated in, we learned more things about ourselves in how we handled the pressure to win and deal with those losses whenever they occurred. In golf every day there was winning and losing… multiple times. And, not to make it sound so serious, mostly I recall more the laughs than any stress or anger after losing.

I think often of those days. The memories of Sammy, Carl, and Dewey…and of the many other people old and young with whom I played golf. I also recall the times I spent at that golf course alone on the local links… lost in my thoughts whether looking for other players' lost golf balls along the river, hitting practice balls into the blue skies with only the wind, squirrels and birds as my witnesses, or simply just playing a round of golf by myself hitting every shot in earnest even though it really didn't matter what I scored.

Invariably in these recollections, the image of my friend Sammy always seems to emerge since he was at the golf course almost as much as I was. During the summers of my youth I probably spent more time with him than I did with my own family. Besides wanting to beat each other every time we played, I recall how easily we laughed and how hilarious we found each other's comments.

There was also something else quite entertaining about Sammy. Everything seemed to happen to him…and too often it seemed or could be interpreted as bad or unlucky. Anyway, that was the way he perceived what was happening in his life. It got so I believed him. I saw plenty of examples. What made him likeable was how he could recover from disaster faster than anyone I'd ever met. It was as if he expected these dire calamities and therefore dealt with them as if they were commonplace. Whether it was the bull snake that struck at him as he laid down his golf bag on the fairway, the breaking of his putter on the practice green in anger before he even teed off that particular morning, the bee that stung him when there were six other guys surrounding him that could have been stung, invariably not getting his candy bar or soda pop after putting coins in a machine, or the complete coincidence of his golf bag strap breaking while carrying his bag at the furthest point from the clubhouse….these occurrences were all just a few of the minor incidents that seemed to constantly happen to my friend, Sammy.

It took someone like Sammy not to see that large bull snake, or having to putt with his three-iron with his broken putter resting uselessly in his golf bag, or having to carry his golf bag on top of his shoulder…like a soldier marching with his rifle…for the remainder of that golfing day after his golf bag strap had snapped. Not only do straps typically not break, but a golfer would likely quit playing, rent a pull cart for the next nine holes, or do most anything else rather than lug a broken golf bag around a golf course in that military manner. But, not Sammy.

Let there be no doubt that Sammy would kick up a storm about each incident before reckoning with it. However, he'd recover. By the next morning he'd gotten money from his folks to buy a new bag, a new putter, or more candy and pop. Maybe that was why I enjoyed Sammy so much. Though he was wailing about his innumerable adversities, he was laughing inside. No problem was that big. Besides, given the number of strange encounters in his life, he also made me feel that my life was thankfully more above average.

Anyway, on that humid July morning, the four of us arrived on our bikes ready for a day of golf at our usual 9:00 starting time. Mondays seemed to start off slower than any other day of the week, so our tee time wasn't precise. It wasn't as if there were other golfers waiting impatiently for the tee box.

Dewey lived the closest to the municipal golf course…about a block away… so naturally he was the last of our foursome to arrive. Sammy and I had gotten to the golf course a half hour early to warm up and practice our putting. The difference between the two of us was that I actually practiced. My friend Sammy parked himself on a bench by the practice green with no intention to lift a club until we were all ready to tee off. Instead he was more interested in telling me of something that had happened to him between the times we departed the golf course the previous evening and yet that morning. It might have been a TV show he'd seen…or maybe something one of his parents had said. Those early morning stories weren't always the most spellbinding.

Carl showed up usually ten minutes before we were to tee off and would warm up briskly while Sammy remained on the bench munching on a candy bar he'd brought from home. It was one of his typical breakfasts…a Snickers bar. That morning Carl arrived on cue and was ready to play with ten quick practice swings and a couple practice putts.

We were already on the tee box when Dewey slid off his bike while it was still moving with his golf bag slung over his shoulder. It was a rather agile move for someone of Dewey's girth. He was a bit overweight for his size and not known for his athleticism. Without a hesitation in his movement, he began walking towards us as his bicycle continued riderless until it slowed and fell into a taller grassy area alongside the practice green. If mistimed the bike often hit a tree before stopping. He paid no heed to either result. The only important factor to him was that the bike would be in that general vicinity when he finally chose to go home.

He never had much to say in the way of greetings on those Monday mornings since he'd only gotten out of bed within the past five minutes. Besides, he'd seen us the day before…and the day before that. To say 'good morning' seemed a bit unnecessary and even superfluous. His only comment after swallowing his last bite of toast was to simply inquire, "Same bet?"

His question about the wager was really not a question, but a statement. Unless something miraculous had happened over the weekend…like one of us coming into some real money… we'd be competing against each other for twenty-five cents apiece. There was a chance to lose seventy-five cents if all three matches were lost during that nine-hole match. However, there would be other bets made to try to balance a foreseeable loss. Therefore, what started as a relatively innocent wager could turn into more money as the round of golf progressed…possibly as much as a dollar won or lost by one golfer!

Dewey's 'same bet' comment typified our feelings that morning. There was no reason to believe that day would be any different than any other of the infinite number of days we'd all played together. We were all twelve or thirteen years old and golfing veterans of two or three years. While Dewey and Carl didn't play nearly the number of rounds of golf as Sammy and I played each summer, they had enough skill to be competitive…and certainly knew a good wager from a bad one.

Regarding the two or three years of links experience, that factor was mighty important as it related to our being accepted at the local golf club. Our undisciplined, but effective golf swings had become more consistent over time. Our comportment on the golf course had also improved. That was important. Without proper behavior and knowledge of the rules of the game, we wouldn't be invited to play along with adults when it was necessary to play with them on the weekends. Our acceptable conduct had thereby resulted in all four of us being considered a few years older than we actually were. Weekends we were always at our best…showing good sportsmanship, being sickly polite, discussing our knowledge of the golf swing with some adults, helping those adults with horrifically poor golf swings, and muffling our laughter after an adult exploded in foul language after a bad shot.

We even played adults for a little money. When we won… which was most of the time…we were paid. When we occasionally lost, the adult would feel so guilty he'd buy us a candy bar and pop with the money we lost. Losing didn't happen often because as kids we knew how to negotiate with the adults. Playing adults for money was a con game and easy money. We'd ask for too many shots or not give away enough shots to a really lousy adult golfer. Either way, most matches were won before we teed off. Sammy and I seemed to know the skill level of all local golfers who came onto our little 'playground'.

Maybe that was also why 'Mondays' were so relaxed. We could let down our façade of acting so mature and get back to being our regular selves in both behavior and language. We weren't completely undisciplined. Needling each other was expected, however, we still could be downright sincere when complimenting one another on a good shot. Sportsmanship was mostly practiced, but it could waver depending on the circumstances in our competitions. While we stayed quiet when each of us was hitting, we were just as apt to break into uncontrolled laughter as offer condolences after a poor or unlucky shot was played. When one of us let go with a flood of swear words or threw a club…something we'd never do on the weekends with adults…the others in the group would fold up in laughter.

Despite all our flagrant immaturity, we did adhere to the rules of golf with more regard than the Ten Commandments. That comparison might not be that noteworthy since there are many more rules of golf than commandments. Besides, we couldn't relate to all the commandments at our age. The numerous golf rules were far easier to remember and heed.

Back on the tee box that morning, it was cooler than normal as we got our game faces on and ready to take our first shots. We were dressed for a very hot day with shorts, various collarless t-shirts, and tennis shoes. Each one of us inspected our golf ball supply in order to choose the best ball to carry out our quest for victory in the coming round.

We didn't notice but Sammy was scrounging into the bottom of his bag apparently trying to find the right ball. We didn't know it at the time, but his choices were limited. One of the three of us should have noticed his growing consternation. After all, we knew this kid better than anyone but his parents… maybe better. I might add that statement was true for each of the four of us. We could put on airs even with our own parents, but not each other.

Maybe it was the peaceful morning. Maybe it was because Carl, Dewey, and I were still a bit sleepy. Or maybe we just didn't expect some calamity to begin brewing for our friend Sammy with the week barely underway.

We should have been more alert. That morning he became very quiet as he prepared for his first shot of the day. That should have been a warning sign.

Sammy always seemed to be the center of attention no matter where we were. He took the most kidding…and fed it back to us. There were always anticipated laughs with him. When he was serious he was funny. When he was angry or frustrated he was especially funny. That morning he seemed preoccupied. He'd usually already be talking as he got ready to hit his first tee shot. It was purposeless chatter, but it always produced snickers or wise comments from the three of us. But, his friendly babble would end with one poorly played shot... which didn't take long. It would be just a matter of time before he mishit a shot to the green, hit the only tree on the fairway, put a slice in his new golf ball with a poor swing...or miss a crucial putt. Then his mood would get foul. His whining would vibrate with profanity and despair. Poor shots would be blamed on everything and everyone but himself. By then, he was at his most entertaining.

Never did he take our jesting as disrespectful or unfriendly. We certainly didn't intend it that way. It did sometimes make me wonder why he didn't. Sammy would let the joking remarks fall off his shoulders like unseen dust. It was remarkable the way he could laugh at himself. And, when not in the mood to laugh after a series of bad shots, his responses to our sarcasm were hilarious enough that he had to break up in laughter as well.

He was funny everywhere...but he was at his funniest when at the golf course. There his misfortunes and disasters were so numerous, so expected and so visible. It could be watching a ball bounce into a hazard or the bird landing a turd on his shoulder or being short of the cup on a foot-and-a-half length putt. Whatever the unfortunate occurrence, it always seemed so normal that it was happening to Sammy.

While getting ready to tee off, Carl, Dewey and I got into an animated conversation about the previous day's Minnesota Twins victory. Typically Sammy would join in on that discussion. With us not paying attention to his anguish, he finally blurted out, "Holy shit, I forgot to bring some more golf balls from home. I only got four balls left in my bag to play with today!"

The three of us couldn't immediately see the problem. Four golf balls were always enough to keep any of us supplied for a day of golf. Then he brought out his small remaining collection for our view... and we winced. Two of the golf balls were white but needed to be washed and another one was more permanently brown than white. It looked older than the four of us combined. His last ball was stained as well but showed a more yellow color. It had a red strip around the middle with the logo 'Range' printed on it. Since our golf course didn't have a 'range' to hit practice shots, it meant that Sammy must have 'acquired' that ball from some other golf course's practice range. Upon closer inspection, the brownish ball had a deep gash in it. It looked fatally injured. The yellowish ball had no cuts in it, but didn't appear round. It likely had been hit so often at a practice range that it no longer could roll straight. Both the brown ball and the yellow one showed enough wear and age to be termed 'unfit' for play. With a cracked cover and no bounce, it would be a waste of time to play with either golf ball. They might fly half as far as an average golf ball and trying to make a putt with either ball would be frustrating if not futile.

What this all meant was that Sammy had but two legitimate golf balls to play with that day. We all knew that minimum number may not be enough for him to complete our day of golf. Frankly it was a fate Carl, Dewey, and I didn't want to ponder. We couldn't imagine being in Sammy's predicament. On the other hand it came as no surprise that Sammy had put himself in this situation.

The three of us retreated from our friend as if he had some kind of disease. Deep down we knew he was in for a trying day on the links. With such a short supply of golf balls, it meant he'd probably have to play more conservatively. Of course Sammy's golf game was not sophisticated enough to have any other classification than 'wild'. It was also not lost on us the possibility of the day getting really funny if he had to resort to playing with the brown or the yellow golf ball.

Sammy finally placed the best of his four golf balls on a tee and proceeded to take a couple golf swings to warm up. Practicing was not one of his favorite pastimes, so it might come as no surprise that our friend's swing was a bit loose. The manner in which he swung typically made his shots not just curve to the right but slice violently in that direction. Habitually, he'd have to aim far left to make room for his ball to curve back onto the fairway. Therefore, on the first hole with the roadway passing by the golf course on the left into the city park, cars or human beings walking along the road would potentially be threatened with Sammy on the tee box. The three of us had seen him play this shot so often we no longer gasped when we saw how far left he was targeted.

With but two playable golf balls and Sam's penchant for catastrophe, Carl, Dewey and I should have suspected his day was already heading down a disastrous path. When Sammy launched that first hit of his day, the direction and trajectory of his golf ball started out like any other opening drive. However, that morning when the ball took off left over the roadway, it failed to slice back onto the fairway. We all watched in horror as the best of his four golf balls began skipping down the road before disappearing over a steep embankment down into the city park below. My initial feeling was one of competitive satisfaction. With the out-of-bounds penalty I was going to be at least two strokes ahead of at least one of my opponents. With Sammy, it meant the bet would be doubled very soon.

Letting go with a few choice words pointed at an unjust God as the ball was in flight, his language changed to a volley of invectives describing waste material as his golf ball skipped over that cliff. Carl, Dewey, and I stood there not saying a word as Sammy was slamming his club at the ground. None of us were the least bit concerned by his behavior. In fact, we were rather enjoying the moment. It was just Sammy being his usual self.

He collected himself and while still muttering some choice expletives, he teed up his second ball and lashed at it not even considering the golf ball might take the same path as his first shot. Similarly, the ball took off again over the roadway with all of our eyes in rapt attention. We all, especially Sammy, held our breath until the ball mercifully began curving sharply to the right bringing it back over the out-of-bound stakes and back onto the golf course. Life was back to normal.

But, was it? Instead of him beginning to talk about some inane topic or another girl he liked as we left the tee box, he grabbed his golf bag, slammed his driver into the bag and walked alone continuing his blue streak of colorful language. There was a new pressure on our friend. He was flabbergasted that he could hit his best golf ball down into the buffalo pen in the city park…and then follow that swing with a shot so ugly he didn't want to claim it.

We all thought he'd be thrilled to have his second ball on the fairway even if he was laying three strokes. It was unlike him to show such fury so early in the round. That was when Carl, Dewey, and I eyed each other with big grins. With one decent golf ball left in his arsenal and two golf balls barely qualified as playable, Sammy was already in a bad mood and the day had just begun. We all suddenly had a collective feeling we were in for a treat that day. We just had no idea how big that treat was going to be.

Had there been any doubt whether Sammy was in a foul mood, it was immediately undisputed when he turned towards us and started on one of his rampages. He cried out, "The God damned greenskeeper…he set the tee markers so they were aimed wrong. He caused me to aim too far left. That old shit should be fired!"

What Sammy of course failed to consider was that the three of us had hit our golf balls between the same tee markers and our drives ended up right down the middle of the fairway. We made that factor abundantly clear as we teased him while walking toward our golf balls. Carl also brought up Sammy's failure to warm up. Dewey taunted him about forgetting to bring more golf balls from home. I simply went with a disparaging remark telling him he was just being a grumpy old turd. I wasn't at my most creative that early in the morning.

Sammy listened to us and couldn't help but chuckle. He then walked away from us with a slight smile towards his penalized second drive mumbling something about the legitimacy of our births. That statement brought us some satisfaction. It was difficult for Sammy to remain enraged. Fulfilling our purpose as his friends, we had kidded him out of his initial poor mood. If it was a typical day, he'd be joining our conversation about the Minnesota Twins after hitting his next shot.

Our anger over a bad golf shot was usually temporary. It was a common trait amongst us four. Each was highly capable of hitting some terrible shots. We had plenty of practice dealing with disappointment and irritation. Carl, Dewey and I tended to control ourselves better than Sammy, although we had our weak times as well. He just expected better results than his skill level allowed and was therefore dissatisfied with more of his shots than we could be with our poor shots.

While our recovery time from a bad shot never took too long, Sammy's recovery was always temporary. His bad shots would multiply and form a trend. Add this to his constant babble about bad luck and bad bounces and his neuroses became more fixed. His friends…the three of us…didn't help. Anytime we witnessed his decline, we happily supplied the salt to his self-inflicted head wounds by agreeing how bad were his misfortunes while exaggerating any good fortune happening to us. We'd speak of getting good bounces or making a lucky putt… positive things Sammy, by his own admission, never thought could happen to him.

Our friend's second shot to the first green mercifully landed close to the putting surface. By the time he reached his next shot he was beginning to settle down. He was only swearing under his breath.

To finish the first hole, all four of us were quiet needing concentration to complete a good score. Sammy was all right until his three-foot putt was misdirected by a spike mark causing his golf ball to miss the hole entirely. He ended up scoring a seven including the two-stroke penalty. He was already three strokes down to each of his opponents…and the three of us were delighted. Marching toward the second tee box, his profanity picked up volume. Making up a three shot deficit along with the lack of control of his golf swing that morning made the quest seem impossible. Knowing what he was thinking, we of course chimed in commenting how unlucky he'd been with his ball being so dramatically impacted by that cleat mark. He was nodding his head disconsolately as if seriously thinking we were being sympathetic…which we were not. Actually, we were pleased how easy it was that morning to get into his head.

The four of us were still talking about the Minnesota Twins game on the second green when things took another turn for the worse for our friend. He three-putted a four- foot putt letting forth with a wail that caused some mourning doves to flutter away. Along with his piercing cry of disgust was the addition of a putter flying in the direction of the next tee box. It landed in some heavy grass.

Carl was unfazed. He deadpanned congratulations to Sammy commenting, "Sammy…that was one of your finest throws. Now, good luck in finding your putter."

It truly was a good throw. I'd seen him heave it higher and longer, but again I played more golf with him than Carl did.

Naturally Carl's goal was to make Sammy even more irate. When our friend held up his finger in response, Carl was satisfied he'd struck the right cord. Pissing Sammy off even more had been achieved.

We waited on the third tee box for our friend. We could hear him muttering to himself while looking for his putter in the weeds. When he finally joined us, the three of us had already chosen a way of further fomenting his malevolent feelings. It was a timely opportunity to propose to Sammy we start a new game for another twenty-five cents for the last seven holes…something always done when one player is hopelessly behind. Not only was his game particularly weak that morning, but so was his mental state. We figured that combination would carry us to another twenty-five cent win.

Surprisingly, Sammy brightened over the idea. He welcomed a new beginning. It was a good way for him to erase the recollection and even the odor of the first two holes. Even though he'd be two-bits down to each of us, his only thought was that he could balance out his losses if he could beat the three of us on the final seven holes.

He grinned in optimistic hope. Carl, Dewey and I knew there'd be a blizzard that afternoon before Sammy would ever pull out any kind of victory...not in the shape he was in.

Grinning, he responded confidently, "Yeh...you're on. Let's double the bet."

I looked over at my other playing companions and they were smiling smugly. We'd all seen our friend disintegrate on the golf course when he got truly mad. With a little prodding we sensed it would be almost too easy to make it one of those kinds of days.

Dewey leaned over to me and sighed, "...like taking candy from baby."

Smirking, I nodded silently. Carl didn't hear our interchange, but knew what the two of us were saying. He smugly nodded as well.

If there had been even one flicker of doubt that our second wagers weren't guaranteed, that concern disappeared with but the next swing by Sammy followed by a gale-force of swear words. Again his expected slicing ball flight...as habitual as a January freeze in Minnesota... went straight left toward the river running parallel to the fairway. The ball showed not the least consideration for curving back toward the short grass. We couldn't see if the ball went into the river, but it didn't matter. Even if he found the ball he'd have a difficult task dislodging the ball from the high grass and brush.

As Sammy trudged down the fairway toward the river, the three of us were now howling as we stumbled along behind him. There was no reason to discuss the Minnesota Twins game anymore. We had plenty of fodder for conversation and laughter just watching our friend crumble.

When Sammy saw his predicament down by the river's edge, the expletives rose above the sound of the flowing water. He was facing the reality that he'd likely lost his second ball...his last decent golf ball. The next ball would be that brownish-colored ball with the severe cut on the outer core.

As he jumped down the river bank in an attempt to find his only real remaining golf ball, he began denigrating himself. He moaned, "God dammit, that was my putting ball. Why didn't I use one of those junk balls in my bag? What the hell was I thinking? Son-of-a-bitch! Where were my brains?"

The three of us were in convulsions. Sammy was at his best when lambasting himself. Odds were against him that he had any chance to win that second bet with yet another lost ball. It would be then that his round of golf would become particularly evil. He'd have to play that cut up, aged brownish-colored ball. Being that it was practically unplayable, the three of us were thrilled.

Disappointingly, though, Sammy found his golf ball. However, the circumstances weren't favorable. His ball was resting about two feet from the river in what appeared to be an unplayable lie next to a protruding rock and a tree root. We stared down at the impossible lie trying unsuccessfully not to crack up. We didn't want to look at Sammy. We knew he was about to explode again and we'd just go back into those convulsions of laughter.

Retreating back up onto the fairway, we left our friend ranting and raving. From twenty yards away we watched him take off his right shoe and sock. The shot required that his right foot stand in the water and his left foot with shoe and sock could at least remain on land, albeit perilously close to the water's edge.

As he addressed his golf ball, he was muttering more words most adults likely would not like to hear from a kid. The cleanest thing he yelped was "God damn the water's cold!"

We tried to remain quiet but the anticipation of seeing something heinous was about to happen made it impossible to muffle our high-pitched giggles. Sammy faced an impossible shot. It would be miraculous if he actually hit the ball. But, to him, his standards were such that he truly believed he could hit the ball back onto the fairway.

Sammy thrashed at his ball and immediately began losing his balance as mud, sand, and grass flew up in the air. To keep from falling face first into the river, he had to recover by pulling his left 'dry' foot back toward the river. He was able to recover his balance, but he cut quite a picture with both feet now firmly implanted in the river bottom up to his knees. His heroic effort had come with risks and those hazards had come to life within seconds. As the water saturated his left sock and shoe, his ball careened off a tree and bounded back toward the river stopping in some tall grass by the river's edge.

Carl didn't help when he shouted, "Hey Sammy, you want us to throw your right shoe and sock in the river so you can have both shoes and socks equally soaked?"

Sammy neither responded nor did he see the humor. He was more concerned about the result of his valiant failed effort.

It should be said at this point that this par-5 hole was long, tough, tight, and intimidating. The river all along the left side of the fairway was like a meandering monster gobbling up golf balls like they were protein. Our friend had barely started the hole and he was already being gobbled up.

Dewey, Carl and I jumped back down the river bank to help our friend once again locate his last 'playable' golf ball. Things hadn't improved. The grass was taller and there were more rocks. We'd all seen some incredibly high scores recorded on this particular hole. In fact, each of us had experienced some of those large scores…unfortunately a number of times. It was just funnier when it happened to Sammy. And, all indications were that our friend was well on his way to a double-figure score.

Again his ball was found in the middle of that thigh high grass predictably next to a rock. We again retreated from the river back to the comfort of the fairway to let Sammy figure out how he wanted to proceed. With our drives all on the fairway, we were in the enviable position of knowing we all had just won our second bet unless our friend pulled off several amazing shots. Given the state of Sammy's game and his temperament, the chances of 'amazing' weren't even in our thoughts.

The profanity now spewing forth from the river's edge was that of legend. Sammy had entered his own new zone of rage. He was short of golf balls; he was about to lose all the second bets he'd made with each of us; and, worst of all his golf swing was completely unfamiliar to him that day. He had no idea where his golf ball was going next. Yet, with the never-say-die spirit of this intrepid young sportsman, our friend was not about to give up. That was assured. He never gave up.

Sammy addressed the ball this time being lucky enough to have both feet on land though his left shoe and sock were sloshing every time he moved. To further unnerve him a snake slithered by his foot. He didn't like snakes…even garter snakes. Lashing at the snake more in rage than fear, his club responded with a loud 'clank' as it made contact with a rock instead of the snake. The slithering creature then made his escape while Sammy examined the damage to his club. Sure enough, there was a nick on the iron head. What followed was another low whine that grew into a deafening roar. The vulgarity was broadcast with the authority of a marine having a bad day. "Shi..i….i…t!" came the cry! We of course were howling once again knowing that Sammy had just gotten his golf clubs new that spring. The injury to the club was like fuel on a fire.

I tried to offer some condolence and shouted to him, "Come on, Sammy, just take a penalty and throw your damned ball up on the fairway. We'll give you a break."

But, he was beyond reason. His only response was more muffled expletives. He slashed at the tall grass and we all were frankly surprised to see his ball zooming forward from the tall grass. It looked like it would make the fairway and potentially be in good position until it hit that thin tree. Bouncing back, the ball bounded toward a huge rock where it exploded like a shot straight back at him. He actually ducked as his ball flew like a shot right past him and out towards the middle of the river. When it finally plunked into the slowly moving water, it was as if the ball was only playing with our friend and had gotten tired of teasing him. Then it surrendered heartlessly with that innocent little splash before sinking down to the bottom of the river.

The blue streak of off-colored words flowing from Sammy's mouth was epic. He was mad at everything…the lost ball, another lost bet, the prospect of playing with two of the poorest conditioned golf balls anyone should ever have in their golf bag.

Sammy had no choice but to put in play the aged brown-colored golf ball. The best thing about this particular ball was that it was noticeably better than his other remaining oblong yellow ball with a cut on its core and the word 'Range' labeled on the red stripe surrounding the ball. Other than that, the brown ball had little bounce and wouldn't go near the distance of a normal golf ball.

Our friend then sloshed up onto the fairway where he threw his third ball of the day onto the short grass. He cared little about the rules of golf anymore now that a double figure score on that hole was pretty much guaranteed.

Ignoring us as we sat on the fairway awaiting his next swing, he tried to dry off his left golf shoe with his wet left golf sock. He didn't use his golf towel as that rag hadn't been laundered in over a year.

Before addressing the brown ball, he looked at us hoping for some compassion. He groused, "God damn it. Look at this worthless ball. It's got a cut right into the very middle. Christ Almighty…I can see the innards."

He gave us a pathetic look hoping we might offer him one of our precious golf balls. That wasn't about to happen. We silently stared back at him with not the least bit of pity.

Our non-verbal response made him whine. "Come on, you guys. Borrow me a ball. I can't play with this thing. It looks more like a turd than a ball."

We looked at each other and knew exactly what each of us was thinking. Carl broke the silence first and said, "Go to hell, Sammy. You'll never pay me back."

Dewey showing no empathy retorted, "I don't have that many balls. Forget it. Play with what you got."

I was more capitalistic and gave him some hope by saying, "How much money you got. I'll sell you a ball."

He looked at me as if a prayer was being answered as he pulled out fifty-five cents from his pocket. He should have known me better. In those days a new ball cost anywhere from $.65 to $1.25 apiece. I had a couple used balls and offered the worst one for $1.00…payment in full up front. I just made the offer because I wanted to hear his irate response.

I wasn't disappointed. His remark again questioned our birthright. He shouted, "O.K., you bastards, I'll play with this beat-up golf ball and I'll whip all of you if you don't rot in hell first."

That was another reason we liked our friend. At times he could be so optimistic when the future looked so dire. Rarely had any of us ever seen this hopefulness actually pay off for him. Most importantly, his rash words also meant he was going to be willing to begin a new wager on the next tee box. After losing two bets on the first three holes, he would be willing to take on a third bet. For the three of us being up fifty cents apiece and the prospects good to win yet another two-bits, the day was progressing quite nicely.

As Sammy addressed his old, brown-colored golf ball, it was Carl who felt compelled to add some angst to the scene. He informed Sam, "Just so you know, this will be your sixth shot."

I then quickly added, "….and you have about four hundred yards left to the green."

Dewey also chimed in. "…and, if you play well the next couple shots you might keep your score below a '10'.

We all thought our quips were hilarious. Sammy's only response was to say something to us that was anatomically impossible.

He then took a mighty swing and watched as the injured ball grazed the grass for almost forty yards and then continued rolling along the ground another forty yards. It was a horrible shot, but the best he'd done so far on the hole...and it even stayed up on the fairway. Sammy, of course, was in no mood to appreciate anything. He was disgusted. Yet, he was not about to give up. We all knew our friend would never surrender. He did not admit defeat easily...or wisely.

Now in hot-tempered silence he picked up his golf bag and marched onward. I called over to him, "Hey Sammy...there's a bright side. At least your bag has to be lighter carrying just one ball."

I'm glad he didn't carry a gun in his golf bag. Carl, Dewey and I remained a safe distance behind him so he couldn't hear our stifled laughter. Truly we were unbearable. His seventh shot flew kind of weirdly to the left and ended up down by the river again. This time his anger was aimed directly at God as he repeatedly told the Almighty what he thought of Him all the way to his next shot.

Adding to Sammy's anguish was that his three mates were playing the hole right down the middle of the fairway. Each time we hit our shots on that long, thin fairway, our golf balls landed safely on the short grass. And each time his shoulders stooped just a bit lower.

Arriving at the spot his ball had dropped over the edge of the fairway into another area by the river, he finally got a mild reprieve. He didn't have to search for this golf ball. It had stopped on some sand and gravel just a few feet from the water's edge with a grove of small trees between his ball and the green. Sammy surveyed his situation. After what he'd been through, he didn't seem too concerned. When he pulled out a wood club indicating that he was going to gamble his next shot would miss those trees, the three of us lost it completely. Through choking laughter, I begged Sammy to consider taking a penalty and throwing his ball up onto the fairway.

Carl even tried to reason with him. He shouted impatiently, "Sammy, for Christ's sake, just chip your ball out onto the fairway. You'll be lucky to make '12' even if you play the rest of the hole decently."

But Sammy was taking no advice. Leaving him to his own devices, we moved away from the river to play our own shots waiting for the predictable surge of foul words echoing from the river's edge. Sure enough, there was a 'swoosh' followed by a ball being tossed around in those trees as if in a pin ball machine. Immediately what followed was his primeval scream of frustration. We were certain Sam had lost his third golf ball.

It turned out not to be true. We heard another swing...and another loud moan. Then another swing and this time the ball came floating out of the deep heavy grass as if it had been thrown. He probably did, but at that point we didn't care. He'd taken enough abuse. We could only beat him once on that hole; that had been done many shots before.

Our friend came sloshing out from down by the river. There was mud all over his shoes, socks, shorts and shirt. His arms were all scratched up. He had the look of a warrior, albeit a defeated one, but at least he held his head high in his attempt to complete the hole.

And, he finally did. We didn't even ask Sam his final score. Carl and Dewey had been keeping track and agreed our friend's score was no better than a '17'… but probably higher. I personally had witnessed a score of '20' while caddying for a woman who hopefully made that round of golf her last one. She smoked a pack of cigarettes on that river hole alone. I didn't think her health could take much more golf.

Like that woman, Sammy was comatose as he marched up the path to the fourth tee box. We showed some mercy and gave him a '17' on the score card without saying any more heartless comments. We figured he deserved a slight reprieve from our obnoxious commentary. Besides, we wanted him willing to take that third bet starting on the fourth hole.

The three of us teed off in relative quiet off that tee box as we closely watched Sammy's mental state. We figured there was a chance we'd have to wait until the following hole before he was stable enough to discuss another wager.

However, I couldn't wait. I offered a gratuitous, self-serving comment that indicated some sense of compassion. I said, "O.K. Sammy, the third hole is over. Let's start a new game so you can win some money back. What do you say?"

Sammy was already down $1.50. In those days that was pretty big money, especially considering he was an unemployed thirteen year old who didn't like to caddy. With fifty-five cents in his pocket, there was a possibility he'd be paying us off for the rest of the summer. What didn't help finalizing a third bet was the reality that the three of us were playing well…even sterling considering our age.

The brown-colored golf ball with a gash in its cover had survived the previous hole. When he teed it up on the fourth tee box, we figured no one in his right mind would wager us. Since there was some question if Sammy was ever in his right mind, he was the one who brought up the third bet as long as we gave him some strokes to balance the disadvantage he had in playing with the injured golf ball. Never before had Sammy asked for strokes. There had been a pride factor. But, that day considering his gross bad luck…and the damaged golf ball… the need for handicap strokes was logical. Frankly the three of us offered no hesitation. We would be playing with 'house' money. Why not give our friend a few strokes. The potential for another 'win' was so ripe. The time seemed right to venture into that dark side of gambling since the upside looked so profitable.

We talked amongst ourselves as Sammy stood waiting to see what was developing. It was that brown-colored ball that finally convinced me to take the risk. Making my voice low and business-like, I offered, "Sammy, I'll tell you what.

Since you're already fifty cents down to me, I'll give you two…no…I'll give you three shots on the last six holes…double or nothing.

Carl and Dewey looked at me as if I was a foreigner speaking another language. They weren't ready to take that high a risk. In their small minds they were contemplating giving Sam one stroke on the last six holes. They couldn't see the rainbow above Sam's head…the pot of gold waiting for us to scoop out some of the coins…the opportunity to make a nine-hole killing that would have Sammy owing us millions….or at least a dollar by the end of the round.

But, it was I, in my appalling greed, who showed them the way. I pointed at Sammy and just shrugged my shoulders. It was my way of telling them the prospect of winning was so probable, the two of them would have to be deaf, dumb, and blind not to understand the high likelihood of victory.

Their problem was a lack of creativity. They weren't as experienced in gambling on the golf course as I was…or even as Sammy was. We just played more golf than they did with different people and varied skill levels. To them golf was played straight up…golfer against golfer. I had learned money could still be made even when I gave my opponent some strokes…or acquired some stroke advantages from golfers who were better or perceived to be more skillful than me. All Carl and Dewey had to do was gaze for a few seconds into Sammy's deranged eyes to see the great potential for winning.

It took a few moments, but they finally came to their senses. Eyeing the brownish colored ball and the peevish look on Sammy's face, they agreed to the same bet…three shots on the last six holes….double or nothing. It was such an obvious chance to win I held my breath hoping Sammy's mind was still not functioning properly. Though a relative veteran on betting games in golf, he was too far gone. I could see he actually felt he had us where he wanted us given our obvious greed. He looked at us disgustedly as if we had no morals and snarled, "I'm playing with this shitty ball. Give me four shots on the last six holes and you're on."

Dewey started to shake his head. Carl rubbed his chin in thought. They sensed it was too much of an advantage for Sammy. I could see it in their unadventurous eyes. In my mind I was ready to give him six shots and triple the bet. In fact I had the strong feeling he could be taken for even more money before the nine holes were completed. I knew my friend well. His mind was fried. His game was out of control. He was in a zone where he couldn't even find the door to exit. I'd seen him in this condition a few other times. After each of those episodes, he was so mad he'd left his clubs in the clubhouse saying he hoped someone would steal them. Then, after paying off his losing wagers, he got on his bike proclaiming he'd never play the game again.

The next day after those couple instances he didn't show up at the golf course the next morning. He would delay his arrival until noon. He'd show up in good spirits and acted like the previous day had never happened. Then he'd tee up his golf ball and have no qualms about playing for our usual bet…a bottle of pop and candy bar…or two-bits. In my experience I could see this day was obviously going to be one of those special days he was again going to quit golf for good.

Holding back responding too quickly to his request for a four-shot handicap, I pretended not to like his request. It was all just a show. Actually I was thrilled. Then afraid he'd change his mind, I quickly agreed. I then said to my other two cowardly friends, "Christ Almighty….Dewey…Carl….it's only money. What the hell…let's give him his four shots apiece and get playing. So what if Sammy wins. We don't want him in debt for the rest of his life!"

I was actually embarrassed over making such a deceitful statement. Sammy wasn't going to win…not with that brown golf ball and the condition of his game. The two of them finally saw the light. In a flash they nodded their agreement saying, "Yeh, what the hell. Sammy, you need a chance to win back your money. We'll give you the four shots."

It was still a risk. The three of us still had to make decent scores. Giving our friend a four-shot advantage was not guaranteed money in the bank, but considering Sammy's situation, the 'pressure' was clearly on him. From Sammy's perspective, though, he looked like he'd just tricked the minister out of the Sunday offertory plate. He snorted as he now more confidently took a practice swing and readied himself for the remaining six holes of golf. He no longer cared that his brownish colored ball had a deep gash in it. He'd even forgotten about his score of '17' on the previous hole. His next shot was going to be the first shot of the rest of his life. Life looked much better once again.

As he took the club back, we could see the fire in his eyes. His body coiled even more than usual as he prepared himself for what would be his hardest swing of the day. His plan was for that pesky ball to go for a long ride. He was going to teach us a thing or two about gambling on the golf course.

It was a worthwhile goal had he not lost his balance at the top of his swing. His awkward movement caused him…as the saying in golf goes…to 'over-swing'. On the downswing he was lucky he made any contact at all with the golf ball. His shot took off very high…like a baseball pop-up…and well left of the 'third-base dugout'…to follow the metaphor. The westerly breeze propelled the ball even further left into the forest…deep, deep into the forest.

The yelp emitted from Sammy seeing his second-to-the-last golf ball take such an unfamiliar path was something I'd rarely heard from any human being least of all from him. It was a sound cultivated by pent up anger, disbelief, and… by that fourth hole…shock. He'd never hit a ball so high and so far left.

Again, it was like a candle that kept re-lighting. The three of us dissolved into freakish, uncontrolled laughter. Carl quite sincerely spat out that he hadn't considered Sammy's worn golf ball could even fly that high or that far.

What followed was the club flying out of Sammy's hand. It flew straighter than his golf shot…like a helicopter blade…and then landed in the fairway about forty yards in front of the tee box. Dewey congratulated Sammy on his most accurate result of the day. Sammy actually didn't hear the barb given the invectives flowing from his mouth.

Grabbing his bag of clubs, Sammy lit out for the woods knowing of his futile chances of finding that brown-colored golf ball. There was no telling what was going on in that brain of his, but it couldn't have been anything hopeful. The pressure had suddenly increased on his minute old new wager. It was likely he was going to have to play the last six holes with that odd-shaped yellow 'range' ball with the red stripe. For added torment, it was just plain humiliating having to play with a ball intended solely for the practice range.

The three of us all hit our second shots on the fourth hole toward the green while hearing shuffling and stifled swear words echoing from high up in the woods. We were about to show some politeness and go over to help him find his ball...or any ball for that matter...when we heard a muffled and distant yet hopeful voice call out. "Watch out...here I come!"

There was a moment of disappointment in our eyes until we heard what was now the familiar swish followed by the ball making square contact with a tree. Another series of profane words bellowed from the confines of the forest but this time they were said with the most sorrowful moan. The three of us buckled over in mirth knowing the inevitable.

Then there was only silence from inside the brush and trees. We couldn't see him, but we knew he was in there someplace. I recovered long enough to yell into the woods, "Sammy, how you doing in there? Are you going to hit or what?"

A whipped, beaten voice sounded meekly from the woods, "I can't find my God damned ball!"

Now even the three of us had to show some pity for our poor friend. Only counting the two-stroke penalty for a lost ball, he'd already used up two of the four shots each of us had given him. Sadly for him, he wasn't halfway to the green...and he was still in the woods. This wasn't just a bad day for our friend. This was torturous.

Carl being more impatient yelled out, "Christ, Sammy, you've got one ball left. Throw it out and hit it."

There was another uncomfortable silence from deep in the trees. Then an even weaker voice cried out, "I don't have another ball worth hitting. This range ball has stains all over it...and it's lumpy."

We were again reduced to tears of laughter. Having no playable golf ball was not supposed to happen to any golfer. But, it was happening to our friend. It was probably best that Sammy could not see from the depths of that thick forest the unsympathetic behavior of his dreadfully unkind three companions.

Dewey finally showed some strands of decency and reached into his golf bag to pull out a couple golf balls. He said to Carl and me, "I've got some extras. I'll go over and give Sammy some balls so we can at least move on."

Carl and I looked at each other. Our eyes were dancing. We both shook our heads at Dewey. "The hell you will," I said. "We made the bet based on the golf balls he had left. A new ball might give him an edge."

Then I paused before saying, "Besides, I've got a feeling this is going to get really good. Sammy is somewhere in space right now. I doubt if he can remember his own name. I say we don't show him any sympathy and see how he does. Let's remember, he's the one who got himself into this predicament. All he had to do was go golf ball hunting like we all do. Instead he let his golf ball supply get down to nothing. Let him suffer a bit. If he gets really pissed and starts walking in, then we'll borrow him a golf ball. But, until that time, let's see what happens."

Carl being more devilish than Dewey saw the humor and nodded his head in agreement. He understood I knew Sammy better than anyone. Sammy and I had already played a million rounds of golf with each other...and we were going to play many millions more. Carl trusted my reading of the situation.

Dewey was more doubtful being the kinder person. He finally chuckled, shrugged his shoulders and put the golf balls back in his bag.

Then he shouted into the trees offering Sam something to consider. "Hey Sammy, stay up in the trees until you find some other golf balls. We'll meet you at the fifth tee box."

Then just to rub it in, he added, "Don't worry. We can start a new game on the next hole!"

This meant that by not finishing the fourth hole, Sammy was going to have to take a loss on the double or nothing bet he had agreed to play just minutes before. He'd be a dollar down to each of us.

A howl came from the woods. "You jackass, Dewey...come on, throw me one of your golf balls."

Carl hollered back smiling, but pretending to be serious, "Go to hell...find your own damn golf balls!"

We all muffled our laughter as Sammy called us a bunch of names that again would be revolting to his mother and minister.

Grinning, we walked on. Words tended to be just words. Rarely were they taken seriously in our little world.

The three of us were lining up our putts on the fourth green when Sammy suddenly appeared at the edge of the woods. He was shuffling slowly along and looking under every bush he passed for a golf ball. He seemed to have calmed down.

When he made it to the green, Carl asked him, "So....did you find a ball?"

Our friend suddenly smiled widely as he took a ball out of his pocket. It looked like a brand new one compared to the brownish ball and the 'range' ball. "Yeh...I found one. I'll take a double bogie on this hole and tee up on the next hole."

There was no give to Carl. He hollered, "Sammy, the hell you will. You couldn't have made a six on this hole even if you'd found your first ball. You'd have made at least an eight on this hole, but probably a ten!"

Sammy knew Carl was right, but had tried to game us anyway. His attempt at claiming a six had been unsuccessful. But that no longer mattered. Sammy had found himself a nice new ball and he was ready to take us on now having no concerns about surrendering the third bet.

He leaped up onto the fifth tee box and announced, "O.K. …new game with all you bastards! I'm down a dollar apiece to each of you. I'm ready to kick some butt. Let's double the bet again and I'll take three shots on the last five holes."

It was a nice quick ploy to try to get us to agree swiftly to the new bet. We were young, but not stupid. I was ready for his desperate attempt at sliding a fast wager by us.

I said to him. "Sammy, we'll give you two shots on the last five holes and play you double or nothing." There was no questioning my methods from Carl and Dewey. They knew a new golf ball was not going to resurrect our friend's game.

Sammy readily agreed. He was happy again as he stood on the tee box ready to let fly his new golf ball. The three of us just quietly shook our heads waiting for the next debacle Sammy would likely have to face.

At that point, double or nothing was like a gift. As far as the three of us were concerned, we'd already won and were thinking of the $2.00 in our pockets. If we had any morals at all we might have not bet with Sammy anymore and let him finish the nine holes of golf peaceably. Since our ethics were not that refined, that thought had never entered our minds.

Sammy showed a factitious confidence as he addressed his newly found golf ball. It wasn't even his turn to play, but we let him hit anyway. The hole was a short par-three with only a line of trees on the left that could cause him trouble. He took another wild swing determinedly not to let the ball go left. This time the ball veered directly right but somehow curved left toward some medium-sized pine trees. At least the ball was still on the golf course. We showed some concern when no one saw the ball bounce down to the ground. Our friend seemed not the least worried. He'd faced hell so far that morning and managed not to fall in. He was still alive. How could anything worse happen to him? No one could lose a newly found golf ball having hit it just once.

Ten minutes later Carl, Dewey and I had finished making our putts on that fifth green while Sammy continued searching for his newly found golf ball in those medium sized pine trees. It had not dropped down to the ground. It had simply disappeared…possibly nestled in a top branch of one of the thick pines. Just dumb luck…bad dumb luck!

Our friend was back in his funk as we moved over to the sixth tee box watching him beat the pine tree branches repeatedly with one of his golf clubs. He seemed beyond any hope of recovery. We now consciously thought of him as disabled…probably permanently. We called out for him to meet us on the next tee box. No longer were we thinking of another wager. He was down $2.00 to each of us. Losses of $6.00 in one day with no income to speak of except fifty cents or a dollar from his folks in weekly allowance, it would take most of the remainder of the summer for him to pay off this debt.

We sat down on a bench and talked about the upcoming Twin's night game with Harmon Killebrew unable to play because of a sore ankle. It seemed hopeless against the New York Yankees. As we lamented the tough game awaiting the Twins, we heard no audible sound from our friend. It was as if he'd run dry of swear words. We only continued to hear the slashing sound as Sammy hit those tree branches over and over again hoping to dislodge the lost ball caught somewhere in those pines.

When he finally approached us, he had in his left hand holding that yellow range ball with the red stripe around it and a pathetic look on his face. It was obvious he was going for the sympathy plea. He was now down so much money he had to wonder if college was still an option. As the three of us had agreed, we maintained a stalwart expression knowing he was going to beg for a golf ball from one of us.

He moaned, "Come on, you guys. Look at this golf ball. It's a damn practice ball that's been hit so many times it doesn't have anything left in it. It's soft as a marshmallow and the damn thing won't roll straight. This ball wasn't any good when it was new."

I looked at Carl and winked. I took the ball from Sam and inspected it before disagreeing. "Sammy, if you wash this ball it might look prettier. The red stripe will stand out so you have a better chance of finding it in the woods. And, if it's really soft, you won't be able to hit it far enough to lose sight of it. Why don't you play with it and see how you do."

Dewey and Carl grinned as Sammy shouted, "God dammit…you guys are just a bunch of crooks. If I have to play with this yellow ball, I want more strokes. I could hit a baseball further than I could hit this piece of crap. I want four shots on the last four holes from each of you…and we'll play for the $2.00 I already owe each of you. Otherwise I'm quitting."

It was like a dream bet. With that yellow ball, Sammy was right. He probably could hit a baseball further.

Dewey grabbed the yellow ball out of my hand and then leaned over toward Carl and whispered, "Jesus, this ball looks like it spent a couple winters out in the brush."

We didn't want Sammy to quit…and truthfully, he didn't want to retreat back to the clubhouse. Given the condition of that golf ball, we should have given him eight shots on the last four holes. Again we were without morals. Greed was our motivator.

I spoke for the three of us very quickly before Sammy changed his mind. In mock sympathy I said, "Sure Sammy, we'll give you a break and give you four shots on the last four holes for $2.00 apiece…just so you have a chance to win your money back."

I almost choked on those last words. The chances of Sammy beating us with that aged, oblong yellow golf ball was as remote as being kissed by the prettiest girl in our class. There was no doubt in our minds our ship had arrived. We might have to wait a year to get the wager paid off, but we'd never owned an annuity before that day.

With the wager re-set, our demeanor returned to normal…truly obnoxious. I said to Sammy before he swung, "Hey Sammy, I don't think you're going to finish this round of golf. I think you're going to lose that yellow one before we complete the last four holes. That'll be embarrassing as all hell. Wait until people hear this story. I don't think I've ever heard of someone having to walk off the golf course because they don't have any more golf balls."

Sammy knew I was pulling his chain. He'd dealt with me before, but my teasing comment was definitely within range of reality. He stepped away with that burning determination renewed in his eyes. He jutted out his chin and growled at me. "Are you all done, comedy man? Maybe I can now take my swing if you'd close that big yap of yours."

Then just to hand out some intimidation of his own, he glowered at Carl and Dewey and snarled, "You bastards shouldn't have given me those four shots. My bad luck is about to even out. I can just feel it."

As he re-addressed his golf ball, Dewey, Carl and I just shook our heads admiring our friend's spirit…as unjustified as it was. He took his swing and surprised us… including probably himself… by making decent contact with the yellow ball. The ill-shaped ball didn't fly very far, but it went surprisingly straight. It was easily the best shot he'd hit so far in that round of golf.

He grabbed his bag and took off for his next shot like he was a combat leader. At the finish of the sixth hole Sammy actually made the same score as Dewey and me… and he even beat Carl by a shot.

We couldn't believe it. Sammy was so ecstatic he practically flew to the seventh tee box. The golfing gods were smiling on him for the first time that day.

The next hole offered a wide open fairway with little chance that a ball could be lost. With his uncontrolled swing and an egg-shaped golf ball, it was another example of two negatives making a positive. His shot limped out onto the fairway. The three of us just shook our heads again not believing his luck. However, I knew him best. I had no confidence he could hold himself together on the last three holes with a four shot lead while playing with an old yellow range ball.

Carl and Dewey became particularly worried and geared up their chiding. Carl kept reminding our friend what would happen if that last yellow ball got lost. He kept repeating, "Yeh, Sammy boy, it doesn't look good about you finishing the round. You lose that pathetic excuse for a golf ball and it's all over. No matter how many strokes you might be ahead of us, you'll have to quit if you don't have a golf ball to finish the round. Damn…that'd mean you'd lose $12 in nine holes of golf…and it all started with a twenty-five cent bet on the first hole. Christ, that's got to be some kind of frinkin record."

Dewey took another angle. Wandering over toward our friend, he said to Sammy, "You know, I think your new way of swinging is really helping. You're starting to hit the ball better."

Dewey winked at me knowing that Sammy had no more a new swing than he had a chauffeur to drive him home at the end of the day. Sammy gave Dewey a vague nod in agreement although knowing damn well his golf swing felt like he'd just begun the game. Every shot was a mystery as to where the ball was going to fly. We knew it and he knew it. Sammy just didn't want to admit it. He knew he'd been lucky on the previous hole…and that the four shot lead we'd given him was precarious at best.

Carl wasn't so certain. He didn't want to see his $2.00 profit disappear. He wouldn't quit his harassment. He inched closer to our friend whispering, "Sammy, we're getting closer to the clubhouse. This would be the best place to lose your last golf ball. You wouldn't have as far to walk."

Sammy mostly ignored the clowning provided by Carl and Dewey, but he was still fragile. Trying desperately to show a positive demeanor, he let go with another wild swing. This time the shot went in the general direction of the green, but took a bad bounce into a greenside bunker. Now his foul language returned with a vengeance. I could see he wanted to wrap his club around a tree had there been one nearby. Instead he simply slammed his iron into the fairway sod burying the iron clubhead in the soft turf. His furor was now aimed at the real culprit in his mind…not himself…but that misshapen yellow golf ball with the red stripe. He called it a 'God-damned whore'. The phrase made little sense to a bunch of thirteen year olds, but we knew it was bad. Besides, he was coming close to using up his entire swearword vocabulary and it was difficult to be more creative.

As we continued hiking toward the seventh green, Sammy calmed down slightly as he watched us play our shots to the green. He seemed to want to change the flow of what had become a horrific day. His mood swing was typical for him. He began telling us about this new girl in town he thought liked him. It was a typical Sammy story…full of optimism as if he was absolutely convinced he was transforming from a skinny kid with glasses, braces, and a face full of freckles into the most attractive guy in our age group. It was just another endearing feature of our young friend, since we knew his tale was mostly fiction but the absolute truth in his fanciful mind.

Dewey sidled up to me and whispered, "She probably said "hi" to him when he saw her someplace downtown and that was all it took for him to fall in love."

I nodded in hopeless agreement.

As we approached the seventh green, the three of us could see where Sammy's yellow ball had landed in the bunker. We immediately began stifling more laughs. His ball was half-buried next to the lip of the sand trap. He'd need a shovel to get that ball out of the trap.

As for Sammy, he was oblivious still lost in his romantic thoughts about that girl. When his voice began to trail off, we knew he'd finally seen his predicament. The only way of addressing the ball was to have one foot in the trap and one foot in the heavy grass beside the trap…a shot he had neither the skill nor the imagination to pull off.

Wasting no time, he readied himself quickly with one foot in the sand trap and the other looking like he'd placed it on a chair. Dewey's giggle began before our friend even took a swing.

The action of Sammy's swing was something to behold. The motion typified someone chopping down a tree on uneven ground. His effort caused him to contact the middle of the ball. It exited the sand trap as if propelled by cannon. For a moment it looked like the ball might hit the flag stick and stop…except that the yellow ball was still rising as it flew ten feet above the flagstick. The ball then sailed over the sand trap on the other side of the green, beyond the nearby eighth tee box, and finally nestling deep in a thicket of weeds, bushes, and grass half way up a hill.

This brought the real Sammy back to reality. The rhythmic expletives flowing from his mouth were poetic. He went charging up that hill past the eighth tee box with his eyes glued to the very spot his range ball had disappeared into the brush. He had to find that ball! Any adult…and I mean any adult… would have been shocked with some of the words exploding from that young kid's mouth. Actually, I was kind of proud I knew someone with that array of cuss words. As he beat away the brush and weeds trying to find his last golf ball, the four shots given him by each one of us were no long a concern. If he didn't have a golf ball, he'd have to forfeit the match. It was bad enough to lose, but the way he would lose would be particularly humiliating…and would certainly move up into the top five 'Sammy' stories of all time.

We calmly putted our balls into the cup and strolled up to the eighth tee box to again wait for our frazzled friend as he continued to hack away in the weeds looking for his yellow range ball. By this time we'd gotten used to the low, guttural flow of profanity in tandem with a golf club chopping away at thick foliage.

His caustic comments now were directed at everyone and everything other than his own golf game. He was irate over his misfortune as he grumbled, "God damn it…that was the worst damned lie in a sand trap I've ever seen. The God-damned greenskeeper should be shot. Don't they ever rake those frinkin sand traps? What do they pay the greenskeeper for …to have coffee up at the clubhouse?"

We just sat there quietly talking and waiting…and occasionally looking over in the direction of our friend spouting off his anger. We were relatively comfortable. It was going to be one of our biggest paydays in our young lives and we hadn't even completed the nine holes. Earning $4.00 apiece in wagers… it was like winning the jackpot.

Dewey then suggested once again we borrow Sammy a golf ball and arrange some kind of bet on the last two holes. He knew opportunities like this to make serious gambling money didn't just roll around every day. We didn't want Sammy to have to walk in from the golf course because he had no more golf balls. Carl and I were inclined to agree showing how our collective gluttony was approaching satiability. Our parents had brought us up as best they could, yet their efforts couldn't work 100% of the time. It wasn't entirely their fault that avarice had taken over our senses. Nonetheless, it was better they weren't at the golf course to witness our disgusting behavior, since we felt no guilt. We could work on improving our moral fiber starting the next day.

And then as if the golfing gods became conscious of our misspent thoughts, a miracle happened. Sammy yelled out in jubilation, "I found it! I found my God-damned yellow ball!"

He sounded too happy for something so insignificant. He was destined to lose. We all knew it.

Sammy then shouted out with some hope and resolve, "…and I got a shot!"

Suddenly we stood up showing some concern. Maybe our friend was going to pull off some kind of lucky shot to maintain his lead on us. We heard a slash as if he wanted to kill someone while simultaneously trying to hit the golf ball. A second later there came a yellow range ball floating high out of the brush as if floating on a cloud. If we hadn't heard the swing, we might have thought Sam threw the ball. We watched as the ball barely made it over the tree by the eighth tee box and looked as if it was going to flop onto the green. It would have been a remarkable shot even amongst the best of golfers if it had.

The problem was that Sammy's shot wasn't remarkable enough. The ball landed in another bunker again stuck against the lip of the sandtrap. Only the top half of the yellow ball could be seen. Bad luck had followed our friend into the brush and weeds and it was holding onto Sammy's leg like a hungered alligator.

The sight of a spirited Sammy charging out of the woods to see the result of a particularly good golf shot was truly heart-warming. That joy and optimism was a testament to the human spirit. But, it would be short-lived.

Then he saw the ball buried on the edge of the sandtrap and his world came crashing back down. That might have been the final revelation as far as Sammy's positive boyhood development was concerned. If he hadn't learned how life could be so unfair in the previous hour and a half, then that shot into the sandtrap had to be the last straw.

Most people at that point would have wondered if life was still worth living. How much could one lone human being take? If ever there'd be a time where golf club shafts would be snapped over a player's knee, this would qualify as one of those times. At the very least we were waiting for a new, more elevated stream of profanity bursting forth from the mouth of our friend.

Strangely, we heard no sound. Sammy didn't let go with his recognizable primeval moan we'd heard all too often that day. He didn't even turn toward the clubhouse where the greenskeeper was having coffee and give him the finger.

He just stood by the sandtrap and stared at the half-submerged golf ball in the sand…as if he was hoping for a piece of lightning to strike him despite there being no clouds in the sky.

He walked into the sandtrap and without taking any time he hacked away at the ball for his fifth shot. The ball didn't move. The word 'Range' on the yellow ball stared up at him as if mocking him for trying to play an actual round of golf with such a sub-standard practice range golf ball.

Carl, Dewey, and I were back to enjoying ourselves as we watched our friend prepare himself for his sixth shot onto the seventh green. This day had become not only profitable, but truly unforgettable…a day destined to be remembered for raucous conversation at golf club bars and class reunions. Even Sammy was excelling beyond his usual bad luck and craziness.

Back to hissing at his yellow practice ball, he took another mighty swing and excavated more sand from the trap…but not the ball. The swing, however, did allow one positive result. The ball was now resting on top of the sand where he had a better chance of hitting it on his next attempt. Unfortunately, his score was mounting with each swing.

With no delay he hacked away for his seventh shot and bladed the ball once again. I began to wonder how much more abuse this poor golf ball was going to take. As the ball shot out of the sandtrap about five feet off the ground, another marvel took place. The yellow ball hit the flagstick squarely and bounced down ending up only three feet away from the cup. Sammy could hit that shot all day for the next ten years and not get that lucky. He now had a chance to make an eight. With our scores of four, he would of course be relinquishing his four shot advantage with still two holes to play, but at least he'd be tied. It was the silver lining if ever there was a silver lining.

But, the seventh hole wasn't over. He pulled out his putter for what he expected to be a routine short putt. What he'd forgotten was that his old yellow ball wasn't round. When he stroked the ball, it veered directly left leaving him another three-foot putt for a nine. How he made that putt, I'll never know, but he did.

As he trudged up the hill to where we were sitting on the eighth tee box, he was mumbling something that was physically impossible for a golf ball to do even if it was human. He was now in a zone even I had never witnessed.

Without delay while muttering to himself, he swatted the yellow ball down the middle of the fairway. He didn't even follow the flight of the ball. Maybe he didn't have the stomach for it.

I finally broke the silence by saying to him, "Gosh, I didn't think that old range ball could go that far."

Even then it was forty yards behind the rest of our drives. He just stared at me with his eyes glazed over as we left the tee box.

He never made a sound all the way down the eighth fairway. Hardly caring, he smashed his next shot close to the green and chipped his yellow range ball within fifteen feet of the hole. Despite the score of nine on the previous hole, he was actually still in the last match only one shot down whether he knew it or not. If somehow he could make that putt, he would be going into the last hole tied with the three of us since the three of us had each scored five.

His putt was absolutely flat, but still challenging considering his oblong golf ball. He stroked the misshapen ball and it bounced along the surface of the green ending up a foot short of the hole. Scoring a five with that ball was within his grasp.

Now all four of us had missed short putts during our short golfing careers, but when Sammy's second putt from twelve inches veered miserable to the right, Carl, Dewey and I ran to the ninth tee box so we wouldn't get hit by a flying golf club.

Strangely, we looked back at Sammy and saw that he hadn't released any tantrum. He'd not said a profane word and his club was not airborne. We even saw him chuckle as he stroked his third putt. This time it rolled unnaturally around the cup. He'd just four-putted from fifteen feet.

Finally tapping in for a score of seven, he was now three shots down to us with one last hole to play. Surprisingly, he still remained seemingly composed. I described it to Carl and Dewey as that Sammy had moved into yet another stratosphere…in a mental state so removed from reality that his senses were either numbed or deceased. His only hope was that his ordeal would soon be over. He could then sit down on the bench outside the clubhouse by the practice green, have a bottle of pop, and collect himself. Sure he'd be twelve dollars down to us, but he had his whole life ahead of him to somehow come up with the money. He had to figure he was going to get a job sometime in the future so he could pay off his debts.

As he approached the ninth tee box, his façade of tranquility was brittle at best. Anything we said or did might set him off…not that this fact would keep us from causing his further decline. After all, he was our friend. Why would we stop?

With but one hole remaining, he'd been spared the ultimate humiliation of not having a golf ball to complete the nine holes. He had to figure he couldn't hit the yellow 'range' ball far enough to lose it on the last hole. Odds were in his favor he'd be able to finish the round of golf.

The three of us, however, had some different thoughts and reminded him of the deep valley of trees and rough on the right side of the fairway…and a high hill of weeds and grass on the left side. Carl added with insincere concern, "God, Sammy, where are you going to aim this shot? No telling where that range ball might fly."

Sam's fidgety manner told us he was beginning to think the exact same thing. Sammy was last to hit after Carl, Dewey, and I launched our drives down the fairway. We watched as he hesitantly took his driver out of his golf bag. With the hazards on both sides, the fairway had to look like a hallway. He took a deep breath as he teed up his old yellow ball with the red stripe around it. Then he stretched as if he needed to relax his body for one last key shot. It was his way of getting his game face back on. Now there was nothing anyone could say that would bother him. He was determinedly visualizing his 'last' golf ball flying straight down the middle of the fairway and past all the hazards on the right and left sides.

This was the point where Sammy's day took another turn…for the worse if that was possible. An expected occurrence for a player having a bad day but showing grit, determination and not quitting might be some kind of reward or piece of good luck…like a good shot or a fortunate bounce.

I knew better. When my friend Sam's luck turned sour, it didn't change back with any great speed. I couldn't predict what would happen, but there was just a continued feeling that catastrophe was waiting out there on the golf course to attack him once again. It turned out my premonition was more imminent than I could have guessed. I should have let him just hit his ball, but I had to squeeze one more drop of blood out of Sammy's horrible day.

I don't know what possessed me, but I threw one more opportunity out there for Sammy to consider before he took his swing. I blurted out, "Sammy boy, I'll tell you what. You're going to owe me four dollars and I'm going to give you a sporting chance to win it back. Since you're still playing with that old yellow ball, I'll give you two shots on this last hole…and we'll play double or nothing. If you win you'll owe me nothing. If you lose, you'll owe me $8.00.

He looked back at me like I was nuts. It was a terrible wager on my part. He and I always played even up for nine holes. Why would I give him two strokes on the last hole…and for so much money? Even Carl and Dewey curled their brow having no interest in making such a crazy bet. They were happy with the $4.00 apiece they were likely going to carry away from this match. This was money for their Christmas fund. With that $4.00 both presents for their Mom and Dad would easily be covered.

As Sam considered the offer, he continued taking easy practice swings. We'd played a lot of golf together and he knew me as well as I knew him. He figured there had to be a catch to the wacky wager. He even had to consider I might be mercifully providing him a 'pity' bet that he could win so he might feel better. But, that thought was ridiculous. He knew me better than that.

Staring at me trying to decide if I was being serious, he saw I wasn't flinching. This only made him madder. I was actually disparaging his golf game with such an offer.

Now he was really pissed. The wager brought him out of his funk. He was going to show me! Stopping his practice swing, he turned to me uttering, "You're on, shitface…two shots…double or nothing."

Sammy no longer even considered the yellow ball as a disadvantage. He simply got a renewed shot of adrenalin sensing I had just given away the farm.

He was certain I was being too big for my britches…and he was going to make me pay for my insolence.

His face was more relaxed as he focused down the fairway visualizing that yellowed 'range' ball taking off from the tee box and following a fluid hooking design that would leave it far down the middle of the fairway. Of course, he hadn't hooked a ball since he'd first begun playing golf, but he was entitled to the dream.

And it was during this dream that his world crumbled once again. He made one last slow practice swing with his angered grin and burning eyes focused on me. Regrettably he was standing too close to his only remaining golf ball and not paying very close attention to its location. Sure enough, on that final practice swing the toe of his club barely grazed that old yellow 'range' ball.

Unfortunately for Sammy, 'barely' was the substantive word. That slight touch of the clubhead to the ball caused it to dribble off the tee box directly perpendicular to where he was aimed. What made the situation especially dire was that the tee box was next to a deep valley of trees, weeds and shrubs that descended down to that same river where Sammy had so many problems earlier in the round. We all waited for the ball to stop, but amazingly it kept rolling…and right toward the edge of that cliff. There was no reason to believe it had enough velocity to actually fall over the precipice. There was no question it had to mercifully stop short of disappearing into the depths below. The ball was even slowing down. With 'mercy' not in vogue that day for our friend, there was the slightest of a downward incline on that part of the golf course that kept the ball barely rolling.

Then there followed a rasping moan of "No..o…o" from Sammy's mouth. It was as if that strange sound actually scared the yellow ball into increasing its speed. Destiny had already spoken to Sammy and there was nothing he could do about the next few seconds. It seemed impossible that yellow ball had enough bounce to reach the edge of the cliff much less topple down into the abyss of poison ivy, shrubs, garter snakes, cobwebs, tall grass and trees. But, it did.

The golf ball rolling so slowly along the hard ground had actually picked up speed with that slight downward slant. It was still rolling hard as it disappeared from view. We could hear the ball thumping against trees and brush as it picked up more speed bounding down that steep hill.

Carl, Dewey and I couldn't believe what we'd just seen. Sammy had just lost his last golf ball…on a practice swing. The explosion of laughter from the three of us was so genuine I swore one of us was going to choke.

Sammy stood on that tee box, a picture of someone passing through hell after having just missed the last exit before entering. His revulsion for life was now absolute. He was so numb with misfortune, he couldn't even react. Even our laughter was nothing more than a distant rumble.

He had just accomplished something so implausible…and so mortifying. He had done what very few people in the history of golf would ever fathom doing… and he'd done it on a practice swing. He'd lost his last golf ball. Unfortunately for him, the event was documented in golf lore having been witnessed by his supposed friends writhing in laughter on the tee box.

Had the occasion ended there, it would have been another great tale. But, there was more. The true character and personality of our friend was yet to be displayed. It was that impulsive optimism…that strong belief that he was better than the circumstances around him…that this day was only a temporary aberration…that life was not over…that things would get better. He was about to show another reason why we enjoyed having him as our friend.

After all his cursing and throwing his clubs, that unfamiliar peaceful look returned that he showed while taking four putts from fifteen feet on the eighth green. While we expected despair and a new level of ferocity never seen before, there was none. Instead he reverted to a coolness that he'd demonstrated only a few times in the years I'd known him.

Without looking at any of us, I could see he was going to try one last attempt at being rational. He reached his hand out with his palm up and his eyes riveted down the fairway. In a calm, measured tone he asked, "I need a golf ball. Will someone please throw me a golf ball from their bag?"

He said it as if he really expected a positive response. We all stood there in silence not moving a muscle. I looked at Carl and Dewey and shook my head. They were thinking the same thing. Sammy wasn't getting one of our golf balls.

Carl spoke for us…maybe more direct than Dewey or I might have said it. He barked, "The hell with you, Sammy. You've lost every ball in your bag and now you want to lose one of ours. Go out in the woods and find yourself some golf balls like we have to do."

While Carl's voice was strident, the curl on his lips gave him away. He had to turn away to hide his laughter. Dewey was barely able to keep himself composed. I didn't turn away. I just stood there maintaining my cool watching my friend deal with the situation. I didn't want to miss one sentence or one movement in this golden chapter of Sammy's travail.

With that rather sharp retort from Carl, Sammy let his arm drop to his side. He just stood there like a statue. It appeared he was out of options. Rationality was gone. Even his own friends were not going to come to his aid.

Still, I knew something about Sammy that the other two guys weren't as aware. Our friend could get very inventive during the sorriest of situations. In the thousands of times he and I had sat by the practice green just talking…or me practicing my putting and he talking…Sammy would mindlessly take a practice swing with or without a golf club. Like any golfer he was always trying to find perfection in his imperfect swing. With a club he'd often swish his swing over a leaf on the ground and envision a golf ball rising majestically into the sky. He'd say, "Ah…there it is…I think I finally have the answer. Let's go play." He actually believed with that one practice swing he'd found the solution to the science of the textbook golf swing.

It was now obvious to me something else was going to happen...something highly unusual for most people, but not necessarily for Sammy. I began to grin. Leaning toward Carl and Dewey, I whispered. "Watch now...don't miss this. He's going to do something."

In the next instant, Sammy's entire posture changed. His mind was of another world. His eyes went blank. Not having a golf ball was of little matter to him anymore.

His tee was still in the ground as he reached into his back pocket. He appeared to be fumbling around for something. Then, with a slight smile, he pulled something out of his pocket and began looking at it. That was when Carl and Dewey got wide-eyed and looked curiously over at me. In Sam's hand was nothing...absolutely nothing. Yet, his eyes looked at the non-object in his hand as if he was holding a large diamond.

I stood there with a full smile now enjoying his every move. It was artful... creative...and proved once again that he was crazy.

Dewey edged over to me and asked, "What the hell is he doing?"

I didn't respond placing a finger over my mouth. Then I whispered, "Just watch...he's completely out of it. He's got a pretend golf ball in his hand and he's going to place it on that tee in the ground. I swear to God...he's going to play the last hole with an imaginary golf ball!"

Dewey and Carl looked at our friend as if they didn't know him...nor did they want to be introduced. Both remained still now slightly concerned they might be part of the cause for Sammy finally cracking up for good.

Sure enough, there he went. He placed the imaginary ball on the tee. Standing back up, he then addressed the make-believe ball. With a deep breath and an enormous swing, the club swished across the grass popping the tee out of the ground. Finishing the swing he held his pose seeming to appreciate the picture of a ball flying off into the sky. His normal voice had returned, but he was speaking only to himself. "Finally!" he declared, "I've been waiting the whole God-damned morning to hit one that good."

Picking up his tee and grabbing his golf bag, he nonchalantly began strolling down the center of the fairway ahead of us and not saying a word. His eyes were glazed and no longer mindful of our existence.

We knew our friend wasn't insane, but he was knocking on the door of the asylum. Momentarily we felt guilty. Maybe we'd carried our kidding and nasty comments too far...and now Sammy was permanently damaged.

We all marched up the ninth fairway silently with Sammy whistling and leading the charge. I'd never heard him whistle. He seemed no longer distressed in the least...despite now being down $16.00... more money than he'd seen in one place in his life.

Carl, Dewey, and I hit our second shots close to the green. Sammy, of course, had hit his 'imaginary' drive longer than any of us by a good ten yards. He studied his upcoming shot to the green though there was no ball on the ground in front of him. He was deciding between a five-iron and a seven-iron. He didn't own a six-iron.

The three of us stood there patiently shaking our heads until he decided on swinging a seven-iron. Finishing his swing he broke out into a smile admiring the flight of the imaginary ball and declaring it one of his finest iron shots he'd hit in years. For a thirteen-year old kid with three entire years of golf experience, his claim had to be quite exceptional. We kind of wished we'd seen the shot.

The round ended with Sammy making a ten-foot putt on that last hole… with no ball. I decided not to make some wise comment about the money he owed me. Carl and Dewey stayed quiet as well. Sammy owed them $4.00 apiece… and me $8.00…figures so high for the times that putting him on suicide watch had to be considered.

But, Sammy was not of the same world at that moment. It would have been a waste of time to even mention the money he owed. I figured to wait until he returned to earth.

As we crossed a small walking bridge to the clubhouse and headed for the pop machine…the typical ending to a round of golf…we didn't notice that Sammy was not following us. In fact he was nowhere to be seen. It was a ritual that we paid off our bets before the next round started. Then there'd be a short respite until we'd finished our bottles of pop before the four of us would head for the first tee box for the next round. New wagers would be proposed and agreed upon. Then the new competition would begin with the previous round hardly a thought anymore.

But our customary rest ended up one person short. Sammy hadn't even crossed the bridge or bought a pop. Dewey pointed across the walking bridge to Sam's golf clubs. They'd been left by the ninth green. It was as if our friend had been grabbed by the Almighty possibly for the flagrant use of 'His' name throughout the last round. Then again we were all guilty of that infraction, so that was discounted.

He'd obviously disappeared into the brush, rough, and trees to replenish his golf bag with golf balls other players had lost. We played as a threesome that next round. Hole by hole we could hear someone thrashing around in the woods. We never saw him, but we knew it was Sammy in the thick of the woods hunting for golf balls.

We wouldn't see him until we finished the second nine holes of golf. After crossing the walking bridge again and grabbing our bottle of pop, there was Sammy coming out of the clubhouse. Without saying a word, he went to the ball washer and began cleaning the golf balls he'd found. He had a satisfied smile on his face.

We wanted to sit back, rest a bit longer, and enjoy our pop before teeing it up again, but Sammy was impatient. He teed up one of his new balls he'd found and shouted over to us. "Come on, you guys. Let's play…how about twenty-five cents for the nine holes?"

It was the same bet we'd always proposed, but he said it as if he was introducing a new game. In fact, he was behaving as if he hadn't even played golf yet that day. Apparently, any memory of that previous 'round through Hell' earlier that morning had disappeared. His eternal optimism prohibited him from remembering it.

Carl, Dewey and I took our last swigs of pop, forced ourselves up from the rusty metal chairs by the first tee box, grabbed our clubs and said to him, "You're on. Let's go."

Sammy then walked towards us with his newly found golf balls in hand and a very happy, contented look on his face. He'd found some beauties and wanted to show them off. We admired his collection of nine golf balls and asked him where he'd found them…as if inquiring where the fish were biting for when we had to go forage for some golf balls for ourselves. We were again just four young kids talking with one another and ready to move forward with another nine holes of life.

We teed off, picked up our golf bags and began marching down the first fairway. Even Sammy's first shot was decent as it started out over the roadway running parallel to the first fairway and sliced back onto the golf course. His customary shot flight had returned. Things were back to normal. Something would be said and we'd start kibitzing or joking or listening to one another's comments about any topic four thirteen-year olds might find interesting.

Strangely, the topic of that first round of golf earlier that day never came up in our conversation. In fact there was not even any mention of the $16.00 Sammy had lost to the three of us in a simple nine-hole match that started with a twenty-five cent bet. Sammy had gone through golfing hell and survived. For that we were pleased. Besides, we knew there would be no point to expect payment, so why ask? That kind of money was only available at a bank. If he robbed a financial institution and got caught, he'd miss school. We didn't want that to happen to our friend.

However, there was another unspoken reason why we didn't expect payment of that wager. It was our way of showing him some respect for not quitting when everything was going so discouragingly wrong. Maybe it was also our hope that if we were ever engaged in the same set of circumstances as our friend had been placed that morning that our immediate friends would exhibit some of the respect we were now showing toward Sammy.

Then again we knew damn well each of us could never be involved in similar conditions. We didn't have Sammy's gift for making a bad situation worse.

In the many years that followed that uniquely entertaining day, I couldn't count the number of times I told that tale to old and new friends about my boyhood friend's playing with an imaginary golf ball. And when I was lucky enough to get back home to play with Carl…or Dewey…or Sammy…and sometimes all three of them…invariably that story would bloom once again. We would laugh until our sides hurt. Sammy laughed just as hard.

Sammy had been to golfing hell…and survived. He'd even showed up later that day to tee it up with us again after he'd resurrected his golf ball supply. As for the $16.00 he lost to us during that one round of golf, I guess Carl, Dewey and I maintained our silence in the name of friendship…and our high regard for his resiliency. The subject of payment was ignored…that day, the next day, the next week….and forever thereafter.